Dion's Dream Girl

Dion's Dream Girl

A small-town, second chance, multicultural, surprise pregnancy, amnesia romance.

Heart's Destiny Book 7

Leah Mae Wright

Copyright

Contents

Dedication

To all the other retired professional wrestlers and car accident survivors out there, who are also dealing with the effects of multiple undiagnosed concussions like me, and to the people who love them enough to help them live with the consequences. Especially my husband, who really should have become a doctor, since he's the one who recognized my head-injury-induced narcolepsy when the neurologists, neuropsychiatrists, neuropsychologists, and concussion specialists all missed it.

Introduction

Dion Davis didn't remember the most important events of his life after helping to rescue one of his fellow wrestlers from a deranged stalker. Truth be told, he didn't remember meeting Allissa, much less helping to rescue her. But he did remember his good friend, Dean Hunter, who just so happened to be Allissa's fiancé, so he couldn't say no when they asked him to be in their wedding.

From what he'd been told after waking up in the hospital with amnesia, he spent a lot of time in Dean's hometown over the last year. So, he hoped his trip to Heart's Destiny for their wedding would bring back a few of the memories he lost. Especially if those memories revealed the identity of the woman he dreamed about nightly since he woke up in the hospital after the altercation with Allissa's stalker. *Jewel. My Dream Girl. My Jewel. She has to be real. Making love to her in all those different hotel rooms has to be my memories trying to come back to me, not just dreams, like the, uh,...guy in the white lab coat thinks they are.*

After almost a year of sneaking around to see Dion without letting on to her matchmaking mother that she'd met *The One*, Julie Burleson was almost ready to announce to the world that they were in love, and possibly starting a family. Then, two days before she was scheduled to see her doctor to verify her suspicion that she was pregnant, Dion was injured while helping to rescue one of their friends from a stalker. After frantically trying to call him in between bouts of nausea at hearing the news, Julie finally got through, only to be told not to call him again because he was blocking her number.

Devastated by the sudden rejection of the man she thought was her soulmate, Julie struggled with her emotions as she tried to move on with her life. Hurt and angry, she didn't want anything to do with him when he returned to Heart's Destiny for Dean and Allissa's wedding, no matter how much her heart and her libido contradicted the thoughts in her head.

But Dion was nothing if not determined. Determined to heal, not only his injuries, but also his relationship with his Jewel. Could this former professional wrestler win the biggest battle of his life — the emotional wrestling match for Jewel's heart? He might not ever be able to step into the squared circle as a pro grappler again, but he planned to spend the rest of his life fighting for his family. Dion knew the most important victory of his life would be winning the heart of his dream girl.

DISCLAIMER: This small-town, second chance, multicultural, surprise pregnancy, amnesia romance contains scenes depicting the physical and mental symptoms experienced after a traumatic brain injury, profanity, and graphic sex scenes. It is intended for adult readers (18+) who are not easily offended.

Author's Note

As I'm writing Dion and Julie's story, I'm pulling a lot of the medical information from my personal experience after suffering multiple concussions. While he only sees one neurologist before the primary care physician recognizes the narcolepsy symptoms, I saw several, along with concussion specialists, neuropsychiatrists, and neuropsychologists. None of those specialists recognized my blackout spells as narcolepsy. NONE! I got lucky that my husband saw a sign about narcolepsy with cataplexy in his sleep specialist's office when he went to be tested for sleep apnea and recognized the symptoms I was having. Because he said something about that sign, I ended up going to be tested, and finally found a medication that works to keep me from falling asleep every time I get overwhelmed.

I normally try to write stories that are an escape from reality to entertain my readers. But with this story, I've tapped into some of my reality in the hope of helping others like me, who might not realize that the sub-concussive bumps to the head they've had over the years, or the whiplash effects they've suffered after car accidents, can all add up to some strange responses in the body.

After a 13 year career in professional wrestling (most of which was as a valet or manager and not in the ring) and multiple car accidents over the years, it only took one diagnosed concussion for me to develop post-concussion syndrome and narcolepsy with cataplexy. So, if any of you recognize some of your own symptoms in this book, especially if you've bumped your head at any point in your life, I hope it will help you figure out which specialists you need to see to get properly diagnosed.

Also, please note, while I've tried to write Dion's portions of the book to show how someone with A.D.D. or A.D.H.D. jumps from thought to thought, I'm writing this while medicated for my A.D.H.D., so it's not completely accurate at the beginning when he hasn't been diagnosed or started medication to treat it yet. Trust me, it's taking long enough to write this book as it is. You don't want me to go off my meds to try to make it more accurate 'cause it would take ten times as long for me to finish it. And more than likely, I'd put in a dozen extra random thoughts that would turn into plot holes we'd never get filled in.

Anyway, I hope you enjoy my brand of crazy. Please buckle up before you get on this wild ride with Dion and Julie.

Happy reading,

Leah

Chapter One

Saturday, October 26, 2019

Julie Burleson sat in her kitchen with her twin sister, Jen, and their cousin, Becky, wishing they weren't trying to convince her to go out that night. With her sister and cousin both being single, they wanted to go into San Antonio for the evening to check out a new club they'd heard about in the hopes of meeting a potential hookup partner for the night.

Technically, Julie was also single, but since she'd started hooking up with Dion Davis the year before, she didn't consider herself as such. Yeah, at first, they'd only joked around about having a future together, but even in their joking there'd been a grain of truth. From their first time getting naked, they'd agreed to be exclusive in their bedroom activities, so she considered herself taken, even though the constant travel of his job as a professional wrestler precluded them from having more than a long-distance, friends-with-benefits situationship for the time being. She knew, deep in her heart of hearts, that she and Dion were soulmates, hopelessly in love with one another, and destined to eventually marry and have a family together.

Not that she would admit to how much they really meant to one another in front of the Matchmaking Mommas of Heart's Destiny, who would instantly start planning their wedding if they got wind of her liaison with Dion. Who was she kidding? The Matchmaking Mommas would do a lot more than just start planning the wedding. They'd incessantly push for instant gratification with the happily ever after, long before Dion was able to retire so the two of them could seriously dive into their relationship.

She'd always enjoyed watching Dion wrestle and thought he was hot, even before she actually met him in person. But when she first

Leah Mae Wright

saw him at the barbecue where the GWA employees, with whom her
cousin Anthony worked, were first introduced to the rest of the
Burleson family, she felt the zing of awareness her elders had warned
her that all the Burlesons felt when they first saw their soulmates.

It was a stark contrast to the way she'd felt when she first met the
boys she'd dated in college. She'd just thought she felt butterflies in
her belly back then. Now she knew what real butterflies felt like, and
that with the real deal, the butterflies were accompanied by feeling like
she was struck by lightning. And since he was already successful in
his chosen career, she didn't think his interest in her was based on how
her last name and family money could be used to his benefit, unlike
the boys who'd pursued her, her sister, and her cousins back in
college.

As she sat there only half-listening to her sister and cousin drone on
and on about this new club, she couldn't help but think back fondly on
her first interaction with Dion. *It's a wonder we didn't set the
paddocks on fire with the way sparks were flying between us that
afternoon.*

Saturday, November 17, 2018

**Julie was in the south bunkhouse, helping prepare side dishes
and desserts to go with all the brisket and ribs her dad and uncle
were fixing in the smoker. When everything was mostly ready,
she'd been sent out by her mother to go mingle with their guests.
She'd stepped outside, thinking she'd either play a round of
horseshoes or take some of the kids over to the stables for a trail
ride. But the sight that greeted her stopped her in her tracks.**

**Dion Davis, the gorgeous African American professional
wrestler known as "Dark Chocolate" by GWA fans around the
world, was on his knees beside the opening of the bounce
house, allowing the little girls her cousin Anthony had just
adopted, and several of their friends, to climb up on his
shoulders to use him as a solid platform to jump off of to be able
to do flips in the air before landing in the bounce house. She felt
her ovaries quiver for the first time in her life, finding his ease
with kids and good-natured attitude even more attractive than his
chiseled physique and sexy smile.**

**She'd already known she was too tall to get in the bounce
house with the kids, so she hadn't ventured over to it earlier,**

when the rest of the family was checking out everything being set up for the party. But she was so drawn to Dion that she ended up walking over to get a closer look, uncaring of how strange it might have appeared to the rest of her family.

While her newest little cousins thought she was there to watch them show off the aerial wrestling moves they were learning, she was really there hoping to get an introduction to Dion. Twelve-year-old Tia hadn't let her "Aunt Julie" down, making the introduction before demonstrating what she called a "backflip splash," where she did a backflip off of Dion's broad shoulders before landing in a belly flop on the giant air mattress that made up the base of the bounce house.

"Yeah, that looks painful," Julie cringed, remembering back to belly flops she'd done into the swimming pool at the park as a kid.

"It's not too bad, as long as you have a partner you trust catching you in the ring," Dion informed her, smiling up at her, as their eyes locked on one another for the first time.

The butterflies in her belly, which she knew were caused by talking to him, suddenly decided to flip and flutter around, just like her newest cousins and their little friends. She unexpectedly felt so tingly, as if she'd been struck by lightning and had the three-hundred-million volts of electricity of the lightning bolt still coursing through her body, that she wasn't sure how she managed to mutter her next words. "Yeah, I think I'll stick to less painful physical activities, like horseback riding."

"Yeah, the guys mentioned that would be an option for today," Dion chuckled, as the next kid climbed up on his shoulders. "Once the kids get tired of practicing planchas, I'll have to find you to take me for a ride."

Julie had to walk away then, not wanting him to see her blushing at the way her dirty mind instantly went to the mental image of her riding him instead of a horse. At the time, she didn't think he'd intentionally used the innuendo because she couldn't let herself believe he could possibly be just as attracted to her as she was to him. And she was most definitely attracted to him. More than anyone she'd ever felt attracted to in her life.

Later that day, when he'd followed through and found her to take him on a trail ride, Julie was grateful she'd put in a tampon for the last and lightest day of her period. She'd needed it to keep her wet pussy from soaking through her panties, riding shorts, and jeans at the sight of that stud in a saddle.

Talking to him that night at the joint bachelor and bachelorette party for Anthony and Kay, Julie found out that Dion had indeed felt an instant attraction to her, too. As they took a turn around the dance floor, he'd confided that he'd finally understood what Anthony had been telling all the guys for the last six weeks about love at first sight and how their family members always fell hard and fast.

While he hadn't actually said the L word in reference to her, Dion had quickly convinced her that his joking around about how they were meant to be together had the potential of being real, confiding, "With you, I want it all. Marriage, babies, the whole nine yards. Hot, sexy times mixed with quiet nights on the couch, cuddling and talking about all our hopes and dreams for the future. I knew you were The One *for me when I felt the exact same thing Anthony described when he talked about seeing Kay the first time. Fate. Destiny. Kismet. Soulmates. Call it whatever you want, but we're inevitable. I felt like I was struck by lightning when I saw you walking toward me at the bounce house earlier. I knew we were meant for each other from that first moment. And I was just more convinced of it when you blushed so prettily at my comment about you taking me for a ride. And the way you're blushing again now tells me that you know I meant a private, naked ride, and not horseback riding."*

She'd felt goosebumps at hearing him compare his feelings to being struck by lightning, since that was exactly how she'd felt, too. Realizing they'd both felt that instant connection, she couldn't deny her own feelings, and had to find out what could develop between them. They'd continued talking about the possibility of them starting to date to see where things might go in the future, until the songs sped up and they decided to leave the dance floor for something to drink. But with him traveling approximately three-hundred-and-twenty days a year with the GWA, and her being tied to her job as the vice president of business diversification and asset management for Burleson Incorporated, neither one of them could figure out how they'd be able to make a real relationship work, especially when they couldn't see each other but a few weeks a year.

That hadn't stopped him from trying for more, though. About halfway through the party, he'd caught her in the hallway outside the restrooms to make his first real move on her.

"Come back to my room tonight," Dion suggested, his voice deepening with desire.

"I can't," Julie protested, even though she desperately wanted to give in. *"I'm not the type of girl who sleeps with someone on the first day we meet, even if it does feel like we've known each other longer."*

Truth be told, she'd wanted to take him up on the offer. But she'd always followed her mother and grandmother's lessons about waiting to get to know someone before sleeping with him, and she wasn't about to change her rules just because she thought he could be The One. Not when getting to know him first seemed so much more important than it had when she'd lost her virginity in college.

"We don't have to do anything but talk," Dion asserted. *"Hell, we can go sit in your parents' living room to talk all night, so you know I won't try anything you don't want."*

"It's not that I don't want you to try anything," Julie backtracked, wanting him to know she was as interested in their physical attraction as he was, even though she wanted to take things a little slower. While she didn't want to get into her history of feeling used by her college boyfriend because of her last name, she did need to communicate her need to know he liked her for her, and not just to get in her pants, or for what her being a Burleson could do for him. *"I just need to take it slow and know it means more to you than a one-night stand. And before you start repeating all that destiny and soulmates stuff you heard from Anthony and spouted on the dance floor earlier, I need to be shown it's true and not just told. You wouldn't be the first guy who's tried telling me what I wanted to hear to get in my pants, so I don't believe it without seeing the effort being made to prove it."*

Dion took her hand then, placing her palm over his heart and covering her hand with his to hold it there. *"Do you feel that?"*

She felt his heart thumping rapidly in his chest and nodded.

"My heart races every time I see you," Dion confided, smiling almost shyly. *"It's never done that with anyone before. So, I already know you mean more to me than anyone else ever has. I don't know how we'll make it work with me on tour and you having such an important job here, but I want to try. That's why I'm willing to go slow and wait for more than a goodnight kiss from you. But I still wanna spend as much time with you as possible this week, so we can really get to know one another outside our physical attraction."*

Julie couldn't deny that he seemed sincere in his plea for more than just the physical with her. But even though she wasn't ready to sleep with him just yet, needing to know for sure that he was her soulmate before she fully gave him her heart, she didn't want him to back off too much on the physical attraction between them, either.

"Who says I'm even gonna give you a goodnight kiss?" Julie teased, stepping in close and pushing up on her tiptoes as she slid her left hand over his shoulder and around his neck while leaving her right hand under his left over his heart. "Maybe I'd rather kiss you now, so I can remember it, instead of waiting until the end of the night, when I'm too drunk to even know what I'm doing."

"I like the way you think, Jewel." Dion grinned as he pulled her closer with his right hand on the small of her back. He slid his hand up her spine, finally resting it on her nape before pressing his pillow-soft lips to hers for the first time. He took his time, warming her up with gentle passes of his mouth and tongue over her closed lips before pressing more firmly and gently nipping at her lips to try to coax her to open for him.

Julie melted into his kiss, unconsciously opening her mouth to the invasion of his tongue before returning his ardent passion. It was unlike any first kiss she'd ever experienced. Primal. Intense. Carnal. A claiming. Transcendent. Transforming her into a state of being she'd never imagined possible. Like the shifters in the paranormal romance books she'd read, she metamorphosed from her normal form of the average, everyday woman into a wanton, sexual goddess, who only existed to mate with this man.

She got so lost in the connection she felt with Dion as they pressed their bodies together that she forgot where she was for a moment, only coming back to earth when she heard her twin calling her name. They quickly separated as Julie warned him, "Nobody else can know about this," before turning to follow Jen back to the table, where the ladies were lining up another round of shots.

Julie tried to shake off her memories of the first day she met Dion to focus on what her sister and cousin were saying, but her mind kept wandering back to the other days that first week, when they kept running into one another at each of the wedding events. *More like Mom and Aunt Hazel kept seating us together.*

Sunday, November 18, 2018

After overhearing the GWA guys giving James Hunter a hard time about a chocolate cream pie line he'd used in a promo he cut against Dion, Julie was curious about how Dion ended up with the Dark Chocolate moniker for his wrestling persona. So, when she ended up sitting beside him later at the wedding shower for Anthony and Kay, she asked him how it came to be his ring name.

"When I was training and in the indies, I always just used my real name," Dion confided, dipping his chin sheepishly, almost like he was embarrassed by his wrestling gimmick. "But then when I started with the GWA, we had to come up with a gimmick other than just a generic wrestler. Since I didn't want to go with the stereotypical gang banger gimmick, and showed up to my first production meeting in a suit and tie, they wanted me to go with a wealthy, ladies' man gimmick. I had no idea how to play wealthy, only owning a suit at the time because Mama Marcel insisted I needed to wear one to church every Sunday."

He paused to tug the cuffs of his classic navy suit and grin at her, showing her that he still followed Mama Marcel's edict about wearing a suit to church. "But in my early twenties, I figured I was doin' alright with the ladies' man part of the gimmick. I was still just using my real name, until one night when I was cutting a promo and popped off with a line about how much the ladies love dark chocolate. The next day, they started billing me as Dark Chocolate, instead of Dion Davis. Hell, it's still kinda cliché for a Black guy to use as a wrestling name, but since I'm pretty much a chocoholic, I like to think of it as a reference to my sweet tooth and not my skin color."

"That's something we have in common," Julie smiled, loving that she'd found the first thing they could bond over besides their physical attraction. "I'm also a chocoholic. To the point that I keep some form of chocolate candy in the dish on my desk, instead of mints like most people in the office have for after lunch."

"Plain chocolate like Hershey's Kisses? Or do you get fancy with Andes Crème de Menthes to make sure you still have fresh

breath after lunch?" Dion grinned as he questioned her candy choices.

"Oh, no, if I'm going with chocolate and mint, I'm filling the candy dish with York Peppermint Patties," Julie grinned back. "But it's seriously whatever I happen to grab on my way to the office. Sometimes it's Kisses, sometimes it's Reese's Peanut Butter Cups, and sometimes it's Hershey's Miniatures, so I can get my fill of Special Darks."

"So, I was right in saying that line about ladies loving dark chocolate," Dion chuckled. "I'll have to get you to share that sentiment with Mama Marcel, 'cause she claims it's not a universal truth, even though it's her favorite kind of chocolate, too."

"And who is Mama Marcel?" Julie was curious about his upbringing, and especially the maternal figure he seemed so fond of as he spoke.

"She was our neighbor when I was growing up." Dion's broad smile dimmed, his expressive face seeming to turn a bit melancholy. "She was my mama's best friend and took care of all of us when Papa died. Then a few years later, when we lost Mama, she finished raising me and my brother, Darius. She's our second mama, who kept us outta the system and from possibly being split up when Katrina hit. Hell, she still keeps Dare outta trouble by acting as the gatekeeper in our condo building."

"She doesn't keep you outta trouble now?" Julie arched an eyebrow at Dion, smiling impishly.

"Yeah, I suppose she does when I'm in NOLA," Dion admitted with a flirtatious grin. "But if she was here right now, she'd be joining forces with your local matchmakers, who insisted we sit together just now, and trying to get us to give her grandbabies."

"Yeah, that was my Aunt Sarah, probably at my mother's insistence, since she's busy with the Newlywed Game," Julie speculated, rolling her eyes at her meddling family's shenanigans.

"Relax , Jewel. I promise I won't bring Mama Marcel around to help with their matchmaking schemes. At least, not until we figure out how to deal with our conflicting schedules to actually take advantage of their efforts to explore the possibilities of our instant attraction to one another."

He might not have brought Mama Marcel to town, but her meddling family and their conflicting schedules hadn't stopped either one of them from wanting to act on the massive attraction they shared. So, after talking about the possibilities several times that week, they'd decided to start seeing each other on the down-low to keep Julie's mom and the rest of the local matchmaking mommas from pushing for them to get married long before either of them was ready.

Dion came to Heart's Destiny whenever the GWA had a holiday break, and Julie met him on the road whenever the GWA had a show in a city where she could schedule meetings with the various branches of Burleson that she managed, or with companies that she wanted to add to the portfolio of the family business. It had been working so well that they hoped to keep it up for a few more years.

They'd assumed Dion would retire from wrestling when he turned forty, so if they kept the spark in their relationship for seven more years, he'd be free to move to her hometown for them to start talking about marriage and babies. She'd be thirty-four then, with over a decade in her current position at Burleson Incorporated, so she thought she'd finally be ready to slow down on her expansion plans for the company and would want to spend more time at home raising their family. At least, until the kids started school and she needed to go back to work full time to show the rest of her family that she was their best option for taking over as the CEO when her father and uncle retired.

It didn't seem that fate agreed with their plans, however, since she was eleven days late starting her period. On Tuesday, the twenty-second, when she'd finally told Dion that she was a week late, he'd been exceptionally quiet as she talked through their options, and how an unplanned pregnancy might need to change their timeline. She chalked it up to his more reserved nature, knowing that she tended to monopolize their phone conversations. But as the day went on and she hadn't heard from him that he was done at the *Halloween Horror* fan expo for them to have some sexy Skype time, she was starting to wonder if he needed the extra time to think about the possibility of becoming a father without her talking his ear off.

Since she knew his primary professional goal was to have a twenty-year career in the wrestling ring, she had to wonder if his recent detachment was because he'd rather give up their relationship and his relationship with their child than retire early. Yeah, she saw his point about how she could take a sabbatical from work and go back to the family business once the children were older, while his career was limited to only a certain time frame in his life. But she still thought they could come to some sort of compromise that would allow her and the baby to travel with him some of the time and him to come off the tour to be with their family some of the time, so neither one of them had to give up their career ambitions.

Unless there's a reason he doesn't want us with him on tour, she thought, hating that she went to the worst-case scenarios in her head. *Like being a parent or admitting publicly that we're in a relationship will cramp his style on the road.*

Damn, I hope he's not being extra quiet lately because he doesn't want to be a father, or at least, not with me, she thought, thinking back to all the pics of him that she'd seen online in the last few months. *He swears those are just fans who've tagged his profiles after getting an autograph and picture while he was out to lunch or whatever, and supposedly they're nothing I should be jealous over. But it seems like the majority of them are with rather scantily clad women. Women who aren't about to be as big as a barn from being pregnant.*

Not that I know for sure I'm pregnant. But come on, the tight pants and tender breasts make it pretty damn obvious, even though I haven't had morning sickness yet. After seeing what Kay, Brooklyn, Amy, and Char have gone through in their pregnancies, I'm sure it's just a matter of time before that symptom shows up, too.

Thinking about how she'd come to the realization that she was possibly pregnant from the signs she'd seen so far brought her right back to why she really didn't want to go out with the girls that night, finally giving her an excuse that she thought might actually work to get her out of it. "You know I'm just gonna make ya'll crazy, and run off any guys ya'll might wanna hook up with, by not drinking and talking through all my feelings about possibly being preggers all night," Julie pointed out. "So, unless ya'll wanna make it a girls' night in with rom-coms and painting our nails, ya might wanna leave me outta your plans."

"Yeah, well, the rest of us aren't as lucky as you are with having Dion," Jen whined, pouting at Julie, as if that would convince her to go. "I'm dying from this dry spell I've been having, and really need to find someone to hook up with this weekend."

Since the GWA had started coming to town regularly, their mom had paired Jen up with Dion's tag-team partner, Liam "Red" Connery, every time she'd seated Julie with Dion. While Jen claimed to not have anywhere near the chemistry with Liam that Julie felt with Dion, she certainly seemed way more upset by Liam's recent Vegas wedding than Julie expected of their just-friends relationship.

Julie thought it had something to do with whatever happened between Jen and Liam in September when their cousin Charlotte got married, back when nobody knew that Liam had married Rylie Long a couple of weeks before. She thought her sister was feeling guilty for trying to step things up from friendship with a man she didn't know was married. Since Liam didn't know he was married then either, Julie didn't think her sister had anything to feel guilty about, even if they'd gone farther than the kiss Jen told her about. Not that Julie had been successful at convincing her sister of that yet.

"She does have a point, though." Becky pointed at Julie as her phone buzzed on the table. "We might have better luck…" Becky's voice trailed off as she looked at the text message on her screen. "Oh shit, emergency family meeting."

Before Julie could ask what Becky was talking about, her own phone buzzed with a message from her dad that said the same thing. They all jumped up and took off toward her Uncle Bob and Aunt Hazel's house, where the Burlesons tended to gather for everything since Memmaw Judy passed away when Julie and Jen were fourteen. While her mom was just as much the family matriarch as her aunt, Julie knew her mom had deferred to Hazel's desire to be the hostess of all family events because she didn't want to risk the damage to her home that came along with such large gatherings.

As Julie, Jen, and Becky ran out of the house, they saw their friend Cait, who was now officially dating their cousin Josh since he'd gotten out of the Navy and moved home, coming out of the house next door. Julie and Jen's brother, JJ, was also coming out of his house on the other side of Cait's. Their other brother, Justin, and his fiancée, Amy, were driving over from their house on the other side of JJ, since she was less than six weeks from her due date with their twins, and their overprotective brother insisted she didn't need to walk that far and risk going into early labor.

As soon as she stepped in the front door of her aunt and uncle's home alongside half her family, she heard Charlotte's newly adopted four-year-old son, Brody, asking why he needed to go up to the game room with Josh's recently found eight-year-old son, JoJo, instead of staying for the family meeting.

Wow! This family is really growing fast with all the adoptions and surprise kiddos showing up recently.

"Because it's an adult meeting," JoJo explained, rushing Brody up the front stairs. "And if we stay down here, they'll have to report to Santa Claus that we've been eavesdropping, and we'll get coal in our stockings instead of presents at Christmas."

Julie couldn't help but smile at the thought of JoJo and Brody talking to her kids about Santa in a couple of years. While she hadn't planned to get pregnant just yet, she had to admit that she was excited about the possibility. Especially with Dion as her baby's father. Whether things worked out for the two of them or not, she'd always have a piece of the man she loved with her, if she was pregnant as she suspected.

Julie couldn't think about that possibility at the moment, however, noticing a somber expression on her dad's and uncle's faces. She took a seat at one of the dining tables with her parents as they waited for everyone to arrive to start the family meeting. Obviously, Charlotte and her husband Ian had come in the back door from their house in between Julie's parents' home and Uncle Bob and Aunt Hazel's home. But it took a little longer for her cousin Bobby, the local police chief, his wife, Brooklyn, and their two-week-old daughter, Maddie, to drive up from their house on the south side of the ranch. That's when she realized that in a couple more months, when Justin and Amy's house was finished down between Bobby and Brook's house and the house Anthony had built for his family earlier in the year, her brother and his family would also take just as long to get to any family gatherings they had at Uncle Bob and Aunt Hazel's house.

I wonder if they're going to conference in Jake from his base in Washington D.C., or Anthony, Kay, and their kids from the hotel in New Orleans, so none of them have to miss this meeting because of work obligations?

"I just got off the phone with Anthony," Uncle Bob informed them once everyone was seated and the two older kids were upstairs. "There's been an incident at the GWA fan expo."

An incident? What kind of incident? Julie wondered, completely forgetting about whether or not anyone conferenced in Jake. *Is this why Dion hasn't messaged me this morning? Is he having to help calm Dean down because Allissa's stalker pulled something else?*

"Anthony, Kay, and their kids are all safe," Uncle Bob continued, unaware that Julie was internally freaking out about whether or not Dion was okay. "So are David, Mandi, Rick, and Patty Hunter. And Allissa's mom, Windy, and her friend, Kandi. And most everyone else, including all the kids with the GWA."

Oh, no! No, no, no, no, no! Most everyone else is safe? That means not everyone is safe. Dear Lord, please protect all of our friends and family there, especially Dion. Our baby needs to know him and not just my memories of him.

"Unfortunately, Allissa was alone in the locker room when her stalker made a move to try to kidnap her. It appears that Dean, Liam, and Dion went in to try and help the security team. And at least one of them was caught in the crossfire between the stalker and the security team."

"Oh, gawd!" Julie cried out, covering her mouth, and jumping up to run out of the room. She beelined for the closest bathroom, unsure if she was sick from worrying about Dion, or if she was having her first bout of morning sickness.

Somehow, she managed to lock the door on her way to the toilet to puke her guts out, not wanting her family to walk in on her right then. If it was just Jen or Becky, it would be okay. Or even Char, Cait, Amy, or Brook. But she didn't want to have to answer any questions from her mom or Aunt Hazel right then. Not that she could while violently vomiting, but whatever.

Once she paused her retching for more than a few seconds, she pulled her phone from her pocket and dialed Dion. When it rang and rang before going to voicemail, Julie hung up and puked again before trying once more to call him. After multiple rounds of trying to call between bouts of vomiting, Julie gave up momentarily, switching apps to check the newsfeed on her phone to see if there was any more information online than her uncle had gotten from her cousin.

She found several stories about there being reports of shots fired at the arena hosting the GWA's *Halloween Horror* show, and about the arena being on lockdown after a shooting, but none of them gave any details about who was involved, or if there were any casualties during the incident. Scared out of her mind for the man she loved, Julie tried once more to call Dion, needing to hear his voice to know he wasn't hurt or dead.

"Hello," he barked when he finally answered the phone right before it could go to voicemail for what seemed like the hundredth time.

"Oh, gawd, D, are you okay?" Julie could barely croak the words out, her voice hoarse from vomiting.

"I'm fine," he huffed. "But I don't have time to deal with another ring rat right now."

"Another ring rat?" Julie went from worried to pissed in less than a millisecond, growling out her words in a low tone to make her anger clear without alerting her family, who were gathering outside the bathroom and knocking on the door to check on her. "I am *not* a ring rat."

"Fine, gold digger, whatever," he snarled. "You're no different from the rest of the greedy bitches in the world. And I've got more important stuff to do than to bother with some ho, who isn't even worth trying to remember fucking. And I'm damn sure not gonna let some slut get away with trying to take advantage of this shitstorm of injuries to make bank. So, do us both a favor and lose this number. I'm blocking you as soon as I hang up, so it won't do you any good to try calling again."

Julie stared at her phone in shock after he hung up on her. *What a fucking bastard!*

As her brain tried to shut down, her stomach rolled again, sending her right back to the toilet to puke some more. The leftover pizza she'd just had for lunch had clearly all come back up, along with the eggs and toast she'd had for breakfast. She didn't know what else was left in her stomach to possibly come up next, but she couldn't stop heaving, even when it seemed like it was just stomach acid she was vomiting.

The whole time she was puking her guts out, her twin sister was on the other side of the door, trying to talk her into either letting her in the bathroom or coming out where the whole family could check on her.

"Come on, Sis," Jen pleaded. "At least unlock the door, so I can hold your hair back while you puke."

Yeah, I can't stop throwing up long enough to go unlock the door, even if I wanted to, Julie thought, hoping her twin would get the message telepathically. She dry-heaved for a few more minutes before flushing the toilet, washing her face, and rinsing out her mouth as she listened to the conversation going on just outside the bathroom door.

"What can I do?" Cait inquired.

"I can take the door off the hinges to get in if you need me to," Josh offered. Knowing her cousin was the jokester of their family and also a former Navy SEAL, Julie wasn't sure if he was serious about knocking down the door or not.

"No," Aunt Hazel objected loudly. "Do not bust that door down, Joshua Bennett Burleson."

"Alright, how 'bout I pick the lock instead?" Josh suggested.

Not wanting to risk him following through with either option, and especially not wanting everyone to try to crowd into the restroom with her, Julie quickly finished cleaning up and opened the door to find Jen, Becky, Cait, Josh, and Charlotte huddled close by, while her mom and Aunt Hazel hovered a few feet away. Seeing the worried expressions on her family's faces, she couldn't hold back her anguish over the conversation she'd just had, even with her meddling mom nearby.

"He doesn't wanna talk to me," she sobbed, paraphrasing the conversation, so she didn't say any of the curse words in front of her mother and aunt. "He said he can't deal with a ring rat that he can't remember, trying to con him out of his money by taking advantage of his injury to claim we're in a relationship. And that I shouldn't bother trying to call him again because he's blocking my number."

The women all surrounded Julie, offering their support through hugs and crying along with her. Julie let the tears flow, needing to let out all the hurt from losing the man she'd thought was her soulmate. *How can the sweet, loving, gentle giant of a man I fell in love with be so cold-hearted and callous to me, when he knows I'm most likely pregnant with his child?*

Maybe it wasn't him who answered his phone? Maybe it was a doctor who's treating him or something? Someone who didn't know who I am, or what we mean to each other?

Julie wanted to believe the tall tale she was telling herself, not wanting to think about the possibility that her probable baby daddy had just rejected her. *But it sounded just like him on the phone, not just someone else from New Orleans, who has a similar accent. Angrier than I've ever heard him before, but it was definitely his voice.*

Since I know he hasn't talked to his brother in over a year, I doubt he would have gone to the hospital to possibly answer D's phone. So, even if they sound alike the way people always say Jen and I sound alike, I don't think it was him. Which means, I've just gotta face the fact that the man I thought I'd spend the rest of my life with, would raise my babies with, just told me not to call him again.

That arrogant bastard! How dare he!

Julie let all her anger and hurt flow freely down her face along with her tears, until she couldn't cry another drop, knowing it would take a long time for her to get over the hell Dion just put her through. Finally, someone's stomach growled loudly, breaking the silence that had descended on the huddle of women as the crying subsided.

"Sorry," Charlotte winced as she rubbed a hand over her small baby bump. "Being called to a family meeting interrupted my lunch prep, and Judy is getting impatient."

"How about ya'll go back to the dining room to wait for an update while I go throw together a late lunch?" Aunt Hazel suggested, smiling sympathetically at Julie and the rest of the women, who'd barely started breaking away from their group hug.

"Thanks, Aunt Hazel," Julie sniffled, wiping her tears with one hand while holding her phone up with the other. "But I got all the updates I need from my online news feed and my brief conversation with whoever it was that answered Dion's phone. So, I think I'm gonna go soak in a nice hot bath and get lost in a good book."

Julie really didn't want to think about reading the next book in the series they were all reading about surprise babies for their book club. Those plots were hitting a little too close to home at the moment, so she decided to ask about changing it up before their book club meeting on Monday evening.

"I know we're supposed to review the newest **Crescent Cove** book on Monday night, but do you think we can switch it up to a paranormal or fantasy romance instead? I know everyone else is into the hot baby daddies right now, but I'm kinda sick of human men at the moment.

So, I'm only gonna read about aliens and vampires and faeries for a little while."

"Absolutely," the women around her chorused.

"I have a whole list of recommendations in the fantasy and paranormal romance category," Becky added with a smile. "Let's head home so I can pull it up on my tablet for you."

Julie nodded her agreement before walking back home with her cousin, twin sister, and their BFF Cait. They picked a series she'd already read by one of their favorite authors before Julie left them talking in her living room to go up to the bath.

As she stripped out of her clothes and filled the tub with bubbles from her favorite bath gel, she started the first audiobook in the series to refresh her memory before the book club meeting, wishing she could transport herself to the parallel universe the author depicted, so she wouldn't have to think about the day she met Dion Davis. Unfortunately, as soon as it got to the first sex scene, she started reminiscing about the first time she made love with Dion, after sneaking out of Anthony and Kay's rehearsal dinner. Because it had been a few years for her and he was well endowed, he'd insisted she rode him when they made love that first time, so she had the control to keep it from being painful for her.

Had sex, she mentally corrected, stopping the flashback before it really got started. *Making love is reserved for my soulmate, whom I'll one day marry. And Dion just proved that's not him, so obviously we weren't making love all those times I thought we were.*

~ ~ ~

"Oh, fuck, yes, Dion!" Jewel cried out as her tight pussy clamped down on Dion's cock as she came. She closed her eyes and threw her head back as the waves of her release washed over her while she rode him. She was the most beautiful woman he'd ever seen with her straight blonde hair falling just below her shoulders as her luscious red lips parted in orgasmic bliss. He wished she'd open her eyes once more, aching to see how the sapphire blue depths had transformed to stormy gray-blue skies in her aroused state. He took a mental picture of her face contorted in ecstasy, planning to draw it later, so he'd always

have that image to look back on, thinking she was the most beautiful woman he'd ever laid eyes on, especially as she came on his cock.

As her movements slowed with her coming down from her climactic high, Dion gripped her hips and bounced her up and down on his dick, not wanting her to stop moving as she recovered from the orgasm. He could feel his spine tingling to signal that he was getting close, so he focused on staring at his large ebony hands on her ivory skin, instead of looking up at her perky little tits or down where his big, black dick filled her tight, pink pussy, trying desperately to hold back his climax until he gave her at least one more.

"Gimme one more, Jewel," Dion commanded as he fucked up into her creamy cunt. "I'll fill you up with my cum just as soon as you gimme one more."

"Yes, Dion, yes!" Jewel screamed, digging her short, unpainted fingernails into his chest as she caught her breath and started to move with him once more. "Come with me!"

Beep. Beep. Beep.

The incessant sound of something beeping brought Dion out of the dream just before he reached his release, causing him to mentally groan as he struggled to open his eyes to find the noise that felt like it was splitting his head in two.

"Turn off the alarm," he tried to mumble, unable to make his mouth work any more than he'd been able to open his eyes. When no sound came out, he attempted to lift his arms, wanting to reach for the phone, or whatever it was beside him that wouldn't stop beeping. Unfortunately, he couldn't move. No matter how hard he felt like he was trying, he just laid there completely paralyzed.

Where the fuck am I? Dion wondered, confused by not being able to move or speak, even though he felt like he was waking up. *And where did Jewel go?*

Dion realized he heard voices, but he couldn't understand what was being said around him as he floated in the strangest state of semi-consciousness he'd ever experienced. He couldn't tell if he was actually waking up or still dreaming. *If I'm dreaming, I wanna go back to dreaming about Jewel. I don't know who the fuck she is, but I was having a whole lot more fun with her than I am now with this pounding headache.*

Aw, hell. Can blue balls cause a headache like this? If so, then I really need to find that blonde-haired, blue-eyed nymph to come finish that ride.

Unfortunately, trying to force himself back into the dream didn't work, only serving to make him feel like he was waking up a little more. After a few minutes, which seemed like at least an hour to Dion, the voices around him started to sound clearer.

"We won't know the extent of your brother's injuries until he wakes up and stays awake, even if he doesn't remember the other times he's woken up so far today." Dion didn't recognize the voice.

"But you said the bullet just grazed him." Dion did recognize his brother's voice, prompting him to try to open his eyes again.

What's Darius doin' here? He's supposed to be back in NOLA, not here in New York. And why's he talkin' about a bullet grazing me? I don't hang out with idiots who carry guns. So, if I'm injured, it had to be a botched move in the ring, not from being shot.

"Dare?" Dion choked the nickname out as he finally got his eyes to open.

"Hey, D, welcome back." Darius smiled, leaning over the bed Dion was lying on and blocking out the bright light overhead. "Man, you scared the hell outta me."

As Dion looked around, he realized he was in a hospital room and the other voice he'd heard was a man in a lab coat, standing on the other side of the bed from Darius. *He must be my...* Dion's thought trailed off as the word for the person taking care of him in the hospital escaped him at the moment. *Fuck, what's the word?*

"Mr. Davis, do you know where you are?" Lab coat man pulled out a flashlight that looked like a pen and shined it in Dion's eyes, holding them open when he tried to close them because the light made his head hurt worse.

"In a hospital?" Dion replied hoarsely, pretty sure he was right. "What happened? Did I botch a move in my match tonight?"

Dion thought he was supposed to have worked a try-out match with the local talent in New York that night, but since he couldn't remember the match, he wasn't about to blame his injuries on the new kid, who was more likely to have botched the move.

"You didn't have a match tonight, D," Darius informed him, shaking his head.

"Yeah, I did," Dion objected, knowing his brother didn't know his wrestling schedule. "Rick asked me to evaluate the local talent in a try-out match at the house show in Madison Square Garden to see if he's someone we want to add to the roster. I can't remember his name, but he's using a mafioso gimmick."

"Mr. Davis, do you know what city you're in?" Lab coat man released Dion's face as he turned off the flashlight.

"New York," Dion answered.

"No, D. We're in NOLA." Darius surprised him by telling him he was in his hometown.

"No, that's not right." Dion lifted his hand to his head, feeling a bandage he hadn't expected.

"What day is it?" Lab coat man was really starting to get on Dion's nerves with all the stupid questions.

"I, uh, I don't know," Dion admitted, his head starting to pound even harder.

"Do you know what year it is?"

"Um, twenty-seventeen?" *Yeah, that's gotta be right, 'cause we just celebrated New Year's.*

The concerned look on his brother's face told Dion that he was wrong once again. *Fuck! Now I really wanna go back to sleep and dream about Jewel.* Instead, he looked around the room, saw a whiteboard with the date "Saturday, October 26, 2019" written on it, and realized just how far off he was in his estimate for the year. He closed his eyes as the people around him continued talking some nonsense he couldn't really comprehend about how he'd been shot and hit his head while rescuing one of the women wrestlers from a stalker. Dion let their words go in one ear and out the other, trying desperately to go back to sleep to get his head to stop pounding.

Unfortunately, sleep was elusive as the nurses and lab coat man poked, prodded, and tested him six ways to Sunday. *Damn it! Why can't I remember what his job is called?*

Fuck! For that matter, why can't I remember what happened to me? Or the last few years of my life?

After the worst case of dizziness when he tried to stand from the bed to get in the wheelchair for them to take him for another test now that he seemed to be staying awake, Dion was glad they planned to wheel him up to the ICU room they decided to move him to while he was still lying in the bed. The world still felt like it was going to spin out from under him as they moved him through the hospital. But at least he knew he wouldn't fall if the vertigo got so bad that he actually passed out.

Damn, maybe if I do pass out, I'll dream about that hot blonde again.

Chapter Two

Sunday, October 27, 2019

Dion didn't feel much better the next morning when his brother got to his room. The Tylenol the nurse gave him for his headache hadn't done much good. Closing the curtains and turning off the lights seemed to help more than anything for the throbbing pain. Because they kept waking him up every couple of hours to make sure he still remembered where he was, the doctor hadn't wanted to give him any narcotic pain killers that might knock him out. And because of his brain injury, he didn't want to give him any of the other over-the-counter pain relievers that might increase bleeding in the brain. *Or was that bleeding from the two places they had to stitch up my head?*

Either way, Dion was just glad he'd finally been able to start calling the guy in the white coat "doctor," instead of continuing to call him "lab coat man" in his head. The nurse had told him that losing words like that wasn't uncommon after a head injury, and that the forgetfulness for things like that would most likely revert back to normal in a week or two. Unfortunately, they couldn't tell him if he'd ever remember the events of his life that had been knocked out of his brain. Or if the dreams he was having were just dreams, or actually his memories trying to come back to him.

Hopefully, the doctor will have a better idea of whether or not I'll get my memories back when he gets here this morning.

"Are you even listening to me, D?" Darius waved a hand in front of Dion's face to get his attention.

"Yeah, sorry," Dion apologized, hating the way he seemed to zone out and miss most of the conversations going on around him since he woke up the day before in the emergency room. "I completely missed what you were saying."

"Yeah, I figured as much with the way your eyes were all glazed over," Dare chuckled as he leaned back in the chair beside the bed. "I was apologizing for being an ass the last year or so."

"Dude, you've been an ass all our lives," Dion smirked, joking with his brother. "Are you telling me that it got worse in the last year or so, and I don't remember it?"

"Damn, D," Dare groaned, shaking his head as his lips turned up in the slightest smile. "I've been feeling guilty as fuck all night for not apologizing as soon as I saw you yesterday. And now you're tellin' me that I don't hafta bother 'cause you don't even remember our fight last year on my thirtieth birthday?"

"Hell, Dare, I barely remember my thirtieth birthday," Dion admitted with a half-shrug as he pointed to the information board on the wall that the new nurse filled out when they changed shifts. "And if the date on that board is right, I'm missing memories for my thirty-first, thirty-second, and thirty-third birthdays. So, you're gonna hafta catch me up on a lot more than just what happened at your birthday party last year."

"Fuck, D, is the amnesia really that bad?" Dare looked worried. Unfortunately, Dion didn't know how to ease his brother's fear when he was just as concerned.

"Yeah," Dion nodded, then immediately wished he hadn't because the movement caused the room to spin. *Maybe I should ask the nurse about more of that other medicine to help with the dizziness?* "When I woke up yesterday, I seriously thought it was January of twenty-seventeen. I remember that New Year's party, and then having a house show in New York the first day back on tour. And then nothing until yesterday."

"You've been doing exactly what the doctor told you not to do, haven't you?" Darius shook his head at Dion. "They said not to try to force the memories, D. You're not gonna get better if you don't follow their instructions."

"What else am I supposed to do when I'm not allowed to turn on the TV, or even look at my phone, and they won't let me sleep?" Dion glared at his brother. "And I wasn't trying to force memories. I was trying to figure out if the hot blonde I was dreaming about banging when I woke up yesterday was a memory trying to come back to me, or just my dream girl. And hoping thinking about her would lead to more dreams about her when they finally let me sleep."

"How'd that work out for ya?" Dare chuckled.

"Well enough, I guess," Dion half-shrugged, not wanting to move too much and risk another bout of vertigo. "She's been in every dream I remember having so far. Unfortunately, I don't remember actually getting to finish the best part of the dreams."

"Damn, D, I don't wanna know about your wet dreams," Darius cringed, his whole body shuddering.

"Then tell me what we fought about, so I can decide if I forgive you or not," Dion suggested for a subject change, knowing that if he laughed at his brother's reaction, the way he wanted to right then because of how ridiculous Dare was acting, it would just worsen his headache.

"Charlene," Dare sighed, dropping his chin to his chest, like he didn't want to make eye contact with Dion.

Dion tried to remember the name, but just like everything else for the last couple of years, he was drawing a blank. "I don't remember anyone named Charlene."

"She was the waitress I'd started dating last summer," Darius explained, finally lifting his head to look back up at Dion in the hospital bed. "I thought she could be the future Mrs. Darius Davis, until I got to the party, where I planned to introduce her to my big brother, and found her hitting on you."

It was Dion's turn to cringe. He didn't remember the incident, but he knew he'd have never let it get that far if he'd known she was Dare's girlfriend. "Please tell me you'd at least shown me a picture of her before then, so I wouldn't have reciprocated the flirtation."

"No, why the fuck would I think I'd need to call dibs before my laid-back brother would make a move on my woman?" Dare shook his head as his shoulders slumped. "Granted, it was obvious that she was the aggressor, and you were just wasting time while waiting on me to get there. But I still got pissed that she chose you over me, so I acted like a bitch and haven't spoken to you since."

"Until yesterday?" Dion couldn't believe that his brother had been so far gone for a woman that they'd stopped speaking to each other over her. And that the silence between them had lasted for over a year.

"Until yesterday," Darius nodded. "When the cop called and said you'd been shot, I realized what an ass I was being, especially since you were just talking to her and hadn't done anything wrong."

"And I didn't reach out to you in the last year to fix things between us?" *Why the hell would I ignore my brother like that?*

"Oh, you called and texted like crazy that weekend when you were in town for the rest of your Labor Day break," Darius snickered. "It was so fucking annoying that I blocked your number for a week or two. When you didn't reach out a month later, when I knew you had a show in town, I figured we'd talk it out when you came home for Thanksgiving. And then you didn't show. Same with Christmas. Hell, you haven't been home for one of your holiday breaks in over a year. And I was too stubborn to reach out to you, when I knew you were in town for GWA shows and staying in the hotel with the other wrestlers, instead of crashing at home."

"Where the hell did I go for my holiday breaks if I didn't come home?"

"Don't ask me." Dare held his hands up and shook his head. "Even Mama Marcel couldn't tell me where you were."

I didn't reach out to Mama Marcel either? What the fuck? There's no way I woulda cut off communication with Mama Marcel because of some bullshit with Dare and whoever he was banging.

Caroline Marcel was their neighbor when they were growing up and had been best friends with their mom before she passed. When they lost their mom, she watched over them from her place next door, and told the school she was their guardian whenever they had to have parent-teacher conferences or permission slips signed. She took care of the guys as if they were her natural sons, instead of just the kids of a former friend. While the boys worked every odd job they could find, Caroline provided the biggest chunk of their living by setting up as a fortune teller in Jackson Square.

A couple of years after that, when Hurricane Katrina hit, she took then nineteen-year-old Dion and sixteen-year-old Darius with her during the evacuation to keep Dare from going into foster care. They started calling her Mama Marcel while they all lived together as a family during the recovery from the storm.

After the city started to come back to life, and once Dion got his break in the wrestling business, he repaid her for taking care of them when they were younger by purchasing a building in the residential area of the French Quarter for them to move back to NOLA. They converted each of the three floors in the historic building into separate condos for the three of them. It was his way to keep their found family together, even though he didn't live there with Dare and Mama Marcel most of the time because of his schedule with the GWA.

While he made more than enough money now to provide for her throughout her retirement years, Mama Marcel still insisted on spending her days telling the futures of tourists in Jackson Square. Dion didn't believe she was psychic in any way, but Darius still let her give him readings at least once a month. Or at least, he did as far as Dion could remember.

"Where is Mama Marcel?" Dion was surprised she wasn't there with Darius.

"Home making a voodoo doll of the security guard who wouldn't let her in to see you last night," Dare chuckled. "And probably getting with her friends to try to figure out how to con her way in here today."

"Why would she have to con her way in?" Dion was confused about why Darius was the only person to visit him in the hospital. *Surely, Rick and half the guys in the GWA woulda come by to see me by now.*

"Because the hospital only allows family members in the emergency room and ICU," Darius explained. "That's why the entire GWA clogged up the ER waiting room yesterday, until I told them I have your phone to be able to send them updates."

Okay, so that's why none of the guys have been by.

"But doesn't Mama Marcel still have that paperwork we made up when Mama died, showing she's our legal guardian? That should get her past that family only rule."

"Apparently, that was only good until we turned eighteen," Dare elaborated with a little shrug. "Now we're gonna hafta look into an adult adoption for us to be considered family. Which we should probably do since Mama Marcel is old enough that she's gonna start having medical issues soon."

"While you've got my phone, call the lawyer and get him started on that," Dion agreed, not sure if it could be done in time for her to be able to visit him while he was in the hospital or not. "Even if it won't be fast enough for her to come see me while I'm in here for another day or two, I don't wanna take a chance on not being able to see her should the worst happen, like with Mama."

Dion and Darius were both teenagers when their mother was hit by a drunk driver and the Black boys had to have Mama Marcel vouch for them being the sons of the white woman in the hospital before they were allowed to see her to say goodbye before she passed. Now that he thought about it, Dion remembered something about her having to show their birth certificates, which listed their races along with the races of their parents, to prove they were not only related, but also that Dare was old enough for the twelve-year-old age cutoff for visitors in the ICU way back then.

"I'll call him first thing in the morning," Darius agreed, just as the door opened and the doctor walked into the room.

"Good morning, Mr. Davis." Dion didn't recognize the new doctor, assuming the doctor who'd treated him in the ER the day before had passed him off to a specialist now that he was in the ICU. He introduced himself, but said his name so fast that Dion didn't comprehend it. "How are you feeling this morning?"

"Not great, Doc," Dion admitted, using the same moniker for the doctor that everyone used for the staff doctor and athletic trainer who worked for the GWA. "The headache isn't really going away and the room spins every time I move my head."

"Yes, the nurse mentioned the headache was why they dimmed the lights in here," the doctor confirmed as he looked at the tablet he held, which Dion assumed showed his chart, so the doctor could catch up on his case. "Any nausea or vomiting?"

"Nausea," Dion confessed. "But luckily I haven't actually vomited, even though I felt close to it a couple of times when I tried rolling over last night."

"Okay, we'll get you something for the nausea and dizziness." The doctor tapped a stylus on the tablet, apparently putting in the medication orders right then. At least, Dion hoped that was what he was doing. "And we'll try a different pain killer, since your scans appear to be clear. Have you had any memories come back since last night?"

"No, not really," Dion sighed, wondering if his dreams were memories he should be telling the doctor about. "I've been dreaming about a girl, though. I don't know if she's someone I met in the last couple of years, or just a figment of my imagination."

"Most likely, you're just dreaming." The doctor shook his head as he looked up from the tablet to make eye contact with Dion. "With post-traumatic retrograde amnesia, your oldest memories might come back, but not until the other symptoms start clearing up. Typically, they'll be triggered to come back by being in certain places, or smelling something associated with them, or possibly even hearing about them. But they won't typically come back in your dreams like that. That's not to say that they can't come back that way, just that it's not likely, especially this soon in your recovery. It'll probably take a couple of weeks of letting your brain rest and recover before talking about past events will help you start to get a few of those memories back. And even then, you'll probably never remember the actual events leading up to your injury."

The doctor went on to tell them the plans for his recovery, including keeping him in the hospital for a few days, while they tried out some different medications for his symptoms, and did follow-up scans of his brain. The only good news Dion heard and comprehended in the whole spiel was that he'd get to sleep a little longer than he had the night before.

Maybe I'll get to finish fucking Jewel tonight, even if it's only a dream and not the memory I want it to be.

<div align="center">~~~</div>

Late that night, Dion gave up his attempts to fall asleep, adjusting his bed so he was lying there like in a recliner instead of lying flat, hoping the different position would ease his headache. Since he wasn't allowed any screen time, he was bored out of his mind after his brother left to check in at the club, Xavier's, which they co-owned and Dare managed, and they'd named after their father. But after taking several naps throughout the day, even boredom wasn't enough to help him fall asleep.

Too bad none of the guys can come up here to fill me in on how the show went tonight. Or better yet, recognize my description of Jewel to tell me if she's someone I've been hooking up with recently.

28

Just that brief thought about Jewel was enough to push him to close his eyes and try again to conjure her image in his mind. *Since all the sex dreams I've been having starring her appear to have happened in hotel rooms, maybe she's one of the new women's division wrestlers that have recently joined the GWA? Or maybe a ring rat I've hooked up with more than once, whenever we're working in a city close to where she lives?*

Just as he almost had her naked in his mind's eye, he heard footsteps and the door to his room opening. He opened his eyes just in time to see Dean Dangerous walk into the room with a woman, who launched herself at Dion. Thankfully, the concussion he'd been told he had wasn't bad enough to slow his reflexes completely, so he was able to sit up and catch her as she threw her arms around him and sobbed.

"Jewel?" Dion momentarily thought she might have found him, only to realize a second later that the long brown hair on this woman didn't match the blonde locks of his dream girl. "You're not Jewel."

"Oh, Dion, I'm so glad you're gonna be okay," the woman he didn't recognize wept on Dion's shoulder.

"Yeah, sweetheart, I'm fine." Dion awkwardly patted the woman's back before looking up at Dean and mouthing, "Who is this?"

"Allissa, Darlin', why don't you give Dion a little breathing room?" Dean pulled a chair over for the woman, apparently named Allissa, to sit beside Dion's bed. Once she was settled, Dean wiped her tears from her cheeks before turning to Dion. "The doc said you have amnesia after yesterday. What's the last thing you remember?"

Dion absentmindedly reached up to touch the bandage around his head with the hand that wasn't attached to his I-V, trying to remember what he thought was his last memory before the incident when he'd been injured. He wasn't sure exactly when it was, but he thought it was sometime after the New York show he'd thought he'd been working when he woke up the day before. "Talking to Rick about teaming up with Red because we lost another tag team to retirement, but I can't tell you who retired."

"Wow, that was like two years ago," Dean pointed out, shaking his head. "So that's why you don't remember Allissa joining the roster last year."

Allissa gasped and covered her mouth, obviously surprised to realize that Dion didn't remember ever meeting her. "I thought the doctor just meant that you don't remember what happened yesterday. How am I supposed to thank you for saving my life when you don't even remember who I am?"

So, she's the wrestler I supposedly helped rescue from a stalker yesterday?

Dean rubbed a hand over Allissa's back to comfort her as Dion reached out with his free hand to take her hand to do the same. He didn't have to know how friendly they'd been in the past to want to reassure her that she was safe and he had no hard feelings about being hurt while helping to keep her that way.

"I don't have to remember you or what happened to appreciate you coming up here to see me. And the doctor seems to think my memory might come back once the headaches ease up and I'm cleared to wrestle again."

"Yeah? How long does he think that'll take?" Dean lifted his chin in curiosity as he voiced the question that Dion wasn't quite sure how to answer.

Dion took a moment to try to remember the treatment plan he'd had to ask Dare to repeat for him a few times earlier in the day. "He wants me to rest for a little while, with no screen time or strenuous activity, for at least a couple of weeks. I'm not really injured enough to need to be in the ICU. They just kept me here to keep the press out of my room while I have to stay for observation for a couple of days." Dion smirked before continuing. "With the GWA having to fly out on Monday and Darius having to work, the doc didn't trust the ring rats who tried to sneak in earlier to follow the concussion protocol."

"Yeah, I imagine not," Dean chuckled, a knowing smile spreading across his face. "Any chance you'll feel up to being in our wedding next month? Or should we plan it farther out to make sure you're all healed up?"

Dion arched an eyebrow at Dean mentioning a wedding, looking back and forth between Dean and Allissa as he realized his former player friend had apparently fallen hard and fast for their new coworker. When he noticed the impressive rock on Allissa's left ring finger, he smirked up at Dean. He desperately wanted to rib his friend about his status as a reformed player, but he wouldn't do it in front of his fiancée.

"I'll definitely be healed up enough to make it to your wedding in a month," Dion assured them, assuming the doctor was right in his timeline for healing from the concussion. "I might need you to come pick me up and drive me there if the doctor doesn't clear me to fly by then. But hopefully, the headaches and dizzy spells will have cleared up enough by then that I can stand up with you for the service."

"I was actually hoping you'd walk me down the aisle." Allissa shocked the shit out of Dion with her declaration. "I know you're way too young to step into the father-of-the-bride role, but since you stepped up and protected me from the man who might be my biological father, it seemed kinda fitting. And you can sit down as soon as we get to the altar, so it won't be too much if you're still having concussion symptoms."

"I would be honored to walk you down the aisle," Dion smiled at Allissa, as humbled by her request as he was confused by the statement about her biological father. He knew he didn't have it in him right then to try to understand any further explanation from her though, so he skipped over asking about the confusing parts of her statement and focused on what he might need to be able to accommodate her request if his injuries weren't completely cleared up in time for the wedding in a month. "And it might be a good idea to be able to sit down through the service, in case the doc's wrong about me being back to normal in a month or so."

"That's how long he said it would take you to heal?"

"Yeah, two weeks of dark rooms and rest, and then two weeks of starting to get up and around with light activity," Dion confirmed, hoping he remembered the info correctly. "Then I'll have to see him to be cleared to fly and increase my activity level."

"Since you remember all that, I'm guessing you remember what's happened since you woke up." Dion tucked his chin in a half-nod, not really sure he remembered everything, since he'd been told he'd woken up several times the day before, asking the same questions multiple times before he finally stayed awake long enough to attempt an ImPACT test, even though he bombed it compared to his baseline test, which was on file with the GWA. "What about your older memories? Have any of them started coming back?"

"Some. Everything's coming in flashes, not like normal memories," Dion explained, looking from Allissa up to Dean, thinking his friend might be able to help fill in a few blanks his brother hadn't been able to help him with since he didn't travel with the GWA. "Darius has been helping me figure out when things really happened, but he can only help with the stuff from before I started with the GWA. Maybe you can help me with the stuff he doesn't know about?"

"Of course," Dean agreed, nodding at Dion. "I'm happy to help as much as I can. What's the first thing you wanna know?"

"There's a woman." Dion looked at Allissa and gave her a slight smile before shaking his head, not believing he'd momentarily mistaken her for his Jewel. "She's about the same size as you, but maybe a little thicker. She's got blonde hair and the brightest blue eyes. Looking into her eyes is like looking at the water in the Caribbean."

"Okay…" Dean drawled out the word in his slow Texas twang. "Jen and Julie Burleson both have blonde hair and blue eyes. Do you remember one of them?"

"No, the only Burleson I know is your friend, the pilot." Dion shook his head before clutching it, the movement causing him more pain and making trying to remember even harder, even the stuff he hadn't lost with the amnesia.

"Yeah, he got married last year, and you came to the wedding," Dean tried reminding Dion, but his head hurt too bad for his friend's words to trigger any memories. "You met Jen and Julie and the rest of the Burlesons then. And every time you're in town for a wedding or holiday, the matchmaking mommas in town seat you with them. Is that possibly where you remember her from?"

"No, her name is Jewel, not Julie," Dion disagreed, feeling frustrated by the pounding headache that made it impossible for him to know if Dean was identifying the right woman or not. "And the memories aren't from weddings or holiday celebrations. They're in different hotel rooms. It's like she's visited me on tour or something, but I can't figure out when or where. I just know she's my girl and I have to let her know what happened, so she can come here while I'm recovering."

"Dude, I haven't seen you meeting up with anyone at our hotels, not even ring rats in the last year or so." Dean looked over at Allissa, as if he was trying to determine if she'd seen Dion with anyone. She shook her head from side to side, which Dion assumed meant that she hadn't seen him hook up with anyone, either. "But I'll ask the guys tomorrow if they remember your girl."

"Yeah, thanks. Darius says I haven't mentioned her to him, either. Which makes me wonder why we're keeping our relationship a secret." Dion closed his eyes and hung his head with a sigh of frustration before looking back up at Dean and Allissa. "Hell, it makes me wonder if she's even real. Or if I'm more brain-damaged than the doc thinks and have completely made her up in my head?"

"I'm sure she's real," Dean asserted, obviously trying to be reassuring. "But maybe you're doin' like Anthony did before he met Kay, and dreamin' about your soulmate before you meet her."

Dion didn't remember Dean's pilot friend talking about dreams like that, but he also didn't remember much more than briefly meeting the man. Growing up in NOLA though, he'd heard plenty of stories about people having prophetic dreams, as well as all the hoodoo Mama Marcel spouted off about having *the sight*, so he wouldn't be surprised if both he and Dean's friend Anthony had visionary dreams about their soulmates.

"Fuck, if that's the case, then I hope my dreams about her come true just as soon as I get outta here," Dion groaned and leaned back on the bed, wishing his friend had been able to confirm Jewel's identity for him.

Dean didn't get the chance to say anything more before the nurse poked her head in the door and informed them their visitation time was up. Dean and Allissa each hugged Dion and promised to text Darius for updates on his condition and keep him in the loop on the wedding plans before they left for the night, leaving Dion to try once more to get some sleep.

Luckily for him, even though he only napped off and on all night like he had all day, Jewel was waiting for him in his dreams. *Too bad I can't stay lucid enough while I'm dreaming to get my dream girl to tell me where to find her.*

Chapter Three

After spending the last couple of days avoiding talking about Dion with everyone she knew, Julie wasn't as excited walking into the Heart's Destiny Clinic as she'd been when she set the appointment. Oh, she was still excited about finding out if she was pregnant, and looking forward to being a mom, regardless of whether or not her baby's father turned out to be Dion, or some nameless, faceless man she'd eventually meet and have a family with in the future. She just wasn't looking forward to the hard conversations she'd have to have with her family if her suspicions were correct and she was currently pregnant.

While she knew her family all loved her unconditionally and would be there for her to lean on during any difficult times she had, either during her pregnancy or while raising her baby on her own, she'd had more than enough of their pitying, sympathetic looks, since she'd broadcast the horrible way her relationship with Dion ended in front of her mom and Aunt Hazel, without ever mentioning that she'd officially been seeing him in the first place. And she knew if she was pregnant, then she'd be in for more and more of those looks as the rest of her friends and family found out about everything that had happened between them.

If only we'd just broken up a couple of months ago, so only Jen, Becky, Char, and Cait would know about my broken heart, Julie mused as she signed in and paid her co-pay. *But if that had happened, I wouldn't be here hoping to find out I'm about to be a mom. And I guess I can deal with a bunch of people pitying me, as long as I get to hold my baby in my arms in a few months. Getting to love my little one will make this hell on earth of heartbreak worth enduring.*

As she looked around the mostly empty waiting room, Julie was glad she'd scheduled the last appointment of the day. That was a trick she'd learned when she first started going to the gynecologist's office in San Antonio for her birth control. Julie had seen whichever OB-GYN was available before Dr. Devon Magnum joined the practice the year before. But after meeting the female physician, she chose to only see her from then on, even staying with Devon when the doctor moved her practice to Heart's Destiny, regardless of the new clinic location no longer being conveniently located near the Burleson Incorporated office for her to just miss an hour of work for appointments. Julie had seen how empty the waiting room was when she got there for the late appointments in San Antonio, and realized that it would probably be the same when she had to start seeing her gynecologist in the same clinic, where she'd seen Doc Hayes as her primary care physician for years. In the small town where she'd grown up, having an empty waiting room was the only way she'd ever have any privacy about why she was there.

Oh, she knew the doctors wouldn't ever share her private medical information. But being seen going into the obstetrics side of the practice by one of the town gossips in the waiting room would guarantee pregnancy rumors would spread all over town before she could make it to the pharmacy to fill her birth control prescription.

Yeah, I highly doubt Devon will be refilling that prescription this afternoon. Of course, Julie had already assumed that based on the fact that she'd been instructed to stop taking the pill when she scheduled this appointment and told them she thought she might be pregnant.

The fact that she'd been on birth control the whole time she'd been seeing Dion was the only reason she thought, maybe, her missing period could be stress related, instead of because she was pregnant. Though if she was really being honest with herself, she'd realize that the only exceptionally stressful situation in her life had occurred in the last two days — a week and a half after her period was due — so stress couldn't be the cause of her missing period.

Once Summer Deere had taken the last of Doc Hayes's patients back to his side of the clinic, Arden Snyder, Dr. Magnum's nurse, finally appeared at the door to the OB-GYN side of the clinic to call

Julie back. They went through the usual pleasantries, reviewed her medical information, and took her vitals before Arden instructed her to go fill a specimen cup with urine.

Julie knew the drill, having gone through the same procedures at each of her annual and birth control appointments for years. So she took care of business and washed her hands before going back to the exam room to wait for Dr. Magnum. As usual, within ten minutes, the doctor knocked on the door to announce herself before entering. What wasn't typical, however, was Arden following her in while pushing a phlebotomy cart.

"Congratulations!" Dr. Devon Magnum smiled as she greeted Julie. "Your urine test confirmed you're pregnant."

Julie was glad she was sitting down as the doctor explained that they would be doing a blood test to check her hCG levels to determine a more accurate due date. *I'm pregnant. Holy. Shit. I'm. Pregnant.*

Julie was numb with shock as she extended her arm for Arden to do the blood draw while Devon ran down a list of things Julie needed to limit or avoid while pregnant.

And Dumbass Dion is the father. No, I can't call him that. No matter how pissed off I am at him right now, he's still the father of my baby. And I don't want to risk my child overhearing me using profanity while referring to the man who provided half of his or her DNA.

I'll just call him Dirtbag Dion for now. And hopefully, by the time the kid is born, I'll be over the anger enough to just call him Dion again.

"For now, we can estimate your due date from the date you started your last period," the doctor informed her, interrupting her thoughts. "That was September seventeenth?"

"Yes, but it wasn't a normal period," Julie explained. "I just had some spotting that day and thought it was because of all the excitement in my family earlier in the month. My cousin got married ten days earlier, and my other cousin had his son, whom none of us knew about, crash the wedding. So, I thought maybe the craziness of the week before might have messed with my hormones or something to make it super light and only last a few hours the one day."

"When was your last normal period?" Dr. Magnum arched an eyebrow at Julie as she looked up from the tablet in her hands, displaying the notes Arden had put in Julie's chart at the beginning of the appointment.

"August twentieth," Julie replied. "And if the online calculators are correct for when my fertility windows were, I'm much more likely to have gotten pregnant the first week of September, when my boyfriend was in town, than I was the first week of October, when I was in Virginia for my cousin's hearing to get custody of his son." She'd also snuck in a night with Dion in Georgia on the thirteenth of October, when she could leave the hotel in Savannah after the GWA vacated the next morning to go to Macon to check on things with Ashbury Enterprises. But she didn't think they could conceive a baby in the two days right before her period was due to start, so she didn't mention that liaison to her doctor.

"Okay," Dr. Magnum nodded as she swiped over to a calendar app and looked at the dates. "It's a little earlier than I prefer to do the first ultrasound, but if you conceived at the beginning of September, then the baby should be about the size of a kumquat and we should be able to hear the heartbeat with a vaginal ultrasound."

A vaginal ultrasound? Like sticking a probe in my hoo-hah, instead of using that jelly stuff on my stomach that Kay, Brooklyn, Amy, and Char have all told me about during their pregnancies? Shit, I hope they use lots of lube. Because while both Arden and Devon are beautiful, neither one of them are my type to help me relax down there. So, I doubt I'll be able to chill enough for that to be any more comfortable than the speculum she uses for my annual exams.

"I'll go get it set up," Arden announced before pushing the phlebotomy cart out of the room.

Once they were alone in the room, Dr. Magnum continued. "If you didn't conceive until the end of September or beginning of October, then the baby should be about the size of a sweet pea and the heart might not be developed to the point where we can hear a heartbeat. Before we do the exam and ultrasound, I want to make sure you understand that not hearing a heartbeat today isn't a bad thing if it's that early in the pregnancy."

"Yes, I understand." Julie nodded, realizing that she was probably going to have to endure the speculum during this visit, too.

Leah Mae Wright

"Okay, then I'll step out and let you get undressed from the waist down," Dr. Magnum smiled as she handed Julie the paper sheet she'd need to cover herself with when she was ready for the exam.

Once the doctor left the room, Julie removed her slacks and panties and sat on the end of the table with the sheet covering her lower body. Dr. Magnum came back in with Arden following her and pushing a different medical cart with a monitor on top, which Julie assumed was the ultrasound machine. Dr. Magnum pulled out the stirrups from the table as Julie laid back and got into the right position to put her feet in them. Then the doctor moved another tray of instruments out from behind the curtain between the door and the exam table to use for the exam.

Yep, speculum time. Only this time, it'll be followed up with an ultrasound dildo.

Julie tried to relax as the doctor did the exam, closing her eyes, and imagining it was Dion touching her instead of the doctor. It was probably completely inappropriate to fantasize about her baby daddy right then, but she had to do something because that little dollop of lube on the speculum just wasn't enough to allow it to slide in easily. And even though she was pissed as hell at him right then, Dion was still the only man she could think of, who actually aroused her enough to get off while using her vibrator, so he had to be the one she thought of right then, too.

She tried to picture one of the many nights they'd met up in a hotel room over the last eleven months, remembering fondly how gentle he always was for their first round after not seeing each other for a few weeks. Dion was well endowed, so he always fingered her or ate her out first, making sure she was relaxed enough to take his big dick without any pain. His first strokes in would be slow and sensual, easing inside her until he was balls-deep. Then he'd hold still to allow her to adjust to his sizable invasion before picking up the pace. Once he was sure she could take all of him, he'd start pounding into her, while swiveling his hips in just the right way to alternate between stimulating her G-spot, tapping her cervix, and applying pressure to her clit with his pubic bone.

Damn, I'm going to miss how fast he could make me come when he did that, she thought, suddenly realizing what a bad idea it was to think about having an orgasm while her doctor had a speculum in her vagina. Though thinking about her breakup with Dion at that moment probably wasn't any better.

No, don't think about him at all! Thinking about Dion is a surefire way to have this exam go wrong, either because I'll get so angry that I'll dry up, or because I'll work myself up into having a little O from the speculum.

Julie opened her eyes to stop any possible Dion fantasies, as Devon dictated her notes to Arden to add to Julie's chart while she finished the exam. When that was done and the speculum was removed, Arden handed Devon a condom covered probe to start the ultrasound.

Oh, yeah, that won't be so bad. Julie stifled a chuckle when she saw the ultrasound probe. *It's barely as big as my first vibrator and like half the size of Dion's dick. So maybe it won't matter that I'm not aroused to loosen up enough for it to fit.*

"That is latex free, right?" Julie double checked, not wanting to break out in a rash if they used a regular latex condom.

"Yes, polyurethane," Devon confirmed, smiling. "With so many people having latex allergies, we've had to go completely latex free in gloves, bandages, and everything else we use in the practice."

As one of those patients who was allergic to latex, Julie was grateful they'd made that switch, so she wouldn't have to worry about asking about it during any of the other procedures she was sure she'd have to endure over the course of her pregnancy, as well as during labor and delivery.

As the doctor held the probe, the nurse opened a small packet of goo that was different from the lube they used for the typical vaginal exam. That's when Julie realized that the gel they used for ultrasounds was essential for more than just allowing the probe to glide across the skin.

I wonder if the ultrasound gel works better or worse than lube for getting that wand to slide in?

She didn't have to wonder for long as Dr. Magnum moved back between her legs to insert the probe.

I'm gonna say better, but it could be because the wand is smaller than the speculum. Or at least, it doesn't crank open like the speculum, which is when it actually gets painful.

Julie turned her head to look at the monitor as Arden fiddled with the mouse and hit a couple of buttons on the keyboard while Devon probed her.

Geez, this feels weird. Like it's a little sexually arousing, but it's also not. Though I suppose it could be more arousing if I were a lesbian. Or had a really hot man as my OB-GYN.

Oh, Gawd. How do women keep from coming if they have a hot OB-GYN they're attracted to doing these exams?

Before Julie could contemplate the scenarios running through her head, the quiet conversation between Devon and Arden permeated her brain. She didn't completely understand all the medical jargon and measurements, but she did understand "separate gestational sacs" and "two placentas" to figure out she was having twins without the doctor specifically having to spell it out for her.

"It looks like both babies were conceived on or around September third," Devon stated with a smile. "Making you ten weeks along as of tomorrow and giving you a due date of May twenty-sixth. But with twins, they could come as early as April twenty-eighth."

"I guess it's not really surprising that I'm carrying twins, since I'm a twin," Julie sighed, trying to figure out where her babies were on the screen. "Hey, since Halloween is coming up in a few days, can you label them as Thing One and Thing Two on the pictures for me to show my family?"

"No, they're babies, not things. They will be labeled as Baby A and Baby B," Devon informed her, not seeming to get Julie's sense of humor.

"Oh, I know they're not things," Julie tried to explain, glad to see that Arden was at least smiling at her silly idea. "I was referring to the characters from **The Cat in the Hat**, thinking the labels could be like their first Halloween costumes."

The doctor looked at her like she'd lost her mind.

"Never mind." Julie waved off Devon's tendency to always be serious and take things literally, knowing it was just a difference in their personalities and not a big deal.

Once the subject was dropped, Arden adjusted something on the machine and the whooshing sounds of her babies' heartbeats filled the room. Devon moved the wand inside Julie, isolating each baby's heartbeat and telling her which one was Baby A and which one was Baby B.

Hearing those little heartbeats suddenly made everything even more real for Julie than even seeing the grainy black-and-white images of her babies on the screen. *Oh, wow! They're really in there.* Julie wiped her eyes before the tears could fall.

Once they finished the ultrasound, they quickly wrapped up the appointment, with Dr. Magnum explaining how she was ten weeks along, even though her babies were only conceived eight weeks ago. Then Arden printed off several pictures from the ultrasound for her before they left the room for Julie to get dressed. As she checked out and scheduled her next appointment, they gave her an insulated bottle bag filled with samples of baby supplies and literature for her to read over later.

They scheduled her next appointment for Wednesday, December fourth, when she'd officially be fifteen weeks and one day along in her pregnancy. Arden informed her that they typically preferred to schedule the appointments every four weeks at this point in a twin pregnancy, but four weeks for her would put the appointment in the middle of the week of Thanksgiving, which was already overbooked because of the holiday making it a three-day week for their office. So, they had to move it out to five weeks instead. And since they'd already filled all the Tuesday time slots for the first week of December, they pushed it to Wednesday, which actually worked out better for her because of Tuesday the third being Brody's birthday. Since it would be his first birthday party as part of the Burleson family, as well as the anniversary of his mother's death, Julie didn't want to risk being late to the party if her appointment ran long or she got stuck waiting at the pharmacy for any reason.

Arden also informed her that if they scheduled her appointments far enough in advance, they'd prefer to schedule them all on Tuesdays, since her date of conception was a Tuesday, making it the day each week when she'd officially change how many weeks along she was in the pregnancy. So Julie had asked to go ahead and schedule her January appointment as well.

We can schedule February, March, and April when I come in next month after I get my new planner to write them in for next year. I'll just jot the one for January down on the twenty-twenty calendar at the front of my twenty-nineteen planner for now, and I can transfer it when I get the new planner sometime between now and then.

When looking at the calendar to schedule the next month's appointment, they opted to go with five weeks again. That kept her from having two appointments in the month of December, as would have happened if they scheduled it for New Year's Eve, and also put her January seventh appointment on the day she was twenty weeks along to be able to schedule the next ultrasound.

Oh, wow, that'll be the halfway mark. But then again, if I'm ten weeks along tomorrow, I guess I'm already a quarter of the way through this pregnancy. Talk about time flying.

As she got in her car to drive to the pharmacy to put in her prenatal vitamin prescription, Julie went back through the dates Dr. Magnum mentioned in her head. *My babies are due May twenty-sixth, but could come as early as April twenty-eighth. Oh wow, I could have my twins on my and my twin's birthday.*

And they were most likely conceived on Tuesday, September third. The day after Labor Day. Oh, yeah, that was the day Dion met me in San Antonio and we went to that hotel for lunch, and for him to do the re-do of saying "I love you" to make it more romantic than the first time. Oh yeah, they were definitely conceived that day. As many times as we fucked that afternoon and then all night, it was kinda inevitable.

Julie couldn't stop herself from thinking back on the day she'd skipped her afternoon of work to christen every flat surface in that hotel suite with Dion. With the way he'd pulled out all the romantic gestures to make up for not being romantic when he said "I love you" the first time the night before, she couldn't stop thinking of her babies as being conceived in love, even if he didn't seem to want to be a father now. And even though her most recent memories of talking with Dion were heartbreaking, she would always cherish the memories of how they'd made their babies.

He made me feel so loved that day, and not just because of saying it so many times. Between the rose petals scattered on the bed, the sensual massages we gave each other, and the decadent treats of champagne and chocolate-covered strawberries, it felt more like Valentine's Day or a special anniversary than just a random Tuesday...

~~~

"Oh, Dion, you didn't have to do all this," Jewel cooed, looking around the room at the things he'd set up before she got there. "It's not some special day that I've forgotten, is it?"

"No, Jewel," Dion smiled at the awestruck blonde as she picked up a chocolate-covered strawberry and held it up for him to taste first. "Just my way of showing you how much I love you."

"You're spoiling me," Jewel beamed as Dion took a bite of the strawberry she held up to his mouth. "But I love you, too, so I'm gonna let you spoil me as much as you want."

Once he had half of the plump ripe berry in his mouth, Jewel popped the other half in her mouth. They each quickly chewed and swallowed, preferring to taste one another to the chocolate-covered fruit.

Dion pulled Jewel into his arms, placing her hand over his heart before dipping his head for a claiming kiss, as she pushed up on her toes to meet his lips with hers. Jewel wound her arms around his neck, as he plundered her mouth with his tongue, enjoying the taste of the tart strawberry mixed with a sweetness that he knew was pure Jewel.

Suddenly, their clothing was gone, and he was eating the strawberries off her nipples before pouring the champagne on her soft, mostly flat midsection before licking it off. After she took a turn eating and drinking from his body, the scene morphed again to him massaging her perky little tits with a tingly oil while stretching her sweet pussy with his big dick. He took his time, telling her how beautiful she was and how much he loved her as he slowly pushed his way into her tight channel, holding still for a moment after each inch he worked inside her to allow her to relax a little more to be able to take the next inch easier.

It seemed like it took forever before he bottomed out inside her soaking wet slit, but his gentle patience was rewarded with the exquisite feel of her pussy fitting his cock like a glove. He barely sped things up as he pulled out and pushed back inside her, wanting to truly make love to her the way his Jewel deserved, until her inner walls clamped down on his cock like a vise and milked him of his cum.
~~~

Next, he had her bent over the table between the half-empty tray of chocolate-covered strawberries and the tray containing two empty champagne flutes and a half-full bottle of Cristal. Dion plowed into her from behind while gripping her firm, heart-shaped ass in his large hands, loving the feel of her tight cunt choking his cock almost as much as he loved her.

"Fuck, I love you, Jewel," Dion roared as he thrust in deep, unable to stop himself from practically screaming his feelings for her as the tip of his dick hit her cervix.

"I love you, too, Dion," Jewel cried out as she pushed back against him, trying to take him even deeper, just as her inner walls started to convulse with her climax.

Hearing her say those words was Dion's undoing. He couldn't hold back his release a second longer, especially with her tight little pussy milking his cum from his cock once more. He plunged into her creamy cunt as far as possible, one last time, shooting his load straight into her womb.

Before the aftershocks wore off, the scene transformed once more, moving them to the shower. Dion stood, bracing himself with his arms on the wall, with Jewel on her knees, sucking his dick.

"Oh, fuck, Jewel," Dion groaned as she took him as far back in her throat as she could without gagging. She applied the perfect amount of suction as she pulled back, stopping with just the head of his cock in her mouth to stroke his shaft with her hands.

He loved the sight of her red lips and delicate, lightly tanned hands wrapped around his big, black cock, as she gave him the best blow job of his life. But it was the way she looked up at him with her heavenly blue eyes darkening to the shade of a stormy sky from being aroused by the act of servicing him that pushed him over the edge until he came down her willing throat.

His little nymph swallowed every drop, licking him clean before standing to allow him the honor of returning the favor. Dion dropped to the floor of the shower, pushing her back against the wall so he could lift one of her legs over his shoulder to open her up for him.

With their height difference, he couldn't stay on his knees like she had to suck him off. Even sitting all the way down on the floor, he still had to bend his head down to be able to lick her sweet, smooth pussy. He swiped his tongue through her slit before moving to swirl the tip around her clit while inserting a finger, then two, into her tight, wet cunt.

"Oh, yes, Dion," Jewel moaned, as he lapped up her juices and sucked lightly on her clit while finger-fucking her perfect pussy. "Yes, just like that. Oh, fuck, I'm gonna come."

Dion doubled his efforts, devouring her like a starving man. His cock throbbed with the need to be inside her once more, but he had to make sure she was opened up enough to take him first. He ran his fingertip over her G-spot as he suckled her clit, taking her over the edge until her pussy gushed.

As soon as her inner walls stopped spasming, Dion pulled his fingers from her cunt and quickly stood, lifting her into his arms and lining up his cock with her pliant pussy. While she was in that hazy, relaxed state of recovery, Dion shoved his dick balls-deep in one powerful thrust, knowing she was feeling no pain at that moment.

Jewel wrapped her arms and legs around him, clinging to him while he gripped her ass to control the way he bounced her up and down on his length. She felt so amazing that he couldn't control his inner beast for long, pushing her back against the shower wall and setting a brutal pace as he ravaged her.

"Oh, fuck, yes, Dion!" Jewel cried out, digging her nails into his back as her whole body convulsed with her next release.

"Mine," Dion growled as he rutted into her like a wild animal, eager to fill her pussy with his cum to mark his possessive claim. "You're. Mine. Jewel." Dion punctuated each word with a powerful thrust into the narrow confines of her body, never slowing in his rhythmic invasion of her soft sex.

"Yes, Dion, yes! I'm all yours," Jewel agreed, continuing to come on his cock. "And you're all mine."

"Fuck, yes, Jewel!" Dion's balls drew up as he spurted jet after jet of his cum deep into Jewel's slippery sheath.

The feel of his hot, sticky cum hitting his stomach woke Dion from the dream.

"Fuck," he groaned, glad his brother had left earlier in the afternoon to go to work that night, so Darius didn't witness his nocturnal emissions. He was also relieved to realize that he'd taken off the hospital gown and kicked off the covers at some point in his sleep, so he didn't have to call the nurse to help him clean up the mess.

Dion moved slowly as he reached over to the table beside him to grab a couple of tissues to wipe up the majority of the cum streaked over his torso. Once he didn't think there was any risk of drippage, he gingerly rolled to his side to sit up.

He had to sit there for a minute to get the room to stop spinning before he could stand. Then he gripped the pole holding his I-V bag, grateful to have it for balance as he walked into the bathroom to clean up a little better.

"I don't care what the doctor says. There's no way that was just a dream," he told his image in the mirror over the sink, finally noticing his short hair sticking up around the bandage on his head and a beard that had obviously been growing for longer than the couple of days he'd been in the hospital. The sight of so much hair had him wondering when he'd stopped shaving his head. "I haven't had a wet dream since I was fifteen years old. So, for them to suddenly start again now, they have to be memories trying to come back to me. And since I know I'm always diligent about wearing condoms, dreaming about fucking her without them shows how important Jewel is to me. Now I just have to figure out how to find her."

<div align="center">~~~</div>

While waiting for the pharmacist to fill her prescription for prenatal vitamins, Julie mentally relived every romantic moment of the day they'd made their babies, from the chocolate-covered strawberries and champagne, which they'd licked off of each other, to the sensual massages on the massage table he'd requested for their room. Then on the drive home, she fantasized about every decadent, dirty way they'd had sex, from the sensual massages leading to languid lovemaking, to him doing her from behind in the living room, to exchanging oral affection and fucking like wild animals in the shower, and finally to making love among the rose petals on the king-sized bed in the bedroom of the suite. As she'd imagined hearing every "I love you" they shared that day, she'd slowly come to realize how each time he'd said those words, it had been a lie.

By the time she got home, where her friends were already gathered for their book club meeting, she was back in the anger stage of her

46

grief over their lost relationship.   But even though she was mad at him, she knew she needed to try to get ahold of Dion to tell him about the babies. She'd wanted to get an update from Anthony about when Dion would be back on the GWA tour to try meeting up with him to tell him before sharing her news with anyone else. But then, after walking down memory lane in her head on the way home, she'd worked herself up to the point that she didn't think she could face him.

Sitting in her driveway and trying to think of how to keep her secret from her friends and family until she talked to Dion, she decided to try calling him one more time to see if he'd actually blocked her number, or if she could tell him over the phone before the girls grilled her at book club. She disconnected from her car's Bluetooth first, not wanting anyone else to overhear the conversation if his voice blared out of her speakers, then dialed his number with the phone to her ear.

When it didn't ring to his voice mail, and instead an electronic voice answered with a message saying, "the person you are calling is unavailable," she knew she'd been blocked from calling him. Which meant that she couldn't contact him to meet up like she'd originally planned, even if she went to whatever city he was in at the moment. It also meant she couldn't take the coward's way out and tell him over the phone the way she'd decided to do a few moments earlier.

Well, then I guess I'll just have to try to keep my announcement limited to my closest family and friends for now. And maybe try again in a few days to see if he's unblocked me, so I can tell him before making a widespread announcement. Supposedly, it's better to wait until after the first trimester to announce it anyway, so maybe I can keep my mouth shut until then.

Before walking into the house, she put her prenatal vitamins in her purse and hid the bag of baby stuff she'd been given at the end of her appointment under the passenger seat in her car, hoping nobody would see it and figure things out before she told them about the babies. Apparently, that was the right move, since she didn't make it up to her room to put away her purse before her friends saw her come in and called her over to where they were fixing drinks before sitting down for the meeting.

Oh, pluck a duck! I didn't think about not being able to drink my normal glass of wine at book club! Shit, and I'm supposed to limit my caffeine intake too, which means I probably can't even have any sweet tea tonight either, since I had three cups of coffee this morning. I should have paid more attention to how much I'm allowed to have each day, so I can figure out how many cups of tea I can have a day if I switch to decaf coffee in the mornings. Hopefully, that's all in the information in that bag I left in the car.

Not that it'll do me any good now. And as soon as I turn down the wine tonight, the girls are all gonna start figuring out that I'm knocked up, even the ones I haven't told about hooking up with Dion. Fuck! Shit! Damn!

Okay, new plan. Bite the bullet and tell them about the babies. Even the women I'm not as close to in this group are capable of keeping a secret from the Matchmaking Mommas, so I can still wait until after the first trimester to make a broad announcement to the rest of the family and the town at large.

"Julie, do you want red or white tonight?" Becky held up a bottle of each to give Julie a choice.

"Yeah, I'm gonna have to stick to lemonade and water tonight," Julie sighed, looking longingly at the wine bottles her cousin was holding up, and stalling on making her baby announcement.

"Are you sick?" Kara Thompson reached over and felt Julie's forehead with the back of her hand, like she was trying to estimate her temperature.

"Not with anything contagious," Julie assured them, pushing Kara's hand away and taking a deep breath for courage. "But I confirmed with Dr. Magnum today that Dirtbag Dion knocked me up, so I can't have alcohol. And since my appointment was this afternoon, instead of this morning, I've already exceeded the amount of caffeine I'm allowed to have in a day, so I can't even have a glass of tea now."

"Whoa! Why are you calling Dion a dirtbag all of a sudden?" Lexi Wilder looked at Julie in shock. "And when did you start sleeping with him without giving us the deets on his magic peen?"

"We've been hooking up since we met last November," Julie admitted to the women in the room who hadn't previously known, feeling guilty for not sharing her relationship with Dion with everyone in the room a lot sooner. "And I started calling him a dirtbag when I called him a couple of days ago and he accused me of being a ring rat, who was after him for his money."

"Seriously?" Kayla Scott's jaw dropped in shock. "And here I thought he was some kind of hero for jumping in to save Allissa over the weekend."

While Julie had avoided talking to anyone about the incident over the weekend, she assumed everyone else in town had been gossiping about it. So, even though none of the online articles she'd seen had mentioned which of his female coworkers he'd been instrumental in rescuing, she assumed Kayla knew it was Allissa because everyone in Heart's Destiny knew about Allissa's stalker issues after the town was asked to be on the lookout for any strangers in town back when she was there for Rick and Fiona's wedding over the summer.

"Yeah, well, as glad as I am that he helped keep Allissa safe, he showed his true dirtbag colors when I called to check on him," Julie huffed, starting to get pissed all over again at having to rehash the conversation where he broke up with her. "And I'm pretty sure it was just because I'd told him about the doctor's appointment last week when I told him my period was a week late. It's way too convenient that he suddenly started being an ass and blocked my number, so I couldn't get through to tell him the test results today."

"What a jackass," Cassidy Reilly scoffed as several of the other women chimed in their agreement, making Julie feel validated in her anger.

It was nice to have the support of her friends while struggling with her broken heart. And she had a feeling she'd really need all of them supporting her as she tried to take care of twins as a single mom.

"Ya'll haven't even heard the best part of it," Julie chuckled wryly. "Because my period in September was only one day of light spotting, Dr. Magnum did an early ultrasound to estimate my due date. And she saw two babies."

"Twins?" Several of the women shouted in unison.

"Yep, I'm not only a twin, I'm a carrier of twins," Julie nodded before swigging a big gulp of her lemonade. She then reached into her purse and pulled out the stack of ultrasound pictures to pass around for all of them to see. "When she started labeling them on the ultrasound pictures, I tried to convince her to label them as Thing One and Thing Two in honor of Halloween coming up this week, but she didn't think that was funny."

"We can get out the markers and glitter pens to change that if you want," Becky offered as everyone cooed over the fuzzy black-and-white images that didn't really look like babies yet.

"So, how far along are you?" Cait questioned as she looked over one of the pictures.

"As of tomorrow, I'll officially be ten weeks along, which I don't understand 'cause they were only conceived eight weeks ago. It makes no sense that they count the two weeks between the first day of my last period and the date of conception as part of the pregnancy, but whatever. At least, it means I'm already a quarter of the way through. And since they're due on May twenty-sixth and twins usually come early, Jen and I might get to share our birthday with my babies."

"That would be cool," Cait said wistfully. "I'd love to share my birthday with my babies."

"When's your birthday, Cait?" Sierra Sadler inquired, arching a curious eyebrow in Cait's direction.

"November nineteenth," Cait replied with a smile.

"Oh, that's only three weeks away," Lexi grinned. "Perfect for a pre-Thanksgiving party."

"Yeah, but there's no chance she'll share a birthday with her baby this year." Kayla looked Cait over, as if she was looking for a baby bump. "And probably not next year, either. With the way the rest of the Burlesons have recently been pumping out babies as soon as they hook up, there's no way she can hold off 'til February before joining the Burleson Baby Boom now that she's with Josh."

"The Burleson Baby Boom?" Becky spluttered as she choked on the drink of wine she'd just taken.

Holy shit! We have been having a baby boom in the family, Julie realized, noting that she was the fifth of them to get pregnant in the last year.

"Yeah, haven't you noticed?" Kayla nodded at Becky. "For the last year, every time a Burleson hooks up with someone, they end up pregnant before they even make it down the aisle, which is miraculous considering how fast your moms can put together a wedding."

"It's not just us, though," Jen objected, shaking her head at Kayla. "There are other babies being born in town besides the babies in our family."

"Yeah, but those are all born to couples who've been together for years," Cassidy pointed out, agreeing with Kayla. "Of the couples our ages who've just recently met and hooked up, it's only the Burlesons making babies almost immediately."

I should have realized this was a pattern when Amy and Charlotte both announced their pregnancies not long after getting engaged over the summer. Not that it would have stopped me from being with Dion to make our babies, but I could have taken extra precautions to make sure we stuck to our planned timeline.

"They're right," Lexi agreed, holding up a hand to count them off on her fingers. "Anthony met Kay, and less than two months later, her pregnancy was announced at their wedding rehearsal. But even though James and Randi got together during that same time frame, they haven't started having kids yet. Then Bobby and Brook got together and less than three months later, her pregnancy was announced at Bobby's birthday party."

"But even though there've been a few couples who've gotten together in the GWA during the same time frame of when Amy and Justin, and Char and Ian have gotten together and announced they're expecting, none of the GWA couples have announced a pregnancy," Kayla added with a half-shrug. "Well, except for Julie, but she's a Burleson, so Dion's GWA anti-baby mojo wasn't strong enough to counteract the super-fertility that runs in ya'll's family."

Yeah, apparently, Dion didn't get the GWA anti-baby mojo, Julie chuckled. *He got the super-sperm capable of defeating my birth control twice in one day.*

"Super-fertility?" Jen rolled her eyes at Kayla.

"She's got a point," Amy admitted, rubbing her hand over her round belly. "Justin knocked me up less than a week after we started having sex."

"I can beat that," Brook giggled. "Bobby hit a bullseye my very first time."

Okay, maybe there is something to the Burleson super-fertility they're talking about. Maybe after these babies are born, I'll have to go back to condoms and my birth control pills to make sure I don't get knocked up again too soon.

Oh, who am I kidding? Since Dion and I broke up, I won't be hooking up with anyone, probably ever again. Or at least, until the kids are grown and off to college, so I can travel again to find someone I haven't known since childhood to hook up with.

"Now I don't feel so bad about only knowing Ian for six months when we got pregnant," Charlotte chuckled.

"I guess the women in our family aren't as fertile as the men," Julie giggled, realizing the male Burlesons certainly worked faster than the guys she and Char had hooked up with. "Since it took Dion almost ten months to get the job done."

"Which brings me back to my point about Cait and Josh," Kayla smirked. "You know Josh is just as virile as his brothers and cousin, so I fully expect Cait to be preggo by the end of the year."

Oh, wow, Cait looks like she's looking forward to making that happen, Julie thought as she studied her friend's reaction to the talk around the room.

"Yeah, I think I'm gonna avoid hooking up in this town," Ashlyn Lawton, Amy's twin sister, chimed in. "I'll stick to my vibrator or go to San Antonio for a hookup from now on."

"Don't worry, Ashlyn," Lexi assured her with a wide grin. "You're safe from the baby bug as long as you don't hook up with a Burleson. So, Jen and Becky are the only ones here who have to forgo man-made orgasms until they're ready for babies."

"Yeah, well, they won't be completely alone. Since Dion's acting like a horse's ass, I'll be forgoing man-made orgasms for probably the next eighteen-and-a-half years," Julie chuckled self-deprecatingly.

"Aw, but no man-made orgasm is gonna feel better than tucking your kids in at night before taking care of yourself." Normally quiet and reserved, Kara surprised Julie with her statement as her lips turned up in a sad smile. "And honestly, between seeing all of you having babies, and reading these **Crescent Cove** baby-making books, I'm kinda thinking I should ask Jake or JJ about donating sperm, so I can take advantage of the Burleson Baby Boom that seems to be happening right now without having to worry about man-made orgasms. I mean, I've been waiting almost a decade for one of those already, so if I have to wait until that unicorn comes to town to have babies, I'll never have kids."

"You really think you're ready to start having kids without trying to find a man first?" Cassidy inquired, arching an eyebrow at Kara. "You sure you don't wanna try going out with us in San Antonio a few times to look for Mr. Right? Or even Mr. Right-Now, who might can give you a man-made orgasm while making the baby you want?"

"Yeah," Kara nodded. "I'm not interested in one-night stands and hoping for a happy accident to conceive my baby. I'd much rather choose someone I know and respect to donate the other half of my child's genetic material. That way, even if it's not a love match, I know I'll be able to have a friendly relationship with the father if he wants to be a part of the baby's life. And since I found out the Walkers are my cousins, JJ and Jake are the only single guys in town, whom I both respect and I'm certain I'm not somehow related to, that I can actually consider as viable options."

"You might could ask Jake, but I think JJ is saving his up for Deanna," Julie blurted, wanting to be supportive of her friend if she was serious about having a baby on her own, while not even thinking about using the word "sperm" in the same sentence with her brother or cousin's names.

"Considering the way Jake's always looked at you, he might even be willing to use his magic peen to give you a few man-made O's while ya'll are trying to make a baby," Lexi added, making Julie cringe at hearing the words "magic peen" and "man-made O's" being used in reference to her cousin.

"But if you go through with having a baby with Jake, don't come complaining to us when your baby starts correcting your spelling before he or she even starts school," Charlotte added, reminding them all about how, all through school, Jake kept trying to correct Kara for misspelling "cakes" when she drew the logo for her mother's bakery when she was only like three or four.

Julie still wasn't sure why Mrs. Thompson had used the name Kara came up with, including the misspelling, when she opened the bakery. But she knew her friend still thought of the Kara's Kakes logo as a special bonding moment with her mom, who'd passed away right after Kara graduated from high school. Come to think of it, that was when Jake finally stopped bugging Kara about it.

Huh? I wonder if Jake was using that as a way to try to flirt with her as a kid? Did he stop doing it because he understood how much the logo meant to her after losing her mom? Or was it just because he gave up on dating her when he went to the Naval Academy? I'm gonna hafta pay attention to how he looks at her next time he's home on leave to see if he's still interested. If so, maybe Kara won't have to forgo those man-made orgasms to have babies after all.

As the conversation around her turned from when the rest of the ladies wanted to think about having families to the books they were actually meeting to discuss, Julie collected the ultrasound pictures she'd passed around. She couldn't resist looking through all of them one more time before tucking them away in her purse and joining in on the rest of the conversation.

Chapter Four

After work on Wednesday, Julie found herself being pulled into a last-minute family dinner. They were meeting because Mandi Hunter had reached out to the Burleson matriarchs to recruit a few more people to help out with scaring the kids of Heart's Destiny, who were brave enough to go on the haunted hayride they were putting on at the bed and breakfast for Halloween. Apparently, between planning for her son's wedding at Thanksgiving and starting the process to build a winery on the previously unused portion of land owned by the Hunter family, Mandi hadn't had time to set up the hayride as early as she usually did each year. And with the route having to change due to the wooded section of land they'd cleared to pave for the drive and parking lot at the building they'd renamed the Heritage House since the previous year, there would be some issues that had to be addressed, instead of just going with the same setup they'd been doing for years.

Considering how many of the Burlesons had become parents in the last year and would want to ride with their kids in the horse-drawn hay wagon, Julie didn't think there would be as many of them volunteering to be ghouls and goblins as there had in previous years. *Hopefully, most of the people who help her out each year already know their roles and when to show up tomorrow, so she can just tell them their new locations on the route and it won't be a big deal that she didn't mention it sooner. And since Josh, Anthony, and Bobby's jobs have prevented them from helping out regularly the last few years, it'll probably only be Justin and Charlotte that we'll need to find replacements for this year.*

Oh, shit! And, unless Mandi has a different job I can do, me!

Leah Mae Wright

Since she'd just found out that she shouldn't ride her horse, Jasmine, because of being pregnant, Julie wasn't sure if she should volunteer or not. In previous years, she'd dressed as the headless horsewoman, wearing a full-head pumpkin mask to ride within sight of the wagon without getting close enough for them to see the large cutouts that allowed her to see what she was doing on the horse. Obviously, that wasn't something she could do this year, but she wasn't sure how else she could help out.

Maybe I can get someone else to trade spots with me and go help with concessions or face painting instead? Julie pondered the possibilities as she took a seat between her sister, Jen, and cousin, Becky, after filling her plate. *But in order to do that, I'll have to tell everyone about the babies, and not just the girls I told at book club Monday night. Guess I won't be waiting until after the first trimester to make that broad announcement, after all.*

Since I'm gonna hafta share it with my gossipy mom tonight to get out of being the headless horsewoman tomorrow, I'm sure everyone will know to ask me about my babies the next time I see anyone in town, without me actually having to publicly announce it like I'd thought.

"So, how's everyone in the GWA doin' now that the stalker's no longer a threat?" Josh's question for Anthony brought Julie back from her mental rabbit hole.

"Mostly okay," Anthony replied with a somber expression. "Ready for the media coverage to die down so the Avington teams can move on to their next jobs, more than anything."

"What's the update on injuries?" JJ inquired.

Julie wasn't sure if she should thank her brother or not for asking the question. On the one hand, she wanted to know if any of their friends were hurt worse than she'd read online, which was just that there were some bumps and bruises but no life-threatening injuries to anyone in the GWA, while the stalker had been killed by the security team on site. But on the other hand, she wasn't sure how to handle her mixed feelings for Dion at the moment, and she didn't want to feel even more confused if Anthony mentioned him in an injury report.

"Dean, Allissa, and Liam are still a little bruised up from hitting the floor when the gunfire started, but they're all fine," Anthony reported. "Dion's the only one who's still in the hospital. He was grazed by a bullet and hit his head on the frame around the toilet stall as he tackled Allissa to save her life. Dean said it was the hit to the head that knocked him out, and that's why they transported him to the hospital."

Oh, gawd! Even though he'd hurt her by rejecting her on the phone, Julie still loved him and hated to think of him as hurt in any way. *He was shot and knocked out! Those don't sound like non-life-threatening injuries to me!*

"In addition to the stitches where they had to sew up the bullet wound and where he busted his head open, he's got a concussion and post-traumatic retrograde amnesia, so he can't remember what happened," Anthony continued. "But when I talked to Rick this morning before we flew out, he said the doctors had ruled out any kind of brain bleed and should be sending him home today."

Thank God. I guess his injuries weren't as life threatening as Anthony first made them sound to me. Now I don't have to feel guilty for being pissed off at him.

Once she knew his injuries weren't so bad that they could have justified his behavior on Saturday when she'd talked to him on the phone, Julie was ready to change the subject. "So, what all does Mandi need us to do at the hayride this year?"

"She's hoping that everyone who's volunteered before will come reprise their roles this year," Julie's mom, Susan, confirmed what she'd assumed would be the plan. "She's been so busy with all the changes at the B and B this last year, and now planning more changes on top of Dean's wedding next month, that she hasn't had time to come up with any new ideas for the hayride, other than planning the new route that doesn't include the area they paved for their expansion."

Damn it! That's what I thought she was gonna say. Guess there's no getting out of telling everyone about the twins now.

"Yeah, I'm not gonna be able to be the headless horsewoman anymore," Julie confessed, looking down at her plate as she pushed her food around, too nervous about her announcement to actually eat any of it.

"Oh, no, that's my favorite scene, 'cause it's not super scary," Aunt Hazel interjected.

"Mine too," Julie's mom agreed, nodding at Hazel before turning to look at Julie. "Why can't you do it?"

"Because I'm not allowed to get on a horse for the next seven months or so," Julie shrugged, lifting her gaze to meet her mom's eyes before continuing. "And after that, I'm gonna wanna spend Halloween with my babies, instead of scaring other people's kids."

"Babies?" Susan's eyes widened as she looked at her daughter in shock.

"Yes, Mom, babies," Julie confirmed, smiling ever so slightly at the excitement transforming her mother's face. "I'm having twins, and they're due in May."

Susan jumped up from her seat and ran around the table, rushing over to pull Julie up into a bearhug as she squealed in delight. "Oh, my precious daughter, giving me two more grandbabies!"

Julie returned her mom's embrace, her smile widening at realizing her family was happy for her, even though she was about to be a single mom. After several more hugs and excited offerings of "congratulations" from the rest of the family, Julie finally got to sit back down and go back to her dinner, not that she felt like eating when she knew the family interrogation was about to begin. They might be happy and supportive, but they were also protective, which meant they wouldn't let her get by without mentioning the man who'd impregnated her.

"So, do we need to go kick Dion's ass once he heals up from the concussion?" Julie wasn't surprised that it was her dad, Jon, that started the overprotective portion of the conversation.

"No," Julie sighed, shaking her head at her dad. "I told him last week that I was going to the doctor this week to find out. And since just the possibility of a baby was enough to scare him off, he's not worthy of being in my life. Or my babies' lives. So as far as I'm concerned, him being injured this week is enough cosmic vengeance for being a jerk to me."

"You're not even gonna tell him he's gonna be a father?" JJ looked pissed as he barked out the question.

"Oh, I'll tell him if he's ever stupid enough to show his face in town again," Julie barked back at her brother, fuming because she wasn't sure if JJ was pissed at her, or pissed at Dion on her behalf. "But when I tried to call and tell him right after confirming everything with Dr. Magnum, I couldn't get through because he blocked my number. When he knew I was going to call him with the results from the test, he blocked me from being able to get ahold of him. So, it's clear he's made his decision and doesn't want to be a part of our babies' lives."

"He's got amnesia after the concussion," Anthony interjected, his tone low, as if he was trying to soothe their tempers, "so he might not remember you or that he was expecting a call from you."

"Oh, yes, he made that clear on Saturday when I talked to him, and he called me a ring rat, a gold digger, a greedy bitch, and a ho not worth trying to remember," Julie scoffed, rolling her eyes at her cousin. "So, hopefully, he legitimately can't remember me because of the head injury. That way I know I won't ever have to worry about him coming around wanting to see my kids. 'Cause I'm not about to let someone who thinks it's okay to talk to any woman like that close enough to teach my sons that it's okay to be that much of a misogynistic ass, or to teach my daughters that it's okay to let men treat them that way."

Julie was fuming by the time she finished her rant. She was so angry that she didn't even care that she'd just cussed in front of her parents and all the kids in the family. All she could do was stare at her plate and count backwards from one hundred, trying to calm herself down and completely missing whatever Kay said to Anthony to cause him to apologize.

"I'm sorry, Julie." Anthony sounded exasperated as he blew out a breath. "I didn't know you were even seeing Dion, much less that he'd said those things. Clearly you got to know a part of him that he never showed the rest of us. And I'm sorry I thought he was a decent guy until now. If I'd have known that was how he treated women, I never would have invited him to our wedding last year."

Julie could tell her cousin felt guilty for being the reason she'd originally met Dion. Which she felt was ridiculous because Anthony hadn't done anything to push her to do more than have a cordial conversation with the man.

"Don't worry about it, Anthony," she sighed. "I wouldn't change a thing about what happened between me and Dion. Even though he turned out to be a colossal jerk, I wouldn't have my babies without having gone through it. And now I know what *not* to look for when trying to find my soulmate."

"Obviously, it's not him if one little hit to the head is enough for him to forget you," Jen added.

"Technically, it was two hits," Tia interjected.

Did his head bounce on the floor too? Julie wondered, missing part of what Tia said as she continued.

"… and one with the frame around the toilet stall."

"I feel like there should be a joke in there somewhere every time someone mentions the toilet stall," Josh chuckled, keeping Julie from asking for clarification of what Tia had just mentioned. "But I feel like he totally missed the mark by not landing with his head in the toilet."

Julie stifled her smile, even as the kids all giggled at the image Josh's words conjured in their minds.

"Are you suggesting we swirly the dude next time we see him for dissin' my sister?" Justin grinned at Josh, who shrugged one shoulder and grinned back.

"Well, they do say the third time's the charm," JJ smirked. "Maybe if we knock him upside the head one more time, we'll knock the sense back into him, and defend her honor, all at the same time."

"Ya'll are gonna leave him alone and ignore him if he ever comes back around," Julie admonished the overprotective men in her family. "I'm more than capable of knocking him upside the head all by myself if necessary. But I'd rather just forget he exists and focus on planning for my babies now."

"Yes, let's get back to planning for the babies," Susan smiled, agreeing with her daughter.

"Have you thought of any name ideas yet?" Char inquired, clearly helping to change the subject.

"I've got a couple of ideas," Julie confided with a smile. "If I have boys, I'm thinking Owen and Kayden. But the only name I've thought of for a girl is Zoe."

"Oh, I love the name Zoe," Becky gushed, nodding emphatically.

"If you have twin boys and name them Owen and Kayden, you're setting them up to be picked on in school," Josh pointed out, shaking his head.

"She is not," his girlfriend, Cait, disagreed, glaring at him. "Those are great name ideas."

"Yeah, if she wants her kids to be collectively referred to as Okayden," Josh snickered before doing a very poor performance of the country rap song, *Okay Then*, by Bubba Sparxxx. He didn't just rap the song like a semi-normal person. No, Josh had to stand up and dance around like a loon the whole time.

Julie had to laugh at her cousin's antics, even though he'd just ruined the only boy name ideas she had for her twins. *Now I've really gotta start praying for girls and come up with more name ideas.*

"Aunt Julie, please don't name your babies Okayden," JoJo pleaded, waving his hand in Josh's direction. "We can't give Dad a reason to do *that*, ever, again."

"Yeah, that's definitely a reason to revoke his membership in the Cool Dad's Club," Bobby chimed in, earning nods of agreement from Anthony, Justin, and Ian.

"You're just sayin' that 'cause we wouldn't let you in the club," Josh teased his older brother as he took his seat once more.

"Why wouldn't you let Uncle Bobby in the Cool Dad's Club?" Maria looked back and forth between her dad and uncles, like she was confused.

"Because when he became the police chief, he got too serious and quit being any fun to hang out with," Josh jokingly replied.

"He gave up any chance of being any kind of cool long before he became the police chief," Becky disagreed, shaking her head. "But so did Josh, Jake, Justin, JJ, and Anthony when they kept telling all the cute boys that we had cooties and couldn't play with them."

"Hey, that's just us bein' good brothers and cousins and protecting you girls from the boys who weren't good enough to date you," Josh argued as all the guys at the table nodded in agreement.

"So, I gotta tell all the boys I'm friends with that Tia and Maria have cooties and can't play with us?" Antonio looked up at Anthony for clarification.

"Yeah, Son," Anthony nodded, smiling as Kay rolled her eyes at him.

"But they don't really have cooties, do they?" Antonio looked worried for his sisters.

"No, there's no such thing as cooties." Tia shook her head at her little brother before turning to glare at her dad. "And if you really want to scare the boys away from us, you should tell them about our menstrual cycles, and how they prepare us to clean up a bloody crime scene every month, so they know we're capable of disposing of their decaying corpses if they ever try anything inappropriate."

"Hey, Dad," JoJo interrupted, pulling on Josh's sleeve. "What's a menstrual cycle? And how does it help Tia prepare to clean up a bloody crime scene?"

Julie burst out laughing, unable to hold it in a moment longer as she watched her former Navy SEAL, badass cousin, turn as pale as a ghost as he struggled with how to answer his son's question. She wasn't the only one who found the situation humorous, as all the women around the table fought to control their giggles.

"Um, Pop," Josh stammered, looking over at his dad at the other end of the table. "I, um, kinda need some of your sage parenting advice right about now."

"Oh, no," Julie's Uncle Bob chuckled, shaking his head, and holding his hands up in surrender to his son. "You're the cool dad, so I'm sure you can handle this one all by yourself."

"Brie-Baby, I can't believe I'm sayin' this, but we're gonna hafta adopt the rest of our kids, so I can guarantee they're all girls," Bobby quipped, looking as nervous as the other men in the room about having to explain menstruation to their sons. "That way you can handle all the birds and bees talks."

"Maybe since you can't be the headless horsewoman tomorrow night, you should dress up as a tampon and tell the horror story of menstruation to scare all the boys instead?" Jen suggested, leaning over to put her arm around Julie and causing them all to chuckle.

"No, that's way too gruesome for the haunted hayride," Julie giggled, loving the way her family took her mind off of Dion.

<p style="text-align:center">~~~</p>

As he struggled to walk up the stairs, when he and Darius finally got home from the hospital, Dion was starting to regret not putting in an elevator when he had the building renovated. And he was really regretting taking the third-floor condo, leaving Mama Marcel the ground floor with Darius just one flight of stairs above her, since he was the one who was in town to take care of her if she ever needed it.

Luckily, all three condos were two bedrooms, so Dion didn't think he'd have to make it all the way to the top floor while feeling so dizzy. Unfortunately, Mama Marcel had her spare bedroom set up for her fortune telling business, so she didn't have to go out to Jackson Square on rainy days. So, Dion still had to make it up to Darius's condo without falling down the stairs from being so woozy.

"Dare, you still got that fold out couch in your office?" Dion inquired, as they were about halfway up the staircase.

"Yeah, why?" Darius looked at him curiously.

"Because I'm too dizzy to make it up more than one flight of stairs before I need to lie down," Dion explained, pausing with a death grip on the banister when the world spun around him.

"Yeah, we can set you up in there," Darius agreed, placing a hand on Dion's back to keep him from falling backwards when he swayed on his feet. "And if this dizziness lasts for more than the two weeks I'm supposed to be monitoring your phone, then we'll hire some movers to swap my office and your guestroom to make you more comfortable 'til you're able to be up in your place by yourself."

"Speaking of what we're gonna do until I'm cleared to be on my own, what are we gonna do when you have to go to work?" Dion knew there was a team of bodyguards that the GWA had left in NOLA to keep him from being bombarded by the paparazzi while he recovered, but they'd only escorted him from the hospital to home and stayed outside to shoo off the papzz as soon as he stepped in the front door of the building. "Can those security guys sit with me, so I know they're big enough to catch me if I start to go out? Or do we need to hire a home health aide or nurse, since it's medical monitoring?"

"I'm not sure, but I'll call the doctor's office in the morning to find out," Darius assured him.

A few moments later, the vertigo seemed to pass, allowing Dion to make it the rest of the way up the stairs to Darius's condo. When they walked in, he was hit with the glorious aroma of Mama Marcel's gumbo coming from the kitchen. Dion couldn't help but smile at the memories that smell invoked, even though they were all old enough memories that he hadn't lost them with his amnesia.

"Mama Marcel," Dion called out, finally realizing why she wasn't waiting downstairs for them when they arrived. "Why'd you go to all the trouble of carrying all that up when we coulda visited in your kitchen before coming up here?"

"And why are you cooking in my kitchen instead of D's?" Darius added, obviously planning for them to stay in Dion's condo, where he had both bedrooms set up as bedrooms with king-sized beds, in case any of the GWA guys stayed over when they were in town.

"How many years have we had the rule that I cook and ya'll clean up?" Mama Marcel shook her head at them as she came out of the kitchen wiping her hands on a tea towel before pointing at Darius. "'Cause that's how many years I've known that if I'd cooked in my kitchen, you'd use the excuse of havin' to take care of your brother to get outta cleaning up." She turned to look Dion over before continuing. "And there was no point in takin' it up to your place 'cause you're in no shape to climb that many stairs. Now gimmie a hug and go sit down before you fall over."

Dion opened his arms for her to walk into them, embracing his adoptive mom for what felt like the first time in years. She looked a little different than he remembered. Her hair was grayer than it had been the last time he remembered seeing her, and she'd lost a little weight, feeling more fragile in his arms than she had previously.

"How come you know he couldn't make it up to his place, but you couldn't tell me where he was the last year?" Darius gave Mama Marcel a curious look.

"Oh, I coulda told you where he was," Mama Marcel explained as she released Dion from the hug and motioned for him to go sit down on the sofa. "I just didn't 'cause he said you needed some time to cool down. And I didn't need to use my gift to know either of those things."

Dion had to chuckle at the exasperated look on his brother's face as he took a seat while watching Dare and Mama Marcel fussin' at one another.

"Yeah, I figured you were still talking to him on the phone all the time," Darius argued. "But nobody said anything about him having a hard time with stairs when they went over his discharge papers while you were on the phone with us earlier, so how'd you know he wouldn't be able to make it all the way up to his place?"

"That doctor said he'd have some vertigo and an unsteady gait for a few days," Mama Marcel reasoned, shaking her head at Darius before moving to sit on the sofa beside Dion. "And that he might feel like he's had too much to drink from some of the medicines. I've seen you stumble up those stairs after a night out often enough to know that if the concussion symptoms amplify the drunk feelings from the medicine, then he really shouldn't've tried walkin' up this far. But you've both got enough of Elena's stubbornness in ya that you wouldn't agree with swapping condos with me for a few days to keep him from havin' to climb those stairs."

"That's 'cause we know how much climbing stairs aggravates your knees," Dion defended his stubbornness about not wanting to put Mama Marcel out for him to stay on the ground floor.

"Nonsense." Mama Marcel swiped her hand through the air. "Since I started goin' to Zumba and yoga with the girls, my knees are fine."

"When did you start going to Zumba and yoga?" Dion couldn't imagine the older woman in front of him going to classes at the gym, like some of the women wrestlers he worked with did on occasion.

"Last year when you sent me on that cruise with the girls for Thanksgiving 'cause you were goin' to your friend's wedding instead of coming home," she replied off-handedly. "Speaking of that cruise, the girls wanna know if we can make that an annual tradition after all the fun we had last time."

"Of course," Dion agreed easily, happy to be able to treat her to some fun trips with her friends after the way she'd stepped up to take care of him and Darius after their mom passed. "But I don't remember setting it up, so you'll have to book it this year and just use my card to pay for it."

"You didn't book it last year," Mama Marcel corrected him. "You had that nice travel agent call me and set it all up. I think I still have her number, so I can call her if I can remember her name. It started with a J, Jan, or Jane, or maybe Janelle?"

"Jewel?" Dion questioned, wondering if the travel agent was the woman he'd been dreaming about since he woke up in the hospital.

"Maybe?" She tilted her head in thought for a moment before shaking it. "No, I think her name is Janelle. I'll have to look in my address book when I go back downstairs later."

"You still tryin' to figure out if the woman you keep dreamin' about is a real person?" Darius plopped down in the chair across from the sofa where Dion was sitting. "Or just your favorite fantasy?"

"Yeah," Dion sighed, already knowing his brother thought she was only a fantasy. After their talks on Sunday morning, both before and after the doctor did his rounds, Dion knew that Darius had been burned too many times by women, who were only using him until someone with a bigger bank account came along, to believe relationships could last longer than a weekend. So, he understood why his brother was skeptical of Dion's belief that Jewel was his soulmate.

Since talking to Dean Hunter on Sunday night, when he and Allissa snuck into Dion's hospital room, and a few of the other guys when they called Dare for updates while he was at the hospital and Dion could talk on speakerphone, Dion was starting to believe that his dreams of Jewel might be more prophetic than actual memories as he'd originally thought. More than one of the guys had mentioned that the pilot friend of the Hunters, whom Dion remembered meeting when he came to a show while on leave from the Navy right after the Dangerous Twins started working with the GWA, had dreamed about his family for a year before he finally met his wife. They'd also informed Dion about how Anthony had been injured in the Navy and started flying the GWA plane after his doctors cleared him.

The similarity between his current situation and Anthony being injured and then dreaming about his wife and their kids made Dion wonder if they'd both had head injuries that knocked loose a little of *the sight* Mama Marcel was always talking about. Plus, when he'd asked the guys if he'd mentioned meeting Jewel, none of them recognized her name. And even though a few of them said the same thing Dean had about Dion being friendly with a set of blonde twins in Dean's hometown, none of them thought he was friendly enough with either of them to have actually done any of the things he dreamed about with one of them.

Since nobody seemed to know who Jewel was, yet they could all tell him about someone who'd dreamed up his soulmate after an injury, Dion was actually looking forward to getting to talk to Anthony when he went to Dean and Allissa's wedding in a few weeks. He wanted to compare notes and see if the man, who'd apparently become a friend in the two years he'd worked with the GWA that Dion couldn't remember, could give him some advice on how to find his Jewel.

"You've been dreaming about a woman?" Mama Marcel reached over and clasped his hand, bringing him back to the moment.

"Yeah, D wants to believe his wet dreams are actually memories trying to come back to him," Dare teased, chuckling, and drawing both of their attention. "I tried tellin' him that if that was the case, then he'd be dreamin' about a bunch of different women, instead of just the one."

"Not if she's his *special one*," Mama Marcel disagreed with Darius before turning back to look into Dion's eyes. "Tell me about her. Not the private stuff you dream about doin' with her, but the woman she is inside that you feel connected with enough for her to reach out to you in your dreams."

"She's my opposite in so many ways, but also feels like she's the missing piece of my soul," Dion confessed, knowing he sounded sappy and would probably be ridiculed by his brother for admitting how he felt about Jewel, even though he wasn't sure he'd ever met her. "She has kind eyes, like you can see in the ocean blue depths that she's a good person, who prefers to take care of others over herself. And when she's excited about something," *or aroused,* "the blue darkens to more of a blue-gray, like the color of a stormy sky."

"She's a white girl?" Dion nodded in response to Mama Marcel's question. "Describe her for me, so I can picture the two of you together."

"She's average height for a woman, a good ten or twelve inches shorter than me. Thin, but fit, not skin and bones, but not super curvy either. Probably half my size weight wise. She has straight, blonde hair that I think she lightens, 'cause her roots are more of a strawberry blonde where the rest is lighter."

"You know, you can tell for sure based on which part of the drapes matches the carpet," Darius interjected, earning a glare from Dion.

Not when there's no carpet, dumbass. Dion wasn't about to mention that Jewel either shaved or waxed her smooth pussy in front of Mama Marcel. Not that he really wanted to share that information with his brother, either.

"You shush and go dish up the gumbo," Mama Marcel reprimanded Darius, pointing toward the kitchen to send him out of the room.

"I'm just trying to be helpful," Dare asserted, raising his hands in surrender as he stood to do her bidding.

Once Darius left the room, Mama Marcel turned all her attention back to Dion. "How does she make you feel?"

"Protective. Possessive. All those caveman things Mama used to claim she didn't miss after Papa died," Dion admitted with a self-deprecating chuckle.

"Well, you are just like your papa, so that's to be expected," she chuckled. "Are you in love with her?"

"Yes, absolutely," Dion answered without any hesitation. "I don't know if the dreams are memories of my time with Jewel, or if they're visions of our future together, but I know she's the woman I'm supposed to marry and have a family with."

"I didn't think you believed in *the sight* to think you could be dreamin' of your future." Mama Marcel tilted her head as she looked at him curiously.

"I didn't," Dion admitted with a half-shrug. "Which is why I keep leaning toward thinking the dreams are memories that are trying to come back to me. But since the doctor said my memories shouldn't come back like that, and nobody I've talked to seems to know who she is, I can't figure out why else they'd feel so powerful. As meaningful as she feels, there's no way I wouldn't tell anyone I was seeing her."

"Oh, I'm sure you told someone," Mama Marcel smiled knowingly. "Just not enough details about her to be useful in helping you track her down."

"I told you about her?" Dion wasn't sure how he knew that, just that he was positive he'd told Mama Marcel more than she was sharing with him at the moment.

"Just that you'd met *The One*," she admitted, her smile dimming at not being able to help him find his dream girl. "And that she was able to meet up with you on the road every few weeks, but didn't want to let anyone know about your relationship yet to keep her family from pressuring you into quitting wrestling to settle down. But you didn't say anything about when or where you met her. You didn't even give me her name, much less a description. Probably because you were afraid I'd go track her down and either scare her off or pressure you for some grandbabies."

"Yeah, I'm so desperate to find her now, I almost wish I'd let you pressure us for grandbabies," Dion chuckled, relaxing his head back on the sofa as the relief of knowing his dreams had to be memories coming back to him washed over him.

"Yes, well, you might not be blood related to me to get my gift of *the sight* to have visions of your future with her," she grinned as she lifted the hand not holding his to place it over his heart. "But I can see your future with her. It'll be a bumpy road getting back to her, but know that your dreams are her spirit calling out to you. They'll eventually lead you back to her."

For the first time he could remember in his life, Dion actually wanted to believe Mama Marcel could tell his future.

Chapter Five

Saturday, November 23, 2019

Considering it was the one-year anniversary of the first time she'd had sex with Dion, Julie couldn't believe she'd let her twin sister convince her to go to the bachelorette party for Allissa, knowing Dion would probably show up for Dean's bachelor party at the same location. When her family and friends started having these joint parties for every wedding the previous year, she'd thought it was a great idea. She'd actually loved having the extra chances to hang out with Dion, when nobody would be suspicious that they were closer than the acquaintances, and eventually friends, that they portrayed to keep the Matchmaking Mommas off their backs. But now that they'd broken up and hadn't even spoken in almost a month, she wasn't looking forward to seeing him again, especially not on a day that would have been special to them if they were still together.

Well, seeing him in person again, anyway. Since she'd left her Google alert set up for any new mention of him online, she'd seen plenty of him in pictures after the day they broke up. The first ones had been of him sitting on a balcony with a bandage on his head that had made her feel bad for being mad at him. Then a few days later, she'd seen more pictures of him sitting on the same balcony, without the bandage and with a beautiful Black woman serving him what appeared to be a breakfast tray. The article that accompanied the pics speculated about whether the woman was a nurse or his girlfriend, taking care of him during his recovery. Regardless of whether the woman started out as his hired nurse, the way she looked at him in the photos made it clear that she was more than willing to warm his bed. Needless to say, Julie's jealous streak had flared to life.

Even as mad as she got over seeing the salacious articles, Julie still didn't cancel the notifications for anytime his name was mentioned online until two weeks later, when the reputable news sources stopped reporting on the stalker incident. As he started being seen out and about in New Orleans, usually with his brother and the flavor of the minute of his female fans, the celebrity news sites pretty much dropped the story. After reporting that his recovery was going well, they'd more than covered the serious news story of the stalker incident, allowing his fans to provide the photographs for anyone still interested, instead of having their reporters and paparazzi following him around. Not that Julie was any less jealous of the fans photographed with him than she had been of the woman who'd taken care of him when he was first injured, which was why she'd had to force herself to stop the notifications.

Seeing the pictorial evidence that he was recovering well had made her briefly wonder why he hadn't gone back on tour with the GWA yet. But seeing there was a medical building in the background of several of the most recent pictures she'd seen, she assumed he had other injuries that weren't reported that required physical therapy to get him back in ring shape.

But even if he's not back to the high level of fitness needed to perform in the ring, his injuries aren't bad enough to keep him from doing most normal daily activities. So, there's no way he'll stay in New Orleans and miss all the wedding festivities this week, she mentally grumbled, wishing they didn't have friends in common, so she wouldn't have to see him so soon.

If it was up to her, he wouldn't come back to town at all, so she'd never have to see him again. But since that probably wasn't an option, she'd hoped he'd stay away long enough for her to have her babies and get her figure back first. But instead of being able to flaunt her body that he'd never get to touch again, she was sporting the baby bump that popped up early because she was carrying twins. And at six-foot-four and two-hundred-and-fifty pounds, their father was bigger than the average NFL linebacker, so she was afraid her babies would be huge when they were born. At least, taking their size from him was what she was using as an excuse for why she was already showing at only thirteen weeks pregnant.

If just thinking I could possibly be pregnant was enough to turn him off so much that he broke things off, he'll probably be disgusted by seeing the evidence of giant twins so prominently displayed.

When Julie realized at the beginning of the month that she could no longer button her tailored business attire, she'd opted to switch to stretchy, but form-fitting, sweater dresses and t-shirt dresses, instead of buying billowy maternity dresses and tops or hideous maternity slacks and jeans. She knew they'd only stretch so far, and she'd eventually have to buy actual maternity clothing, but she was putting it off for as long as she could.

Normally, she didn't care that the pliable dresses clung to her baby bump because she was proud to show it off. She didn't even care that broadcasting her pregnancy worked as a deterrent to men hitting on her, not wanting to even think about dating, while she was still so heartbroken over Dion.

But she hated the thought of him seeing her baby bump and not feeling the love for their babies that she did. So, at that moment, knowing her burgundy sweater dress clung to her new curves, and would show him the baby bump he wanted no part of, made her feel frumpy.

Don't worry, babies. Mommy loves you more than anything else in the world, she silently told her children as she laid her hands over the soft burgundy sweater dress she was wearing, covering either side of her protruding belly to make sure she covered both twins.

Him not loving their babies was even more painful for her to imagine than the realization that he didn't love her. And she didn't think she'd be able to maintain the upbeat, party attitude she was currently trying to project if she saw his disdain — or worse, his ambivalence — in his eyes when he finally arrived at Tully's.

"If this goes sideways when Dion arrives, you've gotta promise to get me outta here," Julie whispered imploringly to her twin as she sat there sipping her mocktail. "I don't wanna be a drama llama and ruin Allissa's party."

Considering the crazy mood swings she'd been having from all the pregnancy hormones, Julie thought it might actually be better if she offered her congratulations to Allissa and Dean right then, so she could leave before Dion arrived. That way, she wouldn't be tempted to lose her temper and cause a scene the first time she saw him after their breakup.

"Yeah, good luck with that," Jen softly scoffed. "Even if we leave right now, you know one of our brothers or cousins are gonna say something to him about the way he treated you. So, there's gonna be drama tonight, even if you're not the drama llama causing it."

Julie didn't have time to make her early escape as she looked up and saw Dion walk into the bar. He looked the same as the last time she'd seen him, impeccably dressed in black slacks and a dinner jacket over a burgundy button-down sans tie, with no visible repercussions of the incident the previous month.

How the fuck did we end up dressed to match tonight? Julie briefly wondered before going back to cataloging everything about his appearance. If he had scars from where the bullet had grazed him or his head was busted open from the fall, either his clothing hid it or his hair had already grown out enough to cover it, so she couldn't see either of them.

I'm surprised he still looks like he's keeping two weeks of beard and hair growth, instead of going back to shaving completely every couple of days, like he did when we first met. But then again, he's probably figured out that I'm not the only woman who likes a little beard burn to remember him by, so he's keeping it to satisfy the ring rats in all those pictures I'm sure are still being posted regularly.

Julie hoped working up a good mad would stop her body from responding to his as blatantly as she had previously. But her hard nipples and wet pussy obviously hadn't gotten the memo from her brain that they weren't supposed to be attracted to him any longer.

No, I don't want him anymore! Julie tried desperately to stop being aroused by the mere sight of Mr. Tall-Dark-and-Handsome, looking down at her now curvier body as she mentally tried to talk her sexual organs into standing down. *It's just the pregnancy hormones making me want to jump his bones.*

At thirteen weeks, I'm officially about to start the second trimester, when all the girls warned me about my sex drive kicking into high gear. I'll go home to use my clit sucker to have a couple of orgasms, and this arousal will all go away.

"Jewel!" Dion shouted as he stalked toward her.

Julie's head popped up as she angrily glared at him, unable to hold back the sudden burst of rage at hearing the endearment he used during their intimate moments. *Oh, hell, no! He did not just call me that. It is not okay to use his pet name for me after all the hideous things he called me last month. He's supposed to have amnesia. He's not supposed to remember me, much less remember the term of endearment he used to call me to try to get back in my panties!*

"No!" Just as he got to the table, Julie held up a hand to stop him from coming any closer, rapidly losing control of her temper. "Don't you dare call me that after ghosting me for the last month!"

"I didn't ghost you, Jewel," Dion asserted, his voice taking on a pleading quality Julie hadn't heard from him before. "At least, not on purpose. I was injured and can't remember how to contact you."

"Oh, I heard all about your injury," Julie fumed, shaking her head at him. She was so angry she felt like her whole body started trembling along with the negative head movement. "From my cousin! When he got home four days later! But he was too late for me to be interested in hearing what happened, since I saw the news reports the day it happened and tried calling you. Do you know what I found out when I called you, Dion?"

Dion shook his head, obviously realizing it was a rhetorical question and not opening his stupidly sexy mouth.

"I was told never to contact you again," Julie seethed. "That you didn't need to be bothered by a *ring rat* trying to take advantage of your injury to con you out of your money. Well, newsflash, *Dark Chocolate*, I'm a Burleson. I don't *need* your fuckin' money. And after being treated like shit when I called, concerned about you possibly being shot, I don't *want* you in my life. Or my babies' lives." Julie pushed her chair back slightly and placed a hand over her belly, as if that could protect her babies from hearing their father's lies. "So, go hang out with your boys in the back, and stay the hell away from me while you're in town this week."

Pluck a duck! That's so not how I wanted to tell him about the babies! But then again, he didn't exactly give me the opportunity to tell him with a cutesy pregnancy reveal and baby paraphernalia scattered around his hotel room when he arrived for one of our rendezvous, either. Or even to call and lamely tell him over the phone because he blocked my number. So, if he has any complaints about how I just sprung the news about our twins on him, they're his own fault.

Dion opened and closed his mouth like a fish out of water for a moment before swaying on his feet.

"Dare, I need to lie down." Dion reached out and clamped a hand on the arm of the man who'd walked into Tully's with him.

"I'm sorry, D. I think I screwed up when I answered your phone while you were in the hospital," the man, whom Julie assumed was Dion's brother Darius based on their similar looks and accents, and Dion's usage of the Dare nickname he'd used when telling her about his brother previously, started as he ushered Dion back toward the door.

She didn't hear everything Dare said to Dion as they left the bar, but she was too mad at the moment to care. Whether it was Dion or Darius that she'd actually spoken to that day didn't matter. Either way, it was obvious that the Davis men had a terrible opinion of women in general and weren't worth wasting her time on.

"Oh my gawd, are you okay, Jules?" Jen looked Julie over, as if she was assessing her sister for physical injuries, instead of the emotional blows that had Julie reeling.

"Was that Dion's brother?" Cait inquired as she turned to watch the two men leave the bar. "And did he just say something about answering Dion's phone while he was in the hospital?"

"Yeah, that was Dion's brother," one of the GWA women confirmed, but Julie wasn't paying attention to recognize which one of them had answered.

Julie closed her eyes and massaged her temples as she tuned out the conversations going on around her, wishing she hadn't let her emotions get the best of her and cause her to make a scene. She wanted to leave the bar right then, but since Dion had just gone out the front door toward where her car was parked, she opted to go to the ladies' room to compose herself first, even though it took everything in her to block out her memories of their first kiss as she walked down the hall where it had happened.

Maybe if I give him a few minutes, he'll be gone by the time I get out to the parking lot, so I won't have to see him again tonight. And I'll do everything I can to avoid him at all the other wedding events I'm sure we'll both be at this week. Since all it took was one mention of the babies for him to turn tail and run away from me, I'm sure he won't bother trying to talk to me again, so that shouldn't be a problem.

She just didn't let herself think about how guilty she'd feel for not making it abundantly clear that she was pregnant with his babies. Or how sad she felt at the way he seemed to reject them by leaving so abruptly.

Not thinking about those things wouldn't change them in any way, but it was the only defense she had against the heartbreak at the moment. *Fake it 'til ya make it, right? I can plaster on a fake smile to get through this week and put off all the emotions of dealing with my broken heart until after Dion leaves town again.*

~~~

Dion hated the feeling of waking up after having one of the spells where he suddenly collapsed. It always felt like his brain woke up, but his body hadn't yet. He could hear what was going on around him, but he couldn't move or speak to acknowledge anything that was happening for several long minutes. And even once he fully woke up after passing out, he had problems remembering what had happened for up to two hours right before he passed out, and often lost more simple words that he should be able to recall easily. Thankfully, the words only seemed to disappear from his memory for a few hours, or maybe a day, before he could recall them again, unlike his memories of the last couple of years, or the events leading up to the passing out spells he hated.

The doctors classified those spells as an unusual symptom of post-concussion syndrome, but they hadn't figured out exactly what they were, or more importantly, how to stop them, yet. They'd tried a few different medications so far, some in the hospital and some after sending him home, including an anti-seizure medication that didn't do anything but knock him out cold for the next thirty-six hours. That had totally freaked Darius out because he couldn't get Dion to wake up during that time, no matter what he tried. Needless to say, Dion didn't take that medication but the one time after being taken by ambulance
~~~

back to the hospital, where they finally got him to wake up before sending him right back home with a different medicine to try.

In the four weeks since his injury, the doctors also tried a couple of different anti-anxiety medications, but not until after Dion pointed out that the spells only happened when he got overwhelmed by not being able to process everything going on around him, or struggled with the aphasia that caused him to have difficulty remembering the right words for things, or had trouble comprehending anything people tried to communicate to him, no matter if it was written down or said during a typical conversation. Those medicines hadn't seemed to do much, if anything, so he'd only been on them a couple of weeks before he gave up taking them.

The only medication the doctors had given him that actually seemed to help prevent any of his symptoms was the one to help with vertigo. He had to take it three times a day and go slow when he was transitioning from lying down to sitting up, or sitting up to standing. But at least, the room spinning feelings were only if he moved too fast now, and didn't make him feel like he was gonna barf every time he turned his head anymore.

He didn't really consider the pain pills for the headaches as effective because they didn't completely get rid of the pain. Besides only partially taking away the discomfort, the headaches always felt twice as bad when the pain pills started to wear off, so Dion avoided taking them, if at all possible.

As Dion laid there trying to get his body to respond, he heard the road noise of being in the car and remembered that he was on a trip to participate in Dean and Allissa's wedding while Mama Marcel was on her Thanksgiving week cruise with her friends. He tried cataloging what he remembered of the trip to see if he could remember the events that led up to him having this most recent spell.

He remembered trying to rest for most of the drive, hoping to get his headache to ease off some before going to the joint bachelor and bachelorette party that night. He also remembered checking into the bed and breakfast that Dean's family owned, where he would be staying for the next few weeks. But he couldn't remember if he'd actually made it to his room before they left for the party.

Since he'd been told that he'd stayed there during every break he had from wrestling for the last year, Dion hoped seeing the place again would trigger his memories to come back to him. Even if it was just a brief sense of familiarity at first, his doctors had told him that being someplace where he'd spent so much time might help his memories return faster. And because they wouldn't release him to fly while he was still suffering from post-concussion symptoms, he couldn't rejoin the GWA crew on the company plane to go to the hotels and arenas, where he'd spent the majority of his time for the last decade plus. So, going to Dean's hometown was his only option for trying to regain any of his memories of the last year.

That was why they'd planned to drive to Heart's Destiny, Texas, in time for the wedding events, and stay through the end of the year. Darius and Mama Marcel were even taking time off to be there to help him, with Darius driving him there and Mama Marcel flying into San Antonio to join them after her cruise.

Okay, if we've already made it to town, why am I waking up from a blackout in the car? Dion wondered as he finally got his eyes to flutter a little. *We left the B and B right after we got there to head over to the party. And I had some flashes of memories as we drove through town.*

"Hey, you finally coming back to the land of the living?" Darius chuckled.

As the sleep paralysis started to lift, Dion opened his eyes and turned his head to see his brother glancing at him from the driver's seat. He opened his mouth, trying to reply, but his ability to speak hadn't returned just yet.

"It's okay, D," Darius reassured him with a slight smile. "I got you outta there before Jewel saw you PTFO like a teenaged girl gettin' to go backstage at a Drake concert."

Jewel was there? Fuck! Talk about shitty timing for one of these blackouts.

"I woulda stayed in the parking lot to wait for you to wake up, so you could go try to talk to her again," Dare explained why they were driving, instead of staying at the bar for Dion to go back and try to get Jewel's number once he woke up. "But a few minutes after we walked out, she came out with another blonde. Only when they got in their car, they drove off instead of just going to get some air and going back to the party. So, I figured you'd rather recover back at the hotel and try again to catch up with her tomorrow at the wedding shower, after we strategize for how to apologize for me fucking things up for you."

"Ha, how," Dion stammered, still struggling to get the words out. "Da, did you fa, fuck things up for me?"

"Shit, you don't remember what happened in the bar, do you?"

Dion shook his head when Dare glanced in his direction, instantly regretting it as the pain in his head flared up.

"Or what I said on the way out?"

Dion decided not to shake his head again as he stuttered out, "Nuh, no."

"Okay," Dare sighed as he pulled into the parking lot at the bed and breakfast. "I guess I'll recap for you. As soon as we walked in, you got this glazed look on your face, like you were having more flashes of memories, just like you had as we drove through town earlier. Then it was like your vision cleared and you saw her, called to her from across the room, and moved faster than I've seen you walk in the last month to get to her side."

Dion smiled, imagining the euphoric feeling of finally seeing Jewel in person after dreaming about her for the last four weeks.

"And let me just say, I can see why you've been dreamin' about her, D. She is smokin' hot."

Dion growled at his brother, not wanting to think of Darius eyeing up Jewel.

"Whoa! Sorry, D." Darius held his hands up in surrender after putting the car in park and turning off the engine. "Just an observation, not me planning to make a move or anything. That little firecracker is all yours. But as soon as you make up with your girl, ya gotta hook me up with one of her smokin' hot friends. That whole place was packed with honeys."

"Get on with your recap," Dion suggested, barely shaking his head at his horndog brother.

"Anyway, she got pissed about you calling her Jewel, so I guess that's just your name for her and not her real name."

Fuck! No wonder I couldn't find her in my phone when Dare gave it back to me.

"And when you tried to tell her that you didn't intend to ghost her, she started ranting about some things I think I might've said to her on the phone when she thought she was talkin' to you."

"What the fuck, Dare?" Dion glared at his brother, furious that Darius had claimed to not know who Jewel was after, apparently, talking to her and pissing her off while he had Dion's phone.

"I didn't know, D. I swear," Darius professed, his expression turning remorseful. "It was the day you were hurt and I'd just had to get hospital security to escort a couple of ring rats out of your room, where they'd snuck in the back way to the ER, while you were off getting that first CT scan, when we didn't know anything more than you couldn't remember shit from the very brief first time you woke up that you still don't remember. Your phone had been ringing off the hook the whole time I was dealing with that shit, so when I was finally alone in the room again, I answered it without looking at the display to know who it was."

"Fuck," Dion groaned, remembering his brother mentioning having to tell off reporters and ring rats who'd tried calling and coming to see him several times over the two weeks he'd not been allowed screen time of any kind.

"Apparently, Jewel is one of the women I lost it with and blocked on your phone. I remember thinking it was weird that the phone asked if I wanted to delete the contact and text thread when I blocked that first number, but then it didn't ask the same thing on any of the ones after that," Darius elaborated. "But I just assumed that selecting yes the first time did the same for all the others. Now I have to wonder if it only asked on the one that you'd actually had saved in your phone and had been texting with, and it was my dumb-ass move that deleted the contact that you've been looking for since you woke up."

"Fuck, Dare," Dion huffed, instantly regretting slamming his head back into the headrest of the passenger seat because it amplified the pounding in his head to the point that it felt like it was about to explode. "Please tell me you explained to her that it wasn't me who said any of the dumb shit you probably spouted off at her before blocking her."

"I didn't get a chance," Dare insisted. "She started talking about being a Burleson, and not needing you, or your money, in her or her baby's life, and you started going out. So, I tried to tell you as I was walking you out to the car, but I don't think she heard any of it."

"Baby?" The world spun as Dion popped his head back up to glare at his brother. "Did you just say she doesn't need me in her baby's life?"

"Yeah, D, she's knocked up," Darius confirmed. "And from the size of her belly, I'm pretty sure it didn't happen in the last month, so it could be your kid."

Dion was stunned into silence as they finally got out of the car and walked into the bed and breakfast.

Jewel's pregnant. And far enough along that she's showing. He wasn't sure how he knew for sure, but he was positive that he was the father of her baby. *I might not remember the last year to know exactly when and how we conceived our little one, but I know, deep in my soul, that we've been exclusive since we met. So, she's definitely pregnant with my baby.*

I'm gonna be a father! Holy fuck!

"We need to figure out how to get her to forgive me for your fuck up," Dion informed his brother as they made their way to their side-by-side rooms on the second floor of the large building the Hunters mentioned expanding into the year before. "Maybe if I run through a few scenarios with you tonight for the different parties and stuff where we might run into her, maybe I can keep from being overwhelmed and blacking out again next time I see her."

"Yeah, I don't know how much help I'm gonna be with that," Darius sighed as they walked into Dion's room. "I'm more than willing to apologize for the stuff I said that day and screwing things up by blocking her and deleting her from your phone. But if her attitude tonight is anything to go by, then I don't think she'll listen long enough to give me the chance to explain."

Dion took off his jacket and hung it in the closet, realizing that they must have only stepped into their rooms long enough to drop off their luggage when they'd stopped at the hotel earlier, since his garment bag was hanging in there, but it hadn't been unpacked yet.

"Well, luckily, we're here for Dean's wedding then," Dion grinned as he sat on the side of his bed and kicked off his shoes. He turned to lean against the headboard and propped his feet up, while his brother sat in the chair in the corner of the room. "She's gonna hafta be cordial at the different wedding events, so we'll get a chance to explain when she won't wanna make a scene."

"We probably shoulda went back into the bar tonight to do some recon. Maybe we can talk to Dean in the morning to at least find out her name before you try to corner her at the wedding shower tomorrow," Dare suggested.

"Her name is Julie," Dion informed his brother, surprising even himself with how positive he was about being correct with that statement.

"But I thought you said it wasn't Julie when Dean and Liam both asked if she could be Jewel?" Dare tilted his head as he studied Dion curiously.

"Yeah, I was still pretty out of it in the hospital when they mentioned how Liam and I kept being pushed toward Julie and her twin every time we were in town," Dion admitted, hating that it sounded like a poor excuse for not remembering her as anything but Jewel. "But the more I think about it, the more it makes sense. Of all the women's names that they've mentioned, Julie sounds the most like Jewel for me to pick it as a pet name for her. Plus, when I described Jewel, Julie Burleson was the first person any of the guys thought of that matched the description. With what Dean said about the matchmakers in town pushing us together, I can see why she'd wanna keep our hookups on the down-low to keep them from knowing their matchmaking was working, which would explain why I didn't mention anything to anyone about us. And you said yourself that she mentioned being a Burleson tonight, so she has to be Julie Burleson."

"I still say we verify that before you screw things up even more by calling her the wrong name," Darius advised, pulling out his phone and clicking away like he was doing an online search for her.

"Yeah, I'm just gonna call her Jewel," Dion decided, not wanting to fuck up by guessing wrong. *But fuck, I'm sure I'm right. Her name is Julie and I'm the father of her baby.*

"But she told you not to call her that anymore," Dare pointed out without looking up from his phone.

"Did she?" Dion grinned, planning to use his concussion symptoms to his advantage for once. "I don't remember that. But I do remember how much it turns her on when I call her Jewel, especially when I'm balls-deep inside her at the time."

"You remember how much it turns her on in your dreams, D, not in real life." Darius shook his head at Dion. "But if you wanna have a chance at winning her back and being a part of your kid's life, you should probably call her whatever she wants you to call her, instead of trying to follow your fantasies. Especially if these articles about how rich her family is are accurate."

"No, those dreams aren't my fantasies," Dion disagreed, ignoring Dare's statement about Jewel's family wealth. He didn't care about whether she had money or not. He might not be able to go back to wrestling to earn his multi-million-dollar annual salary any longer, but he'd invested his money well enough to have more than enough to provide for her and their babies for the rest of their lives without having to dip into her money. "I'm positive they're memories trying to come back to me. Especially now that I've seen this room."

"This room?" Darius motioned to the room around them.

"Maybe not this *specific* room," Dion corrected as he ran a hand over the familiar bedspread. "But we've definitely shared a room or two here. And now I have to wonder if any of the dreams I've had are actually memories of when we made our baby."

"Fuck, man, I can't believe you might be a dad," Darius blurted, his voice lightly tinged with a sense of awe.

"No might about it, Dare." Dion shook his head, feeling even more certain than he had earlier that he was the father of Jewel's baby. "Whether she's currently pregnant or already had the baby and just hasn't lost the baby weight, I'm the dad. Hell, even if she had a kid before we met, I'd step up and be the kid's dad."

"Damn, you're really gone for her, huh, D?" Darius shook his head in disbelief. "It's more than just the voodoo pussy you've been dreaming about, isn't it?"

"Oh, she's definitely got a voodoo pussy," Dion chuckled. "But yeah, it's a lot more than just that. I don't know how to explain it other than I just know she's mine."

"Then we've gotta figure out how to keep you in an upright position long enough to get her to talk to you tomorrow at this wedding shower," Darius declared. "And I'm gonna seriously have to apologize for calling a legit billionaire a gold digger and accusing her of trying to go after your measly millions."

"Maybe if we figure out what triggered the episode tonight," Dion suggested, closing his eyes, and trying to remember walking into the bar earlier, again not comprehending what Darius was saying about

Jewel's wealth. "We can figure out how to navigate those same triggers at the rest of the wedding events this week."

"You thinking things like the crowd, mostly low lighting except for the strobes by the stage, and loud music could be triggers?" Dare inquired.

"Yeah, and maybe the shock at seeing Jewel for the first time," Dion nodded, opening his eyes to look back over at his brother. "Or my brain not making the connection between what she was saying and her appearance to register that she's pregnant."

"Well, if that's what triggered you, then you should be good tomorrow, since you've made that connection in your head now." Dare finally put his phone away.

"Yeah, but if it's the crowd, I may have the same problem at every wedding event this week," Dion sighed, worried that his stupid blackout episodes were going to derail his efforts to work things out with Jewel.

"Any idea what we're gonna walk into tomorrow, so you can prepare yourself to not be overwhelmed within a few minutes of walking in?"

"No clue." Dion shook his head. "I know Dean said I've been to a few of these showers in the last year, but I still don't remember a single one of them."

"Maybe we should call Dean and ask him?" Darius suggested with a quirk of his eyebrow.

"Naw, I don't wanna interrupt his bachelor party for my shit." Dion waved off Dare's suggestion. "But maybe we can call his mom to find out what to expect this week? If she's as much a part of the Matchmaking Mommas Club as Dean thinks, I bet she'd be happy to help me try to get back in Jewel's good graces."

"That's not exactly sticking with her wishes to keep your hookups on the down-low," Darius pointed out, smirking at Dion.

"Maybe not," Dion shrugged. "But if she's knocked up, we can't exactly keep things private for much longer anyway. Besides, all's fair in love and war, and I'm prepared to go to war for my Jewel's love."

Chapter Six

Sunday, November 24, 2019

After crying herself to sleep the night before, Julie hoped to maintain her composure a little better than she had at the bachelorette party as she walked into church for the Sunday service and the wedding shower to follow. It turned out her fake smile the night before only lasted long enough to get her out of the bar and on the way home. No matter how much she tried, she couldn't stop thinking about how badly she'd bungled seeing Dion again, or about how he'd immediately reverted to rejecting her and the babies as soon as she mentioned them. While she wasn't sure she could maintain the façade she hoped to project to keep everyone from knowing how heartbroken she was, at the very least, she hoped to keep her temper in check, so she didn't cuss Dion out in the middle of the sanctuary. But if she had her druthers, she and Dion would stay on opposite sides of the building all day, so she didn't have to deal with her conflicting feelings for him.

She hated that she was still so attracted to him and couldn't stop her eyes from being drawn to him. As soon as she walked into the chapel, she involuntarily stopped in her tracks, waiting to see where he was planning to sit before making her way over to the pews where the Burlesons always sat together.

Down girls! Julie mentally chastised her hard nipples and suddenly wet center. *He's a jerk, remember? We don't like him anymore.*

Unfortunately, her internal admonishments had little to no effect on the way her body responded to Dion's presence in church that morning. Even with him sitting on the other side of the sanctuary with the Hunters and the other GWA wrestlers in attendance for the upcoming wedding, where she could barely make out the top of his head because he was surrounded by men just as large as him, she was aroused by the mere thought of being in the same room with him once more.

Lord, forgive me. I know it's gotta be a sin to be so turned on while sitting in church, but I just can't seem to turn my reaction to Dion off. Maybe you can help me out with that? Like, maybe, help me remember how much he hurt me to help me stay mad enough at him that I can turn my attraction to him off, so I'll be able to stop lusting after him while I'm sittin' here in your house?

Instead of thinking about the phone call a few weeks before to extend her anger, Julie kept thinking about all the other times over the last year that she'd seen Dion in the church she attended every week with her family. She'd thought he was hot in his wrestling tights on television. She'd thought he was even hotter in jeans, a t-shirt, and tennis shoes the first time she'd seen him in person when he came to the barbecue on her family ranch the week before her cousin Anthony's wedding. But seeing him wearing a bespoke suit every time he stepped into the church, and when he met her at his hotels while on tour with the GWA, had never failed to melt the panties right off of her. She finally understood why her mom and Aunt Hazel loved that old ZZ Top song, **Sharp Dressed Man**, because she really did love seeing Dion Davis in a suit and tie.

Julia Elizabeth Burleson, stop thinking about that luscious man and how much fun you had when he removed those suits behind closed doors. Even using her mother's trick of calling herself by her full name wasn't enough to wipe the decadent, dirty thoughts from her head as she sang along with the rest of the congregation, hoping she hadn't accidentally sung the wrong words to the hymns. It wasn't until the preacher finished all his announcements and started his sermon that Julie was able to focus on anything but her memories of her relationship with Dion.

Of course, Pastor Harrison had to pick that Sunday to preach about forgiveness, making it clear that she could only expect God to forgive her if she forgave everyone who'd ever wronged her in any way. Oh, since there were so many extra people there for the wedding shower right after the service, Pastor Harrison had covered it in a sermon about how husbands and wives have to work on their marriages by forgiving each other for the little annoying things they do. But Julie still felt like he was talking directly to her because of the ironic timing of Dion's presence, her prayers, and the sermon.

Seriously, Lord? I ask you to stop me from committing the sin of lust by reminding me of his painful words, and your answer to my prayer is to have Pastor Harrison preach about how I should forgive him?

How am I supposed to do that? How am I supposed to turn the other cheek and give him the opportunity to say those horrible things to me again? Only next time it could be worse, especially if he waits to say them in front of our kids? I have to protect them from learning that type of behavior is acceptable. And I don't see how I can do that if I forgive and forget.

Julie spent the entire service contemplating how she could get over all her feelings for Dion to be the best example she could be for her children. She might one day be able to get past her anger at him to forgive him as the Christian woman she wanted to be should. But she didn't think it could happen while she still felt such a strong attraction to him. Because if she did, then she was afraid she'd fall back into the trap of believing the lustfulness she felt toward him was actually love. And that was a surefire way to set herself up for another heartbreak. One she wasn't sure she could survive a second time.

After the service ended, Julie absentmindedly followed her family to the fellowship hall for the wedding shower that was replacing their typical potluck lunch. They were trying to figure out where they were all supposed to sit when Anthony and Kay were called up to sit with the rest of the bridal party, where they had two rectangular tables pushed together to seat the bride and groom with their parents and everyone participating in the wedding. Aunt Hazel then directed all the kids to go with her, Uncle Bob, Julie's parents, Bobby, and Brooklyn. That made it easy for Julie to sit with her siblings, remaining cousins, and their significant others at a table for ten.

Hum? I wonder if my impending single parenthood made it clear to Mom and Aunt Hazel that they need to back off on their matchmaking for a little while to keep from having another public mistake on their record?

Even thinking that everyone in the room had to be thinking she and Dion were as much of a mistake as she desperately tried to make herself believe, Julie couldn't stop herself from glancing over at him as he sat beside the man, whom she assumed was his brother, at the head table with the rest of the bridal party.

Why does he have to look so freaking delicious in a suit? And why do I keep thinking about how hot he is, and how much I want to feel his arms around me again, instead of how his rejection hurt me?

Thankfully, the conversation at her table turned to the impending birth of her twin nephews, taking Julie's mind off of Dion. Mostly. Knowing she was pregnant with his twins, while talking about how uncomfortable Amy was in the final weeks of her twin pregnancy, really only shifted her thinking to what she was going to experience in a few more months.

"The next eight days can't go by fast enough," Amy declared as she shifted in her seat to place a hand on her low back.

I wonder if I'm going to be as uncomfortable as she seems to be now when I'm that far along?

Oh, pluck a duck! I didn't even think about asking how big a baby Dion was when he was born. At six-foot-four and two-hundred-and-fifty pounds, he's two inches taller and quite a bit heavier than Justin. While Amy and I are almost the same size normally, I have to wonder if Dion's larger size is going to translate to me having bigger babies than Amy and Justin.

Ugh! I really don't wanna be as big and miserable as Amy is now, much less, even more enormous and feeling even more wretched because of having Dion's gigantor babies.

"I can't believe Dr. Magnum agreed to let you go that close to your due date before scheduling you to be induced," Char commented, rubbing a hand over her small baby bump. Her cousin might be farther along than Julie, but her almost twenty-six week, single baby bump wasn't noticeably much bigger than Julie's thirteen week, twin baby bump. "I thought they usually recommended delivering at thirty-eight weeks for twins, even if there aren't any complications."

I'll definitely have to remember to ask Dr. Magnum about that when I go for my next appointment. Delivering at thirty-eight weeks would put our babies' birthday about halfway between my birthday and Dion's. And if I can't have them on my birthday, then I don't wanna push it so close to the due date that they're born on his birthday.

"She originally planned for thirty-eight weeks," Amy replied, grimacing as she continued moving around in her seat. "But that's this week, and with it being Thanksgiving week, she was afraid of being short staffed and keeping us from spending the holiday with the family, if we have any complications."

"Having a small staff that all want to be at home with their families for the holidays is the only drawback we've found to having the birthing center in town," Justin added, rubbing Amy's back, which was obviously bothering her from carrying their twins. "But Dr. Magnum still has privileges at the hospital in San Antonio, so we have a backup plan to call her and meet her there if the boys decide to make their appearance on Turkey Day."

Oh, thank goodness! I'm due the day after Memorial Day, so if we schedule the delivery for a couple of weeks early, instead of letting them go all the way to their due date, then I won't have to worry about a holiday issue with having my babies. Julie absentmindedly rubbed a hand over her belly, feeling calmed by touching the part of her body where her babies rested. *Although, Easter is in April next year, and Devon said the twins could be born as early as April twenty-eighth. But surely, Easter won't be that late in the month, so we should still be good for avoiding a holiday delivery.*

"Is that where everyone had to go to have babies before the birthing center opened?" Cait questioned, looking around the table at the Burlesons who were born in the area.

"Yeah, we were all born in the hospital in San Antonio," Josh replied, grinning at his girlfriend.

"Not all of us," Charlotte chuckled, pointing with her thumb over her shoulder toward the head table where Anthony was sitting with the rest of the bridal party. "Anthony was technically born on the backseat of Memmaw Judy's car somewhere between here and the hospital."

"Seriously?" Amy's eyes widened almost comically at the gut-wrenching prospect of delivering in a moving vehicle. Julie agreed with the horror she saw on her future sister-in-law's face at the thought of delivering their babies in the back of a car driving at highway speed.

"Yeah, seriously," Char confirmed. "I was only three at the time, so I don't really remember it. But Mom told me about it the other day when we were discussing my birth plan."

Leah Mae Wright

"Hopefully, ya'll won't have to go with your backup plan," JJ pointed back and forth between Justin and Amy. "'Cause I have a feeling I'll be the one driving ya'll to the hospital, and I am not cleaning that up off my upholstery."

As lunch was served, Julie decided to grab some plastic drop cloths from the hardware store to keep in the back of her Malibu, just in case one of the pregnant women in her family went into labor and she had to drive them to the delivery. *Maybe I should make sure everyone in the family has one in their vehicle, so none of us will have to clean up our upholstery with all the babies being born into the family in the next few months?*

<p style="text-align:center">~~~</p>

As Dion ate lunch with the rest of the bridal party at the wedding shower, he was glad he'd thought to call Mandi Hunter the night before to ask her what to expect. Walking into the church that morning with so many people that he'd forgotten meeting before was still pretty intimidating, but at least, he'd been able to prepare himself for facing them by getting a general overview of who was most likely to approach him and how they would receive him, so he didn't panic and end up having a blackout episode. He also thought talking to Mandi the night before had given her the opportunity to spread the word around town about him not remembering anyone he'd met in the last couple of years, so they wouldn't overwhelm him by just walking up and talking about something he didn't remember.

After Mandi made a few of the first introductions when they first got to the church, he'd ended up sticking close to the GWA crew that he did remember, and let them introduce him to anyone else from the community that approached him, both before and after the church service. That strategy seemed to be working well, except for the fact that the Burlesons all seemed to be ignoring him. At least, the people he assumed were Burlesons because they were sticking close to Jewel seemed to be ignoring him by avoiding even incidental eye contact with him. And Anthony was mostly being quiet, and only whispering to the petite woman seated next to him, instead of risking interacting

90

with Dion by joining in on the other conversations going on around the table.

Guess I'm gonna hafta suck it up and go introduce myself to them when this is all over. Maybe once they realize that I don't remember any of them but Anthony, and only flashes of my time with Jewel, they'll forgive me for not being there for her and our baby this last month. Though I'm not sure even that will work if Anthony won't even give me the time of day while we're sitting at the same table.

Thinking about Jewel caused him to look in her direction once more. She was still just as beautiful as he remembered in his dreams. But instead of wearing the tailored business suits he removed from her body in his dreams each night, she now wore a purple sweater dress that clung to all of her curves.

Her curves had expanded since the times he'd seen her to create those dream memories, too. Her pregnancy wasn't so far along that she looked like she swallowed a basketball, or a beach ball like the African American woman seated a couple of seats over from Jewel.

Maybe a small football? Like, one of those Nerf footballs that's not quite regulation size for the NFL. I wonder how far along that makes her?

Regardless, Dion ached to run his hand over her little baby bump, wanting to touch her as much as he wanted to feel his child moving inside her. It had taken everything in him not to run over to her the instant she walked into the church that morning. But as much as he wanted to rush headlong into the relationship he knew they were destined to have, he knew he was going to have to take things slow and take the bumps Mama Marcel had predicted for them first.

Thinking of what Mama Marcel had said about his future with Jewel, Dion had to chuckle. He couldn't believe he was starting to buy into her fortune telling after all these years. *I don't know if that's just because she spun it to give me hope for getting back together with Jewel, or if my head injury is worse than the doctors think it is.*

Either way, she's gonna love this town when she gets here next week. And hopefully, she won't cause too much trouble when she starts trying to help out the town matchmakers.

"What's so funny?" Dean arched an eyebrow at Dion from his seat across the table.

"Just thinkin' 'bout how Mama Marcel's gonna wanna move her fortune telling business to town when she gets here next week," Dion confessed with a grin.

"Oh, I wish we'd have thought to have her here for the haunted hayride last month," Mandi pointed out, turning to look at the woman he'd been introduced to that morning as Allissa's mom. "Windy, don't let me forget to get with her next week when she gets here to see if she's interested in booking sessions with the retreat groups we have coming in January."

"Why do I have a feeling Mama Marcel making friends in this town is gonna be a bad thing for me?" Darius looked back and forth between Dion and the two older women at the table.

"Well, you did say you wanna spend some time with the hotties you saw in the bar last night," Dion chuckled, knowing he was throwing his brother on the mercy of the local matchmakers.

"Yeah, that was last night when I thought they were like the party girls in NOLA," Dare defended. "But seein' 'em all in church this morning has changed my perspective."

"Too late, Dare," Dean laughed. "You're on the radar of the Matchmaking Mommas now, so ya might as well prepare yourself for gettin' hitched."

"Just be glad you're meeting them in Heart's Destiny and not out in Vegas," Liam quipped as he put his arm around his reluctant bride, whose name Dion couldn't remember because she hadn't worked with the GWA long enough for him to remember her. "Here the Mommas just manipulate situations, so you'll end up sitting with the woman they wanna match you up with at every public event they can. But out in Vegas, Windy and Kandi will get you drunk and rent a limo to take you to the county marriage license office on the way to one of the chapels, so you actually end up tying the knot."

"Don't listen to them, Darius," Windy argued, shaking her head at Liam. "We just wanted to take some pictures at the marriage license bureau and with an Elvis impersonator at one of the chapels to stir up a buzz on social media, and maybe push Allissa and Dean into getting hitched. But we had nothing to do with any of these yahoos saying 'I do.' That's all on them."

As Dion's coworkers fussed with Windy about her role in their nuptials, Darius turned to his brother and asked, "With you not remembering the last couple years, how do ya know you didn't get married when these guys did?"

"Because Jewel wasn't there," Dion insisted, knowing he wouldn't have even drunkenly walked down the aisle with anyone but her.

"Are you sure she wasn't?" Liam arched an eyebrow at Dion. "It was one of the nights you went to the hotel early, so it coulda been one of the nights she snuck into town to see you without any of us knowing about it."

"Trust me, as often as I've dreamed about those hotel room rendezvous in the last month, if I'd have married her, I'd have remembered it in my dreams," Dion assured his friend, whom he'd had several long discussions with over the last couple of weeks, trying to figure out who starred in his dreams every night. "Besides, both Dare and Mama Marcel woulda known if I got a marriage license in the mail like ya'll did."

Once they'd all seen Dion bomb his reunion with Jewel the night before, Liam had figured out that those hotel hookups Dion was dreaming about had been times when Dion had gone back to the hotel early while everyone else in the GWA had gone out. While they didn't have any hard evidence to back up his theory, they believed Jewel had come to visit him several times while he was on tour over the last year.

"Wait." Emerald Stone, whom Dion remembered working with before he lost his memories, even though he couldn't remember her real name, held up a hand to stop the conversations at the giant square table where all thirteen members of the bridal party sat, along with the parents of both the bride and groom and Darius as Dion's plus one. "Are you saying the only memories you have of the last two years are your hotel room hookups?"

"Yeah, and they're all with Jewel," Dion confessed, hoping Anthony was paying attention to realize how special his relationship with her was, so he'd pass the information along to his cousin. Dion had a feeling that with the way her family was avoiding him, he'd only get the chance to talk to her again if he convinced Anthony to put in a good word for him while her cousin was trapped at the bridal party table with him at each of the wedding events that week.

"And Jewel is Julie?" Amethyst Stone, another female wrestler that he only remembered by her ring name, clarified.

"Jewel is that beautiful blonde in the purple sweater dress," Dion confirmed, lifting his chin in Jewel's direction. "Who is apparently too pissed off to talk to me because of Dare bein' a dickhead when he answered my phone while I was unconscious and having a CT scan the first day I was in the hospital."

"So, it wasn't you she spoke to that day?" Dion assumed the petite brunette to Anthony's right was his wife, but since they hadn't reintroduced themselves, he couldn't be sure.

"No," Dion replied, shaking his head while directly looking into her blue eyes. *Huh? Guess Anthony and I both dreamed about blue-eyed women after being injured,* Dion realized, even though he now knew his dreams weren't prophetic like Anthony's, but memories of his time with Jewel.

"It was me," Darius admitted with a heavy sigh. "And after dealing with reporters calling nonstop and having to get hospital security to remove a couple of women who'd snuck in the back way to his room in the ER, I was a colossal ass when I answered the call. And I followed the angry ass routine with the dumbass move of blocking and deleting her from his phone."

"Lemme guess, D," Crockett chuckled. "You're so chill 'cause Dare got all the hothead genes in your family?"

"Something like that," Dion smiled wryly, not wanting to explain how Darius had also gotten burned by more than one woman who'd fit into that gold digging, ring rat category he'd accused Jewel of being on the phone that day. Unfortunately, the woman Dare had told him about causing them to not speak to one another for the last year wasn't the only woman that had used him to try to get to Dion for his money and fame.

While Dion didn't think Darius's past experiences excused the way he spoke to Jewel while Dion was incapacitated, he hoped that knowing about those events would help her understand enough to be able to forgive both him and his brother. *If only I could get a few minutes alone with her to explain it all.*

Dion turned to look directly at Anthony, hoping to plead his case with Jewel's cousin to help him get an audience with her. "If I'd have been able to answer my phone that day, I woulda begged for her to come to NOLA to help me try to remember more than the few flashes I'd had of her while I was knocked out. I'm hoping that, now that I've found her and figured out who she is besides my Jewel, that we can pick up where we left off before I lost my memories. And I can show her that even when I forgot everything else, I didn't forget how much I love her."

"Oh, wow, that's so romantic." The woman seated beside Dean's twin, James, placed a hand over her heart as she looked at Dion before turning to the woman Dion thought was Anthony's wife. "It sounds like something you'd put in one of your books. A love so strong that even amnesia can't erase it. You'll have all your readers swooning if you pen their story next."

That's right, Dion realized, finally making the connection between the people around him and the things Mandi mentioned the night before when they talked. *Mandi said Anthony's wife is an author and her sister married James.*

Dion couldn't wait for the concussion to clear up enough that he could comprehend things like that when he first heard them, instead of having to make the connections a day or two later to figure things out that he should already know. *Now if I could only remember the names Mandi mentioned last night for the two of them. Well, and everyone else I don't remember meeting in the last couple of years.*

The conversation continued around him as Dion tried to recall the names of the people he hadn't been reintroduced to at the table, not realizing he was missing Anthony's explanation of why he and his family hadn't told anyone in the GWA that Julie was pregnant and Dion was her baby daddy. *Since everyone said I was at their wedding showers here, being here at a wedding shower should trigger my memory to, at least, recall their names, right? Maybe even a few flashes of those wedding showers?*

He was so caught up in trying to remember that he didn't realize how rude he was being by staring into space and not participating in the discussion. Not that it did any good. The harder he tried to remember, the less he actually recalled, and the more his head hurt.

"Hey, come back to earth, D." Darius waved a hand in Dion's face to get his attention. "Ya'll have to excuse my brother. Since the TBI, he tends to zone out like this whenever he gets to thinking too hard, or trying to force a memory."

"Sorry," Dion apologized, realizing he was making more of a scene than was necessary when he could have just asked their names. "I should have just asked everyone I met in the last couple of years to reintroduce themselves, instead of trying to figure out who's who."

"Oh, dear," Mandi gasped. "You did say something about one of your symptoms being that you don't comprehend things as easily as you used to, and I didn't even think about how that would affect you in trying to remember all the names I went over with you on the phone last night. I should have continued with the introductions after church the way I started them this morning. I'm so sorry. I didn't realize."

"No need for you to…" *Fuck, what's that word?* "Be sorry. I'm the one who should…" *I know there's a more appropriate word for being sorry. Why the fuck can't I remember it?* "Be sorry for being a…" *Fuck! I hate this word loss shit!* "Bad guest."

Fuck! Fuck! Fuck! Maybe I should get the hell outta here before this word loss shit gets me so anxious that I collapse and blackout again.

"Dude, you're not a bad guest," Dean argued, shaking his head at Dion. "If anything, we're being bad friends by acting like nothing's changed, when we could be doin' things like extra introductions and talking about the other times you've been here to help you get your memories back."

As they continued eating, Dion was reintroduced to Anthony's wife, Kay, James' wife, Randi, and Liam's wife, Rylie, who used the ring name of Chastity. Emerald and Amethyst reminded him of their real names, Teagan and Aiken, when he pointed out that he only remembered their ring names. Since he remembered Anthony, the Hunters, and the rest of the GWA crew from years before, Allissa from the day she and Dean visited him in the hospital and all their phone calls since, and had been introduced to Allissa's parents that morning, he was finally able to put a name to every face at the table with him.

Dion still wasn't sure why he was tasked with walking Allissa down the aisle for the wedding when she had her dad there. But Grant seemed cool with it, so Dion didn't want to risk bringing up any hard feelings in their past by asking. At least, not while they were in such a public setting.

Maybe I'll get a chance to talk to Dean alone later to find out, Dion reasoned, knowing his brother would probably ask him for details he didn't know when they went back to their rooms for the night.

"So, if you don't remember the last couple of years, you probably don't remember being here for either of our wedding showers." James pointed between himself and his wife and Anthony and Kay.

"No," Dion shook his head. "The church feels familiar, but I don't have any specific memories of being here before."

"The first time was a year ago," Dean started.

"Technically, a year and a week," Anthony interjected, bobbing his head from side to side before turning to smile at his wife. "Since it's our one-year anniversary today."

"Sorry, guys, I didn't even think about ya'll wantin' to spend the day off by yourselves to celebrate today," Dean offered, looking embarrassed at not recognizing the date.

"Don't worry about it," Anthony waved off Dean's concerns. "We've got plans to leave the kids with the grandparents tonight for our private celebration. And we wanna be here for ya'll the same way you were here for us last year."

"Well, we at least need to have an extra toast," Dean suggested, lifting his glass. "To Anthony and Kay. I hope this is the first of many happy anniversaries."

After everyone at the table wished Anthony and Kay a happy anniversary, Anthony went on to tell Dion about their wedding shower, which was the first time he'd stepped foot in the Heart's Destiny Community Church. Unfortunately, hearing the story didn't trigger any specific memories for him.

"Was that the first time I would've met Jewel?" Dion tried desperately to remember what she'd worn to that first meeting as he looked over at her.

"No, that was the day before at the barbecue on the ranch," Kay clarified with a warm smile. "I didn't see the first moment you saw each other, but Hazel and Susan said they saw more sparks flying than horseshoes while ya'll were playing."

"Yeah, I was playing in that game with them and Jen," Liam shook his head. "And I didn't see any sparks, so I think the Matchmaking Mommas were seeing what they wanted to see."

"Dude, none of us knew she was comin' to visit him on the road either," Crockett pointed out, disagreeing with Liam. "So, obviously, they were good at covering their feelings from day one."

"I don't know," Surfer Josh bobbed his head from side to side as he waffled on his thoughts. "I thought he had to be into one of the girls when he followed them over to the horses to go on a trail ride."

"No way!" Darius reached over and slapped Dion's shoulder. "My brother rode a horse?"

Several people at the table nodded, but Dion could only shrug, not remembering if he had or not.

"Please tell me someone got pics," Dare implored, knowing how out of character horseback riding was for Dion.

"Ma might have one that Philippe took," Anthony shrugged, turning to look at his wife for confirmation. "But I don't remember anyone taking pics with their phones that day."

Anthony mentioning phone pics triggered a flash of a memory of sending selfies back and forth with Jewel. Dion wanted to pull his phone out and look through the photo album to find the pictures he remembered, but knew they wouldn't be anything he could look at while still technically in a church and surrounded by people. While he vaguely remembered taking a few when they were together of him riding bareback, they didn't include the horse his brother was asking about.

Damn it! Why didn't I think about looking at my photos on my phone before now to try to remember more about Jewel?

As everyone at the table continued relaying wedding shower stories from the last year, Dion's mind kept wandering back to the pictures he knew he had to have taken and shared with Jewel. Thinking so much about what he was missing with her only reinforced the sense of urgency he felt about needing to speak with her. So as soon as lunch was over and everyone was directed to mingle while they were setting up one of the wedding-shower games, Dion couldn't stay away from her a moment longer.

He walked straight over to the table where she sat with the rest of the Burlesons and their significant others. *Fuck, I should be at that table with her.* Dion knew he couldn't bulldoze his way back into her life, so he tried to infuse a sense of humility into his voice as he reached her side. "Hey, um, Jewel, can we talk?"

"No," Jewel huffed, shaking her head at him. "And I told you last night not to call me that anymore. My name is Julia, and that's what I expect you to call me from now on."

"I'm sorry, Julia," Dion pleaded, aching to have her beautiful blue eyes turn up to look at him. "I know in the middle of the wedding shower isn't really the right time for us to talk. But can I at least get your phone number, so we can talk later this week?"

"You already have my phone number," Jewel scoffed, shaking her head at him again, even though she still wouldn't make eye contact. "If you don't have it in your contacts anymore, try looking in your blocked number list."

"Yeah, about that, my brother…" Dion let his words drift off as he turned to his brother, who had followed him to Jewel's table. "Damn, I should probably introduce ya'll to my brother. This is Darius, but we call him Dare." Dion then turned back to look around the table at the Burlesons and their significant others as he tried to figure out who was whom to introduce them. "I'm sorry, I've been told I've met ya'll before, but after my injury, I don't remember it. So, please forgive me for only being able to introduce you as the Burlesons."

There was a moment of stunned silence before one of the men at the table finally spoke. "Hi Dare, I'm Josh, and this is my girlfriend, Cait."

"Nice to meet you," Dare waved at them across the table.

Just when Dion thought Josh would continue the introductions, the heavily pregnant African American woman at the table cried out in pain and reached over to grab onto the arm of the white man beside her.

Guess that's confirmation that my race isn't a factor in why Jewel's family is giving me the cold shoulder, Dion thought as one of the other women at the table waved over another woman, who was apparently an obstetrician. As the doctor started questioning the woman she called Amy about the possibility of being in labor, Dion took a step back and observed, thinking about how that could be Jewel in just a few months. *We've definitely gotta work things out soon, so I don't miss the birth of my baby.*

"I think that was my first real contraction," Amy panted out, obviously struggling to speak through the pain.

"But you've been having back pain since last night, Sweetheart," her man added. "Could that be the back labor I read about?"

Oh, damn, I should probably be reading all about babies and birth, too, now that I know Jewel is pregnant with our baby.

"It could be," the doctor confirmed. "But your water hasn't broken yet?"

Amy shook her head. "No, I don't think so." She bit her lip and looked at her man before looking back at the doctor. "Unless it can leak out slowly, like only when I laugh or during a contraction?"

"It can, yes," the doctor nodded.

Huh? I thought it was a big deal when a woman's water broke, like a big gush all at once, making it impossible to not know it had happened.

"Then I probably should have called you last night, 'cause I've been wearing pads to catch what I thought was bladder leakage from having two babies sitting on it since we got home from the bachelorette and bachelor party."

Two babies? Fuck! What's that called? It's the same thing Jewel is, so she could be having two babies at once, too.

"Let's get you over to the birthing center, so I can do a full exam," the doctor suggested, causing everyone in the general vicinity to all quickly pick up their things and ask for someone to inform the expectant grandparents to meet them at the birthing center.

Dion wanted to follow along with the Burlesons as they all left the wedding shower, but he wasn't sure why. It wasn't like Jewel was the one in labor. For some reason, though, he still felt like his place was by her side as she welcomed the newest members of her family to the world.

"Come on, D." Darius reached out to lead Dion away from the now empty table. "Let's go watch this game and talk to a few more people to see if they can help you remember some of the other wedding showers you've been to here."

Dion followed his brother over to the table where his boss, Rick, was sitting with his arm around a strawberry blonde woman, his wedding ring glistening under the overhead lights. *Damn! Even the boss got hitched here? I'm missing a lot more memories than I thought.*

Maybe I should let Jewel have the space she seems to want for now and try to get some of my other memories back by talking to the other people in town this week. Hopefully, if I get to know Jewel, uh, Julia, from the perspective of her friends and the people in town who've known her a lot longer than me, I'll be able to figure out how to get her to talk to me without pissing her off even more.

Unfortunately, he didn't get very much socializing done before he felt overwhelmed and had to have Darius take him back to the bed and breakfast to lie down for one of his spells.

<div align="center">~~~</div>

How can he claim he doesn't remember meeting any of us, but he can remember to call me Jewel? That makes absolutely no sense. Julie pondered the brief conversation she'd had with Dion at the wedding shower all afternoon while waiting to go up and see her new nephews after they were born. *Either he remembers me or he doesn't. All the literature I've read on post-traumatic retrograde amnesia in the last few weeks, since Anthony mentioned that was his diagnosis, says that he might get some of the oldest memories he lost back once his brain heals. But he's not likely to get any of the more recent memories back. And he definitely won't get random moments in time spread out over the last year back, like Kay mentioned him talking about at the wedding shower. So, what's he trying to pull with acting like he remembers me, but he doesn't remember anyone else, or even everything about our relationship?*

As soon as they'd gotten to the waiting room at the birthing center, Kay and Anthony had filled everyone in on what Dion believed happened between them the month before, as well as how the only memories he had from the last couple of years were the dreams he had about hooking up with her. Both he and his brother claimed Darius was the one who answered Dion's phone when Julie called, but she wasn't completely convinced yet.

I suppose that could be true, Julie mentally conceded. *But even if Darius was the one who said those awful things to me, Dion could have found me in his contact list or text history to unblock my number and get in touch once Dare gave him his phone back.*

Even if his spotty memory stuff is true, I was listed as Jewel in his phone, so he should have had no problem finding me if he'd really wanted to look. But even if his memories from before the incident in October are spotty, he should have remembered talking to me last night to know not to call me Jewel again. Or to acknowledge the babies that are obvious to anyone who looks at my belly.

But not even asking about them today is just another reason why I should avoid him and not fall for his I-wanna-talk-to-you-because-I've-missed-you schtick. Unless, maybe, he wasn't lying when he said he didn't know how to contact me and really just wanted to get my number, so we could talk about the babies and our previous relationship privately. Like maybe he remembered we were keeping everything about us on the down-low, and he was trying to keep that up, not realizing that I've already outed us to everyone we'd been trying to keep from learning about our secret hookups. But is that because he's trying to respect my wishes? Or because he doesn't want anyone to know he's the father of my babies?

Julie's stomach was in knots from the way she kept going back and forth between wanting to kiss Dion and wanting to punch him. Even when she was trying to tell him off the past couple of days, she'd had to fight her urge to throw herself into his big, strong arms and beg him to make love to her one more time. Even now, while she was working through another angry phase, she couldn't help but wish she could believe him, so they could work things out and get back together.

It's got to be the pregnancy hormones, she decided. *As soon as I have the babies, they'll go away. And I can finally figure out if I love him or hate him.*

"Jerry Thomas and Jonah David Burleson are ready to meet their family," Justin announced as he burst into the waiting room, bringing Julie out of her mental spiral. Her brother was a proud new father with a smile as big as Texas as he rushed them all out of the waiting room and up the stairs to the room where Amy was recovering after giving birth. "They're identical, just like Amy and Ashlyn. Both six pounds and four ounces and nineteen-and-a-half inches long."

Julie couldn't wait to see her new nephews, thinking her brother's boys would be a preview of her own babies. She placed a hand over her baby bump as she mentally talked to her twins, even though she doubted they could hear her thoughts. *Let's go meet your cousins. They're going to either be your best friends, or your annoying overprotectors, just like my brothers and boy cousins were when I was growing up.*

When she got to the room and finally got to hold Jonah, who was wearing the darker of the two blue onesies they'd put the babies in so they could tell them apart, she was surprised to see that his eyes were brown. "I thought all babies were born with blue eyes," she commented as she looked over at Jerry in her sister's arms to see that he also had brown eyes.

She'd known the babies would be paler when they were born than their complexion would eventually turn because of needing the sun to activate their natural melanin. And she thought the same was true for eye color, since it was also partially determined by melanin levels.

"Oh, no, both my girls were born with brown eyes," Andrea, Amy's mother, clarified. "But neither one of them were as pasty white as Jerry and Jonah."

"We were lighter than we are now when we were born, though, right?" Amy questioned her mother, looking back and forth between Andrea and her babies, who were resting peacefully in Julie and Jen's arms.

"Oh, yes, all babies are born lighter than they end up," Andrea clarified, reaching over to lightly brush her fingers through Jonah's black hair. "And once they start growing into their natural complexion, they'll end up having a skin tone somewhere between you and Justin. That's why you're lighter than I am, and I'm lighter than my momma was. We just kept mixin' in those white boy genes 'til your babies came out lookin' like white boys."

"Hey, I'm one percent African, so they could have a small sliver of their Black genes from me," Justin argued, referring to the Southern Bantu People listed on his DNA analysis from the Ancestry site they'd all submitted their samples to at the beginning of the year.

"Oh, please, I have more African in me right now than you do," Julie scoffed, rolling her eyes at her brother. "And my DNA test showed a hundred percent European."

"I know you're referring to your babies," Amy's twin sister, Ashlyn, chimed in with a grin. "But I really wish you'd give me some percentage estimates based on your total body mass while making those babies, so I'd know if Dion's brother is worth takin' for a spin this week."

"Ashlyn Danae!" Andrea scolded her daughter.

Yeah, I'm not touching that with a ten-foot pole, Julie thought, stifling the urge to laugh. *Or even Dion's foot-long-magic-peen pole.*

"What?" Ashlyn gave her mother a confused look. "I'm goin' through a dry spell since moving here. And while ya'll have an obvious preference for white meat, I need to know if I should switch back to dark meat to find a man who's packing the magic peen…"

"Enough!" Julie's dad barked, shutting down the inappropriate conversation, as Julie smiled and shrugged at Ashlyn. "Now is not the time or place for that discussion."

"Sorry, sir," Ashlyn apologized, looking contrite. "I forgot where we are for a moment there."

"I'm sorry, too, Dad," Julie admitted with a little less sincerity than Ashlyn, knowing it was her comment that started their friend down that malapropos path.

"But just so you know, Ashlyn," Julie's mom interjected. "Since he's freely admitting to being the man who said those horrible things to Julie last month, he's got a long way to go to prove he's changed enough to be worthy of dating any of you girls."

"Wait a minute, Mom," JJ interrupted. "Darius acts like a jerk and gets to avoid all your matchmaking ploys? How is that fair? And who do I have to be a jerk to, so I can get outta sittin' with every available woman in town at the rest of the stuff goin' on this week?"

"Oh, please, we're not trying to set you up with anyone this week," Susan scoffed at her oldest son. "We already know you've only got eyes for Deanna and are planning to use the buyout of OK Oil to win her over."

"No, Mom, I'm not," JJ sighed, shaking his head.

Julie thought her oldest brother was protesting a little too much. *He sounds almost exactly like Dion and I did when we didn't want anyone to know we were sneaking around to have sex.*

Thinking about those early stages in her relationship with Dion sent her right back to having lustful thoughts about her baby daddy. Luckily for her, Jonah took that moment to start fussing, obviously not wanting to be held while Julie daydreamed about Dion's magic peen.

"Oh, goodness," she cooed at the baby in her arms. "What's the matter, little man?"

"Did Aunt Julie pinch you, Jonah?" Justin teased as he took the baby from her arms.

"No, I didn't pinch him," Julie defended herself as she watched her brother expertly cradling his son in his arms.

Justin ignored Julie and continued speaking softly to his son as he walked over to the changing table set up in the corner of the room. As the rest of the people in the room continued with their conversations, she watched as her brother deftly changed his son's diaper.

It seemed strange to see her brother in such a domestic role, but it also made her wonder if Dion would ever be as adept at such fatherly skills.

The Dion I knew before would make such a great dad, Julie thought with a sigh. *If he ever acknowledges our babies' existence, that is. And now I really have to wonder if he was trying to set up a private talk to find out what I've shared with everyone and to work out how he can be a part of our babies' lives. Or if he really didn't hear me mention them last night, or what Kay said he seemed to miss when Anthony explained to the GWA crew about not telling them about my pregnancy before they got to town and first saw me yesterday.*

Damn it! I'm going to have to stop being such a bitch to him, so we can actually talk about if he wants to be a part of our babies' lives or not. And, if so, what role he wants to have in our babies' lives. Whether we can work things out to get back together or not, I have to give him the opportunity to step up and be their daddy if he wants it.

Chapter Seven

As she walked into the ballroom at the Hunters' Bed and Breakfast for the town-wide Thanksgiving celebration, Julie still hadn't figured out how she was going to get over her anger and hurt feelings enough to have a civil conversation with Dion, much less how she was going to, eventually, co-parent her children with him if he chose to be a part of their lives. She knew it was irrational to still be mad at him for the things his brother said that day in October, knowing in her heart of hearts that her big teddy bear of a man would never have said those things to her, if he'd been the one who actually answered his phone. As much as she'd tried to paint the Davis brothers with the same asshole brush to keep from forgiving him too soon, Julie knew it was just her hurt feelings that were causing her to keep lashing out at him.

But even when she looked at the situation more rationally, she couldn't help but feel like they could have avoided the whole situation, if only he'd told his brother and closest friends about his relationship with her, the way she'd told her sister and closest girlfriends about her relationship with him.

Yes, they'd originally decided together to keep things on the down-low to avoid any additional pressure from her matchmaking mother. But he knew her twin was in on the secret from day one. And that she'd confided in her cousin Becky shortly thereafter. She'd also told him when she opened up to her other girlfriends over the course of their eleven months together. So, she assumed he understood that she'd be fine with him confiding in the men closest to him. And the fact that he hadn't divulged their relationship to anyone made her feel like he was ashamed of being with her.

Yes, she knew that was partially her fault after the way she'd followed her family mandate to avoid being photographed by paparazzi after Brooklyn's situation had brought them into the national spotlight at the beginning of the year. But there was a big difference between avoiding being publicly photographed, even when she was by herself, and not telling the people nearest and dearest to them that they were closer than just the friendship they let the world see when he was in her hometown, where the paparazzi left them alone. *Or were run out of town by Bobby siccing the rest of the HDPD on them. Whatever.*

Rationally, Julie knew she was mad at Dion for making her feel like a shameful side piece while she was telling her closest confidants that he was her soulmate. But her pride wouldn't let her admit that to anyone, so when her family or friends mentioned him, or tried to talk her into working things out with him, she blamed her pregnancy hormones for her irrational anger.

Apparently, in addition to talking to Anthony, Kay, and the rest of the bridal party at the wedding shower, Dion and Darius had talked to quite a few people after she left with the rest of her family to go to the birthing center. Or at least, to the town gossips, who had spread his side of the story far and wide over the last three days, while she kept herself busy at work to avoid telling anyone how she really felt about everything.

From what she heard as she walked through the ballroom, everyone she knew now believed that Darius was a wonderful brother, who was just trying to protect Dion when he was injured and vulnerable to being taken advantage of by one of the unscrupulous women of the world. The irony that the people who'd known Julie all her life were casting her in the role of the unscrupulous woman seemed to be lost on them.

Feeling so many eyes on her as she joined her family made her wonder how many of her neighbors now thought of her as the horrific harpy, who was punishing Dion for a misunderstanding. Considering she hadn't opened up to anyone about why she was really upset with him, she supposed she couldn't really blame them for thinking that way about her. Not that she really wanted to clear things up so publicly.

Leah Mae Wright

Maybe I should ask Randi how she managed to evade everyone when she snuck back to the ranch last Thanksgiving? Only instead of running out of the room carrying a pregnancy test, I'll run out cradling my baby bump.

Julie still felt a little bit guilty for her part in causing that scene the year before. Oh, she hadn't done anything to cause the pregnancy test to come flying out of Randi's purse in front of the whole town. At least, not directly. But when her sister found the instructions in the bathroom after Randi and Kay came out of the restroom, it had been Julie's idea to return them to Randi's suitcase when nobody would notice, since she was staying at Charlotte's house. She'd had no idea that her attempt to be helpful would lead to Randi freaking out about everyone thinking the pregnancy test was hers and not Kay's.

Darn it! If I'd have thought of it sooner, I could have picked up a test to throw at Dion today. We could have made flying pregnancy tests a funny town Thanksgiving tradition.

As she took her seat with her family, Julie smiled at her quirky sense of humor, knowing she wouldn't have actually done what she was thinking for fear of offending her friend Randi, but still thinking it would have been funny.

I guess, at least, with everyone focused on talking about me and Dion this year, nobody will embarrass Randi by bringing up what happened last year. Not that she really has anything to be ashamed of, since it wasn't her test, and she wasn't one of the ones who ranted and raved and acted like a fool.

Thinking about the events at Thanksgiving the previous year brought her right back to thinking about the first time she met Dion. She'd been with the rest of her family down at the south bunkhouse on the ranch — the one that had since been turned into the second location of the Madeline Ashbury Houses Brooklyn and Bobby were opening across the country to house women and children escaping abusive home lives — when the GWA crew had arrived in a caravan from the bed and breakfast where they were staying.

Like her sister, female cousins, and most of the other women in town, Julie had been excited to have an influx of eye candy in the form of all those hot guys she watched on television every week. She knew her mom and Aunt Hazel would be trying to set them all up to start relationships while the GWA was in town, but she didn't think any of them would work out for her because of their conflicting work schedules. Julie wasn't opposed to meeting *The One* and falling in love, but she'd never wanted her mom to pick her man. Then again, when she was growing up, she hadn't expected her mom to push for her to jump straight into a relationship with a man, either.

It seems ironic that Mom seems to have forgotten the lessons she, Aunt Hazel, and Memmaw Judy taught all us girls about being wary of bulls who give the beef away for free because it's usually rotten.

Unlike most girls, who'd always been told the analogy about guys not wanting to buy the cow when they can get the milk for free to keep them from having sex too soon in a relationship, things were done differently when growing up on the Burleson Ranch. Because they didn't milk their cows, but instead processed them for beef to be sold in restaurants and grocery stores, they'd changed the analogy to better fit with their family business. While they all believed strongly in love at first sight and finding their soulmates, they also wanted the younger generations to take their time to get to know their potential partners instead of jumping straight into bed. And apparently, Memmaw Judy had believed that foodborne illnesses from eating undercooked beef tainted with Salmonella, E. coli, or other bacteria was a better way to reference the risk for sexually transmitted diseases than drinking milk, even though unpasteurized milk could contain some of those same germs.

While Julie had wanted to follow her elders' advice to take things slow, she also hadn't wanted to fall for someone who wouldn't fit into her life, which was why she'd always taken her time before jumping into bed with a man. So, even though she fell head over heels for Dion the instant her blue-gray eyes locked on his umber orbs as she walked across the paddock to where he was playing with the kids by the bounce house, she fought the attraction as much as she could for the first few days. Oh, she couldn't stop herself from being friendly and flirty. But she couldn't ask him to give up his dream job on the road with the GWA to move to town to be with her, any more than she could give up her position with Burleson Incorporated to go on the road with him.

She'd held out for six whole days before she finally allowed herself to enjoy the full physicality of her attraction to him. They'd been sitting together at Anthony and Kay's rehearsal dinner, talking about his travel schedule and holiday plans when she mentioned him coming back to town and getting a room that would be easy for her to sneak in and out of when he had time off for Christmas and New Year's. He'd asked if it was possible for her to sneak into his current room, and she'd taken the challenge to go with him to his room after the dinner started winding down.

Friday, November 23, 2018

"Don't you think someone's gonna notice you not goin' home tonight?" Dion had asked as they slipped out of the ballroom and up the back stairs to his room.

"No, Jen rode with me, so she's taking my car home tonight," Julie explained. "And she'll bring hers and a change of clothes to pick me up in the morning. So, anyone seeing us come home from a donut run will think I've been with her the whole time."

"So, your sister can know about us, but nobody else can?" Dion arched an eyebrow at her as he unlocked the door to his room.

"It's not that nobody can know," Julie clarified, popping up on her toes to peck a kiss on his stubble-covered cheek. "Just nobody who'll tell my mom or Aunt Hazel can know. They're serious about trying to push all of us to get married and start giving them grandbabies. So, if they know we're attracted to one another, then they'll start trying to talk you into retiring from wrestling to move here. Or talk me into taking a sabbatical from work to travel with you."

Julie sauntered past him into the room, twirling around to face him when she got to the end of the bed. "In fact, if they find out I'm the one who invited you to come back here for Christmas, they'll have our wedding planned for before New Year's. So, unless you're ready to say 'I do' and retire to the ranch, we need to keep this between us."

"Would it be so bad for you to take some time off to travel with me?" Dion suggested, stalking toward her after shutting and locking the door behind him.

"Dion," Julie sighed, hating that her next words might end them before they even began. "I love my job just as much as you love yours. So, if starting this is gonna mean you start pressuring me to give it up to be with you, then maybe me coming up here was a bad idea."

"No, Jewel, that's not what I meant," Dion insisted, pulling her into his arms and pressing a sweet kiss to her temple. "I just meant that I wanna see you more often than when I have time off for holiday breaks. Like maybe you could travel with me when you take your vacation time or whatever, so we can make this long-distance thing work until I'm ready to retire. That won't be but a few years, ya know. Since the wrestling business is so rough on our bodies, most of us retire from the ring between thirty-five and forty. So, it won't be long before I'll be ready to settle down and maybe run a gym or something once the kids are in school, so you can keep on being the high-powered executive in the family."

"Yeah, I could possibly do that," Julie decided, leaning her head back to look up at him and smile as she slid her arms around his neck. "In fact, I'd like to meet up with you on tour once in a while, whenever we can coordinate it where I can work with one of our subsidiaries, or scope out a business we're thinking of buying into, in one of the cities you're wrestling in that night. That way we can see each other at least once a month, even when you have a long time between holiday breaks and my family interferes with my vacation time. But we still can't let my mom or Aunt Hazel, or any of their friends know about us."

"Yeah, I'd like that." Dion gave her a dazzling smile. "So, since we're makin' plans to see each other in the future, does that mean you're okay with making this an exclusive arrangement?"

"Most definitely," Julie sighed, pressing her body against his to feel his extra-large erection pressing into her belly.

"Good, 'cause I can't stand the thought of anyone else touching you," Dion growled as he slid his hand down her back to cup her ass.

"Me? I'm not the one with groupies," Julie chuckled as she ran a hand up the previously smooth skin on the back of his head that also now sported a slight five o'clock shadow just like his jaw. "You're the one who's gonna have a problem maintaining our exclusivity."

"Please, I've seen the way all the guys look at you, Jewel," Dion scoffed, shaking his head. "Yeah, I might have to sign an autograph or two for the ring rats who come to our fan expos or catch us out having dinner or whatever, but I doubt I get hit on half as often as you do."

"In case you haven't noticed, Mr. Davis, I live in Heart's Destiny, Texas," Julie smirked. *"Where everyone has known me since birth. And my brothers and cousins made it clear that I'm off limits to every man in town. If I hadn't gone to Austin for college, I'd still be a virgin. Although, since I haven't been with anyone but my battery-operated boyfriend since I graduated three years ago, I kinda feel like I've earned my V-card back."*

"Hmmm, you gonna let me punch that reinstated V-card tonight, Miss Burleson?" Dion wagged his eyebrows suggestively.

"Hmmm, the way you say 'Miss Burleson' makes me wish I had a naughty schoolgirl uniform to wear for a little role play," Julie teased. *"And with the way you shave your head, you do look a lot older than me, so you could pull off the dirty professor role."*

"I'm only thirty-two, Jewel, not that much older than you," Dion protested, grinning as he shook his head at her.

"Really? I thought you said it would just be a few years before you retire at forty?" Julie arched an eyebrow as she questioned his earlier statements. *"Eight years is more than a few. That's two years longer than the difference in our ages."*

"Technically, I'm thirty-two-and-a-half," Dion pointed out. *"So, only seven-and-a-half years before I turn forty. And while my goal is to have a twenty-year career by wrestling until just after my fortieth birthday, I could easily suffer an injury or just feel rundown enough that my performance in the ring suffers so much that I'll decide to retire closer to thirty-five. So only two-and-a-half years before I could possibly turn in my tights. Between two-and-a-half and seven-and-a-half seems like a few to me. And since I now have you as my incentive to retire early, I might not even make it to my thirty-fifth birthday."*

"Yeah, you're gonna have to push that back closer to forty," Julie retorted. *"Especially if you're planning to stay home and be Mister Mom for the first few years after you retire, 'cause I don't plan on taking time off from work to have kids until at least twenty-twenty-five, when I've had ten solid years of work experience. I have to put in my time and prove myself, so I'll be able to fill Dad's shoes as CEO when he retires in another twenty or thirty years."*

Julie placed a hand on her slightly rounded belly as she came back to the present. *Yeah, I shoulda realized a year ago that my planned timeline was doomed to fail. Less than an hour after I made that statement, he took off his clothes, and I could see he was more than virile enough to get past my birth control.*

Magic peen, indeed. The phrase "hung like a horse" finally made sense to me when I first saw Dion's dick. And damn it, I really need to stop thinking about wanting to see it again.

No matter how much she tried to stop herself from thinking about Dion, her gaze kept turning in his direction all through the meal. Even as everyone started finishing the main course and mingling between dinner and dessert, her eyes kept following him around the room of their own accord. It took everything she had to keep her jealousy from showing as she watched several women, whom she'd previously considered friends, appearing to flirt with him.

As she covertly observed Dion making the rounds and talking to the various residents of Heart's Destiny, Julie started to wonder if things between them would be different if she hadn't insisted on keeping their attraction to one another a secret from her mom and Aunt Hazel a year ago. If they'd have been open with everyone about their relationship, and not just her closest family and friends, then Darius might have known about her to call her when Dion was injured, instead of being blindsided by her phone call.

At the very least, if they'd been open and honest with the world about their relationship, she wouldn't be mad about feeling like his dirty little secret. If that were the case, then even if Darius hadn't known about her because of not speaking to Dion for over a year, she might be able to forgive him for the misunderstanding and wouldn't have any hard feelings toward Dion now.

Maybe if I'd have given in and gone on tour with him, instead of just sneaking around for rides on his magic peen, then we could have avoided this whole misunderstanding completely because I would have been at the hospital with him when everything went down.

Even though she was quieter than normal during dinner with her family, all the time she spent thinking made her more open to listening, when her friends finally caught up with her while waiting for their dinner to settle before having dessert. Even though she felt a little jealous of the Thirsty Threesome and the other women in town who'd openly flirted with Dion all day, she knew her true friends would never do such a thing, especially knowing she was carrying his twins. After talking to Dion about his side of the story, her core group of friends all started telling her how sorry both he and Darius were for the things that were said on that infamous phone call.

Everyone suggested she take some time to talk to him, having a one-on-one conversation with nothing to distract them, even the family members who'd been tasked with running interference for her all day. Julie knew she needed to follow their advice, even if she couldn't begin to think about possibly trying to get back together with him yet.

Regardless of anything else, he was the father of her babies. And she had to give him the opportunity to be an active parent to their children if he wanted to participate in their lives.

Maybe Sunday? Or maybe Monday? After the wedding is over and the GWA has left town, so we can find a neutral space to meet without a large audience. But before my doctor's appointment on Wednesday, in case he wants to come to that. If he's even going to be in town past the weekend?

<div align="center">~~~</div>

Friday, November 29, 2019

As he walked into the ballroom at the bed and breakfast for the second time that week, Dion immediately started having more flashes of memories with Jewel. He'd had a couple the day before when he was there for Thanksgiving dinner, but they were mostly replays of his hotel room romps with her that he'd been dreaming about all along, or as they were alone and chatting while on their way to his room, only now he knew which ones were the times he was with her at the B and B, and which ones were at the various hotels they stayed in while he was on tour with the GWA. These flashes of memory were different. They were also the first he could recall having where there were other people present with him and Jewel sitting together and interacting with their friends. As much as he enjoyed remembering all the ways he'd made love to Jewel, these memories of them acting like a couple in public gave him more hope about his potential memory recall, as well as his future with Jewel.

As Dion took his seat and looked around the room, the red and white decorations on every table morphed into royal blue and white before his eyes. He no longer saw Dean and Allissa's rehearsal dinner, but instead he saw a different wedding event when he got to sit beside his Jewel.

"So, when you leave town on Monday, where will you be going?" Jewel's eyes looked sad as she thought of him leaving town.

"We'll fly from San Antonio to Tampa," Dion replied, wishing he didn't have to leave her side. "We'll hit a couple of different cities in Florida before spending the next month going up the east coast until we break in New York for Christmas and New Year's."

"Is that where you'll be spending the holidays?" Jewel tilted her head coyly. "In New York?"

"No, normally I'd head home to NOLA for the holidays," Dion informed her, fighting not to reach over and push her slightly wavy blonde hair behind her ear. "But since I had a fight with my brother last time I was home, I'll probably just hang out with whichever one of the guys doesn't mind me crashing at their place, and call Mama Marcel to make sure she gets the presents I'll send home instead."

"You could come here for the holidays," Jewel suggested, smiling shyly. "Maybe get a room that's easy for me to sneak in and out of?"

Before Dion replied in his memory, the room transformed once more to a different version of red and white decorations. This time instead of sitting and having a whispered conversation with Jewel while the rest of the guests milled about the room, they were sitting down to dinner with Liam, the blonde woman he'd been told was Jewel's fraternal twin sister, the woman he'd been introduced to as Josh's girlfriend, Cait, at the wedding shower earlier in the week, a little boy who looked to be of Hispanic descent, and one of the Burleson couples whose names he still didn't remember.

"When do we get to eat cake?" The little boy looked to the blond man beside him as he asked the question.

"After you eat your dinner," the blond man chuckled, just as a waiter placed a plate of roast beef, potatoes, and baby carrots in front of the little boy.

"Don't worry, Brody," the man assured him. "You only have to eat half of your dinner before you can have cake."

"We'll help you out, little man," Liam told the little boy, whose name Dion now knew was Brody, as he pointed back and forth between himself and Dion. "Pass your plate over here and we'll take half off, so you can see it's not too much you have to eat before getting cake."

"Don't trust him." Dion shook his head at Brody while pointing his thumb at Liam to tease his long-time friend and tag-team partner. "If you pass him your plate now, he'll eat it all before you even get a bite. Eat as much as you want first, and then we'll clean your plate for you once you're full."

"I don't trust either of you." Brody wrapped his arms around his plate, pulling it as close to him as he could without it falling off the table into his lap. "I've seen the way you cheat when you wrestle."

"Smart boy!" Jewel reached around behind Cait to give Brody a high-five, as the rest of the table laughed.

Dion had to smile at Jewel having such an easy interaction with the little boy, knowing she would be a great mom to their kids one day.

He wasn't sure how old the little boy was, but based on his size, he assumed he wasn't old enough to be in school yet. Therefore, Dion was impressed that someone so young had recognized their heel tactics in the ring.

"I only cheat when I'm playing a bad guy on TV," Dion protested, pretending to pout, so he wouldn't look so scary to the small child. "I'm really not a bad guy, I promise."

"Feck!" Liam slugged Dion in the shoulder, his voice taking on the distinct Irish accent he used when in character for the GWA, instead of his typical New Yorker inflection. "You better change dat I to we. I can't be partners wit a clown who throws me oehnder de boehs while defendin' 'imself."

Brody's brow furrowed as he looked at Liam. "Daddy, why's he talking funny?"

Daddy? Either Brody's adopted or he looks more like his mom than his dad.

The blond guy looked confused by his son's question, so Dion stepped in to explain.

"Red's Irish tends to come out at odd times," Dion quipped, garnering chuckles from the ladies at the table. "Especially when he's upset, and right now he's upset that you think he's a bad guy. But we're only pretending to be bad guys when we're wrestling."

"I don't know." Jewel's twin shook her head as she waved her fork at Liam and Dion. "Bugging Brody and not letting him eat his dinner, so he can have cake later, seems like bad guy behavior to me."

"I agree with Jen." The woman beside Jewel's twin reached in front of Brody's dad to pat Brody's arm, which was still protectively wrapped around his plate. "Don't listen to Red Velvet," she instructed him. "They're just trying to trick you into not eating your dinner, so they can have your cake later."

"Yeah, they're such big fans of cake that they use a type of cake as their tag-team name," Jewel added with a giggle.

"We're Red Velvet," Dion blurted, his eyes locking on Liam as the memory faded and he recognized the decorations around the room as transforming back to what they'd been when he walked into the rehearsal dinner a few minutes earlier.

"Yeah," Liam nodded encouragingly.

"Hey, that's something you didn't remember before," Dean pointed out. "But how did you remember the name ya'll started using back in February, instead of one of the other rehearsal dinners you've been to in this room in the last year?"

"It was mentioned in a flash of memory from another time I was in this room. I think we were here for a wedding reception, instead of a rehearsal dinner, though," Dion explained. "There was a little boy at our table and we were talking about cake. And Jewel said something about us being such big fans of cake that we used a type of cake for our tag-team name. I don't remember the name of the woman who actually called us Red Velvet, but I think she's one of Jewel's cousins, or maybe married to or dating one of Jewel's cousins."

"Oh yeah, I remember now," Liam grinned. "That was at James and Randi's wedding reception. Charlotte is Julie's cousin and she married Ian, whose little boy…"

"Brody," Dion interjected, remembering the name from the conversation in his head, since he didn't remember actually meeting him.

"Yeah, we were gonna help Brody clean his plate, so he could have a piece of wedding cake without having to eat all his dinner," Liam chuckled. "And Jen, Julie, and Char were giving us hell about trying to steal his food instead."

Dion noticed Rylie stiffen in her seat beside Liam when he mentioned Jen and wondered why Liam's wife didn't like the other woman. *Wait! I know this. They've gone over all these names with me enough this week that I should remember them all by now.*

Jen. Jen. Jen. Which one is Jen? Jen is Julie's twin.

Fuck! That should be easier for me to remember.

And every time the older women in town paired me up with Julie, they paired Liam up with Jen.

Holy shit! Is that why Rylie doesn't like her? Or maybe she just doesn't like it when Liam mentions her name? Is she jelly? No, that's not the right word. Screw it, I can't think about finding the right word right now. I need to figure out what's going on between Liam and Rylie more than I need to have the right words in my head.

As he closely examined his friend and his new bride, Dion realized that the young Black woman clearly had feelings for her much older white husband.

Fuck! I know Liam said he's got the lawyer who reviews his GWA contracts looking into where he has to file for an annulment or divorce. But doesn't he see that Rylie might actually want to stay married to him?

Dion studied Liam as they ate and gave a few toasts, trying to see if his red-headed friend shared his wife's obvious affection. Unfortunately, he didn't see anything in Liam's behavior to give him a clue how his friend felt about his new wife.

Damn! He's not acting any different with her than he did with Jen when we were pushed to sit with Jen and Julie every time we came to town.

Wait. How do I know that? I've only had the one memory of seeing him sitting beside Jen while I was with Jewel. But for some reason, I get the feeling that we sat with them all the time and always acted friendly and maybe a little flirty, but we never let our true feelings show.

And even in the flashback, when I think I remember talking about Jewel sneaking into my room, we were whispering while everyone else at our table was up dancing or mingling with the other guests. And we didn't even lean in and touch each other then, so nobody would figure out what we were talkin' about.

As the party went on around him, Dion tried to make himself go back to that first flash of memory. He wanted to confirm that they had whispered plans for her to sneak into his room that night, the way he thought the memory had been going when it changed. Instead of picturing those blue and white decorations, however, Dion saw the ballroom decked out in an array of pinks.

"We are seriously gonna hafta rib Rick about having a Pepto Bismol pink wedding," Crockett chuckled as he sat down after holding out a chair for the only non-blonde woman at their table.

"Considering it's Fiona's favorite color, I don't think Rick is gonna appreciate you dissing the pink," the brown-haired woman, whom Dion thought was another of Jewel's cousins, warned, shaking her head at Crockett.

"But by all means, make sure we're around to watch when you mention it to him," Surfer Josh chuckled. **"And maybe wait until the next time we see him sparring to bring it up, so we can watch you get your ass kicked by the boss."**

"Naw, Rick wouldn't risk the show angles by injuring him like that," Dion disagreed, knowing their boss would be much more devious than that. **"But if you do get brave enough to make that comparison to his face, I'd suggest you keep a close eye on your protein shakes."**

"Why would he need to watch his protein shakes?" Jewel looked at Dion curiously.

"'Cause it'd be easy to add some Pepto to the strawberry shakes Crockett's always drinkin'," Dion smirked. **"So, Rick might wanna see if it'll stop Crockett's diarrhea of the mouth."**

"Damn, D, I didn't expect you'd be the one to come up with an idea that demented." Crockett shook his head. **"I've always thought of you as the nicest guy on the roster. But I guess my dad was right when he told me not to trust anyone with a quiet, reserved personality."**

"Why do you think I like teaming with him?" Liam chuckled, pointing at Dion with his thumb. "He comes up with all the best pranks we pull in the locker room."

"Like that oil that made us all tingle when we were doing that photo shoot last time we were in New York?" Surfer Josh glared at Dion.

"Oh, this sounds like a story we need to hear," the blonde beside Surfer Josh, whom Dion remembered meeting at Thanksgiving, but whose name he couldn't recall, giggled as she placed her hand on Josh's forearm.

"We have to do photo shoots at least once a year, so when we were in New York City for TV in May, we stopped by the GWA headquarters for them to get the promo shots to use to advertise the different events over the summer," Surfer Josh explained.

"Only when we do photo shoots, we can't just be in the street clothes for our gimmicks," Liam added, grinning. "We've gotta be in our tights and oiled up, so we look like we're sweating through a fight."

"Peppermint oil," Dion mumbled so low that nobody around him could hear him as his memory transformed from the ballroom where they were talking to the studio set up for photo shoots at the GWA headquarters.

He couldn't recall who all was there for photos that day, but he did remember the makeup artist having to take the sprayer head from the bottle of jojoba oil that she'd misted him down with to the restroom to rinse it out to try to get it to spray more evenly. And while the oil bottle was sitting there uncapped for him to finish rubbing it on his chest and arms, Dion looked through the box of essential oils next to the diffuser on the back corner of the table and put a few drops of peppermint oil in the jojoba oil before she came back to use the oil on the rest of the guys.

After growing up with his mom and Mama Marcel mixing essential oils into carrier oils before selling the little rollerball applicators to tourists, he knew the small amount he'd added wasn't enough to be harmful because the jojoba oil diluted it. But he also knew that even a small amount of peppermint oil felt tingly on the skin, so it was a safe way to freak out the guys.

His memory morphed again to another time he'd used a little bit of peppermint oil in a carrier oil. Only this time, he and Jewel were naked in a hotel room and used it to massage one another. His dick instantly got hard as he remembered rubbing the oil into every inch of her porcelain skin.

Oh, fuck, the feel of her hands on me was fucking amazing, he thought as he tried to regulate his breathing to keep from broadcasting his thoughts to everyone around him. As much as he hated it, he had to let that memory go and try to come back to the moment, so he didn't embarrass himself by jizzing in his pants at his friends' rehearsal dinner.

Instead of tuning back into the party going on around him, Dion's mind morphed into another event in the ballroom. This time, the decorations were various shades of blue, and he was seated at a table with Jewel, Liam, Jen, James, Randi, Allissa's mom Windy, her friend Kandi, and two guys Dion didn't recognize.

"So, I know you two are married," Windy waved her hand at James and Randi. *"But what about the rest of you?"* She turned to motion toward Dion, Jewel, Liam, and Jen, looking particularly interested in Liam's answer for some reason. *"Are you guys married or still just in the dating phase?"*

"Oh, no, we're not a couple," Jen protested, waving her hand between her and Liam.

"But anytime we're in town, Dion and I get paired up with Julie and Jen by the Matchmaking Mommas," Liam explained.

"Oh, so you're just not married yet," Kandi decided, nodding her head as if it helped her understand more clearly. *"Ya know, instead of trying to cram all the wedding stuff into a single week like they did for this wedding, you should let us host your bachelor parties at the brothel next time you come through Vegas."*

While Dion had absolutely no desire to be with anyone other than Jewel, especially not the women who worked in a brothel, he couldn't resist trying to get Jewel riled up by asking about Kandi's idea while Jewel was sitting right beside him. *"What exactly do ya'll do at a bachelor party in the brothel?"*

"Pretty much what we do every night, sugar," Kandi cooed, grinning.

"I've been to bachelor parties at strip clubs," Liam interjected, carrying on the questioning while Dion watched Jewel roll her eyes. *"And while pretty much all of us got a lap dance at some*

point or another, the main event was when the groom was tied to the stripper pole for all the girls to dance on him. Do you do something similar at the brothel? Where the groom gets multiple girls while everyone else watches? Or do the guys all go to separate rooms with a girl for each of them?"

"Either way, it sounds like a good way to piss off the bride, so she calls off the wedding," Jewel muttered disdainfully before either Kandi or Windy could answer.

"Nope!" Dion popped his eyes open and forced himself back to the moment, not wanting to think about a time when he might have pissed Jewel off over something he would never actually do.

"Did you remember something else?" Dion turned to his brother, who had voiced the question that everyone else at the table seemed interested in having him answer as well.

"Yeah, a few more things," Dion admitted, not sure he wanted to get into the details about all the memories that were coming back to him right then. He turned to look at the friends he'd worked with for several years to ask, "Just how many wedding receptions or other events have I been to in this room in the last couple of years?"

"Ours tomorrow is gonna be the fifth wedding reception you've been here for in the last year," Dean replied with a smile. "And you've been at all the rehearsal dinners in this room, too, so your memories could be from any of the nine times we've gathered here for wedding stuff, or the two Thanksgiving dinners counting yesterday, or the New Year's Eve party you attended here last year."

"Or when we used this room to practice two stepping before James and Randi's wedding," Allissa added with a smile. "But Julie wasn't here for that, so you might not remember it, since you only seem to be remembering times when you were with her."

Dion didn't mention remembering a few minutes in the studio in New York, assuming his brain only made that connection because of needing the bridge to go from sitting beside Jewel while discussing the prank in one memory to another memory of using the same oils for sensual massages with her.

"Damn, D, you must really love this girl, if the only memories you're getting back are when you were with her," Darius sighed, shaking his head, "even if they aren't from when ya'll were hookin' up."

"I do," Dion confessed, scanning the room until his eyes locked on his dream girl. "Now I've just gotta figure out how to get her to talk to me again, so we can start making new memories."

Chapter Eight

"Are you sure you want me to do this and not your dad?" As he joined Allissa, and the rest of the women participating in the wedding, in the bridal suite to wait for everyone else to be seated, so he could walk her down the aisle, Dion had to give her one last opportunity to change her mind. "It's not too late for me to go get him to take my place."

"Positive, Big D," Allissa smiled up at him, using the moniker the GWA women usually only called him when they wanted to rile up the other guys, since the nickname was given to him by a ring rat, who'd coined it to describe his dick. "As much as I've loved getting to know Grant the last few weeks, I wouldn't be here if it wasn't for you. So, I want you to be the one to walk me down the aisle."

Over the course of the week in town, Dion had learned that Allissa's stalker hadn't turned out to be her biological father, as she'd feared when she came to see him in the hospital the day after the incident. Apparently, there'd been a rash of people in Heart's Destiny and the GWA doing DNA tests earlier in the year, and Allissa's had revealed her biological father was an eighteen-year-old kid who'd gone with his buddies to lose his virginity at the brothel where Windy Walters worked right before joining the Marines. And Allissa had only recently — since the incident when Dion was injured — connected with Grant Cohen to start getting to know him. Grant coming to town for all the events leading up to the wedding was the first time they'd actually met face to face, but Dion still thought they might regret not having him walk his daughter down the aisle in a few years, once they'd grown closer.

"Actually, I think it was your dad's big D that helped make you," Amethyst pointed out, smirking like she was trying to hold back a giggle.

"Yeah, but he just got laid and didn't know he'd actually made a baby," Allissa disagreed, leaning her head over on Dion's bicep when he sat down beside her. "Big D actually saved my life, risking his own in the process."

"And you probably shouldn't call Dion that where Julie might hear you, 'cause she might get jealous that you're talking about his dick," Emerald added, causing the other women in the room with them to giggle at his expense.

"Since he knocked her up, I think Julie knows better than anyone how big his dick is," Rylie chortled.

Dion suddenly remembered why he'd never dated any of the women's division wrestlers that he worked with. They were as bad, or worse, than some of the guys when it came to crass locker room talk.

"Maybe we should switch the nickname to Big Daddy D?" Randi suggested. "Ya know, since he's gonna be a daddy."

"How about just Big Daddy?" Kay recommended. "That way none of our perverted friends will speculate what the D stands for besides his name."

"How did the rest of the guys get so lucky that they get to wait at the front of the church, instead of walkin' ya'll down the aisle?" Dion wondered aloud, fighting to keep from smiling at the mischievous women around him. "Maybe if your husbands were back here with us, ya'll wouldn't be talkin' about the size of my dick."

"We can't help it." Emerald shrugged nonchalantly. "We're all married to white men, and we all know Black men have bigger dicks."

"Huh? Now I know what part of Anthony comes from his two percent African DNA," Kay quipped, tapping a finger on her chin, and causing another round of giggles among the women.

"T. M. I., woman," Dion asserted, shaking his head at the giggling women, and hoping to stop the rest of them from sharing more than he wanted to know about their husbands, who were all among those he considered his friends. "I don't wanna know how any of your husbands measure up."

"I wonder if ethnicity matters for clit size the way it does for penis size?" Amethyst mused. "You know, since they're formed from the same type of cells in utero."

"I'm not comparing my clit to yours to find out," Emerald snorted.

"I'm not asking you to," Amethyst retorted. "Besides, even if we were to all lift our skirts and measure, six women isn't a big enough sample to compare from race to race, even though we have a relatively even mix of ethnicities represented. But maybe Big Daddy can remember back to his days with the ring rats to give us a bigger sample size. Or at least his opinion on who had bigger clits and who had littler clits."

"I'd rather know if guys prefer a big clit or a little clit," Rylie chuckled.

Dion looked up to the ceiling and prayed aloud. "Dear Lord, please forgive me for whatever sin I committed that earned me the punishment of being a part of this conversation."

"Seriously, D, help a girl out," Amethyst implored him, batting her eyelashes comically. "I need to know if being Vietnamese puts me at a disadvantage for having an appealing clit."

"Sorry, ladies," Dion apologized, tapping his finger to his temple as he used his TBI to his advantage. "Amnesia, remember? I only remember seeing Jewel's in my dreams, so I can't help you."

"You can, at least, give us an opinion on what guys like," Emerald insisted. "Does clit size matter as much as dick size?"

"No," Dion admitted with a sigh. "It doesn't matter. With the right person, none of that superficial shit matters."

Luckily, there was a knock at the door just before the preacher's wife stuck her head in the room to call them out to line up for the processional. As they stepped out of the room and Dion saw Archer Everett and Laci Kirby were waiting with Mrs. Harrison to perform their duties as the ring bearer and flower girl, he cringed. *Hopefully, they didn't hear any of that.*

Once they followed Mrs. Harrison from the bridal suite to the vestibule, she lined them up in the correct order for the women and children to proceed Dion and Allissa into the chapel, so they would each be matched up with their husbands for the recessional.

While Dion wasn't having nearly as many issues with dizziness and vertigo since they'd figured out the right medication for those concussion symptoms, he was relieved to know that once he handed Allissa off to Dean, he could sit down on the first pew with Allissa's parents. As much as he'd love to be able to stand at the front of the church, where he could look out over the audience to see Jewel, he didn't want to ruin any of the photos of his friends' wedding by being caught paying attention to her and not the ceremony.

After everyone else entered the sanctuary, Dion escorted Allissa through the doors and up the aisle. Unlike the day before, when they'd rehearsed the wedding without any music, Dion started having flashes of different weddings as soon as he heard the **Bridal Chorus** start playing. Only instead of seeing his friends as they walked down the aisle, he saw Jewel from her place in the audience at each of the different weddings his friends had mentioned that he'd attended in the last year.

She always seemed to sit in approximately the same location in the church, but her hair and dress changed from ceremony to ceremony. At first, he saw her in a navy-blue dress with her hair down in soft waves around her shoulders. Then she transformed into a burgundy dress with her hair up. Next, she was in a lavender dress, also with her hair up but in a different style than the previous wedding. Finally, she was in a bright blue dress with her hair down and curlier than he remembered ever seeing it before.

As he reached the halfway point between the vestibule doors and the altar, Dion turned to look in the direction he believed he'd find Jewel based on those four quick flashes of memory. Sure enough, she was sitting right where he expected her to be, wearing a dark purple dress and with her blonde hair straight and split down the middle, the way she mostly seemed to wear it in his dreams.

Dion couldn't stop himself from smiling at her. He felt an instant connection to her when their eyes locked on one another, showing him how strong their feelings for each other still were, even if she wasn't ready to admit it just yet. *Fuck! I hope she feels the link between us as strongly as I do.* Unfortunately, he couldn't maintain their eye contact as he had to continue walking Allissa down the aisle to Dean.

He couldn't help but hope she felt that same cosmic connection, wishing for a little wedding magic to convince her to talk to him once all the festivities were over. Even after talking to several of her friends over the course of the last week, he wasn't sure what else might help him get back in her good graces. Trying to talk to her during the various times they were both at a function hadn't worked. Neither had enlisting the help of the bride to try to get the Matchmaking Mommas on his side.

Oh, Allissa had helped him convince both her mom and Dean's mom to talk to their cohorts around town on his behalf. But even though Mandi Hunter claimed to be best friends with Jewel's mom and aunts, they'd all been too busy that week with the various wedding functions, the Thanksgiving holiday, and Jewel's nephews being born to have time for any kind of serious talk.

After placing Allissa's hand in Dean's when they reached the pulpit, Dion sat down beside Allissa's dad. As he watched his friends exchange vows, he imagined the day he'd finally get to stand at that altar with Jewel.

He could clearly see their wedding day in his mind. The bridesmaids would be in purple dresses and carrying bouquets of yellow flowers. The groomsmen would be in black tuxedos with purple ties and yellow boutonnieres. Dion would be dressed similarly, but with both purple and yellow flowers in his boutonniere to match Jewel's bouquet.

I guess the flower stems will have to be enough green to round out the Mardi Gras color theme, 'cause I'm pretty sure she won't wanna go all out with all three colors, or have masks and beads as wedding favors.

Dion imagined standing at the altar as Jewel walked toward him while wearing a flowy, white, strapless wedding dress and carrying a large purple and gold bouquet. The more he thought about it, the more desperate he felt to one day be able to pledge his undying love to her in front of all their family and friends.

Man, I hope she'll forgive me someday soon, so we can still get to that point in our relationship.

<div align="center">~~~</div>

As she'd watched Dean and Allissa say their vows, Julie wondered if she'd ever get to have that happily-ever-after moment in her life. While watching Allissa being walked down the aisle by Dion, there'd been a moment when her gaze had locked with his, when Julie thought she still saw that possibility with him. But as soon as he passed the pew where she was sitting, their brief connection was lost. He'd gone right back to focusing on the task at hand before taking his seat in the front row, where she could no longer see his eyes. And she went right back to feeling as alone as she'd felt for the last month.

Oh, she knew she had her family's support in all things. They'd done a wonderful job of keeping her surrounded and running interference whenever Dion tried to approach her, or one of the busybodies in town tried to maneuver them into interacting for the last week. Even when they didn't understand her need to keep her distance from him for a little while, they'd all still stood by her decision to publicly avoid him to keep from drawing attention away from the lovebirds getting married this weekend. But even with all the love and support her family had shown her, it wasn't the same as that feeling of having a partner in a romantic relationship that she'd so briefly thought she had with Dion.

But was he really my partner when he didn't tell anyone about us being more than acquaintances, who developed a friendship during all of Mom's matchmaking attempts in the last year?

"What are the odds we'll get lucky and not be on the Matchmaking Mommas' radar tonight?" Becky smiled hopefully, as Julie walked into the reception with her sister and cousin.

"Maybe if we rush to sit at one of the tables with the kids, we can fill in the extra seats without leaving any for the guys to be directed toward," Jen suggested as they scanned the room to see where everyone else was sitting.

At the first few weddings they'd attended in the last year, they'd all behaved as their southern mommas raised them and politely sat where their name cards were at each wedding event. But after Rick had swapped around the name cards at Charlotte and Ian's wedding reception, they'd all pretty much ignored the seating arrangements made by the Matchmaking Mommas in an attempt to thwart their misguided efforts.

Since the men they'd been paired up with at every possible function for the last year were all seated at the head table as part of the bridal party, or had recently gotten married, or both, Julie hoped their mothers would back off a little on the matchmaking for the three of them. But knowing her mother and Aunt Hazel as well as she did, she was pretty sure they'd either try seating them with the Walkers or Deeres again, or pick a different set of single wrestlers to match them up with going forward. Well, Jen and Becky anyway. She also knew her mom was hopeful that she'd work things out with Dion, since she was carrying his babies.

"Sweet," Becky exclaimed, pointing to the table where two of her siblings were sitting down with their significant others and children. "Since Antonio is hanging out with Brody and JoJo, there's only three seats available at the table with Char and Cait."

"Perfect," Julie agreed, liking the idea of sitting with her cousin and future cousin-in-law, especially with the kids and guys there to provide some comic relief for the night to help her focus on anything but Dion. They quickly walked in that direction before any of the rest of their family or friends could steal their idea for avoiding being paired up by the Matchmaking Mommas. "Where are the rest of Anthony and Kay's kids?"

Julie knew they wouldn't be sitting with their parents because Anthony and Kay were in the wedding and would be sitting at the head table with the rest of the bridal party. And while Tia and Maria were old enough to go hang out with their friends from the GWA, she knew someone would need to watch over baby Sam.

To be honest, she'd been kind of hoping to volunteer for the job, thinking it would be a good idea to start practicing before her own babies were born. *Plus holding a baby through the whole reception earns me the perks of not dancing or participating in the bouquet toss.*

"Mom has Sam," Becky pointed out, directing Julie's gaze a couple of tables over, where Julie's Aunt Hazel was holding the baby. "And Tia and Maria are sitting with their friends."

As she let her eyes drift off of her aunt, Julie noticed her own parents were seated at the same table with her aunt and uncle. Along with Justin, Amy, and their twin boys, and Bobby, Brooklyn, and their baby, Maddie. "It looks like our folks are gonna be playing musical babies all night," she chuckled, even though she was a little disappointed to not be at the table with all the Burleson kids under six months old to get in on some of that baby holding time.

Playing musical babies would have been a lot more fun than trying to keep from drooling over Dion all night. She hated not being able to control her body's reaction to him. *Why doesn't attraction die when I'm hurt and angry?*

"Hopefully, between being busy with all the new grandbabies and the GWA crew starting to marry amongst themselves, their matchmaking plots against us will slow down," Becky quipped as they settled into their seats.

"Don't hold your breath for that to happen," Charlotte advised Becky, chuckling. "Mom's already asked me about when you're going to start bringing some new prospects to town as part of the cast and crew for your first movie."

"Doesn't she know that we bought that production company in California to get a jump start on making more movies than you could do with your crew at the theater?" Julie had used buying an existing production company, to help Becky get that portion of the entertainment division off the ground faster than starting from scratch, as an excuse to fly out to Los Angeles to see Dion over the summer, so she knew the first few Burleson Entertainment movies were already in production.

She'd actually gone early in the week to work out the production company deal, and then stayed over the weekend to see Dion in both Los Angeles and Long Beach, where she spent the next week working out another deal to add a chain of luxury hotels to the long list of Burleson Incorporated subsidiaries. The plan had been for her to use the need to check out the different hotels and resorts to coordinate more rendezvous with Dion whenever the GWA used one of the hotels that Burleson Incorporated now owned. Unfortunately, it hadn't worked out as planned because Julie wasn't as involved with the day-to-day operations of the individual hotels as she would need to be to have a legitimate excuse to travel to all the different locations. *Thankfully, it was still a lucrative deal that increased our profits for the third quarter, so I didn't have to justify that extended trip to California.*

"No, I didn't have the heart to tell her that," Becky admitted, shaking her head. "If she knew I'm handling most of the meetings I have with the producers overseeing each individual project via teleconference, instead of meeting with the hunky Hollywood guys in person, she'd drive Dad nuts tryin' to get him to make me bring them all to town."

Leah Mae Wright

"I think she still believes you're actually casting each movie personally from our office in town," Cait giggled, referring to the office at the Destiny Playhouse that Becky used as her executive office in her role as vice president of the entertainment division of Burleson Incorporated, and where Cait went to have an office backdrop when she teleconferenced with authors while converting their books into screenplays.

Unlike Julie, who loved traveling to find new businesses to bring under the Burleson umbrella, Cait had issues with agoraphobia after being injured in the same mass shooting a few years back that took the life of Ian's first wife and Brody's biological mom. If it were up to her, Cait would work exclusively from her home on the ranch, the way she had when she first started working with Burleson Incorporated as a housekeeper before she moved over to work as a screenwriter in the entertainment division. So, once they learned of Cait's issues, the whole family had rallied around her to help her expand the places she felt safe going. Now they were all proud of her for overcoming her fear to drive herself to work at the Destiny Playhouse five days a week.

"Yeah, I'm sure she's hoping I'll fall head over heels for a movie star." Becky rolled her eyes. "That's why she's lobbying for us to film **Heart's Desire** on the ranch, which I now have to present as an option to the producer."

"Oh, I doubt she cares if he's a movie star or not," Julie teased her cousin, glossing over the mention of the historical romance by Kay and Brooklyn that Becky and Cait were working on making into a movie. "She'll probably be just as happy if you fall for an unemployed drifter as long as he helps you give her more grandbabies."

"True," Becky laughed.

"Hey, is that what you did, sis?" Jen smirked at Julie.

"No, Dion's not unemployed," Josh stepped in to defend Julie's taste in men. "He's just on the injured reserve list."

"He's not really a drifter, either," Julie added, shaking her head at her sister. Though she was unsure why she felt the need to defend Dion to her sister.

"You don't think all that traveling around with the GWA counts as being a drifter?" Jen argued.

"No, a drifter travels aimlessly and doesn't have a place to go home to," Julie clarified. "Dion has roots in New Orleans and only traveled for work."

"Any chance he'll be replanting his roots here, now that he knows you're pregnant with his babies?" Charlotte's husband, who Julie still called Ian because that was the name he was using when she first met him, even though his sister Cait had reverted to calling him by the name he used before going undercover, posed the question that she had no idea how to answer.

"I don't know what his plans are," Julie shrugged and shook her head.

"That's because you keep avoiding talking to him," Jen pointed out, seeming to switch her opinion of Dion on a dime. "If you'd give him the chance to explain what happened last month and apologize for the misunderstanding, I'm sure ya'll could work things out to get back together."

Julie felt like she had whiplash from her sister's rapid reversal of opinion on Dion. She hated that she felt so disconnected from her twin because of everything that happened with him. Usually, she and Jen were so in sync that they could complete each other's sentences because of having similar thought processes. But that had changed in the last week, with Jen being more open to hearing Dion's side of the story, while Julie was still hurting too much to feel ready to listen to him. Their difference of opinion had started to cause the first rift Julie had ever felt between her and her twin.

They'd argued more than once since Dion came back to town. Jen kept telling Julie to quit being so stubborn and bullheaded, and Julie kept telling Jen that she couldn't understand because she'd never had her heart shattered completely into a billion pieces before, like Julie felt hers was at the moment.

Thankfully, before the current conversation could devolve into yet another argument between the twins, Rick Robertson took the microphone to get everyone's attention while the wedding party made their entrance into the ballroom. While she didn't think she'd ever want to be roasted during the wrestling style introductions he liked to deliver at his employees' weddings, Julie couldn't help but smile at how entertaining they always were.

"First up, we have the couple who kicked off the mass hysteria of all these Heart's Destiny and GWA weddings, Anthony and Kay Burleson!"

"Hey, I can only claim credit for courting Kay," Anthony objected as he twirled his wife around the ballroom. "You've gotta blame all the other weddings on the Matchmaking Mommas."

"Yeah, and your wife is one of them," Rick volleyed back.

"I didn't hear any objections on our wedding night," Fiona yelled across the room at her husband.

"I didn't say I objected, Fifi," Rick backpedaled as he looked pointedly at his wife. "I just said they were the first to fall in love and get married."

Several people laughed at the way the GWA owner had backtracked when it seemed like he would be in the doghouse with his wife, Julie included. When she'd first met Rick Robertson, she'd thought he was too serious and broody for her laid-back and lovable friend Fiona. But now, after multiple times of seeing his more jovial side come out while hanging out with mutual friends, she could tell they were perfect for each other.

As Rick went on to introduce the rest of the wrestlers in the bridal party by the titles they formerly held and how they'd screwed with his storylines over the past few months, Julie let her eyes drift over to the head table where Dion and his brother were already sitting. They had skipped the introductions, even though they were sitting with the rest of the bridal party. Julie had to wonder if that was because of Dion's injuries, or just because he wasn't there with a real date, having his brother as his plus one.

I guess I should look on the bright side and be glad I'm never going to have to endure one of those introductions since Dion and I broke up. Even though he skipped it tonight, I'm sure Rick will come up with a doozy of an introduction whenever Dion eventually gets married. So, I should feel thankful that I won't be the woman roasted with him.

It was kind of weak for a silver lining, but it was the best she could come up with right then. Her mom had always taught her that the best way to get through a bad situation was to look for the good things in life that came out of it. It was a lesson she'd passed down from the Donaldson line of her family tree. That was the line of her ancestors that Julie knew the least about because her mom's parents had passed on before Julie was born.

Thinking about not knowing a set of her grandparents made her realize that was something she was going to have in common with her children, since Dion's parents were both deceased. He had told her that he'd lost both his parents when he was a kid during one of their earliest conversations the week he was in town right after they met, but he hadn't given her specifics of their accidents until one of their later conversations. And even then, he'd focused more on the things he'd enjoyed doing with his parents as a kid than on the circumstances surrounding their deaths.

I know he said both their deaths were accidental — his dad's in a forklift accident on the docks and his mom's from being hit by a drunk driver. But I don't know if either of them had any medical issues before they died that might be passed on to our babies. I should probably ask him about that, so our babies will have a more complete family medical history.

But in order to do that, I'm gonna have to get past my anger and hurt feelings to actually talk to him without lashing out.

Unfortunately, seeing him sitting across the room laughing with his friends, like the fact that they weren't speaking to one another was no big deal, didn't help her quell her anger. In fact, him acting like he wasn't missing her as much as she was missing him just made her madder.

She ended up sitting there fuming about how unaffected he was by their breakup all through dinner and the various speeches. *Maybe I should flirt a little and dance with a few of the other guys here tonight to give him a taste of his own medicine.*

As Dean and Allissa took to the dance floor for their first dance as husband and wife, Julie contemplated whether that was a good idea or not. Unfortunately, she couldn't see flirting and flaunting other men in his face as anything more than a petty attempt to make him jealous as a way to keep everyone from seeing how utterly heartbroken she felt over their breakup. And even though she felt violently angry at him for not realizing how his indifference was hurting her, she didn't want to be *that woman* any more than she wanted everyone to see her as broken. Especially since she was pretty sure he wouldn't care either way.

He can't exactly get jealous over me if he doesn't remember what I thought we meant to one another. And if he sees me dancing with someone else, he might think I've moved on. And if he thinks I've moved on now, he might think I'd moved on before he was injured. And that could lead him to believe the babies aren't his.

Julie brooded all through the special dances, not coming back to the moment until Jen and Becky pulled her from her seat to line up for the bouquet toss. "No, seriously, I don't wanna participate this time," Julie argued, trying to pull away from her sister and cousin as they dragged her out onto the dance floor.

"Sorry, Sis, but if I've gotta do this, then so do you," Jen insisted, not letting go of Julie's hand even as Becky released her.

"Besides, you probably won't catch it anyway," Becky insisted. "I'm sure Dean's family is pushing for Allissa to throw it to his cousin Ashley this time."

"Fine, but ya'll better make sure we're nowhere near Ashley in case she bungles the catch," Julie finally acquiesced, pulling her hand from her sister's grasp, and turning to find Ashley in the crowd to make sure she was as far away from her as possible while still standing on the dance floor.

Unfortunately, turning to try to find Ashley in the crowd meant she took her eyes off of Allissa, so she didn't realize her cousin was dead wrong about whom she planned to target with the bouquet of red roses. She barely caught the flash of red in her peripheral vision in time to turn back toward the bride to catch the bouquet before it smacked her in the face.

Pluck a duck! Julie mentally groaned as she closed her eyes and dropped her head forward, knowing there was no way the garter would go to anyone but Dion after the way he'd been pleading his case to the bridal party all week. *I guess I'm talking to him sooner than I planned, after all.*

~~~

Dean surprised Dion when he pulled him aside after his first dance with his new wife to insist on Dion joining the rest of the guys on the dance floor for the garter toss. Dion had planned to sit it out, not
~~~

wanting to risk any kind of scuffle among the guys that could lead to an accidental elbow to the head, after his doctors had warned him about the dangers of second impact syndrome. But apparently, these things were almost always rigged to go to the next couple the matchmakers in town wanted to push together. And this time it was his and Jewel's turn, so he had to participate.

While he was grateful that everyone seemed to support his efforts to clear things up with Jewel, he still felt hesitant to participate until he saw that Julie had indeed caught the bouquet. It wasn't that he didn't believe his friends would try to rig the toss. But more that he knew there were always things outside their control that could cause the plan to go awry. So, he had to watch and make sure the bouquet toss went the way Dean planned before he decided to take the chance of getting injured again to be paired up with Jewel in the pictures.

"Shit, Dare," Dion warned his brother as they watched the women fill up the dance floor, preparing for Allissa to toss the bouquet. "If Jewel catches the bouquet, then I'm gonna need you to block for me, so I don't take another hit to the head tryin' to catch the garter." Not that he thought Dare would have to step up, since Jewel didn't even appear to be looking in Allissa's direction.

"Don't worry, D," Darius assured him, nodding his head as Allissa took aim and pitched the ball of roses straight at Jewel. "I'll always have your back."

"Thanks," Dion smiled as he watched his woman turn just in time to catch the bouquet before hanging her head as if she was disappointed by making the catch. *Fuck! She's obviously not happy about us being targeted this time around.*

Realizing that Jewel wanted to avoid him so much that she was visibly unhappy about catching the bouquet, and possibly having to be photographed with him after the garter toss, caused Dion to start having the weird feelings he got right before passing out, starting with his lips tingling. *Fuck! Fuck! Fuck! This is the worst possible timing ever!*

Even though he knew Jewel would probably be happier if he snuck out and laid down somewhere until the spell passed, instead of going out on the dance floor to be the man to catch the garter, he couldn't stand the thought of her being paired up with anyone but him for those pictures. So, Dion decided to push his luck, hoping he didn't fall down and hit his head again in the middle of the reception.

As he took his place at the front of the crowd, Dion tried one of the deep breathing techniques the doctor had suggested to push past that overwhelmed feeling and try to keep from passing the fuck out. He closed his eyes and blocked out the way the guys were heckling Dean for turning the chair Allissa was sitting in, so she had her back to the majority of them to keep them from seeing her legs while he retrieved the garter.

He focused solely on inhaling through his nose for a count of four, holding his breath for a count of four, and exhaling through his mouth for a count of four. He didn't even notice when his brother made everyone take two giant steps back from him, trying to give him a safety zone to keep from risking second impact syndrome from an accidental elbow to the head when the guys all reached out for the garter.

Dion just kept focusing on his breath, not even thinking about Jewel, so he didn't risk feeling anxious about how she felt about him at the moment. He had to calm his mind as much as his body to make it through the next few minutes without having an embarrassing blackout spell in the middle of the crowd of men vying to take his place in Jewel's life.

"Yo, Dark Chocolate, you gotta open your eyes to be able to catch this thing," Dean chuckled, alerting Dion that his meditation time was over, whether he was ready or not.

"Ya might just wanna hand it to him, Dean," Darius advised, obviously recognizing how lightheaded Dion felt. "And then help me get him to the nearest sofa to lie down before he goes out like a light."

"Naw, I'm good," Dion assured them as he slowly opened his eyes, feeling like he might have finally beaten one of the anxiety-induced blackouts, since he wasn't slurring his words from trying to talk with numb lips. Reassured when he had full vision, instead of the pinpoint view he usually had right before the darkness finished creeping in from the edges of his line of sight when those blackouts happened, Dion smiled at Dean. He then lifted his hands in front of his chest, giving Dean an easy target to shoot the red and white garter at.

"Damn, guess we shouldn't have bothered even getting up for this one," one of the locals grumbled when Dean looped the garter around his finger and slingshotted it straight into Dion's hands.

"Please, like you'd have half a chance with Julie, even if you'd caught the garter," another local teased the first one.

"Why don't you take the chair for these pictures, Big Daddy?" Allissa suggested, standing, and motioning for Dion to sit in the chair she'd just vacated. "You look a little woozy. Can we get you some water or something to help you feel better?"

"Thanks," Dion smiled as he took the offered seat, grateful to have the support in case the tingling, asleep feeling in his lips came back and that lightheaded feeling got worse. "Just the chair is fine."

"When did you start calling him Big Daddy instead of Big D?" Dean grilled his new wife as they stepped aside for the photographer to call Julie over for the pictures with the bouquet and garter.

"It was something the girls suggested right before the wedding," Allissa explained, lowering her voice to where Dion couldn't hear what else she said as Julie got closer.

Thank you, Allissa, for not rehashing that embarrassing conversation where Jewel can hear you. It wasn't that Dion wanted to keep it a secret from the woman he loved. But more so that he knew he needed to clear up other matters with her first, needing to get out of the doghouse before he risked pissing her off again by telling her how inappropriate some of his former coworkers, whom they were both friends with, could be.

"Alright, Philippe, where do you want me?" Jewel sounded exasperated as she questioned the photographer.

"Since Dion still looks a little pale from overdoing things today, why don't we leave him in the chair and have you sit on his lap," the photographer suggested, directing Jewel to sit sideways on his lap.

Fuck! How am I supposed to keep from freaking her out by getting a boner from finally getting to touch her?

"Can't I just stand beside him?" Jewel proposed, clearly not wanting to have that much contact with Dion. "Or behind him?"

"That's probably safer," Dion muttered, hating that he was starting to feel that darkness creeping in again. "I wouldn't want to risk dropping her if I can't stop the blackout spell I feel coming on."

"Oh, dear, okay," Philippe sputtered, lifting his camera, and starting to snap a few pictures. "If you can just look at each other and smile, I'll make this quick."

After several shutter clicks, Philippe apparently got tired of them awkwardly looking at one another with fake smiles on both their faces. "Alright, Julie, scoot a little closer and put your hand on Dion's shoulder. Dion, put your arm around Julie and both of you look at me and smile."

As they followed the photographer's instructions, Dion felt a strange tingly feeling at every point where their bodies touched. With the way the darkness on the edges of his field of vision receded as soon as she placed her arm around his shoulders and her delicate hand on the shoulder opposite where she was standing, he had to wonder if her touch was somehow healing for him.

After placing his arm around her waist and his hand on her hip, Dion decided to test his theory by looking around the room momentarily. When feeling like everyone was staring at him didn't cause the anxiety to return, Dion smiled genuinely at the photographer for him to take a few more pictures, reveling in finally being allowed to touch the woman of his dreams, even though it was strictly in a platonic manner.

"I know you'd probably rather avoid me the rest of the time I'm in town," Dion sighed as he turned his head to look at her slightly rounded belly that was just below eye level with him sitting down. He caught a whiff of her familiar fruity floral scent, but didn't let it take him out of the moment to one of their memories together. "But I think we have a few things we need to talk about. So, would it be possible for us to meet somewhere tomorrow?"

He couldn't stop himself from reaching out with the hand holding the garter and placing it on her beautiful baby bump. Regardless of where things stood with the two of them, he needed to feel the evidence of his baby resting inside the woman he loved.

"Oh, that's perfect," Philippe beamed before Jewel could reply. "Julie, hold the bouquet up just under his hand."

"Yeah, we can meet tomorrow after church," she conceded with emotion clogging her voice as she followed the photographer's instructions.

Dion couldn't contain his elated smile then, staring at where both their hands rested so close to their little one growing in her belly. Even though he knew she was going to run away from him just as soon as Philippe finished taking their pictures, he knew she couldn't completely shut him out of her life because of their baby.

That opportunity to talk things through with her was all he could ask for at that point in time. But he knew, deep in his soul, that once they started talking again, he'd eventually win her heart.

Chapter Nine

Julie wasn't sure she was really ready for the conversation she was about to have as she walked with Dion out of the church after the service and potluck lunch. But if she was going to force herself to get over her insecurities and invite him to her next doctor's appointment, she knew she couldn't put it off any longer. Yeah, technically, she could put it off another day or two. But since she had to work every day between then and her appointment, and she wasn't sure if Dion planned to stay in town past the weekend, she didn't feel like she had any other choice but to talk to him right then.

"So, do you want to drive somewhere? Or just walk over to the park to talk?" Julie wasn't sure the park provided enough privacy for their discussion, but she also didn't trust herself to fight off her over-the-top physical reaction to him in the enclosed space of a vehicle, especially since she was now close enough to smell the woody aquatic fragrance of his cologne that made her girl parts stand up and take notice. *Versace Man,* she thought, remembering the cologne she'd bought him for his birthday back in May. *No, don't think about how we celebrated our birthdays, or any of the other special moments we had back when we were together. You're here to clear up the misunderstanding and hopefully figure out how to co-parent with him in the future, not fall back into his arms like nothing happened.*

"I'm not cleared to drive yet," Dion shrugged, looking out over the parking lot before turning to look for the park. "So, I either need to stay close enough that Dare can find me to take me back to the B and B, or you'll have to drive and drop me off after our talk."

"Okay, then let's go to the park." Julie pointed in the direction they needed to walk to go around the building to get to the park.

Other than Dion telling Darius to wait for him, they walked in silence, until they cleared the crowd of people continuing to visit with their friends and neighbors on their way out of the church. When they got to the corner of Brahman Boulevard and Quarter Horse Drive, Dion placed his hand on the small of her back to escort her across the streets to the park, which was located diagonally northeast on the opposite side of the intersection from the church.

Julie knew he was just being gentlemanly, but she still felt the tingle of excitement she got whenever he touched her. *No! No, no, no! Do not react to that!* Julie silently warned her traitorous body, even as she wanted to cuddle into his side as they made their way to the nearest park bench to have a seat. *There's no difference between him and any of my male friends or family members, who would all do the same thing with any woman they were walking across the street.*

Unfortunately, she wasn't sure her wet pussy and hard nipples got the memo that he wasn't trying to get to play with them again. Just like they hadn't gotten that memo the night before, when Philippe directed them to pose for pictures and she'd gotten close enough to get another whiff of his succulent scent.

"I'm really sorry for the stuff Dare said when you called while I was in the hospital," Dion apologized as soon as they reached the nearest bench. He waited for her to take a seat before sitting beside her and turning to sit sideways and face her. "You have to know a little of his background with women and what was going on right then to understand why he said those things."

"Okay," Julie drawled, hoping to prompt him to continue his explanation.

Dion took a moment to gather his thoughts, leaving her sitting there quietly when he took longer than normal to fill the silence. He wasn't acting like the confident man she'd known previously, making her wonder if there was more to his injuries than had been reported. *Did hitting his head cause more than just a mild concussion?*

"He was always pretty outgoing and popular with the ladies, even when we were dirt poor as teenagers," Dion finally started. "But then when I got my first big contract and was able to invest in the club he opened, the women who showed the most interest in him seemed to be drawn more toward his status as a business owner and what his income could do for them. Then when I started main-eventing in the GWA, he had more than one girlfriend think she could trade up for money and fame, instead of just money. And even though I had no interest in any of them, the way they acted when I came to town skewed his perception of women."

Julie could almost understand where Darius was coming from that day. But having told Dion about the college boyfriend she'd lost her virginity to, who'd only been interested in her for the Burleson money and a position with Burleson Incorporated when they graduated, she also wondered if he remembered more than he claimed about their time together and was using the similarity between Dare's experiences and her college experiences to sway her opinion about his brother now. But even though she and her siblings and cousins had dealt with being pursued for all the wrong reasons to understand why Dare didn't trust a stranger on the phone that day, none of them had ever deliberately been that cruel to one of their money-hungry suitors to stoop to the level of calling them derogatory names, the way Darius had directed his cruel words at her that day.

He wasn't raised the same way I was, though, she reminded herself. *And his experiences in life weren't exactly the same as mine were in college. So, he's probably not going to react the same way I would.*

Julie remembered back to one of her first talks with Dion, when he'd told her about his brother, reinforcing her thoughts on how Dare would act immaturely. Apparently, one of those women he just referred to was the reason Darius was pissed and Dion had been giving him space for the last year. "I think you told me about one of them. He got pissed because she was hitting on you at his birthday party. And when he refused to speak to you, you decided to give him space to get over it. Did he finally get over it and call you? Or did you break down and call him when you got hurt?"

"I'm not sure who called him when I got hurt." Dion shrugged and smiled ruefully. "But he came straight to the hospital when he heard and acted like we'd never stopped talking to each other. He then had to deal with the hospital to keep the reporters and a few unruly fans out of my room. Apparently, right before you called, there'd been a couple of women who bypassed the security measures at the ER entrance by sneaking through the back way to come into my room from the other side of the hospital. Luckily, I was off being scanned, one of the dozen different scans it seemed like they did that day, so I didn't have to deal with them when I got back to my room. It woulda been an even bigger issue for me to wake up to find them in my room, especially when I was doing good to even remember if it was the first time I woke up or not. But he told me later that they'd been pretty blatant with their claims, all of which I refuted when he showed me their pictures. I might not remember the last, almost, three years, but I was extremely adamant in my description of you as the only woman who had any claim on me."

"I guess he didn't look at my contact picture in your phone when I called," Julie scoffed, knowing if Dion had described her, then the picture that flashed on the screen when she called would have made it obvious that she was the woman he'd been referring to.

"I guess not." Dion shook his head as his lips turned down in a sad frown. "He also seems to think you were the first person he blocked who called my phone. And he started blocking people right after I woke up the first time, which I don't even remember. Apparently, I woke up and had the same conversation with him and the doctor about where we were three or four times before it stuck in my brain to remember waking up earlier in the day."

Dion paused again, obviously thinking more about what to say. So, Julie gave him the time to gather his thoughts, while she tried to imagine herself in Darius's shoes on that awful day, trying to find a way to be empathetic and forgive him.

"Dare is really sorry, too. But he figured you'd need to hear everything from me first before you'd be willing to speak to him so he can…"

Dion closed his eyes as his voice trailed off and his breathing rate increased. He clenched his fists a couple of times as he tried to regulate his breathing, making Julie wonder what was going on with him. Finally, he opened his eyes and released his fists before stuttering out, "So, so he ca-can say sorry, too."

"Are you okay, Dion?" Julie was concerned by Dion's strange behavior, wondering if he was having a panic attack or something because of this conversation. *Or is this part of the reason why he's not cleared to drive yet after the concussion?*

"Yeah," he assured her, slightly nodding his head. "Just having problems remembering the right words sometimes."

"Is that from hitting your head that day?" Julie examined Dion closely for the first time that week, finally noticing the dark, slightly raised scar on the side of his head where his hair hadn't grown back to fill in the space. Because the scar was darker than the rest of his complexion and almost as dark as his hair, she hadn't noticed it until she actually looked closely now that she was sitting on the right side of him to see it. *Guess it's a good thing I stood to his left last night, so I didn't see the scar to feel the need to ask him about it while Philippe was trying to take pictures.*

"Yeah, possibly." Dion rubbed a hand over the back of his head. "Either that or where the bullet grazed me." He pointed to the scar she'd just noticed, indicating it was from the bullet, before turning to let her see the other scar on the back of his head, not quite halfway around the circumference of his head from the bullet wound, where he'd also been busted open when he hit his head.

"So, you had two head injuries that day?" *Oh. My. Gawd. He was literally shot in the head. Holy crap! If it had been more than a graze, he could have died!* Julie felt lightheaded at the realization of how dramatically different that day could have turned out. She didn't even want to think about how close they'd come to losing him that day. *How did I not realize that, when everyone was talking about how he had been hit in the head twice and was grazed by a bullet? Why did I just assume he was grazed on the arm, or shoulder, or something, and his head bounced to have two hits? And how did I not put two and two together to realize that the bullet grazed his head?*

"Yeah," Dion nodded nonchalantly until he noticed Julie's face draining of all color. His expression turned serious as he reached over and took her hand in his. "Are you alright, Jewel? Uh, Julia?"

I could have lost him. My babies could have lost their daddy.

Julie clung to his hand, needing to feel that connection with him, even as she bent forward to try to put her head as close to between her knees as she could get with her growing belly in the way, trying to stop herself from fainting. She focused on taking deep, even breaths, in through her nose and out through her mouth, while Dion used his free hand to rub up and down her back. She waited until the worst of her freak out passed before slowly sitting back up to look at him.

"Promise you won't ever take a risk like that again. Please. Promise me."

"I promise, Jewel." Dion took his hand off her back to reach up and wipe a tear from her cheek that she hadn't even realized she'd let slip from her eye, without removing his left hand from her tight grip. "Unless it's you in the crosshairs of a psycho, I'll leave the rescue up to the professionals from now on."

"No, even if it's me." Julie shook her head, not considering his answer acceptable. "Especially if it's me. Our babies need both of their parents if possible. But if something happens to me, they're gonna need you even more."

"Babies!" Dion smiled, dazzling her with his happiness at talking about their babies.

Huh? I guess he was just waiting until we were alone to acknowledge them.

"Does that mean you've forgiven me and are planning to let me get you pregnant more than once?"

"No." Julie shook her head, confused by how he'd come to that conclusion, considering she'd mentioned their babies as plural the weekend before when he first got to town and ran into her at Tully's Roadhouse. "We're having twins, Dion. Didn't you realize that from how I've referred to them this last week?"

"Twins?" The look of shock on Dion's face as he looked down at her small baby bump was priceless. "Wow! Seriously? How'd I miss that?"

"I don't know," Julie shrugged. "Even if you didn't hear me over the music at Tully's during the bachelorette party, I figured someone in town would have mentioned it to you this last week, since everyone knows I'm having twins."

"Yeah, I went to the parking lot and passed out that first night, so I don't remember anything from then," Dion admitted with a heavy sigh. "Those blackout spells are why I'm not allowed to drive yet. And I'm also still having a hard time understanding everything when I'm talking to people, or there's a lot going on around me. So, if anyone did say something, then I must have missed it."

"You're still having a lot of issues from the head injuries? Not just the amnesia everyone's mentioned?" Julie wasn't sure how long it was supposed to take to recover from something like that, but to her, a month seemed like enough time to start getting back to normal from a concussion. *Damn, I guess not. Either concussions are worse than I thought, or his brain injuries are more complex than just a concussion.*

"Yeah, the worst are the blackout spells," Dion confessed, his shoulders sagging as he leaned his right side on the back of the park bench. "But I'm still having headaches, forgetting simple words I should easily know, and getting confused easily. At least the medicine for the vertigo is working, so I'm not getting super dizzy and feeling nauseous every time I turn my head anymore."

"What does the doctor say about how long it'll take for all that other stuff to go back to normal?" Julie hoped it wouldn't be long, knowing he had to hate feeling stuck in a state of limbo, where he couldn't get back to his career in the ring while he was healing.

"He doesn't have a clue," Dion shrugged. "I could suddenly wake up tomorrow with all my memories back and no more symptoms, or I could be stuck like this for the rest of my life."

"Is there anything they can do to help improve your recovery?"

"Yeah, they've tried a few different meds so far," Dion nodded, smiling regretfully. "Only the Meclizine has actually helped with anything, though. And when I saw him the day before I came here, the doctor seemed to think visiting someplace where I've spent a lot of time would help, which seems to be true. I'm definitely having more flashes of memories here than I was in NOLA."

"So, that's how you knew to call me Jewel, even though you don't remember anything else about me or our time together? Because you had a flash of a memory when you got back to town?"

"Not exactly," Dion grinned. "I've been dreaming about you since the day of, and I always called you Jewel in my dreams. I just wasn't sure if my dreams were memories or not. The doctor didn't think they were, no matter how much Mama Marcel tried to tell him otherwise."

Julie remembered Dion talking about his mother's quirky best friend, who'd taken care of him and his brother after their parents both passed. She loved hearing his stories about the crazy things she told the tourists, who believed she was really a fortune teller.

While neither one of them truly believed she had some kind of special gift to be able to see the futures of anyone she sat and talked to for a few minutes, Dion and Julie had both agreed it was probably best not to introduce her to the Matchmaking Mommas of Heart's Destiny until they were ready to start planning their wedding when he retired from wrestling. Julie was pretty sure that if Mama Marcel ever came to town, more than one of the Matchmaking Mommas would believe her predictions and double down on their plots against their kids.

"How is Mama Marcel?" Julie wondered aloud. "I'm surprised she isn't here supervising your recovery instead of Darius."

"Oh, she'll be here tomorrow," Dion chuckled, grinning. "She's spent the last week on a cruise with her friends. Apparently, after I sent them on one last year, they decided to make it an annual thing. So, she booked it the day after I got home from the hospital, thinking I'd be back to normal and back on tour with the GWA by then. But then when my symptoms didn't clear up and the doctor suggested I spend some extra time here after the wedding, she decided we all need to spend the month of December on vacation."

"So, you're staying at the bed and breakfast for the next month?" *Maybe he'll want to stay in town an extra week to go to the second ultrasound appointment on the seventh of January?* "I guess that means you don't remember us talking about waiting to introduce her to the Matchmaking Mommas here, if she's coming here after the cruise?"

"Yeah, that's the plan for now," Dion nodded. "We've talked about bringing Mama Marcel here before now?"

"Yeah, but it's been a while," Julie let go of her earlier concerns about the fortune teller influencing her mom to push harder with her matchmaking. "It's no big deal. With everything else going on, I'm sure she can't influence my mom and her friends to up their matchmaking efforts any more than they're already plotting."

"Sorry, I wish I could remember everything we've talked about in the last year," Dion apologized, sighing heavily as he dropped his gaze to their joined hands.

"It's fine," Julie waved her free hand through the air. "It's more important that you focus on healing than on what happened between us."

"But part of my healing is getting my memories back," Dion pointed out, lifting his gaze to her eyes as an impish grin spread across his face. "Since you're obviously expecting our babies, I'm pretty sure all my dreams about you this last month are really memories. But now I want to know everything else about our previous relationship, so I can start trying to get us back to where we were."

"Where we were was a long-distance, friends-with-benefits situationship," Julie grumbled, not wanting to go back to that now that there were babies involved. Not that she was ready for him to declare his undying love and propose either, though.

"Really?" Dion arched an eyebrow curiously. "That's not what it feels like to me."

"Yeah, well, you don't really remember any of it," Julie scoffed, unsure why she felt the need to argue with him, instead of trying to help him remember the good times they'd had together. Not that he would argue back with her right then. Especially since it seemed like he'd suddenly started looking through her, instead of paying attention to what she was saying.

~~~

"What are we doing, Dion?" Jewel snuggled into his side as they laid naked in each other's arms after making love multiple times in a wide variety of positions for the last several hours.

"Whatever you wanna do, Jewel," Dion replied, knowing he'd do anything for the beautiful woman he loved, even though they hadn't shared those three little words just yet. He'd known he loved her for months now, but hadn't found the right time to tell her. He knew better than to say it in the middle of making love to her, but the secretive nature of their relationship didn't really give him the opportunity for romantic dates when it would be more appropriate to share his feelings.

"No, I mean, where are we going? How long are we going to keep meeting up in secret before we actually start acting like a real couple? Or are we never going to be a real couple?"

"We're a hundred percent real couple now, Jewel," Dion assured her, turning on his side to face her. Fuck it, I'm done waiting for the perfect setting to say it. *"I love you, Jewel. I don't ever want to be without you. So, I'm more than willing to stop sneaking around just as soon as you tell me you're ready to let the world know we're in love. Hell, I'll retire tomorrow if you're ready for us to start planning the wedding and babies of your mom's dreams."*
~~~

Dion was shocked to realize he meant those words. As much as he wanted to wrestle until after his fortieth birthday to have a twenty-year career in the wrestling business, he wanted to be with Jewel more. Yeah, he'd always love wrestling, but he loved her more. So, he quickly resigned himself to following through with retiring to be with her just as soon as she was ready for them to take their relationship to the next level.

"Seriously? That's how you tell me you love me the first time?" Jewel slapped his chest playfully before continuing. "No big romantic gesture? No flowers? Or anything special?"

"I'll do better next time," Dion laughed, leaning over to kiss her senseless.

"We were in bed at the B and B the first time I said 'I love you' and you got pissed because I wasn't romantic about it," Dion told her as he let the memory of making love to her again fade out, so he could be in the moment with her. "So, I know we were more than just friends with benefits. And it was definitely a romantic relationship, and not a situationship."

"Wait! You remember that?" Jewel looked shocked at him contradicting her.

"I just remembered it," Dion confirmed, nodding. "But before now, I remembered another time in a hotel when I pulled out all the typical romantic overtures of roses, champagne, and chocolate-covered strawberries, and we both said 'I love you' multiple times while making love."

Fuck! She'd better not tell me I was just dreaming that. Dr. Boudreaux might think they're only dreams, but I know they're memories. And based on her expression, she remembers that day clearly, too.

"What days were those?"

Jewel's mouth dropped open as she gaped at him in shock.

"I know they're not just dreams, Jewel. So, please, tell me when they happened to help me remember more," he pleaded.

"The first time you said 'I love you' was on Labor Day, a little over nine months after we started acting on our mutual attraction," Jewel admitted, biting her lip, and looking down at their joined hands before continuing. "And after I commented on how unromantic the declaration was, you pulled out all the stops the next day when we met for lunch at a hotel in San Antonio. That was September third, the day we most likely conceived our babies."

"I knew there was something special about that memory that made it the one I dreamed most often since I was in the hospital," Dion beamed, finally feeling like he was getting somewhere with regaining his memories. "Did I know that before?"

Jewel tilted her head, her eyes narrowing in confusion, like she didn't understand his question.

"Before I…" Dion's words trailed off as he tried to think of the right words. "Did you tell me about the babies, about when we made them, before I, uh, ended up in the hospital and lost my memories?"

"I told you my period was late," Jewel confessed tentatively. "But I didn't confirm I was pregnant, or find out the date of conception, or that we're having twins, until the Monday after you were injured."

She paused and let her eyes drop to their joined hands once more. "You haven't asked if they're yours."

"I know they're mine, Jewel," Dion assured her, reaching up to push her hair behind her ear with his free hand. "I might not remember the first time we met, or when we took each step in building our relationship, but I'm positive we've been an exclusive couple from day one. I knew that I love you and that we're meant to be together before I even figured out I was remembering you, and not just picturing my dream girl and hoping to meet you one day."

"Really? You *know* we've been exclusive for the last twelve-and-a-half months?"

Jewel's angry tone caught him by surprise. He knew he couldn't say for certain that they'd been exclusive for a set number of months because of not remembering much of anything from that time period. But his gut instinct told him he hadn't even looked at another woman since the first time he laid eyes on her. And since he was pretty sure his gut instinct was based on the feelings of his heart and soul, he unwaveringly believed the feeling. Before he could open his mouth to tell her that, however, she was snapping at him once more.

"If we were *so exclusive*, then who's the woman in the pictures that were posted online less than a week after you were injured?"

Dion cringed, knowing she was referring to the paparazzi images the security team hadn't been able to prevent because the sleazy reporters had used telephoto lenses to zoom in on him while he was sitting on the balcony for some fresh air while staying in Dare's condo the first couple of weeks after being injured, when he still felt too dizzy to climb the steps to his or walk downstairs to go outside in the courtyard behind the building. After one of the medications his doctor tried caused him to have to go back to the hospital via ambulance, Dare had hired a nurse to observe him to make sure he wasn't having another adverse reaction to the different medications the doctors tried. Since he'd only had a bad reaction to the one medication, and the dizziness abated when they swapped him over to a different medication for his vertigo symptoms, the nurse had only worked with him for a couple of weeks. But that was long enough for her to have been caught on camera observing him on the balcony.

"That was the nurse Dare hired," Dion explained, hoping Jewel believed him. "She was only there for a couple of weeks, while the doctors figured out which medicines I could take without having an adverse reaction, and I wasn't allowed to be left alone for him and Mama Marcel to go to work. I swear, the only time I had any physical contact with her was when I felt like I was gonna pass out and needed to lean on someone to get someplace safe to lie down."

"To lay down," she mumbled under her breath, causing him to flashback to another conversation they'd previously had.

"We're not lying about anything," Jewel scoffed, turning on her side to face him in the bed. "We're laying on the bed. I don't care what all the English teachers say about being grammatically correct. Lying means 'telling a falsehood' and laying is what we're doing right now. And I only want positive connotations of the two of us in bed, so we're laying, not lying."

"Technically, we're kinda doin' both," Dion teased, reaching over to brush her hair behind her ear. "I mean, keeping us a secret from the Matchmaking Mommas is kinda lying by omission."

"Fine, sometimes, keeping secrets and fibbing a little is necessary to keep from hurting anyone's feelings, especially the feelings of the people we love," Jewel sighed. "But I don't consider stuff like that as lying either. Lying is malicious and evil and I want no part of it. But fibbing is okay if it's done out of love for someone."

Fuck, I love her little quirks like that, Dion thought as he forced himself to come back out of the memory to focus on Jewel and the conversation they were currently having. *And I'll have to remember to say lay or laying, instead of lie or lying, whenever I'm talking to her from now on.*

He could see she was struggling with whether or not to believe him, so he decided to preempt any other questions she might have about photos he'd taken with fans in the last month to keep her fears from festering. "And I'm sure you've seen dozens of other pictures of me posing with fans in the last month, too. But I can assure you, those were only when I was recognized while going to the doctor or vestibular therapy. Considering how long you just said we've been seeing each other, I'm sure we've discussed those situations in the past 'cause they come with the territory of being a professional wrestler."

"Yes, I know," Jewel huffed, dropping her voice to imitate him as she continued. "It's easier and faster to just sign a couple of autographs and pose for a couple of pictures than to be an ass by blowing off the fans, and then listening to a lecture from Rick about professional conduct."

Dion couldn't help but chuckle at her cute impression, even though he hoped he came off a little more gracious toward the fans than she'd just portrayed him with that statement. "My point is…that while I didn't know your name until I came to Heart's Destiny a week ago, I knew I didn't want to be with anyone but you. So, I know for certain that I've been a hundred percent faithful to you since I woke up in the hospital a little over a month ago. And since my feelings for you are so strong that I couldn't fathom cheating, even when I didn't know if you were real, I'm ninety-nine-point-nine percent certain that you're the only woman I've even looked twice at since the day we met."

"Fine," she huffed, rolling her eyes, even though her lips turned up in the faintest of smiles. "You're right. We've been exclusive since day one. Even the first six days when we were fighting not to act on the attraction because of the whole long-distance thing."

Dion wanted to pull her onto his lap and kiss her senseless, celebrating the progress he made toward getting back together with her. Until she dropped a bomb on his mental celebration.

"But with you living in New Orleans, and me living here, that long-distance thing is going to be an even bigger problem with us trying to co-parent than it was when we were just hooking up."

Fuck! Fuck! Fuck!

Dion dropped his gaze back down to their joined hands, unsure if he was more upset with her pointing out the distance between their homes, or with how she'd slotted them into co-parent roles, instead of being willing to discuss them moving forward as a family.

I guess I just have to keep trying to wear her down until she agrees that we can share both of our homes to raise our babies in our perfect, two-parent family. He just hoped that he could keep from being so anxious about their conversation that he could keep from passing out again. At least, until he got back to his room at the B and B, where Jewel wouldn't see how weak he felt at the moment.

~~~

Julie could see she'd clearly burst his bubble of joy over her agreeing with his perception of their previous relationship by pointing out the biggest obstacle they faced, no matter whether he was cleared to go back to work or not. But even if she wasn't as dead set against being a couple as she was trying to convince him she was, the long-distance thing was going to be a problem that they had to face together before they could even start to come up with a co-parenting plan, much less start to navigate a romantic relationship again. So, after giving him a few minutes to brood and comprehend the problem to be able to formulate a plan for overcoming it, she tried a different approach to talking about the issue. "So, when are you planning to go back to New Orleans?"

"New Year's Day," Dion admitted, finally looking back up at her face. "If I stay any longer than that, I'll need to find a doctor here. Or convince my doctor in NOLA to push back my next appointment."

Julie decided to take advantage of him mentioning the doctor again to segue into asking if he wanted to come to her doctor's appointments. "Speaking of doctors, I have an OB appointment on Wednesday, if you want to come. I'm not sure what they'll do then, since it's just my second visit. But on January seventh, when I go for
~~~

my third visit, I know she's planning to do a second ultrasound. So, if you can stay in town that long, you're welcome to come to that appointment, too."

"I'd love to be there for both of them," Dion smiled before his expression turned thoughtful. "But wait, that'll be the second ultrasound? You've already had the first one?"

"Yeah," Julie admitted, taking a deep breath to keep from reverting to her hurt feelings from that day when she'd tried to call Dion, only to face the proof that she'd been blocked. *Let it go, Julie! That wasn't his fault, remember.* "I don't have the pictures with me, but I'll bring them with me on Wednesday if you want."

"Please," Dion nodded, smiling at her. "Um, since I can't drive yet, can you come pick me up on Wednesday for the appointment? Or should I have Dare drive me over there to meet you?"

"I can come get you, so your brother doesn't have to sit around in the waiting room for however long we're there," Julie offered, hoping she could keep herself in check during the short drive back and forth between the B and B and the Heart's Destiny Clinic. Considering they were still holding hands, and she hadn't crawled into his lap yet during this conversation, even when he mentioned remembering conceiving their babies before he even knew the importance of that hotel rendezvous, she assumed she'd be able to keep from jumping his bones while they were alone in her car.

"Thank you," Dion smiled, weakening her resolve. "So, um, since you're willing to let me come to your doctor's appointments, does that mean you've forgiven me for the mix-up with Dare?"

"Yes," Julie returned his smile. "I'm not mad at you for that, 'cause I know it wasn't you who said those horrible things."

"Good," Dion grinned as he slid over closer to her and put his free arm around her shoulders. "I'm more than ready to get back to where we were in our relationship before I got hurt."

"No, we're not there yet." Julie pulled away from him, finally separating their hands as she listened to her head, and not her heart, or her traitorous female parts. "I can forgive you because you weren't the one who said those things, but I can't forget that your brother said them. And he wouldn't have said them if the two of you hadn't been raised to believe it's okay to speak that way to women. So, it's gonna take a while before I can trust that you won't say something similar to me one day, or teach our children that behavior like that is acceptable."

"I would never say those things to you, Jewel," Dion adamantly asserted, shaking his head as he sat up straight.

She knew he was trying to exude confidence in what he was saying. But with their size difference, it felt like he was looming over her, which was rather intimidating. While she didn't fear him in any way, she didn't like the way he seemed to be trying to use his size against her, the same way some of her male business rivals had in the past.

Julie held up a hand to stop him from speaking any further. "Maybe, maybe not," she shrugged. "But it's going to take time for me to see that you're more respectable than that. So, please, just give me that time."

"Okay," Dion conceded, sagging back down into the bench and looking defeated.

"Besides, you need this time to focus on healing and trying to get your memories back," Julie continued. "Not on me or our relationship. I'm not going to cut you out of anything to do with the babies, but we've got a few months before you can do anything more for them than sit beside me at the doctor's office. So, please, use that time to focus on you, so you can be back to a hundred percent when they need you."

"Yeah, okay." Dion leaned forward, resting his elbows on his knees and his head in his hands.

An uneasy silence settled between them, making Julie feel uncomfortable because she had no idea what else to say to him.

After several long minutes, Dion finally raised his head and opened his eyes. "I should probably get back to Dare and go back to the hotel to, um, *lay* down."

"Um, okay." Unsure what else to do, Julie stood when Dion did, not catching the way he used her preferred phrasing instead of saying he needed to "lie down" the way he had earlier in their conversation when talking about his blackout spells.

They walked in silence back to the church, where they separated to go to their different vehicles. As she pulled out of the church parking lot, she watched Dion and Darius turn the opposite direction to go back to the bed and breakfast, realizing she needed to spend some time that afternoon thinking about everything she'd just discussed with the father of her babies.

Since she was sure her family would question her about what all was said when she met up with them for Sunday supper, she hoped to avoid the interrogation by her sister and cousin when she got home. *Maybe I can avoid them by changing into boots and walking out to the paddock to have some bonding time with Jasmine. I mean, just because I can't ride while I'm pregnant, doesn't mean I can't give her treats and pets, so I'm able to stay nice and calm while I'm thinking about everything. Right?*

~~~

After his talk in the park with Jewel, Dion went back to the bed and breakfast to lie down for a bit before he got a call that he had some visitors who wanted to spend some time with him that afternoon. Anthony, Kay, and all four of their children had come over to hang out with him and the rest of the GWA crew, hoping to help him get more of his memories back now that the wedding was over and their time was limited before the GWA would be leaving town again.

While Dion had greatly appreciated all the GWA guys trying to remind him of the events he'd forgotten in his professional career, he especially appreciated that Anthony's daughter Tia was able to help him unblock Jewel from his phone and restore not only her contact information but also all their text exchanges, which apparently contained quite a few photos that hadn't been otherwise saved to his gallery. Not that he could look over any of that while sitting in the library with so many people around. Looking over their history had to wait until he was back in his room, so he wasn't rude to his friends by ignoring them to take a walk down memory lane in his mind.

Instead, he'd pocketed his phone once more and listened to story after story from each and every one of them. In addition to learning about when he and Liam started teaming up and the title runs he'd forgotten in the last few years of his career, he learned about how he'd started hanging out with the Hunters and their lifelong friend Anthony, both backstage and after the shows, and eventually started helping them train Tia to wrestle when Kay and the girls joined Anthony on
~~~

tour with the GWA. He didn't really have any flashes of those memories, though, so it was more like he was relearning his life history from the perspective of his friends than actually reliving it.

When he'd mentioned as such out loud, Tia informed him that she'd be doing some research on memory and brain injuries, trying to find ways to help him get more of his memories back. While he could tell she was clearly smarter than the average thirteen-year-old, he wasn't sure how much such a young teenager would be able to help him, but he appreciated the sweet gesture from the young girl, who claimed he was her favorite wrestler of all time.

With all the outpouring of love he'd felt from his friends, coworkers, and their families that afternoon, he'd had to ask why none of them had informed him that Julie was pregnant with twins in the month that they'd been talking before he came to town to find out for himself. Most of the GWA crew claimed to have not known until they got to town either, with several of them being surprised when he informed them that he and Jewel were expecting twins. It was actually Anthony who'd stepped up and made it clear that he'd been the one to make the decision for his family not to share that news with the GWA crew until Julie shared it herself, inadvertently revealing that Dion had missed that part of the conversation at the bridal shower the week before.

Dion hated that the issues he was having from his concussion had kept him out of the loop for a whole extra week, but he was glad that Jewel had been the one to officially inform him of her pregnancy and that they were having twins. Apparently, she'd had to inform her family earlier than she wanted that she was pregnant in order to get out of riding her horse for the haunted hayride at the B and B on Halloween. So, Anthony wanted his cousin to be able to share the news with everyone else on her own timeline, letting her surprise the GWA crew with her baby bump when they arrived in town.

Dion had thanked Anthony for respecting Julia's boundaries and letting her be the one to tell him about the babies, even though he didn't actually remember the events of his first night back in town to know what she'd said about being pregnant and had to be retold earlier that day. They might not have had the pregnancy reveal that Dion wished they'd had, but at least they were now talking about the babies and their future, and were planning on raising them together, even if she only thought it would be as co-parents for now.

After Anthony and his family left the B and B to go to their weekly family dinner, Dion still felt like he needed to stay downstairs to have one last meal in the restaurant with the rest of the GWA before they moved over to the hotel in San Antonio the next morning in preparation for their show Monday night. While they'd invited him to come hang out backstage, Dion wasn't sure he was ready to be so close to a wrestling ring again after coming to the realization that his career was over.

He'd also gotten several congratulations on becoming a father from his former coworkers, including an invitation to practice taking care of twins from Tank and Tina Olson. He'd had to decline their generous offer to let him babysit their one-year-old twin boys that night for the same reason he'd declined Anthony and Kay's offer to let him hold their infant son, Sam, earlier in the day. Until he got a handle on his anxiety-induced blackout spells, he didn't feel equipped to be responsible for the safety of small children in his care and didn't want to risk injuring them if he had a blackout spell while holding them.

But since Jewel had invited him to stay in town longer than he'd planned to go to her doctor's appointments for their babies, Dion was already thinking of canceling his appointment with Dr. Boudreaux in NOLA and asking for referrals to specialists as close to Heart's Destiny as possible. *I wonder if Dr. Boudreaux's office can give me those referrals? Or maybe I should ask around here in town? Maybe I'll ask Jewel next time I see her.*

With her firmly on his mind once more (*As if she ever left my mind,* Dion mentally scoffed.), Dion pulled his phone from his pocket as soon as he got back up to his room for the evening. He quickly scrolled to his text message thread with her, going all the way back to the beginning of it to review before sending her a text to let her know he'd gotten help to unblock her and restore her contact information.

Seeing the running text thread going back over a year, he was hit with multiple flashes of memory. He not only remembered their text conversations, when they'd shared their likes, dislikes, and several stories from their childhoods, but he also remembered long late-night phone conversations, when they talked about anything and everything they could think of to talk about, really getting to know one another on a deeper level than just their sexual connection. Oh, yeah, he remembered more than a few Skype sex sessions, too, thoroughly enjoying the images of her touching herself on his laptop screen. But he knew the conversations they'd had over the phone and via text were way more meaningful for their relationship.

From the outside looking in, they might look like complete opposites with absolutely nothing in common. But after rehashing their previous conversations with her over text and hearing more about her volunteer activities with the youth center in town, as well as the other causes to which she donated her time and money, Dion knew that wasn't the case. They actually had a lot in common, including their core values, ethics, hopes, and dreams, all of which would provide a strong foundation for them going forward and building their family. And even though he knew it would be an uphill battle to get them back to the point where she'd be willing to consider them a couple again, it was a battle he was more than willing to do everything in his power to win, knowing the best prize was waiting for him when he finally won — Jewel's love.

~~~

After spending some time talking to her babies and her horse, Julie felt a lot more open to spending more time with Dion in the future. She knew it would still take her some time to completely trust him again, but their talk earlier in the day was the perfect first step in starting to clear up the misunderstanding between them. And she could actually feel herself starting to hope for more than just a co-parenting relationship with him in the future. So much so that she'd actually relayed that message to her family when she sat down for Sunday supper, even though she stopped them from discussing her situation with him any further, saying they needed to work things out between just the two of them without any outside influences.

Julie wasn't sure if their talk had been equally beneficial for Dion as it had been for her. But when she got a text from Dion later that night, she was hopeful that he also saw it as the perfect first step toward getting back to the easy friendship she'd once had with him.
~~~

Leah Mae Wright

And maybe, he might also hope that they could eventually be more to one another again one day.

> **Dion:** Finally got some help figuring out how to unblock you & restore your contact & our text messages in my phone. Thought you should know so we can coordinate doctor's appointments or whatever.

> **Julie:** Good to know. I'll pick you up around 4:15 p.m. on Wednesday for the OB appt.

> **Dion:** Perfect. ;)

> **Dion:** Hey, since every dream or flash of memory I've had includes you, can you help me verify that they're real memories? Maybe help me fill in a few more blanks?

> **Julie:** Sure. Is there something you've dreamed about or had a flash of more than once?

> **Dion:** Yeah, but I don't think you're ready to talk about those memories. {Eggplant emoji} {Taco emoji} {Blushing Face emoji}

"Yeah, we definitely don't need to discuss those memories, yet," Julie agreed, assuming he'd been remembering all the times they met up for a hotel hookup in the last year, and not just the two hookup memories he'd sort of shared earlier.

> **Dion:** I was thinking maybe we could start by having you take me to the place where we met, or someplace where we saw each other often. Then, when I'm having a flash of a new memory, you can help me fill in whatever doesn't come back to me.

> **Julie:** Yeah, we can do that. Let's talk on Wednesday to set up a schedule.

"And maybe by then, I'll be able to think of someplace to take him, other than the ranch, Tully's, and his room at the B and B, to jog his memory."

Considering they'd already seen each other at the church and in the ballroom at the bed and breakfast, she wasn't sure they had many other options, unless they traveled the country to bring back the memories of every hotel where they'd met for a hookup. "Yeah, we're going to have to skip any hotel rooms, even here at the B and B. It's going to be hard enough not to climb him like a tree as it is. I wouldn't be able to resist if we take a walk down our sexual memory lane."

> **Julie: Did you have any memories in the park today? We were there on both Memorial Day & Labor Day for picnics & Maria's birthday party.**

> **Dion: Maybe? Was there another part of the park where there was a band set up?**

> **Julie: Yep, & a dance floor. On Memorial Day, you had to show me what Meemaw Hunter taught you in two-step lessons that morning.**

While Julie hoped Meemaw's version of dirty dancing would be the closest they'd come to any sexual references as they texted, she enjoyed spending the rest of the evening starting to remind him of the public conversations they'd had to build their friendship. Texting about their memories in the park soon morphed into rehashing some of their earlier conversations about their likes and dislikes, schooling each other on the different genres of music they preferred, and even him asking about the silly-face selfies they'd sent when they weren't in private to be able to send sexy selfies.

Julie found herself remembering how they'd built their relationship on more than just their sexual attraction as a foundation. Though she wasn't ready to go back to the romance they'd once shared just yet, she could definitely feel the walls she'd built up to protect her heart in the last few weeks starting to fall, one brick at a time.

Chapter Ten

Wednesday, December 4, 2019

After spending the last couple of days exploring the town of Heart's Destiny with Darius and Mama Marcel, Dion had learned a little more about his time in the small town in the last year, especially when he visited the barbershop in town. Apparently, he'd been in for more than one haircut with the local barber on his many visits to see Jewel. And the barber, who had to be pushing eighty yet refused to retire, had been more than happy to clear up Dion's confusion about no longer shaving his head. Walt Scott, the old timer who started Walt's Barbershop long before Dion was born, told him all about how he'd first come into the shop, claiming his girl preferred his hair long enough to be soft against her skin, instead of prickly when he went a couple of days between shaving. While Walt claimed Dion hadn't ever said her name, he also made it clear that he hadn't confirmed or denied who she was when the old timer had guessed his girl was, "that blonde Burleson girl you're always following around like a smitten puppy."

Dion couldn't help but chuckle at how they hadn't been as much of a secret around town as they'd thought, after all. Walt wasn't the only person he'd met the last couple of days that seemed to know all about him and Julia long before he'd come back to town for Dean and Allissa's wedding. He'd heard similar stories in the local ice cream shop, The Creamarie, and the craft supply store, A Stitch in Time, where he'd purchased some sketchbooks and colored pencils for drawing during his free time, like he had with his mom when he was a kid. Thankfully, the proprietors of those businesses all seemed to be geriatric, at least a generation older than Jewel's mom and the rest of the women his friends lovingly dubbed as the Matchmaking Mommas.

At least, that's why he thought they hadn't ever referred to Julia as anything other than "that blonde Burleson girl," or ratted them out to the Matchmaking Mommas as far as he could tell.

After taking a moment to try to set some of those new memories in his brain, now Dion was both nervous and excited as he waited at the entrance to the bed and breakfast for "that blonde Burleson girl" to pick him up to go to her doctor's appointment. He was nervous about going out in public for the first time without his brother there to catch his big ass if he started to pass the fuck out. But he was also excited about learning more about his and Jewel's babies. The fact that she was letting him go with her was a big deal, too.

He might not remember every detail of their relationship from before, but he was sure this was something she wouldn't have allowed him to accompany her to a year ago. *Hell, even a couple of months ago.* So, even though she wasn't ready to talk about them getting back together, he knew it was a small step in the right direction for them as a couple. Combined with the texts they'd started sharing to help him with his memories since Anthony's daughter, Tia, helped him restore Jewel's contact info in his phone, he was positive these small steps would eventually lead them back together.

And hopefully, the OB has enough experience with new dads passing out that someone there will be able to keep me from hitting the floor if it's too overwhelming for me today. Or at least, they'll have someplace for me to lie down if Dare and Mama Marcel are right about me having some warning and not just collapsing like I thought happened. Though, God only knows how Jewel will get me back to the B and B if I go out and stay out for more than a few minutes.

After he'd managed to keep from blacking out at the wedding reception and again at the park while talking with Jewel, Dion had talked to his brother about the spells to get more information about what happened that he couldn't remember, hoping to be able to figure out how to prevent more of them in the future. Apparently, there had been more than one episode over the last few weeks, when Dion had gone out that Dare said it was like he'd fallen asleep and refused to wake up from his nap for a couple of hours. Darius had also informed Dion that he snored during those blackout spells, so it was more like he had anxiety-induced narcolepsy than some kind of seizure disorder like Dr. Boudreaux suspected.

Dion didn't remember what had happened to cause any of the earlier episodes, typically losing anywhere from a few minutes to an hour or more of time before he passed out, but he did recall the tingly, numb feeling lips, weak feeling throughout his body, and darkness creeping in on his vision for the two episodes he'd prevented over the weekend. Once Mama Marcel arrived in town, Dare had her back him up on telling Dion about the episodes from their perspective. Darius and Mama Marcel both told him that he mentioned feeling like he needed to lie down, and complained of his lips tingling or feeling numb right before he went to sleep. So, apparently, instead of fainting suddenly like he'd believed had happened, he always got some kind of warning, and had a few minutes to get laid down before going out. While he wasn't any closer to figuring out a diagnosis, or learning how to stop the blackout spells, Dion was relieved to know that he always had enough warning that he wouldn't just collapse and risk hitting his head again, the way he thought he had when he'd woken up after the earlier episodes.

Hopefully, they're right. So, if I start to pass out today, I won't just collapse without someone around who's strong enough to keep me from hitting the floor and busting my head open again.

Darius and Mama Marcel's assurances that he had early warning signs for those blackouts made him feel a lot better about being able to hold his and Jewel's babies once they were born, too. He'd been afraid that he wouldn't be able to help Jewel take care of their children the way they deserved because of not wanting to risk anything happening to them if he passed out while holding them. He still planned to be careful and sit down to hold them as much as possible, but now he was more confident that he could get them safely laid down in their crib or handed off to another person before he had an episode in the future.

But maybe I should go ahead and find a doctor here to review my case. I don't really want to go back to NOLA when Jewel and our babies are here. Especially since she seemed so dead set against going back to the long-distance relationship we had previously when we talked the other day. And maybe with a second opinion, I can find a doctor who can give me a better idea of how to prevent those episodes altogether, so I don't ever risk our babies getting hurt because I was holding them at the wrong time.

His thoughts of finding a local doctor for a second opinion only increased as Dion saw Jewel pull up in her blue Malibu. The mid-size car wasn't the most comfortable vehicle for a man his size to ride in, but he wasn't about to complain as he slid down into the passenger seat. While it was somewhat emasculating to have to rely on Jewel to drive them to her doctor's appointment, Dion tried to use it as motivation to find someone to help him heal faster, wanting to be cleared to drive again before the babies were due. He didn't care if she wanted to be the one to drive most of the time, but he wanted to man up to be the one to drive her to the hospital when it was time for their babies to be born.

"Thanks for picking me up, Jewel, uh, Julia." Dion smiled at her as he buckled his seatbelt, hoping his slip in calling her Jewel wouldn't upset her before the appointment.

Since everyone else seemed to call her Julie, he didn't really mind calling her Julia, feeling like it was still something special between them because of her only insisting on him using her given name. But one of the drawbacks of his brain injury was that he couldn't always think of it before he spoke, so he often reverted to what he called her in all his dreams because he couldn't think of her as anything but his precious Jewel. And truth be told, he kind of hoped calling her Jewel once in a while would remind her of their intimate moments to start breaking down the walls she had up, which were currently keeping them apart.

"No problem." Jewel smiled at him as she pulled out of the parking lot and drove them through town. "So, I was thinking about the other places in town we could go to help you get some of your memories back."

"Yeah, you come up with any good ideas?" Dion took advantage of her focus being on the road to allow his eyes to wander over her body. He was surprised to see they were dressed to match, hoping it meant something about them being on the same mental wavelength to possibly be a good sign for them getting back together.

While he was in navy-blue slacks and a light blue button-down dress shirt, she was wearing a navy-blue dress that looked to be made out of the same material as some of his thicker t-shirts, with a lighter blue cardigan over it. She looked amazing as always, but he kind of missed the sexy suits she wore in his dreams.

Leah Mae Wright

Those probably don't stretch enough to be maternity wear, though. And I suppose the dresses will allow for easier access for quickies, if we ever get back to the sexual side of our relationship. Not that I can suggest that now, but...

"Not really," Jewel sighed. "Most of our time together was either in the ballroom of the B and B or at church, so you should have already had those flashes of memory last week, if you're likely to remember them."

"I think that might have been most of our platonic time together, but not most of our overall time together," Dion disagreed, grinning as he wagged his eyebrows at her. "But since I know you're not ready to talk about *those* memories yet, I'll happily stick to reviewing the flashes of memory I had this week at the church and the B and B with you for now."

"We can also plan trips to the ranch, Tully's, and back to the park to work on the memories from those places, too." Jewel didn't say anything in response to Dion's reference to their hotel room hookups, but the way she wiggled in her seat as she talked about the other places in town that they could visit together to help with his memories made it obvious to him that she wasn't as unaffected by their sexual memories as she wanted him to believe.

Thank fuck! Maybe it won't be too hard to get her back in my bed after all. Or rather, me in her bed, since we are in her hometown.

"Actually, I think my first flash of memory was the first time Dare drove by here when we got to town," Dion informed her as they drove past the town square. "Did we go to a picnic, or fireworks, or something on the lawn of City Hall? Or did I confuse it with the park we were in on Sunday?"

"Yeah, on Independence Day," Jewel nodded before elaborating. "Since the fireworks are shot off from atop City Hall, they move some of the picnic stuff over here, even though you can still see them clearly from areas of the park without tree cover. Or from pretty much anywhere in town with a wide view of the sky. But we didn't sit together for most of the day. I was with my family and you mostly hung out with the rest of the GWA crew. It wasn't until the fireworks were almost over that you came over to hog the quilt I had laid out on the lawn."

Dion let his mind drift back to that day, remembering sitting and watching her from afar until his need to be close to her became overwhelming. "I came over and teased you about avoiding me all day."

"Yes, and made my mom's day by asking me to give you a ride back to the B and B right in front of her," Jewel huffed as she turned into a parking lot in the center of a U-shaped grouping of three interconnected buildings.

"Shit, did I really? I don't remember that." Dion shrugged when she glared at him. He looked around the car as he recalled reaching over to slip his hand down her shorts to tease her while she drove that steamy July night. "But I do remember being in this car before, now that you mention it."

He'd brought her right to the edge with his fingers stroking her wet pussy, but didn't let her go over until they got back to his room at the bed and breakfast. *Fuck, she was so wet and worked up that we barely had time to shove our shorts down out of the way for me to fuck her against the door of the room.*

"Yeah, we're not discussing that right now," Jewel declared as she got out of the car.

Dion scrambled to catch up to her, barely hearing her mumbling about "being inappropriately aroused right before a pelvic exam," as they walked toward the clinic entrance.

Yeah, I'd better back off now, so the doctor doesn't get the wrong idea. But it is good to know that she's still easily aroused by remembering being with me.

As he looked around, he noticed that the Heart's Destiny Clinic and Birthing Center appeared to take up the majority of two of the buildings, with Pistol Pete's Pizza occupying the lower level of space in the corner where the clinic connected to another building without any signage. With it being a large two-story building taking up a full city block, Dion thought it would make a really cool place for a gym.

It's probably not as vacant as it looks from the parking lot side. I bet all the business signs are on the street side. Unless it's just an office building, like for the doctors who work at the clinic to have a separate space for their files and stuff? I'll have to ask Jewel about it later.

Leah Mae Wright

Since the doctor had informed him that it wouldn't be wise to wrestle again and risk another brain injury, Dion had recently started to think of ideas for businesses he could open once he was cleared to work at all. He'd talked to his now former boss, Rick Robertson, to let him know that he wouldn't be coming back to wrestle, back when they were both in town for the wedding. Rick had suggested he come back to the GWA as a booker once he was cleared to fly, but Dion turned him down, not wanting to be tempted to jump in the ring with his buddies if he was around it all the time.

He'd originally thought he'd start another business in NOLA, in addition to the club he co-owned with his brother. But finding Jewel and learning about their babies seemed like strong signs that it was not only time for him to stop traveling all the time, but also that he was supposed to move out of NOLA. He wanted to be there for every step of the process to make them a family, as well as every milestone the kids had growing up. So, he'd decided to make sure to find something he could do in her hometown to give him something to do when Jewel was at work once their kids started school.

He'd always thought he'd open a gym and fight school when he retired from wrestling. But with his increased risk of permanent brain damage, he'd started to wonder if that was another career option his injury would take from him. Oh, he could still open a gym and do some limited workouts, like he'd been doing at Dean's house since coming to town, but the fight school part of his plan was definitely out.

If I can figure out a way to stop the blackout spells, maybe I can open a day care center, since that's something I didn't notice when we were checking out the town the past couple of days with Mama Marcel? Or hell, maybe even if I don't figure out how to stop the spells, I can still open a day care. That way I can hire some help, so I won't be alone trying to take care of our babies when Jewel goes back to work. And since Heart's Destiny is big enough to have a birthing center, I'm sure there are other parents here who need the services of a day care, which I haven't seen since I've been here.

Or maybe not, Dion decided as he held the door open for Jewel to walk into an empty waiting room. *Where are all the other expectant parents?*

Dion followed Jewel up to the counter, where two ladies in scrubs were waiting for them. One of them was seated at the reception desk, and the other was standing off to the side, holding a tablet in her hand as she talked to the first woman.

"No need to sign in, Julie," the thirty-something year old woman seated at the computer informed them. "You're the last appointment of the day, so as soon as you pay your co-pay, I'm shutting down the system and going home early."

Dion reached into the back pocket of his navy-blue slacks and pulled out his wallet, passing over his credit card before Jewel could get hers out of her purse.

"You don't need to pay for my appointment," Jewel huffed, resting her fist on her hip in indignation.

"Yes, I do," Dion insisted.

"Dion, seriously, like I told you last weekend, I don't need your money," Jewel insisted, pulling out her wallet and trying to get the woman to swap cards with her. "Jeri, please take the co-pay from my account."

"I know you don't," Dion agreed, reaching out to pull back the hand holding her card out to the receptionist. "But those babies are just as much mine as they are yours, so I'm going to pay my fair share of their expenses. And since you've already been to the doctor once, it's my turn to cover the co-pay."

Dion didn't mention that if it was up to him, he'd pay to provide everything for Jewel and their babies from then on. After the gold digger comments Darius had made on the phone with her, though, he knew she'd think he was overcompensating to try to hide sharing his brother's jaded opinions. While Dion knew there were certainly women in the world who'd earned the labels Darius used for them on that fateful phone call, he also knew Jewel wasn't one of them. But she was also too damn independent to accept Dion's inner caveman wanting to be the sole provider for their family.

Dion realized then that he would have to walk a fine line between letting his inner alpha show and giving in when Jewel's independent streak flared up. He didn't want her to feel like he was trying to take over her life, but he also wasn't willing to be her doormat, either.

But fuck, the makeup sex after fighting for control with her could be hot as hell. Yeah, I probably shouldn't mention that I'm looking forward to that just yet, either.

"Fine!" Jewel finally relented, pulling her hand from his to put her card back in her wallet. "But only because I don't want to fight with you about this in public."

"We're not gonna fight about it in private either, Jewel," Dion grinned as Jeri passed him the receipt to sign along with his card. "I'm gonna give you two options for how we cover the expenses for our babies, and I'll gladly go along with whichever one of those two you pick. Either we can split the expenses fifty-fifty, or I'll pay a hundred percent."

Dion scrawled his name on the receipt and passed it back to Jeri before putting his card back in his wallet. Then he turned and bent down to brush his lips over Jewel's forehead. "Just let me know which option you pick, Jewel."

Jewel looked dumbfounded as the two nurses giggled and grinned at him.

"You've got a good man there, Julie," Jeri grinned from her seat. "If he has any brothers, send them my way."

Guess I should pass her name on to Dare when I get back to the hotel.

"For real," the other nurse, who looked to be a few years younger than the one seated at the reception desk, agreed, fanning herself with the tablet in her hand. "Okay, now let's get you back to see Devon, so we can all call it an early night."

Or maybe just bring him up here to meet both of them.

The nurse pointed at the door on the right side of the front counter as she made her way out from behind the desk and around the wall to open it from the other side. Dion followed Jewel through the door, where the nurse introduced herself as Arden after handing Jewel a cup sealed in plastic and pointing her toward the restroom.

Arden escorted Dion to an exam room, where he sat and waited for Jewel to finish what he assumed was a urine test of some sort. He wanted to read the "Pregnancy and Birth" poster on the wall on the opposite side of the room, but apparently, it wasn't just his up-close vision for reading that had changed since his concussion. It seemed his distance vision had also changed enough recently that he couldn't make out most of the words from so far away. And he didn't want to be caught leaning over the exam table to get close enough to read it whenever Jewel, or the nurse, came into the room, so he just sat there in the extra chair, waiting impatiently.

Maybe I should add an eye doctor to my list of doctors to find? Dion wondered if he'd forgotten needing to get glasses over the last couple of years, or if the head injury had impacted his vision, as well as his cognition, more than he'd thought. Since his up-close vision only seemed to get blurry when he tried reading for a long time, or he got anxious about whatever he was reading, Dr. Boudreaux seemed to think it was a concussion symptom that would eventually go back to normal. *I know Dr. Boudreaux said I don't need glasses for some sporadic blurriness, but maybe I should get an actual eye doctor's opinion on that, especially since Dare and Mama Marcel couldn't tell me if I'd needed glasses in the last year before the injury.*

He didn't have to wait long before Jewel joined him in the room. Instead of sitting in the chair beside him, however, she went ahead and climbed up on the exam table for Arden to take her blood pressure and temperature.

After Arden finished asking Jewel all kinds of questions and left the room, Dion decided to ask Jewel about his recent history of vision issues or wearing glasses. "Do you know if I wore glasses anytime in the last couple of years?"

Jewel's face contorted in confusion before she replied, "No, not that I know of. Why?"

"I can't read anything but the heading on that poster from here," Dion shrugged, pointing to the poster on the other side of Jewel. "And it feels like I should be able to read the whole thing. So, I was wondering if I forgot needing to get glasses because my vision changed with age, or if the head injury messed with my eyesight."

"Well, we never discussed eye exam scores, so I can't say for sure," Jewel shrugged, her features softening with compassion as she looked at him. "But I assumed you had twenty-twenty vision, since I've never even seen you pull out a pair of readers like some of my friends have started doing as they hit their thirties."

"Are you having vision issues?" The doctor Dion remembered seeing at the wedding shower over a week before directed her question to Jewel as she walked into the room with the nurse right behind her. She had a concerned look on her face as she looked down at the tablet in her hands.

"No, Dion is, not me," Jewel explained, pointing at him with her thumb.

"Okay, good," the doctor sighed. "I just had to check when I heard you mention readers. While Dads can have some sympathy weight gain, nausea, or even sympathy labor pains, from being empathetic when their partner is pregnant, they don't tend to have the signs and symptoms of complications with the pregnancy, even when Mom is having them."

Huh? Guess it's a good thing I've been going down to Dean's house for those light workouts since I've been in town, so I'm not turning Jewel off with sympathy weight gain, Dion thought before tuning back into what the doctor was saying.

"Blurry vision in pregnant women could be an early sign of gestational diabetes or pre-eclampsia, so make sure you let us know if you start having any vision issues."

"Of course," Jewel agreed as the nurse stepped around the doctor to Jewel's side.

To start off the appointment, Dr. Devon Magnum introduced herself to Dion, while Arden pushed a cart up beside the exam table and took a vial of Jewel's blood. He couldn't help but smile at the doctor having the same name as his favorite brand of condoms, but he kept his comments on the irony of an obstetrician sharing the name of a contraceptive to himself.

Once Arden was done and pushed her cart with Jewel's blood sample on it out of the room, Dr. Magnum took over questioning Jewel about how she was feeling as she did the exam. Most everything seemed similar to the basic physicals he'd had to have regularly as an athlete, other than the questions about morning sickness and vaginal discharge. Dion was glad to hear that Jewel's morning sickness had been minimal and mostly seemed to have passed, except when triggered by certain smells. And that she hadn't had any unusual vaginal discharge.

After warning Jewel that she might have some cramping from her ligaments stretching as the babies continued growing and may even have some false contractions over the next few months, she had Jewel lie back on the exam table and lift her dress to expose her baby bump. Dion couldn't take his eyes off of her slightly swollen abdomen as the doctor pulled out a measuring tape and noted how much their babies had started showing since Jewel's last appointment.

"You may also start feeling some flutters of movement in the next couple of weeks," Dr. Magnum explained as she put away the measuring tape and pulled out a little white box with a probe attached via a spiral cord similar to the old-fashioned phone cords Dion remembered from childhood. She squirted a dollop of some kind of gel on the probe before starting to run it over Jewel's lower abdomen. "By the time I see you again in January, those flutters should be strong enough for you to recognize them as one or both of the babies moving. Ah, there we are. Baby A's heartbeat."

The doctor turned a dial on the white box and a soft thumping sound filled the room. In that moment, the abstract idea of Jewel being pregnant finally solidified in his mind. With its heartbeat pulsing through the air, their baby finally seemed real to Dion. He was so overwhelmed with emotion that he couldn't stop himself from standing up to step closer, wanting to see exactly where their little one was positioned in Jewel's belly. As soon as he reached her side, Jewel reached out and took his hand, smiling up at him as they listened intently to the rapid thumping swooshes of their baby's heart.

"It kinda sounds like Jasmine's hoofbeats when I had her going all out back during my barrel racing days," Jewel giggled.

"Is it supposed to be that fast?" Dion wondered aloud, thinking it sounded more like an exercising heart rate than a resting one.

"Yes, babies' heart rates are twice as fast as an adult's heart rate," Dr. Magnum clarified before moving the probe to the other side of Jewel's belly. "And there is Baby B's heartbeat."

Once again, the soft galloping sound brought with it the realization of Jewel carrying his babies. Dion felt his own heartbeat quicken with the immense love he felt for both of their babies as the second one solidified in his mind.

No doubt about it now. I've gotta find a doctor here to help me heal my brain ASAP, so I can be the daddy they need. Maybe a team of doctors with different specialties, instead of just the neurologist like I've been seeing back in NOLA, so they can fix issues like my vision changes that he hasn't addressed yet.

As the doctor continued to dictate heart rate estimates and other information to the nurse, whom Dion hadn't even realized had come back into the room, for her to note them in Jewel's chart, Dion stood there listening in awe at the various sounds they heard. In addition to the galloping horse sounds of their babies' heartbeats, the doctor also made note of something that sounded like a strong wind to Dion, which she said had something to do with the placentas. But Dion's favorite sound had to be the strong solitary thump he heard when the nurse joked that one of the babies must have punched the probe.

Jewel had smiled and nodded when asked if she'd felt the little flutter. "It was deep though," Jewel elaborated. "More like the way you feel things during digestion, only not where I normally feel that. I don't think I'd have realized it was one of the babies moving if you hadn't heard it with the doppler."

"Well, now you know what it feels like, so you'll probably recognize it more in the future." Dr. Magnum smiled as she lifted the probe from Jewel's abdomen and wiped the gel off. "At fifteen weeks, they're only about as tall as an apple at this point, so most women don't feel movement this early. It's usually week sixteen at the earliest, and may not be noticeable until week twenty-four. But I've found that moms having twins usually feel movement earlier."

"Yeah, I guess double occupancy means they're taking up twice as much space as a single baby, so it makes sense that movement would be noticeable sooner." Jewel lowered her dress as soon as the gel was all wiped off her belly.

Damn, and I was so focused on the babies and looking Jewel in the eyes as we heard their heartbeats that I didn't even look to see what sexy panties she's wearing today.

As they finished up the appointment, Dion realized that was probably a good thing. *It's emasculating enough to have to ask her to drive for these appointments and help me find the best doctors in the area for second and third opinions on my TBI issues. I don't want to give her any reason to think I'm just asking for her help to get back in her panties.*

In addition to not trying to look at her pussy during her doctor's visits, I should probably stop mentioning any of the sexual memories I've been getting back, too, so we can rebuild our friendship first. Then, once she realizes she can trust me again, I can start flirting a little more to get us back to where we were. Or maybe even on a more solid path toward being a family than we had before.

~~~

After they left the doctor's office, Julie finally remembered to show Dion the ultrasound photos she'd stuck in her purse that morning after getting them back from Lakota Deere at the Knick Knack Shack, where she'd taken them to have them blown up and framed for her parents for Christmas. *Maybe I should have done the same for Dion for Christmas? I mean, he won't really have a place to hang them up at the B and B while he's in town, but I bet he's got a place to hang them in his condo in New Orleans when he goes home.*

She knew she was being stingy by only bringing three of the images with her, one of each of the babies individually and one with both of them visible, instead of grabbing the rest of them from home that morning. But she wanted to put them all in the baby book she'd started to log everything about her pregnancy, and she didn't want Dion to think it was okay for him to take more than those three pictures since some of them were similar.

"Sorry, I forgot to give you these earlier," Julie apologized as she handed him the pictures once they were parked at the bed and breakfast.

"You have nothing to be sorry for, Jewel, uh, Julia." Dion shook his head as he looked down at the images. "Wow. I'm just glad you remembered to bring them at all, since I forgot to ask about them."

Julie watched him closely as he reverently ran a fingertip over each baby in the photo of the two of them together. He seemed so different from the man she'd fallen for a year ago, but yet, somehow, he was also still the same. She couldn't quite figure it out because he'd always been more reserved than the rest of the wrestlers whenever they were all together at a wedding or other event in town. *But he didn't hold back his flirtatiousness when it was just the two of us before, so maybe that's why he seems different now.*

"Can we take these in to show Mama Marcel?" Dion turned his head, finally taking his eyes off the ultrasound pictures to look at her imploringly. "And maybe see if Mandi has a copier I can use, so we each have copies of the first pictures of our babies?"

Now Julie really felt guilty for only bringing three of the dozen pictures she'd gotten at the first ultrasound. *I should have realized*
~~~

that he's still the same sweet gentleman I met last year, and not a greedy asshole like his brother came across on the phone with me. My Dion would never insist on taking the originals, so I couldn't put them in the baby book for our kids to have to look back on later. I just have to, somehow, convince my head to separate his actions from those of his brother, so I can get past that pain to see where we go from here.

"Yeah, we can do that," she choked out, nodding her head at him as she turned off her car. "And if there's not a copier here, I can take pics of them and the others I've already put in their baby book with my phone and text them to you."

"You have more than just these three?" Dion arched an eyebrow at her, obviously curious about why she hadn't brought all of them.

"Yes, but I've already taped the others into the baby book," she fibbed, not wanting him to know that she'd held them back intentionally. She just hoped the flush she felt in her cheeks didn't give away her slight falsehood, so she didn't hurt his feelings by confessing the truth. "I just had these three out because I took them to be enlarged and framed for my parents for Christmas. I guess I should have brought the whole baby book to show you today." *And I will later in the week after I actually tape the other pictures into it, instead of just leaving them tucked between the pages.*

"If we can take these in to show Mama Marcel now, I can wait for you to text me copies another time," Dion smiled, not seeming to notice the deception she felt so guilty for that caused her to, uncharacteristically, blush. "But, um, Dare will probably be with her, so if you don't want to talk to him yet, we can wait to show them some other time."

Julie didn't really want to deal with Dion's brother, but since they seemed a lot closer after Dion's injury than they had during the eleven months Julie had known him before then, she assumed she'd eventually have to interact with the man. *I guess it's better to get it over with now, so maybe I can start getting over the issues I have with him without my family around to cause a big scene.*

"It's fine," Julie sighed, resigning herself to trying to be cordial, even if she wasn't really ready to forgive Darius just yet. "I don't expect he and I will ever be best friends, but he is our babies' uncle, so I'm willing to give him the chance to apologize."

"Thank you, Julia." Dion smiled at her before pulling his phone out of his pocket and handing her the ultrasound photos. "I'll just text to find out where to meet them."

When Dare replied that they were on their way down to the restaurant for dinner, Dion gave her another chance to back out of going in with him. "I'd love for you to stay and have dinner with us, but I understand if that's more than you're ready for right now."

Oh, geez, can I really sit down and have a cordial meal with the man who called me all those horrible names just a few short weeks ago?

Julie looked over at the gentle giant she hadn't stopped loving, no matter how hard she tried. Dion was waiting patiently for her to decide, while crammed into the front seat of her car. *Holy crap! He's trying so hard not to irritate me that he didn't even move the seat back to have room for his long legs.*

Holy shit! That's what's different about him! Other than insisting on paying my co-pay at the doctor's office, he's been deferring to me on everything, instead of taking charge like he did before.

Oh, gawd! I hope the head injuries didn't knock the dominant streak out of him. I loved the way we always used that fight for control as foreplay, and I can't imagine we'll be nearly as good together if he stops pushing me to let out my submissive side, or stops playing with my inner brat.

Does he even remember that aspect of our relationship? Or could he possibly be afraid to let his dominant side out right now because I've only allowed him to see my aggressive anger over recent events, instead of letting him see that I still have other feelings for him besides that anger?

Pluck a duck! I have to start giving him a little more, or he's never going to stop trying to placate me to maintain his place in our babies' lives.

"I'd love to stay for dinner," she finally decided, hoping she wouldn't regret it. *This could either backfire big time if I end up fighting with Darius all evening, or it could be a spectacular success if it leads to us all getting along.*

But either way, I have to maintain a little space between me and Dion. I want us to be able to co-parent our babies with ease, but I don't want to let my second trimester sex drive dictate the course of our relationship, and push us to focus on the physical instead of the friendship first.

Dion smiled brightly as he finally got out of the car. She wasn't surprised to see him saunter around the front of the vehicle to open her door as she put the ultrasound pictures back in her purse. When they'd arrived at the doctor's office, she'd gotten out of the car before he could perform the gentlemanly task. But now that she realized how much she missed his dominant tendencies, she knew she needed to let him see a little of her submissive side to bring them back out. And for now, that meant coming up with reasons to waste time, instead of opening her own door.

She also didn't rush ahead of him like she had at the doctor's office, allowing him to escort her into the restaurant area of the bed and breakfast with a hand on the small of her back. She reveled in the tingles that spread throughout her body with his light, innocent touch, even though she wasn't ready to openly admit to how much he affected her just yet.

"Oh, Dion, you didn't tell us you were bringing your Jewel to dinner." They were greeted by an older Black woman, about the same height as Julie, who had to be Mama Marcel. "You are absolutely a vision! I can't wait to hear all about how you and Dion met and fell in love."

Before Julie could correct the woman on her name, or put the brakes on the L-O-V-E talk, she found herself wrapped in the older woman's arms. She couldn't help but smile as she returned the hug, feeling like she was meeting Dion's favorite family member, even though she knew they shared no blood relation.

"Oh, gracious me!" Mama Marcel exclaimed as they released the embrace, crossing herself before reaching out to hug Dion. "Those two little girls are gonna give you gray hair when they're teenagers!"

"What on earth are you talkin' about, Mama Marcel?" Darius had a confused expression on his face as he looked over at his brother and foster mom as they released each other from their brief embrace.

"Jewel is pregnant," Mama Marcel announced.

"Julie," she corrected, earning her a confused look from both Dion and Mama Marcel. "My name is actually Julia, but everyone calls me Julie because it was what my brothers called me as toddlers."

"Julie is pregnant," Mama Marcel reiterated with the correct name, smiling brightly.

"Yeah, we knew that already." Darius shook his head, still looking confused.

He wasn't the only one confused. Julie actually felt like she was in the same boat as Dion's brother for a moment, since pregnancy brain apparently caused her to forget what the older woman had said to trigger Darius's questions.

"With twin girls," Mama Marcel foretold adamantly. "And they're gonna give Dion gray hair when they're teenagers."

Oh! She's put on her fortune teller hat to tell us what she thinks about our babies. I know Dion said he doesn't really believe in her gift, but I kinda hope she's right about this prediction.

"We are havin' twins," Dion confirmed as the hostess came over to seat them. "But it's too early to tell if they're boys, or girls, or one of each, yet."

The conversation stopped as the hostess escorted them to a table. Ever the gentleman, Dion held out her chair as Darius held out the chair for Mama Marcel, seating the women across from one another at the rectangular table. Dion then took the seat beside Julie, while his brother sat beside Mama Marcel.

"And I'm telling you they're girls," Mama Marcel insisted, once the hostess handed them each a menu and left. "Maybe once they're born, you'll finally start to believe in my gift of *the sight*."

"If you're right about them havin' twin girls, I don't think we'll have to wait 'til they're teenagers to see D's hair turn gray," Darius chuckled. "He is getting up there in years, so it won't take much to get 'em to start poppin' out. The first one will probably be the day they're born. Then another ten when he has to change the first diaper. And I bet his head will be a solid silver by the time they start preschool and have little boys in their class."

Regardless of her first impression of Darius from that infamous phone call, Julie found herself smiling at the way he teased Dion. His attitude toward his brother reminded her of her brothers and cousins and how they constantly joked around.

"There will be no little boys in their class," Dion declared, shaking his head. "If there's not an all-girls school around here, then I'll start one for them."

"There's no need for all that," Julie objected, rolling her eyes at Dion. "The schools in Heart's Destiny are amazing. That's where we all went growing up, and where I want my kids to go. Besides, being raised on the ranch with all their male cousins warning the boys at school away from them will be more than enough of a deterrent to dating before they go off to college, just like it was for me and my sister."

"It wasn't your brothers that warned the boys off?" Dion arched an eyebrow at her.

"Oh, yeah, they did, too." Julie nodded in agreement. "But it was my cousin Bobby, as the oldest of our generation, that first started telling his friends that his sisters and female cousins were all off limits. And while JoJo is old enough that he won't ever be in the same school as these two, Brody and Antonio will probably be in fifth grade when they start kindergarten." Julie absentmindedly rubbed her hand over her baby bump as she spoke. "And of course, Sam, Jonah, and Jerry will be in the same grade or one ahead of them, so they'll have more than enough male cousins watching out for them."

"Oh, goodness, Dion said you come from a big family, but he didn't tell us you have so many babies in your family already." Mama Marcel reached across the table and placed her hand on Julie's. "Please tell us all about them."

Julie knew she should be more guarded when discussing her family in public, but for some reason, she felt like she didn't have to be with Dion and his family, even with Darius at the table. So, after recommending the Burleson Beef dishes on the menu when the waitress came by and took their orders, she found herself spewing out a brief history of the Burleson family before listing out all her current living relatives in the Burleson, Avington, and Harper lines, as well as her pseudo cousins, the Whitmans, through her Aunt Hazel's sister, who felt like they were related, even though they shared no biological connection.

"So, of the forty plus people you just listed out, how many of them want to kick my ass for being an idiot on the phone with you?" Darius surprised Julie by posing the question without actually apologizing for what he said that day.

Part of her wanted to pop off with "all of them," but she knew that wasn't exactly true. Besides, she was really trying to keep from making the situation more awkward by lashing out at him. So, she opted to try joking about it, and hoped he got the point and apologized without reverting to his asshole behavior.

"I don't know," she shrugged and smirked. "I haven't taken a poll to find out."

She probably should have stopped speaking then. But for some reason (probably either her bottled up anger toward Darius or her pregnancy hormones), she couldn't seem to control her mouth. Instead, she tilted her head and tapped her chin as if deep in thought before continuing. "But if I were you, I wouldn't worry about most of them. Unless you don't apologize and come to the ranch, where the guys are all armed, ya know, in case of coyotes or rattlesnakes getting too close to the houses or livestock. The only ones who carry guns off the ranch are my cousin Bobby, the police chief, Dougie, who is one of his patrol officers, the Avingtons because of their security company, my cousin Josh, the former Navy SEAL, and maybe Char's husband Ian, since he used to be undercover with the D. E. A. But they're all serious about law enforcement and wouldn't shoot someone just for being a jackass without apologizing, so you're probably safe as long as you don't break the law."

Darius's jaw gaped in shock at her tirade, making him appear to be at a total loss for words. Either that or slightly scared by the mention of so many of her family members being armed.

"Now would be a good time for that apology, Dare," Dion chuckled, obviously understanding Julie's mocking tone the way she intended it.

"You haven't apologized to her yet?" Mama Marcel reached over and slapped the back of Darius's head. "I know you were raised better than that."

"I'm sorry!" Darius held his hands up in surrender, turning in his seat to face Mama Marcel while also leaning back away from her, as if trying to keep her from smacking him again. "I haven't exactly had the chance to speak to her until tonight. And ya'll have monopolized the conversation."

Julie had to stifle a smile when Mama Marcel motioned for him to direct his comments to Julie instead of her.

Darius turned to look at her with a truly contrite expression on his face. "I really am sorry for everything I said to you that day. I was upset about my brother being injured and had just had to call security to escort a couple of, um, unscrupulous women from his room where they'd snuck in, so I wasn't thinking when I answered his phone. I took my anger at them out on you, and you didn't deserve that. And I promise I'll never lash out like that at you or any other undeserving person again."

Crap! I actually believe he means that, so I've got to forgive him. And that means actually trying to do all that stuff Pastor Harrison was talking about the other day, instead of just saying I forgive him and holding onto the anger. That's gonna be a whole lot easier said than done.

Thankfully, she had a moment to think about how to respond as their meals were delivered.

"Thank you." Julie forced herself to smile at Darius once the waitress had left their table, trying to make herself feel the forgiveness she was about to give lip service to. "I accept your apology and will do my best to forgive and forget."

"Good, now let's get back to talking about the babies," Mama Marcel beamed, squeezing Julie's hand once before releasing it to unroll her napkin from around her silverware. "When are they due?"

"They're due May twenty-sixth, but with twins the doctor says they could come as early as April twenty-eighth," Julie informed them, also placing her napkin in her lap before starting to eat.

"Oh, goodness, that's only three days after your birthday, Dion," Mama Marcel gushed. "They could be born on your birthday!"

"Actually, they could be born on either of our birthdays," Julie corrected with a smile, remembering the emerald birthstone necklace Dion had sent her for her birthday earlier in the year. *That's probably something else I can remind him about to jog his memory.*

"Oh, really? When's your birthday?"

"May third," Julie smiled at the older woman's exuberant curiosity.

"Oh, a Taurus! With Dion being a Gemini, the two of you will have to work to understand each other, but your love will be very passionate." Mama Marcel waved her fork back and forth, pointing at Julie and Dion.

Julie felt herself blush at the older woman's comments.

Apparently, she wasn't the only one who felt uncomfortable talking about how passionate their relationship was. At least, she assumed that was why Dion coughed before taking a sip of his tea and changing the subject back to the babies. "Have you thought of any names yet?"

"Only a couple," Julie admitted, realizing she needed to come up with more than just the one she'd decided on for a girl, especially if Mama Marcel's prediction was correct. "I'd thought of Owen and Kayden for boys, but my cousin Josh ruined those by saying they'd be collectively called 'Okayden' and trying to rap the Bubba Sparxxx song, *Okay Then*, when I mentioned them at a family dinner. But I also picked the name Zoe for a girl."

"I like Zoe," Dion smiled at her, rubbing his hand over her shoulder where he'd put the arm he wasn't using to eat on the back of her chair.

"I agree with your cousin," Darius chuckled. "But I'd probably go with Lil Niqo's version of *OK Then*."

"Yeah, even if I end up having boys, those names are out, just so I can avoid a rap-off between you and Josh in my birthing suite," Julie chuckled.

"It's a good thing you're having girls then," Mama Marcel interjected with a grin as she poked Darius. "That way you don't have to worry about hearing this one try to rap. And I love the name Zoe. It's a strong Creole name and perfect to honor your daughter's heritage. Julia is also a Creole name. Do you have some roots out our way?"

"Not that I know of, but even though we did our ancestry earlier this year, I haven't really looked at where all my ancestors lived before coming here to know for sure." Julie shook her head, taking a sip of her tea to wash down the bite of steak she'd just swallowed before continuing. "I think my mom named me after Julia Child, hoping the name would give me some of her culinary abilities, after Memmaw Judy insisted they watch her show while she was trying to teach Mom and Aunt Hazel to cook."

"Oh, goodness," Mama Marcel giggled after swallowing her own steak. "Did it work?"

"Nope, not really," Julie laughed, shaking her head. "I do okay with helping in the kitchen when Mom and Aunt Hazel give me directions, but I'm definitely not a chef. That's why I went to work with my dad, instead of helping cook for all the ranch hands like my mom."

"Well, lucky for you, I made sure Dion and Darius both know their way around the kitchen."

"What's your first name, Mama Marcel?" Julie decided right then to figure out a way to name one of her daughters after this wonderful woman, especially if she turned out to be correct in her prediction.

"Caroline, but you can call me Mama Marcel, just like my boys do."

Oh, I love Caroline as a middle name to go with Zoe!

"Would you mind if I name one of our daughters Zoe Caroline?"

"Oh, you're such a sweet girl," Caroline beamed. "I would be honored if you want to name one of your girls after me. But I really must ask that you also consider the name Elena, after my dear friend and Dion's mother."

"Oh yes, I love the name Elena. Good thing we're gonna have two girls, so I don't have to pick between the two."

"Jewel, uh, Julia has pictures of the babies from the first ultrasound to show you after dinner," Dion mentioned, smiling. "Maybe once you see them, you can help us pick out a middle name for Elena."

"I'm sure you'll come up with the perfect middle name on your own," Mama Marcel assured them with a smile. "Especially if you keep up the tradition of naming your children after the people you love."

We could go with Elena Susan after both our moms. Julie scrunched up her nose, not liking the way their mother's names sounded together. *Or maybe Elena Caroline and Zoe Susan? Or I could let one of my siblings name their daughter after our mom and stick with Zoe Caroline. We've got plenty of time to find a better middle name to go with Elena before the babies are born. And who knows, maybe Mama Marcel will change her mind and have the perfect name idea when she sees the ultrasound pictures.*

Julie wasn't sure how it happened, but she ended up having a great time visiting with Dion's family the rest of the evening. She especially loved how much she felt like they were already one big, happy family. Even Darius.

Chapter Eleven

After talking to Jewel about finding some local specialists to get second, third, and fourth opinions on how he could try to stop some of the issues he was still having from the concussion, Dion took the first available appointment with the general practitioner in town. She hadn't known who all he needed to see, especially specialists that she hadn't had to deal with before, so she'd recommended getting Doc Hayes to refer him to the best in the area. Now Dion found himself sitting in an exam room on the opposite side of the Heart's Destiny Clinic from where he'd gone with Jewel earlier in the week, waiting for Doc Hayes to come into the room.

He felt a little ridiculous having both Darius and Mama Marcel with him for the appointment. But since Dr. Boudreaux hadn't cleared him to drive, Dion couldn't go anywhere alone yet. And even though he'd rather have Jewel there with him, she was at work. Besides, both his brother and Mama Marcel were there in town, instead of being back in New Orleans, simply to help him try to get some of his memories back. So, he felt like he needed to let them tag along to any appointments he had for additional opinions on his prognosis and treatment plans.

Even though he knew they were there because they loved him, it still made him feel like less of a man to have to have them there with him. *Damn it! I'm thirty-three years old. I shouldn't have to be accompanied to the doctor like a three-year-old.*

The worst part was that Dion knew he wouldn't remember everything the doctor recommended if he didn't have someone else there to help him remember. He understood not being able to remember the events surrounding the TBI, and even the amnesia that caused him to forget the majority of the last few years of his life because of the injury. But Dr. Boudreaux hadn't mentioned how much harder it would be for him to remember recent events since the concussion.

When he'd checked in, the receptionist had to remind Dion of her name, even though he'd just talked to her two days before when he was there for Jewel's appointment with Dr. Magnum. Then, when the nurse called him back and took his vitals, Darius had to remind Dion that he'd met Summer at the Thanksgiving dinner they'd attended at the bed and breakfast barely a week earlier. Forgetting people like that made him feel stupid because it was so out of character for him.

"Hey, Dion, it's good to see you again," the doctor greeted him as he walked into the room without giving any of them a chance to respond to his quick knock.

Dion didn't recognize the man, whose graying temples made him look to be about fifteen or twenty years older than Dion. But apparently, he'd met the man before at some point in the last year or so. Regardless, he extended his hand to shake the doctor's. "Sorry, I know you must be Doc Hayes because that's who Jewel recommended I see, but you'll have to forgive me for not remembering when we met before."

"That's quite alright," Doc Hayes smiled. "We've only spoken briefly at a wedding or two in the last year or so, which I didn't expect you to remember after reading over the records Dr. Boudreaux sent over. And since I haven't met your family, I probably should have started by introducing myself. I'm Dr. Eric Hayes."

"Caroline Marcel," Mama Marcel introduced herself, extending her hand to the doctor, when he looked in her direction. "Dion's adoptive mother."

"It's a pleasure to meet you, Ms. Marcel." Doc Hayes took her hand and lifted it to his lips for a brief brush, instead of shaking her hand.

Oh, I'm seriously gonna hafta remember to point out to Mama Marcel that I'm not the only one in the family who's flirting with someone younger and white this week. She may say I got my taste in women from Papa since Mama was younger than him and mostly white, but it'll be fun to pick on her about it being a learned behavior because of watching her all these years.

Darius introduced himself to the doctor while Dion grinned at Mama Marcel. Then Doc Hayes asked Dion to sit on the exam table for him to do an exam as they went over the symptoms he was still suffering with from the concussion.

"It'd be easier to tell you the symptoms that have started getting a little better," Dion chuckled as the doctor examined the two places on his head that had been stitched up six weeks earlier. "As long as I take the Meclizine three times a day, I only feel the room spin when I first wake up and haven't taken it yet. And as long as I move slowly to get out of bed, I don't get the nausea that used to accompany it."

"Well, that's good," Doc Hayes smiled as he pulled a flashlight out of the pocket of his lab coat and shined it in Dion's right eye. "And I'll gladly continue prescribing that for you if you need it while you're in town. But I really need to know the other symptoms Dr. Boudreaux hasn't been able to help you clear up, so maybe I can help you with them."

"The blackout spells are the one I'm most concerned about, 'cause I'm afraid of one of them happening while I'm holding one of the babies after they're born and causing me to drop them," Dion informed the doctor as he moved to examining his left eye. "When I wake up, I don't remember what happened to trigger them, but from what Darius and Mama Marcel have told me, they seem to hit me whenever I get anxious or overwhelmed, which I imagine I'll feel a lot while trying to take care of twins."

"Those seem to have lessened since we got here," Dare interjected as the doctor had Dion follow his finger movement with only his eyes. "He's still had a couple, but they're not nearly as long, and it takes a little more to cause them. At first, he couldn't even go try to find something in the fridge without telling me his lips were tingling and he needed to lie down. Now it takes more than just being confused by not finding what he's looking for, and he was able to breathe through the anxiety at the wedding last weekend to keep from passing out."

"So, when he passes out, he doesn't just suddenly go down?" Doc Hayes turned to look at Darius and Caroline, asking them about the events that Dion didn't remember. "He feels a warning sign?"

"Yeah, I mean, at first, he was dizzy all the time, so I couldn't tell that he wasn't just fainting from that," Darius elaborated. "But since the medicine cleared that up, I've watched him a little closer and noticed that when he gets super anxious or overwhelmed by too much going on around him, it's like his lips start going numb and he slurs his words a little. He's unsteady on his feet, almost like he feels too weak to walk on his own. So, if he has to go very far to sit or lie down, then I have to help him, so he makes it before his legs give out on him. Then he just closes his eyes and takes a nap. Sometimes it's just for a few minutes, and sometimes he'll be out for an hour or two. I was concerned the first time it lasted that long, but then he started snoring, so I figured he was just sleeping it off."

Doc Hayes turned back to look directly at Dion. "Are you tired during the day a lot? And how do you sleep at night?"

"Yeah, I'm always sleepy," Dion confided. "And I don't sleep through the night like I used to at all. It's more like I nap off and on around the clock."

"And this just started since your head injury?"

Dion nodded in response to the doctor's question.

"How do you feel when you wake up from these episodes? Or from your naps?"

"Okay," Dion shrugged. "Rested, I guess. Well, when my body registers that I'm actually awake and I'm finally able to move and talk again, anyway."

"So, you have sleep paralysis when you first wake up?" Doc Hayes arched an eyebrow at Dion. "Is that every time you nap? Or just when you've gotten anxious and passed out?"

"Yeah, that's what one of the nurses in the hospital called it," Dion confirmed, nodding again. "And it only seems to happen when I wake up after passing out. Dr. Boudreaux seemed to think it was a side effect of the brain injury and would clear up along with the headaches, concentration issues, and forgetting simple words after my brain has had time to heal."

"It's possible," Doc Hayes agreed. "But it's also possible that the TBI triggered a condition known as narcolepsy with cataplexy. I'd like to send you to a sleep specialist for a couple of different sleep studies to see if we can avoid misdiagnosing it as syncope or seizures, which unfortunately, I've seen happen a couple of times in my career.

If so, he can put you on something to prevent the narcoleptic sleep attacks, which will make it much safer for you to hold your babies. And if I'm wrong and we can't figure this out before they're born, there are still precautions you can take to be able to hold them without putting them at risk, like only holding them while you're sitting or lying down, and always having someone nearby to take over for you in case you get those warning signs."

Dion felt a little relief at hearing Doc Hayes's suggestions for still being able to be a loving father without putting his and Jewel's babies at risk.

"Hey, maybe I should go back to school to be a doctor," Darius interjected, chuckling. "Since I said you seemed narcoleptic the other day, I'm already doin' better than Dr. Boudreaux at diagnosing you."

"Yeah, Dr. Boudreaux thought I was having seizures." Dion directed his comment to Doc Hayes and ignored his brother. "'Cause I tend to zone out when I'm trying to remember stuff, which he said looked like an absence seizure when I did it in his office." Dion hadn't believed he'd had a seizure then, but there was no convincing his first doctor of that. "That's why he wouldn't clear me to drive yet, 'cause he thought these blackout episodes were just, um…" Dion's voice trailed off as he tried to figure out the right word to use. *Damn it! I know there's a better word than "bigger" to describe it. But, fuck, that's as close as I can think of right now.* "Bigger seizures."

Doc Hayes gave Dion a curious look, obviously recognizing that "bigger" wasn't the correct term.

"I know bigger isn't the right word," Dion sighed, hating that he couldn't come up with simple terms when he used to pride himself on his large vocabulary. "That's the other issue I'm having that's driving me nuts. I can't find the right words in my head and have trouble comprehending conversations and anything I try to read, even though I can tell you that it's a condition known as aphasia."

"Seriously, Doc, he couldn't remember the word *potato* the other day," Darius chuckled, holding his hands up to make an oval shape with his fingers, the same way Dion had the other day when he wanted a baked potato with his dinner. "He held his hands up like this to show me the shape as he described it as oval, brown, and needing to have the dirt cleaned off of it before cooking. Yet when I laughed at him for not being able to ask for a baked potato, he told me I was being vexatious."

"You're being vexatious now, too," Dion grumbled.

"Alright, you've stumped me." Doc Hayes held his hands up in surrender. "What does vexatious mean?"

"Annoying," Dion explained. "And aphasia from hitting my head is even more vexatious than Dare."

"Yeah, I imagine it would be," the doctor agreed, chuckling.

"I suggested going back to picking a new vocabulary word from the dictionary each week the way we did when the boys were in school," Mama Marcel interjected. "It was a habit their mama started when they were little, and I carried on through their high school years. But since it's the easier, more common words that he can't remember, we weren't sure it would help."

"It wouldn't hurt," Dr. Hayes offered, smiling at Mama Marcel before turning to look back at Dion. "But I think you might be better served by seeing a neuropsychologist or neuropsychiatrist and getting their opinion on whether or not speech therapy might be beneficial."

"I'll see whoever you think I need to see, Doc," Dion wholeheartedly agreed. "Jewel, uh, Julia Burleson said you'd be able to refer me to the best specialists in the area and coordinate my overall care plan, so I trust you to send me to the right doctors to be able to fix all this stuff, so I'm able to keep our babies safe once they're born."

"I can definitely refer you to the right specialists and coordinate your overall care, but I can't guarantee we'll be able to 'fix' anything," Doc Hayes agreed, using air quotes when he said the word fix. "But we'll do everything we can to help you get as close to your normal as your brain injury allows. In fact, because I do all the sports physicals for the local schools, I actually have the same software for the ImPACT test that the GWA and Dr. Boudreaux used to assess your concussion status. So, I'd like to reassess you with that today to see if you've had any further improvements since your last appointment with Dr. Boudreaux."

"Test away, Doc." Dion didn't think he'd healed enough in the last couple of weeks to do any better on the test than on the last one he did with Dr. Boudreaux, but he understood that each doctor would want to do their own testing. "Anything to help you figure out how to..." Dion trailed off as he couldn't think of a better word than the one the doctor had already said he couldn't guarantee. Finally, he gave up trying to think of a better term, sighed, and finished his sentence. "…fix me."

"As I said before, this test doesn't really tell us how to fix anything," the doctor clarified, giving Dion a sympathetic look. "It just gives us an idea of how well the concussion is healing. When you see the neuropsychologist, they'll do more extensive cognitive tests that will determine if there are other issues going on that require additional treatments, which may have to be prescribed by the neuropsychiatrist in the same office, or discussed with me and your neurologist to determine the best options for you. But before we set you up for the ImPACT test, are there any other issues you're having that we need to address?"

Dion wasn't sure what the doctor was asking about, unable to remember if they'd listed out all of his concussion symptoms or not. He turned to Darius and Mama Marcel, hoping one of them could fill the doctor in on anything he'd forgotten to mention.

Seeing that Dion wasn't sure how to answer, the doctor expounded on his question. "Any vision issues? Or headaches? Fatigue? Recent short-term memory loss in addition to the amnesia? Irritability? Mood swings?"

"Yes, all of the above," Mama Marcel answered for him before he could comprehend everything the doctor had asked about. "He's also moving a lot slower and seems unsteady on his feet sometimes, like a little old man. It's almost like he's aged fifty years, and he's starting to have a lot of the same ailments my parents did before they passed."

Dion hadn't realized that he was having issues with irritability or mood swings, but both Mama Marcel and Darius pointed them out to the doctor. From their descriptions of when he was short-tempered with them, it seemed to him that the incidents they described were all based on him being frustrated with the blackouts, aphasia, and comprehension issues more than anything. *I'm definitely gonna hafta watch that and get it under control before the babies are born.*

They went on to discuss in detail each of the issues Dion was having since his concussion before Summer took him to another room, which was set up with the computer for him to take the ImPACT test in isolation. Considering how bad his head was hurting after going over everything else with the doctor, he wasn't surprised when he found out he'd actually done worse on the test than he had two weeks earlier in Dr. Boudreaux's office.

When Dion got overwhelmed to the point of having a blackout episode by trying to explain that to Dr. Hayes, he laid back on the exam table and let it happen. After using some kind of smelling salts to wake him up, Doc Hayes reviewed the referrals to a sleep specialist, a neuropsychologist, a neuropsychiatrist, a neurologist, and an optometrist that Dion didn't remember because of losing his memory of most of the appointment before the blackout.

The doctor also explained that he'd decided to have Dion take the ImPACT test first thing when he came back for his follow-up appointment in a month, after seeing the different specialists with whom the Heart's Destiny Clinic staff had scheduled him appointments in the next couple of weeks. Dr. Hayes also switched him to a different headache medication, hoping it would give him more relief without the addiction issues associated with opioids, or the rebound headaches he seemed to get from the meds Dr. Boudreaux had prescribed.

While his physical status hadn't changed, and he still wasn't cleared to drive when he left Doc Hayes's office, Dion was optimistic about finally having a plan for eventually fixing some of his issues. As much as he wanted to get back together with Jewel, he didn't want to push too much toward reestablishing their relationship until he felt like he could be the man she needed him to be, instead of a burden on her life because of his health issues.

Fuck! I hope it doesn't take too long to get me back to normal, so I can actually be Jewel's partner in life, instead of feeling like I'm saddling her with a third kid to take care of, only fully grown.

~~~

Saturday, December 7, 2019

As she drove back to the ranch after picking Dion up from the bed and breakfast, Julie wasn't sure what she'd been thinking when she suggested bringing him to the ranch for breakfast with her family. *Clearly, the pregnancy hormones got the better of me when I made this*
~~~

suggestion the other night. I should have scheduled taking him to the south stables for this afternoon, without breakfast with the family first. Then I could have showed him where we first met without my family reading more into us spending time together today than just a friend trying to help another friend get his memories back.

"So, what all should I remember from where we're goin' today?" Dion smiled at her from the passenger seat, just as she turned onto the ranch and stopped at the gate. "Did we spend a lot of time together here on your family ranch? Or did we try to avoid getting together here, so your family didn't catch us?"

"No, we didn't spend a lot of time together here," Julie replied as she keyed in her code for the gate to open. "First, we're going to my Aunt Hazel and Uncle Bob's house for breakfast. Because Kay, Tia, and Maria already had plans with the Lees on Christmas Day last year, we had a late Christmas party on the Saturday after, so we could open presents with them. And since Kay's sister Randi was dating James Hunter at the time, and Randi's best friend Amy had just moved here to go to work for us at Burleson Incorporated, we ended up inviting the Hunters and everyone staying at the bed and breakfast to come to the party. It's the only time that I know of that you were here other than the day we met, but since we sat together all day, maybe being in the same space while it's decorated for Christmas will bring back a memory or two."

"So, this isn't where we first met?" Dion looked around as she drove through the pastures leading to the cluster of family houses on the northeast corner of the ranch.

"No, that was down at the paddocks between the south bunkhouse and stables, where we held a barbeque to welcome all the out-of-town guests for Anthony and Kay's wedding," Julie explained as she pulled into her driveway to park. "After breakfast, I'll drive you down there to show you the paddocks. But I'm not sure it'll bring back as many memories, since we don't have the bounce house or games set up. And we can't go into the bunkhouse because it's been converted into a Madeline Ashbury Foundation House since then."

As soon as she parked, Dion got out of the car and walked around to open her door for her. He then took her hand to help her out of the vehicle, sending tingles up her arm from the contact. *Why do those always happen? Won't they ever go away?*

Leah Mae Wright

"What's a Madeline Ashbury Foundation House?"

"It's hard to explain," Julie sighed as she pulled her hand from Dion's and directed him toward her aunt and uncle's house. "My cousin Bobby's wife, Brook, started the Madeline Ashbury Foundation to help women and children escaping abusive domestic situations, naming it after her mother. She started with the house she grew up in back in Georgia, and then decided she wanted to be more hands on, so she took advantage of the south bunkhouse needing renovations after a flood to set up the one here. Originally, it was mostly a women's shelter, with the only kids there being the children of the women she helped. But then Bobby worked with my cousin Charlotte's husband, Ian, to bust a human trafficking ring run by a cartel, and one of the kids they rescued was an orphan that Anthony and Kay ended up adopting. So, she realized that there were kids in the foster system who could benefit from the programs she offers through the foundation, too. So, now there are some teenagers who live there too, so they aren't just going to be thrown out on the street when they age out of foster care. The Foundation provides job training programs and any assistance they need with schooling, medical care, therapy, or whatever. Whenever possible, we hire the residents for jobs on the ranch, or in the Burleson facilities here in town, so they can eventually transition to living on their own."

"Wow, that sounds like a great program. Kinda like what Mama Marcel did for us, only for the masses instead of just a couple of kids." Dion looked around as they walked, pointing over his shoulder with his thumb back toward the car parked at her house. "Um, why'd we park at that house instead of the one we're goin' to?"

"Because that's where I live." Julie smiled at the confused look on Dion's face. "I always park there and walk to any of the houses on this part of the ranch. We'll take an ATV down to the south side later, so there's no point in parking here now just to have to move my car again before we go look at the place where we first met."

She decided then to take one of the mules instead of her four-wheeler, knowing she couldn't handle having Dion's arms around her for the ride down to the south paddocks and back. *Nope! If he wraps me in his arms to hold on while we're on a four-wheeler, I'm liable to take off to a secluded spot somewhere to drop my panties and climb him like a tree.*

"Oh, yeah, okay." Dion nodded as if what she said made sense, but the way he looked around as they walked in the door made Julie wonder if he was really listening to her or not. She appreciated him making her feel ignored to help get her libido back in check before she did something she thought she might regret later.

He stopped walking as soon as they stepped into the dining room, where the Burlesons who were in town were gathering for breakfast. They were missing Anthony's family and Jake, but counting the newest babies added to the family, there were still twenty pairs of eyes that all turned to them when they walked into the room.

Julie had thought limiting this breakfast to just the Burlesons, their significant others, and children would keep the crowd from being overwhelming for Dion, since he'd mentioned trying to keep track of so many names during the wedding events being confusing for him because of the concussion symptoms that hadn't yet healed. But the deer-in-the-headlights look he was currently sporting made her wonder if she hadn't limited the crowd quite enough.

Damn it! I knew this wasn't a good idea!

"We can go if this is too much for you," Julie suggested, stepping in front of Dion to see the faraway look in his eyes that made him appear to be looking through her, instead of at her.

He blinked a couple of times before shaking his head and looking down into her eyes. "No, I think I just had a flash of memory. Did I tell you about Réveillon dinners back home in NOLA when we were here before?"

"Yes," Julie nodded, glad she was wrong about why he'd stopped moving, and thankful he was remembering, instead of being about to have one of the blackout spells he'd warned her about. "You said all the people and food reminded you of the ones you had with your parents as a kid, only in the middle of the day, instead of in the middle of the night. And with roast beef and barbeque, instead of gumbo and oysters."

He'd also teased her about not needing the aphrodisiac properties of the oysters because just looking at her from across the room was way more effective for him. But she wasn't going to mention that in front of her family. Based on the way he grinned at her as she felt her cheeks flush at the memory, she didn't think he needed the reminder right then, anyway.

He looked up at the archway into the room before turning back to her. "There was mistletoe in this doorway last time too, right?"

"Yes, but nobody's gone out to shoot some out of the trees on the ranch yet this year," Julie explained why the plant everyone kissed under at Christmas hadn't been hung as a decoration in any of their homes yet.

"Why would you shoot it? It's a plant. Don't you just pick it?" Dion's brow furrowed as he looked at her in confusion.

"Yeah, but it's a parasitic plant that grows up in the branches of other trees, not on the ground where it can be easily picked," Julie elaborated, almost feeling like she was having to explain it to a curious child, instead of the intelligent man she'd previously known. "So, every December, one of us goes out and shoots a few sprigs down to hang with our Christmas decorations. I know it sounds crazy, but it really is the easiest way to get it without risking getting hurt from falling out of the tree by trying to climb up and pick it."

"Everything okay here, Julie?" Julie's overprotective dad stepped up to them, apparently tired of waiting for them to join the rest of the family at the table.

Or tired of waiting to intimidate Dion, Julie thought as she turned to look at her father. *I probably should've been sterner in my warning to the men in my family not to interfere with whatever happens between me and Dion.* "Yeah, Dad, everything's fine. Dion's already starting to remember some bits and pieces of when he was here at Christmas last year."

Dion stood straighter when she said "Dad," obviously trying to make a good impression the first time he remembered meeting her father. He extended his hand to Jon Burleson in greeting. "Thank you, Mr. Burleson, for allowing me to crash your family meal this morning to try to get some of my memories back."

"Is that the only reason you're here?" Julie's dad glared at Dion as he clutched his hand for a brisk but firm shake. "To get your memories back before leaving again? Or are you planning to man up and stick around for my daughter and grandchildren?"

"Dad!" Julie exclaimed, slamming her fists on her hips, and not giving Dion the chance to answer her father. "Right now, Dion's number one priority is healing. And that includes trying to get some of his memories back while we get to know one another again. The twins aren't due until May, so we have plenty of time to figure out how we feel about each other and how we're going to co-parent them. So, don't expect either one of us to be able to tell you how it's going to work out now. Because I honestly can't tell you how I want it to work out. And I haven't had a brain injury. So, there's no way Dion can tell you how he wants things to go either."

"I intend to marry your daughter, sir." Dion immediately contradicted her as soon as she paused to take a breath, smiling at her when she turned her furious glare at him. "I might not remember the day we met yet, but the only memories that have come back to me so far include Jewel. And I'm pretty sure that's because of how special she is to me. She's still hurt over the stuff I don't remember yet, and might never remember, though, so I'm letting her set the pace for our relationship for now. But you don't have to worry about me running off and deserting your daughter or our babies. I'll be making Heart's Destiny my home from now on. I just won't move out of the B and B until Jewel's ready for us to pick a place together."

"I told you not to call me that," Julie grumbled, trying desperately to maintain her anger to keep from letting her heart do a happy dance at hearing he wanted to marry her. It was bad enough that her libido had already taken over thinking for her genitalia, causing her to cream her panties at the thought of being Dion's wife. For her own sense of sanity, she couldn't let any more of her body parts, other than her brain, have a say in what happened between them in the future.

"Jewel, huh?" Jon arched an eyebrow at Dion, completely ignoring Julie's objection to the pet name.

"Yeah, she's precious, like a jewel, so it seems fitting," Dion smirked.

When her dad smiled in appreciation of Dion's explanation of the term of endearment, Julie threw up her hands in exasperation and stomped away. *Great! Now Dad's gonna help Mom with her matchmaking,* she thought as she sat down at the table for breakfast. *Why can't they find a happy medium, where they don't have an opinion either way, instead of either pushing for us to get together or bullying him to defend my honor?*

She intentionally sat across from her oldest brother, hoping JJ would at least support her in thwarting the parental plans to push her and Dion along faster than she was ready to move in their relationship.

Surely, his frustration with the Matchmaking Mommas' schemes will be incentive enough to put him on my side. So, maybe JJ will help me convince everyone else to let us go at our own pace, the same way he's trying with Deanna.

It wasn't that she was absolutely against ever being with Dion again, as her physical response to him clearly proved. She just didn't want to move on anyone else's timeline, especially when she felt so overwhelmed by everything that had happened in recent weeks. On top of not wanting her pregnancy hormones and overpowering physical attraction to him to be the foundation of their relationship, she needed a little time to learn to trust Dion again before she could move forward with him. *Why doesn't anyone else seem to understand that?*

"You know, everyone else marrying into the family has moved onto the ranch," her dad informed Dion as they took the two seats immediately to her left. "The only house that's open right now is the one Justin and Amy just moved out of this week. It's too small for a family of four long term, but it'll work while the twins are babies for the six months or so, it'll take for ya'll to build something bigger."

"Actually, Dad, I was gonna suggest I move into that house, so Julie can have the one I'm in," JJ interjected. "That way she'll have plenty of room for the babies without the girls having to play musical bedrooms to put the babies' nursery next to her room."

"Oh, yes, that will work wonderfully," her dad agreed, not seeming to care if that was where she wanted to live or not. He turned to Dion before describing the house her brother currently lived in across the driveway. "It's three bedrooms plus the office, which is about half the size of the bedroom that used to be there before we converted half of it into a master bathroom. And the attic space is fully finished, so it can easily be left as is for the kids to have a large playroom, or it can be divided up for more bedrooms if ya'll have more kids in the future."

"It sounds perfect," Dion nodded as he slipped his arm around her shoulders. "But only if Julia wants to live there. And I'll still stay at the B and B until she's ready for us to move forward as a couple."

Well, I guess, at least, someone is thinking about getting my opinion on where I want to live. Now if I can just get them all to back off and give me time to think about things, maybe I can figure out what I actually want.

~~~

After what he felt was a successful reintroduction to the Burlesons the day before, Dion looked forward to introducing them to Darius and Mama Marcel at the potluck lunch after church. There'd been a couple of tense moments at breakfast with Jewel's family, the first with Jewel's dad, right after Dion had a minor moment of panic at the thought of Jewel being present when someone was shooting mistletoe out of the trees on the ranch. But once Dion let that pass, listened to what her dad was saying, and made his intention to marry her clear, the older man had made him feel welcomed into the family fold. He'd started talking about options for where Dion could live on the ranch with Jewel and their babies before introducing him to the rest of the family. Then after they'd sat back down after filling their plates, each of her other male relatives had taken a turn at warning him not to do anything to hurt Julie, or they would happily put him back in the hospital. Dion had assured each and every one of them that his primary goal in life was to take care of Jewel and their babies, and that if he ever accidentally did anything to hurt her, he'd gladly stand there and take the ass whuppin' they promised him. After that, they all got along great for the rest of the morning. Jewel hadn't seemed as happy as Dion was at the warm reception he got from her family, but he knew it would take time for her to accept that they couldn't hide their love from the rest of the world any longer. Luckily, he had the patience to wait her out.

A few minutes into the conversation about houses with Jewel's brother, Jon had made introductions, so Dion could finally start trying to remember his previous interactions with the rest of her family. Since he was still having trouble remembering names, especially when he was introduced to multiple people at once, or felt overwhelmed by all the activity going on around him when the introductions were made, Jewel's mom had suggested using the name tags they'd used the first time the GWA crew came to town to meet the equally large group of locals. Since that had been extremely helpful for him the day
~~~

before, he hoped they would continue to use them at church because he was pretty sure he'd already forgotten a few names.

He had recovered a few memories, though. Specifically, talking to Jewel as they ate and opened gifts. He'd apparently screwed up by ordering Mardi Gras masks, beaded bracelets, and t-shirts in bulk to have enough gifts for everyone in attendance, and then buying Jewel a pair of gold, emerald, and amethyst fleur-de-lis earrings. Yeah, he'd still stuck to the Mardi Gras theme, but her earrings were obviously a lot more expensive than the costume jewelry bracelets he'd given to the other women in attendance. She'd covertly hidden the earrings right after opening them and only worn them when she met up with him while he was on tour with the GWA.

Hey, that's something new I just remembered, he realized as he let his mind drift during the church service. He'd remembered her hiding them in her purse at Christmas when they were talking about the gift exchange the day before, but he hadn't thought about when she actually wore them until right then. *Maybe I'll remember more new stuff if I keep reviewing the things I remembered yesterday.*

When he was introduced to Josh's son, JoJo, Dion remembered him crashing a wedding and the GWA guys he was sitting with being surprised that it was a Burleson who had a child he hadn't known about, instead of one of their fellow wrestlers. He'd had to ask Jewel what wedding they'd gone to where they weren't seated together, which led to pissing her off again over the flash of memory he'd shut down a week earlier.

She'd explained in detail how his and Liam's idiotic questions about bachelor parties at a brothel caused a commotion at the rehearsal dinner before Charlotte and Ian's wedding because Dion and Liam hadn't realized the preacher, who was now Rick's father-in-law, was sitting right behind them. That had apparently caused Rick to insist on everyone he employed being supervised by the head of Avington Security, Byron Avington, and his wife, Blair Avington, during the reception, while Windy and Kandi were stuck at the table with all four of the Avingtons' sons and a couple of the other bodyguards who worked for them. Not because he didn't want them matched up with the Burlesons, but more that he was afraid Windy and Kandi would convince them to post more pictures on social media that weren't on brand for their wrestling gimmicks. Considering he knew his friends were still dealing with the aftermath of the first time Windy and Kandi were a bad influence on the GWA wrestlers, Dion agreed it was probably a good move on Rick's part.

Unfortunately, Jewel had been right about him getting more flashes of memory at her aunt and uncle's house than at the location where they first met. She'd tried to tell him to picture the field with a bounce house and horseshoe games set up and filled with people, thinking that might help him remember. But other than a few flashes of her walking across the field in a sexy as fuck pair of jeans, he hadn't been able to picture anything from the first day they met. That led to him getting the song *In Those Jeans* by Ginuwine stuck in his head for the rest of the day, even though she was less than thrilled by his impromptu performance of the song to try to get her to smile.

Since Jewel seemed to be out of sorts after breakfast with her family and his poor attempt at cheering her up had failed, he didn't ask her to review the details about their first meeting with him. Even though he knew hearing about it might help trigger his memories, he didn't want to risk tainting the memory for her by asking her to relive it with him while she was clearly upset with him. Instead, he decided to back off and give her the space she clearly needed, hoping to keep from ruining his chance at getting back together with her in the near future. Having her take him back to the B and B right then, cutting their day together short, had also helped him maintain a little of his dignity by not having a blackout episode until he was back in his room, instead of in the middle of the paddock.

Dion shook off the negative thoughts about his episodes, trying to believe his new doctors would find a way to eliminate them from his life. He didn't believe he'd been lucky enough to find Jewel again, to find out she was carrying his babies, only to not be able to be with her because his spells would make him a burden in her life. The God he believed in wouldn't be that cruel to him. So, he had to believe that his issues would eventually get better, so he could be the man she needed as a partner in life.

Not just her partner, but also her protector, her rock to lean on, and her lover.

Now he found himself wondering how long he needed to stay in the friend zone before he could start moving them back toward the sexual side of their relationship that he desperately missed. Jerking off in the shower was getting old, especially when he clearly remembered how amazing it felt to be buried balls-deep in Jewel.

Holy shit! I wasn't wearing a condom in any of my memories of fucking Jewel. Damn, when did I stop being a stickler for condom usage?

He'd realized before that he wasn't wearing a condom in his dreams about her, but thought that was proof that it was a fantasy and not a memory. Now that he knew they were memories, and not his fantasies or visions of the future, Dion grasped the significance of what that lack of condoms meant for them as a couple.

Only with Jewel, he realized, knowing she would be the only woman he would ever trust enough to go bareback with. *Because she's the only woman I'll ever be with for the rest of my life.*

Dion shifted in his seat, trying to keep his dick's response to daydreaming about his memories of making love to Jewel from being obvious to everyone around him. As he did, he realized that everyone was bowing their heads as the preacher delivered the closing prayer.

Now, I've really gotta get this erection to go down, he thought, closing his eyes as he bowed his head. He quickly pictured himself in the wrestling ring, facing off against the Dangerous Twins. Considering how revealing his wrestling tights were, making wrestling with a hard-on his worst nightmare, the visual worked like a charm, taking him back to flaccid before the pastor said "amen." *Perfect. Instant boner killer.*

Dion joined the chorus of the congregation in repeating "amen" after the pastor and opened his eyes just in time for the preacher to dismiss them from the sanctuary. Along with his brother, he escorted Mama Marcel to the fellowship hall, where he'd dropped off several bottles of soft drinks and a couple of packages of plastic cups on their way into the church that morning.

"Oh, I wish I'd have had a kitchen available, so I coulda made a pot of gumbo, instead of just bringing cold drinks," Mama Marcel fretted.

"Oh, Caroline, if I'd known you wanted to make something, I would've given you free rein in one of our kitchens," Mandi Hunter offered.

"I wouldn't want to get in the way of your staff in the hotel kitchen." Mama Marcel waved off her offer.

"You wouldn't have," Mandi disagreed. "I don't even try to do anything in the kitchen at the Heritage House now that Ashley has the restaurant running so smoothly. But we still have the kitchen in the original B and B that only gets used for the continental breakfast for guests who don't want to go all the way over to the Heritage House for the restaurant. And if you'd wanted to cook when the staff was using it, you could always come use one of our home kitchens."

"Oh, that's so sweet of you." Mama Marcel smiled. "If it won't put you out too much, then we'll have to plan it before next week's service."

"It won't put me out at all." Mandi returned the smile. "But I'll take a good gumbo recipe and lessons on making it as compensation, if you feel so inclined."

"Hey, we want in on that recipe swap," Hazel Burleson interjected as she and Susan walked up on the tail end of the conversation.

"Mama Marcel, this is Julia's mother, Susan Burleson, and her aunt, Hazel Burleson." Dion made introductions immediately, knowing if Mama Marcel got to talking about recipe swapping, he wouldn't get a chance to make them at all. "Ladies, this is Mama, uh, Caroline Marcel, the wonderful woman I told you about yesterday, who took on the task of raising two rowdy teenaged boys when we lost our mama." He pointed around Mama Marcel at his brother before continuing. "And this is my brother, Darius."

The ladies acknowledged his introductions quickly before pulling Mama Marcel over to introduce her to the rest of the Burlesons and Burleson-Campbells in attendance. Dion and Darius dutifully followed along behind them, until Dion broke away from his family to pull out a chair for Jewel and claim the seat beside her.

"I can't believe you just left your brother to fall prey to their matchmaking antics," Jewel giggled, shaking her head at him as they watched her mom and aunt continuing the introductions as they teamed up with Mama Marcel to drag Dare around the room.

"I'm hoping they'll introduce him to enough of the respectable women from around here that he'll realize the ones who've screwed him over in the past are in the minority and don't represent the whole gender." Dion smiled at Jewel as he reached over and pushed a loose lock of hair behind her ear. "Besides, I kinda like the girl they matched me up with, so I'm hoping they'll help my brother find the woman who'll make him wanna settle down, too."

"Dion," Jewel groaned, rolling her eyes at him. "You've gotta stop with the talk about settling down and us getting married. You don't know what's gonna happen when you see the specialists, so you can't say for sure that you're not going to be completely healed and go back to wrestling in a few months."

"Yeah, I can," Dion asserted, taking her hand in his so he could feel her pulse to gauge her response to him. "Even if the doctors figure out how to get all my memories back and do away with all the post-concussion symptoms, I'm not wrestling again. The risks associated with another hit to the head are just too…" *Fuck! What's the right word?* "…much for me to take that chance."

"So, one concussion and you're calling it quits?" Jewel eyed him skeptically. "Those risks are from dozens of concussions, not just one."

"One concussion that was diagnosed," Dion pointed out the fallacy in her logic, lifting the pointer finger on his free hand to make his point before he extended his second finger. "But two hits to the head to cause it. And God only knows how many concussions that weren't diagnosed, or sub-concussive hits that have added up over time from my thirteen years as a professional wrestler, the half dozen car accidents I've been in over the course of my life, or all the fights and roughhousing I did as a kid. Dr. Boudreaux might not've thought it necessary to send me to other specialists, but he did point out my history as being a contributing factor to why I'm not bouncing back from this concussion as fast as I should've. And until another, more educated doctor tells me otherwise, I'm gonna believe his opinion that another hit to the head could be catastrophic."

"Fine," Jewel huffed, conceding his point. "But even if you don't want to wrestle anymore, I know Rick's holding a spot for you as a writer as soon as you're cleared to fly again. So, you could still decide to travel for work, instead of twiddling your thumbs here in town."

"Is that what you're afraid of, Jewel?" Dion softened his voice, hoping to soothe her as he assured her he wasn't going anywhere. "That I'll take a job traveling and will just pop in and out of your life and our babies' lives?"

She didn't respond verbally, but he could see the fear in her eyes and feel the quickening of her pulse. *Damn. She doesn't wanna give me a chance 'cause she really thinks I'm gonna leave again. Is that because we did the long-distance thing already and she knows it's not enough for her? Or is that because every time we parted ways to go back to our jobs, it broke her heart a little, and she doesn't wanna deal with that pain again? Or have our babies feel that pain ever?*

"Because I can assure you that's not gonna happen. I already turned down Rick's job offer. And yeah, that was partially because I didn't think I could handle working with the GWA and not being able to get in the ring. But it was also because I don't want to be that far away from you now that I've found you again. Hell, I don't even wanna go back to NOLA unless you go with me."

Fuck! I shouldn't have admitted that yet. I'm just gonna scare her off if I keep pushing before she's ready.

"What's gonna happen when Darius and Mama Marcel have to go back for work? Are you gonna hire someone to chauffeur you around, so you can stay in town? Or are you gonna move back to the city where you can get a cab or Uber or whatever to go to the doctor and stuff?"

"I'll hire a chauffeur if I have to," Dion declared. "Or maybe Windy and Kandi will have their CouBer service set up by then."

One of the things he'd learned since staying at the bed and breakfast was that Allissa's mom and her best friend were always coming up with ideas for side-hustles, even though they both worked for the Hunters now, helping set up the winery. When they'd heard he wasn't able to drive because of his injuries, they'd decided they needed to start a car service similar to Uber in Heart's Destiny. But they couldn't just look into getting set up as Uber drivers. No, they had to put their own spin on the concept by planning to only hire middle-aged women, who weren't ashamed to admit to being cougars. Hence the name CouBer, as in Cougar-Uber.

"But since we have a great management team running the club, and Mama Marcel is lining up fortune telling gigs with Mandi's retreat groups in January and February, I'm hopeful these doctors will be able to fix me enough that I'll be able to drive myself again before they feel the need to go back to NOLA."

Leah Mae Wright

"Really?" Jewel looked surprised by his adamance that he was staying in Heart's Destiny.

"Yeah, really," Dion smiled, lifting her hand to his lips for a brief brushing across her soft skin. "I know you're not ready to let me back in yet, but I was serious about what I said to your dad yesterday about staying in town to be here for you and our babies. I'll let you set the pace, but eventually, I'll convince you to trust me to be your man. And in the meantime, I'll be the best friend and co-parent you could ever ask for."

He just hoped it wouldn't take her too long to let him out of the friend zone.

Chapter Twelve

Saturday, December 14, 2019

Julie wasn't sure how she got roped into moving into the house her oldest brother had occupied for the last decade. But somehow in the last week — probably with the help of the Walker Construction crews already working on her cousins' houses on the ranch — her family had moved JJ out of the house he'd moved into when he turned eighteen, gone through the whole house to freshen up the paint on all the walls, and refinished the hardwood floors in every room. Thankfully, they had let her pick the paint colors, even though they wouldn't let her paint a single wall because of being pregnant.

It wasn't that she was opposed to moving into the beautiful Queen Anne style brick house her second-great-grandfather originally built in 1906. She actually felt honored to be entrusted with the care and upkeep of the historic house that represented part of her family legacy. She just wished she could take her time moving her things and picking out the perfect pieces to furnish the place that would blend her taste with the historical style of the home, instead of having to get up early on a Saturday to rush around to do it all in one weekend. *Hopefully, Mom didn't go overboard with picking out furniture that I'm going to want to send back because of it not matching my taste. I don't care what she says about dark wood being classic and fitting with the age of the house. White wooden pieces will work better with the various shades of purple and yellow that I've picked for all the walls and trim. And since it was also popular to go with bright vibrant wall paper or paint colors back then, I'm sure there were some people who painted their wooden furniture, too. And even though, more than a hundred years ago, whitewashing was typically done on outside structures like chicken coops and fences to protect them from the weather, I'm sure some people painted their furniture white, too. So, I'm still honoring the age of the house, whether she agrees with me or not.*

Julie's favorite color was purple, and according to her soon-to-be sister-in-law, Amy, yellow was its perfect complementary color. Since yellow was also a primary color, which was one of the main elements she wanted to use for decorating the babies' nursery, it was kind of a no-brainer for her to pick it for the walls of the nursery. Now she just had to make peace with the family members — *cough, her mother, cough* — who disagreed with her choices, starting with changing her mindset when thinking of their interference in her life.

I wonder if there's any truth to that pregnancy-brain stuff that Char mentioned at our last family dinner? If so, maybe I can blame some of my recent irritability on that? I mean, I'm sure everyone's getting tired of me blaming everything on pregnancy hormones, so maybe the different terminology will make it less annoying, even if I'm still whining about the same thing.

No, I'm pretty sure it's still annoying. So, I've gotta quit just reacting and start thinking about stuff from their perspective before I speak. I know even Mom's pushiness with trying to pick out nursery furniture is coming from a place of love. So, I need to return that love in my reactions to her and the rest of the family.

"We've got a lot of family who loves us and wants to take care of us," Julie told her babies as she rubbed her hands over her growing baby bump while walking into her bathroom to start getting ready for the day. "And I'm sure ya'll will love them as much as I do, even though they're crazy for waking us up at the crack of dawn on the one day this week when we could sleep in."

As she got undressed and took care of her morning bathroom needs, Julie realized that her family's plans to move her had started the week before, when she had Dion over for breakfast to help him remember more of his time in Heart's Destiny. "I was probably flustered by his presence, and that's how they convinced me to move this weekend. Crap, I wonder if that means they'll have asked him to come help move me today? Or worse, if they're planning on him moving in with me?"

As she started her shower and shampooed her hair, she thought back over the last couple of weeks and every interaction she'd had with Dion, trying to remember if he gave her any indication that he was in on their plot. When she remembered him saying he'd stay at the B and B until she was ready for them to pick out a place together, she started to relax. But then, as she rinsed out the Tweak'd by Nature Wild Frangi Pangi-Monoi shampoo and replaced it with the conditioner from the same line, she wondered if they would ever get to the point that him moving in with her might be an option.

She gave her babies a running commentary as she examined her feelings and thought about whether or not she was ready to risk her heart on Dion again, while shaving with her electric razor. She figured it wasn't just her heart she'd be risking, so she had to give her babies the chance to offer their opinions. She just wasn't sure if the little flutters of movement she felt every time she spoke were her babies being happy at the thought of their parents getting back together, or their way of telling her to run the other way.

"He's been respectful and gentlemanly every time I've been around him since he came back to town. If you two are girls, that's how I'd want your boyfriends to treat you. And if ya'll're boys, that's how I'd want you to treat the girls you date. But I can't help but wonder how much of that is an act to try to get me to let down my guard."

"But then again, why would he want me to drop my guard? What does he really want from me? I thought at first that it might be the s-e-x that ya'll don't need to know about yet. But other than a couple of mentions of the first memories he had come back to him being when we were in intimate situations, he's kept things pretty platonic. Yeah, he's held my hand and put his arm around me a couple of times, but he's only kissed my hand or my forehead. And while ya'll are way too young to know everything mommies and daddies do together, I'm sure you'll figure out pretty quick, especially living on the ranch with all the lovey-dovey couples in our family, that mommies and daddies kiss more than each other's hands and foreheads."

She felt flutters on the right side of her abdomen and wondered if Twin A was trying to tell her mommy to kiss her daddy. Once she'd rinsed off her shaving cream, she lathered up a washcloth with her favorite Philosophy Passion Fruit Daquiri shower gel and quickly washed her body.

"He's also been pretty insistent that he's staying in Heart's Destiny to be here for the three of us," Julie continued as she rinsed the washcloth first, then the conditioner from her hair, and finally the suds from her body. Once she was finished with her shower, she stepped out and started drying off. "And he's been great with staying in touch via text every day, asking a mix of questions about the two of you and me, like he's trying to get to know me all over again."

He'd also repeatedly told her stories of his past that she'd heard before. Because she knew he didn't remember telling her the first time, she tried not to get irritated by how often he repeated the same things. Unfortunately, she didn't think she'd been as patient with him as she wanted to be, which she was blaming on her pregnancy hormones.

Dang it! I've really gotta stop doing that. No matter how much my hormones change during pregnancy, it's not the babies' fault that I'm acting like a lunatic. She just hoped that she'd go back to normal after the babies were born. And hopefully, the new doctors Dion was seeing would help him recover more of his memories by then, too, so he wouldn't repeat himself so often.

"But other than doing stuff to help him get his memories back, or asking me to stay for dinner after going to the doctor for ya'll, he hasn't exactly tried asking me out, or done anything even remotely romantic. And he was the king of romance when we were together before, so I know he's capable of it. At least, I know he'd normally do that romantic, sappy stuff if he wanted more than friendship and co-parenting with me."

In addition to the day the babies were most likely conceived, Julie thought back to the other romantic things he'd done for her over the last year. He'd sent her flowers at work several times, as well as little thinking-of-you gifts from the various places he visited while on tour. They weren't always expensive gifts, like the jewelry he gave her for Christmas, Valentine's Day, or her birthday, either. Just something that he saw and thought of her, like the variety of teas he sent from his time in England, or the scarf he sent her from Scotland after they discussed her Ancestry results. Julie had to smile at how he'd picked the Davies tartan pattern, since it was the closest he could find to either of their last names and he didn't know which Scottish clan she was descended from.

"Do you think, maybe, he thinks I need more time to get over my anger before he tries any of that again? And if so, how do I show him that I'm pretty much over the anger? How do I make him see that I need him to show me I'm special to him, and not his dirty little secret like before?"

She felt more flutters as she started getting dressed, this time on the left side of her abdomen, and wondered if Twin B was responding to her questions.

Too bad I can't decipher their little kicks into understandable responses. Although, with as upbeat as Dion and I both usually are, I have to assume our kids' attitudes and opinions are more positive than negative.

"I hope we'll be able to tell if ya'll are boys or girls next time we do an ultrasound, so I can start using your names when we talk like this."

Julie hadn't told anyone yet, but now that she was starting to see that Dion wanted to be involved with their kids, she'd decided to name their first son after him. *Oh, I wonder if I'll still need to use the Junior designation after his name, since I'm planning on adding my last name in there, too?* Dion Devereaux Burleson-Davis was a big name for a little boy, but she thought shortening his middle name to Dev for everyday use would give their son time to grow into it. *Surely, it won't be too long a name, even if we have to add a Junior on the end, right? And the only way we'd have to add the Junior is if Dion and I get married and decide to hyphenate all our names, the way Charlotte and Ian did when they got married.*

No! Don't even think about possibly marrying him, Julia Elizabeth Burleson! She mentally chastised herself, knowing she was only going there because she'd thought about the little romantic gestures Dion had done in the past and was starting to get her hopes up that he'd be more romantic again in the future. *Go back to thinking about baby names.*

She also liked the name Dillon if they ended up having twin boys. But like with Elena for her girl's name picks, she hadn't come up with a middle name to go with it yet. *Although, I should probably come up with something soon, so my family doesn't keep pushing name ideas every time one of them catches me alone.* Since she was finished getting ready for the day, she didn't have time to think about middle names right then, though.

"Okay, kiddos, let's go see what Gran and Grandad have planned for this move today." Julie rubbed her hands over her belly as she left her bedroom to go find out the schedule for her move.

"I hope you've already packed anything you might be embarrassed to have seen today," Jen cautioned her when she entered the kitchen to get a glass of orange juice.

"I have," Julie nodded and smiled at her sister, not elaborating on how she'd packed everything from her bedside table and her underwear drawer (minus the ones she put on that morning) the night before. "No way was I gonna take a chance on one of our brothers or cousins opening a drawer to get a better grip on the dresser or bedside table, and accidentally, on purpose, spilling the contents halfway down the driveway."

Julie was relieved to have spent a few evenings talking things out with her sister recently, mending the rift she'd felt over Thanksgiving week when Dion had first come back to town. Apparently, all the conflicting statements and argumentative behavior was Jen's way of trying to get Julie to look at her relationship with Dion from a few different angles to help push them back together. Julie had to pick on her sister then, telling her that she'd inherited their mother's matchmaker gene, since it was coming out long before she was old enough to be eligible to join the ranks of the Matchmaking Mommas, who were all trying to match up their grown children instead of their same-age siblings.

She'd also found out that Jen was a little jealous of Julie finding her soulmate first, but she still loved her enough to want her to be happy with him. Julie, on the other hand, wished she knew how to help her twin find *The One*, so her sister could be as happy as all the rest of the Burlesons who'd found love in the last fifteen months. She might not be back with Dion yet, but she hoped to count herself in their ranks soon, too, and wanted to bring her sister along with her. *Guess we both got some of that matchmaker gene.*

They'd also talked more about how Jen had thought about settling with Liam because of not having felt like she'd met *The One*. Apparently, seeing Liam and Rylie as a couple that week had shown Jen how wrong it would have been if she'd ever tried for more with him without those true-love feelings.

Julie still thought seeing Liam with his wife had caused a little bit of heartbreak for her sister, which was why she was more argumentative that week. But she wasn't about to rock the boat of the new peace they'd found with one another to dissect her sister's feelings further. Even if Jen had feelings for Liam that she didn't want to admit to, as long as he was married to someone else, she'd be better off forgetting about them and moving on to, hopefully, find her one true love.

"Oh, gawd, I didn't even think of them doing something like that," Jen laughed as she rinsed out her coffee cup and put it in the dishwasher. "I was thinking they'd either hide your vibrator or freeze your underwear."

"With Josh home now, any of those were possibilities," Julie chuckled with her sister as she poured the juice into a small glass to take her prenatal vitamin. "So, I made sure to lock that suitcase."

"Oh, smart thinking." Jen dried her hands on a hand towel before hanging it over the bar on the oven door.

"Where's Becky? She didn't go back to bed after knocking on my door to wake me up at the butt crack of dawn, did she?"

"No," Jen assured her, chuckling. "She's already over at Aunt Hazel and Uncle Bob's for breakfast. I just wanted to make sure you had the vital stuff packed before we head over there, too."

Julie took her vitamin and chugged her juice before rinsing the cup and putting it in the dishwasher. "Guess we'd better go have breakfast then. Though I seriously don't understand why we had to get up this early to do this. I only have the stuff in my bedroom to move, so it won't take but an hour or two to move it all, and that's including unpacking."

"You know how Mom is," Jen shrugged as they left the kitchen to walk through the house to their front door. "She wants to get this part over with, so you have time to go shopping this afternoon for the rest of the house stuff."

"I'm surprised she hasn't already ordered everything she thinks I need to have it all delivered this afternoon," Julie groaned, remembering how she and her mom had already butted heads while looking at nursery furniture. Her mom wanted something classic, like the dark wood crib set she kept pushing Julie to pick. Julie, on the other hand, thought white furniture would look better with the primary-colors theme she picked for the nursery. And apparently, they were both too stubborn to pick a happy medium. *I wonder if my babies will inherit that same stubbornness from me that I inherited from Mom?*

As she and Jen walked out the door to go meet up with their family for breakfast before the move, she wasn't as surprised as she should be to find Dion, Darius, and Mama Marcel pulling into her driveway. *I guess, at least, it doesn't look like Dion's stuff is packed up to move in with me today. Unless it's all in the trunk and he's gonna surprise me with it later.*

"No, I think she's planning on sending you and Dion shopping together for everything," Jen teased, walking past Julie to go greet their visitors, as Darius parked, and their doors started to open for the three of them to exit the vehicle. "Hey, ya'll, we're headed over to Aunt Hazel and Uncle Bob's for breakfast first."

"Oh, well, lead the way." Mama Marcel looped her arm through Jen's as they started across the driveway, with Darius following right behind them.

When she saw that he had his heathered-green graphic tee tucked into his jeans, Julie wished Dion would follow along with her sister and his family, so she could get a good look at how well his backside filled out those jeans. Instead, he leaned against the car, giving her plenty of time to read the "Let's Get Cray Cray" slogan surrounding a picture of a crawfish.

Thanks to her time with Dion, Julie now knew that crawfish, crawdads, and crayfish were all terms used to refer to the same crustacean. Though he always pronounced it crawfish, she assumed his shirt was referring to the one pictured as a crayfish. Although, it could also be a reference to the crazy party atmosphere of his hometown. She had to smile at Dion's enjoyment of a play on words.

With his vast vocabulary and how he prides himself on always trying to expand it, I bet the issue he's having with remembering simple words now is driving him crazy. I wonder if there's anything I can do to help him with that?

Dion waited by the car for Julie to catch up before he started walking alongside her, not giving her a chance to ponder how to help him with those issues. "I guess you didn't know your mom invited us to help you move today, huh?"

"No, I didn't know," Julie confirmed in a clipped tone. It wasn't that she was upset that he was there. In fact, she kind of liked that he wanted to help her move. She was just irritated by feeling like her family was making the decisions for her and not letting her act like the twenty-seven-year-old woman she was, who was fully capable of making adult decisions on her own. Add in the pregnancy hormones and she felt like her moods flipped instantly, as if they were attached to a light switch that was easily triggered with just a single word sometimes. "I suppose she also had Bobby assign you a gate code, too, huh? So you can come and go whenever you want without having to let me know you're gonna be here?"

"Yeah," Dion admitted, nodding. "I'm sorry, Jewel, uh, Julia." Dion stepped in front of her, stopping her from walking any farther. "I'll go get Dare and Mama Marcel, and we can all head back to the B and B, if you'd rather not have us here today."

"No, it's not you," Julie disagreed, shaking her head as she reached out to place her hand on his forearm, as if that would stop him from doing what he just said he would. "Or them. I'm just irritated by my family not realizing that I'm a grown woman and want to set my own timeline for when and where I move."

"If you don't want to move, then let's go lock up your stuff, so they can't move it today. We can go hang out someplace else instead, doing whatever you want for fun, where you can just relax and not have to think about anything that upsets you." Dion was so earnest in his suggestion that Julie almost wanted to take him up on it.

"No," she sighed, lightly squeezing the hand on his muscular forearm, as she closed her eyes and enjoyed the feel of his warm strength beneath her palm. "They're right about me needing to move. And I love the house that my second-great-grandpa built, so I do wanna move in there. I'm just tired and irritable because I wasn't able to sleep in this morning, and I can't have coffee to help me wake up."

"Okay, then we'll make sure your bed is the first thing moved, so you can take a nap while we move everything else." Dion smiled and took both her hands in his, lifting them to his lips for soft, sweet kisses before releasing one hand to step to her side. He then walked hand in hand with her to breakfast.

Every time he spoke, Julie felt flutters from both of her babies moving and knew they were happy to hear their daddy's voice. *Yeah,*

I hear you, she thought-talked to her unborn children. *And I know that happy dance is because ya'll both love your daddy as much as I do.*

She just hoped her babies couldn't really hear her thoughts, especially when she realized how arousing it was to have him take charge, and tell her whole family how their plans had changed, so she could get a nap. *I guess demanding I get a nap in is the platonic version of being dominating in the bedroom. Maybe it won't be too much longer before he lets the sexual side of his dominance out, so I won't be creaming my panties for no reason.*

~~~

Dion felt a little guilty for taking charge the way he did as they walked into Jewel's family breakfast. He didn't want her to think he was as demanding and domineering as her family had been to get her to move. But he also didn't want her to miss out on the sleep she desperately needed because of following her family's plans for her life, either.

Besides telling them that Jewel's bed needed to be moved first, so she could *lay* down while they moved everything else, he'd also insisted that she wasn't going to lift a finger other than to point to where she wanted them to put her stuff, which had earned him a nod of approval from her father that he wasn't sure he was comfortable receiving. It almost felt like the older man had nodded to point out that Dion was being as overbearing as he'd been the week before, with talking about moving Jewel without even asking if she wanted to move.

But Dion didn't mean his taking charge to show that he was ignoring her wishes and abilities. If she'd told him she didn't want to move, then he'd have followed her wishes to stop the day's activities. And yeah, he knew pregnant women weren't invalids and were perfectly capable of assisting with the tasks of moving, but he also didn't want to take any chances on her lifting something too heavy and causing some kind of issue with the babies. Especially since there were several men there capable of doing the heavy lifting.

Fuck! I just hope my caveman tendencies to protect and provide for her and our babies don't piss her off too much.
~~~

"I'm perfectly capable of moving my own stuff," Jewel pouted as they sat down with their filled plates for breakfast.

"I know you are," Dion placated her with a smile. "But you're already doing all the heavy lifting with having our babies, so you deserve to sit back and rest, while the people who love you do the rest."

"Oh, Julie, let him have his way," her mom added as she and the baby she was holding joined them, sitting down across from Jewel, instead of at the opposite end of the table with her husband.

Though he still wasn't sure how they told Justin and Amy's twins apart, Dion loved seeing the way all the other babies in the family were passed around. After talking to his new doctors a little more this week to know he could safely hold and help care for his babies, he hoped he'd get a turn holding the other babies in Jewel's family to practice for when his and Jewel's babies were born. His doctors had all agreed that as long as he had plenty of backup to help him learn all he needed about how to care for his little ones, then he shouldn't have any issues with feeling overwhelmed enough to trigger a blackout while caring for them after they were born.

While he'd started listening to audiobooks and letting his Kindle's text-to-talk feature read him books that didn't have audio versions to start preparing for fatherhood without struggling to read while waiting on the glasses he was pretty sure he needed, he knew hands-on experience would be more beneficial for him actually remembering how to do the tasks needed. So, he'd already texted with Anthony and his family to let them know that the doctors had cleared him to hold baby Sam next time they were home in Heart's Destiny, letting him finally be able to take them up on their offer to help him prepare for fatherhood, which he'd had to turn down when they'd visited him at the B and B a couple of weeks ago, after his talk with Jewel in the park. But with their travel schedule with the GWA, Dion thought he might have better luck recruiting Jewel's mom to teach him what he needed to know whenever she was babysitting her twin grandsons.

And maybe she can tell me how they tell them apart in case our twins are identical, too.

"Besides, you're not exactly dressed for manual labor," her mother continued, distracting Dion from asking about holding the babies.

"So, I assumed you were only planning to supervise the move, anyway."

"What's wrong with the way I'm dressed?" Between bites of her breakfast, Jewel looked down at the purple t-shirt dress she wore.

Dion thought she looked beautiful in the vibrant color, which he now knew was her favorite color, and loved how the material clung to her curves to show off her baby bump. He wanted to tell her as much, but the tension between her and her mom made it clear it wasn't the right time for compliments. So, Dion shoveled a big bite of eggs into his mouth, and kept his opinions to himself.

She'd paired the casual dress with a pair of black sneakers and a black cardigan, which she'd hung on the back of her chair once she came inside. Since she was in sensible shoes for walking back and forth between the houses, and not wearing the heels she'd paired with her dresses for work and church, he was as confused as she was about why her mother thought her outfit wasn't appropriate for moving.

"There's nothing wrong with it," Susan cajoled as she gently rocked one of her twin grandsons in her arms. "It's just something you wear to socialize, and don't wear to sit on the bathroom floor while you unpack your toiletries and put them in the cabinet under the sink."

"Yeah, well, I don't want to stretch out the waistband of my favorite yoga pants, and haven't found maternity pants I like," Jewel shrugged. "So, I have a feeling I'm gonna do a lot of things over the next five months that I wouldn't normally do in dresses. Including mopping my bathroom floor, so I can sit on it in a dress."

Dion wished he'd brought some of his workout clothes with him, so he could offer her some sweatpants that were big enough to accommodate their growing babies throughout the rest of her pregnancy, and wouldn't matter if they were damaged by whatever she might sit in or use while cleaning.

Wait. Is that the problem? That she might damage the dress if she sits on the floor after using a bleach cleaner to mop? Or is it that she needs pants to keep from flashing her panties if she sits on the floor?

Dion wanted to voice his questions, but didn't think they were appropriate with both their families in the room. So, instead, he opted to change the subject. "So, um, have you started picking out furniture for the nursery yet?"

"Yes, but I haven't ordered any of it yet." Jewel smiled, obviously glad he'd changed the subject.

"Oh, what nursery theme did you decide on?" Amy questioned as she took one of her sons back from Susan now that she was finished with her breakfast.

"Letters, numbers, and primary colors," Jewel informed them. "I figured that works for boys or girls, while still being vibrant, instead of the drab neutrals that seem to be popular online."

"I still say you're going to regret that sunny yellow wall color when it stimulates the babies so much that you can't get them to sleep," Susan chuckled.

"It's called Fun Yellow, not Sunny Yellow," Jewel huffed. "And it's actually one of the lighter yellows and not the really bright ones that might be overstimulating. I actually picked a lighter yellow to contrast against the darker reds and blues of the bedding, curtains, and art I'm planning on putting in the room. That's why I want to go with white furniture, so again, it contrasts with the darker elements of the room. I'm not just picking it willy-nilly, ya know. Babies need that high contrast of shades to develop their color vision. And everything I've read says that primary colors enhance cognitive learning."

"Oh, I wish I'd have thought of that for Jerry and Jonah's nursery," Amy interjected, before Susan could try to refute Jewel's way of thinking. "But since I already insisted on painting our room in my favorite yellow, I had to let Justin put his favorite light blue on the walls of the nursery. And I don't think the various shades of blue we've used for our science theme provides enough contrast. Maybe I should have let Justin go with the superheroes theme instead to have all those colors."

"Or you could switch out your blue and white periodic table for one that's color coded for the different classes of elements," Jewel suggested. "And as they get older, their toys will be a rainbow of colors to help provide more contrast, too."

Dion continued eating as the women discussed nursery decorating ideas, listening to hear what Jewel wanted for their babies' nursery, so he could go shopping between doctor's appointments the following week. If he could remember what she said she wanted, anyway. *Maybe I should call Mama Marcel over here to help me with the details? But if I do that, Jewel might think I'm planning to take over buying all of it and get pissed. And that's definitely not what I want.*

Deciding that he'd rather use those shopping trips to spend more time with Jewel, he interrupted the ladies' conversation to ask, "Can we schedule a time for you and me to go shopping for the nursery together? Like maybe during your lunch hour while I'm between doctor's appointments this week?"

"Um, I don't know," Jewel sputtered, dabbing her mouth with her napkin before elaborating. "I'm super busy at work this week, trying to get ahead before taking time off for the holidays. And next weekend, we start the festivities for Justin and Amy's wedding, which will be the weekend after Christmas. With so much stuff coming up, I was just planning to go online and order stuff while laying in bed at night, so I don't have to try to schedule shopping time during normal business hours, ya know."

"Oh, um, okay." Dion didn't know what else to say, hating feeling like he was having to push her to spend time with him when she didn't want to. "Well, be sure to send me links, so I can pay for half of whatever you decide to order."

"What doctor's appointments do you have this week, Dion?" Susan changed the subject when she saw how dejected he was by Julie's rejection.

"I'm going to see the neurologist and going back to the sleep specialist for a couple of sleep studies." Dion smiled gratefully at Jewel's mom. "I think there's another doctor I'm seeing this week, too, but I can't remember who."

"I thought you said you went to the neurologist earlier this week?" Jewel looked at him curiously.

"Yeah, I got confused between the neurologist and the neuropsychiatrist. Or was he a neuropsychologist?" Dion sort of clarified, still not being sure what titles each of the multiple people he saw in the same office held. "That was the day I spent all day taking tests that kept triggering episodes, so I had to go back the next day to actually meet with the head doctor. I wanna say the ones administering the tests are neuropsychologists, and the main doctor in the practice is a neuropsychiatrist, but I may have those titles backwards."

"What kind of episodes?" Susan arched an eyebrow at him.

At the same time, Jewel inquired, "What kind of tests?"

Dion decided to answer Jewel first. "Some computer tests, where it told me some words to remember, then I'd have to do something for reaction time, like pushing a certain button whenever the word red appeared in red on the screen, and then it would have me type the three words I was supposed to remember. There was another computer test where I had to identify patterns of dots that it only showed me for a few seconds. Lots of tests where it showed me four or five pictures, then I was supposed to push a button to identify one of the pictures in the original list, only the pictures were of squiggly lines and they turned them different directions, so I had to identify the pattern no matter which direction it was turned. Oh, and the color words got more difficult with having to push one button for red and a different button for blue. Then, not using the computer, there were some tests with blocks that the therapist had me stack to match a picture while being timed. There were some tests where the therapist would tell me to memorize a series of numbers that she said without me seeing them, then I had to do a numbered connect the dots puzzle with pencil and paper before reciting the numbers back to her."

He then turned to her mother and explained his episodes. "I kept zoning out on the computer tests and missing times when I was supposed to push a button. And not being able to remember the words and numbers the therapist told me to remember was enough to get me anxious enough to need to *lay* down and pass out for a little bit. Doc Hayes thinks those might be some kind of narcolepsy, which is why I'm going to the sleep specialist for an overnight sleep study and then a daytime nap study."

"Those are the episodes your doctor back home thought were seizures, right?" Jewel inquired between bites of her breakfast.

"Actually, he thought both the zone outs and the pass out spells were both different types of seizures," Dion clarified. "But the seizure meds Dr. Boudreaux prescribed didn't do anything to stop either one of them. And Doc Hayes actually listed one of the meds as a drug allergy on my records that he sent to the doctors I saw this week because of how long one pill knocked me out."

"Yes, Caroline said something about one of the medicines causing you to be unconscious for so long that you had to go back to the hospital via ambulance." Susan told them all about the conversation she'd had with Mama Marcel about his time recovering in New Orleans. "She also said you were upset when the doctor woke you up because you were dreaming about Julie."

"Yeah, the doctors and nurses in that hospital had a bad habit of waking me up in the middle of the best part of my memory-dreams," Dion chuckled, grinning at Jewel to give her an idea of what he'd been dreaming about without actually mentioning their sexy times together.

"Oh, have you had a lot of your memories come back as dreams?" Susan leaned her elbow on the table, resting her chin on her hand.

"Yeah, in fact the sleep specialist said that since my zone out spells are often when I have flashes of memories, he thinks they might be micro-naps, when I look like I'm still awake, but I've actually slipped into a REM cycle to dream. That's why I have to do the nap study next Saturday."

"Oh, what are those memory-dreams or flashes like?"

Dion tilted his head as he looked at Susan, confused by what she was asking. *She's not asking me to tell her about the dreams of making love with her daughter, is she?*

"Like last weekend, when you just stopped walking as you came in for breakfast, what were you remembering?"

Dion was grateful Susan gave him a specific example, so he could share a memory without mentioning the intimate moments he'd dreamed about with Jewel. "It's kinda like I'm watching a movie of things that happened. That time, being in this same space, I was able to remember bits and pieces of conversations from Christmas last year and pick out what was different in the decorations. I've had several of those episodes since coming to town for Dean and Allissa's wedding. And thankfully, I can usually keep walking or absentmindedly eating when they hit, so I didn't ruin the various wedding events when they happened."

"Oh, I'm sure you getting memories back wouldn't have ruined the wedding events," Susan assured him.

"If I'd have passed out while walking Allissa down the aisle, it might have," Dion chuckled self-deprecatingly.

"You had flashes of memories then?" Jewel looked at him curiously, making him wonder if she thought their special moment during the wedding, when their eyes locked on one another as he walked Allissa down the aisle, was one-sided because he'd been lost in his memories then.

"When the doors first opened, and the music hit me, yeah," Dion confirmed, trying to make sure he worded his next statement correctly to make her realize how special that moment when they connected was for him. "I remembered walking in the chapel and seeing you sitting in the same part of the sanctuary for four different weddings. I can't tell you who got married when, or which wedding you wore the different dresses to, but I distinctly remembered seeing you in a navy-blue dress with your hair down in waves around your shoulders. Then in a burgundy dress with your hair up. Then in a lavender dress, also with your hair up. And finally, in a bright blue dress with your hair down and curly. It's the only memory I have of you with really curly hair. None of the flashes lasted more than a few seconds, but then when I got to that part of the aisle, I was able to look over and see you exactly where I thought you'd be based on those memories. Seeing you then was the most special moment of the wedding for me. Although, I probably shouldn't ever tell Dean or Allissa that."

"You really remember what dresses I wore?" Jewel's expression made it clear that she wasn't sure if she could believe him or not.

"Yeah," Dion nodded and grinned, letting her get away with glossing over his statement about their special moment since her mom was sitting right there. "If they're still hanging in your closet when we go to move your clothes today, I'll point them out to you, and then you can tell me which weddings you wore them to."

"Yeah, they're all still hanging in my closet," Jewel confirmed, smiling playfully. "But you'd better point them out first thing, like while the rest of the guys are taking apart my bed, 'cause I'm definitely taking you up on that offer of a nap while ya'll move my clothes and stuff."

"Guess we'd better hurry up and finish breakfast then, huh?" Dion grinned, glad to see Jewel's smile again, even if he was still stuck in the friend zone.

At least, she's no longer growling about me telling her what to do. So, I'm sure we'll get back to more than friends, eventually.

Later that afternoon, after they'd moved everything from Jewel's bedroom, unpacked everything but the locked suitcase she insisted on unpacking herself after everyone left, and she was lying down for a nap, Dion couldn't stop himself from asking what the plan was for furnishing the rest of the house, as most everyone disbursed to their own houses or headed to their vehicles. While her bedroom and bathrooms were fully functional, they were the only rooms in the large house that he considered inhabitable. From what he could tell, they hadn't even stocked her refrigerator or pantry for her to be able to eat at home yet, so he considered the move far from done.

"There are a few pieces from our place that I think she wants to take with her," Jen replied, motioning for him to head back to the big blue and white Victorian home they'd moved Jewel's other stuff from, as if she was about to show him what else needed to be moved. "But since we tend to host all our book club meetings because of having the most space and plenty of seating for everyone, I think she assumed we'd want to keep everything there."

"Like the purple couch in the den that has her permanent butt print in the cushion from how often she sits on it," Becky added with a chuckle. "And her favorite set of Memmaw Judy's dishes. Shoot, we could probably give her two or three sets of dishes and still never use all the ones we have left."

"You know there's a reason Memmaw Judy had so many sets of dishes, right?" Charlotte rubbed a hand over her baby bump as she walked along with them to the house they'd just moved Julie out of, instead of following her husband and son to her home across the driveway.

"I always assumed it was because she kept losing pieces when they got carried over to the bunkhouse," Jen conjectured with a shrug.

"Nope," Charlotte smiled wistfully, like she was momentarily caught in a happy memory. "She apparently planned on giving us each a set when we got married, but she didn't write down which set she wanted to go to each of us. Pappaw gave me the set he thought she meant for me when I first moved back from college, and I think he did the same for Bobby and JJ. But I don't think he ever said anything to either of our moms about distributing the rest of them, so when ya'll moved in here, you kinda got stuck with all the sets that were still left to mete out."

"Well, then we'll definitely be sorting them out and spreading the dishes around to everyone who hasn't already gotten their set," Jen declared as they walked into the house.

"Starting with Julie's set today," Becky added. "And while we're packing up her stuff from the kitchen, you guys can move all the purple furniture to Julie's, since it'll match her color scheme much better than ours."

Dion looked around at the neutral taupe walls in the den they directed him and Dare to get the purple furniture from, while the ladies went to pack up the kitchen stuff. He definitely agreed that the vibrant sofa, loveseat, and chairs would definitely fit in better with the lavender walls in Jewel's new living room than they did with the brown, white, and orange tribal patterned sofa and loveseat that also occupied the space.

When they saw him and his brother carrying the first piece of purple furniture over to Julie's house, JJ and Josh joined them in helping to move the rest of the stuff that they hadn't known needed to be moved before disbursing earlier.

"What about the side tables and coffee table?" Josh questioned as they put the loveseat down in Jewel's living room.

"No, those were all dark brown and seemed to match the tribal patterned sofa and loveseat we left there." Dion shook his head. "And I think Jewel wants white wood furniture for a higher contrast with the darker elements of the rooms. At least, that's what she said she wanted for the nursery furniture earlier."

"Yes, that's definitely what she wants," Susan agreed, leaning against the doorway between the living room and the hallway from the vestibule as she directed them where to put each piece of furniture. "And now that I see this stuff in here, I agree with her. She definitely needs some lighter pieces to brighten the room up, even with the sunlight coming in from that big, bay window. I know the line she was looking at down at Heart of the Home, so I'll call Honey to see how soon Brent can get it made and delivered for her. I'd planned on sending ya'll shopping for it together this afternoon, but I guess ya'll can do that for artwork or the nursery furniture later. But she needs to have a functional living room, dining room, and kitchen now, so I think it's only right that her father and I provide the things I know she wants as a housewarming gift."

Fuck! I can't even offer to pay for her furniture now that I know her parents want to make it a housewarming gift. Guess I should just take being allowed to help move this stuff for her as the win it is for now. And come up with other ideas for how I can take care of her and our babies later.

"Well, let me know if there's anything I can do to help finish setting up the house for her," Dion offered, smiling sincerely at Jewel's mom. "Like maybe a grocery run to stock the pantry and fridge, or whatever."

"Oh, that's an excellent idea," Susan beamed at him. "I'll go get started on a list while ya'll finish moving over the stuff the girls are packing now."

As Dion went on to help set up her kitchen to make it functional, he thought about other things he could do to help make her house feel more like a home. *Like maybe I could frame some of my drawings for her to hang on the walls?*

He'd picked up sketch pads and colored pencils at A Stitch In Time, the local craft store, a couple weeks earlier when Mama Marcel first got to town and they went exploring. He'd originally planned to just get back into drawing like he'd done with his mom as a kid to give him something to do during his free time, so he wouldn't be bored while he was off work like he'd been back in NOLA. But when he'd mentioned drawing as a hobby to the new doctors he'd seen this week, it had been suggested that he try to draw his memories as they came back to him.

Obviously, she's not gonna wanna hang up the drawings I've done of us making love, but maybe I can come up with some appropriate artwork for hanging in the nursery. Like maybe drawing animals learning to write letters or count to go along with her letters and numbers theme.

While I still might one day give her the sketchbook I've started drawing our naked memories in, I don't think she's ready for that now. But she might enjoy some of the pictures I've drawn of our more innocent, platonic memories. And she might also appreciate caricatures of the babies once they're born, too.

Yeah, I can definitely cover the artwork for her, even if she doesn't wanna go shopping with me for the nursery yet.

Chapter Thirteen

Sunday, December 15, 2019

Julie was glad her family tended to hang out together for meals every weekend, so she didn't have to go back to her house alone to fix dinner. Not that she could do much of her kind of cooking in her new-to-her home until after she took the time to go grocery shopping. While her family had surprised her while she was napping the day before by moving her favorite pieces of furniture, dishes, and kitchen gadgets from the home she'd previously shared with her sister and cousin, and her mom and Aunt Hazel had stocked her kitchen pantry and refrigerator with what they considered staples, she really didn't like the idea of cooking for one. And their staples didn't include the microwave meals and frozen pizzas she had a tendency to live on when not eating with the rest of the family to keep from having to really cook. So, once again, she found herself walking into Aunt Hazel and Uncle Bob's house for Sunday supper and a Skype session to wish her cousin Brady a happy birthday, since he wasn't in town for one of the typical birthday parties they all had on the ranch.

Maybe we can combine Brady and Blake's birthday parties on Friday when the Avingtons all come in from Georgia for the holidays?

The only drawback she foresaw to another family gathering was the questions they were sure to have about why she hadn't invited Dion and his family to join them again, and what was happening between the two of them besides co-parenting their babies. She honestly had no idea how to answer those questions, either. It wasn't that she was trying to avoid him, or intentionally left him out by not mentioning the family meal previously. She was just so overwhelmed by thinking about other things every time she saw him that she didn't think about starting to include him in the weekly family plans. And as for there being more than co-parenting between them, she wasn't sure if it would happen or not.

The day before, she'd been preoccupied with the move, and then kicking herself for her bratty attitude when Dion started dictating what she could and couldn't do to help move her stuff. Considering how much she wanted him to take charge and dominate her sexually, she couldn't comprehend why she'd fought against it when he tried to show a little of his protective instincts toward her and their babies in other aspects of their lives.

Is it the pregnancy hormones? Like, am I an irritable bitch and having massive mood swings because I'm even more hormonal than during the worst PMS I've ever felt before? Like the wackadoodle hormones somehow shut down my brain, so I keep sniping without thinking things through first? And if so, how do I combat the hormones to act more like my normal, rational self?

Or maybe it's just the increased libido kicking in, making me push him until he gives me some kind of sexy punishment for my behavior? Like I was subconsciously hoping he'd insist on spanking me before my nap? We certainly had a lot of fun back in August when we role played the naughty actress intentionally flubbing her lines to get a spanking when we met up in L.A. So maybe I was subliminally trying to remind him of that by being disagreeable yesterday?

Thinking back to how despondent he'd looked when she shot down his plans for them to go baby shopping together really made her feel like the worst bitch ever. Yeah, between work, her volunteering times she'd committed to earlier in the year, and the holidays and weddings coming up, she had a lot on her plate over the next couple of weeks. And he clearly needed to focus on meeting with all the specialists Doc Hayes had referred him to in San Antonio, so he could come up with a complete treatment plan. But she'd also promised him that she wouldn't keep him from participating in anything to do with their babies. And by not letting him have a say in planning their nursery, she felt like she'd already broken that promise.

Damn it! I need to stop shopping online and actually take him to look at cribs and stuff. She realized just how much she'd screwed up, just as she finished filling her plate and followed her cousin Josh into the dining room. Seeing the former SEAL, her train of thought shifted.

Oh, I wonder, since there's so much stuff on the news lately about TBI in the military, if maybe Josh knows someone who's had to go through the same stuff Dion is? If so, then maybe he can give me some ideas for resources for support groups for him. And maybe some for family members and friends of TBI survivors, so I can be a better partner for Dion, too.

As they made it to the table, Julie sat down across from Josh. She would have sat beside him so she could whisper her questions to keep from hearing the opinions of everyone else in the family, but she knew that spot was reserved for Cait, who was still in the kitchen.

"Hey, Josh, I need to pick your brain," she informed him as she placed her napkin in her lap.

"If you need brains, maybe you should wait 'til next week when Jake'll be home," Josh chuckled with a self-deprecating smile.

"No," she disagreed, shaking her head. "I think you're more likely to have SEAL friends who've suffered from TBI, so you're probably better equipped than he is to know how I can best support Dion in his recovery."

"Oh, yeah, probly." Josh nodded as he cut the steak on his plate. "You looking for resources for him or support groups for caregivers and family?"

"Both." Julie cut her steak into small bite-sized pieces as she elaborated. "He asked me for recommendations of specialists in the area a couple of weeks ago, and all I was able to give him was Doc Hayes. And I know Doc has sent him to several specialists, and for cognitive testing and stuff, but I was thinking maybe he'd need to talk to other people who've suffered similar injuries, too. And I'd like to understand the changes in his brain after all this too, so maybe I can keep us from having any more misunderstandings while co-parenting with him."

"Have you been talkin' to Cait about my plans for starting some equine therapy programs next month?" Josh arched an eyebrow at her.

"No, she hasn't mentioned it." Julie shook her head before taking a bite, curious about what her cousin was planning.

"It's something I've been thinking about since I came home," Josh explained between bites. "Even talked to the therapist we've been seeing about doing equine therapy with our family horses, but I'm waiting 'til after the wedding, so I can use my trust fund to start a foundation first. That way I can hire experts to run the programs, since I'm not qualified to do any of it myself."

"Oh, wow, that's a great idea." Julie knew that Josh, Cait, and JoJo had been seeing a therapist to help them come together as a family after all the changes that had happened in their lives in the last year. And since work commitments and pregnancies kept so many of their family members from giving their horses the daily attention they deserved, having the horses participate in the therapy program Josh was suggesting would benefit the horses just as much as it would benefit the humans utilizing the equine therapy services. And maybe even lessen the workload of the ranch hands, who currently had to pick up the slack for the family horses between tasks with the cattle.

"What's a great idea?" Cait inquired as she joined them.

"The equine therapy program I want Dr. Edwards to help us start next year," Josh informed his girlfriend, whom he planned to propose to and marry on the one-year anniversary of the day they met at the end of the month. "I know we were talking about starting with an Ashbury Foundation group and a military PTSD group. Then expanding based on the patients Ariel and Ryan see in their practice, but Julie just brought up a point about people who've suffered from TBI that I hadn't thought about, even though it'll have a lot of crossover with the military group we were already planning."

"Oh, because of Dion." Cait smiled at Julie as she pointed at her with her fork. "Are you going to suggest him starting as one of the first participants in the program?"

Julie nodded and continued eating as her cousin elaborated.

"It'll depend on if he's already seeing a therapist and if they're equine certified," Josh shrugged. "If he's seeing someone equine certified already, I'd love for him to pass along a referral for them to work with our foundation when we get it started. But if he's not seeing someone already, I'd highly recommend either Ariel or Ryan Edwards. They're both going through the process for whatever certifications they need to add equine therapy to their practice, so they might bring him into the program when we get it started. And the next time I talk to them, I'll ask about the caregivers and family members' support groups in the area, and see if that's something else we can add to our programs."

"Thanks," Julie smiled at her cousin and soon-to-be cousin-in-law. "I really appreciate your help."

"So, Dion is definitely planning to stay in Heart's Destiny and isn't going back to New Orleans with his family?" Surprisingly, it was Cait that started the interrogation by her family.

"That's what he says." Julie shrugged, losing her appetite, and starting to push her food around on her plate instead of eating it. "But I'm still not convinced he'll really stick around our small town. After growing up in New Orleans, and then traveling the world with the GWA, I'm sure he'll get bored here eventually and want to go back to his more glamorous life."

"Oh, please," Cait scoffed, rolling her eyes at Julie. "With you and the babies here, he'll be sticking around. Besides, as much as you like traveling for work, he'll get plenty of glitz and glamour traveling with you."

"Considering how he pushed to make sure you have everything you need in your new place, including making Dare take him grocery shopping after we moved the living room furniture and all the kitchen stuff over, I'm sure he's plannin' to stick around," Josh added between bites. "Trust me, as a man who wants nothing more than to love and provide for my family, I recognize that same instinct in Dion. I hope you love him and wanna spend the rest of your life with him. 'Cause if you don't, you're gonna have a damn near impossible task in trying to get rid of him, so you can find someone else."

Dion went grocery shopping? That wasn't Mom and Aunt Hazel? And pushed for all the extra furniture and kitchen stuff to be moved yesterday? Holy shit! Maybe Josh and Cait are right about him? Maybe? But am I ready to risk my heart again by giving him another chance to rip it out?

Julie wanted desperately to believe her friend and cousin. But whether it was residual anger from their previous misunderstanding, or just pregnancy hormones making her skeptical, she still wasn't quite sure she could. Yet.

~~~
~~~

After the last couple of weeks of going to see various specialists, and having multiple sleep studies done on Friday night and Saturday morning, Dion was stuck in a holding pattern until after the holidays. Hopefully, the few changes they'd already made to his meds and treatment plans would be effective, and he'd start seeing the benefits by the time he went back to his doctors in January.

The optometrist had noted definite changes in his vision and prescribed glasses, which Dion immediately ordered. Now, he was just waiting on them to be made and delivered, probably sometime the first week of January. In the meantime, he'd picked up some over-the-counter readers at the drugstore to help improve his drawings, even though they wouldn't do a thing for his distance vision. *I still can't believe I'm gonna hafta wear bifocals to correct both my distance and up-close vision. I swear I thought I'd have another twenty years before I'd be old enough for fuckin' bifocals.*

The neuropsychiatrist had reviewed the findings of the neuropsychologist from the cognitive tests he'd taken and consulted with the neurologist before deciding to prescribe Memantine to help with his memory issues. It was a medication typically used to treat memory issues associated with dementia and Alzheimer's, but according to his new neuropsychiatrist, it also helped with cognitive issues after traumatic brain injuries.

Those cognitive tests also showed that Dion had attention deficit disorder, so the neuropsychiatrist also started him on Adderall. He hadn't thought he'd previously had it because of not being hyperactive. But the doctor explained that the way his mind jumped from topic to topic at a rapid pace was one of the classic signs, and he might not have had as much of the hyperactivity because of his extremely active job as a professional wrestler. Considering his struggles with boredom caused him to be twitchy when he didn't have things to do during the day, Dion could almost see a little of the hyperactivity of A.D.H.D. in the way he fidgeted until he found something to do to keep both his brain and body engaged.

Since Adderall was something the sleep specialist had mentioned might be helpful if his brain injury had triggered the narcolepsy as Doc Hayes suspected, in addition to being the first medication the neuropsych mentioned for the A.D.D., Dion agreed to go ahead and take the medication, even though he couldn't see the sleep specialist to get the results of the sleep studies he'd just had done until after New Year's. Now he was hopeful that when he went in to see the doctors again in a couple of weeks, he'd either already be having fewer episodes because of the medications, or they would have a more definitive diagnosis for him with a clear treatment plan they could put in place.

Of everything he'd been advised to do for his issues, though, he was most intrigued by Jewel's suggestion that he talk to her cousin Josh about the equine-assisted psychotherapy program he was starting on the ranch at the beginning of the year. The neuropsychologist that Dion saw a week and a half before suggested cognitive-behavioral therapy for him to help deal with the anxiety that seemed to trigger his blackout spells. So, when Jewel mentioned the program Josh wanted to start on the ranch, Dion called the doctor's office to see if that was one of his options. The nurse who called him back said the doctor thought it was a great idea, but unfortunately, they didn't offer that service through their office. So, now Dion found himself tasked with finding out more information about the program from Josh to be able to present it to his doctors. And he really hoped they would approve it as a viable treatment option for him, so he'd have another excuse to go to the ranch on a regular basis to see Jewel.

Oh, he'd managed to spend some time there the past couple of weekends. And she'd even given in on going baby shopping with him once earlier in the week. But now that she'd shown him the only two places on the ranch where they'd previously interacted, trying to help him regain his memories, and her move from house to house was completed, he needed to come up with some other options to allow him access to see her regularly. Since she'd pretty much told him to focus on healing both his physical and mental injuries instead of their relationship, asking her on a date like a normal couple was out of the question. So, having his therapy sessions on her family ranch seemed like the best way to get close to her while still honoring her wishes.

He would have asked Josh about the program at the bachelor and bachelorette party for Justin and Amy that Jewel had invited him to the night before. But after the stress of the overnight sleep study Friday night and the nap study Saturday morning, Dion was too anxious to even think about going to a bar where the crowd of people, loud music, and strobe lights might trigger another one of his episodes. So, he'd stayed back in his hotel room and let Dare go to the party to represent the Davises in congratulating the happy couple.

Luckily for Dion, he was guaranteed to see Jewel and her cousin Josh at church every Sunday. So, now he just had to wait for an opening to talk to her cousin about the therapy program. Obviously, that wasn't during the service. Or during the wedding shower for Jewel's brother and future sister-in-law that immediately followed the service and replaced the weekly potluck dinner.

At least, Dion didn't think the wedding shower would be the right time to talk to Josh, until they were given instructions for the Find-The-Guest game as soon as they sat down. There were a couple of printed cards on the tables at each seat, one of which was a list of traits of the guests that was designed to get everyone up and mingling to kick off the party.

Like everyone else in attendance, Dion quickly went through the list and was able to jot down a few names based on what he knew about some of the people in attendance. He had to remember to write "Julia Burleson" instead of "Jewel" on the line for finding someone "who was born in the same month as you," but he was thrilled to remember that they were both born in May — her on the third, and him on the twenty-third. He could easily fill in Darius Davis and Caroline Marcel on the lines about speaking a foreign language and vacationing in the last three months. He could also list his former boss, Rick Robertson, as sharing his favorite television show, which was the GWA's weekly program, *Tuesday Night Takedown*. After those were filled in, he had to get up and mingle to find out if anyone else met the qualifications for the other statements.

And since I've gotta go talk to the other people here, I may as well start with the Burlesons. I'm sure a few of them will match up with these other statements. And if I only catch up with Jewel, I'm sure she can tell me which of her family members to put on each line.

As he walked over to the table where Jewel was sitting with several members of her family, they all stood to start walking around like the rest of the people at the party. He was so blown away by how ravishing she looked in an emerald green sweater dress that he barely managed to step in front of her before she walked away.

He got a whiff of her fruity-floral scent and had a quick flashback to her telling him about the wild frangipani hair products she used as they laid in bed cuddling.

"Are you sure it's a flower they use as the main base for the scent? 'Cause it smells like bananas to me."

"Yes, frangipani is a flower that smells like different flowers, fruits, or spices, depending on which variety it is. This one smells more fruity, probably because there are a lot of other fruity essential oils in the weekly hair scrub and conditioning treatment I used this morning in place of my normal frangipani shampoo and conditioner."

"Yeah, well, I think your normal shampoo and conditioner smells like bananas, too. And since you always smell like bananas, I'm gonna get hard every time I smell bananas now," he chuckled, thinking he'd have to avoid the fruit anytime it was served backstage while he was in his skimpy wrestling tights to keep from embarrassing himself by thinking of her.

"You're breathtaking, Jewel, uh, Julia," he praised, unable to stop the words from tumbling out of his mouth as he pushed aside the memory to stay in the moment with her, so he didn't miss out on the opportunity to talk to her.

"Thank you," Jewel smiled up at him as her cheeks lightly flushed from his compliment.

"Can you, um, help me with some of these?" Dion held up the card for the Find-The-Guest game. "I was able to put you down for the first one and fill in a couple of the others with people I've known from before, but I thought you might be able to help me remember if anyone I've met in town matches the others."

"Oh, um, yeah." Jewel looked down at her card before sharing one of her answers. "I put my parents for the married ten years or longer, but you could pretty much list any of the local couples in their generation for that one. Oh, you speak a foreign language, right?"

"Laissez les bon temps rouler," Dion grinned after spouting off the unofficial motto of his hometown. *Let the good times roll.* "I'm not as fluent as Dare, but I do awrite with the NOLA version of French."

"That's right," Jewel giggled as she wrote his name down on her card for someone who spoke a foreign language, while he wrote down

Jon and Susan Burleson on the marriage line. "You said you knew enough to keep from getting lost in Paris and Marseille back in March, but the locals laughed at your phraseology."

"I was in Paris and Marseille back in March?" *Did we go on a romantic trip to France that I can't remember?* Dion was thoroughly confused by her statement.

"Yeah, I guess you forgot the GWA's two-week European tour with your amnesia, huh? Maybe you can talk to Anthony and Kay while they're home for Christmas, since they went with the rest of the GWA on that tour, and maybe they can help you remember some of the things you did then." She looked back down at the card in her hands before changing the subject. "You can also list them as having more than three children for this game. Oh, and Anthony is left-handed. I listed Kay on the kids and Anthony on the left-handed, so I didn't list anyone twice."

"Thanks, that helps." Dion smiled at her before jotting down the names on the card in his hand. "You can also put Mama Marcel for the vacation one."

"Oh perfect, that's the one none of us thought we'd find." She quickly scribbled down the name. "Oh, and my cousin Jake traveled over fifty miles to be here today. Technically, he's home on leave through New Year's, but since he just got here yesterday, I think it counts."

"Jake's the Burleson I haven't met again yet, right?" Dion was trying diligently to keep them all straight in his head, but between his brain injury and the sheer quantity of family she had, he was having a hard time remembering all the names and matching them up to the individuals.

"Yep." Dion had to smile at how she popped the P on her simple one-word answer. It was another of her quirky traits that he found endearing. "He's standing over there with his twin, Josh, if you wanna meet him again before you use him as an answer on here. They might be able to help you with some of the others, too."

"Sweet. Thanks, Cher." Dion didn't normally use the term of endearment that was actually more popular in the rural areas of Louisiana than in NOLA. But since she'd balked at him calling her Jewel, he thought he'd try out the hypocorism generally associated with his home state the way Darlin' was associated with hers. Since she didn't complain about it before they parted ways, he thought it might be something he could get away with using more regularly.

"Where y'at?" Dare lifted his chin at Dion as they crossed paths moving around the room.

"Awrite," Dion replied, nodding his head in the direction of Jewel's cousins that he was walking toward. "Just goin' to reintroduce myself to the Burleson I haven't met again yet."

"I'll pass by with ya." Darius changed direction to walk with Dion over to where Josh and Jake Burleson were talking with an older couple.

"Yeah, you're gonna have a hard time finding someone else who drives a Lincoln here," Josh informed the older man. "We tend to pick Dodge, Jeep, or Chevy vehicles in our family."

"Doesn't your girlfriend drive a Kia?" Dion assumed the man who just slapped a hand on Josh's shoulder was his brother Jake. Even though he had darker hair and eyes than Josh and was a little bit smaller, there was enough of a family resemblance to verify that was the cousin Jewel had directed him to meet.

"Yeah, and so does Amy," Josh conceded with a nod of his head. "But they're marrying into the family and got their cars without our input."

Josh apparently noticed Dion and Darius walking up, switching his focus to greet them. "Hey, Dion. Darius. Have either of you met my brother, Jake?" He pointed with his thumb at the man Dion had already assumed was his brother before motioning toward the older couple. "Or Kay's parents, Charles and Mary Lee?"

"Yes, we've met Dion a couple of times." Charles extended his hand for Dion to shake.

"But those meetings were before his injury, dear," Mary clarified as she gave Dion a sympathetic smile while he shook her husband's hand. "He probably doesn't remember us."

"No, ma'am, I don't remember meeting you before," Dion agreed. "But I'm happy to meet you now. And introduce ya'll to my brother, Dare, uh, Darius."

"So, did you earn that nickname by being a daredevil?" Charles grinned as they swapped handshakes. "Or is it just a shortened version of your name?"

239

"Probably a little of both," Darius chuckled. "And maybe a little of my friends enjoying the play on words by always daring me to do stupid stuff."

"Nothing illegal, I hope." Charles arched an eyebrow as he sternly looked at Dare.

"No, sir," Darius barked, clearly recognizing the older man as an authority figure.

"You're a bit outside your jurisdiction, aren't you, Sheriff?" Jake smirked at the same time.

"But I'm not outside your brother's jurisdiction," Charles grinned back at Jake. "So as a fellow law enforcement officer, I feel obligated to check out anything that might need to be reported to him while I'm here visiting."

"Yeah, well, you don't have to worry about us," Dare defended himself and Dion. "None of our stupid stunts were illegal. And even the ones that were just too embarrassing to talk about were done back in NOLA and not here."

"Considering you've spent the last month apologizing for the stupid stuff you said to Julie on the phone," Josh chuckled at Darius. "I'm really curious to know what kind of stuff you consider too embarrassing to talk about. Dion, you care to share with Julie's favorite cousins?"

Dion held his hands up in surrender and shook his head. "Don't ask me. Amnesia, remember?" Dion didn't mention that his amnesia didn't cover his teens and early twenties, when he and his brother had more than one embarrassing adventure on Bourbon Street.

"Oh, goodness." Mary dramatically placed her hand on her chest. "Do you even remember what kind of car you drive to find someone to match up with you for this game?"

"Nope," Dion admitted, shaking his head. "Since the doctor hasn't cleared me to drive yet, I didn't even think to ask about my vehicle. I've just been having Dare and Jewel drive me everywhere."

"You drive an Escalade, D," Darius informed him. "Liam brought it back from the arena the day you were injured. It's parked in the garage back in NOLA."

"A caddy?" Jake arched an eyebrow at Dion. "I guess that's okay, since it's still a GM vehicle. But seriously, dude, you might wanna trade it in for something a little less flashy if you ever want Julie to ride with you."

"Really? Why?" Dion was curious about why she wouldn't like his choice in vehicle.

"Because, like all of us, she learned a long time ago not to do anything that causes us to stand out and draw the attention of the paparazzi," Jake explained. "I know your job kinda comes with the fame that draws attention, and that whole stalker situation only amped it up, but that's something we all try to avoid."

"Not that we can avoid it completely when something happens to put Burleson Incorporated in the spotlight," Josh pointed out. "But there's a reason why we live in Heart's Destiny, where Bobby can arrest photographers for harassment and trespassing, instead of hobnobbing with the rich and famous in one of the major cities where we have satellite offices. We might still end up with our pictures on a gossip site once in a while, but by being boring most of the time, we don't typically attract much negative publicity."

"And staying off the paparazzi's radar is vital for some of us," Jake continued for his brother. "Like when Josh was a SEAL and needed anonymity on missions. Or when Bobby and Brook are trying to help someone escape an abusive situation and don't want the photographers alerting the abusers to their location."

"And I'm sure to maintain the privacy of the people coming to the equine-assisted psychotherapy program Julie told me you want to start," Dion nodded along, understanding dawning. "I've been following the guidelines Rick set when he took over running the GWA, but I can see now I might need to get ya'll to school me on the Burleson paparazzi protocol. Especially if I wanna be one of your first therapy patients."

"What guidelines did Rick set?" Jake arched an eyebrow inquisitively.

"To always dress professionally in public." Since he'd left his suitcoat hanging on the back of his chair when he got up to mingle for the game, Dion pointed to the black slacks and green button-down dress shirt and tie he was wearing to make his point. "And to not get caught doing anything stupid. It's okay for the papzz to take our pics as we go in and out of airports, hotels, and arenas, just as long as we don't give them any reason to write salacious stories about us. And all press releases go through the GWA public relations department. He even has a team to handle all our social media to make sure we're all on brand and don't embarrass ourselves or the company."

"So, that's why he was so upset by the Vegas wedding pics." Jake nodded, indicating he finally understood Rick's reaction to the weddings Dion had to be reminded about after waking up in the hospital.

"Yeah, he doesn't care about them getting married." Dion smiled at how he'd seen Rick actively helping the local matchmakers in trying to keep the mistakenly married couples together during the week of Dean and Allissa's wedding. "It was them posting on social media with so many different configurations of couples that contradicted the angles he had planned that pissed him off."

"Yeah, I heard he was behind the conspiracy to make them room with their new spouses when they were all here last month," Josh chuckled. "I wasn't sure if he was joining the Matchmaking Mommas, or still trying to punish them."

"Oh, you didn't see how he was feeding Mandi Hunter ideas for things she could get the couples to do all week to help with the wedding," Dare interjected, laughing along with Josh. "I used to think D's boss was gruff and serious all the time, 'til I saw him helping her deconstruct wedding favors, just so Liam, Crockett, and Surfer Josh could spend a couple of days with their new wives putting them all back together."

"I think he's hoping they'll all stay together," Dion added with a smile. "I haven't heard from the other guys, but Liam called me last night to tell me how Rick had called his folks to make sure they knew he needed to bring his new bride to Christmas dinner."

"Oh, yeah, he's definitely joined the Matchmaking Mommas," Jake chuckled and grinned.

"Attention everyone," Susan Burleson announced into the microphone they had set up at the front of the room. "We have a winner of the Find-The-Guest game. Marie Milton was able to fill in every blank on her card. So, if you haven't met Nana Marie yet, stop by and congratulate her on your way back to your seat for the next activity."

"I guess that means I don't have time to ask you about the equine therapy program now." Dion looked at Josh as he pulled his phone out of his pocket. "Can I get your number to call you about it later in the week?"

"Yeah, sure," Josh agreed, taking Dion's phone to enter his digits. "Or we can plan on talking about it at Christmas dinner on Wednesday."

Dion tilted his head as he looked at Josh in confusion. *Is he inviting me to his family's Christmas dinner? Or just assuming Jewel already invited me?*

"If Julie hasn't already extended the invitation to you and your family, consider yourselves invited now." Josh grinned as he handed Dion back his phone. "We meet at Mom and Dad's place, where you came for breakfast the last couple of weeks, at Noon."

"You joining the Matchmaking Mommas now, too?" Jake punched his brother in the shoulder.

"Naw, I can't be a Matchmaking Momma 'cause I don't have a uterus," Josh asserted, grinning at Dion. "But maybe Rick and I can start our own group to help them out. You think he'd go along with being called the Deputy Daddies?"

"No, but he might go along with the Proxy Papas," Rick's new wife interjected with a grin as she walked up carrying a tea pitcher. "Now ya'll go sit down, so we can serve lunch."

"Yes, ma'am," the four men chimed in unison as they ducked their heads and walked away from where they'd been huddled on the side of the room.

Damn, I should probably get a head count from Josh, so I can do a better job with gifts this year. As he took his seat, Dion pulled his phone out of his pocket and searched for Josh's name in his contact list to send him a text before he forgot.

Dion: How many people are going to be at Christmas? Men? Women? Kids? Need to know how many presents to pick up tomorrow.

Josh Burleson: No clue. But it was such a mess last year that we decided to do something different this year. Just bring one gag gift for each of you for the Grinch game.

Dion: What's the Grinch game?

Josh Burleson: It's something the kids suggested. We're gonna have two circles of people, one for adults & one for kids. We start holding the present we brought & pass them right or left based on when we hear certain words as the Grinch book is read.

Dion: Cool. Thx.

Dion wasn't sure he completely understood how the present exchange would go, but he was looking forward to spending the day with Jewel and her family. *Now I just have to hope she won't be upset by me bringing her a gift separate from the ones for the game.*

He'd had Mama Marcel help him pick out the heart-shaped diamonds and emeralds to go into a Caged-Hearts mother's necklace for her for Christmas, as well as the center three-carat heart-shaped diamond for the engagement ring he was having specially made for her. He knew she wasn't anywhere near ready for him to propose yet, but he had enough confidence in them to plan ahead.

He'd turned the necklace into a piece representing the whole family, and not just their babies, by adding two emeralds for his and Jewel's birthstones, and then picking two emeralds and two diamonds for the babies, since there was the possibility that they could be born in April instead of May. The jeweler assured him that once the babies were born, she could open the heart-shaped cage to pull out the two incorrect stones and have them set on either side of the center stone in the engagement ring. Since the emeralds could represent his and Jewel's birthstones in either piece of jewelry, and diamonds were the traditional stones for engagement rings, he figured it would just help the necklace and ring match, no matter which stones ended up in her ring. He wouldn't be able to modify the engagement ring later for any future children they had, but he could always order more heart-shaped birthstones to have them added to the cage of the necklace if they were blessed with more babies.

Now he just had to figure out how to get her alone on Christmas Day to give her the necklace. *Maybe she'll let me walk her home after the party?*

Chapter Fourteen

Wednesday, December 25, 2019, Christmas Day

After surprising her parents by waking them up to give them the framed ultrasound pictures of her babies, Julie couldn't contain her smile as she finished getting ready for her family's Christmas get-together. She loved the idea of doing a white elephant gift exchange with the twist of the Grinch game, instead of buying something for everyone this year. It not only cut out some of the commercialism of the season and brought their focus back to enjoying time with their family and friends, but it was also a whole lot easier than buying presents for several dozen people who all pretty much had everything already. It also meant she wouldn't have to find room in her closet for more ugly Christmas sweaters and pajamas that she'd only wear once a year. But because she wouldn't get the excitement of being a kid and waking her parents on Christmas morning any longer, she'd opted to do it one last time this morning. Only instead of being excited about the presents she'd open, she bounded into her parents' bedroom to insist they open the present from her first thing.

"I can't wait 'til ya'll are old enough I'll be able to send you across the driveway to wake up Gran and Grandad to join us on Christmas morning," Julie told her babies as she rubbed a hand over her ever-increasing, rounded abdomen. "With as excited as they were to hang up your pictures this morning, I'm sure they're gonna wanna be front and center when ya'll and all your dozens and dozens of cousins start getting excited to see what Santa brings you. Hopefully, ya'll will be early risers on Christmas morning like me, so we'll be first on their schedule of going house to house to watch all their grandkids opening presents. I mean, it seems only fair that we make your aunt and uncles wait 'til later, since they always made me wait to open presents every year on the one day a year that I can't seem to force myself to sleep in."

To this day, Julie still didn't understand why she couldn't ever sleep in on Christmas. It made sense when she was a little kid and still believed in Santa Claus, but not so much once she got old enough to understand the real meaning of the holiday. While she still enjoyed every holiday when she got to spend time with the people she loved, she actually preferred the summer holidays that included barbeque and outdoor activities. She'd even go so far as to say that the Fourth of July was her favorite holiday because of how much she enjoyed the fireworks displays. But she didn't have a problem sleeping in then. If anything, she always slept later, in order to be able to stay up late into the night to watch the fireworks.

"I wonder what ya'll's favorite holiday will be?" Julie continued talking to her unborn babies. "Will you be like me with Independence Day? Or like your daddy with Mardi Gras? Or maybe you'll prefer Halloween or Christmas like most kids? Or maybe you'll be unique like your Uncle Justin, and pick a lesser recognized holiday, like Pi Day for your favorite? Regardless of what your favorites are, I can't wait to celebrate them with you. And hopefully, if things keep going as well as they have recently, Daddy will be celebrating them with us, too."

Julie finished getting dressed, pairing a red t-shirt dress with a white cardigan and black suede, flat-soled boots for a little bit of a pregnant Mrs. Claus look. *If Allissa can pull off the sexy Mrs. Claus look on the* **Christmas Chaos** *pay-per-view, then I can do the pregnant Mrs. Claus look for our Christmas party.* Julie inwardly giggled as she transposed the outfits in her mind and imagined herself exposing her baby bump in the halter-top and skirt outfit Allissa wrestled in at the last big GWA show. *Yeah, even once the babies are born, I'll stick to my more sedate t-shirt dresses. Well, unless Dion and I get back together, and I put on something skimpy just for him. Maybe. On the rare occasion when I can actually start the night with clothes on, instead of stripping down to just my birthday suit like he prefers to sleep.*

She checked her makeup and hair in the mirror one last time before walking downstairs to pick up the wine-bottle puzzle she'd picked up for her white elephant gift. Since she was just walking across the driveway, she stuck her phone in her pocket and left her purse and everything else at home when she walked outside to go to the party.

Julie wasn't surprised in the least to see that someone had invited Dion and his family to the ranch for Christmas dinner as she recognized Darius's car while walking across the driveway to her aunt and uncle's house. *Cool. Now I'll just have to figure out how to get him alone, so I can give him the ultrasound pictures I called and had Lakota blow up and frame for him while she was doing Mom and Dad's, instead of having to track him down at the B and B after the party ends.*

She might not know which meddling member of her family had extended the invite, but she was sure at least one of them thought the holiday get-together would be the ideal time for more matchmaking. *Probably Mom or Aunt Hazel mentioned it to their new best friend, Mama Marcel.*

"Guess you'll get to spend more time with your daddy for Christmas than I expected, babies." Julie ran the hand not holding the wrapped package for the Grinch game over her fluttering belly as she talked to her babies before joining the group entering the house, where she could be overheard. "Though I'm surprised he didn't mention it last week, when I met him at the mall for lunch to do a little nursery shopping."

They'd picked out some of the toys and decorations she wanted, but she hadn't even bothered carrying them in from her trunk because she hadn't ordered the furniture yet to have any place to put them. Dion had insisted on carrying everything to her vehicle, but only after she refused to let him take it all home for her, since she had to go back to work right after their mini shopping spree.

I bet he's going to insist on carrying my stuff home from this party too, she thought as she stepped up on the porch. *Which will be the perfect time to give him his gift from the babies.*

Since they weren't technically a couple again, Julie didn't want to say the gift was from her. Doing that seemed like it might be sending a signal that she wasn't ready to send just yet. But saying the gift was from the babies seemed like a safe way to give him a little something without advancing their relationship past the co-parenting stage to coupledom before she was a hundred percent sure she was ready.

As soon as she walked into the house, she placed her gift under the tree before joining the family members and friends milling about the dining room, including Dion, who looked amazing in a black pinstriped suit with a red shirt and tie. *How on earth did he know I was wearing red today to be able to match me? I swear, he does that way too often for it to be a coincidence.*

Dion was talking to Josh about the equine-assisted psychotherapy programs her cousin was planning to start on the ranch. *Oh, good. I hope that's something that will help him with the emotional and mental aspects of his injuries.*

"Yeah, it's gonna take me longer to get it started than I thought," Josh sighed, shaking his head. "I thought we'd be able to run it in the paddocks here by the family stables, or in the south paddocks that we don't really use for much anymore. Since we're having to buy more horses to have one for each of the kids, I was thinking that moving the horses Bobby, Anthony, and Justin's families use most often down to the south stables closest to their houses would free up space in the current family stable, too. But after talking to the Edwardses last week to find out the requirements for them to bring their clients here, I think I'm gonna hafta build a whole new stable and paddocks with a private entrance and none of our houses nearby."

"Really? Why can't you use the stables and paddocks you already have?" Dion voiced the question Julie was thinking, as she moved a little closer to better hear their conversation over the cacophony of voices around the room.

The closeness also allowed her to enjoy the woody aquatic scent of the Versace Man cologne she'd given him for his birthday earlier in the year. *Wow. I wonder if he realizes I picked out that fragrance for him because of how well it blended with the bodywash he uses?* Julie wondered as her body responded with a heightened arousal level to the mix of the cologne, his bodywash, and his natural musk.

"It's a privacy thing," Josh shrugged. "We can't risk the privacy of the residents at the Ashbury House by having the sessions too close to their safehouse. Not to mention the possibility of one of their previous abusers using this program to find them. And we can't use the family stables and paddocks because the clients won't want to do sessions where anyone in the family could walk up and observe."

"But I thought you said they'd be doing their therapy sessions in groups?" Julie questioned her cousin, tilting her head as she looked at Josh, and trying not to act on the urge to press herself into Dion's side. "Won't they already be observed by the other people in the group? And even if you build a whole new secluded space for them, won't they still be at risk of being observed by the ranch hands or family members, who still have to take care of the horses, no matter where they are on the ranch?"

"Yes, some of the sessions are group sessions, but not all of them. And if we have a location designated as specifically for the program, with restrictions on who's allowed to be there and when, then we're not only less likely to have a HIPPA violation, but we're also less likely to have the clients walk in on a midday make-out session in the hay barn," Josh pointed out.

"Well, if you and Cait wouldn't go make out in the hay barn, then that wouldn't be a problem," Julie teased, knowing from her conversations with Cait that they'd first kissed in a hayloft on the ranch.

"No, we go make out in the baler barn," Josh grinned back. "That's why I had to build a new one, so we could turn the barn where we first kissed into our house."

"If it's not you and Cait, then who's been making out in the hay barn?" Julie was curious about what the ranch hands were up to when they thought nobody was watching, assuming they were the ones getting frisky in the middle of the day.

"You don't wanna know." Josh dramatically shuddered and made a gagging face.

"Oh, yeah, I do," Julie exclaimed, hoping it was the two cowboys she'd been rooting for getting together since she first saw them staring at each other while working with the horses earlier in the year.

"Yeah, you probably wouldn't care, since it wasn't your sister and brother-in-law I accidentally walked in on," Josh scoffed, apparently loud enough for his brother-in-law to hear him.

I probably wouldn't care if I walked in on Jen. Well, depending on who I caught her making out with, anyway.

"My bad." Ian raised his hands in a surrender position as he joined their conversation, causing Julie to need to shift closer to Dion to allow Ian into their circle. "I got the idea from seeing Bob and Hazel come out of there, and I didn't realize it was a space that had to be reserved to keep from being interrupted."

Oh, yeah, I'll definitely avoid the hay barn from now on. I absolutely do not wanna see Uncle Bob and Aunt Hazel making out. That would be as bad as walking in on Mom and Dad. Julie couldn't stop the whole body shudder at the thought. While theoretically she knew the older generation of her family had sex, and she actually liked how openly affectionate they were with their spouses, she was only cool with seeing the chaste kisses they shared publicly. She wanted no part of seeing them if tongues were involved or clothing started coming off.

"And I'm gonna tell you like I told my dad," Josh pointed at Ian. "I'm not taking reservations 'cause I don't wanna know when my family members get their freak on. So, from now on, make sure we've already got the hay we need that day before you go in there. And tie a bandana on the door knob, so everyone else knows not to go in there while you're gettin' busy."

Or just avoid the risk of getting hay stuck in intimate areas where it doesn't belong by avoiding the hay barn, like I'm gonna do from now on.

"Where is this hay barn?" Dion grinned at her as he launched a few questions at Josh. "How do I find out when you're done getting hay out of it for the day? And does it need to be a specific color bandana that we tie to the door?"

"I am not making out with you in the hay barn," Julie protested, though she wasn't sure why. With the smoldering look he gave her, all her female parts started to flutter, clamoring for her to drag him out to the hay barn right that moment. *No. Hay is itchy and rolling around in it is a great way to get eat up with chigger bites. So even sex with Dion's magic peen isn't amazing enough to be worth the risk.*

"Oh, I know we're not there yet, Cher," Dion assured her, softening his smile. "I'm just asking for future reference. Ya know, trying to be prepared for when the time comes that I don't have to lure you under the mistletoe to get a kiss."

Julie was just about to explain why she wouldn't be going to the hay barn with him when she realized he wasn't looking at her anymore. When he looked up and his grin widened, Julie realized she'd mistakenly moved in the wrong direction when Ian joined their discussion. She looked up, and sure enough, she was standing directly under the mistletoe.

Guess my libido is gonna get a little of its way today, after all. Julie had to admit, if only to herself, that she wasn't all that disappointed in the prospect of kissing Dion under the mistletoe. She just wouldn't tell him.

"Damn, Dion, I thought when I warned you not to play with my cousin, that it was implied that you wouldn't use me to trick her into anything." Josh slapped a hand on Dion's shoulder. "But I'm so impressed with that ballsy move that I'll gladly show you where the hay barn is when ya'll get to the point that ya wanna use it."

Dion didn't even act like he heard Josh as he moved closer to Julie, taking her hand, placing it over his heart, and dipping his head toward hers. "Relax, Jewel. It's just a sweet kiss under the mistletoe, not a marriage proposal."

Yet, she thought, knowing he implied the word with his eyes, even if he didn't actually say it. When he lifted her hand to his heart the way he always did when he wanted her to know how she affected him, she couldn't stop her instinctual reaction to him, lifting her lips to his as she felt his heartbeat quicken beneath her palm.

How can this still feel so right? So perfect? Shouldn't we need more time to rebuild our relationship before giving in and acting on our physical attraction?

Unable to wait a second longer, she slid her free hand up around his neck, pulling him down to her, as he cupped her face in his hands to position her for their kiss. The instant their lips touched for the first time in over two months, Julie felt as if the rest of the world disappeared.

He might have said it was just going to be a sweet mistletoe kiss, but the feel of his pillow-soft lips against hers made her crave something much more carnal. And in her little bubble of just the two of them, she didn't see any reason not to open her mouth to deepen the kiss and taste the candy cane he'd obviously eaten just before she arrived.

Dion responded with equal passion, his mint-flavored tongue delving into her mouth as he slid his hands down her neck, over her shoulders, and around her back to pull her body into his. She felt the solid length of his erection against her belly and wished she'd worn heels instead of flats so she could feel him closer to her core.

The sensation of him holding her in his arms again as their tongues tangled made her feel like she was finally home again. Like the piece of her soul that had slipped away over the past couple of months was finally back in place. Kissing Dion made her feel whole again in a way she could never explain.

But all too soon, the applause of her rude family members seeped into her subconscious, bringing her out of her bubble of bliss just before Dion broke off the kiss. She stood there in stunned silence as Dion pulled back from their all too brief embrace.

"Merry Christmas, Jewel."

"Merry Christmas, Dion." Julie wasn't sure her whispered words could be heard over the racket her family made to get everyone to take a seat for dinner. But she was still in such a stupor from the kiss that she couldn't speak any louder right then.

She found herself floating through the motions of joining the celebrations as she contemplated what that kiss meant for her and Dion. The year before, she would have thought it was just another kiss, and not really pivotal to anything changing between them. But after their brief break from their previously passionate love affair, she had to wonder if it signified a shift back out of the friend zone for them. Like the tingling in her lips afterward was her sign that they were officially a couple now, only this time around they weren't hiding the relationship.

Considering it wasn't just her family in attendance who'd witnessed their kiss, Julie assumed it would soon be common knowledge that they were back together. In addition to the Burlesons, Harpers, and Whitmans that always gathered for the holidays, and their passel of new significant others and children, this year they also had the Avingtons that had been added to the family, the Lawtons and Sinclairs that came to be there for Jerry and Jonah's first Christmas, the Lees and Hunters who were all, sort of, related by marriage through Kay and her sister Randi, and even Kay's best friend Deanna, who'd come down to attend all of Justin and Amy's wedding events. Not to mention Dion's brother and Mama Marcel.

Looking around the room that was packed practically wall-to-wall with tables and chairs to fit them all in there, Julie had to wonder if they might need to move all future holiday meals to the ballroom at the B and B to have enough space for all of them. *Gracious, and Becky, Jen, and Jake don't even have dates here today, much less families of their future spouses. Nor do any of our Avington, Harper, or Whitman cousins. Yeah, we're definitely going to need to move to a bigger space once we've all fallen in love and expanded the family.*

While technically JJ didn't have a significant other there either, Julie had already cast Deanna in that role, knowing her oldest brother wanted the woman to be his. *I wonder if he's going to tell her while she's down here visiting that we've been buying out her company for the last couple of months? Or if he's going to wait until we finalize the deal with the last stockholder before telling her?*

Either way, Julie found it much easier to get through the day by focusing on her brother's love life than on her own. Oh, she enjoyed the way Dion stuck by her side all afternoon, pulling out chairs for her and making sure she was comfortable when she had to move out of her seat to set up for the Grinch game. She even reached over and placed his hand on her belly when she felt some strong flutters of their babies' kicking, hoping he'd be able to feel them moving, too. But she stopped herself from thinking about whether or not that kiss meant they were now a couple.

I can worry about all that later. I'd rather grab some popcorn and watch the JJ and Deanna show while they're here together this week.

And yes, I'm gonna completely ignore the fact that I've apparently inherited my mother's matchmaking genes.

~~~

Dion wondered if he'd overstepped when he took advantage of Jewel stepping under the mistletoe hanging in the corner of the dining room to finally feel what it was really like to kiss her, instead of just remembering it in his dreams. *But damn, how was I supposed to resist her with that red dress showing off all her curves and her being so close that her fruity-floral scent brought back so many memories of being with her?* She seemed a little dazed afterward and almost zoned out, the same way he often did when he had flashes of memory, all through the meal they enjoyed. But she didn't balk at him pulling out
~~~

her chair or sitting beside her, though, so he figured he wasn't too out of line in starting to act like the doting boyfriend he wanted to be.

Technically, he wanted to be a whole lot more than her boyfriend, but it was currently the most appropriate word he could think of to describe the role he wanted in her life. He knew she wasn't ready to switch that title to fiancé or husband yet, so he was sticking with boyfriend, even though it felt wrong for someone his age to have such a juvenile title. *At least, it signifies a relationship with her and positions me as more than just her baby daddy.*

Once dinner was over, Hazel directed traffic to get all the dishes moved to the kitchen, and the first load run through the dishwasher, while the tables were moved to open up the space for the chairs to be put in a circle around the room for the strangest present exchange Dion had ever participated in before. The children and teenagers went first, sitting on the floor in the center of the circle of chairs, while the adults sat in the chairs and watched to learn how the Grinch game worked.

Dion made sure Jewel was comfortable when her face looked pained as they took their seats in the outer circle. "Everything okay, Jewel, uh, Julia?"

"Yeah, just thinking the kids are either playing soccer or practicing martial arts, instead of sleeping off the roast beast dinner like I kinda wanna do right now," she chuckled, reaching over to take his hand and place it on her belly.

He didn't feel any movement under his palm, but he enjoyed being able to touch her, so he left his hand there until she told him they'd stopped kicking. *Maybe Daddy calmed them down?* Not that he was gonna ask that out loud and potentially irritate Jewel.

As Jewel looked across the room at her brother and then over to the woman her brother seemed to be staring at on the other side of Anthony's wife, Dion turned to his right to look at Anthony and Bobby, who were each somehow wearing their babies on their chests. "Aren't you guys gonna get in there with the little ones?"

"Naw, this is for the bigger kids." Anthony spoke to Dion while making faces at his son, who was looking up at him and babbling incoherently. "Sam's still too little to play with board games and understand joke books."

"Oh, I bet the other kids will still read the joke books to him, if that's what they end up with at the end of the game," Jewel pointed out.

"True," Anthony chuckled. "But the game is more about enjoying the participation than getting a present, so he's gotta grow up big enough to participate on his own before he can join the other kids."

"And we opened plenty of presents for Maddie this morning that she won't remember, so we're too tuckered out to do more than watch now," Bobby added, running his hand over his sleeping daughter's head, which was sticking up out of what Dion could only describe as a tactical baby carrier.

"Is that some kinda Kevlar baby carrier, so you can take your daughter on patrol?" Dion couldn't stop himself from voicing the question as he compared the solid black baby carrier with D-rings for clipping stuff on the straps that Bobby wore with the fun cartoon airplane covered carrier Anthony wore.

"No, they don't make them out of Kevlar," Bobby pouted. "I looked, but this was the closest I could find."

"I still don't understand why he won't use the pink baby sling I prefer," Bobby's wife, Brooklyn, interjected with a mischievous grin.

"Probably because it's pink," Jewel huffed.

"No, it's because it's a big piece of material that has to be wrapped around weirdly and feels more like baby bondage than a safe way to carry her," Bobby protested.

Dion snorted at the image Bobby painted of the pink carrier, then turned to face Jewel. "If we have girls, I'll wear a pink version of one of these. But I agree with Bobby that I'm not into baby bondage."

"Oh, no, Big Daddy, you're not gonna get off easy with a single carrier like Anthony and Bobby," Kay giggled, addressing him with the nickname the GWA ladies had given him at Dean and Allissa's wedding, which he'd hoped everyone would have forgotten by now. "You're gonna hafta don a twin carrier like the one we got Justin."

Having not seen Justin use a carrier of any kind, Dion wasn't sure what Kay was talking about, but assumed it was a similar concept only designed to carry both babies at once.

"Maybe if Dion uses a twin carrier, he can show Justin that the babies are perfectly safe in it, so he'll actually start using theirs," Jewel's sister, Jen, scoffed as she pointed to where Justin and Amy were each holding one of their twins as they continued watching while Hazel read *How the Grinch Stole Christmas!* to the kids, who were passing presents around their circle.

Damn, I should probably be paying attention to know when we're supposed to pass the presents when it's the adults' turn to play this game.

"What's with the Big Daddy nickname?" Jewel's biting tone stole his focus away from the game before he could figure it out.

Oh, shit. I really don't wanna explain that conversation about my dick size in the middle of a family celebration like this.

"I think it's a GWA thing," Anthony interjected. "For as long as I've worked there, several of the women wrestlers have called him Big D."

"Then when he was the only guy with half the GWA women's division waiting to walk down the aisle at Allissa and Dean's wedding, we decided to change it to Big Daddy now that he's gonna be a daddy," Kay added. "And since he was walking Allissa down the aisle, sorta acting in the dad role for her, even though she'd just found her bio-dad."

"Why did they call you Big D?" Jewel eyed him curiously, clearly implying that she knew it was a dick reference.

Oh, fuck! I've obviously told her the real story before, but now I've gotta figure out how to retell a clean version while we're sitting in the middle of her family.

"Since Dare was a toddler and couldn't say Dion, I've always answered to D, 'cause that's what he called me. It sorta stuck, and eventually, pretty much everybody just called me D," Dion explained, slumping his shoulders at the realization that he was probably going to have to include the dick size reference made by the ring rats who were at the bar when the Big D nickname was first coined, even though he really hoped to avoid it, if possible. "Then when the Hunters first started working with the GWA, Dean and I both answered anytime someone called out for D. At the time, Dean hadn't bulked up as much as he is now, so I was the bigger of the two of us. One night while we were out after a show, someone suggested calling me Big D and using his name instead of just a letter, so there wouldn't be any more confusion."

"Wow, that's a whole different version of the story than the one you told me over a year ago, when I first asked you about the Big D nickname." Jewel clearly looked irritated at him.

"Yeah, well, I didn't think it was appropriate to mention with children present that it was in a bar after a show and first used by ring rats, who were referring to a specific part of my anatomy being big," Dion shrugged, whispering his words to hopefully keep the children from overhearing. "But if you must know everything, the ladies of the GWA opted to change it, so you wouldn't be offended by them continuing to make the reference to my Big D."

Thankfully, their conversation had to stop suddenly as the kid's version of the Grinch game concluded right then. As soon as the kids opened the presents they ended up with at the end of the game, most of them headed upstairs to enjoy them while the adults set up for their round. Apparently, the kids had more of a theme than just the gag gift Josh had told him for the adults, since they all opened some kind of game or book, instead of the toys Dion expected to see.

I guess that's because of the range of ages of the kids? So the older kids wouldn't be disappointed by getting stuck with a little kid's toy? Realizing that the cousins would all be playing those games with one another, it made sense to him that they'd all picked things that were appropriate for all ages. *Damn, maybe I shouldn't have picked that smartphone screen magnifier for my contribution to the gifts. I'm pretty sure I'm the only one here who kinda needs it while waiting on new glasses.*

Because of being distracted by their conversation while the kids played the game, Dion was lost about what to do after the presents were passed out to all the adults participating in the present exchange. While it seemed simple enough to pass the presents to the right whenever they heard the word "who" and to pass them to the left whenever they heard the word "grinch" as the story was read, actually following those directions quickly became difficult for him.

Part of him believed it was the comprehension issues he was having since his injury that caused the difficulty, knowing he was a few seconds behind everyone else in registering the words being read to the group. But with multiple people arguing over whether or not they were supposed to pass the presents when words were said that had "who" or "grinch" in them, like "Whoville," he also realized that having too much sensory information trying to enter his brain at once was also becoming a problem.

Needless to say, Dion felt overwhelmed rather quickly, starting once again to feel the warning signs of an impending blackout. His lips tingled and started to feel numb as his eyelids drooped and the room around him started fuzzing out.

"I can't do this. I need to *lay* down." He was proud of himself for still thinking to use Jewel's preferred word instead of the correct one, as he recognized that he was mumbling the words. But it seemed to be hitting him fast this time, so he didn't have time to determine if she'd recognized the change or not. He was worried that if he didn't hand off the package in his hands and lie down on the floor in front of his chair, he'd either drop the present, or fall out of the chair, or both.

"I got you, Big Daddy." Jewel smiled at him as she turned in her seat to face him, taking the package from his hands, and directing him to place his hands on her belly. "I'll take care of passing the presents. You just focus on feeling our babies moving."

Dion followed her instructions to turn in his seat and put both of his hands on her belly, keeping his eyes glued to the places he touched her as she continued to pass the presents back and forth between her sister on their left and her cousin Bobby on their right.

"Apparently, they wanna play this game by kicking the presents around the circle," she joked, smiling at him as he finally felt the little ripples beneath her skin that she'd been trying to describe to him since their appointment with Dr. Magnum at the beginning of the month.

Still feeling like he needed to lie down, Dion leaned forward and rested his forehead on the curve of her belly, which was finally starting to look rounder, instead of the football shape he thought her baby bump resembled a month earlier. He wasn't sure if he actually went out or not, having some of the symptoms of not being able to move or speak for a few minutes after the fuzzy, need-to-lie-down feeling started to pass, while not feeling like he'd completely lost consciousness or forgotten the events leading up to the spell like he usually did.

"You can stay there lovin' on our little ones as long as you need to, Big Daddy," Jewel assured him as she passed presents from hand to hand over his back, surprising him by continuing to use the moniker.

Maybe touching Jewel and feeling our babies moving inside her is just as healing as when she touched me to stop the episode that I almost had at the wedding last month?

Dion stayed where he was as the numbness and tingling in his lips started to fade, and the rest of the adults in the room finished up the Grinch game. He registered Jewel resting their two presents on his back, since she couldn't exactly open them, or move to put them down anywhere else, while he was still hunched over in her lap and clinging to her belly. With him still unable to move or speak, she had to answer their family members as several of them took a moment to check on him.

As everyone started to give them space by mingling around the room, Jewel lightly stroked his back around the presents she'd sat on him. Her gentle touch comforted him, as he focused on his breathing to try to get the spell to pass faster.

"You okay, D?" Jewel's softly cooed words as she bent down to kiss the top of his head brought him completely back from his episode.

"Yeah, I'm better now." Dion smiled at her as he slowly sat up, lifting his head and hands from her belly now that the babies seemed to have settled down once more. "Thank you, Jewel, uh, Julia. I'm sorry if I caused a scene. But you giving me something special to focus on really did help keep me from hitting the floor and causing an even bigger one."

"No problem," she grinned, handing him the gift in her right hand. "Now let's open these presents and see what we ended up with."

They each tore into the wrapping paper with gusto, laughing when Dion ended up with a pair of lightsaber chopsticks and Jewel ended up with an eight-in-one kitchen tool set.

"Yeah, I might need to trade with someone for this to get used," Jewel laughed.

"I'll trade with you and use 'em," Dion offered with a smile. "But you've gotta keep them at your house for me to come over and cook for you and the babies."

"Deal," Jewel grinned, taking the chopstick box from his hand while still holding onto the kitchen tool set. "I need to see just how well you remember the cooking lessons Mama Marcel gave you."

"If he has forgotten, I'll give him a refresher," Mama Marcel insisted, running a hand over his head as she stood beside them.

"Were you able to completely beat it this time? Or do we need to take you back to the B and B to lie down?"

"I'm good, Mama Marcel," Dion assured his adoptive mother, smiling up at her from his seated position. "Julia and our babies gave me something else to focus on until that overwhelmed and anxious feeling passed." His smile widened as he elaborated. "And I felt our babies move for the first time."

"Oh, Dion, how wonderful," Mama Marcel gushed at him before turning to Jewel. "Are they still moving? Can I feel it too?"

"They're slowing down, like maybe they're ready for a nap, but you're welcome to try to feel them," Jewel offered, turning to allow Mama Marcel to place her hands on her baby bump.

"Alright now, girls, I know you're tired after kicking your daddy to keep him awake, but surely one of you still has the energy to say hi to Mama Marcel." Caroline grinned mischievously before adding. "Come on now, Zoe Caroline, you're gonna be named after me, so I know you're spunky enough to kick my hand. Ah, there it is! What about you Elena? Can you kick my other hand? Or do I need to move it to a better position for you? Oh, wow! Even stronger than your sister. Yep, you're definitely gonna be just as tough as your namesake."

"What's this about namesakes?" Susan interjected, ready to get in on the baby feeling action. "Have you finally decided on names?"

"Just a couple," Jewel admitted sheepishly as her mother's hands replaced Mama Marcel's on her stomach. "But I still need middle names to go with Elena and Dillon."

Dillon? That's a name I don't think she's mentioned before.

"But you have middle names to go with the others you've picked?" Jen joined the conversation, along with a few of the other women in Jewel's family.

"Zoe Caroline is the other girl's name she picked," Mama Marcel boasted, smiling brightly.

"And what's the other boy's name you've picked?" Susan inquired, arching an eyebrow at Jewel.

"Dion Devereaux, like his daddy," Jewel smiled at him. "I'm just not sure if he'll be a junior or not, since I'm planning on hyphenating the babies' last names."

"You want to name our son after me?" Dion was surprised, thinking that might mean she was readier to move their relationship forward than he thought.

Jewel only nodded as Mama Marcel spoke before she could answer him. "Little Dion Junior will have to wait 'til the next pregnancy, 'cause you're having two girls this time."

Her prediction sparked a discussion among the women about Mama Marcel predicting how many babies each of them would have in the future, as well as whether they'd be boys or girls. Dion just sat there observing, trying to picture life with the two girls and then two boys Mama Marcel predicted for him and Jewel.

If she wants to name one of our sons after me, then we really should name one of our daughters after her. Elena Julia? Elena Elizabeth? Elena Jewel? No, I've got it. Elena Juliette. That way it means little Julie, but it isn't exactly like her name, which I know she'll reject. Now I just have to figure out how to convince her of that before the babies are born in a few months.

After a couple more hours of visiting and raiding the dessert table that was somehow set up when Dion didn't notice, the party started breaking up. With several of the people leaving the ranch headed to the bed and breakfast, Dion decided he wanted to hang back and let the road clear, while he finally got Jewel alone to give her the gift he'd been carrying in his pocket all day.

"May I walk you home, Julia?" While he wanted to speak to her privately to give her the Christmas present, Dion hoped he wouldn't have to tell her why he wanted to get her alone while several of her family members were still milling about.

"Sure, but I'm carrying the presents myself," Jewel insisted, holding up the two small boxes between them. "Combined, they're lighter than the wine-bottle puzzle I brought over for the gift exchange, so they're not too heavy for me to carry while pregnant."

Dion raised his hands in surrender as he smiled at his feisty woman. "While I want to take care of you by opening doors, pulling out chairs, and carrying things for you, I would never insult your strength as a woman by insisting on doing any of those things when you'd rather do them yourself."

"In that case, I'll let you carry the Tupperware containers of leftovers that Mom and Aunt Hazel are packing up for me in the kitchen," she smiled at him, pointing him toward the kitchen to grab the leftovers.

"Wow, I'm surprised there was enough left over to divide up like that," Dion chuckled as they walked into the kitchen, knowing he wasn't the only one who'd gorged like a pig all day.

"Oh, yeah, Mom and Aunt Hazel always make sure we cook enough for each person to have at least five servings of everything, knowing with the way we go back and nibble all day, and how the guys double up serving sizes from the get-go, we'd run out of food otherwise," Jewel explained as she stacked several containers in Dion's arms. "Only when they do a head count to figure out how much to make, they count the babies and children as if they're gonna eat as much as a grown man, so we always end up with leftovers."

"That's not true," Hazel contradicted, shaking her head as she sorted more Tupperware containers to go back to the other houses on the ranch. "We never have leftovers of the daily meals we cook for the bunkhouse."

"That's because the hands are all grown folk, who all eat five times the amount of a normal person," Jewel teased her aunt, grinning as she leaned over to give her a one-armed hug.

"And as your babies grow up, you'll realize that they will too sometimes, especially during growth spurts and their teenage years, so we won't always have this much left over to send home with you," Hazel countered, grinning as she returned her niece's embrace before turning to direct her next comment to Dion. "Since you don't have a way to reheat stuff in your room at the B and B, we put your share of leftovers in with Julie's. So, make sure she invites you over this weekend to help her finish them off."

"Yes, ma'am," Dion grinned, glad to have the support of the local matchmakers to help him start trying to take their relationship to the next level. "But if you don't mind, I'm gonna wait 'til we're alone to actually ask her on a date."

"Oh, no, don't do that," Hazel advised him. "You need to ask her in front of a crowd, so she can't turn you down."

"But if we're alone and she says yes, then I'll know she really wants to go out with me, and isn't just saying yes to save face," Dion countered with a sardonic smile. "And if she says no, then I won't be embarrassed in front of a bunch of people, which might trigger one of my blackout spells, kinda like my confusion did during the gift exchange earlier."

"Oh, dear, I wondered what happened." Hazel tilted her head as she gave him a sympathetic smile. "Was it because Tia was reading too fast? Or because so many people were talking at once?"

"Probably a combination of both," Dion shrugged. "But hopefully, all the different tests I did the last couple of weeks will help the doctors come up with a better diagnosis and treatment plan, so being overwhelmed and anxious won't trigger me to pass out like that anymore." He smiled gratefully and nodded at Jewel. "And in the meantime, I just need to hang out with Jewel all the time, so I can stop an episode by focusing on her and our babies."

"Geez, you make me sound like some kind of emotional support animal, like the PTSD dogs some people need to keep from having panic attacks in public," Jewel giggled, grinning mischievously. "Do I have to wear one of those vests that label me as an emotional support human?"

"No," Dion chuckled, shaking his head at her silliness. "Even though I'd definitely prefer kisses from you over having a dog lick my face to calm me down, I don't think my insurance covers emotional support humans."

"Well, good, 'cause I wouldn't want a job where I was paid in kibble anyway," Jewel teased, still grinning. "And I'll still provide the service if we ever go on one of these dates you're hinting at asking me about."

"Well, then ya'll better head on out, so you can ask her on all those dates." Hazel grinned with an impish gleam in her eyes as she shooed them out of her kitchen, so she could continue passing out leftovers to the rest of the family members who'd started filling up the space.

They said several "good evenings" as they made their way through the people still milling about to get to the front of the house. Then they walked quietly side by side across the lawn and driveway to the big brick Queen Anne style home she'd recently moved into. Jewel's house wasn't as big as the plantation style home her aunt and uncle lived in. But with the attic space finished out for a full third story, it was probably twice as big as the Creole townhouse style building Dion lived in back in New Orleans.

Dion juggled the food containers in his hands to open the front door for her, smiling sheepishly when she reminded him that the door was always unlocked. "I know you have the security gate and all, but are you sure it's really safe for you to live here alone without locking your doors?"

"Positive," Jewel assured him as she preceded him into the house. "In addition to the rifle that Dad and Uncle Bob insisted I learn how to use and strap onto my saddle when I go trail riding, I also have a thirty-eight special in my bedside table. So, I'm prepared if someone's dumb enough to get past our security gates and try breaking in."

"I wouldn't call someone capable of getting past the security on the gates, dumb," Dion pointed out, chuckling skeptically as he followed her down the lavender hallway to the kitchen. "Criminal or psychotic, maybe, but I'd think it would take someone with some smarts to get past the security stuff your cousins were talking about earlier."

"No, dumb is the right word," Jewel disagreed with a grin as she opened the fridge and took the first container off the stack in his arms to put it away. "Technologically savvy, maybe, to get past everything Bobby and Jake put in after that reporter climbed the fence back in January. But still dumb to try to break into one of the houses on the ranch. Ya know, since there's at least two guns in every one of them, and most everyone over the age of twelve who lives here has been taught how to properly use them."

"So, does never having touched a gun in my life disqualify me from being allowed to live here one day?" Dion wondered aloud. "Or will your dad teach me, so I can eventually go along with his plan to move in here with you and our babies?"

"Naw, unless you plan on working with the cattle or going on long, solo trail rides, you shouldn't ever have to deal with snakes or coyotes. So, there's no need for you to learn to shoot." Jewel smiled brightly as she finished putting the food away. "And if we ever get to the point where you move in here, you can count on me to protect you from intruders or rogue wildlife."

"Good to know." Dion grinned back at her, not wanting to point out why he'd been taught to steer clear of guns as a Black boy growing up in the city. Instead, he changed the subject, reaching into his pocket to take out her present. "I, um, have a Christmas present for you, but didn't figure you'd wanna open it in front of everyone, ya know, since it wasn't part of the Grinch game."

"Oh, Dion, you didn't have to do that," Jewel protested as he handed her the small box. She placed it on the counter and turned to walk out of the kitchen. "But I did pick up something from the babies for you, too. Wait right there and let me get your present, so we can open them at the same time."

When she came back, she handed Dion a green gift bag with red tissue paper sticking out the top. As she picked up the box with the necklace in it, he felt a little bad at how much nicer her gift bag looked compared to his poor wrapping job.

"I guess I should have left it in the car, instead of carrying it in my pocket all day," he supposed, noticing the wrapping paper looked a little worn on the edges.

"Oh, but if you'd done that, then I wouldn't have these easy spots to tear the paper off," Jewel giggled as she quickly unwrapped the black flip-top box that was just big enough that he didn't think it looked like a ring box. Though from the look in her eyes when she saw the jeweler's logo embossed in the top of the box, Dion wondered if Jewel had the mistaken impression that it was a ring box. "Oh, Dion, what did you do?"

Yeah, I probably shouldn't mention that the engagement ring she thinks is in that box is currently being made and just waiting on two of those stones to be finished once the babies are born. Dion pulled the tissue paper from the gift bag to keep his hands occupied as he figured out how to respond to her question. He recognized that there was something long and flat wrapped in more tissue paper in the bag, but he didn't pull it out yet, opting to focus on her gift first.

"Relax, Jewel. I'm not down on one knee, so you don't have to worry about me proposing before you're ready," Dion assured her as he reached out and flipped the box open to reveal the Caged-Hearts necklace laying on the black velvet insert in the bottom of the box. "It's a mother's necklace, or in this case a family necklace, since two of the emeralds are our birthstones. The other two emeralds and the two diamonds are for the babies. I just didn't know if they needed to be the April birthstone or the May birthstone. So, I had the jeweler put in both, and we can have the incorrect stones removed once they're born."

"It's beautiful," Jewel gushed as she placed the box on the counter to remove the necklace. "But the jeweler isn't going to take back two of the stones so many months later, especially if I wear it daily like I'm thinking."

"No, but she's more than willing to set them in another piece of jewelry." Hoping to get her to drop the subject to keep from revealing that he'd already worked with the jeweler in town, Harmony, to design her engagement ring, Dion pulled the tissue wrapped present from the gift bag and unwrapped it.

"Oh, yeah, and with it being two stones, we could do heart shaped earrings to match the necklace."

She'd had three of the ultrasound pictures she'd texted him blown up and framed in a triptych with the twins together in the middle and their individual photos on either side. "Oh, wow, this is amazing. Thank you, Julia."

"You're welcome," Jewel smiled and held up the necklace he got her. "Will you help me put this on?"

"Of course." Dion placed the triptych back in the gift bag. Then he took the necklace from her hand and motioned for her to turn around, so he could put it around her neck.

Jewel grinned as she spun around and lifted her hair off her neck.

Dion felt like he had two left hands as he fumbled with the clasp until he got it hooked.

"Thank you," she grinned as she turned back to face him, clutching the heart in her hand. "I love it. And since it's a family necklace, I'm guessing you really are planning to ask me out, like you told Aunt Hazel?"

"I am," Dion nodded. "I want us to date like a normal couple, instead of the friends-with-benefits thing we did before. But before I ask you on that first date, I want you to know that the babies make us a family, even if you never want to go out with me again. So, you're stuck with my heart in your necklace, whether you agree to go out with me or not."

"I'm not stuck, Dion." Jewel released the charm on her necklace to place her hand over his heart.

Just like before, when he kissed her under the mistletoe, her hand on his chest triggered another memory of kissing Jewel, making him wonder if he'd always placed her hand there right before kissing her.

"And I'd love to go out with you," Jewel continued, bringing him back to the moment before he could finish kissing her in his head. "But it can't be this weekend. We've got Justin and Amy's rehearsal dinner Friday night and their wedding and reception on Saturday night. Then Josh and Cait's wedding on Sunday night."

Dion hadn't heard anything about Josh and Cait's wedding, so Jewel quickly filled him in on her cousin's plans to propose and marry his girlfriend on the one-year anniversary of the day they met.

"How about New Year's Eve, then?" While he hated the thought of waiting that long to go on their first official date, he hoped he'd at least be able to sit with her at the various wedding events over the weekend to get his Jewel fix until their first official date night.

"We can call New Year's Eve our first official date if you want," Jewel smiled and shrugged. "But I've already bought my dress for the New Year's Eve formal at the B and B, so we'll have to do the date there in front of my whole family and half the town."

"As long as I get to kiss you at midnight, I don't care who else is there," Dion assured her as he took her in his arms. "But maybe we should plan a regular Saturday date night, at least on the Saturdays when there aren't weddings we're already going to, so we can get away from both our families for a little bit."

"I can get behind a regular Saturday date night," Jewel agreed, pushing up on her tiptoes as she wound her arms around his neck. "Now kiss me goodnight and go back to the B and B before your brother and Mama Marcel come looking for you and interrupt us."

"Yes, ma'am." Dion bent his head and took her lips in a passionate kiss, wishing he could carry her up to her bedroom and make love to her all night long. Knowing she wasn't ready for that just yet, though, he maintained control and kept the kiss much shorter and less carnal than he longed for, releasing her, and taking a step back to keep from pushing past her boundaries. He bent down and brushed his lips over both sides of her belly, whispering to their babies, "Merry Christmas, babies. Daddy loves you."

Dion then stood, smiled at his astonished woman, and wished her a "Merry Christmas, Jewel," before picking up his Christmas gift from her, turning, and leaving. He wanted to tell her he loved her too, but he knew she wasn't ready to hear it again just yet.

Leah Mae Wright

But I guarantee, we won't make it past Valentine's Day before we're both saying "I love you" all the time again. And hopefully, it won't take us that long to start making love again.

Fuck! I hope Dare and Mama Marcel are ready to go to our separate rooms when we get to the B and B, so I can deal with this erection I've been fighting to hide all day.

Chapter Fifteen

Friday, December 27, 2019

Julie hadn't been able to stop thinking about the kisses she'd shared with Dion on Christmas. She knew from feeling his rigid length against her belly, both times they'd kissed, that she wasn't the only one of them affected by their flirtatious behavior all day. That made her curious about whether or not he'd gone back to his room at the bed and breakfast to jerk off, the same way she'd practically run up to her bedroom to use her vibrator as soon as he left. She might be telling herself that she wanted to take things slow with him this time around, but that didn't stop her from daydreaming about what could happen if they went back to the warp speed that their previous relationship had progressed.

If only he hadn't had to meet up with his family to go back to the B and B...

Julie had to stop herself from fantasizing about what might have happened with Dion if he'd come upstairs with her on Christmas. She needed to focus and pay attention to what was being said in the Burleson Incorporated board meeting, where she was currently sitting.

Since she'd chosen the business diversification and asset management path for her career, she knew her father considered her the most likely of their generation to step into the CEO role when he and Uncle Bob retired. Technically, her dad and uncle were currently considered the co-CEOs and co-Presidents of the company. Until Pappaw Jerry passed away, they'd been co-Presidents, with Jon running the oil division, Bob running the beef division, and Pappaw Jerry as CEO overseeing everything. When it came time for them to retire — or God-forbid, pass on — she assumed each of her siblings and cousins who were currently vice presidents of the various divisions of the company would be promoted to presidents of their divisions. But since her "division" assisted all the other divisions of the company, she had the vast experience to fill the CEO role more than any of her siblings or cousins, who'd previously focused on only one aspect of the diverse company.

Her twin was the only other member of the family who dealt with as many different divisions of the company as she did. But Jen claimed to never want to leave the human resources department, so Julie doubted Jen would want to step into the role, even as her co-CEO. Which meant Julie really needed to be on the ball in every board meeting to show the rest of her siblings and cousins her competency for being able to take on that role one day. Though she wished she wouldn't have to step into it for another twenty-plus years, and only with her dad and uncle deciding to retire before tragedy struck like with Pappaw Jerry, with Jon and Bob Burleson turning sixty in just a few months, she knew it might be much sooner than she hoped.

"We're in final negotiations with the last shareholder in OK Oil," her brother JJ informed the board. "I'll be flying to Tulsa on January first to meet with him at nine a.m. on the second. I hope to finalize the deal by the weekend to be able to take over operations on Monday the sixth."

While Julie normally took the lead in any negotiations for buying other companies for all the other divisions of Burleson Incorporated, her oldest brother was a bit too much of a control freak to let her handle anything for the energy division. At least, that was what she called him whenever she teased him about not needing her help. Truth be told, he'd been working for the company for a couple of years before her job was created for her when she graduated from college, and even though he was only the VP of the fuel department of Burleson Oil at first, their dad had started teaching him everything he needed to know to take over running the entire oil division when Pappaw Jerry passed away and their father and uncle moved up to co-CEOs, including the procedures for procuring other oil related businesses. So JJ considered these contract negotiations as part of the job he'd been doing all along and didn't hand them over to her like the other division heads had when she started.

"I will be working from the Tulsa office for at least a couple of months as we transition OK Oil into Burleson Energy," JJ continued, laying out a few more specifics of how he intended to set up a management team in Tulsa and personally oversee their training while the company they were purchasing went through a top to bottom rebranding.

Julie knew that all the stuff JJ had planned for OK Oil could easily be handled from his office here in Texas, the same way he'd handled similar acquisitions in the past, sending his team of managers to handle the day-to-day operations of a new asset. But she also knew her brother was planning to take advantage of working in the same office as Deanna Wolfe to finally stake his claim on the woman, which was why he insisted on personally overseeing this one. If she hadn't seen the sparks flying between her oldest brother and Kay's best friend every time Deanna came to town over the last year-plus, she'd be worried JJ was setting himself up for a sexual harassment lawsuit.

Hopefully, JJ's plan will work and he'll finally win Deanna over, she thought. While the older woman had come off as a little abrasive the first time she came to town, Julie had come to like her as she'd lowered her walls a little more each time she visited her bestie. Seeing her laughing and relaxing and being "Aunt Dee" to all the Burleson kids at Christmas, as well as coming out of her shell with the other women in town at the book club meeting they'd had on Monday evening, really made Julie hopeful of having Deanna as a sister-in-law one day. *If they can't make a relationship work while working together daily, then maybe they can both finally screw each other out of their systems, so they can both move on to find their happily ever afters.*

Regardless of whether JJ and Deanna ended up together, Julie wanted both of them to find someone they could love and live a fulfilling life with, while being as joyously happy as she was with Dion.

Geez! A few kisses and some sappy texts to plan a couple of dates and I'm starting to sound as bad as my mother with the matchmaking. Julie absentmindedly played with the heart-shaped cage charm enclosing the heart-shaped birthstones representing her, Dion, and their babies. *We just agreed to date, not get married. Shouldn't I wait*

Leah Mae Wright

to see if we can make it work before I start wanting all my family and friends to find the same kind of love?

Julie shook herself out of her mental rabbit hole as JJ finished speaking, and Becky took over updating everyone on the progress being made by the entertainment division. After informing them that the first couple of Burleson Entertainment movies had wrapped filming, and that post-production was on track for summer releases, Becky outlined the various projects they were working on and what stage of production they were in for the rest of the first ten films they were planning to make.

"And to appease Mom, I invited the producer, director, and location manager for **Heart's Desire** to scout locations in Heart's Destiny for filming, specifically for the ranching scenes," Becky continued after explaining that the movie based on Kay and Brooklyn's first co-written book was in the pre-production phase. "And they surprised me by arriving at my office, while I was driving in for this meeting, instead of waiting until the first week of January like I expected."

"Should we call and warn Ma that they'll be coming by the ranch?" Bobby smirked and chuckled. "Or let them surprise her when she's in the middle of cookin'?"

"I actually have Ashlyn showing them to the B and B and around town while I'm here, and was planning to wait until Monday to show them the ranch," Becky elaborated as she shook her head at her brother. "Ya know, since both Mom and Aunt Susan are probably up to their eyeballs in last-minute wedding prep, and we don't wanna turn them loose to wander around where they shouldn't on the ranch."

Oh, I wonder how she plans to deal with maintaining the privacy of the Ashbury House on the ranch while bringing in film crews?

"Since they'll be staying at the B and B, be sure to extend invitations to the wedding reception tomorrow night," Justin instructed Becky, effectively changing the subject before Julie could pose her question.

"And Sunday night," Josh added with a grin.

"Will do," Becky nodded. "And don't be surprised if they show up at the rehearsal dinner tonight, too."

"So, our mothers will have three opportunities to match you up with them before you even show them the ranch as a possible location for filming?" Julie couldn't help but chuckle at how Becky's attempt to control the Matchmaking Mommas' access to the newcomers in town to prevent being set up seemed to be backfiring on her.

"Well, actually, according to the texts I've gotten from Cait and Nico, I think I'm safe for now." Becky seemed to relax back in her chair as she continued. "The producer is an older man and happily married, traveling with his husband. Ashlyn has called dibs on the director, and they were apparently flirting like crazy during their time in the office this morning. So, obviously, I'll have to tell Mom all about the chemistry between them to make sure the matchmaking is focused on them. But, then again, the location manager is a beautiful, single woman, so I expect they'll still try to fix her up with one of ya'll." Becky motioned toward the single male members of the family as she finished her explanation.

Oh, wow, my conniving cousin obviously hand-picked the people she invited to town. And since she doesn't seem to care that the only single male around our age is showing an interest in Ashlyn, I'm guessing she's met him before and knew she didn't have any chemistry with him.

"Yeah, I'm definitely stopping by the bakery on the way home to ask Kara to be my fake-date for all future weddings and stuff where they might try more of their matchmaking," Jake grumbled.

Julie stifled a laugh, knowing Jake was setting himself up for a fake-dating trope whenever Kay got around to writing the story of "Joe Brown" and "Kiki Thomas" in her **Devine** series. *Oh, pluck a duck! I bet, now that I'm openly dating Dion, her next book is gonna be about Jaelyn Brown and Dwayne Devoe.*

While Julie loved her cousins-in-law and appreciated their talent as writers, she really had to mentally distance herself from the characters in their books because they both seemed to base their characters on people they knew. It was much easier with the historical series they wrote together because changing their names was enough to keep her from seeing her third-great-grandparents, especially since she knew Kay and Brooklyn had no way of verifying that the sex scenes were accurate. It was a lot harder for her to read the contemporary series that Kay was writing, however. Yeah, her cousin-in-law still changed the names, and even the name of the town, but the characters and stories were all very clearly based on the people who lived in Heart's Destiny and worked with the GWA, Julie included.

Kissing Kat, the first book in the ***Devine*** series, was obviously Kay and Anthony's love story, only packaged as Katrina and Anton to give them a bit of anonymity to people outside their community. ***Winning Rhonda***, the second book in the series, was obviously based on Kay's sister, Randi, and James Hunter's story, only changing their names to Rhonda and Jack. And Kay hadn't stopped with basing her books on just her and her sister. No, she'd continued the series with ***Ronnie's Runaway***, which was obviously based on Bobby and Brooklyn, only renamed as Ronnie and Bethany, ***Jazzed for Jamie***, telling Justin and Amy's story using the names Jason and Jamie, ***Claiming Carlita*** for Charlotte and Ian as Carlita and Micah, and her current work in progress, ***Joking with Jeff*** with Josh and Cait portrayed as Jeff and Corina. As one of Kay's alpha readers, Julie had really had to concentrate to picture the characters as strangers, so she didn't get grossed out by enjoying a hot sex scene with characters based on her family members and friends.

At least Julie knew from talking with Brooklyn, Amy, Charlotte, and Cait that Kay had made up most everything in the books, only loosely basing the character descriptions on the real people and only pairing them up with the characters based on the real people they fell for after they officially came out as couples. Julie didn't mind knowing that Jaelyn Brown was her book doppelganger, but she was a little worried about possibly reading Kay's ideas about her sex life with Dion in a future book.

I'm not sure if I want to be one of her alpha readers for that book or not. On the one hand, I could correct anything she gets really wrong about describing Dion in the buff. But if she has a spot-on description of his dick, I might have a coronary from wondering when and how she gained that knowledge.

"Julie, can you help me understand our options for diversifying the services we offer through Avington Security?" Byron Avington brought Julie out of her mental ramblings by specifically speaking to her, after updating the board on the revenue brought in by his subsidiary of the family business.

"Possibly." Julie nodded at her cousin, whom her siblings and Burleson cousins referred to as Uncle Byron because of him only being a few years younger than their dads. "It depends on how you want to diversify. What all do you offer now? And what do you want to expand to offer? Would it be best to learn the ins and outs of those things and offer them with your current staff? Or hire new staff? Or would it be better to purchase a company that already offers those things and merge it into your current business model?"

"Well, when I first started the business, I worked mostly as a consultant with various law enforcement agencies. Then, when the boys joined me in the business, we expanded to doing bodyguard work and corporate security. Now we've got teams to handle a lot of that and the boys help me with the law enforcement side of things," Byron explained, giving her a brief history lesson on Avington Security that she'd heard before when they first merged the Avington family business with Burleson Incorporated, instead of outright answering her questions. "Since we're under the Burleson umbrella now, I'd like to move the Avington headquarters somewhere between here and Heart's Destiny. And while we're doing that, I'd like to purchase enough land to build a training facility. Instead of us working for a bunch of different corporations and handling payroll for the security guards at all of them, I want to train the teams that the corporations hire and pay themselves. I also want to be able to train our bodyguard teams better by running through different scenarios they might run into while working with high-profile private clients. And if we can find a plot of land big enough to set up a few different kinds of training spaces, I want to be able to train hostage rescue teams from various law enforcement agencies, so my boys can quit going on those risky missions."

"And there's not a company you have your eye on that's already doing these kinds of training?" Julie hadn't looked into security training businesses in the past, but she made a mental note to research them when she got back to her office.

"No, there's several places that cover the basic training to get licensed to provide security, but they don't cover the tactical training like we got in the Navy," Byron clarified.

"You thinking about setting up for mission specific training like we did when going in for HVTs with the SEALs?" Josh leaned in, obviously curious about the training programs Byron wanted to offer.

"If we can find enough land." Byron nodded enthusiastically. "That's not something we could do in Atlanta. But I'm thinking we might be able to find five hundred or a thousand acres here that would be perfect for setting up all kinds of scenarios, kind of like a studio lot out in Hollywood, but for military-type training, instead of making movies."

"I don't know," Julie's dad drawled, shaking his head as his brow furrowed in thought. "Plots of land that size tend to stay in families for generations around here."

"The old Gruber farm is going up for auction next month, which I guess is technically next week now," Bobby interjected. "And I can't think of a better place to train people in hostage rescue than someplace we've actually rescued hostages from before."

Charlotte shuddered in her seat as she turned to glare at her brother, probably not feeling comfortable with the reference to where she was held hostage back in April. "While I personally don't want to step foot on that land anytime soon, it would be nice to know it's being used to help fight the cartels and rescue other women and children that are being trafficked."

"How much land is included?" Byron turned to Bobby to ask the question, since he was the one who knew about the auction. "I know we parked a half mile from the house and were already on the farm, but I didn't hear any mention of how many acres they had."

"It's right at five thousand acres, mostly former wheat and corn fields, that the family had sold to what they thought was a corporate farming operation," Bobby explained. "I'm sure that's why it's taken so long for the feds to release it for auction, 'cause they had to double check that there weren't other things being grown in the fields."

"They cleaned up any illegal substances being grown out there, I hope," Julie mused aloud, not wanting to have the company hit with fines or legal issues if they purchased the land.

"Oh, yeah," Bobby nodded. "All seized by the D. E. A."

"You think they'd divide it up?" Byron inquired. "That's quite a bit more land than I think we'll need. And it would be expensive to resod it, so we don't end up with plants growing back that we don't want."

"Everything I've seen has it listed as one parcel," Bobby shrugged. "And the only other commercial property on the auction list for the first Friday of next month is a warehouse on a five-acre lot in San Antonio."

"If we were to purchase it as a Burleson Incorporated property, could we subdivide it between the different subsidiaries and divisions?" Josh spoke up, obviously thinking the agricultural division of Burleson, which he headed up, could use the farmland that the Avingtons didn't have plans for using. "And maybe sell off a section to a charitable organization?"

"You thinking of doing the equestrian therapy out there?" Julie inquired of her cousin. *Maybe that won't be an option for Dion after all, since it's not exactly close to the B and B for him to be able to get a ride there once Darius and Mama Marcel go back to New Orleans.*

"Some of it," Josh confirmed. "The Edwardses can still work with us at the family stable and the Ashbury Foundation group in the south stables and paddocks. But to protect their safety, it's better to work with the other patients somewhere separate from the ranch. Which means, Horsing Around is gonna hafta buy some land, build the necessary facilities, and then buy a few retired horses before the Edwardses can treat more than the Ashbury group, and whichever members of our family that need it, with equine therapy."

Oh, maybe Dion can still work with them on the ranch then? Julie mused, thinking she'd ask Josh about it after the meeting to be sure. *Dion did say the babies make us family, even if we don't end up together. But I don't know if Josh or their therapists will agree.*

"Horsing Around?" Jen chuckled at Josh. "That's what you're naming your foundation?"

"Seems like the perfect name for an equine therapy foundation, don't ya think?" Josh grinned.

Yep, especially for one started by Jokester Josh. And hopefully, that family option will be open to Dion. Surely, his link to the babies is enough to qualify, right? So we don't have to get married before he can do his therapy sessions on the ranch? And he can continue to do it there, even if we don't keep dating in the future.

"We could probably use some of it for a studio lot for the entertainment division, too," Becky interjected, obviously realizing the film production on the ranch would be an issue for the Ashbury House residents without anyone else having to mention it. "Mom probably won't like it as much as having them film on the ranch, but starting with a clean slate like that would be better than trying to disguise the more modern aspects of our homes and ranching facilities to use them for filming a movie set in the eighteen-hundreds. Plus, we won't have to worry about trying to maintain the privacy of the Ashbury House residents."

Julie shook off all thoughts of things not working out for her and Dion as she tried to focus on helping plan for how that land could be divided for use by the different divisions of Burleson Incorporated. She might be setting herself up for another broken heart, but she was determined to remain optimistic about their future as a couple. *But since our sexual connection was always the strongest aspect of our relationship, maybe we should start taking advantage of it to solidify our foundation?*

~~~

Since he wasn't in the bridal party, Dion felt a little strange walking into the rehearsal dinner for Justin and Amy. Yeah, Jewel had specifically mentioned it to him, and Mama Marcel had confirmed they'd all been invited. But it still seemed strange to have dinner with all the wedding guests, instead of just the people who had to participate in the rehearsal and their closest family members.

As he looked around the room to find Jewel, Dion wondered if his unease had less to do with feeling out of place than it did with his trepidation at the thought of having to go through all these big parties if he ever convinced Jewel to marry him. As much as he loved the thought of marrying her and spending the rest of his life raising a family with her, since his injury, he was a lot less excited about being the center of attention at all the festivities leading up to the wedding. Yeah, he'd made it through Dean and Allissa's wedding week with only minor issues. But he wasn't the groom in that wedding.

Fuck! I don't even wanna think about how horrible it would be to have a blackout spell right as Jewel was walking down the aisle. Yeah, when all these parties get overwhelming, I can excuse myself to go lie down, even if it's only on a sofa in the closest parlor if I can't make it all the way to my room. But I doubt she'd still want to marry me if I had to clear out a church pew to lie down in the middle of the ceremony because my emotions overwhelmed me.

Not knowing how to stop the episodes completely was the worst part of the blackout spells for Dion. While his new medications
~~~

seemed to help a little with his aphasia and concentration issues, they hadn't stopped him from feeling like he needed to lie down and pass out at least once a day since he'd started taking them.

He knew the incidents were triggered by being overwhelmed or anxious. But it didn't seem to matter if he was overwhelmed by positive or negative stimuli, and he could blackout from excitement just as easily as he could from anxiety. And while touching Jewel and focusing on her and their babies seemed to help lessen the overwhelmed feeling he got whenever there was too much sensory information for him to process at once, he knew it wasn't feasible to stay glued to her side twenty-four-seven. Especially since he knew he still caused a scene when he had to disrupt whatever activity they were doing to cling to her like a scared little boy, the way he had on Christmas.

Fuck! Should I even think about possibly getting to marry her one day, when I don't know if I'll ever be a whole man again? I don't want to saddle her with my issues, and end up being a burden, instead of her partner in life. And if I can't get some of this shit to stop, then I won't be anything but an albatross around her neck.

Hell, that's probably why she keeps telling me to focus on healing, instead of our relationship, for now. She doesn't want to be with a loser, who can't remember shit, and keeps passing the fuck out for no fucking reason.

But, fuck, I can't stand the thought of not being with her either. And I can't even think about how crazy I'd be if she was with some other guy.

Dion was getting so worked up over his fear of not being good enough for Jewel that he almost triggered one of his episodes. Thankfully, Mama Marcel touched his forearm, getting his attention to point out where Jewel was sitting and waving them over to take the three seats she'd saved for them at her table. He quickly pushed his negative thoughts from his head, trying to force himself to be the man she needed as he made his way to their table.

He was confused when he got to the table and noticed there were only seven chairs instead of eight or ten, like at most of the other guest tables. He was really confused when he noticed that two of those chairs had baby car seats in them. Then he realized Jewel and her sister, Jen, were each holding one of their one-month-old nephews.

Seeing Jewel holding a baby gave him a glimpse of what their future entailed when their babies were born, making him smile. *These doctors better find the right meds to get me back to normal soon, so I can be the man Jewel and our babies need me to be,* Dion thought, trying desperately to banish his fear of inadequacy for the rest of the night, so he could get in some parenting practice. Even though his doctors had all assured him that it was perfectly safe for him to hold babies as long as he had other people around to help him if he started to have an episode, he was still nervous about actually doing it.

"Ah, you convinced your family to let us practice tonight." Dion greeted Jewel with a brush of his lips over her temple before pulling out a chair for Mama Marcel and then sitting down between them.

"Yes, but we've only got the boys for as long as their parents and grandparents are all busy with toasts and stuff," Jewel grinned as she patted the back of the baby she was holding as if she was trying to get him to burp.

"And we only convinced Justin and Amy to let us take care of the boys, instead of having them at the head table with them, because Amy didn't bring her or Justin a change of clothes in case of spit up or diaper leaks," Jen added as she stood and carried her nephew around to hand him off to Dion. "And since I didn't bring a change of clothes either, and ya'll are the ones who need the practice, I'm gonna let you take over with Jerry."

"How do you know which one is which?" As much as Dion wanted to practice holding and taking care of the babies before his and Jewel's were born, he still felt his heart start to race the first time he was actually tasked with holding a baby. Especially since Jerry was fussing in Jen's arms.

"Amy swears she can tell them apart," Jen chuckled, "so she picks two different colors each day for their clothes and tells the rest of us which baby is in what color. Today, Jerry's in green and Jonah's in yellow."

Makes sense, I guess.

"Just be glad I'm a fraternal twin and not an identical twin like Amy," Jewel pointed out, "so our babies most likely won't look so much alike that we can't tell them apart."

"That's good to know," Dion agreed, knowing he'd feel like even worse of a father if he couldn't tell his babies apart.

Dion looked closely at how Jen was holding Jerry, so he could mirror the position as she handed him over. He crossed his arms over his chest, leaving his forearms side by side and with his palms up, for Jen to place the baby in them. "Is there anything specific I'm supposed to do? Some magic trick to soothe him, so he stops crying?"

"Just make sure his head's supported," Jewel pointed out as Jen laid baby Jerry in Dion's arms with his head resting on the crook of his left elbow and his butt on his left palm, leaving his right arm free to move. "And he'll stop crying as soon as Aunt Hazel gets back with the bottles."

"He's so little," Dion observed as Jerry's cries died down once he realized he had someone new to look at. Dion used his free hand to adjust the baby's right arm, trying not to squish it between the baby's body and Dion's as he hugged him in closer to his chest. When he did, Jerry grabbed his finger and moved his arm like he was trying to rattle Dion's finger like a toy. Dion couldn't stop smiling down at the precious little boy in his arms.

"No fair, little Jer," Jen pouted as she laid a white cloth over Dion's left shoulder, much like the one on Jewel's shoulder where Jonah's head was resting. "You wouldn't stop crying for me, even when I tried Aunt Julie's back patting trick. And now you're gonna stop as soon as Dion holds you?"

"Guess you've got the magic touch, D," Jewel beamed, still lightly rocking and patting Jonah.

"Do you think our babies are gonna be this little when they're born?" Dion made faces at Jerry in his arms as his gaze swept back and forth between Jewel and the baby he was holding.

"I'm really hoping they won't be this big when they're born," Jewel cringed. "They were only six pounds, four ounces, and nineteen-and-a-half inches long when they were born, which I think I can handle delivering naturally the way Amy did. Now they're almost ten pounds each, and they've grown two inches in length since they were born. And there's no way I can handle passing one ten-pound baby through my hoo-hah, much less two."

"Is birth weight a hereditary thing?" Dion wondered, knowing he'd been a nine-pound-plus baby, as had his brother.

Jewel's eyes darted to his as she glared at him, making him wish he hadn't spoken his question aloud. "If so, then these two better take after me and Jen."

"Oh, no, you don't want that," Hazel interjected as she walked up carrying two baby bottles. She handed one off to Dion, as Jewel adjusted how she was holding Jonah before taking the other bottle. "Ya'll were so close to the five-pound minimum weight to be able to leave the hospital that the doctor insisted on sending you home the day after you were born, so the excess water weight that babies lose in the first few days wouldn't cause you to have to spend an extra week in the hospital to get back up to five pounds."

Dion watched as Jewel tested the temperature of the milk by holding the bottle between her thumb and last two fingers to drip some out on her first two fingers before feeding it to Jonah. He repeated her process to recognize the milk was lukewarm before feeding Jerry.

"I think she's worried that the twins will be closer to the nine pounds, thirteen ounces Dion was when he was born," Mama Marcel explained, as Dion focused on feeding Jerry, who eagerly suckled his bottle.

"Nine pounds, thirteen ounces?" Jewel screeched, her eyes widening as Dion looked up to see her glaring at him once more. "That's how much Jonah and Jerry weigh now! At almost five weeks old!"

Huh? So, this is how big I was when I was born? Dion realized as he looked back down at the little boy in his arms.

"But twins tend to be smaller, though, right Aunt Hazel?" Jen seemed to be trying to calm Jewel down by enlisting their aunt to verify her way of thinking.

Dion didn't know if twins were smaller or not, so he kept his mouth shut and let the women discuss birth weights and the probable size of their babies. He just kept focusing on the task at hand — feeding Jerry — and tried not to let the anxiety Jewel was obviously feeling amplify his own apprehension to cause him to have a blackout spell.

"Usually, yes," Hazel agreed with her niece. "But if you just go by ya'll's birth weights and split the difference, you'll probably have seven-pound babies, like I did when my twins were born. So, ya'll's babies will be fine, not too big, not too small."

"Don't you dare make any Goldilocks comments about the babies being *just right*," Jewel ordered, using the pinky finger of the hand holding Jonah's bottle to first point at Dion and then at her sister.

"Well, you do have the blonde hair for it," Darius chuckled, raising his hands in surrender when Jewel turned her glare on him. "And I'd think you'd rather I call you Goldilocks than a gold…"

Dare's words were cut off by Mama Marcel reaching over to slap the back of his head.

Luckily, their conversation couldn't restart then as the speeches began. Hazel scurried back to her seat at the next table, just as Jon started the speeches as the father of the groom.

Dion didn't pay attention to what was being said about Justin and Amy. Instead, he watched Jewel and followed her lead to know what to do when the babies finished their bottles. *Ah, that's why Jen put that cloth on my shoulder*, he realized when Jewel showed him how to reposition the baby to burp him.

"You're gonna hafta tap him a little harder than that, D," Mama Marcel instructed when Dion was barely patting the baby's back with two of his fingers. "And don't stay in the same spot. Start at his butt and work your way up to get the gas to go in the right direction."

"But I don't want to accidentally hurt him," Dion protested, worried about how much damage his large hand could do on such a small baby.

"You're not gonna hurt him," Jewel assured him with a provocative smile, which somehow triggered a memory of her naked and draped over his lap as he spanked her.

"You're not gonna hurt me, D," Jewel playfully pouted as she turned her head to look up at him. "But you're gonna hafta slap my ass a little harder if you want me to believe you're actually punishing me for being a brat."

Holy shit! When did we play those kinds of bedroom games? And why the fuck am I just remembering them now, when I obviously can't ask her about 'em?

"Oh, give me your hand, D, so I can show you how hard to tap him," Mama Marcel insisted, reaching over to grab his forearm, and pulling his hand from Jerry's back. She then started tapping her hand on the back of his. "See, this is what you're doing, which is too soft and won't move any gas for the little guy. And this is how hard you should tap him to actually get him to burp."

Dion still only used his fingers instead of the palm of his hand, but he increased the intensity of the taps as Mama Marcel instructed. He also followed her advice to start just above Jerry's diaper and work his way up. He had to tap up the baby's back a half dozen times before Jerry loudly belched, drawing the attention of everyone in the room.

"I think that's my grandson's way of saying it's time for me to cut this speech short," Amy's dad joked before finishing up with his congratulations to the happy couple and passing the microphone to the next person set to give a speech.

As Jerry settled in to take a nap on his shoulder, Dion really looked at everyone seated at the head table for the first time. In addition to Justin and Amy, they had James Hunter and his wife, Randi, and Justin's brother, JJ, and Amy's sister, Ashlyn, acting as their groomsmen and bridesmaids, plus both their parents, Amy's stepmother, and all three of her half-siblings. Dion realized then that the only reason Jen and Julie weren't up there with them was because they'd volunteered to take care of Justin and Amy's babies, while seated at a table between the other parents with small babies in their family and several of their aunts and uncles, who all acted like extra grandparents to all the babies and children in the Burleson family.

While he appreciated having so much backup sitting close in case he had any other issues with taking care of the baby in his arms, Dion realized then just how empty his side of the church would be if he was able to get to the point where he could actually ask Jewel to marry him. Yeah, he'd probably have a few more members of the GWA crew than had come to town for Justin and Amy's wedding. But as far as family went, he only had Darius and Mama Marcel.

Fuck! That's just another way I don't measure up to Jewel and her family. But unlike the issues I'm having since my TBI, there's not a damn thing I can do to fix that.

As Dion once again started to sink into his feelings of inadequacy and worried about never being good enough for Jewel and their babies, he noticed a very distinct smell coming from the baby he was holding. *Great! Even the baby is shitting on my dreams of one day being blessed enough to marry Jewel.*

"Um, Jewel, I, uh, need to trade babies with you," Dion whispered, knowing he had no clue how to change a dirty diaper.

"Oh, no, Big Daddy," Jewel chuckled as she reached down and grabbed a bag from under the chair beside her with a car seat in it. "We're splitting diaper duty fifty-fifty, so that's all on you."

She tried to hand him the diaper bag and send him on his way, but Dion couldn't go along with that. "No, Jewel, seriously," he pleaded, refusing to take the diaper bag from her. "I don't know how to change a diaper. At the very least, you've gotta come show me how to do it the first time."

"Oh, no," Jewel disagreed, shaking her head at him. "You did an excellent job on the diaper changing relay at both of the baby showers you attended this year. So, even if you don't remember them, I'm sure you can do just fine with muscle memory to get you through your first time changing a real baby."

I participated in two diaper changing relays this year?

Luckily for Dion, it seemed that Jonah agreed that it was time for a diaper change, grunting as he, too, filled his diaper.

"We can change them at the same time, so I can watch what you do to know I'm doing it right." Dion grinned at Jewel as she made a face, probably because the smell hit her right then.

"Fine," Jewel sighed, handing him the diaper bag once more before standing. "But you're carrying the diaper bag, and you have to wait in the hall while I make sure the ladies' room is empty before following me into the room with the biggest changing station, so we have room for both of them to be changed at once."

"Absolutely," Dion agreed, looping the strap over his right shoulder since Jerry was still resting on his left. He wrapped both arms around the baby to make sure he didn't risk dropping him, then dutifully followed Jewel as she led the way out of the ballroom and down the hall to the restrooms between the restaurant dining room and the library.

Once there, she stepped into the room, leaving him and Jerry in the hallway. A moment later, an older woman stepped out and smiled at him.

"Go on in, young man," she instructed, holding the door open for him. "Your girlfriend explained everything, so I'm gonna stand guard here to keep anyone else who might need the restroom from being surprised by seeing a man in the ladies' room."

"Thank you, ma'am," Dion smiled and nodded at the older woman as he walked into the room to find Jewel laying out a paper changing pad before lying Jonah down on a long shelf built into one side of the room. He placed the diaper bag on the shelf between them before doing the same with another paper changing pad and Jerry.

"The most important thing to remember when changing boys is that you don't take the old diaper off until you have something to cover them with to keep from getting peed on," Jewel informed him as she started pulling supplies from the diaper bag. "So, we get everything out and ready to use before we even start to undress them."

Dion mimicked Jewel's movements, prepping the new diaper, and laying it on the paper beside Jerry just a few seconds after she'd done the same for Jonah. "Go ahead and get two wipes out, one to make a wee-wee teepee to block him if he starts peeing, and the other to start cleaning him with. You can get more if you need them as you go, but the very minimum you'll need is two."

She went on to instruct him with clothing removal and how to use the first wipe to make what she called a "wee-wee teepee" to protect from a peeing incident, as he removed the soiled diaper while holding the baby's butt off the counter by lifting his feet. Dion ended up needing a lot more wipes than Jewel did to clean the babies up, but he was grateful for the extra wipe trick she showed him when Jerry urinated strong enough to levitate the wipe for a few seconds. "That woulda been all over me if it wasn't covered, right?"

"Yep," Jewel laughed as she finished putting diaper rash cream on Jonah. "Or the wall, or the diaper bag, or pretty much anyone or anything within a three-foot radius. Which is one of the reasons I'm hoping Mama Marcel is right with her prediction that we're having girls."

"Yeah, I hope she's right, too." Dion just didn't mention that he was actually hopeful that Mama Marcel was also correct in her predictions of marriage and more babies in their future. Including the twin boys she predicted to complete their family. *Guess I'll just have to remember the "wee-wee teepee" trick, even if we don't have to use it on our babies for a few years yet.*

Chapter Sixteen

Saturday, December 28, 2019

Julie enjoyed getting some extra baby time in for the second night in a row as she and Dion took care of her nephews while Justin and Amy got married. She had to laugh at Dion insisting on wearing the double baby carrier during the ceremony and after the babies were fed, changed, and back to sleep at the reception. If she'd been asked the year before, she'd have said there was nothing Dion could do to be more attractive to her than he was when they first met. But after seeing him wearing her nephews in that carrier and cooing to them to keep them calm as their parents got married, she had to admit she'd have been wrong. If she wasn't already pregnant, she had a feeling she'd have had an immaculate conception just from the way her ovaries reacted to seeing him taking care of her nephews.

Yeah, I should probably hold off another couple of days before I sneak into his hotel room for some makeup sex, she thought as she sat and enjoyed her dinner at the reception. *'Cause if he keeps doing stuff to make me feel like I'm ovulating, I'm liable to end up carrying quadruplets conceived almost four months apart. Well, if that's even possible, anyway.*

She couldn't believe how much more confident he seemed now in his abilities with the babies than he had the previous night. It was almost like the quiet confidence he'd had in all things before his injury had come back, at least, with regard to taking care of the babies, anyway. *Too bad he's not showing me that sexual confidence again, yet.*

Watching him with her nephews made her think back to the previous night when he hadn't been nearly as competent as he was currently. In fact, she thought she'd seen actual fear in his eyes when he realized he was about to change his first poopy diaper the night before. But this evening, he'd breezed through it like an old pro. And it didn't matter which of the boys they put in his arms, they both stopped fussing as soon as he held them.

Julie actually felt a little disheartened by how much faster the boys calmed with Dion than with her. She intentionally spent time with each of her nephews daily to make sure they felt comfortable with her, hoping it would keep them from being extra fussy in a couple of weeks, when their parents finally took a few days away for a honeymoon. But all her efforts seemed futile when they were much less fussy when Dion was holding them, even though the day before was the first time he'd ever really interacted with either of them.

Maybe when we go shopping next weekend for cribs and stuff for the nursery, I should ask him about sleeping over to help me with them while Justin and Amy are on their honeymoon?

Since they were still in the timeframe after birth that sex was off the table, Justin and Amy planned to postpone their honeymoon until they got the all-clear from Dr. Magnum. And even though Amy could technically be cleared by her doctor six weeks after giving birth, they were waiting until the twentieth of January to leave for their honeymoon, just in case they had to go a full eight weeks to let her episiotomy scar fully heal. Since Julie was positive she'd be able to get her twins' nursery set up by then, with two cribs so each of the boys would have a bed to be able to sleep the way they did at home, she was tasked with overnight duty with the boys while Justin and Amy were planning to be away.

Of course, Gran (Susan) and Memmaw (Hazel) had insisted on taking care of them during the day, both while Julie worked during the week of Justin and Amy's honeymoon and once Justin and Amy went back to work after their parental leave from Burleson Incorporated was over. Julie was pretty sure her mother and aunt would have plenty of help from the rest of the Matchmaking Mommas of Heart's Destiny, volunteering to take care of the babies while they cooked for the ranch hands. But she didn't think she'd have as easy a time convincing Jen or Becky to sleep over to help her with middle-of-the-night feedings and diaper changes.

Yeah, I'll definitely ask Dion to help me that week. He's a lot more likely to be amenable to two a.m. feedings than Jen or Becky. And maybe we can get in some middle-of-the-night sexy time while the babies are sleeping.

Julie was brought out of her rambling thoughts by the emcee calling the single women to the dance floor for the bouquet toss and her sister Jen getting up from their table.

"Aren't you going to join your sister?" Mama Marcel looked at Julie in surprise when she didn't get up to participate.

"Nope." Julie shook her head and smiled as she looked around Dion and the babies strapped to his chest to see Mama Marcel's reaction to her next words. "Dion and I caught the garter and bouquet at the last wedding, so we don't have to participate anymore."

"Dion, you didn't tell me you caught the garter before." Mama Marcel lightly tapped his shoulder, obviously not wanting to jostle him too much, since he was holding two sleeping babies.

"Sorry, Mama Marcel, it just hadn't come up or I woulda mentioned it," Dion shrugged.

"Yeah, based on how that went at Dean and Allissa's wedding, I'm gonna sit it out this time, too," Darius declared, crossing his arms over his chest as he leaned back in his chair.

"Why? What happened at the last wedding?" Mama Marcel looked confused as she glanced back and forth between Darius, Dion, and Julie. "Was there some kind of scuffle for the garter?"

"No, it was rigged based on who the local matchmakers wanted to pair up next," Dion chuckled. "That's why Dean specifically told me to participate. And it was blatantly obvious that it was a setup because of me asking for space to avoid another head injury, and Dean calling out for me to open my eyes to catch the garter, when I was trying to block out everything to keep from passing out."

"So, why don't you wanna do it this time?" Mama Marcel gave Darius a pointed look. "Are you afraid they're gonna match you up with someone tonight?"

"No, I'm pretty sure they already have a couple picked out," Dare explained, shaking his head. "So, it's just a waste of energy to get up when I don't have a chance of catching the garter."

They stopped talking long enough to turn and watch as Amy tossed her bouquet of yellow carnations to her twin sister, Ashlyn.

"Oh, I don't know, Dare," Mama Marcel disagreed with his earlier statement. "Susan told me that Ashlyn was asking about you at the birthing center right after Amy had the boys. And since they were trying to push the two of you together at Christmas, you might ruin their plans if you don't go catch the garter now."

"Don't worry, Dare," Julie assured him. "Ashlyn's not looking to settle down, so even if you catch the garter, she won't want more than a hookup or two while you're in town."

"You sure?" Darius arched an eyebrow at Julie. "I mean, she seems cool and all, but I'm not ready for that whole happily ever after that everyone here seems to be looking for."

"I can't say for certain," Julie shrugged as Dion coughed to cover for calling his brother a liar. *Huh? I wonder what that's all about?* "But since I met her back in February, she seems to flirt with a different guy every time I see her. And while she asked about you a month ago, and has flirted with you a little since then, in that same timeframe, she's also flirted with my brother JJ, a couple of the Walkers, Ryder Deere, and the director, who came to town yesterday to scout out locations for one of the films we've got coming up soon. So, I'm pretty sure she's more interested in having a good time than settling down."

"Well, in that case, I'd better get up there." Darius jumped out of his seat and beelined for the dance floor, where all the men were gathering now that the women were mostly headed back to their tables.

"Wow, Dare must really be into Ashlyn with the way he rushed out there," Jen chortled as she retook her seat at their table beside Dare's now empty chair. "Too bad I'm pretty sure she's more into Cade Starling."

"Who's Cade Starling?" Dion looked at Jen with a confused expression.

"He's the director I mentioned a minute ago," Julie clarified, not revealing that he'd introduced himself as Caden when Ashlyn brought him to the Burleson headquarters the day before and further solidified her choice not to use any version of the name for one of her kids. Not that she had to elaborate with her twin sister sitting at the table with her.

"His name is actually Caden Starling," Jen giggled as she pointed him out, where he'd joined the guys lining up to catch the garter. "But after Josh broke into another bad rendition of the *Okay Then* song in the middle of our offices yesterday, we had to beg him to let us shorten his name to just Cade."

When Cade caught the garter, Julie had to wonder if they could combine his and Ashlyn's names to come up with something that wouldn't make Josh break out into song. "Okay, so are we calling them Ashden or Cadlyn? Which would be least likely to make Josh sing again?"

"Ashden," Jen decided. "Cadlyn still sounds too much like *Okay Then*."

Once again, Dion looked confused. He didn't get the chance to voice the question he obviously had, though, because Mama Marcel did it for him.

"Are you talking about that shipping thing my friends were talking about on our cruise last month?"

"Shipping?" Dion really looked perplexed then, furrowing his brow as he blatantly tried to figure out what Mama Marcel was talking about, and making Julie stifle a chuckle at his expression. "Did you ship something home from your cruise? And what's that got to do with the names Jewel just made up?"

"It's the popular thing with all the kids right now," Julie explained as both Jen and Mama Marcel laughed at Dion's confusion. "Where you combine the names of couples in a relationship. They basically pulled 'ship' from 'relationship' and turned it into the verb 'shipping,' meaning 'combining the individual names of two people in a relationship,' before spreading it all over the internet. Becky can tell you the whole history of how it started with TV show fans who wanted certain characters to get together, but now the kids are applying it to real life couples."

"Okay," Dion drawled, still seeming to be confused as Darius rejoined them, looking a little dejected from not catching the garter.

Damn, I guess I shouldn't have given him any hope there.

"So, like when we shipped ya'll, instead of being Julie and Dion, now ya'll are Julion," Jen clarified. "Tia and her friend Britney started it with all the new couples getting together this last year, starting with Kathony for Kay and Anthony."

"Then there's Jandi for James and Randi," Julie continued for her sister. "Brookby for Brooklyn and Bobby. And my favorite for Justin and Amy…" Julie paused for dramatic effect. "Just Amy. And yes, Tia says it as two words to make it seem like she's cutting Justin out of the picture and just talking about Amy."

"Oh, no, my favorite is Lilie, for Liam and Rylie." Jen surprised Julie by mentioning the couple who basically ended her plans to hook up with Liam by getting married while they were drunk in Vegas. "Because she pronounces it like Lee-Lee, Tia had all the Lees wondering who she was talking about that was missing from Christmas."

"I can't wait any longer," Amy interrupted their conversation, with Justin right behind her. "I need my babies now."

Yeah, there's no way they'll stay out of town for their whole honeymoon in a couple of weeks. Not with how they can't stay away from their babies for more than a couple of hours on their wedding night. If they're still helicoptering this bad in a couple of weeks, I might not even get one night watching my nephews.

Oh well. I'll still enjoy having Dion stay the night.

It was a group effort to take both babies out of the carrier that Dion was wearing, so it could be removed from him and adjusted to fit Amy. Of course, Jonah and Jerry both started fussing as soon as Julie and Jen took them to hold while Dion, Justin, and Amy transferred the carrier. But thankfully, they seemed to settle right back down as soon as they were cuddled up to their mom.

"Thanks a lot, Dion," Justin huffed, though his smile gave him away as not really being irritated. "Now that she's seen the carrier is safe and comfortable for the boys, I'm not gonna get to hold them as much 'cause she's gonna wear them all the time."

"Sorry, man," Dion smiled, not really looking all that contrite. "But it really did make me feel a lot better about carrying them around without worrying about dropping them."

Is that the difference between last night and tonight? He was afraid of dropping them and that's why he didn't look as confident while caring for them? If that double carrier gave him that much more self-assurance, then I guess we'd better add one to our list of things to pick up on one of our upcoming shopping trips.

Once they were no longer responsible for taking care of the babies, Dion asked her to dance, to which she happily agreed. Julie loved being able to spend some time in his arms again, finally acknowledging that she felt mentally ready to add sex back into their relationship.

"So, we're Julion, huh? Does that mean everyone knows we're officially in a relationship now?" Dion's smirk made her wonder if he was on the same page with her and planning to use the relationship talk to suggest spending the night together after the reception was over.

"Yeah, I think that kiss in front of everyone on Christmas pretty much solidified us as a couple in the minds of the nosy Nellies in my family." Julie smiled up at him, as he twirled her around the dance floor. "And anyone they hadn't passed the gossip to before now has probably heard about it tonight."

"And you're okay with everyone knowing we're dating?" Dion leaned down to whisper the words in her ear, almost like he was nervous about how she would answer and wanted to keep the conversation private between them.

Even though they'd talked a little about their previous relationship, she hadn't yet shared her issues with feeling like his secret side piece since he hadn't told anyone about being with her in the past. She didn't really think dancing in the middle of her brother's wedding reception was the right time for the discussion, but Julie knew she couldn't keep her feelings from him if she wanted things to work out for them in the future.

"I'm more than okay with it," she informed him, pulling back to look into his eyes as she confessed her previous fears. "To be honest, I wish we hadn't hidden our relationship before you were injured. I think it would have prevented the whole misunderstanding in October, if you'd told the people you're closest to about me, the way I talked to my sister, cousins, and girlfriends about you."

"Since I hadn't talked to Dare for longer than we'd been together, he still would've acted like a jackass on the phone with you," Dion disagreed, shaking his head at her as their dancing slowed with the seriousness of their talk.

"Probably, but the Hunters or Liam could've cleared things up for us that day," Julie argued. "Or I could have been there with you to introduce myself to him as your girlfriend to keep it from happening. He wouldn't have mistaken me for a ring rat if everyone in the GWA backed up my claim. And I wouldn't have gotten more upset by feeling like your dirty little secret than I did over the phone call with Darius."

"I'm sorry, Jewel," Dion apologized, cutting their dance short to usher her off the dance floor and out to the closest parlor, where they could sit and talk privately. "I don't remember why we were keeping our relationship a secret. But I do know that it wouldn't have been because I wanted to hide my feelings for you. Hell, when I woke up dreaming about you in the hospital, I told everyone I could about you, hoping they'd know who you were to help me find you again."

"I know," Julie huffed, hating that this misunderstanding was all her fault. "I'm the one who insisted we couldn't tell anyone who might let it slip to the Matchmaking Mommas. But even though I didn't want my mom and her cohorts to know, I still confided in Jen from day one, and eventually, Becky, Char, and Cait. And when I realized in October that you hadn't even confided in Liam, who I thought was helping Jen cover for us whenever you were in town, it hurt that you hadn't even told your best friend about us."

"Oh, Jewel," Dion sighed. "If you'd asked me not to tell anyone who might let it slip while we were in town, I never woulda said a word to any of the guys. With the way they are about ribbing pretty much everyone, telling one of the guys, especially Liam, woulda been a sure-fire way for word to get back to your mom. They might not have intentionally leaked the news, but they'd have been trying to irritate me by talking about us while we were here and someone would've inadvertently overheard. So, I'm pretty sure my not telling any of them was more about trying to honor your wishes than any of the reasons you've conjured up in your head."

"I know," Julie sighed. "But just like every other irrational thought or weird reaction I've had in the last four months, I'm blaming my feeling like your shameful side piece on the pregnancy hormones."

"You are definitely not my shameful side piece," Dion chuckled, smiling at her with his love shining through his eyes. "You're my one-and-only piece. And I mean that with both spellings of the word *peace*. You're the only woman who will ever be in my bed, the only woman who will ever own my heart, and the only woman who's capable of clearing the clutter from my mind, so I can feel peaceful. I might not remember everything that happened between us for my feelings to develop, but I know in my heart of hearts that I'm madly in love with you, Jewel, and I will only ever be in love with you for the rest of my life."

Julie swooned at his heartfelt words, feeling so much emotion in that moment that she was speechless.

"Now, to keep you from ever feeling like I'm ashamed of being with you again, let's go back to the reception, so I can make an announcement about how much I love you."

"No," Julie protested, grabbing his arm as he started to stand and pulling him back down on the sofa beside her. "I believe you already. You don't have to interrupt my brother's wedding reception to tell anyone but me."

She wanted to tell him that she loved him too, but she was too afraid he'd think she was just saying it right then because he had. So, instead, she decided to show him how she felt, reaching over to wrap her left hand around his neck to pull him closer as she placed her right hand over his heart and pressed her lips to his.

Dion seemed surprised by the kiss at first, but he quickly succumbed to the passion between them, wrapping her in his arms as he deepened the kiss. Within seconds, Julie found herself under Dion as she laid back on the sofa and they plundered each other's mouths with their tongues.

Unfortunately, no matter how much she was enjoying finally feeling intimate with Dion again, that was also the moment when she remembered Dr. Magnum mentioning her needing to avoid laying on her back after the fourth month of pregnancy. While technically, December was her fourth month of pregnancy, at eighteen-and-a-half weeks along, she considered herself too close to that borderline between the fourth and fifth months to take a chance on potentially decreasing the blood flow to their babies.

"We have to stop, Dion," Julie panted as she turned her head to break their kiss, while moving both hands to his chest to push him up off of her, so she could sit up. "I'm not supposed to lay on my back 'cause it can cut off blood flow to the babies."

As soon as she uttered the warning, Dion practically jumped off of her, gripping her hands to pull her into an upright position. He released her hands and knelt beside her on the floor, so he could place his hands on her belly, almost as if he was trying to check to make sure the babies were okay. "I'm so sorry, Jewel. I didn't know."

"It's fine, Dion." Julie placed her hands over his hands on her baby bump. "It was only for a few seconds, and I'm not really sure if I'm far enough along for it to be an issue yet or not. She said after the fourth month, but I'm just not sure if she meant after sixteen weeks, or four calendar months, since they're actually longer than the four weeks we consider a month for periods and birth control."

"Well, either way, we're close enough that we shouldn't take any chances." Dion brushed his lips across her belly before getting up off the floor and sitting back down beside her on the sofa. "Is there anything else we need to avoid?"

Unsure if he was speaking in general or specifically asking about sexual activities, Julie shrugged. "That's the only sexual position she mentioned, but she also mentioned stopping horseback riding, cutting out alcohol, no more than two-hundred milligrams of caffeine a day, and absolutely no raw meat, eggs, fish, shellfish, unpasteurized dairy products, fish high in mercury, deli meats, hot dogs, cold cured meats, smoked fish, or any unwashed produce."

"Wow, that's a lot of stuff you have to avoid. Is that why you avoided the gumbo and etouffee Mama Marcel brought to the potluck a couple of weeks ago?"

"Yeah, though I know the fish was cooked, I can't remember which kinds of fish or shellfish are considered safe for pregnant women to eat and which ones are considered too high in mercury, so I didn't want to take any chances," Julie fibbed, not wanting to tell him that other than hearing he'd been injured in the confrontation with Allissa's stalker, the smell of fish was the only thing that had triggered her morning sickness. Since she was far enough along that the nausea should start clearing up soon, she didn't see any point in possibly bringing up that horrible day while trying to explain her temporary aversion to fish, when she knew how much he loved it. She didn't want to give him the impression that their babies didn't like his favorite foods and made her sick every time she even smelled them. "I've also had to change the way I order my steaks now, too, 'cause they have to be well done instead of medium, the way my family likes to do them on the grill, or medium-well, the way I like them."

"I bet that seems somewhat sacrilegious on the ranch," Dion chuckled. "Probably as much as not eating gumbo is to those of us from NOLA."

"Exactly," Julie agreed, forcing herself to laugh along with him, even though his words just reinforced her fear of upsetting him by telling him about her pregnancy-induced fish aversion.

"Well, we can fix the gumbo problem," Dion assured her, taking her hand and pulling her up from the sofa. "We'll do a quick online search for safe fish during pregnancy and make sure that's what Mama Marcel uses in the gumbo she's makin' for tomorrow."

And hopefully, I'll be able to stomach a little bit of it then. Since she'd been able to sit with him when he'd had some a couple of weeks before, she was pretty sure it wasn't the smell that would get to her if she had a problem the next day. But she also hadn't exactly brought it up under her nose to take a bite to get the strongest whiff of the fishy odor, so she wasn't certain. *Maybe I can hold my breath every time I take a bite to keep from smelling it and getting sick?*

Or maybe I can push it off another week by insisting on doing the same day of beauty for Cait that we've done with every other bride this last year. Right in the middle of when everyone else is at the potluck.

As they walked back into the reception, Dion did the search on his phone, and Julie wondered how they'd gone from making out like horny teenagers to going back to talk to their families about safe pregnancy foods. When the night ended with only a chaste kiss goodnight before she left to go home alone, Julie had to admit, if only to herself, that she was a little disappointed that he hadn't invited her up to his room, or pushed for more carnal activities now that they'd publicly admitted to being a couple.

Maybe he just wants to do more research on what sexual acts are safe during pregnancy? At least, she hoped that was the only reason he held back that night.

~~~

Sunday, December 29, 2019

Dion had been surprised to see all the Burleson women skip the potluck lunch after the morning church service, causing him to not get to spend that time with Jewel the way he wanted. Them skipping out early also caused Jewel to miss out on Mama Marcel's gumbo yet
~~~

again, even though Dion had verified that the shrimp and crawfish she normally used for the dish were both safe for Jewel to eat while pregnant. But after talking to the guys about how Josh had planned everything, so he could propose and get married on the one-year anniversary of the day he met Cait, he was happy to know Julia was included in the pampering the ladies all enjoyed that afternoon to prepare for the wedding.

Truth be told, he was also a little envious of how Josh had worked things out to avoid a majority of the wedding events they seemed to do in Heart's Destiny, and especially in Jewel's family. But as he spun Jewel around the dance floor for the second night in a row, he was starting to question his thought process on wanting to avoid being the center of attention at events when he could be with her.

He hadn't been lying the day before when he told her how she quieted the jumble of thoughts in his mind to help him feel at peace. Although, he might not have worded it exactly right to explain how it felt in his head when he was with her. Being with her helped focus his brain on how he could best take care of her and their babies. Whereas, when she wasn't by his side, he still thought of those things, but he was also a lot more easily distracted by other random thoughts that weren't nearly as important. Which was why he thought he'd been able to beat back a few of his blackout spells recently by touching her, and focusing on her and their babies.

I should probably ask her to sit with me next time I try to read up on all the pregnancy stuff I tried to look up online last night and this afternoon.

He'd gotten confused after reading conflicting information on different sites about whether or not it was safe to have sex while pregnant with twins. He'd seen the same thing about staying off her back after the fourth month that Dr. Magnum had told Jewel, but it was still just as vague about how many weeks that was, which boggled his mind since everything else about pregnancy seemed to be measured in weeks.

When he got confused trying to figure it out after going to his room the night before, he ended up sleeping off a blackout spell with his laptop in bed beside him. When he'd enlisted Darius's help after the potluck lunch at church, his search hadn't gone any better. He didn't have another blackout spell, but only because Dare had taken him off on a tangent, looking up sexual positions that didn't require the woman to be on her back at any point. And he still didn't know if any of those positions were safe with Jewel carrying twins.

He'd held back on asking her to his room after Justin and Amy's reception the night before because of not knowing what was safe and what wasn't. Since he hadn't been able to figure it out before Josh and Cait's reception, he was pretty sure he wouldn't be able to ask her up to his room once again.

Hell, at this point, we're not gonna be able to make love again until after her next doctor's appointment, when I can ask Dr. Magnum what's safe and what's not. But I have a feeling if I do that, then Jewel will be so embarrassed that she won't let me near her until after the babies are born.

He couldn't worry about that right then, though, because the newlyweds had just stepped off the dance floor to announce it was time for the bouquet and garter toss. Dion escorted Jewel back to their table, taking their seats as the single ladies filled the floor.

"Who do you think the Proxy Papa is gonna target tonight?" Dare inquired, tilting his head toward Josh, where he was standing beside Cait at the edge of the dance floor.

Considering how upset Darius had been the night before when the girl he'd hooked up with on Christmas caught the bouquet and he didn't catch the garter, Dion was surprised his brother was so interested in the next possible pairing.

"Proxy Papa?" Jewel looked at Dare like he was speaking a foreign language that she didn't understand.

"That's what Rick's wife suggested for the name of the group of dads who help out the Matchmaking Mommas at the wedding shower last weekend," Dion explained, grinning at actually remembering the conversation a week later. *Guess that dementia medicine is working better than I thought.*

"Why would Fiona suggest that?" Jewel looked from Dion to Darius. "And why would you think my cousin Josh is part of the group?"

"She walked up when we were talking with Josh and Jake about how both Josh and Rick were doing things to make us think they were joining the Matchmaking Mommas," Dion elaborated.

"And Josh had said he couldn't be a Matchmaking Momma because he doesn't have a uterus, so he wondered if Rick would go along with naming their group the Deputy Daddies," Dare continued for Dion. "I don't know which of those words she had a problem with, but it was impressive how fast she came up with an alternative that was also alliterative."

"Well, she is an English teacher," Jewel giggled, grinning, "so stuff like that should be easy for her."

Dion was so focused on trying to comprehend everything Darius had just said to make sure he remembered it correctly that he missed seeing who caught the bouquet. While his medicine was helping with his memory issues, it hadn't sped up his comprehension of conversations all that much yet.

"Don't bother going up there this time, Darius." Jewel shook her head at Dare while smiling knowingly. "The garter is going to my brother JJ tonight."

"Seriously? I don't even stand a chance with the girl from out of town?" Darius guffawed, clearly playing up his man-whore image to keep anyone else from noticing that he still only had eyes for Ashlyn.

Dion felt bad for his brother, but he didn't have a clue how to help him win Ashlyn over when she seemed to have moved on to her next fling.

"Sorry," Jewel shrugged, grinning as she shook her head at him. "But Mom and Aunt Hazel have been trying to get JJ and Deanna together since the first time Kay mentioned her best friend and it came out that JJ knew her. So, if he's as keen on helping out the Matchmaking Mommas as ya'll just mentioned, then Josh will definitely aim straight for JJ with the garter, since Deanna caught the bouquet."

"How can you be so sure this time, when you had no clue who they'd try to pair Ashlyn with last night?" Dare arched an eyebrow at Jewel inquisitively.

"Because, like I told you yesterday, Ashlyn flirts with everyone, so the Matchmaking Mommas hadn't settled on one specific person they wanted to match her up with, at least, that I knew of. I think that was more Amy wanting to target her sister, and Justin having just seen Ashlyn flirting with Cade on Friday to figure he was her current flavor of the week. JJ and Deanna, on the other hand, are one of the couples they've consistently tried to push together for over a year, so it's kinda a no brainer that they'd want them to catch the garter and bouquet together, especially since all the other couples before me and Dion ended up getting married after catching them."

While he hated how Jewel's words probably crushed Dare's dreams of Ashlyn, Dion liked hearing the track record of successful matches at local weddings and hoped it boded well for him and Jewel to get married one day soon.

"No way!" Darius shook his head at Jewel. "That sounds like an even better prediction record than Mama Marcel. And if it's true, then ya'll should be planning your wedding now."

"What's a better track record than mine?" Mama Marcel and Jen rejoined them at the table after standing up for the bouquet toss.

"Julie's trying to convince me that every couple who catches the bouquet and garter at a wedding here ends up getting married," Dare informed them. "With the exception of her and Dion and the couple that caught them last night. But if their track record is really that good, then shouldn't we start planning Dion and Julie's wedding?"

"I meant it's too soon for us to know if we're gonna get married or not," Jewel protested.

"But it has worked out for all the other couples," Jen interjected, grinning. "Even when one of the kids catches the garter, their dads end up marrying the women who caught the bouquet."

"Point out these couples, 'cause I don't believe it," Dare scoffed, shaking his head.

Damn, he must really be into Ashlyn if he doesn't want to believe last night's pairing will lead to marriage.

"So, Anthony and Kay kicked off this rash of weddings," Jen started, using her fingers to count off the couples who caught the bouquet and garter, then subsequently got married. "They tossed the bouquet and garter to Randi and James, who got engaged less than three months later and married about three-and-a-half months after that. Then when Bobby and Brooklyn got married, they tossed them to Charlotte and Ian, who again got engaged about three months later and married two months after that."

"At James and Randi's wedding, Justin helped set up the bouquet and garter toss to go to him and Amy, so he could propose that night," Jewel continued for her sister. "They waited seven months to get married, but I think that's because Amy didn't want to walk down the aisle while pregnant."

"I don't see why not, since Kay, Brook, and Char all did," Jen giggled.

"Yeah, but they were all early enough in their pregnancies that they weren't really showing yet," Jewel clarified. "Because of having twins, Amy's baby bump popped out early, like mine. And even if they'd planned a wedding for a month after Justin proposed, they'd have been making adjustments to the wedding dress on the day of the wedding because of the daily changes in belly size. So, even if I was certain that Dion and I would work out to want to get married, I wouldn't want to plan a wedding until after the babies are born and I have a couple of months to lose the baby weight. In fact, I'm surprised Amy didn't want to wait until closer to Valentine's Day."

Guess it's a good thing I planned on waiting until after the babies are born to finish her engagement ring with the extra stones from the necklace she's wearing, Dion thought. *Although, after what she just said, I'm not sure that'll be enough time to convince her that we'll last for the long haul, so it may end up being the second anniversary of the day we met when I can finally propose.*

Ugh! All that unsure talk means she probably won't be ready to make love anytime soon, either, even if we get the all-clear from her doctor on the seventh.

"That's only three couples and no mention of kids catching garters," Darius interjected, taking them back to the original subject.

"Technically, there's some controversy over whether Ian or Brody caught the garter at Bobby and Brooklyn's reception," Jewel clarified. "Brody kinda stopped it and dropped it in Ian's hand, since Ian was holding him at the time."

"And that was just the first three weddings," Jen added, going back to counting them on her fingers. "The next one was Rick and Fiona's wedding, where Dean and Allissa caught the garter and bouquet. They weren't even officially dating then, but he still claimed the GWA's Thanksgiving break for their wedding."

"Only because Char vetoed his claim on their Labor Day break for her and Ian's wedding," Jewel giggled. "And when Char and Ian tossed their bouquet and garter, they targeted Cait and Josh, but had Brody help by tossing the garter, which he threw to JoJo."

"That's the wedding I remembered where Josh found out about his son, right?" Dion wasn't sure his new medications were doing much for helping him get his older memories back, but he was pretty sure they were responsible for him being able to recall some of the one's he'd recently remembered and link them to the events mentioned in new discussions.

"Yes," Jewel confirmed. "At that point in time, JoJo had only introduced himself to the kids he played with before the reception as Josh. So, when Ian told Brody to toss the garter to Josh, he tossed it to the kid named Josh he'd just met. Then when Ian told him he meant Uncle Josh, JoJo asked if Brody's uncle's name was Josh Burleson because that's who he was there looking for. It wasn't until after we found out that he was our cousin Josh's son that Cait came up with the JoJo nickname to keep us all from being confused by which Josh we were referring to."

"Yeah, I can see how it would be confusing with father and son sharing the same name." Mama Marcel nodded to show her understanding of everything the ladies had just explained.

"If we have a boy that you wanna name after me, how are we gonna keep everyone from being confused with two Dions?" Dion looked to Jewel, not caring as the rest of the people at the table discussed the couple who caught the bouquet and garter. He just wanted to connect with his Jewel.

"We'll have him go by Dev," Jewel informed him with a gracious smile. "At least, until he gets old enough to complain about it and we have to come up with an idea he likes better."

"Why do I have a feeling there's a story behind that premonition that we'll have to change it later?" Dion leaned in close to Jewel, keeping their conversation between the two of them.

"I may have had a preteen fit about how it wasn't fair that Jennifer was shortened to Jen, but Julie was just as long as Julia," she confessed, rolling her eyes. "When Jen switched to calling me Jules occasionally to be different, I complained that it was still just as long, so there was no benefit to me to have a nickname."

"And Jewel is also five letters, so it's not any better than the nicknames your family came up with," Dion sighed, assuming she still had a problem with pet names that were just as long as her given name.

"Oh no, it's much better," Jewel disagreed. "At least, you used a little creativity when you came up with it, unlike my family, who just changed one or two letters at the end of my name. Besides, I got over the wanting-a-shorter-nickname thing when the boys decided to call me Jeb because my initials are J-E-B. That led to starting middle school with everyone picking on me about it being short for Jebediah and questioning my gender identity."

Her mentioning his creativity in coming up with his pet name for her triggered a flash of memory.

"Relax, Jewel. I promise I won't bring Mama Marcel around to help with their matchmaking schemes. At least, not until we figure out how to deal with our conflicting schedules to actually take advantage of their efforts to explore the possibilities of our instant attraction to one another." Dion was sitting with Jewel at a wedding shower in the fellowship hall at the church while watching Anthony and Kay, their parents, and James and Randi playing the Newlywed game.

"What's with the Jewel nickname?" She arched an eyebrow and tilted her head curiously. "You've called me that a few times since we met yesterday and I wanna know why."

"It's kinda a play on your name." Dion shrugged and smiled flirtatiously. "Plus, your eyes remind me of sapphires. And I think you're precious, like a jewel, so it fits you better than Julie or Jules, like everyone else calls you."

Dion had to shake off the flash of memory to stay in the moment with her, trying to recall what she'd said after mentioning his creativity with coming up with his pet name for her. *Something about the kids calling her Jeb because of her initials...*

"Wow, kids can be cruel," Dion cringed, hating that she'd gone through that. *Damn, I never thought I'd wish I had a different last name, or that I'd taken Marcel as my last name when Mama Marcel stepped in as our guardian. But if I had, then at least she'd be a Jem instead of a Jed if we ever get married.* "How'd you get 'em to stop?"

"I looked at my brothers' and cousins' initials and realized that Bobby's initials are R-A-B," Jewel smirked. "So, I started calling him Rabies and refused to stop until he got everyone to go back to calling me Julie. Since it was his freshman year of high school, he really didn't want it to get around that his nickname was Rabies, so he pretty much laid down the law for everyone to lay off picking on me. Come to think of it, that was also when he started spreading the word that we were all off limits for dating, too. Not that I cared at the time as a sixth grader, who still thought boys had cooties. But now I have to wonder if my lack of dating in high school is all my own fault for going after him with the nickname thing."

"Rabies, huh?" Dion chuckled at her cruel creativity. "I can't decide if ya'll's childhood nicknames were better or worse than what the bullies called me in school."

"What did they call you?" Jewel's eyebrows drew together as if she was gearing up to be angry over the nickname because he'd mentioned it was used by the school bullies.

"Double D's," Dion confided in a low whisper. "You'd think it was because of my initials, but they didn't change it when I pointed out that it should be Triple D's for my initials. I was kinda a chunky little kid, so they were actually using it as a reference to my moob size."

"Ouch!" Jewel cringed on his behalf. "I'm gonna say that's worse, since it was probably wider spread than Rabies or Jeb."

They spent the rest of the evening comparing and contrasting their childhoods. While Dion felt it brought him closer to Jewel, and enjoyed getting to know her on a deeper level, even more than they'd recently covered in their daily text conversations, he couldn't stop thinking about how ill prepared he was to safely progress them to more physical intimacy, instead of just the emotional intimacy they were building with their conversations. So, even though she hinted at wanting to go up to his room after the reception, Dion gave her a chaste kiss and sent her home.

Just the thought of how he could accidentally hurt her or their babies because of not knowing what was safe for them to do sexually while she was pregnant sent him spiraling with anxiety to the point that he recognized the early warning signs for a blackout spell. So, as soon as Jewel left with her sister, Dion asked Dare to walk him up to his room.

I'll just take care of this boner in the shower, again, he thought as he made his way up the stairs with his brother by his side. *Right after I lie down and pass out for a little while.*

Chapter Seventeen

Julie felt more than a little frustrated with Dion's lack of sexual advances since they'd agreed to officially date. After their all too brief make-out session on Saturday, she thought he might be hesitating because of what she'd said about not being able to lay on her back past this point in her pregnancy. Because of that, she assumed he was waiting until he could ask Dr. Magnum what was safe and what wasn't before initiating more than kisses and hugs. So, she'd spent the last two days reviewing all the literature Dr. Magnum had given her at her first appointment, as well as the pregnancy books she'd downloaded to her Kindle, to make sure she knew what they could and couldn't do in the bedroom. Now, as she walked into the ballroom to meet Dion for their date, she hoped having shared her findings in their ongoing text thread would be enough to get him to agree it was time for her to sneak up to his room again.

Yeah, she knew they really needed to continue focusing on rebuilding the friendship portion of their relationship while he was embroiled in various doctor's appointments to try to speed up his healing, so they'd have a strong foundation to build their family on regardless of how life had to change for him because of his injuries. But her cousin, sister-in-law, and cousins-in-law clearly hadn't been joking when they warned her that her libido would crank up to overdrive during the second trimester of pregnancy. Considering her attraction to Dion already had her feeling like a nymphomaniac long before she got pregnant, she was really starting to have a hard time keeping herself from jumping his bones now, especially after feeling his big dick's reaction to her several times since Christmas. So, knowing that she would love him and want him, regardless of whatever physical limitations his injuries caused him to have to deal with in the future, she didn't see any point in wasting time when they could already start enjoying the physical side of their relationship, even if they had to make some adaptations for both of their physical conditions. Now she just had to find Dion to be able to convince him of that.

Looking around the ballroom, where she'd thought she'd find Dion, to see the final preparations being made for the party, Julie was surprised by a change in the standard layout she was used to seeing. Unlike when the ballroom was set up for wedding receptions, when half the space was filled with tables for eight to ten people and the dance floor took up almost all of the other half of the room, with only the head table, cake cutting table, and the band or DJ set up at the opposite end, the setup for the New Year's Eve party included a lot more smaller tables and even some seating areas with sofas and coffee tables, covering about two-thirds of the floor space. There was a stage set up at one end for the live band the Hunters brought in, with the space immediately in front of the stage set up as the dance floor. While that meant they had less space to dance, they could definitely accommodate more attendees with the increased seating.

Julie was thrilled with the option of comfortable seating on the sofas, instead of having to endure another evening in the uncomfortable table chairs required for events with a sit-down dinner. *I wonder if this is some of Windy and Kandi's influence, now that they're officially Heart's Destiny residents and working for Mandi?*

The previous year, when the Hunters held the first of these New Year's Eve parties after opening up the building, which they'd called the Plantation House at the time and had just recently renamed the Heritage House, to accommodate Anthony and Kay's wedding events, they'd stuck with the same setup that they used for wedding receptions. Of course, they also hadn't opened the restaurant for more than just the guests' breakfast, so they needed the tables for the dinner they served as part of the party. *I guess we have to go to the restaurant for dinner this year. I suppose that's why none of the rest of the family was ready to come over for the party yet, 'cause they're having dinner at home first. Not that any of them would admit it when they could joke around about how I was rushing over here early because I couldn't wait to see Dion. If they even know the party doesn't include dinner this year...*

Since it was also their cousin Blaine Avington's birthday, Julie had assumed they'd combine his birthday party with the dinner portion of the evening, serving birthday cake for dessert. Now she had to wonder if her family was planning to meet for his birthday dinner before coming over here and she'd just missed the announcement about the plans due to her pregnancy brain and focusing on her first date with Dion. To double check that she hadn't accidentally dissed her cousin by heading to the bed and breakfast early and skipping a family dinner, Julie pulled her phone out of her small bag and sent a text off to her twin right quick.

Julie: Did you know the NYE party doesn't include dinner this year?

Jen: Yeah, that's why we're eating now, or grabbing something at the restaurant when we get there.

Julie: What about Blaine's birthday dinner & cake?

Jen: No dinner. Bringing the cake to the NYE party. Will probably go to the library or one of the dining rooms to have it like we did for Tia last year, only before midnight instead of after.

Julie: Okay, good. I was worried my pregnancy brain made me miss it.

Julie put her phone back in her purse and looked around, trying to figure out where Dion would expect to find her to start their date.

"I wonder if Daddy knows dinner isn't included this year and is expecting us to meet him in the restaurant instead of the ballroom?" While talking to her babies, Julie ran her hands over her belly, which was covered by the purple stretch satin, empire waist ball gown she'd worn, thinking this would be a more formal event like it was the previous year. "Since nobody's in the ballroom yet, should I check the restaurant first? Or just text him to find out where he is?"

Since the babies seemed to move more during the last question than they had during the first two, Julie assumed they agreed that she should text. So, she pulled her phone from her clutch once more to send off a quick text to Dion to find out where she should meet him.

> **Julie: I'm here in the ballroom, but don't see you. Where are we meeting?**

> **Dion: Sorry. I'm just now leaving my room. Be there in a few minutes.**

> **Julie: They're not serving dinner in the ballroom this year, so the babies think we should meet in the restaurant instead. ;)**

> **Dion: Then let's go feed our babies in the restaurant first. {GIF of baby with face covered in orange baby food}**

"Oh, dear, ya'll's daddy has gone silly if he thinks we're gonna feed ya'll like that," Julie chuckled as she walked back out of the ballroom, heading toward the restaurant in the boutique hotel that the Hunters still called a bed and breakfast, even though in Julie's opinion it had outgrown that designation when they opened the additional building the year before.

Normally, she would have gone out the back way from the ballroom to sneak through the buffet room, where breakfast was served for the hotel guests, to get to the formal dining room for the restaurant. But since she assumed Dion was coming down the main stairs in the grand foyer, she backtracked through the primary ballroom doors and down the hall to the foyer to meet him as soon as he got down to the first floor.

Seeing him confidently walking down the stairs in a bespoke black suit with a purple shirt and tie to match her dress, Julie was glad she'd walked the long way around. He was sex on two legs and she appreciated having the extra time to ogle him without him or anyone else knowing. *Now I've just gotta figure out how to get that sexy man naked again.*

While she knew telling him what she'd learned of her restrictions due to the pregnancy should be enough to ease his trepidation and move them to the next level, she also knew that texting him in those clinical terms hadn't set the right mood for them to rekindle the romantic aspects of their relationship. So, instead of just reiterating her texts by saying, "Hey, just so you know I've reviewed all my restrictions and we're good to go for sex as long as we try out some different positions to find what's comfortable," she planned to be flirtatious all night. Touching him more, slipping innuendos into their conversation, and giving off some come-hither vibes would all be more effective in letting him know she was ready for him to initiate more than a hug or kiss.

And if he doesn't get my hints, then I'll just do like I did our first time together and suggest sneaking up to his room. Hopefully, I can hold off until after our midnight kiss to make that suggestion.

"Wow, Jewel, you're so beautiful, you take my breath away." Dion bent and took her lips in a kiss that was much too impassioned to be considered a typical greeting.

Yeah, we don't need to ring in the new year with the rest of our family members, Julie thought as her hand instinctually covered his heart momentarily before she wrapped her arms around his neck and returned the ardent kiss. She lightly nipped his full lips, hoping to show him that she wanted more of the primal mating they'd done in the past.

It didn't matter that they were standing in the middle of the foyer of the hotel, with the staff bustling around to finish setting up for the party going on that night. To Julie, it felt like they were alone. And nothing mattered more in that moment than her and Dion making love with their mouths.

"Get a room!" Darius teased as he escorted Mama Marcel down the stairs, intruding on their moment enough for Dion to break the kiss.

"I already have a room," Dion grumbled, flipping Darius off as soon as Mama Marcel's back was turned while she greeted Julie with a hug.

Julie grinned at seeing the playful gesture between the brothers as she returned the quick squeeze from Caroline. "And our babies are insisting we eat before we go up to his room for the night," she added as soon as they released the embrace.

"Well, don't let us keep you from your date," Caroline instructed as she pointed over her shoulder in the direction Julie had just come from. "We've got to go set up my space in the ballroom, so I can do a few predictions of the new year's fortunes for the people at the party."

Julie had wondered why Mama Marcel was dressed so dramatically different than her standard attire. She had her hair wrapped in an emerald green scarf with gold-coin fringe that matched the one around her waist. Instead of the fifties-housewife style dresses that Julie had seen Caroline wear to church, or the casual pants and tops she'd worn around town, Mama Marcel was decked out in a long, flowy, purple skirt that matched the corset-style vest she wore over a white peasant blouse. This was obviously her fortune teller getup, which reminded Julie of the pirate wench costume she'd worn to a Halloween party her sophomore year of college, only done in the purple, green, and gold colors of Mardi Gras and with a long skirt instead of the miniskirt Julie had worn that classified her Halloween outfit as a sexy pirate wench costume.

"Oh, I'll definitely have to spend some time sitting with you later to see what all you predict for my friends and family," Julie chuckled, thinking it would be fun to see if Caroline could pick up some of the secrets of the town, which were only coming to light this year after the younger generations in town started doing DNA tests and tracing their family histories to uncover the skeletons their ancestors had tried to keep in the closet.

Julie had heard a few things over the past few months, like how her friend Kara Thompson was somehow cousins with the Walkers and none of them had known until recently, and how the Walkers weren't related to Doc Hayes like they'd thought all their lives. But none of her friends had given her any specific details of the dirt they'd found to figure all that out, so Julie just supported them by being happy for them finding new cousins. Julie had also split a bottle of wine with Kara back in the Spring when those revelations first came to light, trying to help her friend get over the ick-factor of realizing she'd kissed her cousin Leo on prom night almost a decade ago.

Though she'd shared the basics of those things with Dion when they were first discovered in the Spring, from her recent interactions with him, she didn't think he remembered them, or had ever shared them with Mama Marcel. So, in her opinion, if either of those things were mentioned in the readings Caroline gave them that night, then Julie might just start believing in her gift of *the sight*.

Once Mama Marcel and Darius left them to head into the ballroom, Dion escorted Julie into the formal dining room for the restaurant. They were quickly seated at a romantic table for two and placed their orders before making small talk. Julie told Dion about the businesses she was researching to possibly add to the Burleson portfolio, and Dion told Julie about the small improvements he was seeing in his post-concussion symptoms after starting some new medications.

Dion also told her about spending some of his free time exploring Heart's Destiny, specifically looking at the different businesses in town to try to figure out what he could open to contribute to the town once he was cleared to drive and had an idea of what limitations he might have in his future career. "I didn't see a single day care center," he informed her, looking confused. "Surely this entire town isn't made up of single income families, so there's always a parent to stay home with the babies before they're old enough to go to school, or once they start school but aren't old enough to stay home alone until their parents get home."

"I hadn't ever noticed that before," Julie admitted, shaking her head as she tried to think of the options the other families in town used to care for their children. "I know we have the corporate day care centers set up in our headquarters and at each of the office locations for the refineries and various subsidiaries around the country. So, any Burleson employee in Heart's Destiny, whether they work in the refinery, or one of the Gas & Go locations, or even at the theatre with Becky, can drop their kids off at the day care in the refinery offices. And the employees on the ranch are encouraged to bring their kids with them to let Mom and Aunt Hazel act as their extra grandmas, or have the kids stay with Mrs. Mary down at the Ashbury House while their parents aren't able to supervise them while working. And of course, Mom and Aunt Hazel have claimed grandma privileges to keep all the kids that have been added to the family recently. But I have no idea what the rest of the families in town do with their little ones while they work. Unless, maybe, they do the same thing as my friends' parents did when we were kids, either have grandma watch them, or take them to work with them and set them up in an out of the way spot to color or do homework or whatever. And of course, there's the youth center that has after school and summer programs to keep the older kids occupied whenever they aren't in school. We've all spent time volunteering there to teach equestrian skills and stuff, whenever Aunt Sarah needs us."

"Then I guess I don't really need to think about opening a day care center here then," Dion sighed, obviously dejected from feeling like there wasn't a need he could fill in town.

"Maybe not a formal *Big Daddy's Day Care* in the middle of town," Julie half-shrugged and smiled, hoping to cheer him up with her alternative suggestion. "But with the rapid growth in our family, I'm sure Mom and Aunt Hazel would welcome your help on the ranch. Maybe you could start like a home day care there."

"You mean like turn your living room into a day care center?" Dion questioned as the server delivered their meals.

"Maybe not mine, but Mom's or Aunt Hazel's," Julie corrected as she placed her napkin in her lap to start eating her quesadillas. "Since they're the ones insisting on watching all their grandbabies as often as possible."

"How many kids are they taking care of each day?"

As Dion cut into his fish, Julie was glad to realize that the smell didn't seem to bother her as much as it had earlier in her pregnancy. While she would have told him the smell of fish was a problem for her before his injury, she wasn't sure she could afterwards because of how easily his moods seemed to be affected by the littlest things recently. She hadn't wanted to hurt his feelings by making him think their babies didn't like his favorite foods, so she'd blamed her avoiding Mama Marcel's gumbo on not knowing which fish was safe for her to eat. In actuality, she'd been avoiding it because fish of any kind had been the only food that triggered her morning sickness just from smelling it. Now she was hopeful that she might be able to stomach eating it again soon.

"Right now, they just have Brody and JoJo regularly, with Cait there to help them out in the afternoons after she picks JoJo up from school," Julie replied, without mentioning her previous fish issues. "But when Justin and Amy go back to work, they'll have Jonah and Jerry daily, too. Plus, they have Maddie, Sam, Antonio, Maria, and

Tia sporadically, too. Though Tia and Maria are both great with helping with the younger kids, they aren't always home at the same time Brooklyn leaves Maddie with Mom and Aunt Hazel."

"So, two babies and two older kids most of the time." Dion looked deep in thought as he took a bite, contemplating as he chewed. "Well under the ratios of children to caregivers I was reading about online when I was trying to figure out staffing needs for a day care center."

"For now, yeah," Julie agreed, nodding her head between bites. "But then when Char has her baby in February and I have ours in May, they're expecting to get to take care of all the babies while still working with Rosa to cook for the ranch hands and all our big family meals. I'm a little bit worried that five, and sometimes six or seven, babies under a year old might be too much for them, especially on the days when Brody and JoJo are the only older kids around to help them."

"Yeah, I can see your point," Dion nodded before changing the subject. "So, I was thinking instead of just going on our date Saturday night, maybe we can spend the day furnishing the nursery first. I might not be able to drive to the store, but I can carry all the heavy items and help put together cribs and stuff."

Julie was confused about why he was bringing their planned shopping trip up again, as if they hadn't already made those plans. *Did he forget that we already discussed this during our nightly call the other night? Like, is that dementia medicine not working as well as he just told me, and he's not remembering as many of our conversations as he thinks? Or is he just feeling overwhelmed or upset by the conversation about helping Mom and Aunt Hazel with the kids, instead of opening a day care center in town, and trying to come up with something else to talk about to keep from getting too anxious and passing out?*

Should I ask him? Or should I just go along with making these plans again, so I don't embarrass him by pointing out that we've already had this discussion?

I should definitely go along with making them again, she decided. *There's no point in stressing him out and risking him having one of those blackout episodes again. And I'll be sure to ask about how best to deal with situations like this when I go to that caregiver support group Josh found through his and Cait's therapist.*

"Yes, we absolutely need to do that," Julie agreed, smiling at him. "To be honest, I've been a little worried that if I don't hurry up and pick up the antique white furniture I want, Mom will have the dark wood stuff she likes delivered and set up while I'm at work one day."

"That's not what she did with the other furniture for your house, is it?" Dion arched an eyebrow, obviously knowing more about the dining room and sitting room furniture her parents had given her as a housewarming gift than she realized.

"No, she went with the lighter stuff to match what I'd picked for the nursery," Julie confirmed, realizing that she didn't have to worry as much about being gifted the darker stuff after all. "But I think that's only because I'd already told Brent and Honey Deere what I wanted for the nursery, and the Deeres insisted on going with matching pieces when Mom and Dad placed the order for the rest of the house."

They spent the rest of their meal discussing the nursery design, with Dion agreeing to everything Julie wanted. She wasn't sure if it was more of him trying to appease her, or if their tastes really did align as well as he claimed. But at the moment, she was too happy just spending time with him again to nitpick it and risk not getting to spend the rest of the night with him because of a disagreement triggering an episode.

Though maybe I should check with his doctors to make sure he's cleared for sex before we try to do anything other than cuddle all night.

By the time they finished eating and Dion took care of the check, both the restaurant and ballroom had started to fill up for the party. *Hopefully, this will just help Dion bring back some of his good memories of us from last year. And won't be too overwhelming with having more people here than the weddings the last few weeks.*

~~~

"It's almost time, folks," the lead singer of the band announced into the microphone. **"Grab your glasses and midnight kissing partners as we count down the last two minutes of two-thousand-eighteen."**

Dion leaned over and put his arm around Jewel as the wait staff passed out glasses of champagne or sparkling grape juice.
~~~

"I suppose I have to keep this family friendly until I get you up in my room later," Dion whispered in her ear, enjoying the hint of banana in the fruity-floral scent of her hair.

"Sorry, Dark Chocolate, just a quick peck this time," Jewel barely breathed the words next to his ear. "Then we've gotta rush off to the library for Tia's birthday party. But if it's any consolation, she told me she picked a chocolate cake with chocolate frosting because you're her favorite wrestler."

"Yeah, she told me the same thing," Dion chuckled. "But I think it was just to rile up the Hunters. And I didn't have the heart to tell her that she's my second favorite Burleson."

Dion and Jewel both joined in with the rest of the crowd to count down the last twenty seconds of the year, each grabbing one of the noisemakers on the table, which they just had to spin to ring in the stroke of midnight while keeping their lips free for a kiss. Begrudgingly, Dion followed Jewel's directive and kept it to a quick, chaste peck of a kiss, barely brushing his lips over hers before backing away from her to whoop and holler with the rest of the crowd, so nobody around them would realize they were more than friends. "Happy New Year!"

Dion came back to the present just as they found seats on a sofa near where Mama Marcel was set up with her fortune telling table. After helping her sit and then sitting down beside her, he leaned over to whisper-shout a couple of questions to Jewel, speaking just loud enough to be heard over the music filling the space. "Do I have to keep our midnight kiss as short and sweet this year as I did last year? And do you think Tia will kill me for forgetting it's her birthday 'til just now, if I promise to take her birthday shopping next time she's in town since I forgot to get a present in time for her party?"

"You're in luck with Tia," Jewel grinned, leaning in conspiratorially. "They aren't flying out until the second this year, so we're having her party tomorrow evening at seven at Aunt Hazel and Uncle Bob's house, instead of just after midnight like last year, since we're doing my cousin Blaine's birthday cake at some point during this party before his birthday passes and Tia's arrives. And I have access to her Amazon eBook wish list, so you can order something online without having to find a store open on New Year's Day to shop for her."

"Can you drive me over to the ranch for the party? Dare and Mama Marcel are planning on going back to NOLA tomorrow, so I won't have a ride," Dion explained, not wanting to be the first customer for the new CouBer service in town, even though he thought it was only limited to Windy and Kandi driving while they got everything set up to make the business official.

"Yeah, no problem," Jewel agreed with a broad smile. "In fact, if you don't mind me borrowing one of your dress shirts to wear as a dress, I can hang out here until after they leave and then we can head back to the ranch together."

"Yeah, that's fine," Dion nodded. "Or I've got some sweats you can wear if you need something warmer." While he was glad to know he wouldn't disappoint the teenager who'd texted him a few times in the last month, offering suggestions for ways to combat his concussion symptoms, along with stories of their interactions over the last year to try to help him get his memories back, it hadn't gone unnoticed that Jewel skipped over the question about them kissing. *That's fine, Jewel. We can focus on other stuff for now. But we'll definitely be revisiting the kiss conversation later.*

Dion remembered always being friendly with the kids that traveled with the GWA before he lost his memories. But apparently, when Anthony met Kay and her daughters joined the tour, he'd formed a special bond with Tia while helping her train to be a wrestler. When she found out about the extent of Dion's injuries and how his symptoms weren't clearing up as quickly as expected during the week of Dean and Allissa's wedding, Tia took it upon herself to research traumatic brain injuries and the various ways to treat the chronic issues after a TBI. The girl was so freaking smart that Dion wished he could take her to his appointment with Doc Hayes on Monday, so she could offer her suggestions to the doctors treating him, since he'd never be able to remember everything she'd texted him to pass on the information. *Maybe I can just let Doc Hayes read our text thread?*

"And since everyone knows we're dating now, I didn't figure we'd do the friend-kiss like last year." Jewel's words brought Dion back to the moment, causing him to shake off his thoughts about Tia and Doc Hayes to focus on her. "Though before we go up to your room at the end of the night, I have to ask if your doctors have cleared you for the strenuous physical activity that usually happens when the two of us are alone in a hotel room?"

"Yes," Dion declared, smiling broadly at the realization that she wanted to go up to his room at the end of the party. "I might not remember everything from my appointments with Dr. Boudreaux, but I do remember specifically asking if sex was included in the light physical activity he cleared me to do right before I came here."

He'd specifically asked about the safety of sex if he found the woman he was dreaming about, but he didn't think he needed to elaborate more on that with Jewel right then. *But maybe when we get upstairs, she'll need to know what he said about my clean status then?*

Jewel looked around, as if trying to see if anyone was listening to their conversation, before leaning in and whispering in his ear, "Did you describe some of your dream-memories to him to make sure he knew what we do is way more vigorous than the *light physical activity* I'm sure he was thinking of?"

"Technically, I think he recommended having you on top, so I could have my head supported to keep it from jostling around and also keep my part of the movement light," Dion smirked, squeezing her into his side on the sofa. "And since having you on top is also one of the positions recommended in that book you sent to my e-reader, and several of my dream-memories have been of you demonstrating your cowgirl skills, I think we'll be okay whenever you're ready for us to consummate our coupledom."

"Do we have to stay down here 'til midnight?" Jewel ran her hand over his thigh, getting dangerously close to his cock, which was already hardening in response to being cuddled up to her.

"Yes, it would be rude to leave the party before then," Dion informed her, reaching over with the arm not around her shoulders to stop her hand before they went too far in front of an audience.

"Technically, we're being rude now by ignoring all our friends and family members," Jewel cooed before brushing her lips over his jaw. "So, we should probably quit cuddling in the corner of this couch and go do a little mingling."

"Then, by all means, let's go mingle," Dion acquiesced, brushing his lips over her temple as he stood from the sofa before helping her up.

At nineteen weeks pregnant, she wasn't quite halfway through the prenatal phase, but her belly was really starting to round out. After the stuff she'd sent him to read in the last couple of days, Dion knew that their babies were each about nine-and-a-half inches long at that point. So, it made sense to him that she had to be bigger than a woman only carrying one baby at the same point in pregnancy. And apparently, that meant she now found it a little difficult to stand up from some soft surfaces when she couldn't push off on an armrest with her hands. Not that Dion minded taking her hand to assist her in standing.

Hell, I'd pick her up and carry her everywhere if she'd let me. Then she wouldn't have to worry about having trouble standing up or feeling wobbly in her heels because of being top heavy.

That was the other thing she'd complained about recently. Specifically, she mentioned feeling like she had to go buy new bras every other week because of how much her breasts had grown from being pregnant. So much so, that one of their recent text conversations felt like a primer all about maternity clothing and nursing bras. Dion wasn't sure if she'd meant it to be a rant about the drawbacks to pregnancy, or if she was trying to get him to comment on how much her boobs had grown.

Since some of his dream-memories had included him telling her how perfect her perky little tits were, Dion opted not to comment on how he couldn't wait to see her bare breasts now that they were filling out. He loved her, not the size of her boobs, so he didn't want to accidentally say anything that might make her think he wouldn't like them anymore if they went back to being A-cups after the babies were born.

Although he was more than happy with her smaller breasts before pregnancy, as they walked around to make small talk with friends, Dion couldn't help but appreciate her more voluptuous cleavage that filled out the top of her sexy purple dress as much as her baby bump filled out the middle. And with the way she was hinting about going back to his room at the end of the night, he was looking forward to spending some time worshiping every inch of her more curvaceous figure. So, when she stopped to listen to Mama Marcel's fortune telling, Dion had to discreetly adjust his cock in his pants while standing behind her to keep anyone else from noticing.

Leah Mae Wright

"You must be patient, sweet girl," Mama Marcel instructed the proprietress of the bakery in town, Kara, whom he'd met at a couple of events since coming back to Heart's Destiny, as well as when he'd explored the town and stopped into the bakery. "Your soulmate will eventually come home to you, but not this year. At least, not permanently this year. This year is meant for you to spend time preparing for him by nurturing your forgiving heart. You'll not only have to forgive him for leaving for a time, but you also need to forgive the actions of your ancestors to be able to fully love yourself, him, and your newfound family. But start with loving yourself. That's the most important for you this year."

"Did you say something to Mama Marcel about the surprises in Kara's DNA test earlier this year?" Jewel shocked him with the vehemence of her whisper-hissed words as she turned to face him.

"Considering I don't even remember meeting Kara before I was injured, I can't really say for sure," Dion shrugged. "But since Mama Marcel told me I hadn't mentioned anyone here by name before the injury, I'm guessing no."

"Well, then, unless she's been getting caught up on all the local gossip, which is definitely a possibility in this town, then maybe she really does have a gift." Jewel went on to fill him in on how Kara had found out she was cousins with the Walkers after she'd gone her whole life thinking her only blood relatives to have ever lived in the Heart's Destiny area were her parents and paternal grandparents, with three of the four having passed on. "She was really messed up about it because she dated Leo in high school, though she swears they only kissed one time on prom night. And with the amount of DNA she said she shares with them, that would be like me kissing one of my Burleson or Harper cousins."

Dion fought not to growl due to the jealousy that coursed through him at thinking of Jewel kissing anyone but him. At the same time, she shuddered at the thought of kissing one of her cousins, which made him realize how ridiculous he was being for feeling so outraged by a fictitious kiss.

"But I guess them being cousins explains why her dad keeps going after Leo with his gun to keep him from asking Kara out again," Jewel hypothesized as they made their way to the dance floor, where she filled him in on how that had been an issue ever since that fateful prom

320

night while they swayed to the music. She also let him know that she was hoping the way Jake and Kara were fake dating to get the Matchmaking Mommas off their backs at all the town events would lead to the two of them actually getting together because she knew that Kara secretly hoped the "soulmate" that Mama Marcel just referred to would end up being Jake. Apparently, he'd done the typical boy thing of picking on the girl he liked all through school, by teasing Kara about misspelling the name of the bakery when she was a preschooler, among other things. And while Kara had always played it off, acting like she wasn't interested in Jake, more than one person in Julia's family had caught her looking a little too longingly at him over the years, both when they were younger and more recently whenever he came back to town on leave from the Navy.

Dion smiled and listened intently, enjoying being able to hold her in his arms as she talked. He loved listening to her voice, no matter what subject she droned on about. Although, if asked, he'd say he preferred listening to her talk about their babies and their earlier times together that helped jog his memory a lot more than gossip about their friends.

Is it droned or drolled? Dion wondered, unsure if getting two words confused in his head was another aspect of the aphasia from his head injuries, or an improvement from completely losing the words since he'd started his new meds. *I'll have to look it up later. I'd rather focus on flirting with my Jewel now.*

Julie had a wonderful time as the night progressed. It didn't matter what they were doing, whether she was dancing with Dion and enjoying being in his arms, or while she sat with him to have a slice of Blaine's birthday cake and visit with their friends and family while enjoying a refreshing fruit juice mocktail, she felt closer to him than she had doing similar activities in the past, back when they'd had to act like they were only friends. The way he constantly had to be touching her, either holding her hand or draping his arm around her shoulders when they were seated, or holding her close while they danced, made her feel like the Dion she was with during their hotel hookups was back. Only he was able to show his affectionate side

321

publicly now that they were officially a couple that everyone in her hometown knew about.

Even when he'd get that faraway look in his eyes as he had flashes of memories come to him throughout the night, she felt like she had his undivided attention because of the way he'd immediately ask her questions about whatever he remembered. Yeah, he'd done that pretty much every time he had a memory come to him whenever they were together since he'd been back in town, but it seemed like they were hitting him with more frequency this evening than they had before.

In addition to their New Year's kiss and Tia's birthday the year before, he'd remembered several times that they'd danced or sat together in the ballroom with such clarity that he could even describe the different decorations for the various wedding receptions, rehearsal dinners, and holidays. He'd also remembered some of their first conversations when they were getting to know one another that hadn't happened on the Hunters' property, much less in the ballroom, so she wasn't sure how they were triggered.

"I don't get how you can remember talking to me at wedding showers and bachelor and bachelorette parties, but you still don't remember the first time we met," Julie playfully pouted, teasing him just a little. "I thought with retrograde amnesia, you're supposed to get your oldest memories back first, not jump around with what you remember the way you are."

"That's just the typical way it happens, Aunt Julie," Tia pointed out, having joined them where they were seated when she heard Dion was having flashbacks to his memories of being in Heart's Destiny. "But what I learned in the neurobiology classes I've taken this month is that they can come back in a number of different ways. And the brain is capable of completely blocking out the traumatic memories and only allowing the good memories to come back."

"Neurobiology classes?" Julie was blown away by her young cousin's brilliance. "I thought you were doing a degree in pre-law?"

"Yeah, I was," Tia nodded. "But now I'm thinking about changing my major. While I still want to help kids when their parents get divorced, I can do that by helping Aunt Brook with the Ashbury Foundation, without having to be a lawyer. So, now I want to pick a doctorate program that will teach me ways to help people with TBIs."

"Let me guess, brain surgeon," Dion interjected, grinning at the precocious almost fourteen-year-old.

"That's what I thought when she first mentioned it," Anthony chuckled, shaking his head.

"No," Tia denied, making a face at both Dion and her dad as she rolled her eyes. "While the classes I was able to jump in and audit this month were interesting, I couldn't be a doctor who has to actually cut someone open to operate." She visibly shuddered, as if grossed out by the thought. "I'm thinking athletic training or physical therapy, so I can help wrestlers and other athletes recover after concussions and other injuries."

"If you do physical therapy, you'll work with more than just athletes," Dion informed her. "There were people of all ages being treated for all kinds of injuries at the place I went in NOLA for vestibular therapy."

As Dion talked with Tia about the things he had to do in vestibular therapy, Julie turned to her cousin. "I'm surprised you aren't pushing her to do a business degree, so she can run Burleson one day."

"Naw," Anthony disagreed, chuckling. "Since she retains more than I do from reading my books to help me study, she'll be more than prepared for her time on the board without having to actually get a business degree. And we don't want to push her to work for the company if it's not something she's passionate about."

"And we like that she's more passionate about doing something to help others," Kay added with a smile. "Instead of just focusing on how she can make the most money."

Julie almost took Kay's comment as a dig at her for spending her career focused on increasing Burleson Incorporated's bottom line through acquiring more and more assets. At least, until Anthony clarified, "No, she's smart enough to invest her allowance and babysitting money to make all she'll ever need to be able to donate her services in whatever field she finally settles on for her degrees."

"Seriously? She's already investing?" Julie was surprised Tia had the time for that with their travel schedule with the GWA and her college-level classes. But then again, the kid had made time to study the neurobiology of brain injuries in the last month, so maybe Julie shouldn't have been so astonished that she'd started investing the previous year.

"Oh, yeah, she had a higher ROI percentage this year than we did." Anthony motioned to himself and his wife. "And we followed Dad, Uncle Jon, and David Hunter's advice on our investments, instead of researching for ourselves like Tia did."

Julie had also followed what she considered the "family plan" for her personal accounts, which she thought had an excellent return on investment. "Maybe we should have Tia look over all our investments," she chuckled self-deprecatingly.

"I just followed Uncle James and Uncle Dean's advice," Tia informed them with a half-shrug. "After Dion mentioned during training last year that they'd more than doubled his income from the financial planner Rick had referred him to, I figured they'd be the best people to advise me."

Julie hadn't ever inquired about the specifics of Dion's financial status, just assuming he was like most people who saved what they could from their annual salaries, even though she knew he was part owner in his brother's club in New Orleans. She'd just assumed that was his only investment, and now that he was no longer wrestling, it would be his only income. That was why she'd advised him to start with helping watch the kids on the ranch, instead of sinking his savings into a day care center in town, which would require a vast outlay of funds up front that he might not make back in their small town.

Of course, right then wasn't really the time to ask him about his other investments either. Not that she really cared if he was well off or flat broke. She loved him, not his bank balance. Besides, she more than had enough to provide for their family, even if he only ever wanted to stay home and take care of their babies, if things worked out between them the way she hoped they would. Thankfully, Deanna joining their group caused an abrupt change of subject, so nobody else brought it up either.

"Oh, Dee, what's wrong?" Kay looked concerned for her friend, who looked to be holding back tears as she sat on the arm of the sofa beside Kay.

Deanna shook her head and closed her eyes momentarily before replying. "I shouldn't have done that fortune telling," she blubbered, giving up holding back her tears to wipe under her eyes with her fingers. "She said I'm going to have a tragic loss early in the year.

With all Mom's health issues the last few years, I just know she means I'm going to lose her."

Julie felt herself tear up as tiny, little, not quite five-foot tall Kay pulled her five-foot-nine friend into her lap to console her. If they weren't so upset over such a dire prediction, the sight would be comical because of their dramatic size difference.

"Hey, don't stress about anything Mama Marcel said," Dion crooned, attempting to allay their fears. "I've known her my whole life, and she's never been able to predict someone's death before, even with people she was close to, like my parents. To her, tragedies are things like bad hair days or broken nails. Maybe a baseball going through your window. And if she specifically said it would be a tragic loss, she could mean like losing your favorite pair of shoes. But I'm sure she doesn't mean the death of a loved one. NOLA might be known as one of the most haunted cities in America, but Mama Marcel avoids the morbid stuff, especially in her predictions. In fact, I bet she only mentioned this loss because it's supposed to lead you to your one true love, right?"

"That's exactly what she said." Deanna nodded, sliding off of Kay's lap to wedge into the sofa between Kay and the armrest as she turned to look at Dion. "But I don't see how losing anything could lead to falling in love. That just doesn't make sense."

Unless losing your current boss when JJ fires him leads to you finally giving in and admitting JJ is your one true love, Julie thought, wondering if her brother had fed Mama Marcel the prediction to give to Deanna. Thankfully, before she could risk ruining JJ's plans for pursuing Deanna by stating as such aloud, the emcee announced it was time to grab their kissing partners to countdown the final minutes of the year.

They all scrambled for noise makers and glasses of champagne or sparkling grape juice before finally getting settled in and counting down the last thirty seconds to midnight. As Julie turned in her seat to face Dion, she noticed him placing his grape juice glass and noisemaker on the table beside him and wondered if the uptick of noise was too much for him.

He soon alleviated her concern by taking the stuff from her hands, placing her glass and noisemaker on the table beside his, and hauling her into his lap. "Since I get to kiss you for real this year, I want us to be comfortable for it."

Julie couldn't help but smile as he placed her hand over his heart as he joined in on the countdown.

"Ten. Nine. Eight. Seven. Six. Five. Four. Three. Two. One. Happy New Year, Jewel."

"Happy New…" Julie's words were cut off by Dion's lips closing over hers.

While intellectually, Julie knew they were still surrounded by friends, family, and fellow townsfolk, she felt like they were all alone the instant their lips touched. He released the hand holding hers to his chest, wrapping her in his big, strong arms as he ran his tongue over the seam of her lips. The sweet licks soon turned more insistent, demanding entry. She slid her arms up around his neck as their tongues tangled and explored every part of one another's mouths. Julie relished the tangy cranberry flavor of their last mocktail mixed with the savory essence of Dion.

They clung to one another as if they'd been separated for decades as their kiss spiraled toward too obscene for such a public display. Between her love for Dion and her pregnancy hormones, Julie needed to connect with him too much to care who saw them at that point in time.

This kiss felt special somehow, more intense, yet also more poignant than any kiss they'd previously shared. Julie never wanted it to end, and was grateful she'd learned to breathe through her nose while kissing, so they didn't have to stop when everyone around them ceased.

Julie paid no attention to the noisemakers and shouts of "Happy New Year" as she basked in the pure bliss of being connected to Dion on the soul-deep level she'd missed the last couple of months.

It wasn't until Tia shouted over the crowd that they finally came up for air. "Aunt Julie! Uncle Dion! Go to your room!"

"Perfect," Dion grinned as he adjusted her in his arms and stood cradling her to his chest bridal style. "Now that we have our marching orders, we don't have to worry about being rude by sneaking out."

"Dion, put me down!" Julie squealed, even as she clung to his broad shoulders. "I'm too heavy for you to carry all the way up to your room. Besides, we haven't toasted the new year yet, and I need to get my purse before we leave."

"You're not too heavy for me to carry," Dion protested, but he also lowered her feet to the floor. "But I suppose I can wait long enough to toast the new year and let you grab your purse before I take you upstairs."

They did just that, toasting and drinking their sparkling grape juice in record time before saying a general "goodnight" to everyone around them. Julie barely had time to scoop up her clutch before Dion took her hand and started them toward the door. Julie redirected him to the back way out of the ballroom, so they could go up the back stairs, instead of walking all the way through the building to get to the main stairs in the foyer.

"Why do I have a sense of déjà vu sneaking up these stairs?" Dion wondered aloud as he walked hand in hand with Julie up to his room.

"Well, we have snuck up these stairs together before," Julie informed him, grinning at the sexy memories that followed all the times they'd snuck up to his room over the last thirteen months. "A few times, actually. Is it just déjà vu you're feeling? Or are you having a flashback to one of those times?"

"Maybe a little of both?" Dion seemed unfocused as they left the stairs and walked down the hallway to his room. "We talked about whether anyone would notice that you didn't go home and you explained how Jen was covering for you."

"Yeah, that was our first time together," Julie confirmed.

"We also talked about not letting anyone know who might let it slip to your mom or aunt," Dion continued as he opened the door to his room. "And you working in cities where I was on tour so we could see each other more often than my holiday breaks to make the long-distance thing work. And we decided to be exclusive that night."

"Yes," Julie confirmed, smiling at the memory as she walked into his room. "But I already told you that you were right in thinking we'd been exclusive since day one."

"What was day one for us?" Dion questioned as he shut and locked the door behind them before standing in about the same spot he had in a similar room as they'd talked on that first night.

"We met on November seventeenth, but didn't sleep together until November twenty-third." Julie didn't mention how hard it had been to see him again on the one-year anniversary of their first time making love.

"So, I've already missed our first anniversaries," Dion sighed as he pulled her into his arms. "I'm so sorry, Jewel. I hate that I forgot those special dates for us."

"It's fine, Dion," she assured him, wrapping her arms around his neck and smiling up at him. "You're remembering them now, so we can celebrate them in the future. Now, tell me what else you remember from our first time."

"You mentioned earning your V-card back because it had been so long," Dion smirked. "And teased me with role-play ideas when I asked if I was gonna get to punch it that night."

"Oh, you more than punched it that night, Mr. Davis," Julie giggled, feeling as giddy as the schoolgirl she'd mentioned in that role-play idea.

"Then we disagreed about how many years constitute a *few,* while discussing my retirement from wrestling and our future plans to be together," Dion continued as he ran his hands over her back. "And when you planned to take time off from work to have our babies."

"Yeah, not that we're exactly sticking to those plans," Julie chuckled, wiggling to rub her baby bump against him to make her point.

Chapter Eighteen

Wednesday, January 1, 2020, New Year's Day, Just after midnight.

As they stood there in his hotel room, Dion struggled to straddle the mental line between remembering the first night he'd made love with Jewel and staying coherent enough to relay the events of his memories to her in real time. While he'd managed long enough to get to the room, he quickly lost the ability to stay present in the moment and remember all the details at the same time, succumbing to his memories as they played out like a movie in his mind.

Friday, November 23, 2018

"Yeah, you're gonna have to push that back closer to forty," Julie retorted. "Especially if you're planning to stay home and be Mister Mom for the first few years after you retire, 'cause I don't plan on taking time off from work to have kids until at least twenty-twenty-five, when I've had ten solid years of work experience. I have to put in my time and prove myself, so I'll be able to fill Dad's shoes as CEO when he retires in another twenty or thirty years."

"Don't worry, Jewel," Dion assured her with the slightest smirk. "I only wanna practice making babies for now."

He slid her hand down over his heart for her to feel the effect she had on him before kissing her senseless. Their tongues tangled as they dueled over who would control the kiss, going back and forth for several minutes until she conceded and let him be the aggressor.

"Relax, Jewel," Dion commanded as they broke the kiss. "I promise I'll take care of you. You just have to relax and enjoy it."

"Yeah, I have a hard time relaxing," Jewel lightly chuckled. "And especially trusting someone else to take care of my needs. Let's just say I've had too many experiences with men I've dated, or dealt with in business meetings, who are only looking out for themselves. Needless to say, I kinda learned to take charge, so my interests aren't overlooked."

"Well, then it sounds like you've only dated or dealt with selfish little boys before now," Dion smiled, brushing a lock of her flaxen hair behind her ear. "And I'll happily show you how a real man treats his lady. Your wants and needs will always come first for me, even if that means I keep my pants on and just spend the whole night making you come repeatedly."

"Yeah, good luck with that," Jewel giggled, shaking her head at him. "I don't even have multiples when I D-I-Y it with my vibrator. And considering most guys can't make even one happen because I get lost in the random thoughts in my head, I'll be perfectly happy if you can get me to have one O tonight."

"Oh, Jewel, I'll definitely get you to more than one," Dion promised, brushing his lips across her forehead. "From this point on, there's no more thinking for you. Your only job is to feel the pleasure I'm gonna give you."

Without waiting for her to refute his statement, Dion picked Jewel up and carried her to the bed, laying her out for him to take his time undressing her and exploring every inch of her delectable body. It was exquisite torture to languidly expose her porcelain flesh, making sure to run his hands, mouth, and tongue over everywhere but her pink parts to get her worked up and ready before he finally tasted her.

With her lying on her back, her tits seemed even flatter than they were when she was sitting or standing, with only the taut nipples and areolas protruding from her body. Regardless of their small size, they were extremely responsive to every stroke or light pinch from his fingers, and especially to the licks from his tongue and nibbles of his mouth as he took his time worshiping her perky peaks. Dion didn't need more than a mouthful when her taut nipples were such effective indicators of her arousal level.

When he eventually delved between her thighs to lap up her juices, he was rewarded with the sweetest honey he'd ever tasted. After licking every drop from her folds and teasing her slit with the tip of his tongue, Dion finally suckled her clit while using his fingers to start opening her up enough to take his big dick.

After taking his time, stretching her out to take three of his large fingers, he wasted no more time in finding her G-spot, crooking his fingers in a come-hither motion to send her soaring in her first orgasm of the night, all while still working her clit with his mouth. She cried out his name repeatedly, until she was so lost in the euphoria of the moment that her words became unintelligible.

Dion continued to finger-fuck her, licking up the gush of cream she released as she writhed in pleasure. He didn't let her stop with just one, taking her over the edge with his fingers and tongue a couple more times before he finally relented to let her catch her breath.

"Please, Dion, I need your cock now," Jewel begged, panting as she reached for his waistband.

"As you wish, Jewel." He gladly stood to undress himself, eager to give her everything she wanted.

Jewel watched from the bed as he stripped, licking her luscious red lips as he removed his dress shirt to expose his chiseled six-pack abs and powerful pecs. He couldn't tell if her lipstick somehow stayed on, or if her lips were just that red from the added blood flow of their earlier kisses, but he loved the look on her. Her eyes widened and her mouth opened in a shocked expression when he dropped his slacks and his huge cock sprang out of his boxer briefs.

"Don't worry, Jewel," Dion reassured her as he retrieved a condom from his wallet. "We'll have to go slow at first to give you time to stretch, but it'll fit. And we'll start with you on top, so you can control how much you take of me."

As Dion started to roll the Magnum down his length, Jewel stopped him. "Wait! I'm allergic to latex, so you need to use my condoms."

She jumped off the bed and ran to her purse on the table where she left it when they first entered the room. Dion tossed the condom he'd been putting on into the wastebasket beside the bed, lying down to watch her as she rifled through her purse. When she came back to the bed, she handed him three packets from a brand he didn't recognize as she laid down beside him.

Dion didn't know or care what they were made out of as long as he could use them to get inside Jewel, so he quickly opened the first packet and attempted to roll it on. Unfortunately, he barely got it over the head of his dick before it split from being too small for him.

"Fuck," he cursed, pulling it off and rolling to the side of the bed to drop it in the trash. "Please tell me at least one of these is an extra-large."

"No, I think they're all the same, basic size." Jewel bit her lip, looking concerned about their chances of getting to have sex anytime soon.

"Then I need to get dressed and go find a store that sells extra-large, latex-free condoms," Dion grumbled, starting to get out of bed to do just that.

"Or we could, um, go without," Jewel muttered timidly, stopping Dion in his tracks. "I mean, I'm clean, and on the pill, and we did agree to be exclusive, so if you're safe, we don't have to use condoms. But you should probably go wash off first, in case any of the lubricant from the first condom you put on left behind any trace of latex, so I don't end up breaking out in a rash after."

"I'm safe," Dion confirmed, excited about the possibility of going bare for the first time in his life as he got up to go to the restroom to wash off his dick. That was something he'd never even thought of doing with anyone else, but with Jewel, it seemed right. Almost like they were so perfect for one another that having a barrier between them would be a sacrilege. "I've never gone without a condom. And we're tested regularly with the GWA because of the risk of bleeding during our matches, so I know I'm clean and haven't been with anyone since my last test."

Dion came back to the moment as he realized his trip the day before with Dare to the drugstore for condoms had been a waste of time. *I guess I can give them to him,* he thought. *But fuck, it's gonna suck if we have to wait to make love until I can get some that are latex free.*

"We, um, decided to forgo condoms that first night, too, right?" Dion finally settled on linking his hands at the small of her back, so he wouldn't be distracted by stroking her as they discussed the important topic of protection.

"Yes, we did," Jewel confirmed with a sexy smile.

"I know neither one of us has been with anyone else since then to change things. But even though Dr. Boudreaux told me I was clean when he said it was safe for me to have sex again, I don't remember when my last test was. Or if I was exposed to any blood in the ring or when the stalker was shot since then…"

"The last test you told me about was the beginning of October," Jewel interjected, cutting him off. "And you haven't had a bloody match since we met. And while I wasn't there to know for sure that you weren't exposed to anyone else's blood when you rescued Allissa and were in the hospital, I'm sure if you were, they would have notified you, and tested for anything you might have been exposed to then."

"I don't remember them doing any of that, but I can call Dare right quick to make sure that's the test Dr. Boudreaux was talking about," he suggested.

"Again, if it had been an issue, he wouldn't have said you were clean." Jewel shook her head, indicating Dion didn't need to call Darius to double-check the testing dates for his clean status. "So, I don't think we have anything to worry about."

"So," Dion drawled, momentarily hesitating before posing his question because of suddenly feeling so uncharacteristically awkward. "You're okay with us not using condoms? 'Cause I didn't remember your latex allergy until just a few minutes ago, and the condoms I bought yesterday, when I realized this was a possibility, aren't latex free. So, um, we're not gonna be able to do more than cuddle for the next couple of days if we need condoms, 'cause there was a sign up at the drugstore about being closed for New Year's Day."

What the fuck? Now I'm rambling? Is losing my sexual prowess another side effect of traumatic brain injury that nobody told me about?

It wasn't that he worried about not being able to perform in the bedroom, especially with Jewel. His near constant erection while in her presence, and daily jerk off sessions in the shower while fantasizing about her, were proof enough that his dick could get the job done. But unlike before his injuries, when he was more than capable of confidently taking charge in any sexual situation, now he kept second-guessing whether or not she wanted the same thing he did.

"I'm perfectly okay with us not using condoms," Julie cooed seductively as she pressed her curvy body against his, making him feel a little more confident that she wanted to make love as much as he did.

"So, why don't you help me unzip this dress and let's try out a few of those positions from that book?"

"As you wish, Jewel." As Dion unzipped her dress and let it fall to the floor, he mentally flashed back to the first time he'd been naked with her in one of these rooms once again.

"So, I get to be in control this first time, huh?" Jewel cooed as she pushed off the bed to roll on top of him after he'd cleaned up, tossed away the useless, too small condoms, and laid back down on the bed. "From everything we've done up 'til now, I thought you always had to be in control in the bedroom."

"Only so I don't risk hurting you," Dion insisted, grinning as she rubbed her wet pussy over his long, thick dick while pushing up with her hands on his chest to sit straddling him. "And until you're stretched out enough to take all of me, Jewel. After I know you can handle my big cock pounding into you, then I'll take charge again, even if you're still on top."

He gripped her hips to control her movements, proving his point while enjoying the feel of her smooth folds rubbing on the underside of his dick. She tried to wiggle out of his hold to take charge again, whining, "Quit teasing me, Dion."

But he didn't relent until he had the head of his cock lined up with her slick slit. As soon as his tip breached her labial lips, Dion released his hold on her hips and reached up to play with her perky tits. "I'm not teasing you, Jewel. You're the one teasing me by not even taking the whole head before you stopped wiggling your tight pussy down on my dick."

Instead of responding with words, Jewel lifted her hands from his pecs to hold his hands on her breasts, wrongly assuming that he could only control how deep he went if he moved his hands back to her hips. It took every ounce of self-control he had to keep from fucking up into her tight sheath as she languidly lowered herself on his length.

"Fuck, you really did get that V-card back," he groaned as her creamy cunt practically choked his cock from being so tight that she'd only been able to take a third of his length so far.

"Am I doing it right, sir?" Jewel cooed in a breathy, porn-star voice. "Since it's my first time, I need you to teach me how to do it right."

"You're doing it just right, Jewel," Dion assured her as she sank further down him until he felt his dick hit her cervix. He

looked down at where they were joined and noticed there were a couple of inches of his shaft that wouldn't fit inside her yet. Knowing she needed to be even more aroused to take all of him, Dion pulled one hand from her tit to move down and stimulate her clit. "You're fucking perfect, Jewel. So tight you're about to make me come already."

"Oh, no," Jewel protested, lifting up almost completely off of his cock as she ran her hands down his arms and back to his chest. "Not yet, Dark Chocolate. You've gotta show me the same stamina you have in the ring first."

"Yes, Mistress Jewel," he teased, chuckling as she finally increased her pace when he gently rocked his hips to push back inside her. "But only if you show me your skills as a cowgirl."

She grinned down at him as she bounced up and down, taking a little more of him on each downstroke until she finally stretched out enough to take him to the root. He continued circling her clit with his left thumb while using his right hand to lightly knead her breasts and pinch her nipples.

Once he knew she could handle all of him without pain, Dion started fucking up into her slick, wet pussy, matching his thrusts to her bouncing rhythm as she picked up the pace once more. Unfortunately, he hadn't been lying about how close he was to coming earlier just from how tight she felt, so Dion knew he needed to make her come quick or he'd look like an inexperienced teenager when he shot his load prematurely.

"Oh, fuck, yeah, ride me, Jewel. Show me how much you like riding Big D." He didn't have to physically control her body to take charge of their fucking. She responded beautifully to him issuing commands and talking dirty while pounding into her from below. "Come on my big dick, Jewel. Now!"

"Oh, fuck, yes, Dion!" Jewel cried out as her tight pussy clamped down on Dion's cock as she came. She closed her eyes and threw her head back as the waves of her release washed over her while she rode him. She was the most beautiful woman he'd ever seen with her straight blonde hair falling just below her shoulders as her luscious red lips parted in orgasmic bliss. He wished she'd open her eyes once more, aching to see how the sapphire blue depths had transformed to stormy gray-blue skies in her aroused state. He took a mental picture of her face contorted in ecstasy, planning to draw it later, so he'd always have that image to look back on, thinking she was the most

beautiful woman he'd ever laid eyes on, especially as she came on his cock.

As her movements slowed with her coming down from her climactic high, Dion moved his hands to grip her hips and bounced her up and down on his dick, not wanting her to stop moving as she recovered from the orgasm. He could feel his spine tingling to signal that he was getting close, so he focused on staring at his large ebony hands on her ivory skin, instead of looking at her perky little tits or down where his big, black dick filled her tight, pink pussy, trying desperately to hold back his climax until he gave her at least one more.

"Gimme one more, Jewel," Dion commanded as he fucked up into her creamy cunt. "I'll fill you up with my cum just as soon as you gimme one more."

"Yes, Dion, yes!" Jewel screamed, digging her short, unpainted fingernails into his chest as she caught her breath and started to move with him once more. "Come with me!"

He might normally prefer to be the one in charge during sex, but that was one command he didn't mind obeying immediately. As soon as he felt her pussy start to spasm around his rod, Dion shoved deep inside her and let loose. As the waves of his release washed over him, he shot jet after jet of cum straight into her womb.

Dion recognized the flash of memory as the same recurring vision he'd been dreaming about since he first woke up in the hospital. Only now he remembered how she'd collapsed on top of him after their mutual orgasm, the second of her two O's with him inside her, and how he held her as they recovered. He even remembered bantering with her when she called him her "real-life book boyfriend" because he proved that multiple orgasms weren't fictional and referred to himself in the third person as "Big D," which led to him telling her how he'd gotten that nickname.

"While that is an apt description," Jewel giggled as they cuddled in bed with his big D still inside her. "I think I'll stick with calling you D or Dion, so I don't have to explain calling you Big D to my parents."

Shit! I wonder if she's had to explain calling me Big Daddy to her folks this week? Dion wondered as he realized she'd started undressing him while he was zoned out from remembering their first time together. *Yeah, I'll have to ask her about that later. Like long after we see how being pregnant affects her ability to ride me.*

~~~

Julie recognized that Dion was momentarily lost in a memory, so she took her time removing his tie and jacket, while standing there in just her underwear and heels, to give him time to come back to her before removing any more of her clothing. While she was happy that their time together was helping to bring back his memories, she wanted him fully focused and in the moment with her when she revealed her fuller breasts for the first time. He'd always told her that he loved her perky little A-cups and that more than a mouthful was a waste, but she had to wonder if he'd really meant those things when he said them. And the only way for her to know for sure that he wouldn't mind if they shrank back to normal after the babies were born was to watch his reaction the first time he saw her boobs were now solid B-cups and bordering on C-cups.

After draping his suitcoat and tie over a nearby chair, Julie started unbuttoning Dion's dress shirt, watching as the glazed look in his eyes receded. "Did you remember more of our first time together? Or something else?"

"I think I finally remembered everything about our first time together," Dion confessed, smiling seductively. "Specifically, how amazing you looked every one of the five times you came, and especially the two times you came with me inside you before we took a break to recover before round two."

"Is that the most memorable part of that night for you?" Julie wondered, recalling how he'd tickled her funny bone, when he flexed his dick inside her while telling her the story of how a group of drunk ring rats had repeatedly asked to see his big D during one of their club outings after a show right after the Hunters started with the GWA, and then the women wrestlers had somehow gone from picking on him
~~~

backstage by imitating the drunk ring rats that had wanted to see his big dick to calling him Big D as a nickname.

"Watching you come? Oh, yeah." Dion nodded, his eyes smoldering with desire as he ran his hands over her curves while keeping their gazes locked. "You coming while riding me that night was the first dream-memory I remember having in the hospital, and one of the memories that's recurred in my dreams most often since. I was so irritated at first because every time I'd have that same dream, I'd only get through the part where you came before the doctor or nurses would come in and wake me up, so I didn't get to come with you the first couple of days I was in the hospital."

"You know it makes you seem like a perv to be irritated by not getting to come while you were in the hospital, right?" Julie grinned teasingly as she pulled his shirttails from his waistband and finished unbuttoning his shirt.

"Oh, I eventually came while I was in the hospital, usually after one of the other dreams of making love with you that I now know were memories of the day we made our babies." Dion's smile appeared to be somewhat shamefaced, almost like he was embarrassed by his hospital orgasm memories. "But it took a couple of days before they let me sleep long enough to get there. And it was rather embarrassing to have to get the nurse to help me deal with the mess when I hadn't kicked off the covers or stripped in my sleep first. It was like being fifteen years old again and having wet dreams, only they were much more explicit than the ones I had when I was a teen."

Julie couldn't stop the light chuckle that escaped from her lips as she pictured Dion trying to explain how he'd made a mess in his sleep to an older nurse while he was in the hospital. She knew from firsthand experience that Dion was always warm and preferred to sleep naked, without even a sheet covering him. But in trying to be respectful of the hospital staff, she knew he'd probably tried to stay covered while he was there. "So, which was more embarrassing, having them walk in on you in all your naked glory, or having them help you change your sheets and gown to clean up after coming in your sleep?"

"Definitely the clean up after," Dion admitted, shaking his head as he moved his hands up to start unfastening her bra. "If they walked in while I was exposed, I didn't know it because I was asleep, and I was always covered up when I woke up with someone in the room."

Julie assumed the nurses covered him up before waking him to take his vitals, but she couldn't ask to be certain right then because Dion had successfully unfastened her bra without looking. She'd dropped her gaze to his chest as she pushed his shirt off his shoulders, but now she popped her eyes back up to his face, needing to see his reaction to seeing her new curves uncovered for the first time.

Julie dropped her hands, allowing Dion to push the straps of her bra off her shoulders to let it fall to the floor, exposing her breasts. But instead of looking down at her bouncy B-cups, Dion kept his eyes locked on hers as he trailed his hands back up her arms, over her shoulders, and down over her chest to reverently cup her breasts.

"According to that book you sent me, the changes in your body while you're pregnant can either enhance your pleasure or make certain things too uncomfortable to endure." Dion spoke softly as he lightly ran his thumbs over her nipples, causing them to harden and tingle with anticipation of what he would do to them next. "So, as I'm trying to learn what you like all over again, please tell me if I do anything you don't love, so I can stop, even if I can't tell if you like it or not from your body's response."

"You must not have remembered some of our kinkier sexcapades yet," Julie smirked, unfastening his slacks as she continued to stare into his obsidian eyes. She loved the way they turned a deeper hue when he was most aroused. "Or you'd remember that I don't have a problem speaking my mind, even when intentionally being bratty 'cause I know it's gonna earn me a spanking."

"Fuck," Dion groaned, closing his eyes as he rocked his hips to thrust his cock toward her hands, which she was trying to use to push his pants down. "Remind me later to ask you about the memory I had of you telling me to slap your ass harder. As much as I wanna revisit that, I don't wanna get sidetracked now, when I'm finally about to get to make love to you again."

"Oh, yeah, we'll definitely go back to that later," Julie agreed, using both hands just long enough to free his cock from the confines of his eggplant-colored boxer briefs before switching to only one hand pushing them down his legs while the other grasped his erection. She would have commented on the apropos color choice for covering his cock that matched the color of the emoji used most often to represent a dick, but she'd waited too long to be with him again and didn't want to get sidetracked either.

"Fuck, Jewel." Dion's hands fell from her breasts as she dropped to her knees to finish lowering his pants and boxer briefs while starting to stroke his impressive cock.

As he toed out of his shoes and socks, Julie lightly kissed his crown before wrapping her lips around the head of his cock. She sucked and stroked, letting him worry about stepping out of the rest of his clothing while she savored the salty precum already leaking into her mouth. He was so big that it took her mouth and both hands to worship every inch of his long, thick schlong. Her jaw was always sore the next day after giving him a blow job, but Julie loved the feeling, knowing it meant she'd satisfied her man.

"Fuck, you're even more amazing than I remembered," Dion groaned as he gathered her hair in a makeshift ponytail so it didn't block his view.

Julie looked up at Dion as she sucked his cock, delighting in his expression of awe as he focused his gaze on her face. Or rather, on her lips around his cock. He still hadn't really seemed to look at her breasts, making it obvious to her that he didn't care about the size of her tits because he loved her, not her individual body parts.

Hopefully, he'll enjoy the bonus boobs while they last, she thought. *The way I plan on enjoying his big dick for the rest of our lives, even if it shrinks with age.*

She pushed away the memory of walking in on the septuagenarian and octogenarian book club meeting at the B and B, where she'd overheard that little tidbit of TMI, focusing instead on the powerful feeling of control she had as she sucked Dion's cock. She knew he wouldn't let her have all the control for long. At least, the man he'd been before his injuries wouldn't. While she knew some brain injuries could affect an individual's personality and sex drive, she didn't think Dion's had, not from the glimpses she'd seen of the Dion she knew coming through the confused state he seemed to be in when he first arrived in town.

"Fuck, Jewel, that feels so good," Dion growled. "Oh, yeah, just like that. Suck my cock. Get my big dick nice and slick, so I can slide it in your creamy cunt."

She swirled her tongue over the sensitive spot where the head and shaft met, knowing it would drive Dion wild. Sure enough, his dick twitched in her mouth right before he involuntarily thrust deeper, causing his tip to brush against the back of her throat. At his slight loss of control, she smiled around him, just as he pulled back to keep from pushing too far, allowing her saliva to drip past her lips and lubricate his shaft. She glided her hands up and down his base, squeezing and twisting around his cock to mimic the way her inner walls convulsed when she came with him inside her. She continued to bob up and down as she sucked and licked, knowing he wouldn't last much longer before he took charge.

"Stop, Jewel," Dion commanded, stepping back while also lightly tugging her hair to get her to pull her mouth off his cock. "It's my turn to taste you before you ride my dick."

There's my dominant Dion. She couldn't stop the triumph from shining in her expression as she smiled up at him while continuing to stroke his cock. Having him take charge caused her pussy to flood to the point that she felt her juices dripping down her inner thighs.

He released her hair to gently clasp his big hands around her wrists, pulling her hands from his massive member. Then he helped her stand before dropping down to sit on the floor with his upper back against the bed. He motioned for her to stand between his legs, so he could slide her purple silk panties off.

Julie would have been embarrassed by the wetness of the fabric if it was anyone but Dion seeing it. But after his constant praise for how her body responded to him, she'd long since learned how much he loved making her dripping wet. When he leaned forward to sniff her panties just as he got them down to about mid-thigh, then grinned up at her as he pushed them the rest of the way down to her ankles, she knew his sexual proclivities hadn't changed a bit due to the TBI.

"As much as I love the idea of fucking you in nothing but these sexy shoes," Dion crooned as he placed her hands on his shoulders for balance before lifting her left foot to remove her panties and shoe. "I don't think we need anything else that might put you in a precarious position while I eat your pussy."

After placing her bare left foot back on the floor, Dion lifted her right foot to repeat the procedure to fully strip her. He then leaned his head back onto the mattress and stuck out his tongue while wagging his eyebrows suggestively. "Now turn around and step back to straddle me while you sit on my face."

Julie was already aroused, but his deep commanding tone was enough to make her pussy gush once more because of how turned on he made her.

"Yes, Big Daddy," she purred out in a teasing tone as she followed his orders.

As soon as she stepped back and started to sit, he lightly slapped her ass for the insolence, rubbing in the slight sting before gripping her hips to position her where he wanted. She would have mouthed off to get him to spank her other ass cheek, but the feel of his tongue licking through her folds wiped away all thoughts of misbehaving. "Oh, Dion," she moaned at the pleasure of finally having him eating her pussy after two-and-a-half, long months apart.

She placed her hands on her bent knees for balance as he fucked her with his tongue, wishing she could continue fellating his magic peen, which was standing at attention and reaching out toward her. Unfortunately, she didn't think she could mix downward dog and a blow job right then, especially since she'd been warned to be cautious with inverted yoga poses while pregnant because they could increase acid reflux or make her feel short of breath with the babies applying pressure to her internal organs.

Instead of reaching out to stroke the majestic phallus jutting out from his neatly trimmed pubic region, she simply appreciated the view as Dion licked, sucked, and tongue-fucked her to the heights of ecstasy. She knew better than to try to stand before she came. No matter how much she wanted to wait to come until he was balls-deep inside her, he'd long since trained her to come at least once before trying to work his huge cock into her tight pussy.

"Oh, yes, Dion," Julie cried out as his big hands spread her cheeks and he pressed the tip of his nose against her anus to push her over the edge. "Yes, oh fuck, Dion, yes!"

He slurped up her juices, which were pouring out of her as wave after wave of pure pleasure washed over her. Julie was grateful he hadn't let go of her hips, feeling wobbly on weak knees as she slowly came down from her orgasmic high. But even though she didn't feel capable of standing on her own two feet at that moment, she never felt in danger of falling, knowing Dion held her locked in place, even as he switched from long licks and short sucks to sweet butterfly kisses all over her labia.

As she tried to stand to test out her sea legs, Dion adjusted his position to spread more butterfly kisses all over her ass, making her chuckle. "I don't recall ever actually telling you to kiss my ass, but I suppose we can consider this your way of following through on all the times I thought it in the last couple of months."

"Maybe if I do it enough," Dion snickered as he helped her finally stand up. "Then you won't ever have to think it again."

"Maybe." Julie turned, swapping the positions of her feet to continue straddling his torso, only facing him this time. She didn't give him the chance to stand from the floor to move to the bed, lowering to her knees as she reached out and lined the head of his cock up with her opening. "Or maybe I'll just start telling you to kiss my ass, so I can get you to do that more often."

"I'd rather kiss your pouty lips," Dion smirked, pushing her hair behind her ears as he cradled her head in his palms to pull her face toward his. She ran her hands over his pecs, making sure her right hand covered his heart before they kissed. "Especially after you've had them around my cock."

Their lips crashed together as Julie sank down, taking him into her body, one thick inch at a time. She had to go slow, allowing her body to gradually stretch to accommodate his big dick, even after her sex had relaxed from her first orgasm.

Dion pressed his tongue against the seam of her lips, opening her for his invasion as his hands traveled down until he could tweak her nipples. She tasted herself on his tongue, relishing the mix of her sweetness with his salty precum that still coated the inside of her mouth.

Between the carnal kiss and the titty torture, Julie's concupiscence rose to new heights, allowing her inner walls to soften until she finally took all of him. Once fully seated, she rotated her hips, grinding her clit over his pubic bone for the extra stimulation she needed for another quick climax.

"Oh, gawd, Dion," Julie cried out, breaking the kiss as her core convulsed in pleasure. She arched her back as she came, surprised to find the support of Dion's thighs to lean back into since he'd bent his legs while she was otherwise occupied and didn't notice.

"Fuck, yeah, ride me, Jewel," Dion moaned, breathing the words against her skin as he kissed his way down her neck. His lips soon replaced his fingers on her left nipple, sucking it into his mouth before laving it with his tongue. He rocked his hips in time with her rhythm, gently thrusting his cock up into her.

Julie ran her hands over his shoulders and arms, reveling in their soulful lovemaking for their first time coming back together. She loved the way he always took care of her during their first round, holding back his rougher needs until at least round two to make sure her needs were fulfilled first.

That innate need they both had to tend to one another first was why she always tried to take the edge off for him by fighting for control at first, wanting to get him off with her hands and mouth. She knew it had to be difficult for him to hold back his orgasm while waiting for her body to prepare for the intense round of fucking that always left her feeling him for days after. And one of these days, she hoped to actually be successful in making him come first.

Like he'll ever let me have control long enough for that to happen. The closest he's ever come to letting me get him off first was in the shower the day we made our babies. But that was like round three that day, so he didn't really come first, even though I got him off with my mouth before he ate my pussy and fucked me into more orgasms against the shower wall. Maybe we can revisit that later...

Her thoughts trailed off as the exquisite way Dion made love to her pushed everything but what they were currently doing from her mind.

~~~

Fuck, she feels amazing, Dion thought as they gently made love while seated on the floor of his hotel room. While he could push through his heels and bridge up to thrust a little more powerfully than he currently was, since he'd bent his knees and put his feet flat on the floor, he continued to rock his hips in time with Jewel to maintain the slow grinding rhythm that she seemed to prefer this time around. He'd bent his knees to give her something to lean back on in case she needed the back support, and he knew he couldn't sustain that if he gave in and started thrusting harder the way he craved. First and foremost,
~~~

pleasuring Jewel was his number one priority, even when it took every ounce of self-control he possessed to keep from rutting into her tight, slick pussy like an animal, the way his inner caveman coveted.

Even though the books Jewel had referred to him said it was safe to be more vigorous, Dion still felt the need to keep it soft and sensual. He didn't want to take any chances with hurting her or their babies, regardless of whether or not their more carnal activities of the past were considered innocuous. But more so, he wanted to show Jewel all the reverence she deserved as they came together this first time back as a couple. He wanted to show her how much he loved her, putting her first over everyone and everything else in his life.

His goal was to strengthen their emotional connection to one another more than to satiate their physical lust. That's why he sustained their slow pace with gentle, undulating thrusts of his cock while worshiping her more voluptuous breasts with his mouth and hands.

Fuck! Her expanding curves are gorgeous! Dion thought as he kissed his way from her left nipple to her right. He sucked the rosy pink tip into his mouth, lightly grazing it with the edge of his teeth before swirling his tongue around the turgid nubbin.

He took his left hand down to play with her clit as his right cupped her left breast. He lightly pinched her left nipple between his thumb and forefinger while suckling the right, much like their babies would in a few months.

Now is definitely not the time to think about the babies nursing. Dion mentally chastised himself as he rubbed his thumb over her clit, knowing he needed to stay focused on Jewel and her pleasure right then.

He sucked a little harder for a second before popping his mouth off her tit and kissing his way back up her neck. Just as his mouth reached her ear, he whispered, "Come for me, Jewel."

He then pulled back to look her in the eyes, wanting nothing more than to see the look of pure ecstasy on her face as her body convulsed in pleasure from their lovemaking. Their emotional connection was so strong at that point that it felt palpable, like nothing could break their gazes apart right then. Her stormy blue-gray eyes shined with her love for him and Dion knew his brown orbs reflected his love back to her.

Leah Mae Wright

"Yes, Dion, yes!" Jewel cried out, never taking her gaze from his as her inner walls clamped down on his cock with her release.

"Fuck, yes, Jewel." Dion couldn't hold back a second longer, coming simultaneously with the love of his life. With each spasm of her tight pussy, he shot another jet of cum deep inside her.

He reverently ran his hands over her curves, eventually bringing them to her back to rub down and over her ass as they experienced the aftershocks of their soulful bonding. "I love you, Jewel."

"I love you, too, Dion." Jewel pressed her rounded belly and full breasts into his torso as she leaned forward to press their lips together, hugging him to her since there was no room for her hand to cover his heart.

While Dion missed their usual ritual, he also appreciated the way she clung to him with her arms around his shoulders and neck. As he licked into her mouth, he savored the mix of their salty and sweet flavors that still lingered on their tongues from their earlier oral affections.

Tasting the mix of them was enough to revive his only slightly softened cock. He hardened inside her, surprising both of them with his rapid recovery time.

"Wow, already?" Jewel smiled as she broke their kiss.

"With you, always," Dion replied, returning her smile as he hugged her to his chest. "But I can wait for round two if you need a little more recovery time."

"I'm good if you are." Jewel wagged her eyebrows suggestively. "But you've gotta do all the work this time."

"Then move your hands to my biceps and hold on tight with your legs," Dion directed, not wanting to squash her arms between his upper body and the bed, even though the bed was soft enough to give under their mutual weight. As soon as she moved her arms from around his neck, Dion rested his head and shoulders on the mattress and bridged up so his torso and thighs were parallel with the floor. He kept his arms wrapped around her, holding her in place so there was no chance she could fall while he fucked her.

Jewel wrapped her legs around his waist and lightly dug her nails into his upper arms as he lowered his hips halfway back to the floor before thrusting back up into her. He bounced her several times like that, slowly increasing the pace and causing her to laugh with glee.

"I feel like I'm bronc riding," she giggled.

"Really? You're comparing me to a horse right now?" Dion feigned offense, even though he wanted to laugh along with her.

"Oh, please, Big D," Jewel playfully scoffed. "Like you don't know my first thought when I initially saw your cock was that you're hung like a horse. And that's high praise coming from a cowgirl, who's actually seen horses mate to know just how close your dick compares."

"Aw, so that's what that wide-eyed, shocked expression I remembered earlier meant," Dion chuckled, loving that they could banter and laugh with each other in the middle of sex. "I thought you were afraid it wouldn't fit without hurting, but I'm glad to know you were impressed by my cock instead of frightened by it."

"Oh, I'm definitely impressed with your cock," Jewel cooed, wiggling her hips as he continued to buck her up and down on his dick like the bronco she compared him to. "Especially when you hit that spot deep inside me that I can't even find with my vibrator."

Dion put a little extra oomph on his next thrust, grinning as her eyes practically rolled back in her head when he hit her cervix.

"Yep," she chirped as her vaginal walls fluttered around his cock, signaling that she was getting close to the edge again already. "That, that's the spot."

Dion slid his hands down to grip her hips, needing to be able to pull her a little farther off his dick each time he dropped his hips, so he could increase the friction on her G-spot with each deep thrust that allowed the head of his cock to tap her cervix.

After not doing such a vigorous workout in over two months, he knew his hamstrings and glutes were going to be sore the next day from using Jewel as the weight for an exhaustive set of hip thrusts. But he really didn't care at that moment. All that mattered to him right then was making sure he hit all her magic buttons to make her soar to the heights of nirvana while she soaked his cock with her cream.

He continuously repeated the move he'd done in hundreds of workouts over the years, enjoying this sexual version of the exercise with Jewel much more than he'd ever liked doing them in the gym. Especially when she slipped her hand off his bicep to cover his heart right before kissing him through her first climax from round two.

Thankfully, he'd long since mastered breathing through his nose while kissing, as well as syncing his breathing to the exercise by exhaling as he thrust his hips upward and inhaling as he lowered his hips toward the floor, so he didn't have to think about either right then. Instead, he was able to focus solely on the feel of plunging his cock into Jewel's tight, wet pussy.

"Oh, Dion!" Jewel repeatedly chanted his name, barely lifting her lips from his as she convulsed with each wave of her release.

He unleashed the beast inside him then, pounding his big dick into her creamy cunt relentlessly. He didn't slow his rhythm, or lessen the intensity of his thrusts, until he pushed her over the edge several more times.

Finally, he felt the tingling in his spine and balls that he knew all too well as the tell-tale sign of his impending release. "Come one more time, Jewel," he commanded, eager to shoot off his load while she milked his cock with the spasms of her climax. "Come for me. Now. Jewel. One. More. Time."

He punctuated each of his last few words with a powerful thrust, holding deep inside her when she followed his directive. As her pussy clamped down on him in a vise-grip, Dion let loose, painting her inner walls with jet after jet of his white, sticky cum. "Jewel! Julia!"

Dion barely managed to pull her feet off his ass before his hips collapsed to the floor. He felt like every muscle in his body was completely spent as he sat there holding Jewel while gasping for breath, taking several long minutes to recover after their second round of the night.

"I think I need a nap before round three," Jewel teased before Dion could even catch his breath enough to speak.

He only nodded in agreement as she pecked her lips to his before peeling herself off of him. Seeing his cum dripping down her legs as she stood, gave him enough of a second wind to be able to get up and follow her into the ensuite bathroom.

"I think it's my job to clean you up." He reached over her head to grab a washcloth from the stack on the rack behind the toilet before she could.

"I suppose, since you were the one to make the mess," she grinned, grabbing a hand towel just as he turned on the sink.

He adjusted the temperature of the water to warm before wetting the washcloth. Then he dropped to his knees and wiped his cum off her thighs and out from between her legs. Once she appeared as clean as he could get her, he wiped off his dick before dropping the washcloth in the basket in the corner for dirty linens. He then took the hand towel she handed him to repeat the process to dry them both off, always with her first.

"Since you're not supposed to *lay* on your back, how are you supposed to sleep now?" Dion questioned as they walked back into the main room to actually get in the bed.

"On my left side," Jewel informed him as she walked to her normal side of the bed, which would put her facing him if she laid on her left side.

While Dion appreciated that sleeping on their typical sides of the bed would mean she could cuddle up to his side all night, he also remembered that lying on their sides with him behind her was one of the recommended positions for sex while pregnant. "Why don't we switch sides, so I can spoon you to keep you from rolling onto your back in the middle of the night?"

"Did you remember how I always roll to my back instead of cuddling all night?" Jewel eyed him curiously as she walked around the bed to trade sides with him.

"No," Dion smirked as they turned down the bedding, flipped off the bedside lamps, and crawled into bed. "I just figured this would put us in the right position for me to fuck you from behind when I wake up in an hour or two."

"Yeah, you might need to let me sleep a little longer than that," Jewel giggled as he wrapped his arm over her, wiggling her ass against his semi-hard cock. "But that does sound like the perfect way to wake up on the first day of the year."

Too bad I can't wake her up that way every day this year.

"How 'bout I ask if you're awake every time I wake up?" Dion suggested, thinking they could get in another round or two before her typical six a.m. wake-up time.

"And spork me if I'm awake?" Jewel's giggle was cut off by a yawn.

"Exactly," Dion chuckled. "Goodnight, Jewel. I love you."

"Goodnight, Dion. I love you, too."

It didn't take long for them both to fall asleep. And miraculously, Jewel was wide awake and eager for that sporking when he woke up a couple hours later.

Chapter Nineteen

Dion felt almost hyperactively excited about going shopping with Jewel for their babies' nursery, after spending the last two days cooped up alone at the bed and breakfast. He'd ended up spending New Year's Day with her and her family after seeing Darius and Mama Marcel off for their quick trip back to NOLA. But she'd had to go back to work on Thursday and Friday, so they'd gone back to just texting throughout the day and talking on the phone each night after she finally got home from whatever she had going on with her family and friends, or down at the youth center where she volunteered. He'd recently learned that since she couldn't ride the horses while pregnant, she'd switched to teaching a class on the basics of business and economics to the older teenagers in town, instead of the equestrian skills she'd previously gone to the youth center to teach. While he was proud of how she was devoted to giving back to her community, all her commitments left Dion feeling awfully lonely without her at the boutique hotel with him.

Dion couldn't even hang out with James or Dean while he was staying on his own in their family's bed and breakfast, since they'd both gone back on tour with the GWA. And while he felt like he'd started bonding with Jewel's cousin Josh while talking about therapists and the equine therapy program he was planning to start, Dion didn't feel close enough to him to ask about hanging out with him on the ranch while Jewel was at work. So, he'd spent his abundance of free time sitting in the empty ballroom with his sketch pad, trying to draw the memories that came back to him while he was sitting there alone to think about them in depth. He'd remembered several of the more

351

meaningful conversations they'd had about their lives, their likes and dislikes, and how their love had grown from their easy friendship as much as their physical attraction.

He'd also walked out to the Hunters' stables to see if the sight and smell of the horses would help trigger some of the memories of the first time he met Jewel. Since his riding experience with Jewel hadn't been there, just being in that setting hadn't triggered anything. But once he started texting her, and she told him her version of the first time they met, it had come back to him with such clarity that he'd been able to draw her walking toward him at the bounce house in her blue jeans that first day, along with a caricature of himself drooling over her with his heart beating out of his chest as he watched her walking away after their first brief interaction.

He planned to surprise Jewel once he filled up one of the sketchbooks he'd bought on one of his various excursions around town in the last month. Drawing was something he'd picked up from his mom as a kid and made some spending money with as a teenager, drawing caricatures for tourists in Jackson Square. But it wasn't something he'd done regularly as an adult, so even though he'd shared his love of drawing with Jewel during some of their talks that he'd recently recalled, she'd never seen anything he'd drawn before. At least, not that he remembered so far.

I wonder if I ever drew her O face like I thought about doing our first time making love? If so, where'd that drawing go? Surely, I wouldn't have given it to her. I woulda wanted to keep it someplace close, so I could look at it whenever we were apart. But I also wouldn't have wanted to keep it anyplace where the guys could find it to see her in that state. So maybe I didn't ever draw it out to keep that visual private between me and her.

Regardless of whether he'd completed that planned drawing or shared his artistic hobby by giving Jewel previous drawings, now he planned to give her the sketchbooks of their memories once he had them full. Knowing Jewel the way he did now that his memories were returning, he knew she'd cherish those gifts far more than any of the jewelry or expensive items he'd previously bought her.

"So, are Darius and Mama Marcel going to be back in town in time for your doctor's appointment on Monday?" Jewel's question as she drove them to Lytle, where the Baby Bonanza store she wanted to visit was located, brought him back to the moment with her.

"I hope so," Dion sighed, a little worried that Dare would be stuck in NOLA past the weekend. "Since Windy and Kandi aren't quite ready to go with CouBer, the closest car service I was able to find is in San Antonio, and they didn't exactly seem thrilled with the prospect of sending one of their drivers out to Heart's Destiny. So, I'm probably gonna hafta reschedule my appointment if they can't get back in time."

"I still don't understand why they decided to go for such a short trip back," Jewel bemoaned as she slowed down to turn into the mall parking lot. "I thought Caroline had some fortune telling sessions scheduled at the B and B this month, so it doesn't make sense for her to not be here for them, and for your appointments."

"Yeah, but she wasn't planning on them when she came here right after her cruise," Dion explained as she parked the car, "so she wanted to go get her props and stuff to put on more of a show than she did on New Year's Eve. And after talking to the movie people that were in town last weekend, Dare wanted to pitch his club as a possible location for one of their upcoming productions. Since I've decided to stay here permanently, they thought it would be easiest to drive his car back to NOLA, pack up the stuff Mama Marcel needs, and the rest of my clothes and stuff, while Dare's showing the movie people around the club, and then drive my vehicle back here for me. Then once I'm cleared to drive and Mama Marcel's done with her gigs here, they can fly home. Though to be honest, I'm pretty sure Mama Marcel might end up staying here, even when Dare goes back to NOLA to stay."

Even if Mama Marcel didn't stay permanently after coming back this time, he was certain she would the first time she came to visit after the babies were born. She might have only recently become his mama legally, but she was just as eager and excited about becoming a grandma as all the rest of the women in her age range in Heart's Destiny. So, Dion was pretty sure she'd move to wherever Jewel and their babies lived, regardless of whether he'd decided to move there or not.

As he got out of the car and went around to open her door for her, Dion assumed the subject was dropped. But as soon as her car door was shut, Jewel brought it back around to his appointment with Doc

Hayes. "So, what time is your appointment on Monday? If they can't get back in time, then I'll take off work to take you."

"It's at one," Dion informed her as they walked into the outside entrance for Baby Bonanza without having to walk through the mall. "But you don't have to take off work to take me. Mama Marcel said she can fly in Monday morning and get a rental car if Dare gets stuck in NOLA for a few days, trying to work out a deal for the movie stuff."

While he'd much rather have Jewel there than even Mama Marcel or Darius, he didn't want to burden her with his issues when they'd just started to find their way back together.

"Nonsense," Jewel waved off his concern. "We are a couple now, right?"

Dion nodded his agreement, unable to reply verbally as she continued speaking while grabbing a shopping cart and putting her purse in the section where a child would normally sit.

"And as a couple, we're supposed to take care of each other and help each other out when needed." Jewel pushed the shopping cart down the first aisle of baby toys as she continued. "So, there's no point in making your family rush back, when I can easily take you to your appointment, especially since you'll be going with me to mine with Dr. Magnum the next day. And before you try to argue that it's not fair, or try to come up with some way of paying me back, I've already got that figured out, too. Justin and Amy are going on their honeymoon in a couple of weeks, and I'll need your help taking care of Jerry and Jonah for the overnight shift while they're gone. Considering that includes two a.m. feedings and diaper changes for a whole week, plus helping me get the nursery ready in the next two weeks, I'm gonna end up owing you a lot more than one trip to the doctor's office."

"You won't owe me a thing, Jewel," Dion disagreed, even as he looked forward to spending that week at Jewel's house to help her with her nephews. Instead of taking a chance at getting the overwhelmed feeling that triggered his passing out spells by trying to look at every item on the shelves the way Jewel was, Dion focused exclusively on watching her, planning to only comment on specific items if she asked for his opinion. "Especially if I get to cat nap beside you between those bottles and diaper changes."

"Ooh, can we barter diaper changes for sexual favors?" Jewel looked up at him with an impish grin before stopping to compare baby playmats for newborns.

Dion loved seeing her acting more like the playful Jewel he'd gotten to know and love over the last year than the quietly angry version of her he'd encountered when he first came back to Heart's Destiny. "I'm open to bartering. What are you thinking? Something like anal for every shitty diaper I change?"

"You have obviously not gotten all your memories back yet," Jewel scoffed, rolling her eyes at him before putting two different playmats in the shopping cart. "Or you'd know anal is never on the table for bartering. A teasing touch on the outside back there is fine, but nothing inserted because it's an exit not an entrance."

"Damn, who knew amnesia would give a guy hope," Dion teased, covering his heart with his hand momentarily before pointing down to the two playmats she'd picked out. "Why two different playmats? I mean, I know we need two because of having two babies. But shouldn't we get them the same one, so there's not a problem if they both like one more than the other?"

"I can't decide which one I like better, so I figured I'd let the babies decide. If they both end up preferring one, then we'll come back and get a second just like it. And you need to watch your language from now on. While our babies aren't going to repeat what they hear you say yet, the other babies and toddlers in the store today might."

"Oh, okay." Dion ducked his head sheepishly, not pointing out that she'd been the one to start the conversation about sexual favors as a mom with a baby joined them on the aisle. Unable to figure out how to talk about what they'd be bartering while watching his language as they moved on to the next item Jewel wanted to look at, he waited until they were alone in the aisle to continue the discussion. "So, back to the bartering. How about oral for…poopy diapers? And maybe fingering or a hand job if it's just urine? That way, we both get rewarded for every diaper we change."

"You obviously don't know how many diapers a baby goes through each day," Jewel giggled as she put several rattles in the shopping cart. "If we were to reward each other for every single one, we'd both end up with arthritis in our hands and lockjaw within a week. Not that we'll be able to do anything for at least six weeks after our babies are born."

"Seriously?" Dion knew she wouldn't be up for sex right after the babies were born, but he thought he could at least pleasure her in other ways a few days later. "Nothing for six weeks? Come on. It's not like your hands, mouth, or clit will need recovery time."

"Nothing that can cause me to have an orgasm because of the contractions down there," she informed him as they turned down a different aisle to pick out baby bath supplies. "And if I can't have any O's for six weeks, then neither can you. 'Cause just watching yours would trigger mine."

Damn, I hope it isn't too painful to have my sperm backed up in my system for that long.

"Well, um, okay," Dion sputtered, knowing better than to ask if it would be okay for him to jerk off in the shower when she wasn't watching to keep from getting blue balls during the six weeks immediately after their babies were born. "Then what exactly were you thinking for the bartering?"

"Bartering probably wasn't the right word," Jewel hemmed and hawed as she looked at baby bathtubs. "I was thinking more along the lines of a daily or weekly count and rewarding whoever changed the most with getting to pick the quickie position the next time we both have the energy and both babies are asleep at the same time. And I was only thinking about the week we're watching Jerry and Jonah. If we want to do something like that again after our babies are born, then obviously, it'd only be after I'm cleared for that at the six- or eight-week checkup."

"Eight weeks?" Dion groaned. *What the hell? Why'd it suddenly jump from six weeks to eight weeks?* "Remind me to ask our doctors next week how long it's safe to let sperm build up without releasing it."

"Oh, you'll be fine." Jewel lightly tapped his forearm before pointing up at the bathtubs on the top shelf for him to get the one she couldn't reach. "If it gets to be too much, then it'll leak out in your sleep, especially if you keep having those dreams."

"True," Dion agreed as he put two of the bathtubs in the cart.

"We probably only need one of those," Jewel pointed out. "I mean, I can only bathe one baby at a time."

"Yeah, but if we have two tubs, then I can bathe the other one at the same time."

"I guess you're planning to just move in with me when the babies are born?" Jewel arched an eyebrow curiously at him as she loaded down the cart with baby soap, baby shampoo, baby lotion, hooded towels that looked like various animals, and at least a dozen matching baby washcloths.

"I'm not officially moving in until you want me to, Jewel," Dion insisted, taking over pushing the cart now that it was getting heavy as they filled it up. "But I am gonna be there as often as you'll let me, so you're not stuck trying to take care of both of them on your own. Even if that means sleeping on your couch, so I can be there for our babies, if you decide you don't want to be with me anymore."

"You're not gonna be stuck sleeping on the sofa." Jewel rolled her eyes at him. "I just don't want us to progress to living together or whatever, just because of the babies."

"We're not, Julia." Dion gave her a reassuring smile as they turned the corner to the next aisle and she started picking out changing pads and other diaper changing paraphernalia. "The babies are an added blessing, but they're not the basis for our relationship. Even when I couldn't remember your name, or tell if my dreams were memories or premonitions, I knew I loved you. I knew we were meant to be together. I know it seems like an abrupt change to be a couple now after so many months of hiding our relationship, but living together, getting married, having a family with you, those are all things I'm pretty sure I was planning for from day one because of how much I love you. But just like I was prepared to wait to retire from the ring on your timeline before, I'm patient enough to wait to move in and get married now. Fate kinda intervened with my forced retirement and your baby plans, but I firmly believe that we're a strong enough team to be able to roll with those punches and enjoy those blessings. And eventually, we'll hit all the other milestones in our relationship, but only when it works for us."

"I love you, too," Jewel blubbered, stopping in the middle of the aisle to wrap her arms around his waist and rest her forehead on his chest.

Dion returned the embrace, bending his head down to brush his slightly numb lips over the top of her head, and holding her until she regained her composure. He knew it probably looked a bit strange to anyone observing them standing their hugging in the middle of the baby store, but he needed the timeout to deal with his overwhelmed feelings as much as she did. *Probably even more to keep from passing out.*

Once they were both over the tears and minor bout of anxiety, they continued shopping, meandering through the store, and picking a couple of different options for each of the toys and baby supplies they picked out as they continued their conversation about what they wanted for their future together.

"I want all that too, ya know," Jewel mentioned casually, with her back turned to him as she looked at baby toys. "The living together, getting married, and being a family you mentioned earlier. I want all that with you, too. But we've got all the time in the world, so there's no need to rush toward our happily ever after. We can take our time and enjoy each phase of our relationship at our own pace."

"Yeah, I agree," Dion nodded, pushing the cart behind her as she strolled through the store, picking out more toys. "I'm really enjoying the dating-and-preparing-for-our-babies phase now."

"Me, too," Jewel smiled, turning to hold up a couple of stuffed animals for Dion to pick which one he liked best.

"Get them both," Dion insisted, unable to deny her or their babies anything they might want.

They didn't set any exact dates or plan anything concrete, but Dion was relieved to know that they were on the same page for wanting to be a family with all the usual trappings of living what Jewel called their "happily ever after."

Thank fuck! Now I don't have to worry about her saying no when I finally get her ring from the jewelers and can pop the question. At least, not if I wait long enough for her to be ready to start talking about dates for moving in together first.

~~~

After a very successful trip to Baby Bonanza and a stop at Heart of the Home to get Brent Deere to deliver the custom-made baby furniture she'd picked out, Julie finally understood why Dion had dressed in
~~~

navy-blue slacks and a classic white button-down, instead of wearing something more casual for their shopping trip. He hadn't wanted to leave in the middle of putting everything away in the nursery to go back to the bed and breakfast to change clothes for their date. And he also hadn't wanted to seem presumptuous of spending the night with her by bringing a bag with his clothes to change into at her place. Instead, he'd just rolled up his sleeves to try to keep from messing up his clothes as he moved stuff around until she was satisfied with the placement of everything in the nursery.

Now they mostly had the nursery ready for her and Dion to watch her nephews overnight while Justin and Amy were on their honeymoon, with the exception of the rocker she'd picked out. Dion had nixed the glider that she'd chosen because he was right at the maximum weight limit that it could hold, so he couldn't safely sit in it while holding a baby. Plus, he pointed out the need for two of them, so they could both rock one of their twins at the same time. Now, in order to finish setting up the nursery, he had two gliders ordered in a larger, sturdier version of what she wanted, so they could both sit and rock a baby at the same time without worrying about whether or not he sat in the correct chair. And Brent was confident that he could build and deliver them before the twentieth, when Justin and Amy left for their honeymoon.

She also still had to wash all the bedding and the unisex baby clothes they'd already bought for their babies. But she had plenty of time to do that, even if she waited until after her ultrasound appointment on Tuesday to wash everything together after picking out some gender specific clothing for her babies, if Dr. Magnum was able to determine their biological sexes during that visit. Not that she had time to think about any of that as she hurriedly freshened up and changed for her date with Dion.

He'd surprised her by getting recommendations from her family and making reservations for an upscale restaurant in San Antonio. Needless to say, she had to change out of her t-shirt dress and sneakers to put on actual dress shoes and one of the nicer maternity dresses she'd recently broke down and bought. Luckily, she'd straightened her hair that morning, so she just had to run a brush through it and add a little makeup for more of a nighttime look than her usual natural look.

When she got downstairs after getting ready, she found that Dion had gone out to her car to get his suitcoat that he'd ditched first thing that morning. Apparently, he'd also had his red tie stashed in a pocket somewhere because he'd donned it for their date.

She'd picked a navy-blue dress and white wrap, thinking that would make them match. But now she wanted to go swap her navy kitten heels and white wrap for their counterparts in red to add the same pop of color he had.

"Wow, you look amazing, Jewel," Dion gushed, not giving her the chance to retreat and change her shoes and wrap.

"Thank you," she smiled, suddenly wishing she could just take him upstairs and strip him from his suit, instead of going to dinner. "So do you."

She grabbed her keys off the hook in the kitchen as they made their way through the back of the house and out to her car in the detached garage. As always, Dion was ever the gentleman, opening doors for her and making sure she was secured in the car before getting in the passenger side.

"So, other than texting me, what did you do the past couple of days to keep from getting bored at the B and B?" Julie wondered if he'd gotten one of the Hunters to take him somewhere in town, or if he'd vegged in front of the TV more than he'd told her about.

"You know I checked out the stables," Dion mentioned, reminding her about the text conversation they'd had while she was at work, when he'd asked her all about the day they met and his experience going horseback riding. "I also called that therapy group Josh recommended to see if there was anything I could do there to prepare for when they start offering equine therapy."

"Was there?" She didn't think they'd have him try to do anything like that on his own, but she supposed they might want him to start getting comfortable being around horses.

"No, not really." Dion shook his head, which she only noticed through her peripheral vision because of focusing on driving them to San Antonio. "But I was able to set an appointment to meet with them on the thirteenth for my first therapy appointment. That one will be in their office. But when I mentioned being referred there by Josh for equine therapy and that we're dating, they said I might be able to set my future appointments to be at your family stable as early as the next week."

"Huh, I guess they're planning to start Burleson family and Ashbury Foundation sessions as soon as the licensing goes through," Julie mused aloud. "Instead of waiting for Josh to finish building the Horsing Around facilities on the land we just bought yesterday."

Bobby had told them about the land auction just in time the previous Friday for them to attend and win the bid for the old Gruber farm a week later. They were still dealing with all the legal red tape to divide the land up among the agricultural and entertainment divisions of Burleson Incorporated, Avington Security, and Horsing Around, so Julie knew it would be a few months before Josh had all his ducks in a row to get his foundation fully up and running. But she was glad to hear that Dion would be able to get into therapy a lot sooner than that.

"What land?" Dion turned to look at her with a confused expression on his face.

Julie ended up spending the rest of their drive into San Antonio explaining the issues Josh had uncovered regarding using the stables on the ranch for all the therapy groups he wanted to help, as well as how they'd found a way to deal with them by purchasing the farm land. Dion was fascinated with the plans for using part of the land for training security and law enforcement personnel, part of the land for growing crops, part of the land for a studio lot for the movies they'd started making, and part of the land for the equine therapy program.

"I hope our babies get their intelligence from you," Dion informed her as they exited the car to walk into the restaurant. "You've gotta have like a genius IQ to be able to be so well versed on all aspects of the different divisions of your family business."

Julie felt herself blush, appreciating how Dion complimented her on her brain, not just her looks like most guys did. He probably didn't remember it, but he'd complemented her intelligence in the past as well, commenting on her vast vocabulary and ability to discuss a large variety of topics several times over the last year. Their long talks about everything from pop culture to ancient history had been one of the reasons she'd fallen deeper in love with him. Now she felt the need to remind him that he was just as brilliant as he thought she was, only he'd gained that knowledge through self-study as opposed to going to college like she did.

Unfortunately, she didn't get the chance to say anything right then as the hostess at Biga on the River greeted them.

"Oh. My. Gawd. You're Dion Davis!"

Geez. Fangirl much? Julie thought as the overly made-up woman fawned over Dion without even acknowledging that Julie was standing there with Dion's hand on the small of her back.

Dion just smiled, offering the woman an autograph, and getting roped into a selfie before she finally escorted them through the restaurant to their table. Julie's eyes rolled so hard, she was almost afraid they'd get stuck looking at the back of her head.

She could clearly see that Dion wasn't flirting back with the hostess, but she still couldn't stop feeling jealous of the little bit of attention he gave the woman. She knew he was reverting to his standard behavior when dealing with fans because it was second nature to him after thirteen years in the wrestling business. Besides, his affable, friendly personality was one of the attributes that first drew her to him over a year before. But regardless of all that, she still hated having to share him with his female fans.

"Sorry about that," Dion apologized, pulling out her chair and brushing his lips over her temple.

Julie took her seat, but didn't say a word as the hostess still hovered. Once Dion sat down, the hostess finally handed them menus. Well, "handed" was probably an oversimplified, much too polite description of the way she tossed Julie's menu down on the table in front of her. And based on the way the woman bent to practically shove her cleavage in Dion's face to actually place his menu in his hands, Julie was pretty sure she'd be trying to sneak her phone number to him before they finished their meal.

Dion shook his head as the hostess finally left them alone. "The last six weeks in Heart's Destiny have spoiled me so much to being just a normal guy again that I didn't even think to ask for discretion when I made the reservation."

"No biggie." Julie shrugged, ready to drop the subject, so they could enjoy the rest of their date.

Unfortunately, as she looked over the menu for their appetizer options, she realized she wasn't as over the morning sickness phase of her pregnancy as she thought. The grilled wagyu burger and bread service were the only things that even sounded palatable in the appetizer list. And she was pretty sure it would offend the chef if she asked to have the burger cooked well-done. The rest of the options were either seafood items, which she wasn't sure she could handle smelling without getting sick, or things she was grossed out by even thinking about, like escargot and foie gras, which would most definitely make her puke if she saw them on their table.

Oh, pluck a duck! I'm gonna hafta tell Dion about my morning sickness triggers.

"Um, D, I have a confession to make," she mumbled, hating that she was probably going to hurt his feelings.

Dion placed his menu on the table to give her his full attention. "Okay."

Julie followed his lead, placing her menu down to look him in the eyes, even though she really wished she could stay hidden behind the menu when she saw the wariness in his expression. "When I told you that I haven't had much morning sickness, I wasn't completely honest with you. I mean, I haven't really had much compared to the other pregnant women in my family, but the few bouts I did have were really bad, like violent and explosive."

Dion visibly relaxed as he smiled at her. "That's okay, Jewel. I don't need a play-by-play accounting of every episode. I'm just glad that part of the pregnancy is behind you, so you don't have to suffer through it anymore."

"Yeah, well, that's the thing," Julie admitted sheepishly. "It's not really behind me. It's just, kinda, only triggered by certain things, so I can avoid it as long as I avoid smelling them, or seeing stuff that makes me nauseous. And, um, pretty much everything on the appetizer list falls into one of those categories."

Dion looked down at the menu laying open in front of him, obviously recognizing that most of the appetizer items were seafood of some type. "That's why you've avoided Mama Marcel's gumbo."

"I'm sorry," she apologized. "I didn't know how to tell you that our babies apparently hate all your favorite foods."

"Naw," Dion laughed, shaking his head and grinning at her. "They're probably just upset whenever they smell seafood because they're getting all their nutrients through their umbilical cords and don't get to taste that gumbo goodness."

Julie relaxed then, realizing she'd been worried about offending him for no reason. She'd let her early pregnancy bad experiences with rude chefs, who didn't like having their culinary practices questioned, and seeing Dion almost pass out whenever he felt anxious or overwhelmed, skew her thoughts about talking to him about her pregnancy-induced food aversions. Seeing him respond the same way he would have prior to his TBI, she felt rather foolish for not being one-hundred percent honest with him all along.

"So, which appetizer do you think you can handle? The burger or the bread service?"

"The bread for sure." Julie returned Dion's affectionate smile. "The burger sounds amazing, but I'm not sure how the chef here will react to ordering it well-done."

"You've had to deal with chefs who didn't want to follow the safety precautions for pregnant women?" Dion appeared irritated when she nodded in response to his question.

"Yeah, even Ashley at the B and B questioned my well-done steak orders until I told her about it being a pregnancy thing." She didn't mention that Ashley had only questioned it because of knowing Julie for so long that she'd recognized it as out of character for her to order anything but medium-well. "And I've pretty much quit going to business lunches, since having a few issues with chefs, right after I found out about the babies. It's just too much trouble to spend half the meeting time sending my food back, and then arguing when they refuse to cook it longer."

"Well, we'll make sure to explain why up front. And if they have a problem with following the necessary safety precautions, we'll go somewhere else," Dion declared, just as their waitress showed up.

"Good evening. I'm Monique, and I'll be your server tonight," she greeted them as she placed water glasses on the table before actually making eye contact. As soon as Monique glanced in Dion's direction, it was obvious that she was going to fangirl just as much as the hostess had. "Oh, wow, Dark Chocolate! I'm such a big fan! Please tell me they were lying when they announced your retirement!"

Why couldn't I have been wrong in that prediction?

Because that girl's so obvious that you don't even need my gift of "the sight" to know she's gonna chase after every good-looking guy who looks like he can afford the lifestyle she wants within a hundred-

mile radius. Julie imagined Mama Marcel's response as if she was sitting there with them, blocking out whatever Dion was discussing with Monique.

Oh, for crying out loud! Seeing these girls tonight makes it a little more clear why Dare felt like he had to fend off gold diggers while Dion was incapacitated. I guess only spending time in public with Dion in Heart's Destiny has clouded my judgement of how much they've had to deal with thirsty women. Though I suppose, even there, we have the Thirsty Threesome to show that not all women are scrupulous. Only BJ, Jackie, and Melody know better than to hit on a man when he's out with another woman.

Of course, you'd think most women in Texas would know better than that, on account of our reputation for having more armed residents than any other state. But I'm sure when she looks at me, Monique doesn't see the woman who grew up on a ranch and had to prove I was just as tough as my brothers and cousins.

She probably also doesn't realize that I'm pregnant with Dion's babies. She just sees a fat chick that she doesn't think will be any competition for his affections because she's thinner, yet still has bigger boobs than me.

Seriously, those things have got to be surgically enhanced. Either that or she's wearing the world's greatest bra. Would it be rude to ask her? I mean, I'd kinda like to know where to get a bra that would make me look like I have bigger boobs that aren't saggy after nursing my babies. So, if it's the bra that's making her breasts look that appealing, then I really wanna know where she got it.

"Jewel, do you know what you want to order for dinner?" Dion's question brought her out of her head and back to the moment.

"Um, no, I didn't get that far on the menu," she admitted, picking up her menu to look again.

"I'm guessing you either want the ribeye or the tenderloin." Dion pointed out the options on the menu. "Honestly, I'm pretty sure you want the ribeye because it's bigger, but I'm not sure about the sides it comes with, in case some of the alcohol didn't cook out of the sauce."

"Yeah, I'm not a fan of mushrooms right now either, so I'll go with the tenderloin," Julie decided after looking closer at the menu items he'd just mentioned. "Well-done."

"And I'll take the same," Dion announced, handing his menu over to the waitress. "And again, if there's a problem with cooking our beef to a minimum internal temperature of one-hundred-and-sixty degrees, let me know before turning in the order, so we can go somewhere else for dinner."

"Of course," Monique smiled at Dion, not taking her eyes off him as she took the menu from Julie's hand. "And I'm sure it won't be a problem."

"Thank you," Dion dismissed the server.

"If there's anything else you need, Dion," the waitress purred, reaching out to place her hand on Dion's shoulder. "Just let me know."

A barf bag, so I don't puke on her massive rack to get her away from my man, Julie thought, grateful the woman finally walked away. She hated the jealous feelings coursing through her right then, unsure where they came from since she'd always been fairly self-confident in the past. *Is it the pregnancy hormones? Or do I need more time to get over all the fears that cropped up from seeing Dion taking pics with other women while we were broken up? Either way, I need to figure out how to stop these jealous urges to get violent with these women who keep hitting on him.*

Dion reached across the table and unballed the fists she hadn't realized she'd made as Monique finally walked away from their table. "Relax, Jewel, I may not be much of a celebrity anymore, but I'm sure I still have enough clout to get our steaks cooked to the right temperature."

Well, I guess that's one benefit to having to deal with his fangirls.

"And if the chef's not a wrestling fan to want to cater to my special request, then we'll just drop your last name and threaten to cut off their beef supply, if they're not willing to follow the safety precautions for pregnant women." Dion's smirk broke the tension, causing Julie to chuckle along with him.

"You realize I don't handle the beef distribution to even know if we supply the beef for this restaurant, right?" Julie squeezed Dion's hands, realizing they'd somehow ended up holding hands across the table after he unballed her fists.

"Well, then hopefully, we won't have to bluff our way through then," Dion chuckled and shrugged. "And maybe we should get a list from whoever in your family actually handles that to know which restaurants we need to stick with in the future to have that as leverage."

"That would be a sales manager in the beef division, a few levels down from Josh and Uncle Bob." Julie shook her head at him, knowing she'd never take things that far to get a chef to do what she wanted. "Though I'm sure Uncle Bob knows every place we supply in the beef and agricultural divisions, even though he's turned the supervision of them over to Josh."

"How did Josh go from being a Navy SEAL to running the beef and ag divisions of Burleson?" Dion tilted his head curiously. "Those seem like two radically different jobs that would be hard to transition between."

"Like all of us when we were teenagers, he spent his summers working in the different divisions to learn all about the company from the bottom up. The boys all actually had to spend time working with the cattle doing the dirtier jobs that we girls were smart enough to get out of, though," Julie chuckled, remembering back to her teenaged threats of becoming vegan because if she worked with the cows she'd adopt them all as pets. "When it came time to move from working on the ranch to working in the office, Josh insisted on working in the beef and ag divisions just long enough to learn how to do the different jobs in those areas before going back to working on the ranch. Even now, as the VP of beef and ag, he spends half his time on the ranch, just like Uncle Bob."

"What did you do those summers to get out of working on the ranch?"

"I threatened to adopt all the cows as pets and only eat vegan," Julie admitted with a chuckle.

"Yeah, I guess that would do it," Dion laughed along with her. "So, what did you do instead?"

"Filing and secretarial work, mostly," Julie shrugged. "I actually moved around the company more than my siblings or cousins. They all seemed to have certain areas that interested them more than others, and once they got to those divisions, they stayed there. Whereas, I went through every department, learning as much as I could about each aspect of our business before moving onto the next division. I get bored easily, and knew I didn't want to be stuck only focusing on one section of the company for my whole career. So, when I graduated college and wanted to start working full time with the rest of my family, I suggested starting the business diversification and asset management division. This way, I get to research new industries regularly to keep from getting bored while helping the business grow, and provide jobs to people all over the country, and not just our little section of Texas."

"Like I said earlier, you're fuckin' brilliant to be able to remember all that stuff." Dion smiled at her, causing Julie to blush at the praise.

"Not as brilliant as some of the other people in my family, but not afraid of the hard work it takes to look like I am." Julie smiled and shrugged, appreciating the compliment, but not really feeling like she deserved it. She quickly turned the conversation to the roles of the rest of her family in the company, so she wouldn't feel like she was taking all the credit for the group effort it took to keep everything running smoothly in the multi-billion-dollar business.

They continued talking about the different jobs her various family members did for Burleson Incorporated until Monique delivered their appetizers. Surprisingly, their burger was cooked well-done, as were their tenderloins when they were delivered a little later.

Damn, Monique might be a little too flirty, but I can't fault her for her customer service.

"I wish I had my sketch pad with me to draw you right now," Dion mused as she cut into her meal.

Julie remembered him talking about drawing caricatures as a teenager and immediately pictured him drawing a caricature of her pigging out at his offhand comment. "Yeah, I'm not sure I'd wanna see how much I look like Miss Piggy while eating for three," she quipped. "No matter how much I want to see some of the caricatures you told me about drawing as a teenager."

"You don't look like Miss Piggy," Dion chuckled. "But you do have that pregnancy glow everyone talks about. And that's something I haven't captured in the drawings I've done recently."

"You've been drawing recently?" Julie was curious about what he'd been drawing, wanting to see how talented he was.

"Yeah, I picked up some sketchbooks in town a few weeks ago," Dion admitted sheepishly, almost like he was embarrassed about taking up drawing again, now that he had so much free time while not working. "I've been drawing my memories to get them to come in more clearly. But after today, I'm thinking maybe I should start drawing some of the new memories we're making, too, so I don't forget them."

"Do you think drawing them will help the memories stick in your head better than taking a picture?" Julie wondered if the mind-body connection of physically capturing the image with his hand to put it on paper would help him retain the memories more than having the picture to look back on later.

"I don't know," Dion shrugged before putting down his fork to take a sip of his water. Once he swallowed and put his glass back down, he continued. "But drawing my memories has helped me remember more details about certain things, so maybe it would. And I can always take a picture now with my phone and then draw it later while looking at the photo to see if it helps the details stick in my brain better."

"Well, then by all means, snap away," Julie suggested, placing her fork down to pose for him to take a picture without looking like the glutton she felt like right then. "But you've gotta show me the drawing when you finish it."

"I'm actually planning to give you the sketchbooks of our memories when I fill 'em up," Dion admitted as he pulled out his phone and snapped her picture.

"Dion, have you been drawing dirty pictures of me?" Julie leaned across the table and whispered her question, not wanting any of their fellow restaurant patrons overhearing them.

"Maybe a few," Dion smirked. "But those are in a separate sketchbook that I only draw in when I'm alone in my room, so nobody else gets to see us the way I remember us in my head."

"Oh, so I'm not alone in those sketches?" Julie teased him, reaching across the table to hold his free hand with hers. "Is that because you wanna make sure that if anyone does see them, they'll know I'm taken?"

"Maybe," Dion admitted in a low tone, grinning seductively. "And maybe because I like the way your pussy looks when it's stuffed full with my cock."

"Oh, we're definitely going back to your room tonight so you can show me those sketches," Julie declared just as Monique came back to their table.

Leah Mae Wright

"Can I get ya'll any dessert tonight?" Monique's eyes seemed to lock on Julie and Dion's joined hands. "Maybe a dark chocolate mousse for Dark Chocolate?"

"No, Dion's all the Dark Chocolate I can handle eating tonight," Julie quipped, grinning suggestively at him without looking over at the server.

"Yeah, girl, if I were you, I wouldn't want anything else, either," Monique giggled, placing their check on the table before turning to walk away. Julie wasn't a hundred percent certain, but she thought she heard Monique mumble something about a "lucky bitch" as she moved across the room to another table.

Yeah, I'm a very lucky bitch indeed, Julie thought, reveling in how Dion kept his focus on her without even acknowledging the other woman. *And I'll be even luckier when we get back to the B and B and I get him in all his naked glory.*

~~~

Dion was nervous about showing Jewel his sketches as they walked up to his room at the bed and breakfast. To be honest, he was surprised he'd mentioned them to her before having them all completed to the point that he could give her one of the sketchbooks. But after seeing how uncomfortable she was with the women at the restaurant flirting with him, he wanted to make sure she knew he only had eyes for her. And what better way to do that than to show her how he saw her by showing her the sketches he'd done of her from his memories?

Hopefully, she won't think I'm a total hack as an artist, he thought as he unlocked the door and escorted her inside. As she kicked off her heels and sat down on the bed, Dion went to his computer satchel and pulled out the two sketchbooks devoted to his memories with Jewel before joining her.

"Keep in mind that before this last month I haven't drawn much since I was a teenager," he warned her as he handed over the book of sketches from their non-sexual memories together first, holding back the book of nudes that he drew from his memories of their sexual escapades in various hotels. "So, some of these are pretty rough from being so out of practice."
~~~

"I'm sure they're way better than anything I could draw," Jewel disagreed with his self-deprecation as she started flipping through the various wedding scenes he'd drawn from his memories during his first few weeks back in Heart's Destiny. She stopped on one of the two of them dancing with a blue and white wedding cake in the background that he'd drawn after being texted a photograph from Anthony and Kay's wedding. "Wow. These are amazing. Like you should frame some of them and put them in an art gallery, amazing."

"Naw, I'm definitely not that good an artist," Dion scoffed, shaking his head. "Besides, I doubt there's much of a market for drawings done with the same colored pencils kids use in elementary school."

She flipped to the caricature of him watching her as she walked across the paddock on the first day they met and started laughing, probably at how he'd shown his heart beating out of his chest. "I thought it was the head that was supposed to be bigger than the rest of the body in a caricature, not my butt. That looks like it should be the cover art for Sir Mix-a-Lot's greatest hits."

Dion knew better than to start singing **Baby Got Back** right then, but it was very tempting. He hadn't even thought about how he'd emphasized her ass, using the same heart shape that was beating out of his chest as if they were connected.

"Flip the page and you'll see where I did the big head in the one where you were walking toward me," Dion instructed before explaining the first drawing. "But in all my memories of you walking away from me, or even just walking in front of me, it's become clear that I've had a fascination with your sexy ass since that first day. And if you recall, it wasn't **Baby Got Back** that I was inspired to sing when I first started getting back my memories of the day we met."

"Please tell me you didn't sing **In Those Jeans** in front of my nieces and their friends when I walked away from the bounce house that first day." Jewel's eyes bugged out as she gave him a pleading look.

"No, I didn't sing it in front of the kids," Dion laughed. "Even though my thoughts that day definitely ran along the same lines as the lyrics. But since I was out in public when I drew that, I had to emphasize my heart beating out of my chest, instead of the boner I had from how much I wanted in your jeans, which I was tryin' to hide all day."

"I wondered why you suddenly had to go sit at one of the picnic tables, instead of continuing with the wrestling practice the kids roped you into." Jewel flipped the page, looking at the other pictures he'd drawn of watching her play horseshoes and on the horse in front of him during the trail ride her texts had helped him remember.

"I'm surprised none of the guys figured out how instantly into you I was after I risked permanent injury to my balls just to have that view for a little while," Dion quipped, making her smile. "Though now that I remember how painful horseback riding is, I'm not so sure about doing equine therapy anymore."

"Yeah, I was a little surprised you were so interested in it in the first place, considering how uncomfortable you were around the horses before," Jewel admitted.

"Really? Then why'd you suggest it?" Dion wondered, surprised she'd push for him to participate in her cousin's program if she knew he wasn't comfortable with the horses previously.

"Because I saw how Cait integrated petting and grooming them into her healing process last summer, and I thought you'd do like she did and slowly get more and more comfortable with horses, too." Jewel shrugged. "Besides, I thought you looked hot in the saddle, so I was hoping you'd eventually learn to love riding as much as I do."

"Yeah, I'll always prefer having you ride me." Dion grinned and wagged his eyebrows suggestively. "And to be honest, the main reason I was interested in doing the equine therapy on your family's ranch was to get more chances to see you back when you were still leery of going out with me again. But now that we're back together, and since you'll probably be teaching our kids to follow in your rodeo queen footsteps, I'll just have to remember to put on a jockstrap before learning all I can to keep up with ya'll on the back of a horse."

"I'll get you some padded riding shorts like we all wear under our jeans," Jewel grinned. "According to my brothers, they're a lot more comfortable than a jock strap and they protect the backside as well as the front. Ya know, come to think of it, they could be the reason you remembered my butt being curvier in my jeans that first day."

"Seriously? Why didn't anyone tell me to get a pair of those shorts when I bought my cowboy boots?" Dion had a quick flash of standing in a western store looking at a wall of boots, when he assumed he'd gone shopping to buy the cowboy boots he hadn't recognized in his closet until he remembered wearing them a couple of times while he was in Heart's Destiny. *But I was wearing sneakers in my memories of going horseback riding that first day. When did I buy cowboy boots?*

"Why the fuck didn't you take us all shopping for cowboy gear this morning instead of just Red, so we wouldn't look so outta place here?" *Dion punched Dean in the shoulder as they stood around a table in a bar with country music playing while their friends danced.*

"Sorry, man, didn't think you'd really need it. And honestly, I thought it would make Red look like a tool, so we could rib him about it." *Dean held his hands up in a placating gesture.* ***"But we can go Monday to get ya some boots and Wranglers if ya want."***

"Dean took me shopping for cowboy boots," Dion announced as he let the memories fade. "I'm not sure when, but I think it was sometime in that first week when we all came to town for Anthony and Kay's wedding. He also helped me find jeans that would fit over the boots, so I didn't look like a douchebag wearing the boots over the ankles of my jeans. Why didn't he mention the padded shorts then?"

"If I had to guess? Probably because Dean thought it was funny to pick on you about icing your groin after riding that first time," Jewel giggled. "Either that, or he doesn't know about them because of not being as big into the rodeo as some of the other guys from around here."

"Yeah, next time I'm down at his house for a workout while he's on tour, I'm gonna hafta check his drawers," Dion grumbled, plotting how to rib his friend if he figured out that Dean had intentionally withheld that vital piece of information. "And if I find padded riding shorts, I'm gonna rub them down with itching powder right before they come home next, so I can invite him to go for a ride and get a little revenge."

"Yeah, if you have access to itching powder, you'd better stay away from my underwear," Jewel warned, wagging her finger at him as if she was scolding a misbehaving child.

"I promise, Jewel, it won't come anywhere near you or your sexy undies," Dion swore, holding his hand up as if he was being sworn in to testify in court.

"Speaking of sexy undies, I'm assuming the drawings of your memories of my sexy undies are in that sketchbook instead of this one?" Jewel pointed to the book he still held with the one she'd been looking through.

"Sorry to disappoint, but these are all nudes," Dion smirked, finally handing her the sketchbook he kept hidden in his suitcase whenever he carried his satchel with his art supplies out in public. He didn't even want to take a chance on one of the hotel housekeepers seeing it on his bedside table and flipping through it, so he was diligent about making sure it was covered by his clothing, knowing they weren't likely to snoop through his things to come across it.

"Oooh, gimmie." Jewel dropped the first sketchbook on the bed and reached for the one in Dion's hand, grinning mischievously the whole time.

Dion handed over the book, moving the other one to the bedside table and watching as Jewel got her first look at his dirty drawings. Her eyes widened as she saw the first picture of her riding him from his perspective as it happened. As she flipped the page to the next image of him doing her from behind, she licked her lips as her eyes turned that stormy gray-blue that let him know she was getting turned on.

Neither of them said a word as she looked over image after image of all the different ways he'd remembered making love to her. Since he had more time to draw in this book when he was alone in his room and couldn't sleep at night, there were a lot more sketches finished in it than in the one she'd already looked at.

"Wow, Dion, this is like a graphic novel of all our hotel hookups," Jewel whispered in awe, starting to wiggle her hips, as if she was trying to get a little friction on her clit from how aroused she was by his drawings. "And I don't care what you say about them being drawn with the same colored pencils used in elementary schools, these are good enough to go in a museum. Though maybe not the ones that show my face, so I'm not recognizable to any of my friends or family who might see them."

"The Museum of Sex, maybe, but not a reputable art museum," Dion chuckled, knowing he'd never submit nude drawings of Jewel for any kind of public exhibit. *But if she thinks they're that good, maybe I could do some different drawings to start an art gallery in town. That would be something to keep me busy once our kids are in school without risking another head injury. And it would provide a place for other local artists to sell their work. Maybe even a place to bring in some art teachers to give the kids in town something else to do.*

"…and considering how many of these are you doing me from behind, I think they reinforce what you said earlier about how much you like looking at my ass."

"Sorry, my brain went off on a tangent about helping other local artists by opening a gallery in town, and I missed the first part of what you just said." Dion cringed as he apologized, hating how he sometimes still kept jumping around inside his head and hadn't focused exclusively on Jewel.

"I said it's a good thing doggie style is one of the recommended positions for pregnant women, 'cause it's obviously your favorite position based on these sketches, which are proof positive that you love looking at my ass." Jewel smiled seductively at him as she rephrased her previous statement. "And after looking at these, I think it's time to put the sketchbooks away and see if it's still your favorite position."

Dion didn't remember her being quite so sexually aggressive before, but he had to admit, as he watched her stand from the bed and start to undress, he kinda liked it now. *But in my memories, she does like to challenge me for control at first, just long enough to get me to respond in kind and wrest all control from her. Is that what she's doing now? Trying to push the button to activate my inner caveman, who likes being in charge in the bedroom?*

Well, damn, Jewel, I'll be happy to give you what we both seem to want. Right. Fucking. Now.

Dion stood too, picking up the sketchbooks and putting them away before turning back to her and ordering, "Stop, Jewel. I get to unwrap you tonight."

Thankfully, she'd only set aside the white shawl she'd had over her shoulders and started lowering the zipper on the side of her navy-blue dress, when she complied with his command. Dion stepped over to her, removed her hands from the zipper, and lethargically lowered it himself.

He then bent and lifted the hem of the dress, not believing that the spaghetti straps over her shoulders would allow the zipper to open enough for the neckline of the dress to pass over her baby bump. He pulled the dress up and over her head, draping it over the chair she'd already placed her shawl on. Even though he intended for her to wear another pair of his sweats and one of his t-shirts home the next morning, the same way she had on New Year's Day, he didn't want to damage the dress, in case she wanted to wear it again.

Dion appreciated the view of her standing there in only her navy-blue strapless bra and matching lace panties, wishing she hadn't kicked off her heels, so he could have her stand bent over the bed with her pussy almost the perfect height to line up with his cock. *Fuck it! I'll just have her put them back on after I help her lose the lingerie.*

"You're gonna do exactly as I tell you for the rest of the night. Right, Jewel?" Dion reverently ran his fingertip over the swell of her breasts.

"Yes, Dion," Jewel purred breathlessly, her nipples hardening enough to be visible through the layers of lace over satin comprising her bra.

Dion used his left hand to loosen his tie while reaching around with his right hand to unfasten her bra, letting it drop to the floor. Once he removed his jacket, Dion took his time undressing one handed while using the other hand to tease and tantalize Jewel, knowing the anticipation would amplify her arousal.

Unfortunately, once he'd completely unbuttoned it, he had to have both hands to remove his shirt and drape it over the same chair as her dress. But even without his hands on her, he knew he could turn her on with only his words. "Fuck, Jewel, I can smell how much you want me and I've barely even started touching you. I bet if I were to slip my finger under those panties, I'd find you dripping wet."

He looked down and sure enough, there was already a spot on the crotch of her underwear that was so much darker than the rest of the panties that it was almost black instead of blue. "Damn, your pussy's so wet, I don't even have to check 'cause you're already dripping through your panties. Is that all for me, Jewel?"

"Yes, Dion, only for you."

Dion could tell she was fighting not to move, even though he'd never issued that command. His memories of another time when they'd played dominance games flashed before his eyes. Knowing that must have been when he'd insisted she stay still while he teased her, he pushed the memories aside to stay in the moment with her and enjoy the real thing instead of his memories.

"Damn right, it's only for me," he growled, letting his possessive side out to play. "No other man will ever even see what's mine, much less touch you or turn you on, 'cause I don't share."

"As long as you remember I don't share either," she snarked, momentarily breaking her submissive character.

"You don't have to worry about that, Jewel." Dion grinned as he looped his fingers in the sides of her panties. "I'm just as much yours as you're mine. I love you. Forever and always."

"And I love you. Forever and always," she agreed, pecking her lips to his cheek as he bent to lower her panties.

While Dion knew they'd said they loved one another before, he wasn't sure if they'd ever exchanged the words "forever and always" previously. But in that moment, he knew he meant them as a solemn vow for how long their love would last. As soon as she stepped out of her panties, Dion stood and took her right hand in his left as he wrapped his right arm around her, placing her hand over his heart before kissing her passionately to seal their promise.

As tempting as it was to lift her up and try out standing sex as a pregnant position option, she'd requested doggie style. Even if that wasn't one of his favorite ways to fuck Jewel, he could never deny her anything she asked him for, especially sexually. So, he released her from the kiss and gave her a choice as he toed off his shoes and socks and unfastened his pants. "You wanna put your shoes back on and bend over the bed standing? Or do you wanna be on your hands and knees while I fuck you from behind?"

"Normally, I'd be irritated by you asking me that, instead of just telling me to do what you wanted," Jewel pouted, propping a hand on her hip playfully. "But considering I know you think the shoes make it hotter, and would pick that if you weren't thinking of my comfort level, I'm not gonna complain about you not being as domineering as normal. Instead, I'm gonna thank you for giving me the option of getting on my hands and knees, so I don't have to try to squeeze my swollen feet back in those shoes tonight."

"Then get in position, brat," Dion demanded, lowering his voice to sound more commanding, even though he couldn't help but smile at her cheekiness. *And I'll rub your feet later to help with whatever swelling you're having from being pregnant.*

As she turned and climbed up on the bed, Dion shoved his pants and boxer briefs down, stepping out of them as he moved behind her. He reached out with one hand to lightly slap her ass as he stroked his cock with the other. He knew prepping her to take his big dick was going to be a one-handed job this time because of needing the tight grip to keep himself from plunging into her before she was opened up enough to take him.

Jewel wiggled her ass, taunting him enough to get him to slap her other ass cheek before he swiped a finger through her soaked slit. He worked the digit into her tight opening as he spread his precum over his shaft.

"Fuck, I can't believe how tight you are, even after I've filled your creamy cunt with my big dick so many times."

"Kegels," Julie giggled, wiggling her hips as he fucked her with his finger. "Lots and lots of Kegels. The girls have already warned me to get into the habit of doing them daily, so I can get everything to go back to normal after the babies stretch me out when they're born."

Dion didn't want to think about the fact that he was about to stick his dick in the same hole his babies would use as an exit. Too much of that visual would only make him worry about the possibility of hurting their babies by fucking his woman. And since the books all said it was safe and not harmful to the babies, he refused to let his unfounded fears derail their lovemaking.

He inserted a second finger, slowly starting to stretch her to be able to take his massive member. "Fuck, you're so hot, Jewel," he groaned, precum dripping from the end of his cock from how turned on he was by watching her wet pussy open up for him.

"I wish I could see…" she moaned, dropping her head as if she was trying to look between her legs. "Guess you'll have to draw it for me later, since I can't see around the babies now."

"I will definitely draw it for you later," Dion promised as he pushed a third finger into her slick opening, targeting her G-spot as he massaged her inner walls to prepare her to take him. Keeping one finger targeting that swollen bumpy spot on her vaginal wall, he scissored the other two fingers to open her up.

"Oh, Dion, that feels so good," Jewel whimpered, rocking her hips to fuck herself on his fingers. "But I want you inside me before I come."

"I am inside you, Jewel." Dion smiled, knowing she meant his cock and enjoying making her ask for exactly what she wanted before giving it to her.

"Not your fingers," she groaned, still wiggling her hips seductively. "I need your big dick inside me. Please, Dion."

"Only because you beg so beautifully." Dion pulled his fingers from her creamy cunt, lining up the engorged head of his cock before leisurely pushing inside her.

Jewel rammed her hips backwards, trying to take more of him than she was fully ready to accommodate. Thankfully, Dion knew her tricks and pulled back just in time to keep from accidentally hurting her. He gripped her hip with his left hand while slapping her ass once more with his right. "Be still and take what I give you, Jewel. Or I'll jerk off on your sexy ass and leave you without an orgasm the rest of the night."

She whimpered in frustration, but stilled all her movements. Surprisingly, she didn't voice her objections to his suggested punishment in an attempt to earn more swats.

Dion rubbed the slightly pink area on her ass to soothe the sting before moving his hand over to grip both sides of her hips. He held her in place as he gradually squeezed back inside her, stopping every inch or so to let her adjust to his girth. He used his thumb to spread some of her cream up over her anus, knowing it turned her on to have him tease her back entrance, even though she claimed she never wanted to try anything anal.

Once he was fully seated inside her, he started describing his view, praising her for how sexy she was and how amazing it felt to be inside her as he started thrusting and retreating. It didn't take long before her pretty, pink pussy started spasming around his cock. She cried out his name repeatedly as she flew over the edge.

Dion loved how easy it was to make her come once he got her to quit fighting for control and let him take care of her. He remembered how she'd confided in him about how hard it was for her to come before they met, explaining that she just had so much going on at work that she couldn't get out of her head to let go, no matter if she was alone or with a previous partner. He'd quickly found the things that worked best for getting her out of her head and focused on him and what they were doing.

First things first, he had to let her talk, to get out any extraneous thoughts that popped into her head as they were getting started. Then he kept up the talk, but started narrowing it down to dirty talk and things that set the scene for whatever role play ideas that struck their fancy. At the same time, he'd start exerting his dominance to take control, so she could fully relax and just enjoy the pleasure.

Sometimes it took two or three orgasms to get her to turn it all over to him. But other times, like right then, only one was necessary before she became so pliable that he could let loose a little.

As she softened and sighed in pleasure, he amped up the intensity, starting to pound into her harder and faster, his balls slapping against her clit, until her words became unintelligible as anything other than "yes, Dion," chanted repeatedly, as her climax seemed never ending. With her tight cunt clamping down on his cock like a vise, Dion couldn't hold back his own release, shooting spurt after spurt of cum deep inside her.

"Oh. Fuck. Yes. Jewel. Julia. Mine." He punctuated each word with a powerful thrust and a spray of his jizz, praying he was painting the outside of her womb and not getting his cum anywhere near their babies.

As Jewel collapsed down onto the bed on her stomach, Dion pulled out and flopped down beside her, lying on his side facing her. "Fuck, I'm gonna need a minute to catch my breath before I can go get a rag to clean us up."

"Don't worry about it," she panted, turning her head to face him with a brilliant smile. "I'm not sure I'll be able to move out of this position before morning."

"Is that okay for the babies?" Dion assumed lying on her stomach could be just as bad as lying on her back.

"I don't know if it's okay or not, but since I can't feel my legs yet, I can't do anything about it right now."

Not wanting to take any chances, he sat up and gently rolled her onto her left side.

"Thanks." She smiled at him as he stood to go to the bathroom to get a washcloth and hand towel to clean them up.

Her eyes were closed when he returned with a wet washcloth and a dry hand towel, so he deftly cleaned between her legs and returned the linens to the bathroom before cleaning himself. She still hadn't moved when he returned the second time, so he scooped her up into his arms and moved her to lay in the middle of the bed with her head resting on a pillow. He then crawled in behind her and cuddled her until her breathing evened out in sleep.

Unable to go to sleep himself, Dion finally gave up an hour later. He tucked her in under the covers before moving over to the desk and drawing the pictures she'd asked for at the beginning of their lovemaking that night.

Once they were done, he left the sketchbook open on the desk and crawled back into bed, holding the love of his life as he finally drifted off for a short nap.

Chapter Twenty

After his talk with Jewel on Saturday about his appointment with Doc Hayes, Dion called Mama Marcel to let her know that she didn't have to hop on a plane to rush back to Heart's Destiny. Since Dare was still entertaining Ashlyn Lawton and the movie people who'd traveled from Heart's Destiny to New Orleans the week before, Dare and Mama Marcel were spending another few days in NOLA before coming back at the end of the week. Dion wasn't quite sure how Ashlyn had ended up going on that location scouting trip, but he was pretty sure there was some kind of a love triangle forming between his brother, Ashlyn, and Cade Starling. *Maybe I should suggest texting the Inglemans to Dare, so maybe him, Ashlyn, and Cade can form a successful threesome the way Reid, Tait, and Kori have? If he and Cade are doing like I think they are, and making Ashlyn choose between them, then that might be the only way to keep my little brother from getting his heart broken.*

It still seemed strange to Dion that the last time he remembered talking to the Inglemans before his injury was when their son was just a baby, but he'd met both of their children, four-year-old Xander and nine-month-old Talia, when they were in town for Dean and Allissa's wedding back in November.

Hopefully, now that he has all the results of my tests last month, Doc Hayes will be able to come up with a plan for helping me get more of my memories of wrestling and hanging out with my GWA friends back, Dion thought after he finished the ImPACT test and walked back to the exam room where Jewel was waiting on him. *Yeah, my memories with Jewel are the most important for me to get back, but I'd kinda like to remember the good times with the rest of my friends, too.*

"How'd it go?" As soon as he walked into the room, Jewel put down the magazine she'd been flipping through while waiting for him.

"Better than last time," Dion informed her as he sat down beside her in one of the two guest chairs in the exam room, instead of getting on the table the way he had to when Dare and Mama Marcel were both with him. "But I don't know how much of that is because of the new meds, and how much is because of taking it first thing this time, instead of feeling overwhelmed by the rest of the appointment when I took it at the end last time."

Summer knocked once on the open door as she joined them to take Dion's vitals, having let him take the computer test even before the basics of a doctor's appointment. Once he'd answered all her questions and she'd logged everything in his chart, Doc Hayes joined them, carrying a stack of papers, which he immediately started reviewing right after the pleasantries of greetings concluded.

"Your ImPACT scores are much better this time, surpassing your highest scores with Dr. Boudreaux, but they're not quite back to your baseline scores with the GWA." Doc Hayes seemed satisfied with the results, smiling as he handed the printout of the results to Dion. "Your verbal memory composite seems to have improved more than your visual memory composite, but I'm sure that will be rectified once you get your new glasses. Did the ophthalmologist's office give you an idea of when they'll be ready?"

"Yeah, they're supposed to call me this week when they come in," Dion informed the doctor, passing the ImPACT test report over to Jewel when she leaned in, trying to read it over his shoulder. None of those different numbers actually meant anything to him, so Dion was fine with just knowing that his scores were improving and letting her see if she could make heads or tails out of them.

"Good, I'm sure you'll find wearing them all the time will help your headaches, too, so hopefully, you won't need the painkillers nearly as often." Doc Hayes nodded.

"His glasses are for his distance vision?" Jewel questioned, tilting her head curiously as the doctor continued nodding. "That's why he has to wear them all the time, right? But will they help him when he's trying to read his phone or whatever, and seems to have trouble finding the sweet spot for how far away it is to see it clearly?"

"Actually, I'm so old I'm getting bifocals," Dion admitted with a heavy sigh, feeling ancient for having to get what Mama Marcel called "granny glasses" instead of just single vision lenses. "And when you saw me trying to find that sweet spot to read this weekend, it was because I'd left my drug-store readers, which the eye doctor suggested I get to get me through the holidays, at the B and B with my art supplies, 'cause I've only been wearing them while drawing."

"I'm not an eye doctor of any kind, so I couldn't tell you what he was getting even if I had his eyeglasses' prescription in front of me," Doc Hayes chuckled. "But I'm pretty sure the need for bifocals is completely because of the head injury and not because of age. In fact, it wouldn't surprise me at all if your vision improves as your brain heals a little more over the next couple of years."

"Well, that's good to know. Maybe I'll be able to go down to ones with the drug-store readers like Mama Marcel, so she'll quit telling me that my two-point-fives are for people way older than her."

"Hopefully," Doc Hayes agreed. "I've read the reports from the neurologist and neuropsychiatrist, so I know they've added a couple of new meds to help with your memory and concentration issues. How do you feel they're working for you?"

"So far, they seem to be helping." Dion shrugged, unsure which of the new meds was responsible for the slight improvements with the aphasia and comprehension issues he'd recently noticed. "I was surprised when the neuropsych said I've had A.D.D. all my life. I always thought I was just really good at multitasking, and since I wasn't hyperactive, the way I switched from topic to topic faster than anyone else I knew was more of a skill than a disorder. And when I think back on my teenage years, when I had to rush through drawing caricatures to be able to switch from one person to the next every fifteen minutes or so, it was actually beneficial. But now, since starting the Adderall, I can literally focus on the same picture for hours, so I think it's actually improved the quality of my artwork."

At least, that was the reason Dion believed his skills hadn't rusted from lack of use for the last fifteen years or so.

"You draw?" Doc Hayes looked surprised at Dion's revelation.

"He's an amazing artist," Jewel gushed. "You should see some of the pictures he's drawn of the things he's remembered in the last month."

"Don't listen to her, she's biased," Dion grinned self-deprecatingly. "I'm an okay artist, just good enough to make a little side money drawing caricatures for tourists back when I was a teenager. The only way my drawings would ever be shown otherwise would be if I opened my own gallery, 'cause nobody else would be willing to hang them up. And if I do that, I'd want to focus on showcasing other local artists who are way more talented than I'll ever be."

"Can a brain injury like Dion's knock the self-confidence out of someone? 'Cause I swear, Dion was not this humble when I first met him," Jewel teased, smirking mischievously.

"I'm still cocky in all the ways I need to be," Dion quipped back, hoping to cover for the self-assuredness he'd recently lost with a little innuendo. Dion didn't really think he was less confident in most things, just that he needed to find his new limits for certain abilities and his triggers for the blackout spells to be able to prevent them going forward. Once he knew those things, he knew he'd go back to the same level of quiet confidence he'd always exuded.

"That can definitely happen," Doc Hayes informed them. "Especially when the injury impacts job prospects, or takes away the ability to continue in a job that's so closely linked to a person's identity, such as any form of professional athletics. But therapy can help deal with that, along with doing other things you've always found enjoyable, like drawing. I saw a referral for therapy in the neuropsych records. Did they specifically recommend art therapy? Or did you just start drawing again on your own?"

"I actually bought the supplies and started drawing whenever I was bored before I saw any of the specialists you referred me to. But art therapy was one of the types of therapy the neuropsych mentioned," Dion clarified, nodding. "But I don't actually have my first appointment with a therapist until next Monday. And I didn't think I had to be in their office to start drawing the things I'm remembering since coming to Heart's Destiny, so I picked up a couple more sketchbooks just for my memories while checking out the town one day last month."

Dion didn't mention that he wouldn't feel comfortable showing a therapist the sexual drawings he'd done from his most prevalent memories, which was why he'd bought several different sketchbooks to make it easier to keep those sketches of his intimate moments with Jewel private.

"Excellent. And has drawing the memories helped more of them to come back?"

"I don't know if it's drawing them, the medicine that's supposed to help with my memory, or just being in the same places where the memories happened and talking about them with Jewel that's helping," Dion admitted with another half-shrug. "But at least ninety-five percent of the memories I've recovered are of times when I was with Jewel. And the few memories I've gotten back when she wasn't present in them, I've been talking to her or about her when they come back. Do you know why that is? Or what I can do to get back some of the memories I've lost of the couple of years before I met her with my other friends and family members?"

"Unfortunately, there's no rhyme or reason for when and how memories come back," Doc Hayes sighed. "But spending time where they happened and with the people you want to remember most are definitely the right steps to getting them back. I know that hasn't been possible with your wrestling memories because of not being cleared to fly yet. But considering the improvements in your most recent tests, and how well controlled the vertigo and headaches are now, I think we can lift that restriction. I still don't want you getting in the ring if you go visit the GWA on tour, but that might help you with some of those memories."

"What about driving? Will that be possible once I get my glasses? Or do we still need to clear up the blackout spells first?" Dion was anxious to be able to drive again, wanting to get more of his independence back, as well as wanting to be able to drive Jewel to the hospital when their babies were born.

"Yes, we need to get those under control first, but they aren't blackout spells," Doc Hayes clarified. "The reports from the sleep specialist show they are indeed narcolepsy episodes."

"But there are medicines to treat narcolepsy, right?" Jewel inquired, her voice rising in a hopeful lilt.

"Yes, there are," Doc Hayes returned her smile before directing his next comments to Dion. "In fact, the Adderall you've been taking is one of the first things we try. Have you noticed any lessening of the episodes since starting to take it?"

"Honestly, no," Dion shook his head. "The episodes I've been able to prevent have all been when Jewel gives me something else to focus on when I get that overwhelmed, anxious feeling. And that happened just as often before I started taking the Adderall as it's happened since."

"Okay, then we'll call and get Dr. Khan on the phone to set up a more advanced treatment." Doc Hayes pushed a button on the phone to call Jeri at the front desk to set up the call and ring back to the exam room they were currently in.

It only took a few minutes before they had the other doctor on speaker-phone discussing treatment options. Apparently, the most effective treatment involved a substance so controlled that only certain doctors were allowed to prescribe it, and each patient had to be enrolled in the REMS program to have it overnighted from the only pharmacy in the United States authorized to dispense it.

Unfortunately, all the red tape to get Dr. Khan to prescribe Xyrem and his insurance to cover the outrageously expensive medication was extremely overwhelming for Dion. So anxiety inducing that even reaching over to place his hand on Jewel's belly to try to feel their babies wasn't enough to stop the tingly, pins-and-needles feeling in his lips as they started going numb, or the darkness that creeped in on the edges of his vision, signaling the beginning of one of the episodes. Luckily, he managed to give his verbal authorization for Julie to deal with the company handling his health insurance coverage, both doctors, and the specialty pharmacy on his behalf before he laid down on the exam table to take a narcolepsy nap.

Julie's heart ached for Dion when he reached over and placed his hand on her belly as the pharmacist, insurance representative, and sleep specialist discussed all the paperwork steps they had to take to get him started on his new medication while on speakerphone with them and

Doc Hayes. She wasn't sure if it was the rapid-fire discussion that he found confusing because of his comprehension issues since the TBI, the outrageous price of over six-thousand dollars per bottle, with him needing as many as three bottles per month, that was mentioned when the insurance representative wasn't sure if it was covered on his COBRA plan, or her earlier idiocy of bringing up his self-confidence issues that triggered his episode. But it was very clear that focusing on their babies wasn't enough to stop him from passing out this time.

Upon hearing the cost per bottle, Julie immediately went into business mode, wondering if she could talk her family into buying the company that manufactured it, so they could get the cost down for people who couldn't afford to pay out of pocket when their insurance didn't cover the medication. Doing a little mental math, she quickly realized that at over eighteen-thousand dollars a month, the yearly cost of this medication would be over two-hundred-thousand dollars, which was almost equal to half her yearly salary as a board member and vice president at Burleson Incorporated. While technically, she could afford to cover the cost of Dion's medication, doing so would severely cut into what she had to invest for their children's future, as well as her annual charitable donations. And she still had no idea about Dion's finances to know if he could afford it or not. But seeing Dion's eyes glass over and start to droop, she knew she couldn't think about that right then, needing to focus on taking care of him instead.

"Jewel, can you remember all this for me, so I can do, wha-whatever, later? I need to lie, uh, lay down," Dion implored her, slightly slurring his words as his eyelids fluttered, signaling how hard he was fighting to keep from passing out, even as he remembered to change his wording to satisfy her quirk about laying instead of lying.

Wow, even when he's fighting his narcolepsy, he's still the most thoughtful man on the freaking planet.

"Let's get you up on the exam table," Doc Hayes directed, jumping from his seat to help her shuffle Dion over to the long, padded table, which reminded Julie of a massage table without the attachment for laying face down, on the other side of the room. "And are you giving Julie Burleson your verbal authorization to act on your behalf while we finish setting up your medication?"

"Yes," Dion choked out as he crawled on the table without waiting for Doc Hayes to cover it with the paper on the roll attached to the end.

He barely got laid down before his eyes fully closed and his breathing evened out in sleep.

"What's going on?" Julie wasn't sure which disembodied voice made the inquiry, but thankfully, Doc Hayes took charge to reply while she stood beside the table to keep an eye on Dion.

"Apparently, this discussion was overwhelming enough to trigger Dion to have a cataplectic sleep attack," Doc Hayes informed the rest of the people on the conference call. "But before he went out, he verbally authorized his girlfriend, Julie Burleson, to act on his behalf, so we can go ahead and get him started on Xyrem and wake him up afterward."

"As I was saying earlier, in order for us to cover this medication, Dr. Khan will need to fill out our prior authorization form and submit copies of Mr. Davis's sleep study results," the person whom Julie assumed was the insurance representative continued, not seeming fazed by Dion having a narcoleptic episode. "Mr. Davis will also need to send in the paperwork and premium to convert his previous policy to a COBRA policy."

"Wait," Julie interjected, confused by why his health insurance hadn't already been converted to a COBRA policy since he was injured in October and unable to work since then. "Are you saying his insurance hasn't already converted to COBRA? He was injured and taken off the GWA roster back in October."

"The Galactic Wrestling Association continued covering his premium through December thirty-first," the representative replied. "We mailed Mr. Davis everything he needed to convert the policy on December first, but haven't heard back from him. So, technically, he's not covered at all right now. But as soon as we get the premium and paperwork back from him, we'll reinstate the policy and start the prior authorization process to cover this new medication."

"And you probably sent that paperwork to his address in New Orleans, so he hasn't seen it since he's been here in Heart's Destiny for the last six weeks." Julie stepped away from a peacefully sleeping Dion to get her purse out from under the chair where she'd previously been sitting, reaching into the side pocket to pull out her phone. She quickly sent a text to her sister, needing to know if she could add Dion to her company health insurance any faster than they could get the COBRA paperwork resent and his previous policy reinstated.

Julie: How long does it take to add a domestic partner to our company health insurance? With us still being in the open enrollment period, I don't need any documentation to add him, right? Any chance you can add Dion to mine effective today?

Jen: You have until 1/15 to add him without having to provide legal documentation. After that, you'll either need to provide a domestic partnership agreement, proof that he's moved in with you, or wait until the babies are born to show their birth certificates as the qualifying event to add him. Why? Are you finally giving in & letting him move in?

Julie: We haven't talked about it. But I thought it might be faster to get him covered for his new meds than waiting on his old insurance company to resend his COBRA info to Heart's Destiny instead of NOLA & reinstate his previous policy.

Jen: Shit! Ya'll are at the doctor now, right?

Julie: Yes, & they want to start him on a drug that costs over $18,000 a month. I can cover it to get him started while waiting on the prior authorization to go through, but he'll be pissed when he wakes up & finds out.

Jen: When he wakes up? Did he pass out when he heard that price?

Julie was irritated by her sister wanting to carry on a long conversation while she was sitting in the doctor's office, listening to the conference call going on without her input. Thankfully, the doctor, pharmacy, and insurance company were all just exchanging fax numbers to be able to deal with all the paperwork on their end. But still, she needed to know if she should give them her insurance company information or not.

Julie: Something like that. Can I add him to my policy or not?

Jen: I'm starting the paperwork now. Call me with his SSN as soon as you can, so I can get them to push it through ASAP. May not cover today's visit, but should be effective by the end of the week to get his new meds.

Julie: Thanks Sis!

Julie shoved her phone back in the side pocket of her purse and grabbed her insurance card out of her wallet before interrupting the conversation once more. "Actually, ya'll need to send all that prior authorization stuff to my insurance company instead."

"Excuse me?" Once again, Julie wasn't sure which disembodied voice was speaking through the speakerphone.

Geez, do none of these people employ women? At least, if they weren't all men talking with similar accents, I might be able to figure out who I'm talking to for part of this conversation.

"My company benefits extend to domestic partners, so I'm having Dion added to my policy," Julie explained, not getting into the details about how her sister had negotiated a plan with their insurance company to cover all their employee's loved ones, regardless of gender, relationship, or legally recognized union when they were added during the open enrollment period. "It'll get him covered faster than having the COBRA paperwork resent to him here in Heart's Destiny and having to send it all back in to be processed."

"Since Mr. Davis will be using another insurance company from now on, I'll wish you all the best of luck in this matter and leave the call so you can continue." The insurance representative clicked off before any of them could thank him for his help.

Yeah, I probably pissed him off by cutting his company out of those COBRA premiums. Oops. Hopefully, Dion won't be too upset by me making this decision for him.

Leah Mae Wright

"I don't know if he'll be covered by the end of the day today or the end of the week, but his policy number and stuff will all be the same as mine, so I can go ahead and give it to ya'll now, if you want." After verbal agreements from Dr. Khan and the pharmacist, Julie gave them the information from her insurance card, so they could go ahead and start submitting everything.

And hopefully, Jen will have everything set up soon enough that my insurance company won't reject the paperwork when they send it in, claiming they don't have Dion listed on a policy.

"We actually have a quick start voucher we can use to send Mr. Davis his first month free, so once we verify his new insurance information, he can go ahead and get started on the medication while waiting on the prior authorization to go through," the pharmacist informed her, explaining that the prior authorization process was time consuming for everyone, so the company implemented this program to keep all their patients from having to delay treatment, regardless of income level. He also mentioned that they had a bridge program to provide up to four months of medication at no cost to the patients when their insurance changed or their prior authorization had to be recertified.

Huh? Maybe we don't have to buy the company to help make it more affordable after all.

"Excellent. What do I need to do to get him set up with that?" Julie hoped his verbal authorization a few minutes earlier was enough for her to be able to handle all the paperwork to get the medicine shipped out soon, regardless of whether she had to pay the eighteen-thousand dollars or they used this voucher program.

"We have to go through Mr. Davis's medical information, allergies, et cetera, have a counseling call with him and one of our pharmacists, and have him go on our website to electronically sign some forms. Since we have his verbal authorization to talk to you about everything now, we can go ahead and get started with filling in whatever medical information you know, but without something in writing authorizing you to sign on his behalf, we'll have to schedule the online forms and counseling calls for when Mr. Davis is available."

With Doc Hayes and Dr. Khan's help, Julie quickly relayed what little she knew of Dion's medical history. The doctors filled in some of the blanks she couldn't from their records for Dion, which she made mental notes of in case she had to use it again in the future. She also looked over Doc Hayes's shoulder to see that his hospital records from New Orleans showed that he had tested negative for any bloodborne pathogens, since they weren't sure if he'd come in contact with the stalker's blood or not. With a sigh of relief at knowing her instincts had been correct about his clean status, she then wrote down the web address for the site he needed to visit and what forms he needed to fill out and sign electronically. With how easily the process overwhelmed him today, she planned to sit by his side as he made the calls for the counseling and filled out the forms, just in case he had any comprehension issues crop up while going through them.

Once everything was handled to the best of her ability, Doc Hayes disconnected the call, got out the smelling salts, and woke Dion up, so she could take him back to the bed and breakfast. It was a different experience watching him wake up after his sleep attack than it had been when they woke up together in bed after spending the night together. While she hadn't expected cuddles and kisses in the middle of the doctor's office, like was the norm for their morning after routine, seeing him barely open his eyes and stare into space without otherwise moving or speaking was somewhat disconcerting.

"It's the sleep paralysis," Doc Hayes assured her, reminding her of one of the symptoms of narcolepsy. "It may take up to fifteen minutes before he can move or speak again. But that'll give me time to get his chart updated with his new insurance information and all the details for today's visit. So, ya'll can relax for as long as you need without us having to kick you out to bring the next patient back."

"But he is awake, right?" Julie ran her hand down Dion's arm, clasping his big hand in hers when she reached it.

"Yep, and can hear everything we say, so now's the time to take advantage of having a captive audience if you wanna try out some bad jokes when he can't even groan about 'em." Doc Hayes grinned as he tossed the capsule he'd broken and put under Dion's nose to wake him up in the garbage can before washing his hands. "Dion, I wanna see you back here in three weeks. That'll give you a week to get the Xyrem shipped to you, so you'll have two weeks on it before reporting back how it's working for you. And you're good to go as soon as you feel up to it. But please, lay there as long as you need to, 'cause Julie and I combined aren't strong enough to carry you out to her car, so we need you to be able to safely walk out on your own."

"Thanks, Doc. I'll make sure he schedules his next appointment on the way out." Julie smiled as her family practitioner left the room. She turned her gaze back to Dion, who looked up at her with big, puppy-dog eyes. "I guess now's the time to tell you that I added you to my insurance, so you can't complain about it."

After a momentary flare of confusion, Dion's eyes hardened, letting her know he was just as irritated by her covering the cost of his insurance as she'd assumed he'd be.

"I know, I know, you wanna pay your own way and not have me cover your expenses." Julie raised her hands in surrender as he groaned, as if he was trying to verbally object, but couldn't until the sleep paralysis passed. "But it was either add you as my domestic partner on my company policy, or wait on your former insurance company to send you the COBRA paperwork again, and then wait however many weeks it takes them to reinstate your policy once you filled it all out and sent them the first month's premium. This will be effective by the end of the week, if it's not effective by the end of the day today. And it's only, like, an extra hundred dollars a month to switch to a family plan on my insurance, which I was gonna hafta do when the babies are born, anyway. But COBRA policies are more than double whatever you were paying through the GWA. So, even if you want to reimburse me the difference in what I was paying and what will now be deducted from my check, I've probably saved you at least five-hundred dollars a month. And I know you're now covered by the best health insurance policy Jen could find."

Dion blew out a breath through his nose, barely getting his mouth to move enough to croak out, "Thanks, Jewel."

"Yeah, don't thank me yet," Julie teased, smiling at him. "You still have to sit through a counseling call with the pharmacist and fill out some online forms to get your first shipment of Xyrem free while we're waiting on the new insurance to kick in and go through the prior authorization process."

"Fra-free?" Dion stuttered, still struggling to speak, even though he'd managed to squeeze her hand.

"Yeah, apparently this prior authorization process is such a pain that it causes delays for everyone, so the company has this program to go ahead and get patients started on the medication while waiting for it to get approved. They just have to verify your new insurance info before they can use the voucher to send the first shipment." Julie almost joked that it was similar to a drug dealer giving away free product to get people hooked, like she'd seen on numerous police procedurals on television, but considering the active ingredient in his new medication was GHB, she decided the joke was inappropriate. "And if it's gonna stop these sleep attacks the way Dr. Khan claims, then I think you need to get on it now and not wait for the insurance to approve it."

"Yeah, you're right." Dion finally started sounding more like himself, slowly moving his extremities, almost like he was making sure he could move again, before rolling on his side to start to sit up.

Julie released his hand and stepped back out of his way, so he could push himself up to sit on the side of the table. They talked for a few more minutes about the medication and his next steps, waiting until he felt steady on his feet to be able to walk out of the exam room.

They scheduled his next appointment with Doc Hayes for January twenty-seventh, with Dion insisting on paying the cost of the whole appointment, instead of the estimated co-pay with his new insurance, since they weren't sure when it would go into effect. As they drove back to the B and B, Julie called Jen through her car's Bluetooth system, so Dion could give her his social security number and answer any other questions she had to be able to add him to Julie's policy.

"So, um, I'm officially using your address now, huh?" Dion smirked after the call with Jen disconnected. "Is that just for this, so I can be listed as your domestic partner? Or do I need to actually put in a change of address with the post office and move my stuff from the B and B?"

"I don't want you to move in for *this*, any more than I want you to move in for the babies," Julie grumbled as she turned onto the Hunters' property, her irritation at having their timeline dictated by outside influences amped up to the Nth degree. "I think we need to date for a little while longer before we decide if we're ready to move in together. But as you said on Christmas, the babies make us family whether we're a couple or not, so I think that qualifies us to use the domestic partner clause to get your health insurance."

Leah Mae Wright

"I'll keep using the address at the B and B for now then." Dion reached over to take her hand, pulling it to his lips for a quick kiss. "But for the record, you're welcome to spend the night with me here anytime, not just after our Saturday date nights."

"Yes, well, right now I'm just coming up to help you navigate the Xyrem website to fill out these forms and schedule the counseling call." *And if that takes up the rest of the afternoon, I suppose I could stay for dinner and spend the night. I mean, that is why I packed an overnight bag and put it in my trunk before going to work this morning. He just doesn't need to know that yet, so he doesn't get any ideas about it meaning more than it does.*

A few hours later, after handling as much of the process for getting his medication as they could until his new insurance was verified by the pharmacy and they completed the counseling call they'd scheduled for Wednesday afternoon, Julie and Dion opted for an early dinner before retiring to his room for the night. She knew, if she really wanted to take things slow with him, she should probably go home for the night and wait until their Saturday date night to spend the night with Dion again. But no matter what she thought about wanting to deliberately build their relationship before living together, her heart and her female parts kept overriding her brain. At least, this time, she'd planned ahead and brought an overnight bag, so she wouldn't have to wear another set of Dion's workout clothes home the next morning to change before going into work.

She'd actually tried to return his sweats and t-shirts after wearing them home the past two times she'd spent the night with him. But Dion insisted she keep them to have something big enough to accommodate her growing baby bump on the days she needed to wear pants to clean her house, instead of one of the nice maternity dresses she'd bought. So far, she'd only worn his t-shirts to sleep in on the few nights she'd actually spent at home.

She didn't have the heart to tell him that the only housekeeping she usually did was running her dishwasher and wiping up any messes she made daily. Since the Madeline Ashbury Foundation House opened on the ranch the previous year, the Burlesons hired some of the women who lived there to clean all the houses on the ranch. It gave the women a way to earn a living while staying safe from their previous abusers behind the gates of the ranch, until such time as their abusers were no longer a threat and they'd trained for the careers they wanted while compiling a nest egg to be able to purchase a home of their own when they moved on to those careers.

When she packed her overnight bag with a couple days' worth of clothes for work, she thought about packing his sweats and t-shirts to return them and explain why. But she liked the feeling of wearing his things so much that part of her didn't want to give them back. It was just too comforting to have something of his wrapped around her body when he wasn't physically in her bed to hold her.

She'd also known better than to pack anything to sleep in when she planned to spend the night in Dion's bed. The first time she'd traveled to meet him while he was on tour with the GWA, her pajamas never left her suitcase. He'd taught her the benefit of sleeping in the buff multiple times over the last year, so she hadn't ever packed pajamas to spend the night with him again.

I wonder how he'll deal with needing to sleep in clothing of some sort after the babies are born? Or in a couple of weeks when he helps me with Jerry and Jonah?

As they brushed their teeth and she washed off her makeup, preparing for going to bed, she decided to ask him, knowing they needed to plan ahead. "So, what are we gonna do about your whole naked sleeping thing when we have to get up for two a.m. feedings in a couple of weeks?"

"I guess we'll do like we've done in the past when we had to answer the hotel door for room service." Dion shrugged, like it was no big deal. "Put on a robe before opening the bedroom door."

After putting his toothbrush away, Dion pecked a kiss on the top of her head and left her in the bathroom. Julie finished washing her face, put away her things, and wiped down the counter where they'd splashed water before stepping back out into his room. She found him already naked, cleaning off the dresser and moving the few things, like his wallet and watch that he normally left laying there at night, over to the table under the television.

"But what about when our kids are older and come running into our room in the middle of the night when they have a bad dream, or to wake us up on Christmas morning?" Julie stopped at the closet where she'd stashed her overnight bag after hanging up the dresses she'd brought with her to wear on Tuesday and Wednesday, planning to put her dirty clothes back in it as she took them off.

Dion walked up behind her and lifted the hem of her dress before she could pull it off. "Well, then maybe you can sleep in some of these dresses, or nightgowns that are similar," he suggested, his deep voice causing goosebumps on her flesh as he pulled the loose dress up over her head. "With no panties, so I have easy access, but you're still modestly covered when the kids come in. Come to think of it, you can continue wearing these dresses all the time, instead of going back to your pantsuits once the babies are born, so I'll always have easy access for a quickie."

Julie shook her head at him, knowing he couldn't see her eye roll at his sexual scheming.

"And I'll learn to sleep under the covers or in a pair of loose workout shorts that I can easily shove outta the way when I wanna fuck you in the middle of the night."

"Yeah, you start under the covers with me now," she teasingly scoffed as he dropped her dress on his pile of dirty clothes at their feet. "But by the time we wake up, you've kicked them off the bed, so we're both uncovered."

"That's 'cause you make me so hot that we don't need 'em," Dion replied, running butterfly kisses over her shoulders as he unfastened her bra. He slipped the straps down her arms before dropping it on top of her dress. He then kissed his way down her back to squat down and remove her panties.

"Well, since it's been over a year and you haven't broken the habit of kicking off the covers, maybe you should start sleeping in shorts now, so you'll have plenty of time to get used to them before the kids are able to walk." Julie wasn't sure how she managed to get the words out as Dion's titillating touches and feather-soft kisses amped up her arousal level to the point that she couldn't think about anything but making love with him any longer.

She turned to face him as he slowly stood, trailing his hands and mouth up her body to continue his erotic torture. She placed her hand over his heart as he brought their lips together for a passionate kiss. As the woody aquatic fragrance of his cologne surrounded her, she relished the taste of mint and man, tangling their tongues in a primal dance.

Dion's large erection pressed against her center as he gripped the globes of her ass and lifted her from the floor. Julie instinctually wrapped her arms and legs around him, clinging to him like a monkey in a tree as he carried her over to set her on the dresser. He stepped out of her embrace to position her right on the edge, so he had full access to her pussy without the flat surface she was sitting on getting in his way. *Ah, so that's why he was cleaning it off. My kinky man has plans for another position we can try.*

"I'll start trying to sleep in shorts when I sleep over at your house when your nephews are there," Dion muttered against her skin as he broke the kiss and trailed his lips and tongue down the column of her neck. "And after our babies are born. But only when we're sleeping somewhere with children present. If it's just the two of us, I want full access to every part of you, Jewel."

"Yes," Julie panted out her agreement as he caressed up her torso until his hands and mouth met at her breasts. He cupped her mounds in his palms, teasing one nipple with his mouth while pinching the other between his finger and thumb. He lightly twisted the tip, just enough to be stimulating but not painful.

She still couldn't tell if he preferred her more voluptuous curves while she was pregnant or the perfect mouthfuls he'd called her breasts before. But she appreciated the way he still gave them the same loving affection as he had previously. As they were even more sensitive during her pregnancy, she was especially grateful for the way he'd lightened up with his pinches and nibbles, ensuring she only felt pleasure from his touch and never pain.

"Oh, Dion," Julie moaned in pleasure as he suckled her, already feeling close to the edge and he hadn't even touched her pussy yet.

Dion pulled his head back, popping his mouth off her breast to move to the other one to repeat the exquisite treatment. Julie hoped there was enough varnish on the wooden dresser to protect it from the gush of fluid between her legs from how much she enjoyed having Dion play with her breasts.

"One of these days, I'm gonna make you come just from sucking on your sweet tits," Dion declared after popping off her other breast. He then kissed his way down her body, reverently worshiping her belly before kneeling to drop his head between her spread legs. His hot breath blew across her clit just before he swiped his tongue through her folds.

Julie was pretty sure that would only be possible while her libido was increased and her breasts were their most sensitive during the second trimester of pregnancy, but she was too aroused to mention it right then. If she did, then he might go back to her breasts to attempt it immediately. And she needed the decadent feel of his tongue on her pussy too much at that moment to risk him changing his plans.

Having released her hold on him so he could move down her body, Julie felt at a loss for how to touch him to show him how much she wanted him. She just kept running her hands over his shoulders and head, since he'd dropped his arms between his torso and the dresser to hold her thighs open with his big hands on either side of her pussy.

"Play with your tits while I eat your pussy." Dion lifted his mouth just long enough to issue his command before sucking her clit between his lips and plunging his thumbs inside her. He swirled his tongue around the engorged nub as he stretched her pussy by pulling his thumbs in opposite directions while massaging her inner walls.

Julie followed his directions, lifting her hands to cup her breasts while rubbing the pads of her thumbs over her turgid nipples. She looked down to watch as he sucked, licked, and finger-fucked her, noting that his eyes were glued to her chest. *Oh, he likes watching me touch myself for him.*

She let the heavy mounds fall as she released them from her palms, lightly trailing her fingertips over the swollen flesh to tease him before pinching her nipples between her thumbs and forefingers the way he had earlier. Dion hummed against her clit, encouraging her to continue with the treatment he preferred. Then he doubled his efforts, devouring her like a starving man until she squirted her release into his mouth.

"Oh, fuck, Dion," Julie cried out as she came, unable to stop chanting his name as her orgasm washed over her like the waves of the ocean crashing against the shore. It wasn't until she started to come down that she realized that while she was drowning in pleasure, Dion was actually in danger of literally drowning from the abundance of arousal she'd squirted in his mouth. "Oh, Dion, are you okay?"

"Way better than okay," he grinned, wiping his mouth with one hand, and gripping his dick with the other as he stood. "And I'll be perfect just as soon as I get inside you."

"Yes, now," she pleaded, gripping his upper arms to pull him closer as he lined up the head of his cock with her slit and slowly sank inside her. She wished he would have plunged in hard, deep, and fast, filling her with one stroke, and fucking her with abandon. But she knew her gentle giant would always be careful with her at first and work his way up to more intense coupling to keep from hurting her or their babies.

Dion cupped her face in his hands and kissed her passionately, sharing the tangy sweet taste of her juices as he worked his way inside her until he was balls-deep. He then pulled her a little farther off the edge of the dresser, probably making sure he wouldn't slap his balls against the hard wood when he got up to speed.

Julie wrapped her arms and legs around him once more, needing to feel him skin on skin, almost as much as she needed to feel secure, now that she was precariously balanced on the edge of the dresser. They continued kissing, telling each other how they felt without words, as Dion pulled back and thrust in once more.

Julie rocked her hips against his, even though she couldn't move much without slipping off the edge of the dresser. Dion's hands trailed over her body, tantalizing her with his touch as he escalated the intensity of their copulation. He thrust harder and faster, eventually gripping the globes of her ass to lift her from the dresser, so it wouldn't be in their way any longer.

Standing in the middle of the room, he bounced her up and down his length, until she tore her lips from his to cry out his name once more as she came with wild abandon. Her whole body shuddered with each wave of her release, her core muscles spasming in the same rhythm to milk the cum from his cock. Dion plunged in deep one last time, holding still as he emptied himself inside her with a guttural groan. "Julia!"

Julie came so hard, she felt like she was floating through space in an other-worldly realm. Feeling connected only to Dion, she rested her head on his shoulder as she recovered. When her soul came back to earth, she had to wonder how he'd managed to walk across the room and sit down on the bed without breaking their connection. "Wow, that was…"

"The best ever?" Dion smiled, turning to brush his lips over her temple.

"Definitely in the top five," she teased, lifting her head just enough to brush her lips over the scruff on his jaw. "But the massage oil that made everything tingly the day we made our babies is still number one."

"Hmmm, do I need to get some more of that?" Dion massaged her back in a manner similar to the way he'd rubbed her down on the day she'd just referenced.

"Maybe, but we'll have to limit where we use it, 'cause I don't think my nipples can handle that right now." Julie relaxed into Dion, feeling so comfortable in his arms that she drifted off to sleep before they'd fully recovered and cleaned up.

Chapter Twenty-One

As she sat on the exam table in Dr. Magnum's office, Julie had to admit, if only to herself, that she agreed with Dion about the easy access of the dresses she'd started wearing all the time since being pregnant. Only instead of just thinking about how he'd have easy access for a quickie anytime and anywhere, she was also thinking about how the doctor would have easy access for doing ultrasounds and exams. Even if she had to have another vaginal ultrasound or pelvic exam, she'd just have to remove her panties, instead of getting half undressed like when she wore pants. *And yet, before now, I'd only thought about how it was more convenient to go to the bathroom because of how much pressure the babies are putting on my bladder.*

It was a good thing she had to give a urine sample first thing every time she came to the doctor. With the weight of two babies pressing on her bladder, she'd barely been able to hold it until she was called back after driving to Heart's Destiny from work and picking up Dion before going to the doctor's office. And she'd literally gone to the bathroom right before she walked out of the building when she left work.

"Do they do blood and urine tests at every visit?" Dion questioned as Arden left the room after taking her vitals and drawing her blood.

She didn't have the chance to reply to Dion because of the knock on the door right before Dr. Magnum walked into the room. She pushed the ultrasound cart in with her, not waiting for Arden to finish submitting Julie's blood for testing to bring it this time. "Good afternoon, Julie. Dion."

"Good afternoon, Dr. Magnum," Dion greeted the doctor as Julie said a quick, "Hi, Devon. Hope we aren't making your office feel overrun with Burlesons this week."

Dr. Magnum gave her a confused look as she positioned the ultrasound cart beside the exam table.

Not wanting the doctor to feel as flustered as she looked, Julie elaborated. "Charlotte mentioned having an appointment yesterday, and Amy said she has her follow-up after having the twins at the end of the week. So, I figured with seeing so many of us this week, it must feel like we're monopolizing your practice."

"Oh, no." Devon shook her head and smiled as she walked around the cart and unwound a cord from the back of it. "While I do have several members of your family as patients, even your family isn't large enough to monopolize the practice."

As the doctor plugged in the machine, Dion jumped up from his seat to move around to stand between Julie, who was already on the exam table, and the wall. He took her hand, bringing it to his lips for a quick kiss as they anxiously awaited seeing their babies.

Dr. Magnum didn't start with the ultrasound, however, instead asking questions about how Julie was feeling and how much movement she'd noticed from the babies.

"They seem to move more at night than during the day," Julie informed the doctor. "Does that mean our babies are going to be night owls?"

"Not necessarily," Devon explained. "They have no sense of night or day at this point. They're just more active an hour or two after you eat, when those nutrients hit their systems. So, if you're like most people, who eat more in the evening when you're off work, having snacks after dinner or right before bed, then they'll be more active later in the night."

She went on to instruct Julie on kick counting to learn their babies patterns throughout the day, telling them it could be a useful tool to monitor the babies' wellbeing as the pregnancy progressed. "And you're right on target with weight gain, which is another indicator of how well your babies are growing."

Julie was relieved to hear that, previously thinking gaining twenty pounds in twenty weeks seemed a little excessive. "It's not too much? I have to admit that I was a little worried when I found out Charlotte's gained about the same amount of weight as me, even though she's three months farther along in her pregnancy."

"Charlotte's only having one baby, so she only needs to gain twenty-five to thirty-five pounds," Dr. Magnum pointed out. "But with two, we want you to gain between forty and fifty-five pounds. And if you gain a pound and a half every week for the rest of your pregnancy, you'll be right on target for where we want you when the babies are born."

Maybe I should have asked Amy how much weight she gained with the boys, instead of just comparing my weight gain to my currently pregnant cousin.

Once they were finished discussing her weight, Dr. Magnum asked Julie to lay back on the exam table and lift her dress. She then pulled out her tape measure and measured the size of Julie's baby belly, taking her own notes since Arden hadn't come back in the room. Then she picked up the ultrasound probe and squirted the gel on the end before running it over Julie's abdomen.

As she went through the anatomy scan, Devon quietly clicked buttons on the keyboard to measure the babies' growth as Julie and Dion watched the screen to see their babies now that they were actually starting to look like babies, even in the grainy black-and-white images.

"Look at that little face," Dion gushed, squeezing her hand. "I knew the little blobs in the last ultrasound pictures were our babies, but now they actually look like babies."

Before Julie could pop off with a snarky comment about him expecting them to look like puppies the way she was thinking, Dr. Magnum asked, "Would you like to know the sex of your babies?"

"Yes," Julie and Dion answered in unison, smiling at each other before looking back at the monitor to see as the doctor scanned farther down on Baby A's body.

"Holy shit, my boy takes after me," Dion blurted, obviously thinking Baby A had a penis.

"That's the umbilical cord," Devon corrected him, causing Julie to start laughing, as the doctor repositioned the probe to show the baby's genitals. "And Baby A is actually a girl."

"Are you sure?" Dion leaned over Julie, trying to get a better look at the screen, since he didn't have his glasses yet. "'Cause that looks like a dick to me."

"Yes, I'm sure," Dr. Magnum replied as she clicked a button on the keyboard. "A baby's penis is much smaller than the umbilical cord."

"Don't worry, D," Julie chuckled. "I'm sure you'll be able to see Zoe's vagina on the pictures once you get your glasses." *I'll have to remember to ask him if he needs me to take him to pick them up when we leave here.*

After taking a few more measurements of Zoe's body parts, the doctor turned up the sound and repositioned the probe to show them her beating heart.

"Oh, wow, I didn't realize we'd be able to see her heart beating like that." Julie was entranced by the image on the screen as they listened to the galloping hoofbeat sounds filling the room.

"Amazing," Dion breathed out in awe. "That's our little girl."

As Dr. Magnum finished her assessment of Zoe and moved on to start the scan and measurements of Baby B, Dion leaned down to brush his lips across Julie's forehead. He then closed his eyes and rested his head on the exam table beside hers as he took a few deep breaths.

"You okay, D?" Julie was worried that his excitement at seeing their babies for the first time could feel as overwhelming as anxiety and trigger one of his narcolepsy sleep attacks. She turned to look at him instead of at the monitor, reaching over to place her hand on his jaw to comfort him.

"Yeah, Jewel, I'm fine." Dion covered her hand with his, but he didn't open his eyes. "Just need a minute to get used to these emotions before I find out if Baby B is Elena or Dev."

A couple of seconds later, he opened his eyes, pecked her lips with his, and stood back up to watch as Devon showed them their other baby. When she got to Baby B's face, Dion spoke once more. "Can you tell if they're identical or fraternal from this scan? 'Cause they look identical to me."

"Because your babies each have their own placenta, the only way we'd be able to tell from this scan is if Baby B is a boy. Then we'd know they are fraternal." Dr. Magnum explained as she moved the probe to look at the baby's genitals. "But since Baby B is also a girl, we'd have to do an amniocentesis or chorionic villus sampling to test their genetics before they're born. But since I don't see any abnormalities in either of your daughters on the ultrasound, I'd recommend you wait until they're born to do less invasive tests, if we can't physically see the differences between them."

Julie momentarily got mentally sidetracked by the thought of doing one of the prenatal tests that would require inserting a large needle into her abdomen and almost missed the revelation of their second baby's sex. "Wait. Did you say Baby B is also a girl?"

"Yes," Devon nodded, matter-of-factly.

"Now I really have to start thinking of middle names for Elena," Julie mused as she looked at their second daughter on the screen. "And maybe take Mama Marcel's predictions more seriously in the future, since she told us they're both girls a month ago."

"Yeah, she's never gonna let us live that down now," Dion chuckled.

When Devon looked at them with a confused expression, they quickly filled her in on the night Julie met Mama Marcel, as well as Caroline's history as a fortune teller. "And now I'm gonna follow her advice and look at the names on our family tree to give Elena the same middle name as one of our loved ones."

"I think we should name her Elena Juliette," Dion suggested, surprising Julie.

"Juliette? As in, little Julie?" She arched an eyebrow at Dion. "Don't you think it would seem a little narcissistic to name one of my daughters after myself?"

"No, 'cause I'm the one who wants to name her after you," Dion disagreed. "Just like it's not narcissistic on my part for you to want to name one of our future sons after me."

Damn it! I'm gonna hafta give in and let him have his pick for Elena's middle name if I want him to go along with my plans if we have twin boys in the future like Mama Marcel predicted. But I don't have to let him know that just yet, so I can have a little fun teasing him with other name ideas for a little while.

"What if I wanna name her Elena Dion?" Julie quipped, unable to hide her grin. "I mean, until I met you, when I thought of the name Dion, I thought of Dionne Warwick, so it's kind of a gender neutral name. And since we don't know if we'll have more than these two babies, it guarantees I get to name one of them after you."

"Dionne Warwick spells her name with two N's and an E, so it's not the same name," Dion protested, shaking his head at her. "It just sounds the same, so the male and female versions are homophones. Besides, you just said we have to believe Mama Marcel's predictions now, so you're still gonna wanna name one of the boys after me."

Before Julie could continue the verbal foreplay, Dr. Magnum turned up the volume on Elena's heartbeat, drowning them out and drawing their attention back to the screen to see the strong heartbeat of their second daughter. *Well played, Doc. Well played.* Julie had to smile at the always sensible, serious doctor, taking control of the room without having to say a word.

They soon wrapped up the appointment, leaving with another dozen or so photos from the ultrasound. As Dion snapped pictures of each of them with his phone, Julie set her next two appointments with the doctor for February fourth and March third. She also learned that in March, her appointments would start being scheduled every two weeks, instead of the every-four-week rotation they were scheduled on now. So, she went ahead and scheduled the two others after that for March seventeenth and March thirty-first.

As they walked out of the clinic, Julie caught a whiff of the cheesy goodness of Pistol Pete's Pizza, causing her stomach to growl loudly. "I think your daughters are craving pizza," Julie joked, rubbing a hand over her belly as she used the other hand to grab Dion's, so she could pull him toward the pizza place beside the clinic in the corner of the building where it connected to the building housing the local dentist and optometrist. "Is it too early to go into Pistol Pete's and sit down for dinner? Or should I just order a pie to go, eat a slice now as a snack, and save the rest for dinner later?"

"If our daughters want pizza, then it's time to sit down and eat pizza," Dion replied with a grin. "And if anyone says anything about it being too early for dinner, then we'll just call it lupper."

"Did you just invent a new meal time?" Julie laughed at the way he'd combined lunch and supper. "And if so, does it replace my afternoon snack at three? Or is it an additional meal I get to eat every day?"

"Since you're eating for three, and have been instructed to gain a pound and a half a week for the next twenty weeks, I say you need to just make it an extra meal every day." Dion smirked as he opened the door to the pizza place for her to enter. "So, what do Zoe and Elena want on their pizza?"

"Tomatoes, spinach, and pineapple," Julie declared, still not understanding the strange cravings she'd started having since finding out she was pregnant. "And maybe we should get it to go, so we can stop at the Creamarie for a chocolate milkshake to go with it."

"Yeah, we need two large pizzas to go," Dion ordered when they got to the counter, visibly swallowing, like he might have thrown up a little in his mouth at the thought of her pizza and milkshake combination. "One pepperoni, and one with tomatoes, spinach, and pineapple."

"Deep dish," Julie added, smiling gratefully as she leaned into Dion's side. *Such a good man. Zoe, Elena, you girls better pay attention to all the little things like this your daddy does. And when it comes time for you to start dating, don't settle for any man who isn't willing to swallow his disgust and order your outlandish cravings without saying a word about how gross they sound.*

Once he paid for their pizzas and they sat down to wait on them to be made, Dion surprised her with his next comment. "So, before we go to the Creamarie, you have to tell me how Nana Marie knew about us before the rest of the Matchmaking Mommas."

"Have you recovered more memories than you've told me about?" Dion shook his head, answering her question in the negative without verbally saying a word. "Then how do you know Nana Marie knew about us over a year ago?"

"Because I talked to her last month while out exploring the town," Dion stated with a half-shrug. "But even though she claimed to have known about us all along, she wouldn't tell me about when I met her before, saying I needed to wait and let those memories come back on their own. So, is it true that she knew all along? And if so, how'd you keep her from gossiping about us with the rest of the ladies in town?"

"Oh, yeah, it's true," Julie nodded, smiling at the memory of first introducing Dion to Nana Marie at the town-wide Thanksgiving dinner way back when she was fighting not to give in to her desire for him. "I actually introduced you to her on Thanksgiving that first week, before we became more than friends. Right after the introduction, you got called away by one of the guys, and she grilled me about the attraction that was obvious to her. I admitted to being attracted, but told her I wasn't planning on acting on it because I didn't want Mom to claim credit for finding me a man. Then two days later, she pulled me aside at Anthony and Kay's wedding reception to let me know I could talk to her about my new boyfriend, since I wasn't ready to talk to Mom yet. She's really good at keeping secrets and great at giving advice, even if it can get a little TMI at times."

"Why do I have a feeling I don't wanna know how it can get a little TMI?" Dion arched an eyebrow at her, clearly fighting a smile.

"It's not too bad," Julie smirked, looking around the room to make sure there were no children close enough to hear her. "I mean, if it wasn't for her openness about discussing things, I wouldn't have learned that ice cream BJ trick you like so much."

Julie could laugh about it now, but she'd actually cringed when Nana Marie had mentioned it was helpful to numb the throat by blowing an extra-large ice cream cone before going down on a big dick. She'd actually pulled Julie into the back office at the Creamarie to demonstrate the technique, giving Julie her own extra-large chocolate cone to practice on. Of course, Julie couldn't practice for laughing so hard, so she'd asked if it would be okay to just spread the ice cream on Dion's dick for them both to experience the cool, numbing effect. To which, Nana Marie had decided that might be the best option, "since cold causes shrinkage, and that might be necessary to swallow a really large dick."

Dion's eyes widened as he obviously had a flash of memory from one of the times they'd tried it, making her wonder if he was remembering her telling him about that conversation with Nana Marie. "Yeah, we're gonna get some extra ice cream when we stop for your shake. Only I'll be eating it off of you tonight, Jewel."

"Oh, you are, are you?" Julie practically purred the words, wanting to tease him as much as he was teasing her by running his finger over her forearm as they sat across from each other at the small table off to the side of the room. "Are you planning to torture me for any reason in particular? Or is it just because you think we'll both enjoy it?"

"Oh, I think we'll both enjoy it quite a bit," Dion nodded, a sexy grin spreading across his face. "But I'm also not gonna stop until you agree to let me pick Elena's middle name."

Julie wasn't sure she could wait long enough to get their food and actually eat it before demanding he get started on plying her with sexual favors to get his way. "We should probably do that first before waking the girls up by eating."

"Don't worry, Jewel," Dion smirked, just as they called his name to collect their pizzas. He stood and picked up the two boxes, leaning down to whisper in her ear as they walked out to the car. "We can silence your growling stomach by playing with our food before, during, and after the erotic torture I have planned for you tonight."

Sorry, Elena, I guess your middle name is gonna be Juliette, after all.

Dion hadn't been teasing about his plans as they left Pistol Pete's Pizza. He didn't say another word about it as they drove to the Creamarie and picked up her shake, a couple pints of ice cream, and a cup of hot fudge sauce. But as soon as they got to his room at the B and B, he commanded her to strip for a naked dinner while he arranged their pizzas, her shake, and a bottle of water on the desk, and put away the ice cream for a little while later.

Julie excitedly followed his directions, eagerly stripping off her clothes as she watched him do the same. Normally, she would have playfully argued with him or done something a little bratty to challenge him for control. But she was too eager to experience his dominance to do anything other than sink into her submissive role. Once they were both naked, he sat down in the desk chair and pulled her onto his lap.

What on earth does he have planned? Surely, he doesn't think he can make eating pizza sexy just by having us eat naked, even with me sitting on his lap while we eat.

"Clasp your hands behind your back and keep them there. If you move them, I'll get one of my ties from the closet and bind your wrists, so you can't disobey me." Dion kept a firm hold on her hip with one hand as he picked up a slice of her pizza with the other. As soon as she complied with his directive, he held the slice up to her lips for her to take a bite. "I'm thinking one slice each for now, then we can take the ice cream and hot fudge to the shower for easy clean up after playtime. And once we've finished dessert and you've given in and agreed to let me pick Elena's middle name, we can come back and finish our dinner."

"Yes, Sir," Julie agreed after swallowing her first bite of pizza. *Oh yeah, having him feed me while we're both naked is a lot sexier than I thought it'd be. Now, I'm gonna hafta figure out how we can do this without having anyone walk in on us, if and when he finally moves to the ranch.*

Dion took a bite of his own pizza before holding her shake cup up, so she could sip from the straw. Julie wasn't sure what it was about sitting there silently while he hand-fed her that she found so arousing, but based on her diamond hard nipples and dripping wet pussy, it obviously turned her on, even though he hadn't yet touched her in a sexual manner.

Since they only ate one slice of pizza each, which was just enough to stave off the hunger pangs, it didn't take long before he closed the pizza boxes, picked her up, and carried her to the bathroom. Julie's heart raced at not being able to wrap her arms around his neck to feel more secure, but it also felt like keeping her hands clasped behind her back showed how much she trusted him. Like physically showing she trusted him not to drop her, demonstrated her deeper trust that he wouldn't break her heart again.

I hope he understands just how much I trust him.

Dion sat her down on the widest part of the ledge surrounding the built-in bathtub before stepping back out of the bathroom to go get the supplies. With the edge of the jetted tub only being about a foot away from the wall, there wasn't much room for her hands at the small of her back without making her feel like only half her backside was secure on the tiled surround.

"May I release my hands, Sir?" Julie posed the question as soon as Dion stepped back into the room, carrying the last of her milkshake stacked on top of a pint of ice cream in one hand and the cup of hot fudge and a couple of plastic spoons in the other. "I promise to leave them by my sides, but I feel like I need to scoot back some, so I don't slide off into the tub."

"Yes, Jewel, you may," Dion replied with an appreciative grin as she moved her hands from behind her back and scooted her butt up against the tiled wall. "And as a reward for being such a good girl and leaving them in place until you had permission to move them, I'm going to let you decide which one of us gets to eat our dessert first."

Yes! Finally! I get to suck him and get him off first this time!

"Well, then I guess we should follow tradition and say it's ladies first," she cooed in her most genteel tone of voice, as he placed the items in his hands on the ledge beside her and stepped into the tub.

"Oh, Jewel, I'll let you go first, but sucking my cock isn't gonna convince me to give up naming our daughter after you." Dion shook his head, appearing disappointed in her trying to use his own game against him.

"I don't expect it to change your mind, Sir." Julie smiled up at him. "In fact, I'm willing to concede the middle name choice for both Elena and our future son Dillon to you, so we can just enjoy playing tonight without any ulterior motives, other than showing our love for one another."

"So gracious," Dion smirked, reaching out to push her hair behind her ears. "I think you're just trying to butter me up, so you can use your hands to put the ice cream and hot fudge on my dick instead of trying to hold the spoon in your mouth to spread them on me."

Julie couldn't stop her eyes from widening and her jaw from dropping as she realized how he intended her to try to get some ice cream and hot fudge on his dick before sucking him off. Thankfully, she quickly recovered, deciding to use her milkshake instead. "I hadn't even thought about needing my hands, actually," she admitted with a triumphant smile.

Leaving her hands on the tile, Julie twisted her upper body to lean over and close her lips over the straw in her shake. She sucked on the straw until she could taste the first drop of chocolate on her tongue, which she used to cover the end of the straw to hold the shake inside. Then, using only her lips, she pulled the straw from the cup, turning to place the other end over the head of Dion's cock and pulling back her tongue to let the contents of the straw drizzle over his dick. She then turned and placed the straw back in the cup, so her mouth was now unencumbered.

"Very creative, Jewel," Dion praised her as she licked the shake from his shaft. He ran his fingers through her hair, pulling it back into a makeshift ponytail, so it didn't fall in her face or end up in the way of her sucking his cock. "Too bad that's not what we're having for dessert."

Julie just shrugged, licking up the last of the shake before trailing her tongue along the vein in his cock that ran up the underside to the super sensitive spot just below his crown. As Dion shuddered in response, she lapped up the precum oozing from his tip before closing her lips over the bulbous head and sucking him to the back of her mouth. The mostly melted shake didn't do much to numb her gag reflex, so she couldn't swallow as much of him as she wanted. But Dion didn't seem to mind that she could only bob up and down on the first few inches of his long, thick dick.

"Oh, fuck, Jewel," Dion moaned, his hand holding her hair giving the illusion that he was controlling her, when in actuality she was the one in charge right then. "Fuck. Use your hands. Jerk my cock while you suck me dry."

Julie reached out with one hand to wrap it around his base, wanting to obey his directive. She also reached over with her other hand to scoop some of the chocolate sauce up with her fingers, making sure it wasn't too hot before spreading it on his shaft.

Surprisingly, the hot fudge sauce was too sticky to work well as lube for giving him a hand job. So, Julie popped her mouth off the end of his dick, needing to lick it all off before replacing it with the ice cream.

"Fuck, Jewel, I love the way you tease me with your tongue," Dion groaned, rocking his hips, like he couldn't stop himself from thrusting, even though he wasn't actually inside her. "But I really need inside your pretty mouth."

Julie smiled as she finished laving off the fudge and dipped her hand in the ice cream. She was pleasantly surprised to see he'd brought the natural vanilla bean instead of the dark chocolate ripple. While she loved both, the hot fudge sauce would be too much on top of chocolate ice cream that already had ribbons of fudge running through it. Whereas the natural vanilla bean was the perfect complement to the fudge sauce she'd already consumed. She quickly spread it over the head of Dion's dick, dipping out more to put on his shaft as she sucked his cock to the back of her throat.

"That's it. Fuck, Jewel, that feels so fucking good," he grunted, lightly thrusting, so as not to push past what she could take. "Swallow my cock. Eat all your dessert, like a good girl, and I'll wash it down with my cum."

Julie wished it didn't take both hands to completely encircle Dion's dick, wanting one free to touch herself. She was so turned on by sucking his cock that she knew it would only take the lightest touch on her clit to send her soaring over the edge with him. She looked up at his face, imploring him with her eyes as she sucked and stroked.

"Fuck, you like sucking my cock, don't you, Jewel?"

Julie tried nodding, but she wasn't sure if he could tell the difference between her nod and the way she was already bobbing up and down on his dick.

"Yeah, show me how much you like it, Jewel. Come, Jewel. Come from sucking my cock, while your needy little pussy drips from being empty." Dion's deep commanding tone pushed her over the edge, making her pussy clench around nothing as her climax astonished her, at the same time Dion held her head still and started shooting his load down her throat. His dick was so far back in her mouth that she couldn't even taste his salty cum mixing with the ice cream and chocolate sauce on her tongue. "Oh. Fuck. Yes. Jewel."

Once he stopped shuddering with each aftershock, Dion pulled his dick from her mouth, released her hair, and dropped to his knees. "Put your hands by your sides, Jewel, and spread your legs. Now it's my turn to eat your pussy for dessert."

"Yes, Sir." Julie happily complied with his instructions, eager to find out how many times he was going to make her orgasm with his mouth and fingers before finally fucking her in the shower.

Holy shit! Five! My man is freaking amazing with his tongue!

It turned out that five was added to her list of lucky numbers that night, along with one, two, and seven. One from them each coming once from her sucking his cock. Five from the five orgasms he gave her while finishing off the ice cream and hot fudge by eating them off of her. Two from the two times they came at the same time, the second of which was from him fucking her from behind while she was bent over in the shower. And seven from the seven total orgasms she had before they went back to finish their pizza before going to bed.

He is indeed my real-life book boyfriend. The only man capable of making me have multiple O's. And it's pretty amazing that he's able to have multiples with me, too.

~~~

Friday, January 10, 2020

After it took a couple of days to get his new insurance verified and the prior authorization for his new medication started, Dion had to hang out in the front lobby of the B and B most of the day to be able to sign for his first shipment of Xyrem. When he'd sat with Jewel and gone through the counseling on the phone on Wednesday, he'd learned that the generic name of sodium oxybate was another name for the active ingredient gamma-hydroxybutyrate, commonly known as GHB. Because it was such a highly controlled substance, it had to be signed for by someone over the age of twenty-one, who physically had to show their photo identification before they could sign for it. While technically, he knew that whoever was at the front desk could sign for the package from FedEx, Dion didn't want to inconvenience them if they didn't have their driver's license, or other photo identification that showed their date of birth, on them while working. Not to mention the fact that the controlled substance classification being emphasized so strongly by the pharmacist made him feel like he needed to maintain a chain of custody, as if that box was evidence in a criminal case, to ensure it wasn't misplaced, or accidentally handed over to someone who might use the drugs inside for nefarious purposes. And with no idea what time the FedEx driver would arrive at the bed and breakfast, Dion went to the lobby as soon as he got the text notification that the box was out for delivery at eight o'clock that morning. He then stayed in the lobby until the box was finally delivered at four o'clock that afternoon.

Luckily for him, Meemaw, PopPop, and Mandi Hunter all took turns making sure he had meals and company while waiting until Mama Marcel and Darius arrived back in town that afternoon, when
~~~

they took over keeping him company and filling him in on their trip to NOLA. So, even though he had to stay close to the front desk to be able to show his identification to the delivery driver, he wasn't bored at any point in the day. In fact, he now had a few more sketches in his sketchbook, including one of Dean proposing to Allissa on the day Dion was injured, thanks to the Hunters helping him remember the scene backstage.

He felt a little bad about stopping them before they gave him any specific details about the incident in the women's locker room. But he had no desire to remember the scary tragic parts of the day, choosing to focus on recovering only his happy memories. As long as he knew Allissa was safe and her stalker had been dealt with, he was happy with not knowing the specifics of how it all went down.

Looking back on his life, he realized he'd always been the type to only focus on the good and let the bad go. It might not work for everyone, but that was his way of fighting the depression he could have easily fallen into several times in his life.

For instance, he focused on remembering the happy times with his parents as a child. Things like playing football with his dad, or drawing with his mom, stuck out in his mind, while he glossed over the notifications about their accidents, and going to their funerals. When he thought back to when Hurricane Katrina hit, he remembered the road trip with Mama Marcel and Dare, not the destruction of their homes, or losing everything they hadn't thought to take with them when they evacuated.

Evacuating to Houston actually turned out to be a blessing for him, leading to him training to become a professional wrestler. He'd worked part-time at the front desk of a local gym in New Orleans before the hurricane, while studying to become a certified personal trainer with the hope of making it a full-time gig, so he could quit his other side gigs. Then, when they had to stay in Houston for months afterward, he found another gym job, completing his certification program to become a full-time personal trainer. But unlike the gym where he'd worked in NOLA, which was mostly utilized by local business people before and after work and on their lunch breaks, the gym in Houston was where the talent for the local independent wrestling promotion worked out. Once the promoter saw him working with a personal training client on the proper form for weightlifting, he'd quickly recruited Dion to train to wrestle, appreciating his physique as marketable in the wrestling business. Less than a year later, Dion signed on with the GWA, and he finally made enough money to be able to move his brother and Mama Marcel back to the city they loved and wanted to help rebuild.

After watching wrestling with his parents as a kid, Dion like to think they were watching over him from Heaven, pulling strings back then to help him get into the business. It wasn't just keeping him safe during life threatening situations or helping him start a lucrative career that he credited to them watching over him either. He believed that they'd used their knowledge of God's plans to guide him and the people he loved in how they responded to those events because it was their teachings while they were still with him in his childhood that shaped his perspective, so he could see the silver lining that came from tragedy.

If Hurricane Katrina hadn't hit New Orleans, he probably would have been satisfied with just becoming a personal trainer and supplementing his income by drawing caricatures for tourists. While a career as a personal trainer would have been fulfilling, in the aftermath of Katrina, he'd have struggled to get by when they went back to NOLA. Instead, the time he spent training to wrestle gave him the capability of earning millions each year in the squared circle. Millions he'd reinvested and multiplied, so he could donate the equivalent of his yearly salary with the GWA back to his community, wanting to help his fellow New Orleanians, who hadn't been as lucky as he was back then.

He also thought of Hurricane Katrina as a blessing because he wouldn't have ever met Julia if he hadn't worked with the GWA. He loved her so much that he couldn't imagine he'd ever have felt complete without her in his life. And he couldn't believe his blessings were about to multiply with the birth of their babies. *I sure hope Mama and Papa are still watching over all of us 'cause I know they'd have been excited about becoming grandparents in a few months.*

Now he wanted to look back on the day he was injured and remember the happy parts of the day, while considering the injury as a blessing in disguise, much the same way as he looked at his evacuation during Hurricane Katrina. Yeah, being injured had caused some wrinkles in his relationship with Jewel, but it also forced him to retire from wrestling long before he probably would have otherwise. If he hadn't been injured, he and Jewel probably would have had much bigger issues, like arguing over which of them would give up their job so they could raise their family together when she got pregnant sooner than they'd planned.

While he'd told her he'd retire sometime between his thirty-fifth and fortieth birthdays, Dion knew he'd really been thinking of wrestling a little past turning forty, so he could have a twenty-year-long career with the GWA. He also knew that even with her having a decent salary as a vice president in her family business, his multi-million dollar annual contracts with the GWA meant he'd earned more money each year as a wrestler than she did as a vice president in her family business.

Wanting to build a sizable nest egg for their family, he also knew he would have really pushed her to take a sabbatical from her family business to travel with him from the time their babies were born to when he hit that twenty-year mark and retired from wrestling, especially since he knew her job would always be there waiting for her. And trying to dominate Jewel outside the bedroom to get his way would have most likely led to the destruction of their relationship, and possibly estrangement from his kids.

Thankfully, that won't be an issue now, Dion decided as he put in some of the finer details on the drawing he'd started that afternoon. Now that he was alone in his room after dinner, he wanted to finish the proposal drawing to have it framed for his friends as a sort of "thank you" for their roles in getting him to Heart's Destiny to reconnect with Jewel.

His brother banging on his door startled Dion out of his chair. "Open up, D! I'm crashing with you tonight!"

"What the hell, Dare?" Dion grumbled, stomping across the room, and flinging open the door to see his brother standing there in a pair of pajama pants and a t-shirt. "You trying to yell loud enough the whole town of Heart's Destiny can hear you?"

"No, just wasn't sure if I'd catch you before you took your new meds or not," Dare insisted, walking into the room without being invited. "So, I figured if it had already knocked you out for the night, then I'd have to yell to get you to wake up enough to let me in. We really should have asked for connecting rooms, so it would be easier for me to keep an eye on you when you start new meds like this."

"That woulda meant sharing a bathroom, which woulda been more of a pain than it was worth," Dion reminded his brother, who tended to hog the bathroom like a teenaged girl. Only instead of soaking in bubble baths or spending hours on complicated hair and makeup routines, Dare sat on the toilet like it was his throne and he was King Shit. Dion had to smile at the memory of the nickname he'd given his brother as a teenager. "Unless you want me to draw an updated edition of the King Shit comics I started the last time we had to share a bathroom."

"No, absolutely not!" Dare glared at him. "They need to stay in whatever watery grave they ended up in after Katrina."

Ironic that I just thought about my silver lining from back then and now Dare is talking about his. Dion chuckled as he went back to his seat at the desk to finish the shading on his latest sketch. "Why do you suddenly wanna crash here and not in your room next door? Can't get Ashlyn to come join you?"

"Don't even go there, D," Darius warned Dion, shaking his head.

"I'm telling you, ya really should talk to Tait and Reid, then see if sharing her is something you and Cade can agree on," Dion reiterated to Darius, knowing his brother's attraction to Ashlyn was more than the fling he portrayed it to be.

"Yeah, we tried the sharing thing while we were all in NOLA." Dare shook his head like it didn't work out well at all. "It was fun and definitely ranks up there as my number one sexual experience, but I'm not cut out to just be their extra dick whenever we're all in the same town."

"Damn, sorry, Bro." Dion didn't know what else to say to his brother, wishing he had some words of wisdom to help ease Darius's broken heart. "So, why are you coming to hang out with me in my room, instead of hitting up the local bar?"

"Because I need to make sure you don't have another bad reaction to a new medicine, like you did when we first brought you home from the hospital," Dare finally explained, making himself comfortable on Dion's bed. "And since this one is supposed to make you sleep, I wanna make sure I can wake you up in the morning and don't have to take you back to the ER. So, when are you planning on taking it?"

"Ten o'clock, or whenever Jewel lets me know she's home from her book club meeting, whichever comes first. Well, if it's at least two hours after I ate when she calls me, so maybe as early as nine-thirty." Dion put away his art supplies, knowing he needed to focus on his conversation with his brother. Besides wanting to give his brother his undivided attention, Dion also knew he wouldn't do his best work on the sketch if he didn't focus on it exclusively.

"Book club? Damn, we really have landed in suburbia," Dare chuckled. "So, why didn't you go with her to hear everyone else's thoughts on that baby book ya'll have been reading?"

"Yeah, that's not the book they're discussing," Dion snickered, remembering the sex scene Jewel had read to him over the phone the night before, when she'd insisted on going home to prepare for the meeting tonight, instead of spending the night in bed with him again. "It's some rockstar romance. And apparently, the only guys they allow at their meetings are Nico and Philippe, so they can compare book dicks to the real thing without making boyfriends or husbands jealous."

"So, being gay makes Nico and Philippe immune to being jealous when their husband is comparing their dick to book dicks right in front of them?" Dare looked as skeptical as Dion felt at Jewel's excuse for not allowing straight guys at their book club meetings.

"Hell if I know." Dion shrugged.

"I bet it's just that the girls wanna gossip about who's getting dick and who isn't," Darius scoffed.

"All I know is what Jewel told me," Dion admitted, holding up his hands in surrender, placing his hands in the perfect position for doing air quotes as he explained what Jewel told him about her book club meetings. "Which is that the meetings always seem to devolve into a discussion about 'magic peens,' who they know that has one, and which of them are benefiting from getting some, until one of their brothers or cousins are mentioned and they have to cut the discussion off to avoid gagging."

"Maybe we should start our own book club for the guys to compare voodoo pussies," Dare suggested, grinning. "Think Jewel will give you a reading list to help us get it started?"

"Only way to find out is to ask her," Dion smirked, pulling his phone out to text Jewel, not wanting to forget to mention it when she finished her meeting and called him. "Even though I won't be able to brag about hers if we invite her brothers and cousins to join us in this book club."

> **Dion:** Hey, Dare wants us to start our own book club to be
> able to talk about voodoo pussy the way ya'll talk
> about magic peens. Can you recommend any books
> like you read from last night to get us started?

> **Jewel:** Yeah, there are a few authors I've read who use
> that term, including Kay and Brook. I'll start sending
> you books on your Kindle when I get done here. Then
> we can read them together & act out our favorite
> scenes. ;)

> **Dion:** Know anyplace around here we can act out that
> rocky amphitheater scene you read me last night?

> **Jewel:** Maybe? When we discussed it tonight, Kay &
> Randi told us about a rocky outcropping on the
> Hunters' property where Randi & James recreated their
> 1st date, which included park sex much like that scene.
> Not an amphitheater, but close enough for role play.
> {Eggplant emoji} {Taco emoji} {Sweat droplets emoji}

> **Dion:** We'll have to get more details to see if we can find
> it. {Tongue emoji} {Taco emoji}

"Are you seriously sexting right now?" Dare barked. "While I'm sitting right here? Shouldn't you be reading all about your meds to get ready to take 'em instead?"

"You really expect me to pass up the chance to sext my girl just because you're here?" Dion arched an eyebrow at his brother, fighting the urge to roll his eyes like Jewel would have if she was there. "Besides, I was kinda hopin' she'd get done with her meeting early enough I could ask her to bring me a measuring cup to mix it up."

"A measuring cup? What the fuck?" Dare's face contorted in confusion. "What kind of medicine did they give you that you have to mix it up before you take it? Aren't you just popping a sleeping pill of some kind?"

"No, it's a liquid, and each dose has to be mixed with a quarter cup of water," Dion explained, getting the box it came in out of the closet where he'd stored it and pulling out the paperwork that came with the medication. He tossed the papers on his brother's lap before putting the box down on the desk. "Read that. It explains everything."

As Dion sat back down, his brother started flipping through the first booklet Dion had handed him. While Darius read, Dion took off his glasses and rubbed his eyes. Adjusting to wearing bifocals wasn't as easy as he'd expected. *Maybe I should have picked the lined version instead of the no-line version, so I could clearly see which part of them I'm supposed to look through based on what I'm doing.* Going from using the bottom portion to see the paper where he was drawing when Dare got to the room, to using the top to be able to see to walk across the room, made his eyes feel funny. Almost like he was using muscles he hadn't ever needed before, or maybe his brain was processing the visual signals differently than he had previously. But either way, it made his eyes feel itchy after a few hours of wearing them.

"Holy shit, D! You're taking GHB?" Darius shouted, smirking when he got Dion's attention. "That's one of the date-rape drugs we have to watch out for in the club. Hell, maybe I should take you to Julie's for the night, or have her come be the one to watch you tonight, so ya'll can do a little role play. And I can avoid any implications about my kinks that could be drawn from being around that shit."

"Don't even joke about a date-rape kink, Dare," Dion warned his brother. Yeah, he and Jewel liked to role play their fantasies once in a while, but neither one of them had fantasies about drugging and raping one another.

"Sorry, D. You know I wouldn't joke about it in the club. But I also know you'd never use it for reprehensible reasons, so I figured I was safe joking around with you," Darius apologized, holding up his hands with the paperwork still clutched in one.

"Yeah, I know." Dion smiled at his brother to let him know they were cool. "Just maybe don't mention what I'm taking outside this room, so nobody thinks we're into that shit."

"Yeah, I get it," Dare agreed. "So, are you supposed to take this once or twice each night?"

"Twice." Dion reached into the box and got out the two medication bottles he was supposed to use to prepare both doses before lying down for the night, holding them up to show his brother before dropping them back in the box. "Seems strange to drink it out of a pill bottle after it's mixed up, though."

"So, they provide the bottles for you to mix it up in, but not the measuring cup to be able to mix it with the right amount of water?" Dare scooted over to the edge of the bed, sitting up as close to the desk as possible, so he could peer into the box.

"They provide the special syringe to measure the medicine, and even an alarm to wake up for the second dose, but not the water or a measuring cup for it," Dion elaborated with a shrug. "You'd think as much as this stuff costs, they'd provide everything and we wouldn't have to mix it up ourselves. But I guess once it's mixed with water, it's only good for so long, so they can't ship sixty pre-made doses. And the gallon of water it'll take to mix up a month's worth wouldn't fit in this box."

Their discussion was interrupted as Dion's phone rang with Jewel flashing on the screen. "Hey, beautiful, you home?" Dion answered as Dare tossed the paperwork back in the box and walked over to the mini fridge to get out a bottle of water.

"Yeah, I'm home," Jewel replied over the phone. "Wasn't sure if I'd get you or your voicemail. Since you quit texting, I thought you might have already taken your medicine."

"Naw, I was waiting on you to call first, so I could ask if you have a quarter-cup measuring cup I can borrow to mix it up." Dion hoped she could hear the invitation to his room in his tone of voice without him having to expressly say the words while his brother was listening to his side of the conversation.

"Don't listen to him, Julie," Dare shouted loud enough for Jewel to hear him from across the room. "He wants you to come give him his date-rape drugs and take advantage of him when they knock him out."

"Oooh, fun times! Does that mean I get to be in charge in the bedroom from now on?" Jewel laughed, making Dion glad he was holding the phone to his ear and hadn't put her on speaker. He didn't need Jewel giving Darius more ammunition for his inappropriate sense of humor.

"No," Dion replied, not wanting to say anything his brother shouldn't overhear.

"Yeah, we'll see about that," Jewel giggled. "You can't exactly run the show if you're out cold, Big Daddy."

"I knew I shoulda asked Meemaw or Mandi if they could lend me a measuring cup today," Dion grumbled, feigning irritation with his voice, even though he was smirking at her playfulness. "Then I coulda mixed up my meds and taken them earlier without having to listen to either one of you giving me shit about 'em now."

"Oh, please, you love it when I act bratty, so you can spank me," Jewel popped off, seeing through his ruse, even though she wasn't in the room with him.

"Yeah, I do." Dion's smile widened, loving the images she was putting in his head.

"I'm not sure if I wanna know what she said to put that look on your face or not," Dare commented from where he'd sat down on the other side of the bed. "Part of me wants to have you put her on speaker, so I can hear the dirty talk. And the other part of me wants to go hide in the bathroom 'til ya'll are done, so I don't see my brother with a boner."

"Nope, no boners allowed tonight," Jewel quipped in his ear.

"You're only saying no boners allowed 'cause you're not here to enjoy mine," Dion bantered back.

"Exactly," Jewel agreed with a giggle.

"Then you really should be the one here observing his reaction tonight, Julie," Dare pointed out, obviously not realizing he was talking over Jewel. "'Cause GHB increases sex drive and lowers sexual inhibitions, so he's liable to pop a boner, even with me in the room."

Yeah, I doubt the GHB will have more of an effect on my sex drive than Jewel does without even trying.

"Oooh, I wonder if it has as much of an effect on libido as second trimester pregnancy hormones?" Jewel mused in his ear.

"Obviously, your second trimester pregnancy hormones aren't having that much of an effect, or you'd be on your way over here with a measuring cup right now," Dion teased her.

"Seriously? Pregnant women are hornier during the second trimester?"

Dion nodded in reply to his brother's question at the same time Jewel shouted, "So much hornier!"

Dion had to pull the phone from his ear before she busted his eardrum, placing her on speaker, even though she didn't need to be on speaker for Darius to hear her last statement. "Obviously not, since you aren't on your way over here for me to alleviate your need."

"Nope, I'm staying home and playing with my big girl toys until we know how that medicine affects you. I don't want to be disappointed if you fall asleep within five minutes of taking it and we don't have time to play. Or worse, if it's one of the drugs that has an opposite effect on you because of the A.D.D. like the Adderall, so instead of increasing your sex drive, it'll decrease it."

"Wait, certain drugs have an opposite effect on you?" Darius looked confused by Jewel's statement, surprising Dion that he'd focused on that part of what she'd said, instead of making jokes about the possibility of him not being able to get his dick up. "Is that why we've never been successful at getting you drunk?"

"Yeah, I guess. The A.D.D. medicine they put me on is basically speed, which is a stimulant for most people. But instead of increasing my heart rate and blood pressure and making me feel jittery, it's more like taking a chill pill for people with A.D.D., so my brain slows down to where I can focus on one thing at a time, instead of bouncing around from topic to topic." Dion didn't know if the attention deficit disorder had anything to do with why he'd never even felt a buzz when he drank alcohol or not, so he didn't bother trying to expound on his reply to that part of Dare's questions.

"So, if you chill out on speed, does that mean you'd get hyper instead of mellow on weed?" Darius smirked as he posed his asinine question.

"I don't think anything would make Dion physically hyper," Jewel chimed in over the phone. "But it might exacerbate the A.D.D. by making his brain hyperactively switch topics and be easily distracted."

"Not that it matters, 'cause I'm not gonna try it to find out," Dion added, wondering how they got so far off on a tangent from the discussion about his actual medication. "Now, how 'bout ya'll help me figure out how to measure the water I need to mix with my Xyrem, so I can take it before tomorrow."

"Use one of the shaker cups you mix your protein shakes in," Jewel suggested. "They have markings on the side for measuring ounces, so that should make it pretty easy without having to go buy a set of measuring cups when H.E.B. is already closed for the night."

"I thought about that," Dion confided. "But the smallest measurement is six ounces, and I'm only supposed to mix it with two ounces of water."

"So, guesstimate it," Jewel recommended. "If you can draw people to scale, you can easily eyeball dividing those six ounces into thirds."

"She's got a point, D." Darius nodded in agreement with Jewel.

Dion wasn't sure it was as simple as she believed due to the curvature on the bottom and the slight tapering of the sidewalls of the shaker cups he used. *But it's only for one night. I can go pick up a set of measuring cups tomorrow to make sure it's exact going forward.*

"Fine," Dion conceded, leaving his phone laying on the desk to go get one of his shaker cups out of the cabinet above the mini fridge and a bottle of water from the refrigerator before walking back over to measure out and mix his medicine.

"You're supposed to be in bed when you take it, D," Dare pointed out as Dion used the syringe to pull up the correct dose of medicine to put it in the first empty bottle.

"I'm just mixing it now," Dion sighed. "Not taking it yet."

He repeated the process to dispense the medicine into the second empty bottle before capping and putting the unused Xyrem back in the box. Then he estimated where the two-ounce line would be on his shaker cup and poured the water to that imaginary line before transferring it into the medicine bottle with the first dose of Xyrem. He repeated the water measurement and addition to the second dose before closing both bottles and swirling them to mix the medication with the water. Once both doses were prepared, he placed them and the alarm on his bedside table, and took the syringe to the bathroom to rinse it out.

"What's goin' on? Ya'll are bein' awfully quiet," Jewel complained from the phone.

"Just watching him mix this up, so I can get a visual for what to watch out for in the club," Dare answered her as Dion walked back over to put the syringe in the box and put his medication away in the closet.

It had to be stored in an upright position in a cool, dry place, so Dion felt like keeping it in the shipping box in the closet was the best way to keep it in his hotel room. Plus, stowing it there, he could cover the box with his dirty clothes when he left the room, so the housekeeping staff wouldn't see it. At least, he could until laundry day when he bagged his dirty clothes up and dropped them off at the front desk for the laundry service. While he trusted the people he'd met in Heart's Destiny, he didn't know everyone who worked for the Hunters to know he could trust them with knowledge of his medication. *I'll just put the Do-Not-Disturb sign out on laundry day, so I won't have to worry about housekeeping seeing my meds.*

"Do you guys have those straws to test for these kinds of things in the club?" Jewel inquired.

"We don't have the straws, but we do have test kits on hand," Dare elucidated, filling Jewel in on all the safety procedures they'd implemented since opening the club.

While his girlfriend and brother talked, Dion decided to go ahead and get ready for bed, walking into the bathroom to empty his bladder and brush his teeth. Once that was done, he stripped off his clothes, dropped them in the bottom of the closet, and picked up his phone on the way over to lie down in bed.

"D! Dude!" Dare squealed like a girl as Dion walked past him. "At least put your boxers back on. I don't need to see your dick hanging out all night."

"Yeah, it's my room and I sleep in the nude," Dion scoffed as he flopped down on the bed. "If you don't wanna see it, maybe you should go back to your own room, so I can have phone sex with Jewel before taking my meds."

"Nope, no phone sex tonight," Jewel argued from the phone he'd laid on the bed beside him. "In fact, I'm gonna say goodnight now, so you can go right to sleep after setting the alarm and taking your first dose. I love you."

"Goodnight, Jewel. I love you, too," Dion replied, waiting for her to hang up the phone before placing it on the bedside table and picking up the alarm that looked a lot like the kitchen timer in Mama Marcel's kitchen back in NOLA. He set it for four hours, knowing he could turn it off early, if he woke up anytime between two-and-a-half hours later and when it was set to go off, to take his second dose of medicine.

"Seriously? You're not gonna put your boxers back on with me sleeping in the bed beside you?" Dare glared at Dion from where he stood at the end of the bed.

"Nope. 'Cause you're not gonna sleep in here." Dion smirked at his brother as he picked up the first dose of Xyrem to take it now that he was lying in bed. "If you're that worried about being able to wake me up, take my extra keycard, so you can get back in here in the morning. But you seriously need to go sleep in your own room."

As Dare turned to pick up the keycard from the table under the television, Dion drank his first dose of Xyrem, gagging from the saltiness of the solution. He couldn't control the involuntary contortion of his face as he swallowed the vile medication.

Guess I should have expected a salty taste with sodium in the generic name. "Fuck," he groaned, wishing he had a soda or something to chase it with to get that horrible taste out of his mouth. "That tastes more robustly brackish than the water in Lake Pontchartrain."

"It can't be that bad or it wouldn't be easily covered up by whatever froufrou drink it's put in by the slimeballs using it to drug women," Darius laughed, obviously finding Dion's disgusted facial expressions funny.

"Yeah, I don't care what it's mixed with," Dion scoffed. "There's no way it wouldn't be noticeable that the drink was spiked from one sip. Hey, toss me those mints by my wallet on the dresser. I gotta do something to get this salty ass taste outta my mouth."

Dare continued laughing, but thankfully, he tossed the mints to Dion. "It can't be that bad."

"You remember when Mama made us gargle with saltwater when we had a sore throat as kids?" As Dion popped two mints in his mouth, Dare nodded in response to Dion's question. "It tastes like that mixed with some kind of chemical."

"Is it as bad as asparagus jizz?" Dare was laughing so hard he could barely get the words out.

"I don't know about asparagus jizz," Dion chuckled around the mints in his mouth, not wanting to know if his brother had first-hand knowledge of how that tasted or not. "But it's worse than the residual of mine I've tasted from kissing Jewel after a blow job."

"So, if it was added to a blow job shot, would the girls just think it tasted like the real thing?"

Dion shook his head at his brother's inappropriate humor. "Sometimes I wonder what happened to warp you, little brother," Dion chortled. "Now get outta here, so I can let this medicine work and get some sleep."

Dare turned off the lights right before he walked out the door. Dion turned onto his side, plumping up the pillow under his head as he waited for the Xyrem to make him sleepy. He closed his eyes and thought about Jewel, hoping to relive some of their memories in his dreams.

Unfortunately, all that did was make his dick hard. Which he didn't feel like he could do anything about because of not knowing when the medication would kick in and make him fall asleep. "Damn it. I'd jerk off, if I wasn't afraid I'd fall asleep before having time to clean up."

He tossed and turned, trying to think of anything but Jewel to get his cock to deflate, so he could get comfortable enough to go to sleep. Unfortunately, nothing seemed to help. "I shoulda insisted on kicking Dare out to have phone sex with Jewel before taking my meds."

After more tossing and turning, Dion gave in and palmed his cock. "Five to fifteen minutes to fall asleep, my ass," Dion grumbled, noticing the timer had counted down over an hour already when he started stroking his dick. "If it's gonna take this long to knock me out, then I'm gonna brush my teeth immediately after taking it from now on. And I'll still have time to fuck Jewel before falling asleep."

At least, he thought he'd have time. Considering he fell asleep after only a few passes of his hand over his cock, and before he was anywhere near coming, he couldn't be sure.

Chapter Twenty-Two

After spending the afternoon touring art museums in San Antonio with Dion before a more casual dinner on the RiverWalk, Julie was thrilled with the results of his first night on Xyrem. He hadn't had a single episode all day, where he appeared even slightly overwhelmed or anxious, much less overwhelmed or anxious enough to stop whatever they were doing to focus on something else to try to prevent a narcoleptic sleep attack. She'd thought it would take a few days for his body to adjust to the medication before he saw a reduction in his daily episodes, especially since the doctor and pharmacist had both mentioned how he'd have to titrate up to the final dose for it to be most effective. Granted, it was only one day, but it was a day when they were out in public, where he could easily be triggered.

Although, she supposed as she brushed her teeth to get ready for bed, *there isn't much crossover between the patrons of art museums and professional wrestling fans, so maybe not being recognized and accosted for autographs all day could explain part of his ability to be more relaxed today. It'll be interesting to see if the medicine works to keep him from having an episode at Char's birthday party on Monday, when there's more chaos going on around us, like there was on Christmas. Or if he can get through three days in a row of stressful situations, like the last week of the month when he has a doctor's appointment on Monday, Antonio's day-late birthday party on Tuesday when Anthony, Kay, and their kids get home from working with the GWA, and Brooklyn's birthday party on Wednesday. Yeah, that week will definitely be the best test of how well this medicine is working for him.*

Leah Mae Wright

Julie was also interested in seeing how he acted while on the medicine. He'd told her earlier that it took him over an hour to fall asleep after taking the first dose the night before, so she was curious about the way he acted in that hour. She'd assumed it would make him sluggish or appear drunk the way she'd seen it portrayed on TV crime shows, like **Law & Order: Special Victims Unit**. But after what Dare said the night before about it increasing sex drive, she had to wonder if it would have that effect on him. And if so, what would an even more sexually aroused version of Dion look like?

Constantly hard? Even more multiple orgasms? Fucking like the Energizer bunny until we're both chafed raw?

Yeah, she was in the middle of the constantly horny part of her pregnancy, but Dion already matched her pretty well in libido level. So, she was slightly worried she wouldn't be able to keep up with him if his sexual desire spiked any higher.

Guess I'll find out in a few minutes, Julie thought as she finished her nightly routine and walked out of the bathroom to crawl in bed.

Dion had just finished mixing up his meds and placed the two doses on his bedside table along with an alarm, stopping to give her a peck of a kiss on the top of her head as he walked to the bathroom to rinse out the syringe he used to draw up the Xyrem and squirt it into the medicine bottles for mixing with water. When he returned, he put the syringe in the box his medication came in and returned it to the closet.

As Julie got comfortable under the covers, she was surprised to see Dion sit on the side of the bed and take his first dose without going to brush his teeth and get undressed for bed first. "I thought you were supposed to be in bed for the night when you take that?"

"Yeah," he choked out, making a face after swallowing the solution. "But since I didn't fall asleep in the five to fifteen minutes it claims, I figured I have enough time to brush my teeth and get that disgusting taste out of my mouth before it makes me too sleepy to walk back to the bed. At least, I think I can this week. I'll have to play it by ear when I titrate up to the next dosage level on Friday."

Yeah, he can probably do that now with the initial week being only two-point-two-five grams per dose. But I bet by the time he gets to the fourth week on it, when he's worked up to four-point-five grams per dose, he'll be out in those five to fifteen minutes they told us about and won't be able to brush his teeth then.

As he stood and walked into the bathroom, Julie questioned him, speaking loud enough for him to hear her even when he turned on the water. "What does it taste like?"

"Like they mixed ocean water with some kind of chemical," Dion called back, the end of his sentence slightly garbled by him starting to brush his teeth while still talking. She heard him rinse and spit several times before he continued. "Have you ever gone swimming in the Gulf of Mexico and accidentally gotten water in your mouth?"

"Yeah, pretty much every summer when we went down to Padre Island when I was a kid," Julie chuckled, ignoring the sound of him urinating without closing the bathroom door. Thinking back to those trips when her Burleson cousins visited their maternal grandparents and she and her siblings tagged along, she was easily able to imagine the taste of the salty gulf water, even though it had been at least a decade since she'd accidentally opened her mouth right before being hit with a wave.

"Okay, imagine that, only right after an oil spill when the beaches were closed from the water being contaminated," Dion elaborated as he ran the water in the sink once more, presumably to wash his hands. "It's not actually oily, since oil and water don't mix and it's easy to see you just got some of the water near the oil, not that you're drinking some of the oil. Or maybe you're drinking the water where the oil's been cleaned up, but it flavored the water it was previously floating on. Like you can taste that it's more than just saltwater, but it's just a trace of something chemically."

Julie cringed at the thought of drinking oil-spill water, finally understanding the grossed out expression on Dion's face when he took his medicine a few minutes earlier. "If that's what it tastes like, how on earth are creeps able to use it as a date-rape drug?"

"No clue," Dion shrugged as he dropped his dirty clothes in the bottom of the closet. He then turned off the lights as he made his way to the bed. "In fact, I told Dare last night that I thought it would be very noticeable from only a small sip of a drink spiked with it."

"I guess, maybe they could get away with putting it in a margarita with a salted rim," Julie mused, thinking of the only drink she knew of where a salty taste wouldn't be an obvious giveaway as she rolled onto her right side to face him while they talked.

"Possibly," Dion agreed as he crawled into bed, rolling to face her, and opening his arms so they could cuddle as they talked. "And I suppose the tequila would probably cover up the chemical aftertaste. But considering how adamantly that pharmacist warned me not to drink alcohol while I'm on this stuff, it's kinda scary to think about it being used in something like that."

Julie scooted in close, thinking about how glad she was that Dion didn't drink all that often when she'd heard those warnings. He'd never been much of a drinker the whole time she'd known him, saying there was no point in drinking something he didn't like the taste of when his size prevented him from ever getting a buzz, even when he'd tried drinking an entire bottle of whiskey on his twenty-first birthday. She'd eventually found some fruitier wines that he'd liked enough to have a glass or two when they met up for their hotel hookups, and of course, he'd had a glass of champagne at special events. But for the most part, he usually stuck to water or other non-alcoholic beverages most of the time.

Since his injury, he'd even gone with the sparkling grape juice instead of champagne at the New Year's Eve party and most recent weddings they'd attended, saying he didn't want to risk spiking his headache from even one glass of champagne. Apparently, his migraine-like headaches were really bad right after his injury and his neurologist had given him a whole list of things to avoid to keep from triggering them, including alcohol, foods containing nitrates, and even chocolate.

When Dion told her about having to forgo chocolate, which was his go to sweet flavor of choice, Julie had been skeptical of his ability to follow his doctor's orders. Considering she hadn't seen him skip it since he'd been back in town, she'd actually called him out on disobeying. He then informed her that it was the only potential trigger food he'd added back into his diet. And luckily, he'd had no ill effects from it. In fact, his headaches were greatly reduced after Doc Hayes changed the medication he took for them, so now he didn't have rebound headaches when the drugs wore off like he did with the medication he'd been on previously.

While his headaches had tapered off dramatically, and seemed to be mostly triggered by his anxiety, he was still avoiding most of the things on that list. And she had a feeling his love of red beans and rice would cause him to add beans back to his diet next. Not that she could ask him about that right then because she was too distracted by the way he'd stopped talking to let his hands and lips wander over her body.

As he fondled her breasts with his free hand and rubbed her back with the hand attached to the arm she was using for a pillow, Dion kissed his way from her temple down to her ear to whisper, "Aren't you supposed to be on your other side?"

"Yes, the left side is the recommended sleeping position," Julie conceded as she brushed her lips over his slightly longer than normal beard, which seemed to be due for a trim. "But I can't kiss you when I have my back to you, so I thought we might try a more traditional side-by-side position before the babies get too big for this to be possible."

"Hmmm, smart thinking," Dion agreed, moving to line them up a little better for kissing before pressing his lips to hers.

Julie covered his heart with her hand as they kissed, enjoying the feel of his strong heartbeat under his thick pectoral muscle. As Dion licked across her lips, Julie opened her mouth to allow his invasion, savoring his minty taste. *Guess I should be grateful he brushed his teeth after taking his medicine, so I don't have to endure that horrible aftertaste he mentioned earlier.*

As Dion trailed his free hand down her body until he reached the apex of her thighs, Julie ran her hands over the smooth umber planes of his chest, swirling her fingertips around the turgid tips of his nipples, which reminded her of tiny western coneflowers for both their shape at the base of his pecs and their deeper brown color than the rest of his rich sepia skin. She felt her own nipples harden along with his, knowing her body's response was more from the way he was teasing his fingers through her folds than from enjoying touching him, even though she did relish seeing his response to her touch.

She left her right hand on his chest, unable to move it much while laying on that side. With her left arm free, however, she ran it down over the ridges of his abs until she reached the neatly trimmed patch of hair on his lower abdomen at the base of his dick. She tormented him with her touch by only allowing the back of her hand to graze his cock as she traced each line defining his abdominals, wondering which of them would give in first to move beyond the lightly teasing touches to more satisfying forms of foreplay.

Me, Julie thought as they continued making out like teenagers, unable to stop herself from wiggling her hips, trying to entice him to actually touch her clit or insert a finger. *'Cause I don't have nearly as much patience as Dion.*

She tore her lips from his to beg, "Please, Dion, I need you inside me."

"Hmmm," Dion moaned as he finally penetrated her with first one, then two, of his large, talented fingers. He pressed his thumb against her clit, swirling it lightly while deftly zeroing in on her G-spot to work her right up to the edge.

Julie quit teasing him then, too, wrapping her hand as far around his thick cock as she could before starting to stroke his shaft from base to tip. She spread the precum oozing from his dick down the length, using it to lubricate her movements, so her hand could easily glide over the velvet soft skin covering his hard-as-steel rod.

"Fuck, Jewel," he groaned, his dick twitching in her hand as she jerked him.

"Yes, please, fuck Jewel," Julie agreed, rocking her hips as he inserted a third finger into her dripping wet channel. She couldn't tell exactly what he was doing with his fingers to open her up enough to take his big dick, but she loved the way he applied the perfect amount of pressure with his thumb on her clit, swirling it to spread her arousal and push her over the edge to float on an orgasmic high.

Dion bucked his hips, rutting into her hand when she stopped stroking him to have an out-of-body experience as he finger-fucked her through her first climax of the night. Her whole body convulsed as he used his tactilely talented extremities to play her body like an erotic guitar.

"Oh, yes, Dion," she moaned in pleasure, realizing as she started to come down from her orgasm high that he was being much quieter than normal. He lifted his thumb from her clit and gradually slowed his finger-work inside her, bringing her back down to earth gradually. The hand on her back had also stopped moving, so she opened her eyes to see if he was starting to fall asleep from his medicine.

His eyes were closed, but he still managed to pull his fingers from her sex, tug his cock from her hand as he grabbed it, and line his dick up perfectly to slide inside her. Dion rocked his hips, gently making love to her at a leisurely pace.

Surely, he's still awake, right?

"Dion?" She spoke against his lips as she planned to kiss him some more if he was still awake.

"Hmmm," was his only response, even though he continued his slow, steady strokes of his cock into her pussy. The hand he'd used to finger-fuck her rested on her thigh, which was draped over his hip to allow him access to her pussy. But he didn't caress her with it, or even grip her thigh to hold her leg in place. Both hands were just still, much like most of the rest of his body. Only his hips and cock continued actively moving, while his chest passively expanded with each steady, even breath he took.

Holy shit! He's asleep. Well, everything but his dick is asleep, anyway. How on earth is he still hard enough to fuck while he's asleep?

Duh! The same way guys wake up every morning with a hard-on, she mentally told herself, unable to stop rocking her hips in time with his thrusts because of how amazing he felt inside her.

But can he still finish while under the influence of this medicine? Or should I stop now, so I'm not taking advantage of him while he's incapacitated, and try this again in the morning?

Somehow, even in his sleep, Dion managed to flex his dick inside her to hit that special spot only he'd ever been able to find, causing her to moan in pleasure as her inner walls fluttered in the beginning stage of another orgasm. No matter how she worried about being perceived as using him in that moment, she couldn't stop her body's response to his, having another small orgasm from his tender, slumbering copulation.

Hell, should I wake him up, so we can finish without me feeling like I'm a date-rapist? Can I even wake him up when he's on this stuff?

Feeling guilty for her little O without his knowledge, Julie tried to pull away, thinking she'd roll onto her left side, go to sleep, and plan to finish when he woke up the next morning. She barely pulled back an inch before Dion wrapped his free arm around her, tightened his grip with the arm she was laying on, and held her tightly against him, so she couldn't get away.

He's sleep-fucking me. Julie couldn't help but chuckle at the absurdity of the situation. *Is it wrong that I'm so turned on by not being able to stop him right now?*

And really, who's raping whom here? He's the one who's been roofied, but I'm the one who can't overpower him to stop it. And technically, we both consented before he took his meds, so I don't think either one of us are really being raped right now. Maybe we haven't verbally expressed our consent each and every time, but making love is pretty much the point of spending the night together. So, is it really wrong to just enjoy it? Even if I have to tell him about it tomorrow 'cause he can't remember the sleep-fucking?

She didn't have the chance to think it over and answer her own questions as Dion's unhurried, tender thrusts slowed even more, until he finally stopped moving altogether. His tight embrace slackened as his limbs finally succumbed to his deep slumber.

Yeah, we're gonna hafta make sure we make love before he takes his meds from now on, Julie decided as she brushed her lips over his once more. She pulled back just enough for his still hard-as-a-rock cock to slip from her body before rolling over to sleep on her left side, spooning with her super-sleepy man. *And we should probably discuss what I'm supposed to do next time he tries to sleep-fuck me.*

Unfortunately, they didn't have that talk before she woke up mid-orgasm a few hours later with him sporking her. *I guess it's okay if we're both asleep when it starts and we both come,* Julie chortled once the aftershocks subsided, getting out of bed to grab a washcloth and hand towel to clean them both up. *But if all he's capable of doing after taking his medicine is rolling over and sleep-fucking, then I might need to try to talk Jen into helping me with the babies' middle-of-the-night feedings.*

~~~

Sunday, January 12, 2020

Dion felt extremely groggy when he woke up, only vaguely remembering waking up with only thirty minutes left before his alarm was set to go off and taking his second dose of Xyrem. He knew he
~~~

turned off the alarm before it went off, so it wouldn't wake Jewel. But he wasn't sure if he'd only dreamed about cuddling up to her from behind and making love to her, or if it had actually happened. Considering he awoke holding her in his arms with his cock nestled between her ass cheeks, he knew at least part of the cuddling actually happened. Although, that could've been him acting out what he was dreaming, or just their natural tendency to cuddle whenever they slept in the same bed.

Guess we're gonna hafta have our first awkward morning-after conversation, after all, he mused, suddenly remembering how they'd easily settled into a routine whenever they spent the night together in the past, not even having an awkward conversation the morning after their first time together. *Who'd have thought after a year of normal, easy conversations on the mornings we woke up together, our first uncomfortable morning-after conversation would be because I can't remember what all we did last night and want to make sure it was all consensual?*

Fuck! What if it wasn't consensual? I mean, I know we both wanted it before I fell asleep. But what if I got too rough in my sleep and she couldn't get me to wake up to stop?

Fuck! Fuck! Fuck!

I hope I haven't screwed things up between us by hurting her in my sleep. We shoulda discussed possible issues with this medicine a little more before sleeping together while I'm taking it.

"Quit thinking so loud," Jewel mumbled, wiggling her ass against his cock. "Either go back to sleep, or wake me up the same way you did in the middle of the night."

"I'm sorry, Jewel," Dion apologized, not quite comprehending the second half of her statement, and only registering that he'd woken her up. He brushed his lips over the top of her head before releasing her from his arms and rolling onto his back. As much as he wanted to cling to her to get through this conversation, he knew he couldn't touch her while working up the courage to ask if he'd been inappropriate in his sleep. "I didn't mean to wake you up in the middle of the night. Since I woke up and it was still a half hour before the four-hour mark after taking the first dose, I went ahead and took the second dose and turned off the alarm, hoping it wouldn't disturb your sleep."

Jewel rolled to her right side, presumably wanting to face him while they talked. But Dion kept his gaze focused on the ceiling, unable to face her as she told him how he'd screwed up.

"Dion, I wasn't complaining about you waking me up. I was pointing out that I like having you wake me up with orgasms much better than waking up when you tense up from whatever negative thoughts are running through your head."

"I woke you up with an orgasm in the middle of the night?" *Fuck! I must have acted out more of my dreams than I thought. But at least, if she was able to come from it, then it doesn't sound like I got as rough as I was dreaming about. Unless I got rougher later?*

"Yeah, a really good one too," Jewel grinned, reaching over to place her hand on his jaw and turn his head toward her, forcing him to face her as she told him about his transgressions. "I have to admit, I wasn't sure what to do when you fell asleep in the middle of the first round, kinda feeling like I was taking advantage when you didn't stop thrusting, even though it was obvious you were unconscious. But later, when round two started while we were both sleeping, I figured it was cool since we were both asleep and we both came."

"You weren't taking advantage, Jewel." Dion shook his head as he rolled onto his side to pull her into his arms once more, reassured that she didn't seem to be traumatized by him misbehaving in the wee hours of the morning. "If I ever fall asleep in the middle again, I want you to keep going until you come, whether I do or not. At least, that's what I want if you're still enjoying it. If I act stupid and get too rough, I'd rather you do whatever you have to do to stop me, so I don't hurt you or our babies."

"I don't think there's any risk of you getting too rough, no matter how out of it you are from your meds," Jewel giggled and grinned, running her hands over his pecs. "If last night is anything to go by, your movements are too sluggish to be anything but super gentle. While I might have laughingly called it *sleep-fucking* in my head, it was more like *sleep-sensual-lovemaking*, minus the extended eye contact and whispered words of love that normally happens when we slow things down."

Dion let out a relieved breath, glad to know he hadn't done anything to put her or their babies at risk in his altered sleep state. "Thank fuck," he groaned as he pressed a kiss to her forehead. "But promise me, if I try anything you don't want, or can't do, like right after the babies are born when you'll need to heal, promise me that you'll gouge my eyes, or knee me in the nuts, or whatever you have to do to wake me up to stop."

"I'm not gonna gouge your eyes, or knee you in the nuts," Jewel scoffed, shaking her head. "This medicine might increase your natural desire, but it doesn't change your innate personality to the point that you'd try to force me, or hurt me in any way, so I don't think brute force will ever be necessary." She paused and smirked mischievously for a moment, trailing her hand down his body until she reached his dick before continuing. "Although, you do make a good point about right after the babies are born, when I'm gonna hafta abstain for six to eight weeks. Maybe we should look online for cock cages, so we can keep Big D locked up during the only time sleep sex is off limits."

Dion was so entranced by her stroking his cock that her suggestion didn't register for a moment. "Wait," he grumbled when he realized what she'd just mentioned. "What do you know about cock cages?"

"Only what Ashlyn told us about them when she was talking about the new items on her website at our book club meeting on Friday." Julie's eyes flashed with excitement, making Dion a little nervous about what she was about to say next. "She also told us about living out her why-choose fantasies with Cade and Dare while in New Orleans, so I figured if your brother was open to cock cages, you might be, too."

"Whoa, slow down. I'm gonna need some help unpacking that statement." Dion reached down and stilled her hand on his cock, needing some of his blood to flow back to his brain, so he could comprehend their conversation. "First of all, let's not assume that I'm into any of the same stuff Dare's into. Not that I really wanna know if my brother is into having his cock caged."

"Yeah, sorry, that'd be TMI if we were talking about one of my brothers, too, so I shoulda known not to mention it."

"Now, I'm guessing *why choose* is the new term for having a threesome, since that's what Dare mentioned they did the other night."

"Not exactly." Jewel shook her head before elaborating. "It's the term used for the romance book trope of a permanent ménage. And since Kay was able to Skype into the book club meeting, she asked Ashlyn all kinds of questions about how it worked, probably so she can write their book in her *Devine* series, if they end up making it work long term."

"Yeah, I wouldn't hold your breath for that one," Dion chuckled wryly. "Dare said he felt like their extra dick, so I'm not sure they're ready to settle down in a permanent ménage, even though I suggested he talk to the Inglemans about how they make it work, so he could try to do the same with Ashlyn and Cade. Or something similar that works better for their dynamic since Dare's not bi like Tait and Reid."

At least, Darius wasn't bisexual as far as Dion knew. But then again, he'd never thought his brother would be open to sharing his woman either, so what did he know?

"Well, hopefully, they'll figure out how to make it work. 'Cause Friday night was the happiest I've seen Ashlyn since she moved down here. And that's really saying something, since Ashlyn's a pretty upbeat person most of the time already." Jewel resumed stroking his cock before changing the subject. "But enough about them. We need to decide what we're gonna do to keep Big D outta trouble when I have to abstain."

"Sorry, Jewel, I don't think a cock cage is the right answer for that problem," Dion smirked, thrusting into her hand as he trailed his hand down her back and over her ass, so he could finger her pussy. "But since your pussy is gonna be off limits, maybe we could get you a chastity belt to wear while I fuck my hand for those few weeks. Or your hands…"

Dion let his words trail off as he stroked his fingers through her creamy cunt, hoping to entice her to offer more suggestions of things they could do to maintain their physical intimacy during her recovery time.

"Oh, no," Jewel protested, shaking her head. "If I can't come then, neither can you. Besides, I was gonna suggest you going to get your dick pierced a day or two after the girls are born, so we'll have similar recovery times and we can find out if what some of the girls have said about pierced peens is true."

"Yeah, I think I'd rather try the cock cage," Dion groaned, not even wanting to imagine the pain of having his dick pierced.

"But the girls claim the piercings make sex even better," Jewel argued.

"And I really don't wanna know which of our friends have firsthand knowledge of those claims," Dion quibbled, hoping to change the subject once more by plunging two fingers into her soaking wet slit. "I'd rather pick up where we left off last night when I fell asleep. I believe we were in about this same position."

"Hmmm, we were," Jewel agreed, smiling at him, "so we could kiss while making love."

Dion was glad he'd remembered to pop a mint in his mouth after taking his second dose of Xyrem in the middle of the night, so hopefully, his morning breath wasn't nearly as bad as it could have been. Instead of replying to her statement, Dion dipped his head and pressed his lips to hers, not wasting any time before running the tip of his tongue over the seam of her lips to request entry.

Though Jewel eagerly opened for him, Dion took his time, savoring every lick as he inserted a third finger into her tight pussy to prepare her for taking his cock. Jewel moaned in pleasure, rocking her hips in perfect rhythm with the strokes of his fingers, even as she continued jerking his dick.

"Need you inside me," she panted breathlessly as they broke for a few quick gulps of air. "Now, please, Dion."

"Yes, Jewel," Dion agreed, pulling his dripping wet digits from her slick sheath, draping her top leg over his hip, and positioning his cock to slide home in one steady thrust. As he plunged his cock inside her slick sex, he lifted his fingers to his mouth, licking her cream from his digits before giving her a taste of herself in their next kiss.

Their kiss was as impassioned as their lovemaking, with Jewel sucking the remnants of her arousal from his tongue much like she'd previously sucked his cock. Her ardent enjoyment of their coupling only increased Dion's desire, causing him to buck his hips harder and faster as he rutted into her bare pussy like a man possessed.

As he felt her inner walls start to flutter with her impending release, Dion pushed in deep and flexed his cock to brush the tip around her cervix, knowing it would push her over the edge. *Huh, maybe I should look into the different dick piercings and see if one of them will enhance this move? Surely, it won't be as painful as childbirth, so I can endure it to show my solidarity with her then. Hell, it'd be worth a little bit of pain on my part, if it enhances her pleasure.*

"Fuck, yeah, come on my cock, Jewel," Dion growled, barely lifting his lips from hers, and forcing himself to keep thinking about getting his dick pierced to keep from blowing his load too soon, as her pussy clamped down on him like a vise and her whole body started spasming in wave after wave of orgasmic bliss. He barely maintained control as he fucked her through it with a steady, pounding rhythm.

"Oh, yes, Dion." Their breath mingled as she continuously chanted his name as she came.

As much as he wanted to kiss her again, he loved hearing his name on her lips too much to interrupt her. So, Dion bided his time, extending her orgasm by caressing her clit with the pad of his thumb until the peak caused her words to be incoherent. Then he devoured her with a claiming kiss, holding her close and trapping her hands between their bare chests.

Dion reveled in the feel of her short nails pressing into his pecs, knowing she'd lost control enough to mark him as hers with ten perfect little crescent moon indentations. *Too bad they'll be gone by the time we get out of the shower.*

When she finally came down enough for her body to go limp, Dion picked up his pace, repeatedly plunging his cock into her soaking wet pussy until they were both right back on the brink. "Come for me again, Jewel," he commanded as he pulled back from their lip lock to gulp in more air than he could consume while breathing through his nose.

"Come with me, Dion, please," Jewel begged as her core convulsed around his cock with the first waves of her next release.

Dion's spine tingled and his balls started to draw up, signaling his impending explosive orgasm.

"Yes, Jewel, I'm gonna fill your pussy with my cum," Dion declared, unable to hold back his climax a moment longer, as her creamy cunt milked his big, black dick of every last drop of his jizz. "Take it all, Julia. All that cum, just for your tight little pussy. Fuck! Julia!"

Dion pushed in as deep as he could go, practically fusing their pelvic bones together as jet after jet of his thick, sticky semen shot out of his cock into her pliant pussy.

"Yes! Dion!" Jewel screamed as their bodies convulsed in an explosive, simultaneous climax.

One benefit of lying on their sides while making love was that they didn't have to worry about him crushing her as they collapsed in orgasmic bliss while the aftershocks washed over them. They laid there for several long minutes, waiting until they'd both caught their breath and adequately recovered before Dion extracted himself from her body and rolled to get up.

He walked into the bathroom to take his morning medication and empty his bladder before going back to the bedroom. Since his vertigo medicine hadn't had time to take effect yet, Dion didn't feel safe picking Jewel up and carrying her to the shower the way he wanted to. So, he had to settle for helping her up from the bed, and letting her lean on him if her legs were still too wobbly from her multiple orgasms to be able to walk normally to the bathroom.

"Come on, Jewel," he coaxed her with a smile as he took her hands in his to help her stand. "We've gotta hurry in the shower. Otherwise, we're gonna still be naked when Mama Marcel comes to bang on the door and get us up for church."

"Yeah, we definitely don't need another repeat performance of you yelling loud enough for all of Heart's Destiny to hear about why we won't answer the door, like on New Year's," Jewel giggled as she stood.

"It worked to get 'em to go away and come back an hour later, didn't it?" Dion shrugged as they walked back to the bathroom together to get ready for the day. Well, after round two in the shower.

Chapter Twenty-Three

Dion was more than a little nervous about helping Jewel with her nephews overnight while her brother and sister-in-law were on their honeymoon. He was thrilled that she'd asked him to stay with her on the ranch this week to practice for when their twins were born, but he was afraid he wouldn't be much help with his medication knocking him out when he needed to be awake to help her.

Maybe I can figure out a way to time my meds, so I wake up for their feeding time and don't take that second dose until the babies are back to sleep?

Dion didn't know exactly what Jerry and Jonah's sleep schedule was, even with the information Susan and Hazel gave him earlier that day about their feeding and changing routine. But he'd done enough reading about babies during his downtime, while Jewel was at work and he didn't have doctor's appointments scheduled in the last couple of months, that he was pretty sure they slept for two to three hours at a time. Since he typically started to wake up about three hours after taking his first dose of Xyrem, he was hopeful that he could take it when they went to sleep, wake up to help take care of them three hours later, and still take his second dose before the four-hour mark.

Since he'd only been taking it for ten days, though, and he never actually got out of bed when the alarm went off for his second dose any of those ten days, he wasn't sure how coherent he'd be during that hour. And since the second dose each night seemed to knock him out much faster than the first, especially since he'd increased the dosage to three grams each on Friday after the first seven days as directed, he was afraid he still had enough of the first dose in his system when he took the second dose to be too groggy to safely change diapers and feed babies.

Maybe I should have woken Jewel up on one of the nights when she stayed with me at the B and B after our dates, so she could decide how much to have me try to do between doses.

She'd only spent the night with him twice since he'd been on the new medication. And after the first time when he didn't remember sleep-fucking her, Dion had tried to be very careful not to wake her up in the middle of the night the second time. She might not have complained about him acting out his dreams that first time, but he didn't want to make it a habit to disturb her sleep, even if he somehow managed to only wake her up with orgasms.

Lord knows, the babies are gonna wake her up often enough after they're born, he thought as he did a quick taste test on the red beans and rice he made them for dinner. He turned the heat off under both the beans and rice, not wanting to scorch them while he finished frying the okra and waited on the oven timer to go off for the cornbread.

Wanting to give them a glimpse at the full experience they could have living together after their babies were born, Dion had his brother take him grocery shopping and drop him off at Jewel's house early in the day, so he had time to do a quick soak of the beans while he was hanging out with her family before going back to her house to actually make their dinner. He wanted to surprise her by having dinner ready when she got home from work, even though he'd had to tell her he'd already be there, so she didn't go try to pick him up at the bed and breakfast.

Spending the day on the ranch also gave him the chance to spend some time with her family while she wasn't around. Some of that time had been with her cousin Josh to learn more about the animals on the ranch and coordinate with his therapist to do his first equine-assisted therapy session later in the week. But the majority of his day had been spent with Jewel's mom and aunt, helping with the babies, and modifying his favorite recipes to work with their current dietary restrictions, while hearing more stories about Jewel's childhood.

He'd also asked what Susan and Hazel knew about Jerry and Jonah's sleep schedule, and for their advice on how he could best help Jewel with caring for the babies, without skipping his medication to stay awake for middle-of-the-night feedings. While they were extremely helpful with confirming his assumption about the babies sleeping up to three hours at a time, unfortunately, other than volunteering to stay with Jewel in his place, they didn't have a clue what to do if he was too groggy to help her when the boys woke up at two in the morning.

I wish I'd have thought to ask Doc Hayes about that at my appointment a couple of weeks ago. Guess I'll have to ask him next week when I go for my recheck, so maybe I'll be more prepared for after our babies are born.

"What is that delicious smell?" Jewel called out as she walked into the house. "Am I finally getting to taste your cooking, D? Or did Mom and Aunt Hazel send you over with extra that they made today?"

"It's a vegetarian version of red beans and rice, since neither one of us need the nitrates in the andouille sausage that's normally in the recipe, and fried okra," Dion informed her as she walked into the kitchen, assuming she could see for herself that he was doing the cooking. "Unless you're smelling the cornbread in the oven."

"Vegetarian?" Jewel snorted as she walked up behind him and wrapped her arms around his waist, pressing her body into his back. "Yeah, that's definitely all you. No way Mom or Aunt Hazel would skip the meat when they're cooking. They'd have a revolt of all the ranch hands if they did."

"Actually, after helping me modify my recipes today, I think they're making this same version of red beans and rice tonight, only as a side dish instead of the main dish," Dion pointed out. "I even helped them set up a shrimp boil out at the bunkhouse before I came over here to start cooking."

"And you didn't plan on shrimp for us?" Julie poked her head under his arm as he spooned the last of the okra out of the oil to rest on a plate of paper towels, so it wouldn't be too greasy when they ate it.

"Nope," Dion smiled, as she reached out, picked up one of the first pieces of okra he'd made that had already cooled down some, and popped it in her mouth. "Until you tell me the girls aren't gonna make you puke at the smell of seafood, I'm not gonna subject you to anything like that."

"But you shouldn't have to give up some of your favorite foods just because I can't stomach them yet." She moved away from him to get out plates for them to start dishing up their dinner.

"I'm not giving them up completely," Dion elaborated as the oven timer went off. He grabbed a potholder from the drawer beside the stove before pulling out the cornbread and turning off the oven. "I'm just not eating them around you, so the smells won't make you nauseous. And I brushed my teeth an extra time after my shrimp boil late lunch, so I'm not risking Zoe and Elena's wrath by having shrimpy breath when I kiss you."

Once everything was turned off and his hands were free, he did just that, stopping her from walking to the table with the silverware she'd gotten out, so he could welcome her home properly. He took the utensils from her hands and placed them on the counter, held her right hand in his left over his heart, and pulled her in close with his right arm wrapped around her as he pressed their lips together. Julie slid her left hand across his chest and over his shoulder, finally resting her palm on his nape, and eagerly opening her mouth as they deepened the kiss.

As much as he wanted to pick her up and place her on the counter to make love to her right then, Dion knew he'd have to wait. Her parents would be bringing her nephews over right after dinner for them to start their shift of childcare. And even if it meant having blue balls all evening while waiting until the babies went to sleep, he couldn't take the chance of having Jon and Susan walk in while he was balls-deep in their daughter.

Reluctantly, Dion finally broke the kiss. "Sorry, Jewel, we've gotta hurry and eat before the boys get here."

"We don't even have time for a quickie?" Jewel questioned as Dion reached over to get the silverware and return it to her hands.

"Fuck, I really want to," Dion groaned, pointedly looking down to emphasize his point with the visual of how his erection was fighting the confines of his jeans. "But since we didn't set a specific time that your parents will be bringing the boys over, I don't wanna take any chances that they'll walk in right in the middle, ya know."

"Oh, good point," Jewel giggled as she looked down at his crotch before turning to finish setting the table.

Dion dished up their plates as Julie filled a couple of glasses with lemonade. Soon they were sitting down to eat and discussing the things they'd each done that day.

"Yeah, if you spend every day this week helping Mom and Aunt Hazel, don't be surprised if they try to recruit you to take over cooking duties for all the hands," Jewel pointed out after he told her where he'd spent most of his time that day. "Especially if everything you make tastes as good as this meal."

"Yeah, maybe I'll pull out my sketch pad tomorrow and draw as they're working," Dion mused, not wanting to get roped into cooking daily. "Maybe if I draw them a few pictures of their grandkids, they won't be too disappointed to find out I don't love cooking enough to wanna make it into a job."

"Oh, wow, you've got them pegged already," Jewel laughed, nodding at his suggestion. "They're both so grandbaby crazy that just might work. Especially if you draw pictures of them with their grandkids."

"Oh, yeah, that's definitely doable," Dion agreed. "I'll just hafta remember to bring my new sketchbook tomorrow, so I can start on the drawings while they're monopolizing the babies."

"They didn't let you get in much practice today?" Jewel arched an eyebrow at him as she shoveled a forkful of red beans and rice into her mouth.

"Only when they were otherwise occupied with cooking when the boys first woke up from one of their many naps," Dion confirmed. "But hopefully, I'll get plenty of practice time while we have them overnight."

Mentioning their upcoming childcare duties reminded Dion that he needed to discuss how to work around his medicine with her. "Speaking of, I'm wondering if I should delay my second dose of Xyrem to be awake for their two a.m. feeding time, or if I should skip it altogether, since it knocks me out so well that I'm afraid I won't be able to wake up for their six a.m. feeding. Honestly, I'm a little worried that I'll still be a little groggy at their ten a.m. feeding time, since Dare had to bang on my door to wake me up at ten this morning."

"Are those the times Amy listed on the schedule she was supposed to write up for us before leaving?"

"I guess." Dion shrugged. "Those are the times your mom told me today. Apparently, they're pretty regimented to eat and have diaper changes every four hours, at ten, two, and six, around the clock, with extra diaper changes in between as needed."

"I didn't realize they were that consistent." Jewel shook her head. "But if they are, then I think you should just adjust your meds to eleven and three. You seemed to wake up easily enough on the mornings I've been with you since you started taking it, so I'm sure I'll be able to wake you up. Well, if their crying over the monitor doesn't do it first. And if I absolutely can't get you to wake up when I need help, I can call Jen or Mom to come help me."

Dion really hoped she was right in saying she'd be able to wake him up. *Fuck! I really don't want my presence here to be more of a burden on her, especially when I'm supposed to be helping her. And I really don't want her to hafta call someone else to help because I'm still asleep.*

~ ~ ~

Julie thoroughly enjoyed her evening playing house with Dion and her infant nephews. It was nice to come home from work to find he'd made dinner, so she didn't have to heat up something from the freezer, or go eat with the rest of her extended family. *Damn, my man's a good cook too! I could seriously get spoiled to having him cooking all my meals. Or gain, like, a hundred pounds, instead of the fifty Dr. Magnum suggested during this pregnancy.*

After dinner, he'd surprised her with a king cake that he'd apparently talked Kara into adding to her menu, so he wouldn't have to miss out on them while spending Carnival season outside of New Orleans. Her parents had shown up with Jerry and Jonah just as they were about to cut into it, so after a few extra minutes of playing with the babies until they started getting sleepy, they'd cut a couple extra pieces and had dessert with her parents while the boys slept off their evening milk stupor.

When her dad found the plastic baby hidden in his piece of king cake, Dion had to explain the traditional meaning. He also told Jon about needing to order a day in advance to get a king cake from Kara's Kakes, since it was now his responsibility to provide the next one the four of them ate together.

Leah Mae Wright

Hopefully, Dad will actually call Kara in the morning to place the order he was talking about for enough king cakes for everyone to have a slice at church on Sunday, since there's no way she can make that many of them in a day. I should probably pop over to his office in the morning to remind him of that, Julie decided as she walked back downstairs after checking on the babies, who were still sleeping soundly in the nursery.

Technically, she'd already known they were fine, since they had the baby monitor in the dining room with them as they visited with her parents. But having Dion in her kitchen when she got home from work, and then her parents bringing the boys over and staying for dessert, had thrown off her normal nightly routine. So, as soon as her parents left for the night, she'd needed a moment to go up to her bathroom and wash away the stress of her workday.

She'd just peeked in at the babies when she first went upstairs, instead of actually going over to risk disturbing them by getting close enough to the cribs that they could see her, knowing Dion still had the baby monitor with him downstairs to see if they needed anything, whether she went in the room or not. Then she spent a few minutes washing off her makeup, changing out of her work clothes, and putting on her nightgown, robe, and fuzzy slippers before heading back down to help with the kitchen cleanup.

When she walked back into the kitchen to see that Dion had already finished most of the chores, she worried that she'd taken more time to herself than she thought. And felt more than a little guilty for leaving all the housework to him. "Did you leave anything for me to do?"

"Nope." Dion grinned as he finished wiping down the counters before rinsing the dishrag and draping it over the sink divider to dry. "I figured we've probably only got…" Dion's voice trailed off as he looked at his watch and licked his lips. "…a thirty-minute window between now and when the boys wake up, so I wanted to make sure we have all of it to do a few dirty things, instead of cleaning the kitchen."

"Oh, you wanna do dirty things, huh?" Julie stepped up to Dion and ran her palms over his chest, wishing he'd already removed his t-shirt. "What kind of dirty things did you have in mind, D?"

"I was thinkin' of setting you up on this counter and eatin' your pussy as my second dessert," Dion suggested, gripping her hips to lift her into position. Once she was seated, he tugged on the belt of her plush, royal purple robe to open it, exposing the plum-colored nylon and spandex chemise she wore under it. "But seeing this sexy lingerie, I might just have to skip that and go straight to pushing it up outta my way and fucking you while you're still wearing it."

"Yeah, you shoulda moved it outta the way before you sat me up here," Julie chuckled, grinning at how much he seemed to like her nightgown, especially since he'd been so adamant throughout their whole relationship that he preferred having her totally nude for their sexual escapades. "But I suppose there's a learning curve for having to deal with clothes after I've spoiled you by always being naked for our carnal activities."

"I believe I've had to remove hotel robes in the past." Dion arched an eyebrow as his lips turned up in an enigmatic smile. He ran his hands up her thighs, only slightly lifting the hem of her chemise. "And I've also peeled you out of your professional pantsuits a time or two, so I'm sure I'm perfectly capable of pushing your gown and robe out of the way while you stay right where you are."

"Ah, but when you've removed my clothing before, I was usually standing up to make it easier, not sitting on them like I am now. Or I was naked under the robe, so opening it was enough if I was already seated somewhere you wanted to play," Julie argued, smirking playfully as she opened her legs to give him access to step between them. "And we didn't have to worry about preventing any bodily fluids from getting on my clothes and making wearing them for feeding babies into an uncomfortable situation immediately after."

"Damn, I didn't even think about that." Dion shook his head, conceding to her way of thinking. He stepped back, and once again, lifted her by the hips to place her back down on her feet. "Now turn around, Jewel, so I can get this robe off you before we waste any more time."

"Yes, Sir!" Julie playfully saluted him before turning around and dropping her arms, so he could remove her robe.

"Smart ass." Julie could clearly hear the mirth in Dion's voice as he draped her robe over the counter beside the baby monitor. "Bend over and hold on to the counter, Jewel. This is gonna be hard and fast."

As Julie followed his directions, she heard him lower the zipper on his jeans right before the rustling of fabric indicated that he'd pushed them down out of his way. Once she'd hinged at the hips to bend at a ninety-degree angle and rest her head and arms on the kitchen counter, Dion lifted the hem of her nightgown and pushed it up onto her back, revealing the fact that she hadn't put on any underwear when she changed her clothes.

"Such a naughty girl, walking around the house without any panties on," Dion crooned as he kneaded her bare ass with his big hands. "You know what naughty girls get, don't you, Jewel?"

"Yes," she replied breathlessly, anticipation of her reward for being naughty, amping up her arousal. "Naughty girls get fucked."

"Yes, naughty girls get fucked," Dion repeated the words he'd previously used, whenever they'd role played one of their fantasies, several times in their previous hookups over the past year-plus.

He might have claimed it was going to be hard and fast, but as was always the case with Dion, he took his time fingering her first to make sure she was wet and ready to take his massive member. He teased her first by smearing her arousal from her clit to her anus before finally inserting his digits to start spreading her open for his cock.

Julie lifted her head, placing her palms on the counter to push back against him, eager to show him she was more than ready by fucking herself on his fingers. Her blatant attempt at taking control earned her a single swat on her ass as he pulled his fingers from her pussy. Julie didn't mind though, as the slight sting quickly morphed from pain to pleasure as he massaged it in.

"Behave yourself, Jewel. You know I'm in charge now, so you just need to stand there and be my good girl. And take what I give you."

With his free hand, Dion lined up the bulbous head of his dick with her dripping wet slit. He swirled the crown through her folds as he stroked his length with his hand, coating himself in her cream before impaling her on his cock with one swift stroke.

"Oh, yes, Dion," Julie cried out, loving the sudden fullness of having every inch of him inside her. She couldn't have stopped her hips from bucking in time with his powerful thrusts if she'd tried, needing the rough intensity their most recent lovemaking had lacked. "Fuck your naughty girl. Take me so hard, I'll still feel you inside me tomorrow."

Not that she really minded that he'd been gentler since they got back together in deference to her pregnancy. Dion always made her feel loved and cherished, ensuring her needs were always met first, no matter how they made love. But she'd missed some of the wilder hotel room romps they'd had earlier in their relationship, so she reveled in having him give her a little taste of their dirtier desires now.

"Fuck, yeah, Jewel, I'm gonna take my tight, pink pussy so hard tonight, you're gonna feel your big, black dick for at least a week," Dion growled as he plowed into her from behind. "Fuck, I love how tight and wet you are. You feel so, fucking, good on my cock."

"You feel even better inside me," Julie cooed, trying not to get distracted by the feeling of her larger than normal boobs hanging down and bouncing in a way she hadn't noticed before. It wasn't an exceptionally painful feeling, but it wasn't entirely pleasant either. Just different enough to be conspicuous now that she actually had womanly breasts, instead of the "pancakes" on her chest that she'd been teased about as a teenager, or even the "perfect mouthfuls" Dion had called her A-cups that she hadn't really sprouted until her early-twenties.

After only a brief moment of insecurity brought on by her thoughts distracting her, Dion was able to bring her back to the moment with his continuous dirty talk, which mostly consisted of him complementing and praising her while sprinkling his prose with liberal uses of the variations of the word "fucking" utilized as an adverb.

"You're so fucking hot, Jewel."

"So, fuckin' sexy."

"Your pussy feels so effing amazing on my cock, Jewel."

"I fuckin' love you, Jewel."

"I fuckin' love you, too, Dion," Julie returned his carnal declaration of affection as she felt her orgasm building in her core with each forceful thrust of his dick into her sex. It only took a few more strokes of his shaft over her G-spot while his tip tapped her cervix for her to fly over the edge. Her explosive climax felt like it shattered her into a million pieces. Pieces that only Dion could put back together. "Oh! Yes! Dion!"

"Fuck! Jewel! Julia!" Dion pounded into her one last time, holding himself deep inside her as he filled her with his seed.

Julie was barely able to bend her arms to use them as a pillow on the counter while she enjoyed the aftershocks of her dynamic release. Dion bent forward behind her, barely allowing his torso to rest on her back by holding himself up with his hands on either side of hers on the counter as he, too, recovered.

Oh, I hope the boys can wait long enough for us to catch our breath before they wake up, she thought as she faintly heard her cell phone ringing from her purse, which was still sitting on a side table in the dining room. Since it wasn't the baby monitor making noise, she decided to ignore it, needing a few more minutes before she'd be able to move.

"You should probably get that," Dion suggested as he pushed off the counter to stand to his full height before pulling his spent cock from her body. "Since that's the third time I've heard it ring in the last few minutes, I think it might be Justin and Amy calling to check on the babies."

"You really think they're interrupting their honeymoon to call me?" Julie reluctantly stood up just as her phone stopped ringing. Dion got a clean dishrag from the drawer and started to wet it to clean them up. "Especially when it's almost time for the boys to wake up for their ten o'clock feeding?"

"I'm just guessing based on how many times they called your mom earlier today." Dion held his hands up in a placating gesture momentarily before dropping them to quickly wipe her up.

He barely had time to complete the task before her phone rang once again. Julie left him to clean himself up, walking through the butler's pantry to the dining room to get her phone from her purse and answer the call. She had to chuckle when she saw Amy's name flash on her screen. *Oops! I guess he was right after all.* "Hi, Amy. How's the honeymoon going?"

"Oh, my, gawd, Julie, what took you so long to answer the phone? Are the boys alright?" Julie felt a little bad for worrying her sister-in-law by not answering earlier. "We've been trying to call for almost twenty minutes. I was about to call Susan to come check on you."

"The boys are fine," Julie quickly replied as she rejoined Dion in the kitchen, wanting to put Amy at ease before explaining the delay in answering. Or rather, giving her a modified version of their activities that left out the sexual escapades. "They're still sleeping peacefully, as they've been since shortly after Mom and Dad brought them over here for the evening. Dion and I were cleaning the kitchen while watching them on the baby monitor, and I didn't hear my phone, since it was in my purse in the other room."

"You're just now cleaning the kitchen? It's almost ten o'clock. You should be getting their bottles ready and changing their diapers by now, not just now finishing cleaning up after dinner."

"Well, Mom and Dad didn't bring them over 'til after seven," Julie elaborated, hoping to not have to mention the time they spent having sex. "Then we played with the boys for a few minutes before putting them down for bed. And we visited with Mom and Dad while having king cake for a late dessert, putting us at almost nine when they went home." Julie just didn't mention that Dion had cleaned as he cooked, so it only took a few minutes to put their dessert dishes in the dishwasher and wipe down the counters.

"They're not following the schedule, Justin," Amy complained, her voice muffled, like she wasn't talking into her phone to direct the words at Julie. She was obviously fretting about spending her first night away from her babies, so Julie hoped to reassure her by telling her how they were getting back on schedule now.

"You've gotta blame Dad for them not going to bed at seven, 'cause he's the one who insisted on spending extra time playing with them before bringing them over here this evening. And we're getting back on schedule now. In fact, Dion's making their bottles as we speak, so we can go up and change and feed them right at ten. From what I've been reading, doing a dream feed on nights like tonight will help them learn to sleep through the night."

"A dream feed?" Dion mouthed the words at the same time Amy voiced them.

"Yeah, it's where you don't wait for them to wake up to feed them," Julie explained while motioning for Dion to get started preparing the bottles. "It keeps them on schedule while they maintain a state of semi-sleep, so they don't think it's time to wake up and play. It's supposed to help both the babies and the parents get more rest."

While Julie listened to Amy explaining dream feeding to Justin, Dion pulled two bottles from the fridge and turned on the faucet to start warming them. She figured it was best to let him do the majority of the work on this scheduled feeding and changing, then she'd set an alarm for fifteen minutes before two to get up and do all the tasks that Dion might still be too groggy to do for the babies next feeding and changing time. And if he was absolutely too out of it to walk into the nursery, then she could use the double carrier to take them both into her bedroom, where they could all four lay on the bed. *Surely, he'll wake up enough to hold a bottle, right? I mean, he wakes up enough to take his medicine and suck on a mint without choking before falling back to sleep, so he should be awake enough to hold a bottle for fifteen or twenty minutes before he takes his second dose of medicine.*

After deciding that what Julie called "dream feeding" was the same thing their pediatrician recommended, only the pediatrician didn't use the same term, Amy asked to switch to a video call, so she could see her boys before going to bed. Julie quickly threw on her robe before she happily switched the call, aiming her phone at the baby monitor as she and Dion walked upstairs to get started on changing diapers and feeding babies.

Once they were in the nursery, Julie felt more like a videographer as she aimed her phone at Dion while he changed both diapers like an old pro. Justin and Amy cooed to their babies, wishing them sweet dreams before signing off, so Julie could put the phone down and hold Jonah to feed him.

Once she was in one rocking chair, giving Jonah his bottle, and Dion was in the other rocking chair, feeding Jerry, Julie finally broached the subject of setting a schedule for their daughters. "What do you think of staggering the feeding and changing schedule for the girls?"

"What do you mean?" Dion gave her a confused look, wiping Jerry's chin where he'd drooled a little milk out.

"Like changing and feeding one of the girls thirty minutes earlier than the other," Julie elaborated. "Trying to take care of both of them at the same time seems impossible for only one person. So, I was thinking that if we stagger it by thirty minutes, then it won't be a big deal if you're too out of it from your meds to get up for a two a.m. feeding."

"Yeah, I suppose we can do that." Dion nodded, but he looked down at Jerry the whole time, not looking up to meet Julie's eyes. "If the girls let us. If not, then I'll just have to go off the meds 'til they're sleeping through the night."

"But it's working so well, you can't go off of it for several months like that," Julie argued, not wanting him to revert back to having sleep attacks several times a day, especially since he hadn't had a single one since starting the meds.

"I'll talk to the doctors next week then," he huffed, setting Jerry's empty bottle aside and lifting him to his shoulder to burp him. "And get their recommendations for how to modify my dosing schedule to be able to wake up and take care of our babies. And if it turns out that I'm not able to find a way to make it work, then I'll get Mama Marcel to come stay with you to help you at night if you need it. Or hire an overnight nanny or whatever."

As soon as Jerry burped, Dion stood, put him in the crib to continue sleeping, and walked out of the nursery.

Great! I just pissed him off by trying to come up with a better plan than trying to be Supermom or having him stop taking the medication he needs. Maybe I should try staggering ya'll's next feeding and changing time, so I don't have to try to wake him up at two.

Unfortunately, after she finished feeding Jonah, burped him, and put him back in the crib, she almost forgot to change the alarm she'd already set on her phone to wake her up fifteen minutes before the boys were due to wake up for their next feeding and changing time. She went to her room to find that Dion had already gone through his nightly routine and took his first dose of medicine. He was laying in her bed, wearing a pair of workout shorts, with his eyes closed.

"I'm sorry," she said as she walked by the bed to get to her bathroom, knowing the meds hadn't had time to knock him out yet. "I didn't mean to upset you."

"I'm not upset, Jewel," he sighed, opening his eyes to give her a wan smile. "At least, not with you. I'm just frustrated by how my injuries and the medications to treat them are altering my ability to be a good dad. And I don't like not being able to be a normal parent. Not being able to sacrifice my sleep for our babies, like my dad did for me and Dare."

"You know you're gonna be a great dad, regardless of whether you sacrifice your sleep or not, right?" Julie sat down on the bed beside him, needing to touch him to reassure him. "Our daughters aren't gonna remember who changed their diapers or fed them in the middle of the night. But they will remember all the other things you're gonna do with them as they grow up to know how much you love them. Besides, we have a couple of different plans to try before we just give up and call someone else in, so you can stick to your normal dosing schedule."

"Really? I thought the only plan was for me to hold off on taking the second dose until after they've been changed and fed at two."

"Yeah, well, while you were covering most of the tasks earlier while I played videographer for Justin and Amy to see the boys, I figured I could do all that at two, and use the double carrier to bring them both in here to lay them in the bed to feed them. Even if you're not able to walk into the nursery because of still being half asleep, I figured you'll be able to wake up enough to hold a bottle. And then I can put them back in the double carrier to burp them and carry them back to the cribs." Julie shrugged after outlining her other plan for later that night and remembering to reset her alarm. "And if you can't, I can sit up in between them to hold both bottles at once, if I have to. It's not impossible to have one person taking care of twins at the same time, just a little harder than having help."

"Well, hopefully, my plan will work, so you don't have to shoulder the burden for both of us," Dion yawned, drawing out his last word as his eyes drifted shut.

"I don't mind. And I'm sure over the course of our lives, there'll be times you have to cover for me while I'm at work or whatever, so it'll all even out in the end." She wasn't sure if he heard her or not, since he seemed to have fallen asleep. So, she leaned over and pecked his lips with hers before going to brush her teeth and go pee for what seemed like the millionth time that day.

"Girls, you really need to quit kicking my bladder like it's a soccer ball," she chuckled as she crawled into bed and placed her phone with the alarm set on her bedside table.

"They're practicing for kicking teenage boys in the nuts," Dion mumbled in her ear, rolling over to spoon her. He placed his hand over her belly. "But you girls should let Mommy rest now. You can practice more tomorrow."

She felt his lips brush the back of her head. "Goodnight, Jewel. Love you."

"Goodnight, Dion. Love you, too." Julie snuggled in, hoping to fall asleep as fast as he did, so she could get almost three hours of sleep before waking up to take care of Jonah and Jerry. And possibly Dion.

When her alarm went off to give her fifteen minutes to go warm up the babies' bottles, she was surprised to see Dion sitting up in bed, trying to wake up enough to go into the nursery with her. She turned on the bedside lamps, thinking the light might help him wake a little more than just sitting up in the dark. "Stay here and just try to wake up a little more while I go down and warm up the bottles," she directed Dion as she put on her robe and shoved her feet into her fuzzy slippers.

"Hmmm, 'kay," Dion slurred, nodding as he fought to keep his eyes open.

She went down to the kitchen to warm up two more bottles under the running faucet, wishing she'd thought to take the two from earlier down to put them in the dishwasher, so it could have run overnight. *Oh well, I'll put all four of them in there after feeding the boys this time. And they'll still be clean and ready to fill in the morning.*

Since Amy had a hard time making enough milk to breastfeed the boys exclusively, they'd already had to supplement with formula. So, Julie wondered if these few days apart, when the boys were exclusively drinking formula, would be long enough for Amy's milk to dry up, or if she would pump and dump all week to try to continue breastfeeding when they returned from their honeymoon.

If Justin can keep her from coming home early, that is.

As she held the bottles of formula under the flow of warm water, she had to wonder if her naturally small breasts were capable of growing enough to provide adequate nutrition for her twins. Or if she would have the same kind of issues with milk production that Amy had. She also wondered if Kay and Brooklyn didn't have as much of an issue with milk production as Amy because they had bigger boobs to start with, or if it was because they each only had one baby to feed.

I know they say breast is best, but if I have as much trouble breastfeeding as Amy's had with twins, I think I'd rather just give the girls formula. At least, then I'd know they were getting enough nutrients. And if they get their appetites from Dion, then Lord knows, they're gonna need a lotta milk, probably more than I can make.

She pulled the bottles from under the tap and tested the temperature on her wrist, rinsing the milk off her arm before turning off the tap. She dried off the outside of the bottles before heading back upstairs.

She peeked into her bedroom to see that Dion had moved to sitting on the side of the bed, instead of just sitting up in the middle of it like he'd been when she got up. When he saw her, he stood and staggered out of the room to follow her into the nursery.

"Just sit down, D," Julie instructed as she sat the bottles down on the table between the rockers, thinking he looked too wobbly on his feet to move one of the babies from the crib to the changing table, much less capable of actually changing a diaper at that moment. "I'll get them changed first before we decide if you feel safe enough to feed them in the rocking chairs, or if I'll need to move them to the bed."

Dion nodded instead of verbally replying, practically falling into the chair when he reached it. Julie picked up Jerry and carried him to the changing table, efficiently changing his diaper without waking him up.

Dion rubbed his eyes and yawned, clearly fighting the effects of his medication. But when she finished changing Jerry, he held out his arms for her to hand him the baby. "I'm good to feed him here. But after he burps, we're gonna hafta wait for you to finish feeding Jonah to put him back in the crib 'cause I don't feel stable enough to carry him while walking."

"No problem," Julie agreed, placing Jerry in Dion's arms before going to pick up Jonah to change his diaper and feed him.

She had to laugh when Dion started singing to the boys about playing with a ding-a-ling. "What on earth are you singing? And why do you think two in the morning is an okay time to sing something so inappropriate to my nephews?"

"It's not inappropriate," Dion smirked, chuckling lightly and obviously waking up a little more than he'd been a few minutes before.

"You don't think singing about playing with your junk is inappropriate when babies are present?" Julie narrowed her eyes at Dion as she sat down to feed Jonah after changing his diaper.

"I'm not singing about playing with my dick," Dion scoffed, still chuckling. "It's an old Chuck Berry song, *My Ding a Ling*, and it's about playing with bells on a string that were a present from the songwriter's grandma when he was a little boy."

"And how do you know an old Chuck Berry song?" Julie was curious about how this silly song ended up in Dion's repertoire, when he usually listened to current R & B.

"My dad used to sing it to me when I was a little kid," Dion half-shrugged. "And I figured singing to the kids would help me stay awake now, so I started singing the song Papa sung most often, 'cause it's the only sorta kid's song I can remember all the words to right now."

"Well, then by all means, please teach me the words, so I can help you carry on the tradition with our kids," Julie beamed, knowing they were probably in for some strange looks from the older ladies at church, when their children started singing *My Ding a Ling* at some point in the future.

Unless he doesn't remember this in the morning...

No, this is too funny not to tell him about it. And it'll be even funnier in a few years when our girls invariably find the most inappropriate times and places to break out in song.

~~~

Monday, January 27, 2020

Since Julie was at work and Mama Marcel was telling the fortunes of a group at the bed and breakfast for some kind of retreat, Dion only had Dare with him when he went to see Doc Hayes for his follow-up appointment. That was fine with him, though, since he felt like his memory was getting better since he'd started his new meds. Maybe not his memories of what he did in the middle of the night when he was on Xyrem. But the Memantine had definitely helped with retaining his memories of recent conversations and daily interactions, keeping him from repeating them to the point that they became an annoyance to his family and friends. So, he didn't feel like he needed someone to go to the doctor with him anymore to remind him what was said later. *And hopefully, since I haven't had any blackout spells since starting the narcolepsy meds, Doc Hayes will finally let me know*
~~~

my driving restrictions are lifted, so I won't hafta have anyone tagging along just to drive me from now on.

He still had the occasional episode when he'd zone out while having a memory come back to him. But since those had slowed down considerably since he'd gotten back most of his memories of his previous visits to Heart's Destiny, and only seemed to happen when he concentrated to try to get the specific details right as he was drawing them now, he didn't think those would be a problem while he was behind the wheel. Now he hoped to convince his doctors of that, so they'd revoke that driving restriction.

His only worry about this appointment was if his issues while helping with nighttime feedings for the babies would change the doctor's mind about keeping him on Xyrem. He knew going off of it wasn't an option because the episodes coming back would put the babies at more risk while in his care during the day. Not to mention that going off of it would definitely mean he couldn't drive. But he also knew not remembering what he did to help with Jerry and Jonah in the middle of the night the previous week wasn't ideal either.

Granted, he had more recollection of the events of the middle-of-the-night feedings at the beginning of the week, when his dosage was only three grams per dose, than he did on Friday and Saturday, when he'd started his third week of titrating it up. But if he couldn't remember anything from the nights when he took three-point-seven-five grams per dose, when Julie had left him in bed and brought both babies into her room, so she could lay them down and just have him help hold a bottle while he slept through it, then he knew he'd never remember helping with their babies once he got up to the full dose of four-point-five grams per dose each night, which he was supposed to switch to at the end of this week. If he could even help with his and Julie's babies while taking that much of the sleep medication. Which was why he wanted to talk to his doctor about maybe going back down to the initial two-point-two-five grams per dose he'd been on for the first seven days, or even the three grams per dose he'd been on for the second week, when he'd started falling asleep faster and wasn't too out of it when he woke up three hours later, instead of continuing to titrate up to the maximum dosage.

Dion recognized the single knock on the door, which seemed to be standard for both of the doctors at the Heart's Destiny Clinic, right before Doc Hayes stepped into the exam room.

"Good afternoon, Dion, Darius," the doctor greeted them with a smile and a nod in each of their directions. "Where are the lovely ladies who usually accompany you to my office?"

"Sorry, Doc, just us ugly guys today," Dion chuckled. "You know how those strong, independent women are. Both of 'em insisted on going to work instead of comin' with today."

"Hey, who you callin' ugly?" Dare gave Dion a dirty look, and probably would have punched him in the shoulder if he'd been sitting within arm's reach instead of on the exam table. "I happen to think we're a couple of good lookin' guys, not ugly."

"I'm not weighing in on that point," Doc Hayes chuckled, holding his hands up in surrender, with some paperwork clutched in one hand and a tablet computer in the other.

"Is that my ImPACT test results?" Dion wondered aloud, eager to get on with the appointment.

"Yes, and your scores this time were excellent," the doctor confirmed. "You're back to the baseline the GWA sent me, so I think it's safe to say the majority of the concussion symptoms have resolved. That's not to say that you won't still have some symptoms from post-concussion syndrome, but for the most part, your brain has healed."

"That's good news," Dion grinned. "Is that from the medications we added last month? Or from just giving it more time to heal?"

"Probably a combination of both," Doc Hayes informed him. "But we're gonna leave you on the meds, so the symptoms don't come back as part of the post-concussion syndrome. I still don't recommend you do anything to risk hitting your head again, but these scores basically indicate that you're no longer at risk of second impact syndrome, at least from this incident."

Dion was relieved to hear that, knowing that second impact syndrome often led to death. Yeah, he could still suffer from it in the future, but now it would take more than one blow to the head for a second impact syndrome diagnosis.

"Now, tell me how you're doing on the Xyrem," Doc Hayes instructed Dion. "Have the sleep attacks decreased any since you've started taking it?"

"I haven't had one at all since I started taking it," Dion proudly stated. "The first week, when I started out at two-point-two-five grams per dose, it took me about an hour to fall asleep after I took it. But I clearly remember waking up to take the second dose, even though I didn't know if some of the things I did in my sleep were real or just dreams."

"What do you mean?" Doc Hayes furrowed his brow as he leaned forward, resting his elbows on his knees.

"Like the night Julia slept over, I couldn't remember if we had sex, or if I just dreamed about having sex with her," Dion admitted sheepishly, wishing his brother wasn't sitting there listening to this conversation.

"Damn, I bet that led to an awkward morning-after talk," Dare chuckled.

Dion turned his head and glared at his brother, not deigning to confirm his assumption. "We actually talked it out and decided to make sure any amorous activities take place before I take the first dose from now on, so I don't fall asleep in the middle anymore. But that's not really what I'm worried about being a problem on this stuff."

"Then tell me what you are worried about," Doc Hayes suggested, skipping over any awkward sex talk.

"The second week, when I bumped it up to three grams per dose, and the first couple nights of this third week, when I went up to three-point-seven-five grams per dose, I was staying at Julia's to help with her twin nephews while their parents were on their honeymoon. We wanted to get a little practice in before our twins are born, so we'd know what to expect for middle-of-the-night feedings and diaper changes and stuff."

"Okay…" Doc Hayes nodded as his voice trailed off, encouraging Dion to go on.

"Well, I adjusted the times on my meds, so I could take the first dose right after their ten o'clock feeding and wake up three hours later for their two o'clock feeding and still have an hour to get both babies changed and fed before I had to take my second dose. And that worked okay while I was on the three grams per dose. I was able to wake up enough to sit in a chair and feed one of the babies, even though I felt too groggy to feel safe carrying them while walking across the room. Jewel was able to do the stuff I couldn't do safely and supervise while I was holding and feeding the babies, both at two and at six the next morning, when I really struggled to wake up. And I even remember singing *My Ding a Ling* to the babies while feeding them to stay awake, though I did have to confirm with her that I actually sang it and didn't just dream it."

Dion paused long enough to suck in a deep breath before continuing. "But as the week went on, my middle-of-the-night memories get fuzzier. Jewel had to tell me about conversations we had that I was apparently having while I was asleep. And since Friday, when I went up to three-point-seven-five grams per dose, I'm falling asleep so fast that I don't even have time to brush my teeth to get that nasty taste out of my mouth. Jewel had to help me back to bed from the bathroom, and I was absolutely no help to her for taking care of the babies for their two a.m. feedings. Apparently, I recognize that it's time to take the second dose when the alarm goes off, but I'm taking it without remembering waking up to do it, or doing anything to get rid of that nasty aftertaste. So, I'm hoping you can tell me it's okay to go back to the two-point-two-five or three grams per dose, instead of continuing to titrate up to the max dosage of four-point-five grams per dose, so I can actually be helpful to her when our babies are born, and not wake up still tasting it."

"Is it really that bad a taste? I thought it just tasted like saltwater, at least from what I read about it."

"Yeah, it's saltwater alright," Dion chuckled, thinking the doctor's assessment was a weak understatement. "Like I imagine the water in the Gulf of Mexico tastes after an oil spill, with a salty chemical after taste. That's why I prefer having that fifteen minute window when I can get up and brush my teeth or suck on a mint without risking choking on it in my sleep."

"Yeah, I see your point." Doc Hayes nodded his agreement. "And you didn't have any sleep attacks, even on the lower doses? From what I understand, they titrate up that first month because the lower doses aren't considered effective, especially for someone your size."

"No, I haven't had any sleep attacks," Dion confirmed. "I have still had those little zone-out spells when I'm recalling memories, but I almost have to force them now, instead of just having them hit me all of a sudden, since I haven't gone anyplace new that might trigger a memory this month."

"Yeah, I think we determined with your sleep studies that those were micro-naps and not narcolepsy episodes," Doc Hayes explained, double checking his notes in Dion's chart on the tablet he'd placed on the desk. "Those can happen to anyone, whether or not they have narcolepsy, just from being tired. You just got lucky to dream about your memories when you've had them. But because they aren't narcolepsy episodes, the Xyrem won't necessarily clear them up. Although, I'm sure that as your overnight sleep improves from taking the Xyrem, they'll happen less often."

"So, when I'm forcing the memories to be able to draw the details of them, I'm not really having a micro-nap and dreaming now?"

"Probably not. If you can still hear the people around you or other things currently happening to recognize the delineation between the present moment and what you're trying to picture in your mind, then you're still awake, not having a micro-nap." Doc Hayes made some notes in Dion's chart on his tablet.

Dion was relieved to find out he wasn't really having either kind of episode now that he was getting close to seven hours of sleep every night, instead of just taking a half-dozen catnaps.

"Because of the FDA restrictions on that drug, Dr. Khan will have to make that adjustment to your prescription, but since the lower doses seem to have controlled your episodes, I don't think it will be a problem to go back to one of the lower dosages." Doc Hayes turned and picked up the phone in the room and called one of the other people in his office to get him in touch with Dr. Khan.

While they waited for the phone to ring back to them, Dion decided to tackle the other issue he wanted to know how to deal with next. "So, um, Doc, since I'm not having those narcolepsy episodes since starting the Xyrem, when will I be allowed to drive again?"

"Since I'm not a specialist in that area to know the laws regarding driving with a narcolepsy diagnosis, I'll have to check with Dr. Khan to be certain, but I think as long as it's controlled with the lower dose of medication you want to take, then you should be good to start driving again now."

Doc Hayes was interrupted by the phone ringing, so he placed it on speaker to consult with Dr. Khan. Dion had to repeat his recent experiences at the different dosage levels with the sleep specialist on the phone, but they soon had confirmation that he could go back down to three grams per dose, which was considered the lowest effective dosage, and that his driving restriction was lifted. He wasn't allowed to drive within six hours of taking the Xyrem, but since he knew he still felt groggy for eight hours after taking that second dose every night, he just planned to schedule later appointments, so he wouldn't have to drive anywhere first thing in the morning.

At least now I can drive for my date nights with Jewel. And hopefully, when the time comes to have our babies, Jewel won't go into labor within eight hours of me taking my middle-of-the-night meds.

Chapter Twenty-Four

Now that Dion was cleared to drive again, Julie got to enjoy riding as a passenger in his Escalade while they went out for their weekly date night. It was a nice change of pace after she'd had to drive for all their previous dates and outings since his traumatic brain injury, and actually made her feel like they were finally able to be a normal couple. Not that she had a problem with driving for their dates when he couldn't, as was evidenced by how she'd driven him back to the B and B earlier in their secret relationship, whenever he'd ridden somewhere with one of the other wrestlers but then hung out with her. But she knew there was a difference between him choosing to split a rental car with his coworkers while he was in town, which necessitated having her drive on occasion so they could spend some time alone instead of with their mutual friends, and him not being allowed to drive because of a medical issue. She knew that being told not to drive had felt emasculating to him, and she was glad to see that he clearly felt more like his old self now that he could drive again.

She also knew that he still had limitations from his injuries and the medications to treat them that made him feel like less of the man he'd been before. While she didn't see him as less than in any way, shape, or form, she knew having to deal with the consequences of his injuries, and the limitations caused by his medications to treat those injuries, made him feel that way.

She hoped that the week they'd spent basically living together while caring for her nephews had shown him, as much as it had her, that they really could have their happily ever after. Yeah, they both had their work cut out for them to find modifications for how to deal with things like middle-of-the-night baby care. But she knew their love for one another was strong enough to adapt however necessary, so they could have a long life together with their happy family.

They just had to keep the lines of communication open between them, and plan for those things in advance if they could, so they could have their dream life together. And the first step to that was to give him the opportunity to do more of the things he enjoyed in life that made him feel like his old self, while having backup plans in place to accommodate the changes in both their lives now.

Julie was convinced that if anyone was capable of living happily after a brain injury, it was Dion Davis. And she felt blessed to be the woman at his side, as he tackled these new challenges and found ways to prove to himself that he was still the same man. The wonderful man she loved and wanted to spend the rest of her life with, having children, a few pets, eventually having grandchildren and great-grandchildren, and growing old together. Seeing him drive for their date night was only one of many baby steps to living that dream.

Since his medication had proved to be effective in preventing his narcoleptic episodes, even during the three days at the beginning of the week when he had stressful events to attend, they'd decided to attempt a return trip to Tully's Roadhouse after having dinner at Millie's Diner. Dion hadn't wanted to go back there sooner because of worrying that the lighting and music had played a part in why he'd had that episode on his first night back in town. But now he considered Tully's the ultimate test of his medication, so they planned this trip back there for a time when some of their friends and family could be there to help her get him back to the B and B, if he did have another incident. Not that Julie thought they'd really need the assistance, since she had full faith in his medication's efficacy.

And if it doesn't work, then I'll enjoy getting behind the wheel of his sweet ride, she thought as he parked in front of Millie's. *And we'll try again another time, after we go over what worked and what didn't with his doctors and our therapists, and come up with another plan.*

As he walked around the vehicle to come open her door, Julie appreciated the opportunity to ogle him. Dion was dressed in dark-washed Wrangler jeans, a burgundy button-down, and cowboy boots. *Holy shit! He makes a hot cowboy!*

She'd seen him in cowboy boots and Wranglers before, since he'd worn them to a few of the bachelor and bachelorette parties they'd gone to at Tully's in the past. But since he didn't wear them on a regular basis, and hadn't worn them since he'd come back to town in November, she'd almost forgotten how great he looked in the standard attire of the country boys she grew up with, instead of his usual big city style. He was so freaking hot that he practically melted her panties off as he helped her down out of his SUV.

I didn't even realize he had Wranglers and cowboy boots here in town. But maybe they were included in the stuff Dare and Mama Marcel brought him from NOLA last month, and I just didn't see them, since he didn't exactly rush to unpack those boxes when I stayed over with him then.

"Ya know, you should really wear those boots and jeans next time you have an equine therapy session," Julie mentioned casually, as they walked hand in hand toward the restaurant, thinking she'd like to see him in them more often. "And any other time you're on the ranch around the stables."

She'd missed his sessions the last couple of weeks because of being at work when he did them, but from what he'd said, they'd gone well. As were the lessons Josh was giving him on caring for the animals outside of his therapy. Julie was looking forward to the time after their babies were born, when she'd be home on maternity leave to be able to take part in some of that time with him, too. Especially if she could get him to dress the part to fuel her Cowboy Dion fantasies.

"Yeah?" Dion arched an eyebrow at her, obviously recognizing her sexual thoughts from her expression as he leaned down to whisper in her ear, so nobody else could hear their conversation. "Is that because you think they're more appropriate than my sneakers? Or do you have a cowboy fantasy you want me to fulfill for you?"

"Maybe a little of both," Julie admitted with a grin, as he opened the door to the diner for her to enter first. "But only with you in the role of hot cowboy."

"Howdy, ya'll," Jane greeted them as they walked in, preventing them from continuing the flirtatious conversation. The forty-something-year-old mixed-race woman was actually the granddaughter of the original Millie who'd opened the diner, but she'd managed it for as long as Julie could remember and had inherited it when her grandma passed about ten years back. "Seat yourselves anywhere."

"Thanks, Jane," Julie smiled at the proprietress, knowing one of the wait staff would be over to actually take their order, since Jane mostly stayed behind the counter to be able to quickly go back and forth between the kitchen and the dining room to supervise everyone who worked for her.

Dion looked at Julie before looking over the booths that lined the front windows of the diner. He then looked at the more standard tables and chairs between the booths and the counter before asking, "Do you prefer a booth, or a chair you don't have to scoot into?"

"I know I'm getting rounder every day, but I think I can still fit in a booth for a few more weeks," Julie teased, pointing to the empty booth just before the large, round banquette in the corner for large parties. That last booth seemed to have the table set a little farther from the bench seats than the others. She assumed the extra elbow room in that one was because of the oversized group table beside it throwing off the spacing along the front of the restaurant, but she'd gladly take advantage of the additional clearance while she could to have a more comfortable, padded seat than the small, round, wooden chairs at the other tables.

"I didn't mean to imply you wouldn't fit," Dion sighed as they scooted into opposite sides of the booth. "I just know you've complained about how hard it is to get up off of soft surfaces, and I wasn't sure if the scooting would be a problem or not."

"I know. I was just joking around," Julie reassured him as she reached across the table and placed her hand over his. "And honestly, if I gain as much weight as Dr. Magnum wants me to, then fitting my baby belly in a booth is gonna be a problem during the last month or two before the girls are born. I just hope I don't get so big that I end up needing two of those chairs to hold up the massive spread of my hips." Julie pictured herself sitting on two of the chairs, with one butt cheek on each chair, and stifled a giggle at the ridiculous image in her head, though she didn't stop her smile at Dion.

"I don't think your hips are gonna spread nearly enough to need two chairs," Dion chuckled, shaking his head at her as he turned his hand over to hold hers.

"Yeah, well, with the way my panties are starting to feel tight, I'm not so sure," Julie sighed, knowing that her low-rise bikinis didn't come up far enough in the front to be stretched out over her baby bump. So, feeling them digging into her hips had to be because her hips were already spreading to accommodate the babies when it came time for them to pass through the birth canal.

"You should have told me this earlier, Jewel," Dion pointed out with his lips turning up in a sexy smirk, "so we coulda spent the afternoon lingerie shopping."

She didn't get the chance to tell him that she'd needed the afternoon for her waxing aftercare, as Jane's teenaged daughter, Rianna, walked up to their table, introduced herself, and delivered their water glasses, silverware, and menus. Not that Julie needed the menu, since Rianna also announced the catfish special that Julie instantly started craving.

Huh? That's different. And hopefully, a good sign that I can actually start eating fish again without getting sick.

"I'll take the special," Julie proclaimed, handing the menu right back to Rianna, without even opening it, as her stomach growled in anticipation. "With an extra order of hush puppies and a large lemonade."

"I guess the girls are no longer protesting seafood?" Dion chuckled, grinning at Julie as he handed his menu back to Rianna as well. He only partially turned to face the teenager as he placed his order, never really taking his eyes off of Julie. "I'll take the same, including the extra hush puppies, just in case two orders aren't enough to fill up our babies."

"I'll get that put right in," Rianna smiled shyly before turning and race-walking back to the kitchen, making Julie wonder if the teenager had a bit of a crush on Dion, or was just intimidated by his celebrity status.

"No, the girls are no longer protesting seafood," Julie confirmed, smiling at Dion as he turned his full attention back to her without seeming to notice the young girl's possible crush. "At least, I don't think they are, considering how I instantly started craving it when Rianna mentioned it. In fact, I'm now looking forward to finally getting to try Mama Marcel's gumbo tomorrow at the potluck after church."

"Guess it's a good thing she didn't head back to NOLA with Dare this morning then."

"Is she staying in town permanently now? Or still planning to go back to New Orleans?" Julie knew Dion had gotten used to having both Dare and Caroline around all the time in the months since his injury. So, now she worried how much he'd miss them, if they both went home while he stayed in Heart's Destiny. She also worried that missing his family would mean he'd eventually start planning trips to visit them. Trips she wouldn't be able to take with him because of her obligations at work and travel restrictions later in her pregnancy.

"No, she's just planning to stay long enough to do some readings for the couples retreat at the B and B over Valentine's weekend, and then she's planning to head home just in time for Mardi Gras." Dion's smile faded, demonstrating the feelings Julie expected from her sweet, sensitive man. "But she's planning to come back just as soon as I call and tell her you've gone into labor to help us however we need when the babies are born."

"I'm sure Mom's already worked her into the schedule of helpers she's putting together for us for that first couple of weeks, when we're trying to get into some kind of routine," Julie chuckled. "Which is probably why Mom was so adamant about insisting I pick out furniture for the guest bedroom, so whoever she ropes into overnight duty will have a place to crash."

They paused their conversation as Rianna delivered their lemonades. But Julie could still see that the way the discussion had turned seemed to deflate Dion's earlier good mood.

Is that because of how much he's gonna miss Caroline and Dare? Or because he doesn't like the idea of Mom, Aunt Hazel, Caroline, and whoever else they rope into helping out, staying over, and seeing him while he's loopy from his Xyrem?

"While I hate that my issues and meds make me pretty much useless for middle-of-the-night diaper changes and feedings," Dion sighed, breaking eye contact to look down and pick at a chip in the edge of the table. "I'm really glad you've got such a great support system to help with all that."

"You're not useless for that stuff," Julie scoffed, squeezing his hand to try to get his attention focused back on her. She wanted to see his eyes when she said her next words, so she'd know he truly heard her.

Once his gaze lifted back to hers, she continued. "Last week was the perfect trial run with Jonah and Jerry, which just proved that getting into a routine with the babies and your meds is actually possible. Yeah, it might be tough at first with needing to get the girls on a schedule like the boys are already on. But with you going back to the same dose you were on at the beginning of last week, I know we'll be fine with it. Probably a lot sooner than everyone thinks it'll take to get into a routine because of already having multiple game plans tried out."

"Yeah, but that was with babies that are already on a schedule," Dion pointed out, looking sad, even though he did, at least, maintain eye contact. "Newborns aren't going to sleep as long as two-month-olds, so I'm still worried about being too knocked out to be helpful when they wake up only an hour or two after I've taken my meds. And worrying about all the possible ways things can go wrong makes me feel like I'm gonna fail as a father."

"You are *not* going to fail as a father," Julie declared adamantly, squeezing his hand. "Seriously, last week proved to me just how great we are at being able to adapt as necessary to take care of our babies. I might have to do the double-carrier trick to bring them to the bedroom for feedings at the same time. But if I'm able to breastfeed, then I'm gonna hafta figure out how to feed them at the same time anyway, even when you're wide awake and able to help me. So, it's not that big a deal. And they won't remember who feeds them and changes their diapers anyway, so they'll still know you're a great dad from all the other stuff you're gonna do with them when they're actually old enough to remember."

"Yeah, you said that last week," Dion sighed, nodding as his lips turned up slightly. "And I'm trying to stay optimistic about you being right about all that. But sometimes it's mentally challenging to feel like I'm less capable than I was before. Ya know?"

He remembers that conversation? Maybe his meds really are helping him with his memory after all.

Come to think of it, he hasn't repeated a conversation with me since New Year's Eve. So, yeah, that memory medicine really is helping.

Julie knew it wouldn't matter to her if the medicine hadn't worked at all. She would have just repeated the conversations as needed because of how much she loved Dion. They might not have exchanged vows yet, but she already felt committed to loving him "through sickness and health, 'til death do they part." But she also knew how frustrated he was by feeling like he was forgetting more of his life, so she was thrilled for him to have found something effective for delaying the dementia-like symptoms he was having, even if his TBI history meant he was likely to have a recurrence of them later in life.

"Yeah, I know," Julie agreed, wanting to validate his feelings, while also building up his self-confidence. "We all feel inadequate at times, but that's why we have partners to help us when we struggle. And I wouldn't want anyone but you as my partner because I know just how well our strengths and weaknesses line up, so we can each carry the load for the other when necessary. And let's be honest, I'm getting the much better end of this whole deal. Yeah, I'm gonna do a little more for our children in the middle of the night, but you're gonna do a lot more for them than I will during the day once I go back to work. Plus, you have to pick up the slack for my inability to cook more than the basics. And you're gonna hafta do that stuff for like decades, where I'm only gonna have like two or three years, when our kids will be babies and toddlers, that I'll be able to carry the load for middle-of-the-night feedings and diaper changes."

Dion chuckled and smiled just as Rianna arrived with their meals, not giving him the chance to refute her statements. As soon as the plates were on the table, Julie dug in, closing her eyes, and moaning in pleasure at the first taste of her catfish filet.

"Maybe we should take this meal to go," Dion chortled, grinning when Julie opened her eyes to look at him, "so nobody else gets to see your O face from eating it."

"Sorry, not sorry," Julie grinned before popping a hush puppy in her mouth. She quickly chewed and swallowed the sweet, deep fried, cornbread ball before continuing. "Do you realize just how long it's been since I've been able to eat fish of any kind? Like four months. That's like a third of a year, which might not sound like a lot, but it feels like forever when you can't eat one of your favorite foods."

"I'm sure our daughters thank you for your sacrifice," Dion quipped, unable to hide his roguish smile, even as he closed his mouth around his fork to take his own bite of the delicious fish.

Leah Mae Wright

When he looked at her like that, with so much heat in his eyes that the room temperature seemed to jump by at least ten degrees, she started questioning why she hadn't asked him to move in yet. *I love him. He loves me. We've both said we want to be together for the rest of our lives. So, why am I still just packing an overnight bag for our date nights, instead of asking him to move in?*

When I really think about it, it seems kinda silly to pack a bag and stay with him at the bed and breakfast just a few miles from my house. Am I waiting for him to pop the question before suggesting we move in together first? What if he's waiting to pop the question because he wants us to live together first to make sure we're as compatible as it feels every time we spend the night together? Was last week not enough to show him that?

"So, now that you can eat seafood again, what do you think of going to NOLA with me for a few days, so I can show you my favorite restaurants and give you an authentic Mardi Gras experience? From what the other guys have said, it'll be about the right time for me to take you on a babymoon before you're too far along to fly."

Dion's abrupt topic change brought Julie back out of her head, putting thoughts about how to ask him to move in with her to the back of her mind. *No point in thinking about that when he's already trying to plan to go back home to New Orleans.* Hating that her inner voice sounded like a shrew, trying to keep him away from his family, she decided to deflect the negative thoughts and maintain her happy mood. *Hopefully, him saying he wants to make it a babymoon for me means he does think of it as a vacation from our normal life and not a way to try to talk me into moving to where he feels most at home. And I do want to go see where he grew up, so I can better understand him.*

"I thought Mardi Gras was about getting drunk and flashing boobs for beads, not exactly the right atmosphere for a babymoon," Julie joked, grinning, even though she didn't really feel like it. "I mean, I can't exactly get drunk this year, but I suppose now is the best time to show off the goods to get the most beads."

"Technically, it's about consuming the last of the meat and other unhealthy things in the house that we give up for Lent starting on Ash Wednesday," Dion corrected her misconception. "Though that does include alcohol, and for some people, sex, we can still have a great time celebrating with just the decadent foods that you're allowed to eat while pregnant. And I'll buy you all the beads you want, so nobody else gets to see your perfect mouthfuls but me."

While Julie appreciated that he referred to her boobs the same way he did before her pregnancy enlarged them, she wasn't so happy about hearing that he might give up sex for Lent. They'd had a few conversations about the differences between his Catholic faith and her non-denominational religious upbringing, but they hadn't really gotten into the details of how he practiced his religion. *That's gonna totally suck if he has to abstain for forty days before the babies are born, and then we have to abstain again for my postpartum period.* "Wait, you don't give up sex for Lent, do you? I think I would have remembered if you said something about that last year."

"Not always, but I have in the past," Dion shrugged. "When I was a teenager, I only gave it up if I didn't have a girlfriend at the time. Then working with the GWA, it was kinda hard to have a serious relationship, so I abstained quite a lot, even when it wasn't for Lent, just to avoid some of the more aggressive ring rats."

"Like you expect me to believe you didn't enjoy your fair share of one-night stands with ring rats during your wrestling career," Julie scoffed, lightly chuckling.

"When I first got in the business, yeah, but that got old pretty quick," Dion admitted with another nonchalant shrug. "I can't say for sure how long it was before we met that I quit having random hookups altogether, but I do know they were very few and far between in twenty-sixteen, which is the last year that I can clearly remember giving up sex for Lent. And honestly, you'd be the one to know about last year, since I don't remember the specific dates we were able to meet up then to know if any of them were between Mardi Gras and Easter or not."

"You were in Portugal on Mardi Gras last year," Julie informed him, trying to remember what he'd said about the celebration back then. "And you said it was almost like being back in New Orleans because of the costumes and parades you saw while you were there."

"And did we meet up between then and Easter?"

"No," Julie shook her head. "Between the GWA's European tour, the northern loop of the US, and a Canadian tour, you spent most of the Spring in places I couldn't justify flying to for Burleson business, so it was the day after Easter before I was able to meet up with you in Austin."

"So, I guess I did give up sex for Lent last year." Dion shrugged once more before going back to eating his meal.

"But we did have Skype sex several times then," Julie pointed out, whispering so nobody else in the diner would hear her, and wondering if their Skype sessions counted as sex or not. "Unless you don't count mutual masturbation as sex."

"Yeah, I'm not sure if that counts or not," Dion chuckled. "I mean, in previous years, I didn't count solo sessions, which was the only way I was able to make it through the full forty days. But if we were on Skype and watching each other, I think that might count."

"Are you planning to give it up this year?" Julie bit her lip, hoping he'd say no.

"Absolutely not," Dion declared vehemently. "With me staying with you to help with the babies, it'll be hard enough to abstain while you're healing. There's no way I can give up our date nights for forty days three months before the girls are due, too. So, unless Dr. Magnum tells us we have to stop because of something to do with the babies, I plan on making love to you every time you'll let me, right up 'til you go into labor."

Julie smiled as wide as she could without opening her mouth as she savored her next bite, reveling in the fact that he wanted her as much, and as often, as she wanted him. She might not know for sure that he'd be happy living in the small town of Heart's Destiny, but she was sure that wherever he wanted to live, he loved her enough to want her with him.

"But you're still giving up meat for forty days, right? Is it gonna be a problem if I'm still insisting on steaks and burgers and stuff then 'cause the babies are making me crave 'em?"

"Yeah, I'm giving up meat, but only on Ash Wednesday, Good Friday, and every Friday during Lent," Dion explained before going into a much more detailed explanation of the practices of his Catholic faith than he had in the past, helping her understand that the religious fasting tradition didn't actually mean going completely without food the way she'd always thought.

After hearing the way weddings were so much different in the Catholic church from what she'd grown up with in a non-denominational church, Julie had to wonder if Dion would want to bring in a priest to officiate, if and when they ever got married. *Surely, he won't expect us to replace all the pews for ones with kneelers, so everyone's able to kneel during the ceremony? Will he? And will I have to convert so I can take communion during the wedding? Or will he be okay with just adding a couple of the Bible readings and hymns, but otherwise sticking to what we normally do here instead?*

I guess we'll figure all that out, if and when we get to that point in our relationship. And hopefully, we'll actually take the time to plan for whatever changes to the norm have to be made, instead of rushing through planning the wedding like Mom and Aunt Hazel have for everyone else in the family. And in the meantime, I'm just gonna enjoy my time with Dion and put off worrying about all that stuff as long as I can.

~~~

As soon as they walked into Tully's Roadhouse, Dion was hit with a barrage of memories. It was like a slideshow flipping through his brain, showing him image after image of his time there with Jewel, drowning out his earlier feelings of inadequacy that she hadn't completely quashed at the diner earlier. He saw several different versions of her dancing on the same dance floor he could clearly see to his left, both with him and when her friends filled the dance floor with her for line dances. He pictured Jewel playing pool at the tables he could see through the archway into the back room, all while wearing the same outfits he'd just envisioned her dancing in. And most vividly, he remembered Jewel pressed against a door that seemed to fit into the décor of the bar, possibly the door of a bathroom or storage room, as he plowed his hard cock into her tight, wet pussy.

"We've been here a lot, haven't we?" Dion turned to look at the large wooden bar on the right side of the room, noticing the hallway that led to the back area of the bar, where he assumed the restrooms were located.

"Yeah, a few times," Jewel confirmed, nodding as she held his hand. She stood still beside him, not directing him to any particular
~~~

part of the bar, or to where their friends and her family were hanging out, almost like she was waiting for him to decide which memories he wanted to relive first. "Starting with the day we met, when we had our first kiss here."

Her words must have triggered something in his brain, causing him to pull her along as he walked past the bar to find the spot in the hallway that he could clearly see in his mind. *What day did she say that was again?*

Saturday, November 17, 2018

"Come back to my room tonight," Dion suggested, not recognizing his own voice because of how much it seemed to have deepened with his desire for Jewel.

"I can't," Julie protested, slightly shaking her head. "I'm not the type of girl who sleeps with someone on the first day we meet, even if it does feel like we've known each other longer."

"We don't have to do anything but talk," Dion assured her, knowing he would never pressure her to do more than spend time with him. "Hell, we can go sit in your parents' living room to talk all night, so you know I won't try anything you don't want."

"It's not that I don't want you to try anything," Julie backtracked, giving him hope that he might, at least, get to do more than hold her in his arms while they danced that night. "I just need to take it slow and know it means more to you than a one-night stand. And before you start repeating all that destiny and soulmates stuff you heard from Anthony and spouted on the dance floor earlier, I need to be shown it's true and not just told. You wouldn't be the first guy who's tried telling me what I wanted to hear to get in my pants, so I don't believe it without seeing the effort being made to prove it."

Dion took her hand then, placing her palm over his heart and covering her hand with his to hold it there, leaning back against the wall, so she felt free to walk away from him at any time. "Do you feel that?"

So that's when I started putting her hand on my heart every time I kiss her, Dion thought as he momentarily paused the flashback before jumping right back into it.

She nodded.

"My heart races every time I see you," Dion confided, hoping she found his smile reassuring. "It's never done that with anyone before. So, I already know you mean more to me than anyone else ever has. I don't know how we'll make it work with me on tour and you having such an important job here, but I want to try. That's why I'm willing to go slow and wait for more than a goodnight kiss from you. But I still wanna spend as much time with you as possible this week, so we can really get to know one another outside our physical attraction."

Julie looked at him pensively at first. Then her luscious red lips tilted up in an impish smile.

"Who says I'm even gonna give you a goodnight kiss?" Julie teased, stepping in close and pushing up on her tiptoes as she slid her left hand over his shoulder and around his neck while leaving her right hand under his left over his heart. "Maybe I'd rather kiss you now, so I can remember it, instead of waiting until the end of the night, when I'm too drunk to even know what I'm doing."

"I like the way you think, Jewel." Dion couldn't stop himself from using the term of endearment in reference to how her bright blue eyes sparkled like sapphires, grinning as he pulled her close with his right hand on the small of her back. He slid his hand up her spine, finally resting it on her nape before pressing his lips to hers for the first time. He took his time, warming her up with gentle passes of his mouth and tongue over her closed lips before pressing more firmly and gently nipping at her lips to try to persuade her to open for him.

It didn't take much coaxing before she melted into his kiss, opening her mouth to the invasion of his tongue before returning his ardent passion. Dion felt tingles throughout his whole body from the carnality of the kiss, especially every point where her body made contact with his. He lost himself in Julie, feeling like their souls were connecting even more than their lips and tongues. Kissing Julie was an out-of-this-world experience, like nothing he'd ever known before.

Mine! *Dion thought as he kissed her, knowing deep in his heart that they were soulmates, destined to be together forever.* Julie Burleson is the woman of my dreams, meant to be mine, forever and always. My Jewel.

Unfortunately, the moment he wished could last forever was interrupted all too soon by a woman's voice calling out, "Julie!"

They quickly separated as Julie warned him, "Nobody else can know about this," before turning to walk away, leaving him standing there with a steel rod tenting his slacks.

"Yeah, you might not wanna let anyone know about us yet, Jewel, but eventually, I plan on walking down the aisle with you, so everyone knows you're mine."

"It was right here," Dion declared as he came back from the memory in his head, turning to lean back against the wall in approximately the same spot he remembered. "I was trying to convince you to let me take you home, so we could spend more time getting to know one another, and hoping for a goodnight kiss. And you told me you didn't want to wait until you were too drunk to remember kissing me."

"Yeah, you were really laying it on thick with the soulmates stuff that night," Jewel chuckled as she leaned in close and lifted both hands to his chest. "Telling me how you finally understood what Anthony was talking about when he described falling in love at first sight with Kay because you felt like you'd been struck by lightning when you first saw me. But you took it a little too far with explaining your earlier sexual innuendo about us going for a naked ride and not on horseback."

"Damn, realizing you're *The One* must have done a number on my head to cause me to make a rookie mistake like that," Dion chuckled self-deprecatingly, as the conversation on the dance floor came back to him in living color.

"You're gonna hafta learn to Texas two-step if you plan on dancing with me more than once," Julie goaded him, grinning sexily as she stepped into his arms the first time.

"Well, then, you'd better teach me how to Texas two-step, 'cause I plan on dancing with you regularly for the next sixty or seventy years," Dion declared, hugging her close before letting her pull back and set the boundaries between them.

"Fine, I'll teach you," she agreed, eyeing him skeptically. "Technically, you're supposed to lead, but I'll try to do it for now 'til you get the steps down. But since I'm going backwards, I'll need you to make sure I don't run into anyone." She directed him which foot to use for each step of the two-to-one rhythm of

the dance, insisting on only touching where they held hands, with his free hand on her waist, and her free hand on his shoulder. Once they finally seemed to get into sync with one another, she circled back to address his earlier comment about how long they'd be together. "Only for sixty or seventy years, huh? Not forever?"

"I suppose it could be forever, if our ghosts dance together after we spend the next sixty or seventy years together here on earth," Dion shrugged, smiling suggestively at the beautiful blonde he wanted to hold closer.

"Don't tell me you've fallen prey to the Matchmaking Mommas and their plans to marry off all my siblings, cousins, and me," Julie scoffed, shaking her head at him.

"I don't know anything about the Matchmaking Mommas," Dion assured her. "But I was instantly attracted to you when I first saw you earlier, like we're destined to be soulmates. And while I'm not ready to commit to marriage, or anything serious like that yet, I would like to get to know you better, so we can see where things might go between us."

"Oh, no, you can't have it both ways," Julie objected to his statement, laughing at him. "After saying you think we'll be together for sixty or seventy years and are destined to be soulmates, you can't say you're not ready to commit to marriage or anything serious."

"Yet," Dion inserted, making sure she understood how he felt. "Just because I can see us getting to the point that we live out our destiny and become inseparable, doesn't mean I'm ready to retire and ride off into the sunset with you right now, cowgirl. Unless you agree that we're destined to be soulmates and you're willing to travel with me while I finish out my planned twenty-year career in the ring?"

"I'm the vice president of business diversification and asset management at Burleson Incorporated," Julie scoffed, rolling her eyes at him, even as they sparkled like sapphires in the flashing lights on the dance floor. "And eventually, I plan on taking over as CEO from my dad and uncle. So, no, I'm not willing to follow you around the world like a groupie. Besides, I'm not so sure you're right about us possibly being anything more than acquaintances, who find each other attractive when we run into each other at weddings and stuff."

"Oh, we're definitely more than acquaintances," Dion assured her, pulling her in closer than she'd previously allowed, so he

could get a closer look at those sapphire eyes. My Jewel, *he thought as their gazes locked on one another. "For the last six weeks, I've heard Anthony gushing about how he felt when he first saw Kay, and how your family members always fall in love at first sight, when they first meet their soulmates, but I didn't understand it, much less believe it, 'til I first saw you this afternoon. Then it all made sense. You and me," he lifted his hand from her hip to motion between them as he spoke, "we're meant to be together for the rest of our lives. You might not want to admit it yet, but we're the real deal."*

"The real deal, huh?" Julie laughed, shaking her head. "And when did you come to that realization? For that matter, why should I believe this isn't just another line to try to get in my pants, like I've heard from a dozen other guys in the past?"

"'Cause I'm not like any of those guys," Dion assured her, lightly squeezing the hand he'd placed back on her hip. "Do I want in your pants? Hell yeah. But that's not the only thing I want with you, Jewel. With you, I want it all. Marriage, babies, the whole nine yards. Hot, sexy times mixed with quiet nights on the couch, cuddling and talking about all our hopes and dreams for the future. I knew you were The One *for me when I felt the exact same thing Anthony described when he talked about seeing Kay the first time. Fate. Destiny. Kismet. Soulmates. Call it whatever you want, but we're inevitable. I felt like I was struck by lightning when I saw you walking toward me at the bounce house earlier. I knew we were meant for each other from that first moment. And I was just more convinced of it when you blushed so prettily at my comment about you taking me for a ride. And the way you're blushing again now tells me that you know I meant a private, naked ride, and not horseback riding."*

"Just because I'm attracted to you and might eventually be convinced to let you in my pants, doesn't mean we can make the relationship you're talking about work between us," Julie argued, shaking her head at him once more. "As a wrestler, you're on the road more than Anthony, so I don't see how we could ever spend any time together."

"Yeah, I have a brutal schedule, traveling approximately three-hundred-and-twenty days a year with the GWA, but we can still see each other every time I get off for a holiday break," Dion countered, hoping to win her over. "And if we start by dating whenever I'm not on tour, then we should have a good, solid

foundation for our relationship to figure out how to spend more time together in the future."

"Don't worry, D," Jewel assured him with a sexy smile, bringing him back out of the memory. "You redeemed yourself with that first kiss later that night and were right back to your smooth self by the next day. I honestly don't know how I held out for almost a week before giving in and succumbing to your charms."

"Yeah, I don't know how I survived that week either," Dion smiled, pulling her close and wanting to recreate their first kiss. "In fact, I don't know how I'm gonna survive going back out to the bar to hang out with your sister and cousins the rest of the night, when all I wanna do is recreate the memories I'm getting back here and now." He couldn't resist thrusting his hips at her, so she could feel how hard he was from being so close to her while remembering their first kiss.

"Oh, really?" Jewel smiled up at him with mischief lighting up her blue eyes, which seemed to be turning from their normal sapphire to the stormy gray sky that indicated she was getting aroused. "Well, I think we can maybe spend a few minutes recreating that first kiss before we go hang out with everyone."

Dion covered her right hand over his heart with his left, wrapping his right arm around her to pull her in as close as possible. Jewel slid her left hand up over his shoulder and around to his nape, pushing up on her tiptoes, just as he dipped his head to press their lips together.

Once again, it was like the rest of the world disappeared as their souls connected on another plane of existence. Dion savored the sweet taste of her cherry red lips before deepening the kiss to explore the hidden recesses of her mouth with his tongue. Jewel met him lick for lick, seeming to be as lost in their own little world as he was from the carnal preamble to the rest of the night's events.

Unfortunately, their passionate kiss was cut all too short by Jen hollering, "Julie, Dion, ya'll are supposed to come hang out for a bit before you sneak off to make out!"

"Guess we should have snuck into the storeroom to relive the memories of what we did at Fiona and Rick's bachelorette and bachelor party," Jewel teased as they broke the kiss, her eyes flashing with even more of that stormy gray he knew signaled her arousal.

Leah Mae Wright

Once again, her words triggered a memory of them heading to the restrooms just a couple of minutes apart to sneak off for a quickie and hoping nobody noticed. "What day was that?"

She barely had time to answer him before he drifted back there in his mind.

Saturday, June 29, 2019

"Jewel?" Dion whispered the pet name he'd given her as he lightly knocked on the door just past the restrooms, where she'd told him to meet her.

"Hurry, get in here and shut the door before anyone else comes down the hall," Jewel instructed him as she opened the door and motioned for him to enter the small space.

Dion gladly followed her directives, barely noticing the shelves of bar supplies and extra stock of non-alcoholic drinks as he shifted around to pull Jewel into his arms. Since there didn't seem to be a lock on the door, he quickly decided to press her back against it to keep anyone else from being able to come in the room and interrupt their make-out session.

Before Dion could pick Jewel up, however, she had other plans, lightly pushing him back as she leaned against the door and reached under her dress to slide her panties down her legs. She quickly stepped out of them, sticking them in his pocket to keep them from getting dirty on the floor of the storeroom, so she could put them back on afterward. "Gotta keep these clean to contain any drippage when we head back out to dance," she informed him as she looked up at him with an impish gleam in her blue-gray eyes.

"Fuck," Dion groaned, quickly unbuttoning his jeans, and shoving them and his boxer briefs down his thighs, freeing his hard cock, which seemed to grow an extra inch from the thought of his cum dripping down her legs while they danced. "I hope you're ready, Jewel, 'cause I don't think we have time for much foreplay."

He pushed her dress up to her waist and ran his fingers through her dripping wet pussy, knowing he needed to give her at least one orgasm before she could take more than the head of his big dick. As he inserted first one finger and then two, Jewel wrapped her hands around his cock, spreading his precum down his shaft to lube him up for a sweet hand job at the same time he targeted her G-spot with his fingers.

"Then let's not waste time with foreplay," Jewel insisted, releasing his dick to place her hands on his shoulders and jump up to throw her legs around his waist. "Fuck me now, Dion."

Dion quickly pulled his fingers from her tight channel and caught her, gripping her ass with both hands to lift her up above his cock, so he could obey her command. "We'll do it your way this time, Jewel," he smirked as he pressed the head of his cock into her wet heat. "But when we get back to the B and B later, I plan on punishing you for taking charge now by withholding your orgasms during an extended foreplay session."

"Yes, Sir," Jewel panted, as he pushed inside her to the hilt, amazed by how easily she took him after only a few passes of his fingers to get her wet. "Sorry, Sir."

Dion chuckled and covered her mouth with his, knowing they needed to limit the noise they made to keep from being overheard by anyone going to the restrooms right outside the storeroom. He kissed her passionately as he pressed her upper back against the door, hoping the brutal pace he set wouldn't cause the door to bang in the frame and draw attention to them.

He soon lost himself in the tight glove-like feel of her pussy clenching around his cock, no longer consciously aware if they were making too much noise or not. Nothing else mattered but the exquisite experience of having Jewel come multiple times on his big dick before he finally exploded in ecstasy inside her.

"Come on, D," Jewel implored him, bringing him out of the memory by taking his hand and pulling him down the hallway. "Let's go let everyone know we're here, and hopefully, they'll leave early so we can recreate a few more memories later."

Dion was slightly disappointed at not being able to enjoy those memories right then. But as he followed the sway of her hips, appreciating how she filled out the eggplant-colored dress she wore, which almost exactly matched his shirt, he had to admit that he was looking forward to spending the rest of the evening with her, even if part of that time included mingling with friends before he could get her alone and naked again.

~~~

Julie hated that she couldn't take advantage of Dion remembering their storeroom antics from the previous year as she watched the feelings of euphoria cross his face in the hallway at Tully's. But as much as she wanted to pull him back to the storeroom right then, she knew if they dawdled any longer before joining her family and their friends, then they'd definitely get caught in the act of reenacting the memory. So, she did the responsible thing and insisted they go hang out, dance, and play a game or two of pool.

After stopping back at the bar to order her a mocktail and Dion a bottle of water, they joined Jen, Becky, Josh, Cait, Charlotte, and Ian at a table in the back room. Apparently, JoJo and Brody were having a sleepover with Memmaw and Pappaw, so their parents could all go out. And being the good friends they were to Dion, her family had chosen a table in the back, where the music wasn't as loud, hoping to decrease his chances of having an episode.

"You alright, D?" Josh asked as soon as they took their seats.

"Yeah, just got sidetracked by memories hitting before we could order our drinks and head back here," Dion replied with a smile.

"Oh, please!" Jen rolled her eyes dramatically. "They were making out in the hall between the bar and the bathrooms when I found them."

"Reliving our first kiss after he remembered it," Julie explained to her family, leaning her head on Dion's arm as a few of their friends joined them.

"Not the only memory I hope to recreate tonight," Dion teased, brushing his lips over the top of her head as he pulled her hand onto his leg, holding it there with his, so she couldn't explore a little higher on his thigh to tease his dick.

"I can get behind recreating a few memories here," Ian agreed, wrapping his arm around Charlotte.

"Yeah, well, there'll be no recreating the night Judy was possibly conceived while I'm too big to fit in the storeroom," Charlotte disagreed, not lowering her voice enough for only Ian to hear her over the music the way she seemed to think she had.
~~~

"Are you saying Judy was conceived in the storeroom here at Tully's?" Becky gasped, her eyes bugging out as she gaped at her sister in shock.

"It was either here during James and Randi's bachelor and bachelorette party or the next day at church," Ian gloated, smirking when Char blushed and tried to shush him.

"Wait, ya'll disappeared at the same time at Char and Ian's party," Becky pointed out, waving her finger at Julie and Dion. "Did ya'll conceive the twins in the storeroom here, too?"

"No, Jewel told me the time I remember hooking up in the storeroom here was at Rick and Fiona's party at the end of June," Dion replied. "And our twins weren't conceived until the day after labor day."

"And we couldn't use the storeroom at Char and Ian's party because it was already occupied," Julie added, unsure who among their friends and family members might have utilized the space then. *Although, now that I see how Jen's trying to look inconspicuous right now, I have to wonder if that was when she told me she'd kissed Liam. And if they did more than kiss, since apparently Dion and I aren't the only ones who've hooked up in there.*

"Don't look at us," Josh insisted, shaking his head, and motioning between himself and Cait, as everyone else at the table looked around, trying to see who might have hooked up in the storeroom on the last day of August. "We weren't together until after Char and Ian's wedding."

"And I wasn't comfortable enough out in public for a quickie in the storeroom here until Dean and Allissa's bachelor and bachelorette party," Cait added, blushing, and covering her mouth when she realized what she said.

"Damn, I knew Leo said he had a problem with not being able to restock during those parties, but I didn't realize it was 'cause the storeroom is the hot hookup spot now," Aiden Walker chuckled. "Not that I'll be using it, since it seems like it's only for couples who end up getting married, or having babies, or both. And I don't plan on doing any of that anytime soon."

"Just don't hook up with Jen or Becky and you should be safe," Kayla warned Aiden, giggling lightly. "Since it just seems to be the Burlesons having a baby boom recently."

Leah Mae Wright

"Yeah, I'm not touching that conversation with a ten-foot pole," Luke Walker chimed in. "So, how 'bout them Mustangs? Anyone think the new team can make it to the finals this year?"

As the guys delved into a conversation about the new ice hockey team in San Antonio, Julie convinced Dion to take a spin on the dance floor to reenact a few more of their memories from the various joint bachelor and bachelorette parties they'd both attended. Since the only ones he hadn't attended in the last year-plus were Bobby & Brooklyn's and Justin & Amy's, they had lots of memories of dancing together to recall besides the first night they met, when they attended Anthony & Kay's joint bachelor and bachelorette party.

Not that she really wanted him to remember the few minutes they spoke at Dean & Allissa's party. Since they'd worked everything out, she kinda felt bad about being such a bitch to him that night, especially since she felt like her tirade, when they saw each other again after a month of no contact, was what actually triggered his narcoleptic episode.

"I'm sorry for the way I acted when you first came back here," Julie apologized, hiding her face in Dion's chest, and fighting the tears that she blamed on her guilt being amplified by her pregnancy hormones. "If I hadn't been such a bitch that first night, then you might not have had that episode."

"Hey, Jewel, don't cry," Dion crooned, releasing her hand to lift her chin, so she had to look him in the eyes. "None of my episodes were your fault. Yeah, the narcolepsy is triggered by anxiety, but you've never caused me any anxiety, unless you count when I was afraid you were merely a figment of my imagination before I came back here as anxiety. It was mostly sensory overload that triggered all my narcolepsy naps, not you or anything you might have said that night."

"You can't tell me that being yelled at to leave me alone in the middle of a crowded bar with music blaring and dance floor lights flashing didn't add to the sensory overload," Julie argued, shaking her head, and stopping their slow two-step in the middle of the dance floor. "If I'd have been a bit more empathetic to your injuries and given you the chance to explain what happened from your perspective, then maybe we could have moved back to the back room or down the hall to talk, instead of prolonging the sensory overload, and prevented you having a sleep attack right then."

"No, I don't think so," Dion countered, moving them off the dance floor and out of the way of the other patrons, who continued dancing. "If I was bombarded with memories when I first walked in here that night the way I was tonight, then there wasn't anything anyone could do to stop the episode, even if the music and lights were turned off. You've gotta understand, back then, it didn't take much of anything to trigger the blackouts, even something as simple as looking in my refrigerator and not being able to figure out what I wanted to drink. And it was actually a few days later when I realized I was having memories come back when I wasn't in bed sleeping, so I imagine having that many memories trying to hit me at once probably triggered my body to go to sleep. And would have triggered me regardless of where I was when it happened. So, it was absolutely *not your fault*."

He sat down in the nearest chair, pulling her onto his lap before hugging her close. Being wrapped in his big, strong arms made Julie feel safe in a way she hadn't even realized she'd needed, assuaging her guilt whether she deserved it or not. She snaked her arms around his torso, basking in the comfort he gave her.

"Besides, until I started my narcolepsy medicine, the only way to stop those episodes was touching you, so that should prove that you were my cure all along, and not the cause of any of them." Dion kissed her temple before resting his cheek on the top of her head. "But if you want more proof of just how perfect you are for me, I think we might be able to sneak off to the storeroom, so I can give you a *long, hard* example of how you keep me from having a narcolepsy episode better than even my meds."

Julie couldn't help but laugh when she felt his dick twitch under her butt. "I thought you said you wanted more with me than just getting in my pants?"

"Yeah, I love you and want everything with you, Jewel," Dion asserted, as she lifted her head from his chest to look into his eyes, which suddenly gleamed with mischief. "But I figured, since you technically aren't wearing pants, it'd be okay to get in your panties, too."

"I do love it when you get in my panties," Julie drawled, pulling her right hand from behind his back to place it over his heart. "Almost as much as I love you."

They pressed their lips together in what started out as a sweet way to show their affection. No kiss between Julie and Dion could stay sweet for long, however, so she quickly pulled back before it got out of hand in front of an audience of her family, friends, and the Saturday night regulars at Tully's Roadhouse.

"I'm not sure how much sneaking we might be able to do right now," Julie teased, grinning at the man she planned to spend the rest of her life with, even if that life included extended trips to New Orleans to keep him from missing his family and hometown. "But if we can't make it to the storeroom without being caught, maybe we should head on back to the B and B…"

Julie's thought was cut off as Dion stood, lifting her in his arms at the same time and causing her to squeal as she threw her arms around his neck to hang on for the ride. "AAAHHH! Dion, what are you doing?"

"Checkin' to see if the storeroom's free first," Dion replied as he carried her across the bar toward the hallway. "And if not, then you need to think of a secluded spot we can go parking on this side of town, 'cause I don't think we'll be able to make it all the way back to the B and B."

"If the storeroom's not free, the code to the gate for the trails is three-eight-two-five," Leo Walker informed them from behind the bar just as they got to the hallway. "And if the numbers are too hard to remember, you can look at the letters on the keypad and use the corresponding numbers to spell out fuck."

"All these years," Julie laughed as Dion arched an eyebrow and changed direction, heading for the door. "I've avoided the trails, thinking my brothers and cousins wouldn't ever let ya'll give me the code. And all along, I coulda probably guessed it, if I'd ever tried."

"Tell the truth, Jewel," Dion chaffed, grinning, and wagging his eyebrows suggestively. "You were just saving this first for me, your soulmate."

"You've got me," Julie agreed, chuckling as she released his neck with one hand to rub it over her baby bump. "I've saved all the rest of my firsts for you, Dion. Especially the important ones." And she didn't just mean having babies…

Chapter Twenty-Five

Friday, February 14, 2020

On her way home from work, Julie stopped at the Heart's Destiny Birthing Center to see the newest member of the family born that morning. Since she had plans with Dion for later that night, she'd actually left the office early to have time to spend with her cousin Charlotte and baby Judy before going home to get ready for him to pick her up for their date. When she got to Charlotte's room, Julie was surprised to see that she wasn't the only Burleson who'd apparently had the same idea. With the exceptions of JJ, Jake, Anthony, and Anthony's family, who were all out of town at the moment, all of the Burlesons and Burleson-Campbells were either already there or arrived shortly after Julie, filling up the large birthing suite.

Julie had learned at her appointment ten days earlier that the birthing suites were designed to be a blend of a hospital labor and delivery unit and a holistic birthing center. Unlike most birthing centers, which weren't set up for surgical or neonatal care and would have to transfer higher-risk patients to actual hospitals for at-risk deliveries, the Heart's Destiny Birthing Center was set up like a small hospital so they could provide those services. And Doc Hayes hoped to eventually hire other professionals and expand until they had a full-fledged hospital.

But in the meantime, the birthing suites were set up more like the comfortable rooms used for births in non-hospital settings, with a second bed for dad to be able to spend the night with mom and baby, and plenty of seating scattered around the room, so the entire family could be present during an uncomplicated birth, if the expectant mother wanted them there. And the only time anyone technically had to leave the suite was if there was a complication that required the mother to be wheeled down to the surgical suite for a C-section.

Technically, having twins was considered a high enough risk pregnancy that the doctor had told her she'd be in the birthing suite for most of the time she was in labor, but would be wheeled down to the surgical suite when she was dilated to ten centimeters, just in case things changed suddenly and the second baby had to be delivered via C-section. So, if she wanted, the rest of the family could wait in her birthing suite, instead of the waiting room downstairs, while she and Dion were in the surgical suite to have their daughters. Since she hadn't been told that when any of the other babies in her family were born in the last eight months, Julie assumed her cousin, sister-in-law, and cousins-in-law had all chosen to only have their spouses in the room with them for even the early stages of labor.

Although, since she went into labor in the middle of the night, I suppose Kay could have left it open for us to come in whenever we woke up and found out she was in labor. But then when she had to have a C-section with Sam before any of us made it up here, we weren't given any instructions where to wait. I'll have to ask her when she gets back in town next week.

I should also ask Dr. Magnum if there's a way I can set restrictions on who is, and who isn't, allowed to come back here when I'm actively in labor. I mean, I wouldn't mind having any of my family visit while I'm just having the early contractions. But once my feet are in the stirrups for Dr. Magnum to check how far dilated I am, I think Dion's the only guy I'd want back here 'cause my dad, uncles, brothers, and cousins really don't need to see my lady parts. And I know they won't be able to go back when we're wheeled to the surgical suite for me to start actually pushing them out, so it won't be a big deal if they wait in my birthing suite.

Unless…when would I attempt nursing them the first time? I don't want any of the guys in the room for that either. But it might be nice to have my mom, Jen, or any of the rest of my girl tribe there when my daughters are born and to help me with learning to nurse my babies. Yep, I definitely need to ask about limiting who can come into the birthing suite.

Julie shifted in her seat, trying to find a position where the girls weren't resting on her bladder and making her feel like she had to pee every five minutes. With only a little over three months left in her pregnancy, her belly was really starting to round out, making her feel like she looked farther along than she was at twenty-five weeks. But since she was finally past the seafood aversion she'd experienced early on, she wasn't going to complain about feeling like she was carrying two big, Dion-sized babies. At least, not until she actually reached the third trimester and got so big that she was miserable and needed help doing everyday activities, like tying her shoes because she couldn't bend over far enough to reach them.

"I can't wait 'til it's my turn in that bed," Julie sighed, rubbing her hand over where her daughters were kicking.

"How far along are you now?" Amy inquired as she rocked one of her twin sons, while Justin held the other. They still looked so much alike that she couldn't tell which was which without asking for the onesie color code her brother and his wife had picked for that day, even after spending a week taking care of them overnight and being the one to pick the color code for their clothes first thing each morning. She'd just assumed that nobody else had mixed up their colors when they'd cared for them during the day and went by what color they were wearing when she and Dion took over to determine which baby was which when she assigned new colors for the next day.

"Twenty-five weeks," Julie smiled. "Finally in that sweet spot between the morning-sickness phase and the too-big-to-tie-my-shoes phase."

"Oh, I remember that phase," Brooklyn giggled. "I think it was Bobby's favorite part of my pregnancy."

"No, that was the second trimester, horny phase," Bobby corrected, leaning over to kiss his wife's temple as she held their daughter, Maddie.

"Yeah, exactly," Brooklyn confirmed with a slight blush to her cheeks.

"That phase does fall right in between the morning-sickness phase and the too-big-to-tie-our-shoes phase," Charlotte confirmed, smirking at Ian. "And it seems to be the favorite phase of most men."

"That's the phase Anthony called the hobbit-sex phase, when I first talked to him about Amy being pregnant," Justin chuckled. "'Cause it's when pregnant women want sex before breakfast, after breakfast, elevenses, as a nooner, as a mid-afternoon snack, before dinner, after dinner, and as a midnight snack."

Julie couldn't disagree with that assessment, even though she wished she wasn't hearing about it from her brother, or that her cousin had coined the term. Apparently, nobody else in the room could disagree either, most of them chuckling, including her.

"So, um," Josh spoke up as the laughter died down. "While we've got most everyone here, we wanted to let ya'll know that we're adding another Burleson baby to the family in August."

Oh, wow! Due in August? That means she got pregnant in, like, November or December. How on earth did Cait keep that a secret for so long?

"Oh my goodness! Really?" Hazel beamed as she rocked baby Judy in her arms.

"Yes, really," Cait giggled as she pulled a stack of ultrasound pictures from her purse and passed them around the room.

"Michael Ian Burleson-Campbell, don't you dare laugh!" Charlotte shouted from her hospital bed, pointing at her husband as she gave him a dirty look.

"Sorry, Princess, I can't help it," Ian chuckled as he stood up and walked over to hug his sister, Cait. "Congratulations, Caitir. I can't wait to meet my next nephew or niece."

"Thanks, Mikey." Cait quickly returned the brief embrace, referring to her brother by the nickname he'd used prior to changing his name when he was evading the cartel and before he moved to Heart's Destiny.

Once they released the hug, Ian shook Josh's hand to congratulate him on his impending fatherhood. "Your little one will be the lucky number thirteen to help me win a bet with Charlotte."

"What?" Josh looked confused by Ian's mention of a bet.

Julie was a little curious about what they were talking about, too, but she was more eager to see the ultrasound pictures of Cait and Josh's baby, so she didn't ask any questions, assuming either Josh would ask them, or Charlotte and Ian would explain without anyone having to ask.

"You may have won the bet, but this just proves I was justified in naming Judy after Memmaw," Char huffed, as Ian walked back over to her bed and brushed his lips over her forehead.

"Ya'll are gonna hafta explain this one to the rest of us," Bobby pointed to Char and Ian.

Or Bobby will ask the questions for us, Julie thought just as the first of the ultrasound pictures reached her. She looked down at the tiny little black-and-white blob that she could now recognize as a baby after seeing the same stage of pregnancy in her own ultrasound pictures, only half listening to the rest of the conversation.

"Does this have something to do with the dreams you had about Memmaw last year?" Becky asked Charlotte.

"Yes," Char confirmed, nodding at Becky. "And while trying to distract me during labor, Ian bet me that Josh and Cait would be the ones to have the thirteenth of the great-grandbabies Memmaw told me she'd have by Christmas this year."

"Wait a minute, I'm lost," Josh interjected, still looking confused. "What dreams? And when did you talk to Memmaw about us all having kids? Hell, we were all still kids when she passed away."

"I didn't actually talk to her about it when we were kids," Charlotte explained. "But last year I had a bunch of dreams where she sat on the side of my bed and talked to me about the future of our family. She told me I'd met my soulmate and was going to give birth to a daughter within the next year. And then within a couple of months, I found out I was pregnant, so I decided if she was right about the baby being a girl, I was going to name her Judy after Memmaw."

"It was Char's way of getting back at Memmaw for proving her wrong about prophetic dreams," Becky elaborated, reminding Julie of the conversation they'd had on the same subject while moving Anthony's family into their new home on the south side of the ranch back in April of the previous year.

"Anyway, she also told me that she'd have thirteen great-grandbabies by Christmas this year, and three dozen great-grandbabies by the time we're all finished falling in love and having babies," Charlotte went on. "At the time, I thought there was no way we'd get to thirteen kids added to the family in less than two years, 'cause Anthony and Bobby were the only two of us who'd gotten married, with Anthony adopting Tia and Maria, and then both Kay and Brook announcing they were having babies. I didn't think there was any way we'd go from four to thirteen without everyone else getting married by the end of the year."

Charlotte held up both hands, but only put up four fingers, as she started counting off the rest of the kids being added to the family. "But then Anthony and Kay adopted Antonio, bringing the total up to five." She extended her thumb on the first hand. "And then I found out I was pregnant right before Justin and Amy announced they were having twins, so the total jumped to eight." She extended three fingers on the other hand. "A couple weeks later, Brody asked me to adopt him, making it nine. Then we found out about JoJo, ten." Char held up both hands with all her digits extended before reaching over for Ian's hand to use his fingers to add the next three. "Then Julie made her Halloween announcement of twins, bringing the total up to twelve." Ian extended two fingers on the hand Char had pulled over by hers. "And now ya'll just announced number thirteen." Ian extended another finger. "So, now I have to wonder if Memmaw really had to have visited me in my dreams to tell me the exact number of great-grandkids she'd have by Christmas."

"I just hope I get a few more from the twenty-three that are yet to come than I did from the first thirteen, so I can have as many grandkids as Hazel," Julie's mom giggled. "And hopefully, things will work out with JJ and Deanna, so they can give us the first of the next batch at the beginning of next year."

Julie looked over at her twin sister, Jen, and single cousin, Becky, and wondered if one of them would beat JJ and Deanna to the maternity ward. Or if Jake would have an accidental baby while in the Navy like his twin brother, Josh. Considering she was pretty sure Kara wanted to make the fake dating she and Jake were doing every time he was home on leave into something real, Julie hoped Jake wasn't taking any chances of history repeating itself. *Unless she got brave enough to ask him to be her sperm donor like she mentioned back in October, and he's exclusively giving it to her now?*

"Yeah, I wouldn't hold your breath on that hope, Mom," Jen scoffed. "From the HR complaints I've been told to expect since JJ's been in Tulsa, Deanna's just as likely to sue him for sexual harassment as she is to go on a date with him."

"Well, then I guess we need to focus on finding your Mr. Right next, so you can help me catch up in the grandbaby count," their mom teased. "Jon, are there any men who work for OK Oil that would be good candidates for Jen's Mr. Right? Maybe we need to send her up there to personally deal with any HR issues JJ's been causing?"

"Yeah, I'm just as likely to fall for some office worker in Tulsa, as Becky is to fall for the leading man in one of the movies filming here in town later this year." Jen rolled her eyes. "And neither one of us have any plans to participate in the Burleson baby boom anytime soon."

"Yeah, and if I was interested in finding my Mr. Right, I can one-hundred percent guarantee he won't be Rafe Kincade," Becky added, mentioning the actor that was recently cast as the male lead, Jeremiah Brown, in *Heart's Desire*, which would be the first project filming in Heart's Destiny. "So, you'll be better off trying to figure out which of the previous procreators are ready to have more kids than to look to those of us who are still single for your next grandbabies."

Yeah, you won't fall for Rafe Kincade, Julie thought, stifling a snicker. *That's why you dragged Jen and I to see both of his action-adventure films last year, when none of us are big action-adventure fans. Either you're protesting too much because both our mothers are in the room, or you're really pissed about whatever bad press he's gotten recently that's led him to try to change his image by signing on for a role in a historical romance.*

"It won't be us," Bobby pointed out. "We're focusing on helping way more kids than we could ever adopt by expanding the Ashbury Foundation for the next few years before we plan on having or adopting baby number two."

"It won't be us either," Justin added, shaking his head at their mother while pointing back and forth between himself and his wife, Amy. "We wanna get the boys walking, talking, and out of diapers before we'll even start thinking about expanding our family, so Amy went right back on birth control as soon as Dr. Magnum okayed it."

"Don't look at me," Julie tacked on when her mother's gaze landed on her. "I still have to birth the girls before I can even think about having more babies. Besides, after having Jerry and Jonah overnight for a week, I agree with Justin and Amy about needing to have the first two walking, talking, and out of diapers before giving them siblings."

Although, since I got pregnant while on birth control, maybe I should talk to Dion about doubling up the protection by using

501

condoms too, when I'm allowed to have sex again after the girls are born.

I should also probably talk to him about moving in with me before they're born, so I can have help getting him up and in the car if I go into labor while he's out cold from his narcolepsy meds. Not that having him there to keep from having someone else in the family trying to track him down at the B and B when I go into labor is the main reason I want him to move in, but it's definitely a big perk.

Although, it's been a while since he's said anything about us getting married or moving in together, so maybe he'd rather have his space. I mean, when we talked about his insecurities about his helpfulness during middle-of-the-night feedings a couple weeks ago, he implied that he'd be staying with me once the babies are born. But he certainly hasn't pushed to move in.

As the rest of her family fussed about which of them would have babies next, Julie went back over the various discussions she'd had with Dion, or that her family had with Dion back at the beginning of December, when they ignored her protests because they weren't back together yet, trying to figure out why he hadn't mentioned any kind of timeline for progressing their relationship past the one or two nights a week that they spent together in his hotel room.

It was obvious how well we worked at cohabitating when he stayed that week with me to watch Jerry and Jonah. And since he said he plans on marrying me when he first re-met Dad back in December, shouldn't he be making plans to pop the question and suggest moving in now, so we can have our nightly routine down before the girls are born?

But then again, he was also the only one who seemed to be paying attention to my cues then. And he did specifically say something about not moving in until I'm ready. Maybe he's waiting for me to give him the green light before popping the question?

Well, shit! It's Valentine's Day. What better day to tell him I love him and want him to move in with me? What better day for him to say yes to moving in, and then top my declaration of love with a marriage proposal? Hopefully, he's already bought the ring and has just been carrying it around, waiting on me to let him know I'm ready.

Armed with a plan for giving Dion her extra garage door opener as an additional Valentine's present on top of the Godiva chocolate gift basket she'd planned to put together for him when she bought one of every gift box in the Godiva store on her lunch break the day before, Julie wished Judy a happy birthday, gave Charlotte and Cait congratulatory hugs, and excused herself from the family gathering. She left just in time to pick up everything else she needed for Dion's Valentine's surprise, get home to put it together, and get ready before he picked her up for their date.

~~~

Dion spent the last couple of weeks really focused on building up his self-esteem, wanting to be the confident, competent man Jewel needed him to be, now that he felt like he'd reached the point in his recovery where he felt like he was as close to his old self as he could get. That meant he did extra sessions with his therapist, both in the office and on the ranch, between spending every free moment he could with Jewel when she didn't have work or other obligations, going to his follow-up doctor's appointments, spending time with Susan and Hazel to increase his confidence in caring for children before his and Jewel's were born, looking into the various options for opening an art gallery in town, and actually spending time drawing.

In addition to drawing his memories with Jewel, which he now only did when he was in his room alone so he could keep the pieces private, he'd started drawing more commercial art pieces, such as landscapes and the various buildings around Heart's Destiny while he was out and about in the community. While he planned to give some of his memory drawings to the people he cared about, most of which would go to Jewel, he didn't really want his private memories with her on display for all the world to see in the gallery, even the ones that weren't sexual in nature.

Not that he planned to put that many of his own pieces on display there, except at the beginning, when he was still trying to find local artists to showcase in the space. So far, he'd only learned the names of the art teachers in the local schools, which had only happened after talking to Charlotte and Ian after working with Brody and JoJo on caricature drawing during his time helping with the childcare on the ranch the week before. But hopefully, once he finalized a deal with
~~~

Tully Walker for gallery space in one of the downtown buildings, he'd be able to talk them into displaying their work and introducing him to their best students for him to be able to add the work of more local artists.

While his therapists seemed to think focusing on displaying his own artwork would help his self-esteem most, Dion knew that once the twins were born, he wouldn't have time to devote to drawing as much as he'd need to in order to keep the gallery full. So, he was already putting plans in place to turn the gallery over to a manager, knowing he'd actually get more personal satisfaction from providing a full-time job to someone in the community, and possibly several people when cleaning crews, framers, and various suppliers were given more work, as well as a way to sell their artwork, and hopefully make a living from their passion projects, to countless other artists in the area.

While Dion enjoyed drawing, he didn't consider it a passion project. It felt like more of a way for him to remember the things his brain injury tried to take away from him, while honoring the lessons he'd learned from his mom as a child. While he might still struggle some with feeling worthy of living his dream life, with Jewel's constant reassurance, he was getting closer to believing they could have a near-perfect life together. A life where he could spend all his time working on improving himself while focusing on his passions.

Drawing and opening a gallery were nice hobbies to round out his life, but his true passion projects would always be loving Jewel and their children, spending quality time with his family, and passing on the life lessons he'd learned over the years to the next generation. While he might not be able to do everything he wanted to do in order to be the perfect husband and father, he loved Jewel and their children enough to keep trying, knowing she'd accept his shortcomings and love him anyway.

Drawing our memories for Jewel is just one of the ways I plan on showing my love for her, he thought as he drove to the ranch to pick her up for their Valentine's Day date. *And hopefully, the massive amount of love I have for her and our babies will make up for my medical limitations. I might not be able to roughhouse with the kids, or teach any of them to wrestle, or stay up for stuff that happens in the middle of the night, but I'm more than capable of showing my love for them in other ways. Especially the more romantic ways with Jewel.*

Trying to make the first Valentine's Day he clearly remembered spending with Jewel extra romantic, he had flowers and a sapphire tennis bracelet to give her to start off the night, followed by reservations at the Heritage House restaurant in the bed and breakfast for dinner and the Sweetheart's Dance in the ballroom, with plans to finish off the night in his room with sparkling grape juice, various chocolates and chocolate-covered fruits, and giving her the sketchbook he'd completely filled with drawings of their intimate moments, letting her choose which scenes she might like to recreate.

He would have made reservations at a restaurant in San Antonio and skipped the Sweetheart's Dance to spend the whole evening alone with her, but he didn't want to take a chance on another flirtatious server or hostess putting a damper on their night. Spending part of their evening with whomever among her family and their friends who might attend the Sweetheart's Dance would be a much better experience than getting irritated by the fans that seemed to interrupt almost every date they had outside of Heart's Destiny.

As he parked and walked up to her door, carrying the flowers in one hand and the gift box in the other, Dion wondered what they'd done for Valentine's Day the year before. *Since we were trying to keep our relationship secret, did we even celebrate it together? And if so, did I do better or worse with the gifts and romance than I have planned for tonight?*

Jewel surprised him by opening the door before he could figure out how to knock or ring the doorbell with his hands full. "Oh, Dion, how on earth did you manage to come up with purple flowers when most people are going with red or pink for Valentine's Day?"

"I had a nice long conversation with Florence at the flower shop about the different colors and meanings of various flowers when I was drawing the courthouse and downtown buildings a couple of weeks ago." Dion shrugged, walking in her door as he handed her the vase containing a mix of purple flowers, including roses, tulips, irises, calla lilies, and a few others that Dion didn't remember the names of at the moment. "And told her I wanted a bouquet in your favorite color that represented love, romance, devotion, and happiness for Valentine's Day."

He knew there were a lot more meanings behind the flowers, like royalty, elegance, grace, and pleasure, but he didn't figure he needed to list them all out for her right then. If she was really curious, they could go by the flower shop the next day to ask Florence about all the different flowers she'd used in the bouquet and their individual meanings.

"Well, they're absolutely beautiful," Jewel gushed, smiling up at him. "Thank you."

She carried the vase straight to the dining room table as he closed the door behind them, wanting to have her open the other present before they left for dinner. "I hope you like the other present I have for you, too," he mumbled as he followed her through the sitting room to the dining room, handing her the box containing the bracelet as soon as she placed the flowers on the center of the dining table.

He was nervous about not having picked a bracelet that matched the necklace he gave her for Christmas or the engagement ring he'd special ordered, which was still at the jewelers just waiting on the extra stones from her necklace once the babies were born. Considering the only other jewelry he'd remembered getting her so far also contained emeralds, he probably should have stuck with the same stones. But when he saw the sapphire bracelet, it reminded him too much of her typical eye color for him to pick anything else. While he loved how her eyes turned more of a stormy gray when she was aroused, he also loved the brilliant blue they were most of the time. So, he hoped the dazzling blue stones in the bracelet would show her how he felt.

"I'm sure I'll love it," she beamed, setting the box down on the table to grab a similarly shaped, if slightly larger, box and the largest gift basket Dion had ever seen from a side table to hand them to him. Seriously, the wicker basket was as big as a laundry hamper and wrapped in cellophane, so she could place the box on top to use both hands to pick it up. "Just as I hope you'll love your gifts."

Dion quickly took the basket, worried it was too heavy for her to safely lift while pregnant. He peered through the cellophane around the gift basket to see several different boxes of assorted chocolates as he placed it down on the table and waited for her to open the bracelet before he opened his gift box from her.

Guess we were at least thinking along the same lines on something tonight. Dion smiled, stifling a chuckle as he thought about the chocolate assortment waiting in his hotel room for them for later that night. Seeing the chocolates must have triggered a memory from their last Valentine's Day together, or at least, the day closest to Valentine's Day that they'd met up in a hotel room.

"I didn't figure you'd have room to carry the flowers and teddy bears most people exchange this time of year while you're on tour," Jewel smiled as she handed him a heart-shaped box of chocolates, *"but I knew you'd love the chocolates."*

"They're perfect," Dion grinned, taking the box. *"Now I wish I'd have thought to get you some too, so we'd have enough to share."*

"Oh, Dion, it's beautiful," Jewel gushed as soon as she got the box opened, bringing Dion out of the memory. "But now I have to go change my necklace and earrings to the ones you got me last Valentine's Day, so I'll match."

"I got you sapphire jewelry last Valentine's Day?" Dion really wished he could remember more of how they'd celebrated.

"Technically, we celebrated a few days before Valentine's Day last year, on Monday the eleventh," Jewel explained as she pulled the bracelet from the box and motioned for him to help her put it on. "'Cause you were in a city without a Burleson subsidiary for me to have an excuse to go see you on the fourteenth. So, while I hosted a Galentine's Day party with my sister, cousins, and single girlfriends, you and a few of the other single wrestlers volunteered to watch the kids of the married wrestlers, so they could celebrate. But it wasn't a big deal that we didn't get to do more than text on the day of, since you were in town for the pay-per-view in San Antonio the weekend before. Unfortunately, I was stuck in Georgia negotiating for Burleson to buy Ashbury Enterprises after Brooklyn's dad was arrested."

Dion wished he had a calendar in front of him to figure out the dates as she told him the whole story about Brooklyn and her family issues that had been national news the year before, but he didn't really care about all the drama at the moment. He was more interested in hearing about when and how they'd celebrated Valentine's Day instead.

"Anyway, it was a whole big thing," Jewel went on, waving her hands around as she talked. "But I basically only got back in town in time to watch you wrestle the Sunday before Valentine's, then we all went out to eat after the show to celebrate James and Randi getting engaged in the middle of the ring, so we didn't get much alone time that night. Which was why I scheduled meetings with our auto dealership division in Houston for the next day, so we could have our early Valentine's celebration on Monday evening, when you were able to leave the arena early because of not being scheduled to wrestle."

"And what did we do for Valentine's then?" Dion wondered aloud, sneaking in his question when she paused to take a breath.

"We ordered in room service and exchanged gifts," Jewel replied with a wide grin. "Only I felt lame for just getting you a heart-shaped box of chocolates when you gave me a sapphire earring and necklace set, which I'm going to go put on right now, so I match."

She darted out of the room and up the stairs before he could get a word in edgewise, leaving him standing there unable to open his presents until she returned. *Good to know being pregnant hasn't zapped her energy level even the slightest,* he thought with a chuckle as he sat down in a dining chair to wait for her return.

So, I got her sapphire jewelry last Valentine's Day, too? Guess I subconsciously remembered that when I went shopping this year to get another piece to match. Thinking about the jewelry she mentioned helped him flash right back to the previous year.

Monday, February 11, 2019

"Oh, Dion, these are gorgeous!" Jewel gushed after opening the box containing the sapphire earrings and necklace.

"I wasn't sure if you'd like the stones or not, since they aren't your birthstone or your favorite color," Dion explained as he watched her eyes turn from the brilliant blue they normally were to the stormy sky blue-gray that he hoped only he ever got to see. "But the blue reminded me of your eyes, well most of the time. But I've never seen a gemstone that matches the blue-gray your eyes turn when you're aroused."

"Can you help me with the necklace clasps?" Once again, Julia brought him out of the memory as she bounded back into the room with her earrings changed and holding the sapphire necklace out to him.

"Of course," Dion agreed, taking the necklace, and opening the clasp as she turned around and lifted her hair. When he slipped it around her neck, he noticed that it was more of a choker, while the caged-hearts necklace was long enough for the charm to sit just above her cleavage. "Since the chains are two different lengths, you could leave them both on if you want."

"Oh, good. Then I don't have to take our family necklace off," Jewel agreed, dropping her hair and turning around after he got the choker clasped around her neck. "Now open your presents."

"Yes, dear," Dion repeated the two words her father had told him he would need to say most often to maintain the peace and harmony in their relationship. "Do I need to open the chocolates first, so you can have a few to tide you over 'til dinner? Or the box first?"

"Well, I did get one of every gift assortment in the Godiva store, so there's plenty there to share," she giggled as she nodded toward the extremely large gift basket. "But I actually snacked on a few from the box that's still up in my bedroom 'cause it wouldn't fit in the basket, even without using the filler I bought, wrongfully thinking the basket was too big for all of them. So, I can probably survive without anything else until dinner."

"In that case, I'll open the box first," Dion chuckled at her admission of keeping a box of chocolates for herself. Not that he minded. While he loved chocolate, he loved watching the enjoyment she got from eating it even more. So, all things considered, he was probably going to feed her at least half the chocolates in the basket anyway.

As he picked up the box to start unwrapping it, Jewel bewildered him by pulling out the chair beside him and using it to balance as she kneeled on the dining room floor. *Holy shit! She's down on one knee. Damn it! She's not the one who's supposed to propose! And I can't yet, 'cause her engagement ring won't be ready until after the babies are born!*

Fuck it! If she proposes, then I'll say yes and explain why she'll have to wait for her engagement ring.

Dion tried to hide his nervous excitement as he tore the paper from the box. He wasn't sure he was quite as successful hiding his confusion when he got the box open to find a black gadget with a silver clip on the back and gray buttons on what he assumed was the front. *Is this a remote for something? Or maybe a garage door opener?*

"Big Daddy, will you move in with me, Zoe, and Elena?" Jewel looked up at him imploringly with her hands on her belly covering their babies. "I would have given you a key to the house, but since we never lock the doors, I don't even have one of those. So, I thought the garage door opener for you to be able to park in my garage was the next best thing."

"Yes, I will happily move in with you, Jewel," Dion replied, grinning with relief that she'd found a way to move their relationship forward without stealing his thunder by being the one to propose marriage. "But please, don't teach our daughters to call me Big Daddy. You can call me that in the bedroom if you want, but I'd rather not have anything I associate with the size of my dick coming out of our daughters' mouths."

"Deal," Jewel laughed as Dion bent down to seal their new relationship status with a kiss.

He kept the kiss chaste and brief, placing the garage door opener on the table before gripping her under her arms to lift her from the floor. "Now, do you want to stay one more night at the B and B and move me in tomorrow? Or do you wanna skip the Sweetheart's Dance and move me in tonight right after dinner, so we can celebrate Valentine's Day in *our* bedroom?"

"We're gonna hafta skip the dance and move you tonight," Jewel decided. "'Cause I spent all the time I had after visiting Charlotte and baby Judy at the birthing center this afternoon, trying to get all your chocolates in that basket without stacking it too tall to cover it in cellophane, and didn't have time to pack an overnight bag."

"Then we should probably take some plastic containers with us to pack up the assortment of chocolate-covered fruit and truffles I have waiting in my room, so we can leave the trays they came on at the B and B." Dion knew he could probably take the silver trays and return them later without upsetting Mandi Hunter, but he didn't want to take a chance on damaging them by washing them wrong and tarnishing the silver, or forgetting to return them in a timely manner if they didn't eat all the fruit that night.

"So, I wasn't the only one who thought of chocolates this year," Jewel giggled once more, heading into the kitchen, presumably to get the plastic containers.

"No, I have a feeling we'll still be eating the chocolates we bought for tonight in three months when the babies are born," Dion chuckled, pocketing the garage door opener to put it in his Escalade before following Jewel to the kitchen to get what they needed to move him in and start living their lives together from then on.

~~~

Julie knew her parents would probably wonder why she hadn't made it to the Sweetheart's Dance as she'd told them she would. But as she carried in the last Tupperware container of chocolate-covered strawberries, which Dion only allowed her to carry in because she promised to only carry one Tupperware container at a time, while he moved the last of his luggage up to their now shared bedroom, she figured they could wait until the next morning to find out she'd spent the evening moving Dion in with her. She was too anxious to get everything unloaded and unpacked to take the time to text them now, eager to find out what the other surprise he'd mentioned having for her at bedtime was, and hoping it was a proposal. Now that she was ready to commit to moving their relationship forward, she wanted to be able to start planning a summer wedding, so she wouldn't feel rushed to do it, the way everyone else in her family seemed to throw together weddings in only a month or two.

She didn't have a preference for the cut or style of her engagement ring, knowing from the previous jewelry gifts that Dion had given her that she'd love whatever he picked because of how in sync their tastes were. While she wasn't sure many people would know it from just looking at the two of them, their tastes in most things were pretty similar. Yeah, they had different favorite colors, foods, and songs, but for the most part, they were both open to enjoying the other's favorites whenever they didn't perfectly align. But with the important stuff, like their ethics and priorities, things like loving each other and their families, and especially their sexual compatibility, they were perfectly attuned to one another.
~~~

Which was why it didn't surprise her one bit, when Dion hunted her down in the kitchen within a few minutes of carrying his bags upstairs, assuming he'd rushed through throwing his bags in the closet, and only unpacked what he needed for later that night. "Grab whatever chocolates and fruits you want to eat tonight," Dion commanded as he grabbed two champagne flutes from the cabinet, obviously as eager for the sexual part of their celebration to commence as she was right then.

"I think we'll stick to the chocolate-covered strawberries for now, and save the rest for when I'm not so full from dinner," Julie decided, not wanting to take the time to go through the different containers to put an assortment of truffles and fruits on a plate, which they might have to bring back down to put away if they didn't eat it all. Not when she could just carry up the one container that was already in her hands, and close it up without having to come back downstairs, if they got sidetracked with other things before they finished off the strawberries.

Dion veered off into the dining room instead of heading right back upstairs with Julie, ripping through the cellophane on the gift basket she'd put together for him to grab one of the assorted boxes of Godiva chocolates before quickly catching up with her on the stairs. "I wanna make sure we enjoy some of both our chocolate gifts tonight," he admitted with a grin as she looked to see which package he'd picked.

Of course, he picked one of the dark chocolate assortments first. For someone who freely admitted his ring name was trite and cliché, he certainly seems to love feeding into it with his choice of sweet treats. But since I know it's his way of taking back his power and laughing his way through life, instead of letting the haters and bigots get to him, I wouldn't want him to ever change.

When they got to the top of the stairs, she could see there was only low light coming from the bedroom, which made more sense when they stepped into the room and she realized he'd turned on and arranged a couple dozen flameless candles on every flat surface in the room. On the dresser, there was a bottle of sparkling grape juice, which he promptly opened as soon as he sat down the champagne flutes and box of chocolates in the space he left free of the flameless candles.

Julie put the Tupperware of chocolate-covered strawberries down beside the chocolates and took the flat, wrapped box he pulled from beside the dresser. She felt a little disappointment that it wasn't a ring box, but she covered her chagrin with a broad smile, assuming he'd framed one of his drawings for her due to the size and weight of the box.

He probably just doesn't have the ring yet, she assumed as she unwrapped the package in her hands. *I bet he didn't think I'd be ready to get engaged this soon, so he hasn't picked it out yet. No big deal. Now that we're living together, I'm sure he'll realize I'm ready soon enough.*

As soon as she got the paper off the box, Dion took it from her to throw away in the wastebasket beside the bed. When she lifted the lid to the box, she realized the extra weight of the present wasn't because of a frame around one of his drawings, but because he'd put a whole sketchbook in the box. *Why would he give me a whole sketchbook? Doesn't he need some of these drawings for the gallery he's planning to open?*

"This book was always meant to be for our eyes only, Jewel," Dion explained without her having to verbalize her questions. "From the first day I started drawing in it, I always intended to give it to you when I filled it up. At the time, I thought I'd finish the other one first and give it to you to help remind you of our good times together to help me win you back. Then once I got you to start talking to me again, I'd give you this one to move us along, back to what we had before. But then we were able to work things out before I could finish filling up either one of them, so I showed them to you long before I finished even half the drawings."

Dion paused long enough to shrug sheepishly. "So, when I finished this one just in time for Valentine's Day, I figured it was perfect timing to give it to you. I thought you might want to keep it in your bedside table to be able to flip through and pick your favorite memories of us that you might want me to recreate."

Julie lifted the book from the box and flipped the pages to see the drawings he'd added since the last time she looked at the ones in the first quarter of the book. He'd not only added more of their hotel room hookups from their past, but he'd also added their more recent rendezvous, like their backseat banging on the trails across from Lover's Lanes, the local bowling alley, and their ice cream antics at the bed and breakfast.

   While she would definitely be having him reenact those memories in the years to come, she thought back to the earlier times they'd incorporated champagne and chocolates or chocolate-covered strawberries into their foreplay, thinking they were more appropriate for Valentine's Day. She flipped back through the book until she found the drawing of her laid out on a massage table with the strawberries strategically placed over her intimate areas for him to eat them off of her, knowing that had to be from the day they conceived their babies, when they'd enjoyed eating and drinking from each other's bodies before covering them in massage oil. The next page had him laid out on a bed with her pouring the champagne on his abs before licking it off. She wondered if he realized they'd only used the bed for that activity on their early Valentine's celebration the year before, learning to move food play to surfaces that were easier to clean up after that, like the vinyl massage table or a large bathtub or shower enclosure.
   "I think we should combine a few of these," Julie finally decided. "Since we don't have a massage table here, like we did in the hotel on the day we made our babies, and my belly is too round to hold more than a navel-full of that grape juice, we'll definitely need to be in the bathtub for easy cleanup after, so we don't have a repeat of sleeping in sticky sheets, like we did in Houston for our early Valentine's last year."
   "Wait," Dion pointed to the drawing of him in the bed with her pouring champagne on his abs, "so this was on Valentine's last year? I knew it was a different day than the time we did similar activities on a massage table, but I didn't realize it was when we celebrated Valentine's Day before."
   "Yes, two different days," Julie agreed with a smile as Dion looked down at the drawing. "Last February, we used the chocolates I gave you, and we only ordered the champagne from room service. Then in September, you ordered chocolate-covered strawberries and champagne from room service."
   "And I preferred the chocolates, so I could open them up and spread the filling on your nipples before licking it off," Dion remembered, grinning as he took the sketchbook from her hands and placed it on the bed before handing her the two flutes of sparkling grape juice he'd

poured. "I was frustrated with having to chew the strawberry and swallow it before going back to licking you."

"Yeah, I suppose liquids and lickable foods work better for food play," Julie chuckled, remembering some of the same frustration with having to stop teasing Dion with her tongue to chew the strawberries back in September, as he put the chocolates on top of the container of strawberries and picked them both up, along with the bottle containing the rest of the grape juice. "We might be able to smear the fillings from the chocolates on one another, but I think we should save the strawberries for eating after to replenish our energy before round two."

"You are a brilliant woman, Jewel," Dion praised her, brushing his lips over her temple as he put the food items back down on the dresser before picking up just the box of chocolates and ushering her to the ensuite bathroom, which had been added when the house was updated several years before JJ moved in there.

Since her family had tried to maintain the same style as the house that had been built in 1906, the master bathroom had a clawfoot tub similar to the tub in the main bathroom, which was between the two smaller bedrooms that she'd designated as the nursery and a guest room for now. But instead of installing a shower head over the clawfoot tub like in the main bathroom, they'd built in a separate tiled shower in the corner behind the tub, since they had the extra room from taking half of the fourth bedroom for the closet and bathroom remodel. While she would prefer to rinse off in the shower, where she had a handheld sprayer attachment, after their food play, there wasn't room in the shower for either one of them to lay down. To be honest, she wasn't sure there was room for Dion to fully lay down in the tub, even though it was the biggest clawfoot tub available at the time it was installed.

Yeah, there's no way we're both gonna fit in there and have room to move, much less lick this stuff off each other. Shoot! While I'm pregnant, we're gonna be doin' good to just squeeze us both in there to soak and snuggle.

"On second thought, maybe we should wait to do this once the babies are born, and we can get a massage table and some plastic to put down to protect the floors," Julie suggested, motioning toward the bathtub before setting the two glasses on the vanity and rubbing her hands over her protruding belly. "'Cause I don't wanna take a chance on getting stuck in that tub, which I used to think was huge, but now looks way too small for the two of us and the twins."

Dion placed the chocolates and the bottle of grape juice on the vanity beside the glasses before placing his hands over hers to still her nervous movement. "I wasn't planning on getting in the tub, Jewel. You can't lay on your back right now, and I'm too big to lay on my back in that tub, so I was planning on doing what we could while standing, or kneeling, in the shower."

"Oh." Julie felt foolish for not having come to the same realization sooner, but any embarrassment she might have felt was quickly forgotten when Dion slid his hands down her sides to lift the hem of her red maternity dress. She lifted her arms as he swept it up over her head before dropping it in the hamper in the corner of the bathroom.

"Fuck, you're gorgeous, Jewel," Dion growled, his dark brown eyes roaming over her red lace bra and panties that she'd picked up specifically for that night.

With the way her body was changing with her pregnancy, she wasn't sure she'd still fit in them by the next week, or if her post-pregnancy body would ever fill them out once she lost the baby weight. But the heat in his gaze as he looked her over made them worth every penny she'd spent, even if she only got to wear them the one time. *Especially if the way he's looking at me right now means he wants to rip them off me. As wet as my panties are right now, they're pretty much ruined anyway, so he may as well destroy them.*

"And you're wearing way too many clothes," she retorted, deflecting the compliment as she reached up to remove his red tie before unbuttoning the matching shirt.

"You're welcome to remove them," he smirked, holding his arms out for her to remove his cufflinks next.

She placed the tie and cufflinks on the jewelry tray on the vanity before unbuckling his belt and pulling his shirttails from his black slacks. As she pushed his shirt from his shoulders, exposing his powerful torso, she hoped her hard nipples didn't tear through the lace cups of her bra. *Or maybe if they do, then Dion will get the message that this set is already ruined and fair game for tearing off me.*

After tossing his shirt in the hamper on top of her dress, Julie couldn't resist running her hands and mouth over Dion's defined pecs and abs. "How are you staying in such great shape when you're not wrestling or working out with the rest of the GWA anymore? Aren't you supposed to be gaining sympathy pregnancy weight with me?"

"I've still been going to Dean's house to workout at least every other day," Dion admitted, gripping her hips and toying with her panties. "But now that I'm living here and not at the B and B, where I was close to Dean's house most of the time, I should probably come up with a new routine, something I can do here or in town instead."

"I have a yoga mat and resistance bands you can use," Julie offered before trailing her tongue over his left nipple while squeezing his right pec with her hand. "But I don't know if that will be enough to help you maintain this muscle mass."

"No, I'll need to keep lifting weights for that," Dion informed her as he dipped his head to spread butterfly kisses over her collarbones. "Maybe while I'm looking at gallery space in town, I'll also have Tully show me places that can easily be turned into a gym, too, since that was my original plan for after I retired from wrestling."

"Something co-ed, so I can come workout with you to get back in shape after having the babies?" Julie wondered aloud as she moved her hands down to unfasten his slacks.

"Not just co-ed, but all-gendered, so none of our friends would ever feel unwelcome," Dion assured her before kissing his way up her neck as he slipped his fingers in her panties to tease her outer lips.

"Gawd, I love the way you're always so accepting and think of things like that," Julie cooed, trying not to get too lost in the feelings he was evoking before getting her next words out. "You should probably talk to Jen about how we can update our HR policies at Burleson to make the company more inclusive like that. Maybe even talk to Dad about how you plan to handle all-gendered restrooms and locker rooms, so we can make some upgrades to our buildings as well."

"Hmmm, yeah, but later." Dion sucked her neck, just below her ear. "Right now, I just wanna focus on us, celebrating our first night officially living together."

"Agreed." Julie pushed Dion's black slacks down off his hips, making sure to catch the waistband of his black boxer-briefs at the same time to free his massive erection.

His hand slipped from her panties when she squatted down to remove his pants and boxer briefs. But Dion still somehow managed to unfasten her bra while toeing out of his shoes and socks and stepping out of the rest of his clothing. While she was on her knees, she reached for his cock, completely forgetting their plans to use the sparkling grape juice and chocolates as part of their foreplay.

"Oh, no, not yet, Jewel," Dion chastised her, pulling her hands from his cock and helping her stand back up. "We've gotta finish undressing you and get in the shower first."

Julie stepped out of her shoes as Dion slid her panties down her legs, preserving them for her to try to wear another time. "I guess I shoulda told you that it was okay to rip this lingerie off me 'cause I'm not sure I'll fit in it for more than tonight."

"Guess we'll hafta plan that caveman-ripping-your-clothes-off fantasy for another time." Dion grinned as he stood back up and turned her toward the shower. He quickly opened the box of chocolates and grabbed a handful of them, picking up the flutes of grape juice in the other hand before following her into the shower, which neither one of them turned on. He placed the two glasses on the bench at the back of the shower, along with most of the chocolates, before dropping to his knees to draw on her body with the one he still held in his hand.

He drew hearts on her belly with the outer layer of chocolate, which apparently melted at body temperature, before moving up to her breasts to spread the white creamy filling over her nipples. When the first piece didn't go as far as he wanted, he picked up another and continued the same process until the majority of her torso was covered. Then he finally started the exquisite torture of licking it all off of her. She was so turned on by the whole experience that she had multiple mini O's as he sucked and licked her sensitive nipples, even though he'd barely touched her pussy earlier and didn't so much as graze her clit with his fingers as he licked off the candy.

By the time he cleaned off her breasts and belly, Julie didn't think she could handle him repeating the process with her pussy, knowing she'd explode in a massive orgasm from the first pass of his fingers spreading the chocolate or filling over her needy nub. "Dion, please, let it be my turn now."

"But I haven't gotten to your sweet center yet," Dion teased, trailing a single finger over the top of her mound.

She stilled his hand, not wanting to go over the edge with the massive orgasm she knew was coming until his dick was buried deep inside her. "That'll hafta wait for later. I'm too close and don't wanna come again until you're inside me. So, if I'm gonna eat any of this chocolate off of you, I need to do it now. And as soon as I'm done, you'll need to do an imitation of the Flash with how fast you get cleaned up and stick your dick in me."

"If you need my dick that bad, Jewel, I'm more than happy to wait for you to lick me later." Dion smiled suggestively as he motioned for her to turn around. "In fact, I think I need to sip my knock-off champagne from the small of your back to rinse down the candy I just ate before we do anything else. So, maybe you should bend over and put your hands on the bench, so you're in the perfect position for me to fill you up just as soon as I quench my thirst."

Julie didn't argue, feeling way too eager for the fucking that would follow his quick sip. As soon as she was turned around and bent over in the proper position, Dion poured a little of his sparkling grape juice on her low back, right above the crack of her ass, and bent over to lap it up. She hadn't realized her low back was that much of an erogenous zone until she felt Dion's tongue there, swirling around to get every drop and turning her on to the point that her pussy felt like a leaky faucet.

Oh, she knew she got tingles throughout her whole body whenever he placed his hand on the small of her back as he escorted her places. But she'd thought that was just from liking the way he seemed to claim her by doing the alpha move she'd previously thought was just a gentlemanly gesture. Having him lick her low back was damn near orgasmic.

"Can't wait, Dion, please," she begged, trying to hold off her release until he was inside her. "Don't wanna come until you're inside me."

Dion chuckled as he lifted his mouth from her low back. "Then I guess I won't torture you by making you wait." As soon as he stood, she felt him run the blunt head of his cock through her soaking wet folds, brushing her clit with just enough pressure to start the first waves of her orgasm before slowly pushing his dick inside her. "Fuck, Jewel, you're dripping wet. Is that all for me?"

"Yes, Dion, yes!" Julie cried out, amazed he was able to penetrate her when her inner walls were trying to push him out from the intensity of her release. "All for you. Always all for you."

Julie lost the ability to speak as Dion matched his pace with the intensity of her climax, slow as he had to fight the contractions of her body and speeding up as her body relaxed while she came back down the other side.

"Fuck, Jewel, I love the feel of you coming on my cock," Dion groaned, pounding into her like a man possessed as she floated in that state of nirvana only he could take her to, where she didn't have to think, or do anything, but feel him moving inside her. "How many times do you think you can do that before I fill your pussy with cum?"

Julie was too lost in her afterglow to respond, happy to let him count the orgasms for both of them as he took her up and over the edge again before she'd caught her breath. She was so far gone for Dion that she lost count of the times he got her off before he finally exploded, filling her with jet after jet of his semen.

Their multiple mutual climaxes drained her so completely that she felt like she might have momentarily passed out from lack of oxygen to the brain. Either that or he really had transported her to another realm, one where she felt like she was floating on a cloud while wrapped in his arms as they both recovered. When she came back into her body, she found herself cradled on his lap as he sat on the bench in the shower.

Huh? Guess that floaty feeling was him picking me up and moving me onto his lap, so I didn't fall over while in my orgasm coma.

"You really should eat some of these chocolates, Jewel, and drink some juice," Dion instructed as he held the full glass of grape juice to her lips, "so you can replenish your energy."

Julie opened her mouth, allowing him to tip the glass up for her to drink a little juice. She swallowed just enough to keep from feeling parched before he took the glass away, probably because he didn't want to give her more than she could handle. "I think I now understand what some of the girls mean when they talk about orgasm comas."

"Well, maybe we should save those for when we're in bed, so neither one of us have to worry about falling while trying to get there when they hit us." Dion chuckled as she wondered if her floaty feeling earlier from him picking her up and turning them around in the shower before sitting down felt anything like he had when the higher dose of his medication kicked in before he made it back to bed after brushing his teeth at night. "And just to be safe, I think I'm gonna wash you off right quick before moving both of us to the bed for the rest of the night."

"Yeah, hopefully, you can do that without me having to stand up," Julie teased, grinning at her man before brushing her lips over his strong jaw. "'Cause I still can't feel my legs, so I don't think I'm gonna make it to bed any other way."

"Don't worry, Jewel. I got you," Dion assured her, brushing his lips over her temple as he reached across the shower to grab the handheld sprayer and turn on the water. "And I'm looking forward to taking care of you by carrying you to bed quite regularly for the rest of our lives."

Julie couldn't imagine anything better than the future he'd just described.

Chapter Twenty-Six

As Dion took Jewel on an eating tour of New Orleans — starting the day with beignets at Café Du Monde and planning on ending the evening with fried chicken at Willie Mae's Scotch House — he wished he had her engagement ring ready to propose while they were in his hometown for Mardi Gras. Since he'd moved in with her a little over a week before, she'd dropped a few hints that she was ready to accept his proposal and start planning their wedding, making him start to second-guess his plan to wait until after their daughters were born to pop the question. Being back in NOLA also made him wish he'd already had her ring finished. He couldn't think of a better way to ask her to be his wife than to get down on one knee in Jackson Square while listening to a zydeco band as one of the parades passed by behind him. At least, not until they tried to get through the parade traffic to walk alongside Decatur Street from Café Du Monde to Jackson Square and were spotted by reporters already out to cover the festivities.

Dion had intentionally planned to show Jewel around the French Quarter from midmorning to midday, knowing it would be less crowded earlier in the day than it would be in the late afternoon and evening, when everyone started gathering at the bars and other party spots on Bourbon Street and around the French Quarter to celebrate late into the night. But even though he'd thought to have them dress inconspicuously — her in one of her purple maternity dresses and sneakers, and him in sneakers, jeans, and a Mardi Gras t-shirt — to keep from drawing attention to them by going out in costume, he'd made the mistake of not looking at the parade routes online to make sure they wouldn't get caught up in one of the many crowds of parade watchers or have to cross over a parade route to get to the places he wanted to show her.

He'd never had a problem with being able to walk through any of those crowds before, or even with cutting across a parade route, considering how slow the floats actually traveled. But with his height, he could clearly see over the heads of most of the people out celebrating to look for openings to weave his way through. With being almost a foot shorter than him, though, Jewel didn't have that luxury. She was also a good hundred pounds lighter than him, even with the weight she'd gained so far while carrying the twins, which put her at greater risk of being injured if she got caught up in a crowd surge.

Fuck! I shoulda realized how the crowds have changed in all the years that I've been traveling with the GWA and not able to be home for Mardi Gras. And I really shoulda thought about how dangerous this could be for Jewel and our babies, Dion berated himself as he pulled Jewel into his side, and they made their way closer to the parade route, so she could see more than the backs of the heads of the people in front of them. *We'd have been better off watching from the balcony at home. Yeah, we wouldn't have seen the parade because of not being on the route, but she'd have seen plenty of people in costumes walking around the neighborhood to get an idea of what this part of Mardi Gras is like, without being at risk of being jostled too much.*

In his lack of thinking ahead, Dion unfortunately didn't realize the paparazzi would be scoping out the area, too, probably to find the best places to set up to catch the majority of the city's most notable revelers later on that night in the sights of their cameras. *Or maybe to cover the parades, in case anyone famous happens to be on a float today?*

And apparently, after the events of the previous October, he wasn't as low-ranking of a D-list celebrity in his hometown as he'd thought. Either that, or the reporters who had dubbed him a "hometown hero" back in October were now pissed at him for having skipped town for the last three months, instead of sticking around to give them something to gossip about, and were now trying to make their next story by bringing attention to him. And there was no way he could shrink himself down to not be noticeable when he was more than half a foot taller than the average American male. *Fuck! Who knew not being the tallest person around when I'm in Heart's Destiny, or hanging with my former coworkers in the GWA, would spoil me to thinking I wouldn't stick out like the Jolly Green Giant while we're here in NOLA for the week?*

"Dion! Where have you been the last three months?"

"Dark Chocolate! When can we expect to see you in the GWA again?"

"Dion! Who's the woman with you?"

"Dion!"

"Dark Chocolate!"

"Blah, blah, blah…" was all Dion could hear with the continuous shouts trying to get his attention, even as they were drowned out by a zydeco band playing in the parade only a few feet away. He had to block it all out and come up with a better plan for protecting Jewel and their unborn daughters. *Why the fuck didn't I insist on bringing Dare with me today to help protect her? Or call her cousins to set up a security detail before this trip?*

The paparazzi's shouted questions as they snapped picture after picture were annoying, even before they drew the attention of a few wrestling fans, who suddenly swarmed him. The questions about his career and personal life were soon overshadowed by fans of all ages screaming his name and asking for autographs.

Fuck! Fuck, fuck, fuck! Dion desperately tried to quickly map out an escape route to get Jewel back to his condo without being followed, but he felt completely ill-equipped to get her out of the crowd safely. *If I'd have known it was gonna be like this, instead of my usual semi-anonymity in NOLA, I woulda hired everyone Avington Security could round up to come with us. Or maybe I'd have just stayed in Heart's Destiny to keep Jewel and the babies as far away from this crazy ass shit as possible.*

"Sorry, guys, no autographs right now," Dion deflected the fans, ignored the continued shouts of the reporters, and held Jewel even tighter to his side as he turned around and tried to push through the parade watchers to get back to the relative safety of the café to call for assistance.

"Are you okay, D? You're not about to take a nap on me, are ya?" Jewel clung to his side with her arm around his waist as they inched their way back through the mass of bodies he ignorantly hadn't expected to have to deal with so early in the day.

Only Jewel would be asking about me right now, when she's clearly the one of us most at risk of getting trampled.

"I'm okay," Dion tried assuring her, grateful his medicine seemed to be working well enough for this incident not to trigger a narcolepsy episode. At least, not yet, anyway. "Not taking any naps, unless you want one when we get back home."

That's it. Deflect. Think about being back in that king-sized bed, cuddling with Jewel for a nap, he silently told himself, trying to banish all thoughts of possibly passing out to keep it from manifesting into reality.

"Why do I get the feeling we wouldn't get much sleep, even if we were able to snap our fingers and teleport back to your condo right now?" Jewel smiled up at him, smirking playfully, and obviously trying to get his mind focused on sex with her, instead of their current situation.

Damn. How'd I get so lucky? To find the perfect woman, who knows me so well, and instinctually knows how to redirect my mind when I start getting anxious?

"Probably not," he chuckled, grinning at her before turning serious to apologize. "Sorry, Jewel, if I'd have realized it would be this bad today, I never would have suggested this, or would have asked your cousins for a security team to come run interference for us, at least."

"Yeah, well, you can make it up to me when we get back to the condo," she grinned in response, licking her lips, and giving him all kinds of dirty thoughts about licking her.

"Definitely," he agreed, already planning the different positions she'd be most comfortable in for hours of him pleasuring her in his mind. At least, until the yelling around them infiltrated his brain once more.

Among all the shouts of his name and questions about his career and injuries, Dion heard a loud feminine voice shout, "Oh my gawd! She's one of those Burlesons who used their oil money to start making movies!"

Dion wasn't sure if it was one of the paparazzi that identified Jewel, or just a random tourist, who followed enough celebrity gossip to recognize Julia from the press releases that had gone out when the

Burlesons announced the acquisition of the production company that Burleson Entertainment bought the year before. *Not the time to remember those, Dumbass,* he mentally scolded himself as he pushed away his mental pictures of her and her family that were online back then. But whether she was part of the paparazzi or just a random gossip junkie, the woman's shouted announcement was enough to change the tone and direction of the paparazzi's bombardment of questions.

"Is that why you're meeting with her, Dion? To get cast in a Burleson Productions movie now that your wrestling career is over?"

Seriously? Why would anyone think something like that?

"Are you only with her for her family money, Dion? Didn't you save anything you made with the GWA?"

Oh? So, now I've gone from "hometown hero" to "greedy, gold-digging gigolo" in the course of a few minutes? Surely, Jewel knows this shit isn't true.

"I would never," Dion asserted, imploringly looking only at Jewel, and not acknowledging the crazy people who'd basically blocked them in and kept them moving at a snail's pace to prevent him from getting Jewel to safety.

"I know you wouldn't," Jewel replied before he could even finish his sentence. "I learned a long time ago not to listen to the idiotic ideas of the media. Especially paparazzi putas, who make stuff up to try to get more money for their pictures."

Thank fuck! Dion relaxed a little at knowing they were still okay and weren't going to have another misunderstanding because of the accusations of the paparazzi. *Or the paparazzi prostitutes,* he chuckled at her usage of the Spanish term, wondering if she thought it would be less likely to be understood by the people around them than if she'd used the English or French term.

He felt bad enough for not protecting her better this morning. He didn't need any other obstacles thrown in their path when he was doing a bang-up job of causing enough on his own, so he tried to block out the rest of the things being shouted around them. Not that he was completely able to act like he didn't hear some of the vile things being shouted.

"Of course! That's gotta be the only reason he'd hang out with a fat, white chick, instead of hookin' up with a sista from NOLA."

Dion had always prided himself on maintaining his cool and never losing his temper, even when he was being taunted by bigots and assholes. He knew all the shit they spewed just reflected poorly on their character, and not his or Julia's, which was why he ignored the taunts accusing him of being a gold digger or trying to sleep his way into a movie role. But when he'd normally just walk away and leave the assholes to their idiocy when they shouted derogatory things at him, he couldn't stand for it when they insulted his Jewel.

"Enough!" Dion shouted, stopping in his tracks, and turning in the direction of the last voice that clearly permeated his brain, pulling Jewel around with him since she was still plastered to his side. He planned to verbally put them in their place, while hopefully, securing his and Jewel's way out of the crowd without having to physically defend her honor and risk her or the babies getting hurt. "Julie is not fat. She's beautifully pregnant. You don't know anything about Julie, or me, so you have no idea what's really goin' on between us. But I can guarantee you it has nothing to do with her family money or my choice of future careers. I will not be pursuing acting, whether for Burleson Entertainment or anyone else, because, after my injuries, there's no way I can memorize the scripts necessary to be an actor. But if you really need all the juicy gossip on my dating life, even though I've retired from wrestling and stepped out of the spotlight, I'll gladly give you the scoop if it'll get all ya'll to back off and let us pass without further incident."

As he glared at the crowd between them and the parade, he thought he recognized one of the women still aiming her camera at him and Jewel. *Is she the one who identified Jewel? And how the fuck do I know her?* But he didn't have the chance to scour his memory for the information because the crowd all turned, drawing his attention back toward the parade, where a half-dozen local football players just jumped off their float to come to his and Jewel's rescue. At least, Dion assumed that was why his old friend Jamal added his voice to those shouting his name.

"Yo, D! Dion, effin', Davis!" Jamal Fontenot, whom Dion had known since childhood, and who'd gone on to play professional football, led the charge of his teammates from the stopped parade float to where Dion and Jewel were basically trapped in the horde of Mardi Gras carousers and paparazzi.

The throng parted like the Red Sea, as if Jamal was the second coming of Moses. Considering how precarious Dion felt their situation was right then, he'd gladly play the role of an Israelite and follow his old friend. *And maybe even give Jamal a new nickname by the end of the day.*

"Why don't you and your girl come ride on our float for the rest of the parade?" Jamal inquired as he and his teammates got close enough to surround Dion and Julia.

"Dark Chocolate, don't forget to give us that scoop before you go!"

Dion looked down at Jewel, who was still quietly standing by his side and following his lead. After not realizing how dangerous the situation could get before they left the condo that morning, he didn't feel worthy of her unconditional trust at that moment. But he was sure as fuck glad to have it, knowing she'd have to really trust him to follow him right then. He knew getting on a float with a couple dozen professional football players would be extremely intimidating for most people, but it would also be the safest place for Jewel and their babies until they could escape the crowd and get a ride back to their NOLA residence. "Feel like riding on a float to see some more of my hometown?"

"Sure," Jewel grinned before her smile slightly dimmed. "But I don't have any beads to throw out."

"We've got you covered, little lady," one of Jamal's teammates, whose name Dion didn't know, replied before he could.

"And you did promise to give these reporters our story before we go," Jewel added with a mischievous smirk.

"Only if you're okay with being in the spotlight for a bit," Dion smirked back, unsure if what he planned to say would be breaking the Burleson press protocol or not.

"The Matchmaking Mommas already know all about us, so we might as well tell the world," Jewel shrugged, still grinning.

"Alright, but we're gonna hafta walk and talk, so we don't hold up the parade," Dion pointed out as Jamal and his teammates flanked him and Jewel to start walking toward the float as he addressed the reporters. "Julie Burleson and I have been exclusively dating for the last fifteen months, almost a year before I was injured and retired from wrestling. I'm not with her because of her family, her money, or even how gorgeous she is, but because she stole my heart with her intelligence and wit back when my travel schedule with the GWA kept us texting and talking on the phone way more than we actually got to see each other. And, like I said before, she's not fat. She's pregnant with my twin daughters, who are hopefully gonna look a lot more like her than me."

"I actually hope the girls look like a mix of both of us," Jewel giggled, grinning as the papzz continued following them and snapping pictures. "But if they can get their size from me, instead of coming out already halfway to the size of toddlers when they're born like D, that'd be great."

"Are there wedding bells in your future?"

"Absolutely," Dion shouted back at the reporter while smiling widely at Jewel. "But she's already told me it won't happen 'til after the girls are born and she has time to lose the baby weight and fit into a smokin' hot dress."

"When are the babies due?"

"May," Jewel replied for them. "So, if he wants a wedding anytime this summer, he needs to get on with planning an amazing proposal now!"

Fuck! Yeah! Too bad I have to wait until I know if the girls are gonna be born in April or May to have the extra stones removed from her necklace to finish her engagement ring. But I guess, even if the girls aren't born by the first of May, I can go ahead and remove the diamonds then to have her ring ready in time to propose on her birthday a couple days later. Maybe with breakfast in bed? Or should I do it in front of her whole family at her birthday party? Or maybe I should just play it by ear, in case the girls decide to come on her birthday to change my plans?

The shouted questions continued following them as they got on the float, but they were quickly drowned out by Jamal introducing Dion and Julie to the entire starting lineup of the New Orleans Gators. It also helped that the float started moving as soon as they were all on board, leaving the reporters behind.

"Now we've gotta get a few jerseys and stuff to wear to support the Gators before football season starts," Jewel gushed, as they were each handed an armful of beads to toss out.

"Yeah, you have a big family who'll wanna root for us, too?" Jamal practically shouted at Julia over the music blaring from the speakers of the float behind them, as they all tossed strands of beads to the people lined up along the parade route. "We can hook you up with enough swag for all of 'em when the parade's over, if ya want."

"Well, I do have a big family," Jewel confessed sheepishly, getting an ornery look in her eyes. "But they're all fans of the Houston Herefords, so I doubt they'd appreciate anything like that. Although, if you can beat the Herefords again when you face them next season, it might keep my brothers and cousins from talking too much smack about Dion and I wearing our Gators gear."

"Considering how we dominated the cows this season, I don't think that'll be a problem," Jamal chuckled.

"Oh, I love how ya'll call them the *cows*," Jewel giggled. "My brothers and cousins used to get so mad whenever they heard that, saying they were obviously bulls 'cause the players are all male. It was so funny when Uncle Bob corrected them by pointing out that their mascot didn't have genitals, so they could either be heifers or steers, but not bulls or cows."

"Wait," Jaden Collins, the quarterback for the Gators, interjected from the other side of Jamal. "I thought cows were female and bulls were male, and their mascot was female 'cause it doesn't have horns. What are these other things we should be calling them instead?"

"Actually, whether or not cattle have horns depends on the breed and both male and female cattle can have horns. Herefords don't have horns, which is why that's what we have on the ranch, so nobody's in danger of being gored. And technically, you're right about cows being female and bulls being male, but in order to be a cow, a female has to give birth. Before that, she's a heifer. And steers are male cattle that have been castrated." Jewel gave them all a quick lesson on the terms he'd recently learned since spending so much time on the ranch. "But typically, people who don't work with them regularly to need to differentiate to know what pasture to put an individual animal in just calls them all cows. So, if you were to call them heifers or steers, since their mascot doesn't have genitals, either to show it's a bull or to show it could have given birth, only ranchers and people like me, who've grown up on a ranch, will know what you're talking about."

"I'd know what they meant," Dion pointed out, chuckling as he tossed a string of beads out to a kid along the parade route.

"Well, yeah, 'cause you live on a ranch now, and have listened to Josh drone on and on about the cattle in the different pastures he's taken you out to draw," Jewel agreed, tossing out way more strings of beads than he was, since he couldn't take his eyes off of her long enough to toss more than one string every few minutes. "But up 'til the last month, you wouldn't have known either."

"True," Dion agreed with a chuckle. "Now I also know that you have Herefords on the ranch where we live, but there are Angus cattle on some of the other ranches producing Burleson Beef."

Dion had gotten completely lost when Josh tried explaining the differences in the breeds. He knew it had something to do with the marbling of the meat and the coloring of the cattle. But even with Josh offering to take him to one of the other ranches to draw some of the Angus cattle, he didn't think he'd be able to tell one breed from the other just by looking at them the way Josh apparently could.

"Oh, we've gotta take some time in the off season to come see D out on the ranch," Jamal laughed. "Julie, you've gotta be one hell of a woman to get one of us NOLA boys to live out in the sticks among the cattle."

"Damn right she is," Dion agreed, putting his arm around Jewel, covering her cleavage with the beads strung on his forearm, pulling her back to his front, and staking his claim before his old friend tried to steal her away. "And she's all mine, so if you get brave enough to come visit, you're gonna have to limit your flirting to her single sister, cousin, and friends. And stay away from my dream girl."

"Oh shit, no, we gotta stay away from visiting then," Jaden interjected, shaking his head. "Julie's safe to flirt with 'cause she's happily taken. But if we go out there and meet single girls like her, we might end up havin' to go play for the heifers, so we can settle down like you have. And even amazing country girls like Julie wouldn't wanna stay with us if we traded to a losing team like that."

Jaden's words triggered Dion to have a momentary sense of fear of losing Jewel because of being unemployed, until he realized that with his investments and various ventures like the gallery he was planning to open, he could still provide for their family without having to go to a normal job daily. "Naw, the really good ones, who love with their whole heart like Jewel, don't even care if we're unemployed." He brushed his lips across her temple. "Right, Jewel?"

"Nope, not at all," she agreed with a teasing smile, turning her head to brush her lips across his jaw. "I'm happy to be your Sugar Momma as long as you stay home and be Mr. Mom."

"Aw, but I'm smart enough to let Tia advise me on my investments this year, so I can be your Big Daddy and won't need a Sugar Momma," Dion teased Jewel back. "Unless you're talking about the sugar in the ice cream you use for…"

"Yes!" Jewel reached up and covered his mouth with her hand to stop him from talking about blow jobs in front of the football players on the float with them. "That's exactly the type of sugar I'm talking about! Which you won't be getting if you keep sharing details in front of my new friends."

All Dion could do was laugh, grateful for the way this outing was turning out. And especially for the woman in his arms, who he knew he would spend the rest of his life loving, laughing with, and raising a happy family with, no matter what else came their way. Dion had found his dream girl, and he planned to enjoy every minute of the time he was blessed to have with her.

~~~

As she laid in Dion's king-sized bed resting before dinner, Julie reflected on how much of a blast she'd had celebrating Dion's favorite holiday with him in his hometown. Yeah, the mob scene that morning had been scary for a bit, but more because she was afraid Dion would have a narcolepsy attack when they couldn't get out of the crowd than because of the rabid fans and paparazzi surrounding them. *And after the way he jumped off the float to come get his childhood friend to come hang out, and rescued us from the crazies, Jamal is now on my short list of possible middle names for Dillon, if and when we have the twin boys Mama Marcel predicted for us in a few years.*

Once they'd gotten on the float, they'd both relaxed quite a bit, negating any worry she had about Dion's narcolepsy flaring up. She'd had a ball getting to know the football players they met that day, hearing stories about Dion growing up with Jamal, sharing the story of how she and Dion met and fell in love, tossing out beads to the kids
~~~

along the parade route, and hopefully, keeping those kids from seeing the rowdier women, who'd flashed their boobs at the guys for beads.

While there had been more than a few women along the parade route who'd called out Dion's name before flashing their breasts, Julie had quickly realized that he wasn't paying a lick of attention to them. Any feelings of jealousy she'd previously felt were quickly quashed by the way he kept his focus on her, keeping some form of physical contact between them at all times, even when he looked away from her to talk to one of the guys on the float or toss the occasional strand of beads to a little kid. And he only tossed beads to the kids, the same way she had, making it clear that they were both on the same page with keeping things family friendly on the float.

When she quickly ran out of the first batch of beads Jamal had looped on her forearm, Dion let her pull the ones from his arms to toss out, going so far as to load up both arms before caging her in with his body pressed to her back to give her double the ammunition to toss. Having him pressed against her all morning also made it clear to her, and everyone around them, that he was claiming her as his, much like he had with the reporters and paparazzi that had hounded them that morning. Her family might not normally like a lot of the limelight that came with their wealth and status, but she knew they'd all be proud of how he'd handled the press and proudly declared them a couple to the world.

Once the parade was over, they'd exchanged contact information with Jamal, Jaden, and a few of the other guys, with Dion promising to send the guys autographed GWA merchandise in exchange for the autographed jerseys she and Dion were given while having seafood gumbo for lunch with the team at Dooky Chase's Restaurant. She'd originally thought it was a strange name for a restaurant, reminding her of what Memmaw Judy had called a bowel movement when Julie was a small child. But apparently, it was named after the original owner, who'd opened the restaurant in 1941, so she quickly understood the sentimental significance of the name and felt really bad for her initial thoughts.

The restaurant was also a historical landmark (at least, in Julie's opinion, even if it wasn't officially designated as such by anyone with authority for making such things legally recognized) for how many pivotal members of the civil rights movement met there to discuss the issues of their time. In addition to being one of the Black-owned businesses where African Americans could cash their paychecks back in the days of segregation, when there were no Black-owned banks in the area, it was also the first art gallery in New Orleans for African American artists.

Julie felt exceptionally humbled to be able to eat in a place so rich in history. While she thoroughly enjoyed every place Dion had taken her to eat so far, Dooky Chase's Restaurant was by far her favorite. She could clearly see how the restaurant and the family who owned it had influenced Dion, and had such a positive impact on his life.

I wonder if he might want to have a restaurant component to his gallery in Heart's Destiny as a way to pay homage to his roots here in New Orleans? Lord knows, we need more restaurants in town. But I don't know who he could get for the chef, since I know he doesn't want to be the one to cook all the time.

After lunch, they'd gotten a car service to take them back to Dion's condo, which he was now calling "their place in NOLA," before calling Uncle Byron to get a recommendation for a local security team. *I still don't know when he thinks I'll have the time to redecorate and convert "our" guest room into our kids' bedroom for when we come here on vacations, like he was talking about last night. Unless he thinks we're gonna get the bodyguards he hired to help move furniture after following us on a shopping trip later this week?*

Luckily, Avington Security had a bodyguard team in the city, who had just finished a job nearby over the weekend and were sticking around to enjoy the Mardi Gras festivities while waiting for their next assignment. So, once Miller and Knight arrived at the condo, they were able to go on with their original plans to visit Jackson Square and walk around the French Quarter to see the sights once the official parades were done for the day, at least in that part of town.

While, technically, the streets weren't blocked off for parades in the French Quarter any longer, there were so many residents out walking from party to party that it was actually faster to walk than to drive anywhere. And while she was less nervous about walking from the condo over to Jackson Square than she'd been that morning once they had Miller and Knight with them, she was glad Dion had insisted on only walking around Jackson Square for a little while, instead of spending half the day walking all over the French Quarter as he'd originally planned. They'd still had plenty of time to listen to a band and give her a feeling of the atmosphere he'd grown up in, while shopping with street vendors and checking out local artists, who used the park as their studio space. But they didn't get caught up in any of the late-afternoon carousing over on Bourbon Street.

They'd seen Mama Marcel in her natural element, which led to Dion telling her stories about his mom, Elena, having set up right beside Mama Marcel to sell her art and various other items throughout his childhood. They'd also gone for a ride in a horse-drawn carriage that Julie had thoroughly enjoyed. Though it would have been a lot more romantic if they hadn't had the two big, burly bodyguards tagging along.

While they'd donned Mardi Gras masks to try to blend in a little more with the rest of the revelers, they'd still run into a few fans who recognized Dion. Thankfully, they were much more laid back and respectful than the paparazzi were that morning, so it wasn't a big deal for him to sign a few autographs and take a few pictures. Surprisingly, the majority of them had seen the reports from that morning already, and actually asked Julie to join them in the pictures, too.

One young woman even asked for Julie's autograph instead of Dion's, claiming the badass business woman was more her type of hero than any professional athlete. After talking with her for a few minutes to learn she was a local college student working on a business degree, Julie had added her Burleson Incorporated email address to the paper where she'd signed her autograph, telling Tanisha to send her a résumé when she got closer to her last semester, so she could get it in the right hands for internship and job opportunities.

While she'd had a great time, all that walking was exhausting at twenty-seven weeks pregnant with twins. So, they'd ended up sending Miller and Knight to pick them up an early dinner and retired to Dion's condo long before the party really got started down on the streets of NOLA. She'd fallen fast asleep as soon as they'd laid down earlier, right after the bodyguards left, but she knew Dion was planning to give them the rest of the night off.

Since Dion lived on the third floor of the building he'd had restored and converted into three separate condos, they could safely go out on the balcony to listen to the music that never seemed to stop from the various parties going on all around them, without needing the bodyguards to stay with them to keep them safe. So, once they brought back Dion and Julie's fried chicken dinners, Miller and Knight would be informed it was time for them to go enjoy the festivities, with complimentary drinks and food if they happened to stop in at Xavier's, the club Dion and Darius co-owned and named after their father.

Julie wasn't sure if they would need the bodyguards the rest of the week while they were in town, or if the crowds were only a problem earlier because of it being Fat Tuesday. But she figured it was best to keep them on call, and let Dion decide if they were needed when they went to Mass for Ash Wednesday, or any of the other places he wanted to show her until they went home to Heart's Destiny on the weekend.

Now that I'm up from my nap, I should probably go find him to find out the plan for the rest of our time here, Julie thought. *Though I really wish he'd have stayed in bed with me, I suppose he had to get up to answer the door when Miller and Knight brought our dinner. And we should probably eat it before doing what I'd want to do if he was here in bed with me, anyway.*

Julie stretched languidly before getting up and padding in her stocking feet over the hardwood floors to the restroom, needing to relieve the pressure the girls were putting on her bladder before she did anything else. Once that was done, and she'd washed and dried her hands, she made her way out to the living room, taking a moment to appreciate the family photos and original artwork on the exposed brick walls before noticing Dion was standing out on the balcony.

Based on his skin tone, Julie had been surprised when Dion first told her that his mother was mostly Caucasian, thinking he'd been pulling her leg after she'd shared her DNA results in the Spring of the previous year. She'd begrudgingly started to believe him when he showed her his DNA results later in the year that showed he was thirty-five percent French, and claimed that the extra fifteen percent of his African DNA, over the fifty percent he inherited from his father, had to account for every bit of his mother's DNA that wasn't French to give her an olive complexion that never burned in the sun. But looking at the pictures he had on the walls from when he was a little kid, she could clearly see that the shape of his eyes and ears came from his mostly white mother, while all the rest of his physical traits were the spitting image of his African American father. *I wonder if that means our daughters could come out looking more like one of us, instead of being beautiful medium-brown-skinned mixes of both of us?*

I suppose Jonah and Jerry do look a little more like Justin than Amy. But is that because they're boys? Like maybe that's why Dion and Darius also look more like their dad, too? And since we're having girls, they'll look more like me? And when we eventually have boys, they'll look more like Dion? Why can't they all look like a combination of both of us?

I mean, besides wanting them to look like both me and Dion, I want all my kids to have the added sun protection of more melanin than I have, so they aren't as at risk as I am of burning or getting skin cancer from all the time I know I'm gonna teach them to like spending out in the sun, she pouted, feeling overly emotional at the prospect of their kids not obviously being a visual representation of their love.

"Jewel, what's wrong?" Dion seemed to appear out of nowhere, suddenly by her side instead of doing whatever he'd been doing out on the balcony. He cupped her face in his hands, turning it up to look at him while he wiped below her eyes with his thumbs. "Why are you crying?"

"I don't want our daughters to be pasty white like me," she sobbed, throwing her arms around his waist, and burying her face in his chest. "I want them to look like both of us, not more like me, the way Jonah and Jerry look more like Justin, and you and Darius look more like your dad."

"I'm sure our daughters will be a beautiful mix of both of us," Dion assured her, wrapping her in his big, strong arms and brushing his lips over the top of her head. "And Jerry and Jonah clearly got their hair and eyes from Amy, so I don't think they really look more like Justin."

"Yeah, but I'm talking about their complexion, not their individual features," Julie elaborated, lifting her head to look into his deep umber eyes. "I know Amy's mom, Andrea, keeps saying they're turning more khaki-colored than when they were born, but they still look almost as pale as Justin to me, not golden-brown like Amy. And after seeing how much you and Dare look like your dad, I'm worried that all boys are gonna look more like their fathers and all girls are gonna look more like their mothers. Which means our poor girls are gonna suffer through painful sunburns and looking like lobsters anytime they forget to reapply sunscreen, like I do."

"I think you might be exaggerating a little," Dion chuckled. "I mean, I know I don't remember every day we spent together before I was injured, but I think you looking like a lobster would stand out enough to come back to me pretty easily."

"Fine, maybe I don't go full-blown lobster anymore, like I did as a kid," Julie conceded with a sigh. "But I do get a little pink the first couple days after being in the sun before I start to tan."

Before Dion could reply, she started ranting once more, feeling like a crazy woman for losing her shit the way she was, but being completely unable to stop it. "And I want our girls to look like a mix of the two of us, with more of a golden-brown or copper skin tone, so they don't ever feel the need to torture themselves with tanning beds, or risk looking like the Great Pumpkin with artificial tanners, to keep from looking washed out in pictures. And don't even get me started on the skin cancer risk of being as pale as I am!"

"If our girls are born with your creamy complexion, then we'll get Justin and Amy to start working on developing a sunscreen with an artificial tanner that doesn't look orange," Dion suggested with a smirk. "I mean, I know the R and D lab at Burleson is supposed to be focused on automotive chemicals, but I'm sure they'll happily switch it over when you point out the skin cancer risk for their boys, too."

"Are you laughing at my fears for our daughters?" Julie pulled a little farther back, even though Dion still kept his arms loosely around her.

"No, Jewel, not at all." Dion shook his head, keeping his expression neutral, obviously not wanting to set her off any more than she already was. "But you have to admit that making sure the girls put on more sunscreen is a much easier thing to do to protect them than preventing the racism they'll have to face if they get their complexion from me."

Julie felt like a colossal moron for not thinking about how Dion's perspective would differ from hers because of their different upbringings and racial breakdowns. "I'm sorry. I wasn't thinking," she muttered, hugging him tight and burying her face in his chest once again. "I hate that you ever had to deal with that kind of stuff. And I know that part of the reason I don't think about our kids possibly having to deal with it in the future is because I've never been discriminated against because of my race. But honestly, I don't think any of my African American, Native American, or Hispanic friends who grew up in Heart's Destiny ever have either. That's one of the reasons I love my hometown so much and want to raise our children there, so I don't have to worry about racism affecting our babies."

"I know, and I agree." Dion brushed his lips over the top of her head. "But we're still gonna hafta teach them how to deal with it when they go off to college or travel to other parts of the world."

"What's the point in being rich and famous, if we can't prevent our kids from having to deal with idiots once they're grown up and go off to explore the world?" Julie pouted, realizing just how sheltered she'd been all her life. *Geez! He must think I sound like a total spoiled brat right now. And how wrong is it of me to want to spoil our children the same way?*

"I don't know about being famous, since I'm really trying to step out of the spotlight now that I've retired from the ring," Dion chuckled. "But hopefully, our wealth will at least give us and our kids more of a voice to lead future generations in breaking the cycles of racism in the world."

"I hope so," Julie agreed. Though she wasn't sure what she could do to help change things on a global scale the way it needed to be changed, she was really glad she'd have Dion by her side to help her protect their children and prepare them for whatever they'd have to face in the future.

While she'd always thought it was the things they had in common that would bring them closer together, she was starting to realize just how much their differences would also be beneficial to them in the future. Because of their unique perspectives of life, he'd be able to teach her the things she'd never realized her children would one day need to know, like how to deal with racial discrimination, and she'd be able to help him with issues he might not have thought of before, like how their daughters would need to know how to defend themselves from sexual assault or harassment. While she wasn't exactly looking forward to the hard topics they'd have to address as their children grew up, she knew they'd get through it all with ease because Dion was her perfect partner, with whom she looked forward to spending the rest of her life.

"Now, how 'bout we quit stressing about the stuff we aren't gonna hafta deal with for a few years and enjoy some of the best fried chicken you'll ever taste?" Dion suggested, smiling down at her as he wiped away the last of her tears.

Before she could verbally respond, her stomach growled loudly, clearly speaking for itself. "I guess the girls and my stomach agree with you," she chuckled, stepping out of Dion's arms to head into the kitchen, where she assumed he'd stashed the food.

"I actually have it set up on the balcony," Dion redirected her, placing a hand on the small of her back to guide her out to where she'd seen him earlier. "I was just coming to wake you up to eat it while it's hot, but I guess the guys ringing the doorbell, or us talking for a couple of minutes, woke you up instead."

Since Julie didn't remember hearing either the doorbell or voices, she assumed it was the bell that woke her, and she hadn't heard their voices over the water running when she was in the bathroom. "I guess," she shrugged as they stepped out onto the balcony, where he had a table set with the Styrofoam containers containing their food, along with silverware, napkins, a couple bottles of water, and two glasses of whichever mocktail he'd apparently mixed up for them. "And what are we drinking with this amazing fried chicken?" *And is that where you've hidden my engagement ring for a proposal tonight?*

"You can't experience Mardi Gras in NOLA without having a Hurricane, even if it is a non-alcoholic version," Dion grinned, pulling out a chair for her to take a seat. "So, before we got here last night, I had Dare stock my fridge with everything but the rum that he uses to mix them up at Xavier's, and I mixed us up a pitcher while you were napping. It's a combination of orange juice, lime juice, passion fruit juice, grenadine, simple syrup, and lime sparkling water."

Though he didn't mention it, he'd also garnished the top of the glass with a toothpick holding a slice of an orange, a slice of a lime, and a maraschino cherry. Unfortunately, while she thought that would have been the perfect place to stick an engagement ring, there wasn't anything sparkly on either of their drinks. "Sounds delicious."

Guess I'll just have to wait to find out what he thinks is the best way to surprise me to pop the question. Hopefully, he won't build up the anticipation too much longer.

After Dion sat down and said a prayer, Julie opened the Styrofoam container in front of her and pinched off a bite of the chicken. She popped it in her mouth and promptly moaned in pleasure from the foodgasmic taste. "Oh. Wow! This really is the best fried chicken I've ever tasted."

"I'm glad you like it," Dion grinned as he also dug into the food. They spent a few minutes eating in silence before Dion changed the subject to the events of that morning, looking a little nervous as he did so. "So, how do you think your family is gonna react to our impromptu interview this morning?"

"They'll be fine with it," she reassured him, placing her free hand on his in the center of the table. "I mean, we didn't exactly reveal anything they didn't already know, and what we said this morning isn't much different than what will be released with the girls' birth announcement, or our engagement announcement, if and when you get around to proposing. So, there's nothing for them to be upset about."

"There's no *if* to that statement, ya know." Dion pointed at her with his fork as he turned his other hand over under hers to hold her hand while they ate and talked. "I'm definitely gonna be proposing. But since you'd already said you don't wanna get married until a couple months after the girls are born, I figured I have time to plan the perfect special moment for us to get engaged."

"You know I don't need anything super flashy or like the grand gestures in romance novels, right?" At least, she hoped he knew her well enough to know that she preferred the simple things in life and only needed the two of them together to make every day special. She'd say yes to his proposal, no matter what, even if he didn't bother with picking out a ring beforehand. "Anytime we're together is special to me."

"Yeah, I know," Dion smiled between bites. "And for the most part, I agree that every minute we're together is precious. But I only plan on getting down on one knee to ask you to be my wife one time, and I wanna make sure I do it exactly right."

"I'm kinda surprised you didn't plan it for today," Julie admitted as she sipped her virgin hurricane, "with as much as you love Mardi Gras and it being the first time we're celebrating it together here."

"No, I admit I thought about it," Dion confessed with a slight shake of his head. "But while it woulda been cool for me, it's not something special for both of us. I think it needs to happen on the ranch, in our home where we'll be raising our children, so we can point to the exact spot where I proposed when we're telling them about it later in life.

Not here in a place that's too small for us to even vacation in once we have more than just the girls."

"You're really okay with living on the ranch, instead of buying a bigger place here?" Julie hated that she still felt the need to have him reassure her that he wouldn't want to move home to New Orleans, but she couldn't stop herself from posing the question. "You're not gonna get bored living in Heart's Destiny?"

"Bored living with you and our children? Hell no!" Dion chuckled, putting down his fork before picking up his drink and taking a swig before continuing to speak. "And I love our home, especially after your dad told me all about your family history and who built it. I love the idea of passing that legacy down to our kids. And the attic is huge, so we could put four more bedrooms up there to make room for a half dozen kids if Mama Marcel was short sighted in predicting we'll only have four."

"You've been spending too much time with my mother," Julie laughed, shaking her head at him as she loaded her fork with another bite of food. "And I'm gonna tell you the same thing I told her when she started in on wanting more grandbabies. I have to birth these two first before I can even think about having more. And I want the girls walking, talking, and potty trained before we even think about getting pregnant again. So, be prepared, Big Daddy. After the girls are born, I'm going back on the pill, but you're also gonna hafta start wrapping Big D up, so we have double the protection, since one form of birth control clearly wasn't enough for us."

"I guess that means I need to start researching latex-free condoms to figure out which ones will actually fit on Big D," Dion smirked.

"Yeah, you're probably gonna hafta order them online, since neither the pharmacy nor the grocery store in Heart's Destiny stocks anything but the standard size in latex-free," Julie informed him between bites.

"I'm sure they'll add them to the inventory if they get a request for them." Dion shrugged as he forked up his last bite of food.

"Yeah, well, I wasn't about to deal with the rumors that woulda started if I'd have requested them back when I was shopping for them before we met," Julie pointed out. "It was bad enough having to make sure to go through the right line to check out, so nobody said anything about me buying the regular size."

"So, I guess that means you don't wanna be there when I go to the store and ask for the manager to put in my request?" Dion snarked with a mischievous grin. "I'm sure they'll understand the need when I tell them about how their standard size failed to stay in one piece going on, especially if we go in together before the babies are born."

"Oh, you are terrible!" Julie chuckled, imagining the look on the grocery store manager's face if Dion insinuated their girls were on the way because of the condoms she'd bought in his store being too small and failing. "Doing something like that would give Mr. Adkisson a heart attack! Especially since his daughter, Jackie, has a bit of a reputation in town for being promiscuous."

"Well, then he should definitely want to stock a bigger variety of sizes in latex-free condoms to keep her safe," Dion shrugged. "I mean, even if she's not allergic to latex, one of the men she fucks might be, so it's better to be safe than sorry."

"Yeah, you can go by yourself to make that request if you want, but I don't wanna even think about who else might benefit from the expanded selection of condoms in the H.E.B." Julie cringed at the thought of discussing the habits of one of the Thirsty Threesome with Jackie's father, ready to change the subject as she stabbed her last bite of chicken with her fork. "Besides, we won't need them for another four or five months, so we should really focus on enjoying being able to go without for a little while longer."

"Is that your way of suggesting we move to the bedroom before dessert?" Dion arched an eyebrow at her as he finished off his hurricane.

"Tonight's the last night we get king cake for dessert, isn't it?" Julie pouted, thinking she'd miss the sweet treat if she had to wait until the next January to eat it again.

"Traditionally, yeah," Dion confirmed. "But some places make it year round. And if you get a craving for it, I'll make you one whenever you want. But before we eat any tonight, I'd rather get a taste of you. And I believe I promised to shower you with Mardi Gras beads, too."

"Oh, yes, please," Julie agreed, downing the last of her hurricane, so they could quickly clean up from dinner and head to the bedroom.

While she didn't get the proposal she'd hoped for that night, she did enjoy the way he incorporated Mardi Gras beads into their lovemaking when they went inside and got naked. He teased her with them first by running them over her most intimate areas to amp up her arousal before following them with his mouth to have his first dessert of the night. Then, with the beads scattered across the bed while she rode his cock, he rewarded her by looping a strand of the plastic baubles around her neck after every orgasm.

It might seem silly to anyone outside their two-person bubble, but in Julie's opinion, cherishing the way they showed their love for one another as they played with those inexpensive trinkets as if they were precious jewels was just more proof of how perfect they were for each other. And even though she was more than ready to start planning their wedding and the rest of their future together, she wasn't about to nag him about it to get him to rush the proposal. She'd rather enjoy living every moment with Dion, knowing her perfect-for-her man would surprise her by dropping to one knee when she least expected it.

Epilogue

Julie awoke after only a couple hours of sleep with what she thought might be more Braxton-Hicks contractions. She'd had a few episodes of them over the last month as she settled into the routine of life on the ranch with Dion. They'd both freaked out when they first started happening. At least, until everyone around them, who'd previously had babies, and Dr. Magnum, repeatedly informed them that Braxton-Hicks contractions were a normal and necessary part of being pregnant. Now, she wasn't too worried about being woken up by the strange sensation, hoping she'd be able to get comfortable to get some more sleep, even if she couldn't get them to stop by changing positions like she'd been taught to try. Unfortunately, instead of just feeling the momentary tightening of her abdominal muscles that she'd experienced with her previous episodes of Braxton-Hicks contractions, this time that tightening was accompanied by pain in her low back that wasn't alleviated by pulling her knees up and adjusting the pillow she put between her knees when she slept.

Does that mean this is a real contraction? Not Braxton-Hicks? Like, I might actually be going into labor?

No! No! No!

I knew I should have asked Dr. Magnum if we were getting to the point that we'd need to stop having sex to keep from inducing labor when we were in her office on Tuesday. But I had to get sidetracked by the size estimates she was giving us from the ultrasound and forgot. And because I thought we were still okay for another week until my next appointment, I had absolutely no objections to making love with Dion before bed tonight, uh, last night.

Leah Mae Wright

On Tuesday at her appointment, right after informing them that she'd have weekly appointments for the rest of the pregnancy, Dr. Magnum had done another ultrasound to estimate the size of the babies. She said it would help determine how much longer they needed to stay in utero to keep from having as high a risk of low birth weights. But when Dr. Magnum did the measurements and estimated the babies to already be over seven-and-a-half pounds each, Julie freaked out, thinking they'd both be over nine pounds like Dion if they waited another month to have them. Unfortunately, her doctor hadn't agreed that it would be okay to go ahead and induce her labor at thirty-six weeks.

I guess the girls agreed with me that they've fully developed and are ready to be born. And lucky for me, if I'm actually in labor now, then they're still small enough they might not rip me a new one coming out.

But, damn, they really need to wait a few hours, so Dion's medicine can wear off before we have to drive to the birthing center.

Seriously, girls, we can't have labor start now. Not while your daddy is sound asleep from his meds. Zoe, Elena, ya'll need to listen to Mommy, and be good girls, and stay put for at least a few more hours. We've gotta give Daddy time to wake up 'cause he really wants to be the one to drive us to the birthing center.

Julie wasn't sure if her mental pep talk to her daughters would be effective or not, but she really hoped it would. Yeah, she knew she could call any member of her family who lived around her on the ranch to help her get Dion up and give them a ride to town. But she also knew how important it was to him to be the one to drive her to the birthing center to deliver their babies. And she really wanted to give him that opportunity, even though he was still making her wait to build up the anticipation for his proposal.

Geez, I hope he doesn't think while I'm in active labor is the best time to propose!

As the contraction passed and the pain subsided, she reached over to grab her phone off her bedside table to note the time. *Twelve-thirty. Two-and-a-half hours after Dion took his first dose of Xyrem. Shit, that means I need to stay awake now and tell him not to take the second dose, just in case these contractions are the real thing.*

If he skips the second dose, then he'll be safe to drive by four a.m. So, as long as the contractions stay more than five minutes apart until then, he'll be able to drive us to town. But if I fall asleep now and he takes that second dose at two, it'll be eight in the morning before he can drive. Maybe I should move it off his bedside table, so he won't take it if I fall asleep in the next hour and a half?

She gingerly lifted Dion's arm from around her midsection, wanting to let him sleep as long as possible from the one dose, so hopefully, missing the second dose wouldn't cause him any issues the next day while they were in the delivery room. After sliding his hand down behind her to rest on the bed, she carefully pushed herself up into a sitting position, so she could then use both hands to push off the side of the bed to stand up.

It only took her a couple of tries to stand up and feel stable on her feet, without her big ol' belly causing her to be off balance and flop back down in a seated position, as it often did recently. But once she made it up, she waddled around to Dion's bedside table and picked up both bottles that he used for his nightly Xyrem. She knew he normally rinsed them both out in the morning before putting them back in the box in the bathroom cabinet until it was time to make his doses for the next night, but she didn't bother rinsing the empty bottle before putting it and the full bottle for his next dose back in the box in the bathroom cabinet.

Hopefully, even if I'm asleep when he wakes up, he won't think to get up and look in here for it, when it's not sitting where he put it on the bedside table. And even if I forget to tell him that I put it away, he'll be able to find it easily when he's gathering everything we need to take to the birthing center, so he won't have to miss his medicine, if we have to stay at the birthing center a few nights.

Once that was done, she emptied her bladder again before going back to bed. As she wiped and noticed some of Dion's semen had leaked out of her from their earlier lovemaking, she cringed at the thought of her babies having to come through the rest of the residual still inside her.

Oh, how embarrassing! I don't even want to think about asking Dr. Magnum about rinsing that out with some kind of saline solution to keep it from getting in the girls' eyes, noses, or mouths during birth.

Leah Mae Wright

What am I thinking? Any of his semen left inside me will probably be washed out when my water breaks. Right?

When she tossed the toilet paper in the toilet, she noticed a clump that seemed a little darker than the rest of the white semen floating around it, possibly tinged with blood.

Is that the mucus plug they warned me about? Or is there something wrong with Dion's swimmers? Considering the rest of it looks normal, I'm guessing that's the mucus plug. At least, I hope it's the mucus plug.

Huh? Who knew it would look like dark, lumpy cum? Maybe I should ask Devon or Arden to give me a better description of it, so I can confirm that's what I'm seeing now. Hopefully, I'll remember to do that later.

Julie momentarily thought about Googling it, but quickly decided she wasn't brave enough to look at those images on her phone. Seeing what was probably her mucus plug was gross enough. She had no desire to see anyone else's online and risk making herself nauseous while in labor.

Right now, I need to try to get a little more rest. And hopefully, laying down will slow the contractions enough that we won't have to wake anyone up in the middle of the night to meet us at the birthing center.

As soon as she laid down, Dion pulled her back into his arms, resting his hands on her belly, his left at the top and his right down low, exactly where one of their daughters kicked. She pulled her extra pillow between her knees and used the ring on the back of her phone like a kickstand to set it up where she could see the clock on her lock screen without having to lift her head from Dion's bicep. She'd still have to reach over and tap the button on the side of her phone to see it when the screen timed out, but that wasn't as much of a hassle as actually having to pick it up to see the screen.

Unfortunately, even though she closed her eyes and tried to get her rest, she couldn't fall asleep because she was just too anxious about whether or not that one painful contraction was really labor, or just a stronger Braxton-Hicks contraction than she'd ever had before. *Maybe I should have waited until I had more than one before I moved Dion's Xyrem? I'm gonna feel like the biggest idiot on the planet if I make him skip a dose of medicine for a false alarm.*

But after Dr. Magnum mentioned that the babies seemed to be dropping to prepare for birth when she measured my belly and did the ultrasound on Tuesday, I'm pretty sure this could be me actually going into labor, and not just Braxton-Hicks. That one contraction was certainly more painful than those have been for the last month. But then again, she also said that first-time moms usually have that drop and can lose the mucus plug as much as two weeks before actually going into labor, so maybe it's still just false labor?

If it's false labor, maybe I should put Dion's medicine back on his bedside table, so he can take his second dose like normal. But now I'm afraid that as soon as I do that, I'll have another painful contraction that could cause my water to break, or start having multiple contractions at regular intervals, just as soon as he takes that second dose. And if this turns out to be our daughters' birthday, Dion will be devastated if he can't drive us to the birthing center.

She'd been going back and forth about getting up and putting his medication back on his bedside table and randomly tapping the button on the side of her phone to check the time for about forty-five minutes when she finally had a second painful contraction.

Okay, yeah, this is definitely the real deal, she decided as the pain spread from her back around her sides and rippled from her ribs to her pubis. She watched the clock on her phone and saw that it lasted long enough for a minute to flip, but since she didn't have the phone set up with the seconds showing, she couldn't be sure exactly how long the contraction actually lasted. *But at about forty-five minutes apart, I should have plenty of time for Dion to wake up and be safe to drive before they're close enough together that we need to go into the birthing center. Right?*

She laid there reviving the screen and watching the clock for another forty-five minutes, resolved to having him skip his second dose of medicine and help her time her contractions until it was safe for him to drive them to the birthing center.

Just as his alarm went off at two a.m. to take his second dose, the third contraction hit, feeling even stronger than the first two. She gripped his wrists and didn't let him roll away from her to turn off the alarm, needing to communicate that he couldn't take his meds, but having to breathe through the pain before she could verbalize an explanation.

"Jewel, what's going on?" Dion's voice sounded pained and frantic as he growled out the question in her ear. As her abdominal muscles tightened under his hands, Dion must have felt the movement and figured out what was happening. "Oh, shit, Jewel. Are you in labor?"

Trying to maintain the deep, cleansing breath pattern she'd learned in the Lamaze classes she and Dion had taken in April, Julie could only nod in response until the contraction passed.

"Okay, keep breathing," Dion instructed as he tried extracting his wrists from her grip. "Let me turn off this alarm, and then we'll figure out what we need to do to get to the birthing center."

Once she knew he understood the need to not look for his medication, she released his wrists and let him roll away from her while she kept breathing, in and out, slow and steady.

Dion shut off his alarm and turned on the bedside lamp. She felt the bed move as he stood, just as the contraction eased off and the pain subsided, what felt like a full minute after it had started.

"The contractions are forty-five minutes apart," she told him as she heard him rustling around in the closet and knew he was getting dressed. "And that was only the third one, so we have a few hours before we have to go to the birthing center."

"That's good," Dion called out from the closet. "'Cause even if I skip my second dose of meds now, I'm not sure I'll be safe to drive for about four more hours."

"I know you've said you don't feel like the six-hour recommendation to wait before driving is enough when you've taken two doses, but do you think it might be okay to go by what the doctors and pharmacists suggested after only taking one dose?" Julie was pretty sure it would take more than two hours for her contractions to progress from forty-five minutes apart to the five minutes apart they were supposed to be when they'd been instructed to head to the birthing center, if she started having contractions but her water hadn't broken. But she wanted to have a plan in place if the contractions got closer together or her water broke in less than four hours, if Dion still felt unsafe to drive until eight hours after taking his only dose that night.

"Maybe," Dion muttered as he came out of the closet, fully dressed and carrying her go-bag and one of the maternity gowns she'd bought specifically for wearing to their daughters' birth. Since she couldn't be sure she wouldn't have to change out of it if she was wearing the gown when her water broke, she'd bought two, putting one in the go-bag and leaving the other folded up in the top drawer in the closet to put on for the trip to the birthing center. "To be honest, this has me excited and amped up enough that I feel like I'm wide awake and safe to drive now. But I know that's just from the adrenaline spike and will go away just as soon as I calm down."

"I'm not putting that gown on until after my water breaks and I get cleaned up, or the contractions are close enough together that it's time to go to the birthing center, whichever comes first," Julie informed Dion, pointing at the gown he laid over the bag, which he'd placed on the bench at the foot of the bed.

"I'm just getting everything together, so I don't have to go hunting for stuff when it gets closer to time," Dion assured her before turning back to the closet to grab their shoes and socks. Once he had everything ready and waiting, either on the bench or on the floor beside the bench, Dion crawled back into bed behind her to cuddle. "Is there anything else I can do for you now? Maybe fix you something to eat, since they won't let you have anything after we get to the birthing center?"

"Are you awake enough to make me some cheeseburger macaroni?" She wasn't sure if his homemade macaroni and cheese with ground beef mixed in was really the best thing to eat while in the early stages of labor, especially if there were issues with delivering the girls naturally and she ended up having to have a C-section. But as soon as he mentioned food, it was the only thing she craved.

"I can make you some cheeseburger macaroni," Dion agreed, brushing his lips over the back of her head before getting back out of the bed. "Do you want to come downstairs with me, so I can help you time the contractions, or do you wanna just lay here and try to rest up while you can?"

"I'll go ahead and come down," Julie decided, reaching out to him to get him to walk around to her side of the bed. "But you've gotta help me up, 'cause I think I used my quota of successful standing attempts earlier, when I moved your medicine back to the bathroom cabinet."

Dion turned his head to look at his bedside table, apparently just noticing that his meds were missing when she mentioned it. "Damn, I realized you were in labor and didn't even look for it," he chuckled as he took her hands and helped her stand.

"Yeah, well, I wasn't sure if I'd be able to go to sleep between contractions or not," Julie explained as he helped her put on her fuzzy robe and slippers to walk downstairs. "And I didn't want to take a chance on you taking it while I was asleep and not being able to drive us to the birthing center before ten in the morning."

"Smart thinking," Dion praised as he put on his glasses and pocketed both their phones. "Now let's go get you set up somewhere comfortable before the next contraction hits."

"I was kinda thinking of covering a kitchen chair with plastic to make the clean-up easier if my water breaks while we're eating and waiting for the contractions to get closer together."

"Is that why you have a bunch of plastic drop cloths in the cabinet in the mudroom? I thought they were for protecting the floors after the babies are born and you're able to lay on your back again for our kinky food play."

"Yeah, I bought extra to have on hand for that," she agreed with a grin, remembering back to their Valentine's Day celebration, when they'd had to improvise in the shower. "But after hearing about Anthony being born in the back seat of Memmaw Judy's car, and seeing the destruction of the upholstery on one of Aunt Hazel's dining chairs when Brooklyn's water broke, I figured they'd be good to have on hand for protecting our vehicles and furniture when I went into labor, too."

Considering her next contraction hit just as they reached the bottom of the stairs, barely thirty minutes after the last one, Julie was glad that she'd been prepared. Dion held her up, breathing along with her until it passed, so they could keep walking into the kitchen. He then stepped out to the mudroom to get one of the drop cloths from the cabinet where she'd stored them to cover her dining chair before starting to prepare her final meal before delivering their babies.

Guess it's too much to ask you girls to wait two more days, so we can share a birthday, isn't it?

~~~
~~~

Dion was exhausted after only getting about three-and-a-half hours sleep before spending the last twelve hours trying to take care of Jewel while she was in labor. He followed every instruction Jewel, Dr. Magnum, or one of the nurses gave him, rubbing her back, feeding her ice chips, and basically doing anything else he could do to make her more comfortable while she went through the pain of early labor. But most of his instructions had come from Jewel and her family, as the doctor popped in and out of the room, running back and forth between the birthing suite and her normal daily appointments down in the clinic. Jewel's mom and sister had been in the room earlier, too, but he only took advantage of the backup long enough to run to the restroom, not wanting to miss a moment of their daughters' birthday. Susan and Jen had just left about thirty minutes earlier to grab a late lunch, after the doctor popped in the last time, telling them Jewel was only dilated to eight centimeters, so it would still be a little while before the girls were born. Still, he didn't want to go eat when Jewel couldn't, so he stayed, even though he could probably, at least, use a cup of coffee to help keep him awake.

Or maybe not, since caffeine hasn't ever really helped me wake up. Guess it's one of the things, like Adderall, that has an opposite effect on me because of the A.D.D. Maybe I should call the sleep specialist and have him talk with the neuropsych to figure out how to wake my ass up, so I don't fall asleep while Jewel's in labor.

He knew Jewel had it much worse than he did, having been up an hour and a half longer than him and enduring the pain of contraction after contraction for over thirteen hours. He was just glad she wasn't also having to fight off the excessive sleepiness of narcolepsy that, apparently, one dose of Xyrem a night wasn't effective at combating.

Luckily, her contractions had stayed far enough apart for long enough that he was safe to drive before they had to leave the house that morning. Unfortunately, her water hadn't broken until they were on the way to the birthing center, so she'd had to be uncomfortable riding in her wet birthing gown and robe while sitting on a plastic tarp that couldn't fully cover the seat without blocking the seatbelts. Jewel had to change into another birthing gown when they got to the birthing center. And now he had to figure out how to clean amniotic fluid and blood from the seatbelt, carpet, and crevices in the upholstery of the front passenger compartment of his Escalade. *And maybe buy her a new fuzzy robe, if I can't get the blood and amniotic fluid out of hers.*

Dion was proud of himself, however, for not passing out when he saw way more blood between Jewel's legs than he'd ever wanted to see. Once he got her cleaned up and changed, however, he made sure to stick to his position up by her head for the rest of the day, and avoided looking under the sheet every time the doctor examined her, knowing he wouldn't be so lucky to avoid passing out if he saw any more of the bloody part of giving birth.

"Are you seriously yawning like you're bored by the birth of our daughters?" Jewel growled, barely loosening her vise-like grip on his hand as the most recent contraction passed. Considering he could see them on the monitor and could tell she was in the least painful time between contractions, he wondered if she was still squeezing so hard in an effort to wake him up.

"I'm not bored, Jewel. I'm just really sleepy." Dion tried placating her as he wiped her brow with the washcloth in his free hand and stifled yet another yawn. "I didn't realize just how much it would affect me to skip that second dose of Xyrem."

"Yeah, well, if I'd have known it was still gonna take this long, even after we got here, I'd have let you take it," she moaned as the next contraction started much sooner than he expected.

"Breathe, Julia," he instructed as she tightened her grip once more, holding her breath, instead of following the Lamaze breathing they'd learned a couple weeks earlier.

"You breathe, Dion," she barked, making him wonder if the medication they'd injected in her I-V earlier had worn off, or if she was in that transition phase Dr. Magnum had warned them about, when the pain would be the worst and she would be the most irritable. "And maybe grab a catcher's mitt 'cause I think Zoe is ready to make her entrance into the world." Jewel huffed and puffed for a few seconds before pushing his hands away from her. "Seriously, go look and see if your daughter's crawling out of my hoo-hah already, 'cause I seriously think the first baby is ready to be born, whether Dr. Magnum gets back up here in time or not."

Dion didn't really want to look, but he knew better than to argue with Jewel when she was clearly distraught. Still, he took the time to push the nurse-call button before slowly moving down to the end of the bed to lift the sheet covering Jewel's lower half.

"Oh, shit!" Dion exclaimed when he saw dark curly hair matted down with blood between the spread lips of Jewel's pussy. He was both horrified and enthralled by the sight. While he hated the thought of Jewel hurting from having her pussy stretched over something bigger than his cock, he couldn't deny how meaningful it was to see his baby coming out of her body. "Somebody get the doctor in here now!"

He didn't have a catcher's mitt. Hell, he didn't even have gloves on like the doctor and nurses who'd been in and out of the room all morning. But he still placed his hands between Jewel's thighs, so he could catch their daughter if she came the rest of the way out before the doctor could get up to the room and in position for the delivery.

"Oh, wow, yeah, let me page her, and let her know there's no time to move to the surgical suite," the nurse babbled from the doorway behind him. Since he couldn't look away from the top of his daughter's head as it breached Jewel's vagina, he couldn't tell if it was Carlee or Savannah, since they'd been alternating which of them came in to check on Jewel all morning. "Don't push yet."

"I can't stop it!" Jewel squealed, just as he heard the door swish closed, and then rapidly open once more.

"Alright, Dad, I'm gonna need you to move back up to support Mom," Carlee instructed as she wheeled a cart full of instruments up beside him at the end of the bed and put on a clean pair of gloves.

Everything moved fast then, with the nurse moving Jewel's feet into the stirrups and dropping the end of the bed down out of the way, just as Dr. Magnum arrived. As the doctor and both nurses worked quickly to get scrubbed up and put everything they needed in place, Dion moved back up to Jewel's side and took her hand.

"I love you, Jewel," he crooned, bending to brush his lips over hers as a way to distract her from pushing.

He wasn't sure if it worked or not, but hoped so based on her breathlessly panted, "I love you, too."

"Alright, Julie, we're going to have you push on this next contraction," Dr. Magnum instructed as she did something under the sheet that Dion could no longer see from his new position.

Dion wrapped his right arm around Jewel's shoulders to support her as she crunched up to push, holding her hand in his left, so she was still able to squeeze tight as the contraction hit. Some people might call him a wimp for standing on her weaker left side and letting her squeeze the bedding with her dominant right hand, but since his right hand was already sore from spending most of the day on the opposite side of her bed, he figured he was just evening out the pain. *And maybe preventing her from breaking my right hand during the most painful part of the delivery, when she's obviously squeezing harder than she was earlier,* he thought as the sweet sound of his daughter crying for the first time filled the room.

"Baby A, born at two-twenty-three p.m.," Dr. Magnum announced as she laid the baby on the towels they'd spread on Jewel's abdomen and chest just a few moments earlier.

"Zoe Caroline Burleson-Davis," Jewel corrected as Carlee wiped the baby down with the towels.

"Wow, she's beautiful, just like her mother," Dion praised in awe as he brushed his lips over Jewel's temple. He would have kissed her properly, but he was unable to take his eyes off the baby, whose golden-brown skin tone was only slightly darker brown than Jewel's porcelain skin got when she tanned in the summer sun. Once the nurse wiped away the blood and amniotic fluid, Dion could tell her hair was lighter than it appeared when she was crowning earlier, too. Zoe's medium-brown hair wasn't nearly as light as Julia's blonde locks, but it wasn't as dark as his either. She was the perfect mix of the two of them.

"Dad, do you want to cut the cord?" Dr. Magnum looked at Dion as she held out a pair of scissors.

"No, I'll leave that to the professionals," Dion choked out, afraid he'd somehow screw it up by cutting the wrong place and end up hurting either Julia or Zoe. *Or I could see more blood from the cord and pass the fuck out. And I don't wanna take a chance on that happening and making me miss Elena's birth.*

As the doctor did her thing, Dion kept his eyes trained on Julia and Zoe, trying to figure out which features the baby got from each of them. He was truly thankful their daughter seemed to resemble Julia more than him, believing her delicate features were much more suitable for a pretty little girl than his wide nose and fuller lips. Though it was obvious her brown eyes were clearly from him.

Once the doctor had clamped and cut the umbilical cord, Carlee wrapped Zoe in the towels. "Give me a few minutes to get her cleaned up, weighed, and measured, and I'll bring her back to you after your second baby is born."

Dion watched Carlee carrying Zoe over to a station set up on the other side of the room, not wanting to lose sight of his daughter, even as Savannah placed more towels on Julia's abdomen to prepare for the birth of Zoe's twin. But when Jewel had another contraction and squeezed his hand once more while moaning in pain, he refocused on her, talking her through the breathing and praising her for her strength as she went through the whole process all over again and gave birth to their second daughter.

"Baby B, born at two-thirty p.m.," Dr. Magnum announced.

"Elena Juliette Burleson-Davis," Dion declared as their second squalling daughter was placed on Jewel's abdomen to be cleaned up by the nurse. Elena had the same golden-brown skin tone as her sister, but her hair was lighter than Zoe's, as were her eyes. He just wouldn't mention that her nose and lips looked a little more like his than her twin. "And with blue eyes just like her momma, I think we definitely picked the correct daughter to name after you, Jewel."

"Oh, no, I did not need to see that!" Jen yelled from the doorway before turning and leaving the room once more. But Dion and Jewel both ignored her as both of their eyes were locked onto their daughter.

"Yeah, but since brown is the dominant gene for eye color, her eyes will probably change color over time to match yours," Jewel protested weakly as the doctor and nurses took care of Jewel and their daughters, with Savannah wrapping up Elena and taking her over to another station beside where Carlee was working with Zoe.

"True," Dion, sort of, conceded, smiling because he knew something she didn't. "But since my mom had blue eyes, it's possible that I passed on a blue-eyed gene to Elena just like you did, so her eyes could stay blue."

"Genetics are weird," Jewel giggled, then winced in pain from whatever Dr. Magnum was doing between her legs. Dion knew she had to do something with the placentas, so he didn't want to look to find out what she was doing right then. "Ow! What are you doing down there, Devon?"

I wonder if Jen saw the placentas coming out and that's why she got grossed out and bolted?

"Sorry, just a local anesthetic, so I can sew up a small perineal tear without hurting you anymore," Dr. Magnum explained, not looking up from where she was working.

Dion felt queasy from just the thought of Jewel's pussy tearing from giving birth to his babies. *Is that because they took after me and are a lot bigger than Jewel was when she was born? Should we have done something different to keep that from happening?*

"Guess it's a good thing the girls came early and didn't keep growing for the next three-and-a-half weeks," Jewel scoffed, just as Carlee brought Zoe back over to them, "so it's not a big tear."

Yeah, I guess she was right when she said they were developed enough to deliver the other day when Dr. Magnum said it was still too early to induce labor.

"Dad, you wanna hold Zoe first while Mom's getting sewn up?" Carlee held Zoe out to Dion, who quickly released his hold on Jewel to place his arms in position to hold his daughter for the first time. Carlee gently laid the baby, who was wrapped in a white receiving blanket with pink and blue footprints all over it and wearing a tiny pink hat, in Dion's arms. "She's seven pounds, thirteen ounces, and twenty inches long."

"Hi, Zoe, I'm your dad," Dion whispered in awe to the beautiful baby in his arms. As soon as Carlee stepped out of the way, Dion scooted in closer to the bed and adjusted his hold on the baby, so Jewel could see her better while still lying on the delivery table. "And that beautiful woman is your mom."

"Hi, Zoe," Jewel cooed, reaching out to run her finger over the baby's cheek.

A few minutes later, after the doctor finished everything she had to do and put the bed back to where Jewel could stretch her legs out normally, and Savannah had taken care of cleaning up Elena, the other nurse carried Elena over and placed her in Jewel's arms. "Elena is eight pounds, two ounces, and twenty-and-a-half inches long."

"Hello, Elena," Dion cooed, looking into their other daughter's blue eyes, and deciding that her mix of his and Jewel's features was just as beautiful as her twin, just slightly different. "I'm sure you girls already know each other from hanging out together for the last several months. But I'm your dad, and that beautiful woman holding you is your mom."

Doing a little mental math based on the six ounces per week that Dr. Magnum had told them to expect their babies to gain toward the end of the pregnancy, Dion realized that both the girls would have been well over nine pounds, if they'd stayed in utero until closer to their due date. *Damn, hopefully, Jewel won't figure that out and decide she doesn't want to take a chance on our boys being even bigger and really ripping her open when they're born.*

"You owe me one heck of a push present after your big babies ripped me open," Jewel teased, grinning at him after kissing Elena's pink hat covered head. "I'm not sure the diamonds that need to come out of my necklace are big enough for the earrings I need to represent these big, beautiful girls."

Guess I'll be looking at some big ass, emerald earrings when I go get those diamonds taken out of the necklace and set in your engagement ring then.

"Don't worry, Jewel, I'm sure I'll find something appropriate when I take your necklace to the jewelry store this weekend," Dion assured her, not wanting to give her any hints about the ring already waiting for her.

And stopping by Flora's Flowers while I'm waiting for the diamonds to be transferred to see if they have the May birth flower in stock, or if I'll just need to pick the most colorful assortment of roses they have to bring back up here after my short shopping trip.

Once the doctor, nurses, and staff finished clearing the room of the various things they'd needed for the delivery, and brought in two clear bassinets for the girls to sleep in, as well as a second bed for him, they set him up with the paperwork to fill out for the girls' birth certificates and let him know that he needed to alert the family whenever he and Jewel were ready for the rest of their visitors to join them in the suite to meet their daughters. Jewel insisted on trying to nurse the girls before anyone else was allowed back there, so he waited until they'd spent a few minutes trying to get each of them to latch on and Jewel had freshened up before going to relay the message to the family.

When he got to the waiting room, he was surprised to see that Susan was holding a cold compress to Jen's head as she bent over a trash can, where she'd apparently lost her lunch. "Um, I was gonna tell ya'll to come back and meet the girls, but if you're sick, I'm not sure…"

"I'm not contagious," Jen protested, cutting him off before taking the washcloth Susan was using as a compress and wiping her mouth with it as she sat up. "I'm only sick because of seeing what looked like raw liver coming out of my sister's hoo-hah instead of a baby."

"And I told you, that was the placenta, not one of the babies," Susan corrected Jen with a sigh of exasperation before turning to direct the rest of her comments to Dion. "I didn't get but a glimpse of one of the babies because of having to keep Jen from puking in the hall, but I'm assuming they've both been born now, so we can go back and see them?"

"Yeah, they were both already born before I heard Jen start to come back in," Dion explained, nodding at his future mother-in-law. "But there's a lot more stuff they have to do after the delivery to get everyone cleaned up and stuff."

"Now that we know Julie actually had babies and didn't just pass raw liver, tell us all the details," Hazel quipped with a grin as she took Dion's arm and insistently pulled to get him to lead them all up the stairs and back down the hallway to Jewel's room. "Names, weights, how we're supposed to tell them apart, we need to know it all."

"Zoe Caroline was born first," Dion started as he let Susan and Hazel lead the group back to the birthing suite. "She weighs seven pounds and thirteen ounces, and is twenty inches long. And Elena Juliette weighs eight pounds and two ounces, and is twenty-and-a-half inches long. Zoe has brown eyes and medium-brown hair. Elena has blue eyes and light-brown hair. So, I think it'll be a lot easier to tell them apart than it is with Jonah and Jerry. And I may be biased 'cause I'm their dad, but I think Zoe and Elena are the two most beautiful babies on the planet."

He didn't mention anything about their other features and how they were a mix of him and Jewel. But he assumed they'd each make those assessments on their own, the same way he had when he first saw each of his daughters. His assumption was proven correct just as soon as they got back to the room, with everyone gushing about his beautiful family.

Dion knew he was truly blessed to be the lucky man who got to love Julia Burleson for the rest of his days. *Now, I just need to take advantage of all the extra help she has up here right now to sneak off to Jeweled Destiny to get the ring that will tie her to me permanently.*

~~~

Sunday, May 3, 2020

Even though she'd only napped off and on all night between getting up to take care of Zoe and Elena, Julie woke up early on her twenty-eighth birthday, feeling strange because of not waking up in the same place as her twin. Even when they were in college in Austin, she'd roomed with Jen, and just like when they were growing up, the first thing Julie did was go wake up Jen to wish each other a happy birthday. She'd planned to do the same this year, even though it wouldn't be exactly the same, since she'd moved into a different house on the ranch and was now living with Dion, instead of her sister. But since she was still in her room at the birthing center, instead of just a couple houses down from her sister on the ranch, she couldn't follow through with the tradition for the first time in her life.

Even with Dion asleep on the other bed, and both of the girls in their individual bassinets wedged between them, she still felt like she was missing an essential part of her being because Jen wasn't there. So, while Dion and the girls slept on, Julie grabbed her phone to call her twin. As soon as she double-checked that Dion, Zoe, and Elena were all sleeping soundly and wouldn't need her for a few minutes, she snuck out of bed and walked into the ensuite bathroom to keep from disturbing them while talking to Jen.

She emptied her bladder, washed her hands and face, and brushed her teeth and hair before sitting down on the chair at the vanity and dialing the number. *I seriously need to get one of these chairs for my vanity at home.*

"Happy birthday!" Jen exclaimed in lieu of a greeting before Julie could get the same words out.
~~~

Leah Mae Wright

"Happy birthday," Julie laughed, realizing it was the first time Jen had successfully said the words first because Julie usually shouted them as she opened Jen's bedroom door before her sister was fully awake.

"Are my nieces still as peacefully asleep as they were when I left last night?"

"Well, they're back to peacefully asleep after waking up every couple of hours all night." Julie stifled a yawn as she recalled how Dion had only woken up enough to be helpful one of the three times the girls had cried when they woke up since he took his ten p.m. dose of medication the night before. "But I expect them to wake up again in the next thirty minutes or so, so don't be surprised if I have to cut this call short to go nurse them again."

"Oh, yeah, I completely understand," Jen chuckled. "Gotta keep those baby bellies full. Are they still gonna let you come home today? Or do we need to plan to bring our birthday party up to you this evening?"

"As far as I know, we'll be released sometime today. Since the girls are doing much better with nursing than I expected, and don't seem to have any issues from being born early, I don't expect Dr. Magnum to suddenly come up with a reason to keep us here."

"Cool. Then I'll make sure everyone here knows to just wait on ya'll to get home, instead of trying to come up there and possibly missing you. Unless, does Dion need one of us to relieve him, so he can go pick up whatever he put those diamonds in for your birthday present?"

Dion had taken advantage of the whole family being there to help her on the afternoon the girls were born to take her necklace to the jewelers and have the extra stones removed. He'd also picked up a larger pair of heart-shaped emerald earrings for her as a push present, along with a vase filled with two dozen assorted colors of roses interspersed with lily of the valley, the May birth month flower, instead of the typical baby's breath.

But even though he'd brought her family necklace back with just the emeralds in the heart-shaped cage, he hadn't given her any other jewelry that utilized the two diamonds he'd had removed from the charm. When she asked him about it, he'd told her she'd just have to be patient and wait to get her birthday present on her birthday, not on their daughters' birthday.

"If so, he hasn't said anything about it. But I'll have him call you if he says anything about it before we get discharged." Julie barely got the words out before she heard one of the babies start to fuss from the next room. She quickly stood, walked out of the bathroom, and back into the room where she'd left her little family sleeping. "Gotta go. One of the girls is ready for her second breakfast."

"'Bye sis! Give the girls a kiss from Auntie Jen."

"Will do," Julie agreed before disconnecting the call and dropping her phone on her bed as she watched Dion sleepily undress Elena to change her diaper. Elena might have gotten her blue eyes and strawberry blonde hair from Julie, but she'd clearly gotten her appetite from Dion. She was always the first one to fuss when it was feeding time and consistently nursed longer than Zoe.

"Will do, what?" Dion asked as she squeezed in between the beds to kiss each of the girls' heads. The kiss was just enough of a distraction for Elena that she stopped fussing and didn't end up breaking out in a full-blown crying fit, like both girls had in the middle of the night, when Julie had to spend too much time changing diapers before nursing them.

"Give the girls a kiss from Auntie Jen," Julie replied before crawling into her own bed to position the nursing pillow and open the cups on her nursing gown to get ready to feed the babies. "She's planning to let everyone know we'll be home later today, so we won't be overrun with visitors while we're trying to get discharged. But she said to let her know if you need her to come up here for a bit, so you can go pick up my birthday present, since you didn't go back for it yesterday."

"I didn't have to go back for it yesterday 'cause I already have it," Dion informed her as he finished changing Elena and handed her over to Julie to start nursing.

Julie positioned their daughter on the twin nursing pillow, so she could latch on to her right breast, while Dion moved to change Zoe before she fully woke up and started fussing too. "I guess I'm gonna hafta wait until after the girls are fed before I get to open it?"

"I thought you'd want to open it at your birthday party, so your whole family can see it." Dion deftly changed Zoe's diaper as he spoke, not looking Julie in the eye for her to be able to read his expression.

"If it's jewelry, I can wear it to the party and they'll all still get to see it," Julie playfully pouted, too excited to see what he'd done with those diamonds to wait until that evening when they'd have the whole family together for her and Jen's birthday.

"Well, I suppose I could go back to my original plan to give it to you with breakfast in bed this morning," Dion stated as he finished changing Zoe and lifted her from the bassinet. He gently laid Zoe on the nursing pillow to position her at Julie's left breast as he continued. "Even though I can't exactly make you a stack of pancakes with birthday candles stuck in them like I'd intended."

"How 'bout we do the present this morning and I'll take a raincheck on those pancakes for tomorrow morning when we're home," Julie teased, grinning at him as their daughters both nursed while she lightly rubbed their little backs.

"I suppose we can do that," Dion grinned as he disposed of the girls' dirty diapers. "Even though this isn't exactly the romantic atmosphere I was hoping for when I give you this present. But you're gonna hafta wait a few more minutes while I go wash up."

Dion stepped out of the room to the ensuite restroom, taking his duffle bag with him. Julie heard the water turn on in the restroom and assumed he was just going to wash his hands and maybe brush his teeth, like she had while she was in there a few minutes before. But when the sink turned off and the shower turned on, she realized he had more planned than she thought.

I guess he's planning to shower and get dressed first, instead of just washing his hands? Julie couldn't help but chuckle at the way he was stalling in giving her the birthday present he'd been teasing her about since Friday evening. *I suppose he thinks I'm gonna wanna do the same after nursing the girls, and wait until they're back to sleep, so I'll have my hands free to open the present? Silly man, he must not realize that my keeping a hand on each of the girls while nursing is just because of wanting that physical contact with them, not because it's actually necessary with the pillow supporting them. And he really must not realize that I'm capable of multitasking to open presents while feeding the girls at the same time.*

She heard the shower turn off just about the time Zoe released her left breast with a huge yawn. "Oh, goodness, what a big yawn," she cooed down at her daughter, waiting to see if Zoe would root around again, or if she was done eating for the time being. When Zoe closed her mouth and looked around with her big brown eyes, Julie assumed her daughter was full for now. "Guess I shoulda had Daddy hand me a burp cloth before he went in the bathroom."

She closed the cup on her nursing gown to cover her left breast before picking Zoe up to burp her. She was only on the second round of back pats before Dion came back out of the restroom, dressed in dark gray slacks and a lavender button-down dress shirt. She assumed the steam that followed him out of the restroom was why his clothes didn't look as wrinkled as she'd expected from being packed in a duffle bag.

"Guess I wasn't as fast as I thought," Dion smiled sheepishly as he dropped his duffle on the sofa on the other side of his bed. He dug into the diaper bag and pulled out a burp cloth, which he laid over his shoulder before coming around the bed to take Zoe and finish burping her.

"No worries," Julie smiled up at him as she handed off Zoe. "The bassinets are close enough I coulda safely put her in it before burping Elena. And if they weren't, I coulda done like I did in the middle of the night and laid her back on the pillow until the nurse answered the call button to push them up against the bed again."

"You shoulda woke me up," Dion sighed as he started patting Zoe's back. "Even if I was too out of it to safely hold the babies, I coulda pushed the bassinets up against your bed without getting out of mine."

"Yeah, it was when you'd helped with changing them before handing them to me to nurse," Julie explained as Elena finally got her fill of colostrum and released her breast. "But neither one of us thought to have you push them back up before you laid down, and then you fell right back to sleep. The only way I coulda woke you up right then woulda been to yell loud enough I'd have also woken the girls and probably everyone else up here, so it was better to just use the nurse-call button."

"Do you think we should get some bedside bassinets for the house?" Dion handed her a burp cloth for her shoulder as she fastened the cup covering her right breast before picking Elena up to burp her.

"And have them sleep in our room until they sleep long enough to sync up their sleep schedule with my med schedule, so you don't have to try to get out from under the nursing pillow to put on the double carrier to take them to their cribs?"

"That's a great idea," Julie agreed, wishing they'd thought of it before the day they were taking the babies home, so they wouldn't have to make a trip to one of the larger towns around them with Heart of the Home closed on Sundays. "But I don't know how we'll have time to go to Baby Bonanza to get them, and get them put together, when everyone expects us to go straight to either the potluck after church or mine and Jen's birthday party when we leave here, depending on what time we get discharged."

Dion laid Zoe in her bassinet after she belched. Then he pulled his cell from his pocket and swiped the screen. "I'll have Dare and Mama Marcel go right after church to pick them up. And if we get out of here early enough, we'll skip the potluck to go put them together."

"And if we don't get out of here until late this afternoon?" Julie continued patting Elena's back until she finally burped as well.

"Then Dare and Mama Marcel will put them together for us." Dion shrugged, like it was no big deal, as he put his phone back in his pocket and picked Zoe back up. "Besides, as soon as Mama Marcel tells Susan where she's going, they'll probably convince Brent Deere to open the store and let them pick up the bassinets he has already put together to match the rest of our furniture."

"I guess we shoulda listened to him when he suggested getting them too, instead of just going with the cribs," Julie realized as she adjusted Elena in her arms, so she could move the nursing pillow and they could have a little playtime with their daughters.

"Probably," Dion chuckled as she crossed her legs to give him room to sit on the end of her bed. He sat down with one leg bent up on the bed and the other foot flat on the floor, so they were facing each other and each had a baby in their arms, where the girls could turn their heads to see each other and both their parents. They spent several minutes making silly faces and talking to the girls before Dion surprised her by standing back up. "Ya know what? I'm not gonna wait for breakfast in bed. I think it'll be even more special if the girls are awake and part of this, even though we're not at home like I'd planned."

"Part of what?" Julie questioned as Dion dropped to one knee and pulled a black jewelry box from his pocket.

With Zoe cradled in his left arm, Dion lifted the box in his right hand and flipped it open to reveal a three-stone diamond ring with all three stones in the shape of hearts. The large center stone was flanked on either side of the gold band by the two smaller heart-shaped diamonds he'd had removed from her family necklace two days earlier.

Oh! Wow! Yeah, it is better with the girls awake, instead of having them asleep in the bassinets while he proposes over a plate of runny eggs.

"I love you, Jewel. I know it's taken a while for me to get back all the memories of how we fell in love, and all the quirky little things I love about you, like how you put peanut butter on your pancakes, think everyone and everything looks better in purple, and refuse to say lying instead of laying because you don't like the negative connotation, even though you're brilliant enough to know it's grammatically incorrect, and especially how you strive to find the silver lining in even the worst of situations. Your joyousness and the way you graciously show your love for others have truly been a blessing to me, and I know they're traits I'm gonna love seeing you teach our children. I wanna spend the rest of my life as the father of your children, your partner in life, your best friend, your lover, your man, and especially as your husband. Julia Elizabeth Burleson, will you marry me?"

Julie couldn't help but giggle like a giddy schoolgirl as she nodded her head, too caught up in the perfect moment to speak.

"Please, Mommy, say yes to marrying our daddy." Dion raised his voice in a chirpy falsetto as he pretended Zoe and Elena could already talk.

"Yes," she choked out through her laughter, shifting Elena to her right arm, so she could extend her left hand for him to put the ring on her finger. "Yes, yes, yes, I'll marry you, Dion!"

Dion had to place the box down on her bed to get the ring out one handed, but he managed to get it on her finger without much of a delay. He then stood and leaned over to seal their engagement with a kiss, being careful not to bump the girls' heads into one another.

Even though they could only hug each other with one arm while holding their daughters, she still felt like they were intimately connected as he briefly deepened the kiss. Unfortunately, due to the awkward position on the bed with the girls between them, they had to keep it short.

Dion returned to his previous seated position on the end of the bed and looked back and forth between her and their daughters. "So, what do you say, girls? You ready to help Mommy and Daddy plan our wedding?"

"You do remember that I want a couple of months to plan everything and get back in shape first, right?" Julie grinned at him.

"Yeah, but I figured that would work out perfect to plan it for when the GWA is on their Independence Day break, so my half of the church won't be so empty," Dion grinned right back. "In fact, when I called to tell Rick that the girls were born so he could pass the news on to all the guys, I asked when they'll be on break to help us narrow down the days. They'll be coming to town on July third and not leaving until the thirteenth, so I'm thinking either Saturday the eleventh or Sunday the twelfth. Whichever you prefer."

"Saturday the eleventh," Julie decided. "I don't want to cut the nails, hair, and makeup as close as we did when Josh and Cait got married by trying to squeeze it all in after church. That works out much better when we can get started first thing in the morning to give everyone time to get ready without risking messing something up before the ceremony."

And I guess I'll end up getting roasted in one of Rick's introductions after all. Not that Julie minded even the least little bit.

Several hours later, after taking advantage of the girls nap time to eat breakfast, shower, and change out of her nursing gown into a purple wrap dress, which would still allow her easy access for nursing them the rest of the day, they were finally discharged. When they got home, they weren't the least bit surprised to find the girls' bassinets were already temporarily replacing the bench at the foot of their bed.

At least, not nearly as surprised as they were when they got to Jen and Julie's birthday party to find out they weren't the only couple announcing their engagement to the family. *Oh, I can't wait to hear all the details of how that happened,* Julie thought as she sat down to dinner with her family to hear JJ and Deanna's story of their time in

Tulsa. *And maybe Mom will be so busy trying to plan two weddings in the next two months that she won't have time to pressure any of us to give her more grandbabies.*

Yeah, right, she mentally scoffed while smiling knowingly at Dion, who was wearing a pink double carrier with both their daughters snuggled in against his chest. *More like she'll take advantage of all the fittings and appointments to pick flowers and cakes and stuff to drop even more hints. And poor Jen, as the only single sibling left, will be bombarded with a shit-ton of prospective husband suggestions.*

Next in the GWA

Mistakenly Married?
Galactic Wrestling Association Book 3

What happens when the Galactic Wrestling Association celebrates a little too hard after a successful show in Las Vegas? Too much drinking that leads to a night several of the wrestlers have completely forgotten. Especially when one of their meddling, matchmaking mommas instigates an excursion to take pictures at a local wedding chapel.

The photographic evidence on social media of thirteen inebriated performers stopping at a wedding chapel caused quite an uproar, making them wonder if some of their angles needed to be rebooked. But with all of them waking up in their own rooms at the hotel the next morning, with only vague memories of what had happened, they all believed they'd stayed outside the chapel, as the pictures indicated.

Until a few weeks later, when Rylie Long checked her mail while the GWA was in her hometown for a show, and learned that what happens in Vegas doesn't always stay there. Finding out she'd actually married Liam Connery that night in Vegas was a shock. She hadn't wanted to let on to anyone in the company that she had a little crush on the older wrestler. Now she had to figure out if she wanted to take advantage of their situation to see if her little crush could turn into more.

When Rylie took her marriage license to the arena to inform her boss, several of her coworkers suddenly scrambled to check their mail to find out their marital statuses as well. Apparently, Rylie and Liam weren't the only GWA wrestlers who got mistakenly married.

Teagan Shields and Josh Parker also got married while drunk that night, as did Aiken Pearson and Brent Crockett. Now they all had to figure out how they wanted to handle the legalities of their situation, while the GWA bookers reworked their angles to try to control the celebrity gossip. Would any of them stay married? Or would they get divorced? Or have their marriages annulled? And how did the fact that none of them had their legal residences listed in the same state as their spouses, or the state where they got married, factor into their options?

Taking the time to meet with attorneys and determine the requirements for each of their situations was difficult with them traveling with the GWA. Especially when their coworkers conspired to keep them together by pairing the three couples in the bridal party for Dean and Allissa's wedding, so they couldn't go home for their Thanksgiving break.

DISCLAIMER: This multicultural, age gap, forced proximity, friends-to-lovers, drunk Vegas marriage, sports romance contains profanity, graphic sex scenes, and references to infertility issues. It is intended for adult readers (18+) who are not easily offended.

Next in Heart's Destiny

<u>Destined for Deanna</u>
Heart's Destiny Book 8

JJ Burleson met the woman he knew he was destined to marry a few years ago. They spent a wonderful week together at a conference, with JJ planning to propose before it ended and bring her back to his hometown. But for some unknown reason, Deanna Wolfe ended their fling before he could get the words out, leaving him heartbroken.

Deanna had fallen head over heels for JJ when she first met him. But after a whirlwind week with him, she had to end things because she knew she could never give him the family he wanted in the future. She went home and tried to make herself forget the younger man who'd stolen her heart, but it was difficult when her boss at OK Oil kept going head to head with JJ for deals they both wanted for their companies. While she never had to see him, it was still difficult for her to hear his name whenever Burleson Incorporated won a contract her boss wanted.

When JJ's cousin married Deanna's best friend, their longing for one another only got worse because she could no longer avoid seeing him whenever her friend invited her to family events. Especially when she learned that their breakup led him to study the kinks they'd both been curious about years ago.

Somehow she managed to keep her secrets, if not her distance, from JJ for over a year after they ran into one another again. But when

Burleson Incorporated bought out OK Oil, JJ moved out of his small hometown to take over as her boss in Tulsa. Fighting their destiny was a lot harder when she had to report to him daily as his executive assistant.

DISCLAIMER: This second chance, older woman, younger man, he falls first, office romance contains profanity, graphic sex scenes including BDSM, and flashbacks to an abusive past, pregnancy loss, and forced infertility, as well as a hostage situation when her former abuser breaks out of prison and comes for revenge. It is intended for adult readers (18+) who are not easily offended.

Books by Leah Mae Wright

Heart's Destiny Series

Galactic Wrestling Association Series

About The Author

Leah Mae Wright lives in Florida with her husband and fur babies. Her head has been filled with romantic stories for as long as she can remember, beginning with fairy tales as a small child growing up in Oklahoma and carrying through to countless ideas of her own throughout the years, as she has moved around to live in several different states. Now that her children are grown and life has slowed down, she's letting them out of her head, so they can join the libraries of her fellow fans of romance. Leah's literary world is a wonderful place that has no Covid, no real politicians, and a few unreal towns. Her favorite part about her characters living in her literary world is knowing that they are guaranteed a happily ever after.

You can keep up to date with Leah's future book plans at:
www.leahmaewright.com –Be sure to sign up for the Newsletter to receive emails about new releases, sales, and freebies.
www.facebook.com/LeahWrightAuthor
www.amazon.com/author/leah_wright
https://www.instagram.com/leahmaewrightauthor/

https://www.pinterest.com/LeahMaeWrightAuthor/

Provide your feedback to the author at:
Leah's Literary World Facebook Group
LeahWrightAuthor@gmail.com
Leah@LeahMaeWright.com

You can also review Leah's books on Amazon, Goodreads, Bookbub, and Fictiondb.